Mariners of Gor

GOREAN SAGA

Mariners of Gor

John Norman

OPEN ROAD
INTEGRATED MEDIA
NEW YORK

Copyright © 2011 by John Norman

978-1-4976-4495-3

This edition published in 2014 by Open Road Integrated Media, Inc.
345 Hudson Street
New York, NY 10014
www.openroadmedia.com

Mariners of Gor

Chapter One

Late One Night, in a Tavern in Brundisium

And he spoke.

"I sailed on the great ship," he said. "Yea, the ship of Tersites."

"It was lost at sea," said a man.

"It sailed over the edge of the world," said another.

"Listen," he said. "And I will tell you a story."

"For paga," laughed a Merchant.

"We have heard such stories," said a fellow.

"You are a liar," scoffed the taverner.

"A thousand ships come and go, in the great harbor of Brundisium," said a fellow. "There are a thousand stories."

"But not of the ship of Tersites," he said.

"No," said a fellow, "not of the ship of Tersites."

"There is no such ship," said a man. "Tersites was mad, fled from Port Kar."

"I hear 'banished'," said another.

"The ship was never built," said a man.

"It was built," averred the fellow.

"No," said a man.

"In the northern forests," he said.

"Absurd," laughed a man.

"And debouched onto Thassa from the Alexandra," he said.

"Have you seen it?" asked a man.

"I berthed upon her," he said.

"Liar," said the taverner.

"What happened?" asked a man.

"That is my story," said the man.

It was a small tavern, *The Sea Sleen*, only yards from the water, declining by a steep slope to the southern piers. It was late. Tharlarion-oil lamps hung on their slender chains, three to a lamp, adjusted variously, table to table, from the low, beamed ceiling. Most had been extinguished, as tables were vacated. The few lamps remaining alit put out little light, the wicks shortened to conserve fuel. There were no musicians. The dancing sand was empty. Given the nature and paucity of its custom, *The Sea Sleen* could afford to hire musicians only at the height of the season. It was now the second month in autumn, called in Brundisium the month of Lykourgos. The harbor was not now much trafficked. Mostly coasting. Until the arrival of the stranger, it had been muchly quiet. One might have heard the clink of a goblet now and then, the scraping of a wooden trencher on a low table, sometimes the crack of a kaissa piece being struck down on a board in an aggressive move. Outside, away from the portal, down the slope a bit, if one listened, one could hear the water lapping against the pilings, where the vast glory of looming Thassa, in the darkness, deigned to touch the small works of men. *The Sea Sleen* was not one of the higher, larger taverns in the great port of Brundisium, such as that of the Diamond Collar, the Joys of Turia, the Dina, the tavern of Chang, that of Hendow, or such. Her patronage was mostly that of ruffians, mariners between voyages, their coins now mostly spent, left in the higher taverns, drifters, wanderers, peddlers, exiles, some mercenaries, willing to unsheathe their blades for a bit of silver, or a fight. The stranger sat cross-legged at one of the small tables. Several were gathered about him. One could not see his face well in the half-darkness, but the reddish outline marked his place. Most of those about him were muchly in darkness. Some held cups of paga. The trenchers had been gathered in, and the kaissa boards had been folded and put away, the red and yellow pieces in two shallow drawers, fixed in the board, one on each side, one for each color. This is not an unusual arrangement in taverns. Commonly, however, kaissa boards are simple, straight boards, and the pieces are kept separately, in boxes or sacks. Members of the Caste of Players are recognized by their red-and-yellow-checked robes, the worn board slung over their shoulder, the sack of pieces at their waist. Depending on the Player, they will give you a game for as little as a tarsk-bit, as much as a golden tarn disk of Ar. It was said that Centius of Cos had once played in Brundisium.

"If you have a story to tell, for a drink," said the taverner, "why not tell it toward the upper city, against the outer walls, in a landward tavern, say, the Diamond Collar?"

The stranger was silent. Then he said, "I want paga."

"I will tell you," said the taverner. "You were ejected elsewhere, thrown into the streets, and stumbled downward, bewildered, blindly, mad, knowing nothing else, stumbling from door to door, until you would reach the piers."

"And then Thassa, dark, cold Thassa," said a man.

"Paga," said the stranger.

"Do you beg?" inquired the taverner.

"No," said the stranger, and the taverner, alarmed, sensing danger, stepped a bit back, but recovered himself, almost immediately.

The stranger was a large, spare man, with roughened hands, perhaps hardened from the oar, or from hauling on lines. He was clad in little more than rags. He did have a dirty mariner's cap. I did not think it unlikely he had indeed ventured upon Thassa. Those hands, I did not doubt, might close about a man's throat, might break a man's neck.

"I will pay," said the man.

"You have coins?" inquired the taverner.

"No," said the man.

"Extinguish the lamps," said the taverner to his man, who stood behind him.

The other tables were empty now, as their occupants had left, or had gathered with us, about the stranger's low table.

The only lamp remaining lit then, of the hanging lamps, was the one in which we could see the outline of the stranger's face. A bowl lamp did glow at the serving table, near the kitchen gate, near the paga vat, near the goblets.

"I can pay," said the stranger.

"With what?" inquired the taverner.

"I will tell you a story," said the stranger. His eyes had a wild, feral look.

5

"We are closing," said the taverner. Then, looking to his man, he gestured toward the stranger. "Eject him," he said.

"Where will he go? What will he do?" asked a fellow, a Scribe from his robes, of shoddy, faded blue.

"Thassa," said a man, I think a mercenary. "Dark, cold Thassa."

"Perhaps," said a man.

"No," said the stranger. "No."

"Come along, fellow," said the taverner's man. "There is garbage outside, in the sewer troughs." He put his hand on the stranger's arm.

"Do not touch me," said the stranger, quietly, politely, rising unsteadily to his feet. His voice was courteous, almost gentlemanly. But the taverner's man did not mistake the tone of that voice, and removed his hand from the stranger's arm.

"It is time to go," said the taverner's man, gently.

"I will leave," said the stranger.

"I would hear his story," said a man.

"I will buy him paga," said another.

"No," said the stranger.

I had not realized how large he was until he stood.

"We are closing," called the taverner, suddenly, loudly, impatiently, for two figures, cloaked, hooded, stood at the portal, now within. They had entered silently. None of us had noticed them, lest it was the stranger.

I think he had noticed.

"So," said the stranger to the two newcomers. "You have found me."

Neither of the newcomers spoke, for their kind is efficient. They do quietly, and swiftly, what they have come to do. In such situations speaking is unnecessary, and sometimes dangerous, as it costs time. A moment of indulgence, of clever vanity, can cost one one's life. There are caste codes pertaining to such matters.

This was not a typical hunt, I gathered, in which the tunic is worn openly, the sign emblazoned publicly upon the brow, the prey helpless, cornered, as vulnerable as a vulo.

The cloaks parted and two crossbows, together, the quarrels set, were smoothly, swiftly raised.

At the same moment, the stranger bent down, seized up the

small table, and flung it upward, and two quarrels splintered halfway through the wood. The stranger's hands disappeared within his sleeves, and each hand emerged, a dagger in hand. The newcomers cast down the bows and, together, reached within their robes to unsheathe blades, the common *gladius*, but the cloaks, hitherto so convenient in concealing their caste, their intent, their weapons, cost them an unencumbered draw, and the stranger was at them, table flung aside, daggers like striking osts, moving twice, and the newcomers half fell, half stumbled, outside the tavern, into the darkness, the street outside, probably neither realizing for a moment that they had been killed.

"Did you see?" asked the taverner's man. "They wore the dagger."

"Yes," said a fellow.

That had been obvious only when the hoods had been disarranged in the stranger's attack. When hunting, it is common for members of the black caste, the Caste of Assassins, to paint a black dagger on their forehead.

We waited within the tavern, and, in a few Ehn, the stranger returned.

He jerked the quarrels from the small table and cast them to the side. He then righted the small table and resumed his place, sitting cross-legged, behind it.

"They were Assassins," said the taverner, shuddering.

"What did you do with them?" asked a man.

"Thassa accepted them, as she would not accept me," said the man.

"Bolt the door," said the taverner, uneasily.

"Who are you," asked a man, "that those of the black caste would come secretly, silently, upon you?"

The stranger was silent.

He replaced the two daggers in the sleeve sheaths of his tunic.

"What is your story?" asked a man.

"It has to do with the ship of Tersites," he said.

The taverner turned to his man. "Bring bread, and meat, suls, and tur-pah, and fruit, for our guest."

"And paga," said the stranger.

"And paga!" said the taverner, admiringly.

We were patient, while the stranger fed, voraciously, as might have a starving sleen. When he had emptied his trencher twice, the taverner's man set a goblet of paga before him.

"Is this how you serve paga?" inquired the stranger. He now seemed a different man, one ruddy with vigor and power.

The taverner gestured to his man, and the man hurried away, going behind the serving table, passing through the gate to the kitchen. Shortly thereafter, we heard the bright flash of bells.

The girl was quite beautiful, but that is not unusual in a tavern, even one of cheap, reduced custom, in such a district of the port, so near the waterfront, yards from the southern piers, such as *The Sea Sleen*. Musicians are expensive, but girls are cheap. In a paga tavern one may rely on the quality of the girls, more so, I fear, than on the quality of the food, or paga. They are, of course, taken from the block with the satisfaction of customers in mind.

She knelt, appropriately.

With the back of her right hand she rubbed her eyes, removing a residue of sleep. Clearly she was uneasy, and did not understand the meaning of her summons, this late, the tavern muchly empty, the group gathered about the small table, the stranger, in rags and mariner's cap, before whom she knelt.

Under his gaze she widened her knees further.

She noticed the table.

She looked at it, frightened.

Clearly she was curious as to the condition of the table, the two ruptured, splintered gashes, the wood burst inward, as though struck by twin spikes, in its surface. She did not, of course, speak, nor inquire.

Her collar was a simple, flat metal band, light, close-fitting, with the lock, as is common, at the back of the neck. In this fashion, the front of the collar, if engraved, may be easily read.

"She is clothed," observed the stranger.

"Of course," said the taverner. "This is a high tavern."

Two of the men about laughed.

It was true that she was clothed, in a fashion. She wore the common camisk, a brief rectangle of cloth slipped over the head, belted with a double loop of binding fiber. The camisk was of thin, clinging, yellow rep-cloth. It was ragged and soiled. The tavern, you see, was not truly a high tavern. If she stood, it would fall midway to her thighs. It was closely belted, as required, a bow knot at the left hip, where it would be convenient to a right-handed master. The double loop is to allow for an adequate length, enough for a variety of ties.

In the high taverns, girls are often silked, often belled, sometimes jeweled. In low taverns they often serve nude, sometimes chained. The silks of tavern girls, of course, are quite unlike the silks of free women, which are cumbersome and concealing, even to veils. The silks of tavern girls are usually brief and diaphanous. There is no mistaking them for free women. Obviously masters have dressed them, to the extent they have been permitted clothing, for the pleasure of men. In the low taverns, the chaining, though perfectly secure, as all Gorean chaining, is largely for aesthetic purposes, the obduracy of chains, in their way, enhancing and setting off, by stark contrast, the softness and beauty in their clasp. For such girls, chained or not, and others like them, marked and collared, there is no escape, no more than for any other form of domestic animal.

"Reveal yourself," said the taverner.

Slowly, carefully, kneeling, the girl undid the knot at her left hip. She removed the binding fiber, drawing it loose, and then, slowly, carefully looping it, put it to her left, beside her, at her left knee. She then, after a moment's hesitation, lifted the camisk away, gracefully.

"Ah," said the stranger, pleased.

The girl shuddered and then folded the camisk. She worked carefully, head down. She put the folded camisk also to her left, but a bit behind her. She then lifted the looped binding fiber and placed it neatly on the camisk, centered. In this way, though to her left, her clothing, slight as it was, was behind her. It was not between her and her master's customers. Her beauty was thus placed forward, and prominently displayed. She was well bared. Similarly, the looped binding fiber, a bit behind her, on the folded camisk, was where a man might easily have lifted it, and wrapped it about her neck, several times, from behind; similarly it was about even with where her wrists would have been, if they had been crossed behind her, for binding. The square was approximately a foot Gorean. Sometimes, as a punishment, girls are forced to remain in place, standing on such a bit of cloth. It is not easy to do, after a time. A misstep or loss of balance must be reported to the master, and is commonly met with a stroke of the switch. The coils of the looped binding fiber, in their circularity and width, suggested the encirclement of a collar, one for a small throat, that of a female. And certainly they were reminiscent of the multiply stranded, temporary collars, tied shut, sometimes put on captures, particularly on stripped free women, the stripping and collaring serving to make clear their transient status, prior to an appropriate marking and collaring.

There is little in a paga tavern which does not have, in one way or another, its meaning.

The girl lifted her head.

"You are crying," said the stranger.

"Forgive me, Master," she said.

"She has not been long in the collar," said the taverner.

"She is barbarian, is she not?" asked the stranger.

"I fear so," said the taverner, "but she is not without interest, I trust."

"Paga, Master?" asked the girl.

"What is your name?" asked the stranger.

The girl cast a frightened look at the taverner. Then she said, "I have no name, Master. I have not been given a name. Forgive me, Master."

"Yes," said the stranger. "Her accent is clearly barbarian."

"Some men," said the taverner, "enjoy the accent. It makes their barbarian status clear, and thus gives their mastery, in its perfection, an interesting and exotic flavor. As they are barbarians, one's relationship to them is uncomplicated. One need not be concerned with their treatment. One may treat them as one wishes."

"One's relationship to collar meat, of any sort," said a fellow, he I took to be a mercenary, "is uncomplicated."

"Who is concerned with collar meat?" said another. "They are all the same, Gorean or barbarian. One will treat them as one wishes."

"I think," said another, "it is even more delicious to take a Gorean woman, one of those haughty she-sleen, so arrogant and lofty in their pride, so pretentiously superior, and strip them and teach them the collar."

"The terrified lips of either sort, pressed supplicatingly to your feet, are pleasant," said a fellow.

"Yes," said another.

"Would you like a name?" asked the stranger.

"That is at the pleasure of masters," whispered the girl. "It will be as they wish. I am theirs, to be named or not."

As such as the girl are domestic animals, they have no name in their own right, no more than other domestic animals, say, verr, tarsk, or kaiila. One such as she would commonly bring more than a verr or tarsk, but far less than a kaiila.

"Many barbarians learn to speak a fluent lovely Gorean," said the taverner.

"I understand so," said the stranger. I gathered he might have known instances of such.

"You had a name in your former life," said the stranger.

"Yes, Master," she said. A tear coursed down her cheek.

"It is gone," he said.

"Yes, Master," she said.

"Would you like to name her?" asked the taverner.

"Is she any good?" asked the stranger.

Obviously such considerations might affect the quality and nature of a name.

"The fires have begun to burn in her belly," said the taverner.

One of the men laughed.

The girl put her head down, trembling, shamed.

I suspected that the fires had, indeed, begun to burn in her belly. I wondered if she knew, now, how much, later, their prisoner she would be. Compared to them how feeble and imperfect would be the bars of cages, the weight of shackles.

"Paga, Master?" she asked.

"Yes," he said.

She rose gracefully, backed away deferentially, and then turned, and hurried to the serving table.

The tavern was muchly dark, but we could see her outline at the serving table, in the light of the tiny bowl lamp. She wiped out a goblet with a cloth, set it beside the vat, lifted the lid from the vat, and dipped the goblet in the amber fluid, filling it. She then put the goblet down, replaced the vat lid, and, to the sound of the bells on her left ankle, approached the table. She knelt at the side of the table, rather before the stranger. She widened her knees and put her head down. She had both hands on the goblet.

"Paga, Master?" she asked, again.

The girl was lithe, slender, dark-eyed, dark-haired, well breasted, sweetly thighed, with an inviting love cradle. Her hands and feet were small.

The soft glow of the tiny lamp, the single lamp, on its chains, hanging near the table, glinted on the metal goblet, and the close-fitting, narrow band encircling her neck.

"Yes," he said.

"Yes, Master," she whispered.

She pressed the metal of the goblet to her waist, and then, gently, but unmistakably, to her breasts, after which she lifted the goblet, regarding the stranger, frightened, over its rim. She then kissed the goblet, and licked it for a moment with her small tongue, and then kissed it again, tenderly, lingeringly, supplicatingly, and then lowered her head between her extended arms, lifting the goblet to the stranger.

The stranger took the goblet, and regarded the girl. She knelt back.

"Nadu," whispered the taverner, and the girl went to position, back on heels, knees wide, back straight, the palms of her hands down on her thighs. She kept her head down. Commonly, in nadu, the head is up, the gaze straight ahead, that the beauty of her features be displayed, and that she be in a position to better detect the slightest nuances of her master, either in tone or expression, but neither the taverner nor the stranger exacted this small adjustment. Tears ran down her cheeks, some falling to the floor, between her knees.

"I think," said the stranger, "I shall name her."

"If you wish," said the taverner. He could later, of course, do what he wished with the name, removing it, or changing it.

"Let her, for the time," said the stranger, "be Talena."

Men cried out in protest.

The girl looked up, her hand risen before her mouth, in terror.

"Never! Never!" said the taverner. "That hated name is no longer spoken. It is to be heard no more."

'Talena', it might be noted, was at one time a common name on Gor, much as dozens of other names. To be sure, it was a high-caste name, rare amongst the lower castes. But even so, it was not unknown in the lower castes, and I have encountered it even amongst the Peasants, the fundamental caste, the "Ox on which the Home Stone rests." It was rare as a slave name until after the fall of Ar, and the rise of Talena of Ar to the throne of Ar, placed on the throne as a puppet Ubara by the occupying forces of victorious Cos and Tyros, the major maritime Ubarates of Gor, abetted by numerous mercenary companies. It was only after that time that some masters outside of Ar, in various far cities, and even as faraway as Cos and Tyros, in their contempt for the new Ubara, regarded as having betrayed her Home Stone, might place that now-contemptible name upon some slaves, usually deficient or temporarily lacking slaves, as a punishment name. Well then might they strive for a name with less affinity to the whip. In Ar itself, to name a slave 'Talena' was deemed an act of sedition, punishable by impalement. For many years Ar had been ruled by the great Marlenus of Ar, a giant of a man, mountainous in boldness and power, yet famed as much for subtlety and cunning. Marlenus was ambitious, despotic, and imperialistic. Known Gor stood much in fear of him. This Talena was once his daughter. It seems that long ago, during the Planting Feast of Ar, a bold tarnsman, thought to be from the north, seized the Home Stone of Ar, which catastrophe brought about the temporary downfall of the Ubar, who fled from the city with chosen men. In the disruptions and chaos ensuing upon the loss of the Home Stone, leagues of cities, enemies to Ar, under the leadership of an Assassin, Pa-Kur, marched on the troubled, disunited city. His "horde," as historians would come to speak of it, lay encamped outside her walls, poised to breach her defenses, ready to enter, sack, and burn the city; all seemed lost; but Marlenus, somehow abetted in his return by a figure now thought by many to be mythical, a Tarl of Bristol, which city we do not know, entered and rallied his city, and the invading horde was resisted and routed. Pa-Kur may have perished, but this is not known, as the body was never found. This Tarl of Bristol, if such a figure ever existed, supposedly companioned Talena, daughter of the Ubar, but appears to have deserted her. Much is unclear. Somehow, it seems, she was apprehended by Rask of Treve, perhaps in trying to return to Ar. Ar and Treve are mortal enemies. One may well suppose it was quite a coup for Rask of Treve to have his collar on the neck of the daughter of Marlenus, inveterate foe of his city. She was kept in his tents for a time, but then it seems that the fancy of the mighty Rask was taken by a mere slave, a blond barbarian collar slut, named El-in-or. In any event, Rask, perhaps in amusement, or to show his contempt for her, gave Talena as a braceleted, leashed slave, to Verna, a panther girl of the northern forests. The shame of Talena infuriated proud Marlenus, obsessed with his name and honor, particularly as it became clear, later, in the northern forests, when Talena was put up for sale, that, hoping to be freed and returned to Ar, she had begged to be purchased, a slave's act, for in such an act one acknowledges that one is property, a slave, and may be purchased. It seems she was purchased by Samos of Port Kar, First Captain of the Council of Captains of Port Kar, and later came into the possession of another captain from Port Kar, Bosk of Port Kar, who freed her. Earlier he had been crippled in the northern forest, the victim of poisoned steel. Talena, freed, in contempt and arrogance, permitted to a free woman, ridiculed and scorned her benefactor, and insisted upon being returned to power and glory in Ar, which matter was arranged by this fellow, Bosk of Port Kar. Perhaps, as he was chairbound, he thought he would get little good out of her in a collar. In any event, Talena was returned to Ar. This Bosk later, it seems, obtained access to an antidote which, administered, reversed his affliction. In any event, later, at the time of his mysterious disappearance, he was a noted, high captain in Port Kar. To be sure, much is obscure, and rumors vary. I have heard more than one account of such events. The fate of Talena, however, seems more clear. She was returned to Ar, but Marlenus, in view of the shame she had brought upon his house, both in the matter of Rask of Treve, and her actions in the northern forests, removed the stain upon his honor by disowning her. No longer then, disowned, was she his daughter. Accordingly, when she arrived in Ar, she was not returned to glory, to position and power, but removed from public sight, being sequestered, for most practical purposes, imprisoned, in the Central Cylinder. Thus, let the shame brought upon the name and honor of Marlenus of Ar be hidden away, if not forgotten. Later, Marlenus, on a hunting trip to the Voltai Mountains, was injured in a fall from tarnback, which injury impaired his memory. No longer did he know himself to be Marlenus, Ubar of Ar. He, ignorant of his true identity, was captured by Trevans, or perhaps delivered to them by traitors. Still not knowing his true identity he later escaped from Treve and made his way back to Ar, believing himself to be of the Peasants, and he lived for a time in a village in the vicinity of Ar, as one Peasant amongst others, accepting their hospitality, working in their fields. Meanwhile, Talena, in her disgrace and fury, conspired with malcontents and traitors who, given the absence of Marlenus, and the unsettled conditions in the city, wished to come to power in Ar. A conspiracy was formed, abetted by propagandas contrived to paralyze and confuse the citizens of Ar, propagandas promoting self-doubt and guilt amongst her citizens for the successes and glories of Ar's past, propagandas including belittlings of danger, and representations of enemies as allies and friends, intent upon the best interests of the city. The eventual outcome of these machinations, hailing policies of concession, appeasement, and surrender as victories of beneficent statecraft, as demands of an overdue justice, was the conquest of Ar, and her occupation by Cosians, those of Tyros, and large numbers of mercenaries. The walls of Ar, mightier even than those of southern Turia, were dismantled by duped, rejoicing citizens to the music of flute girls, and betrayed, fallen Ar would be systematically looted and exploited for months. Talena, smug with the spears of invaders behind her, sat regally upon her father's throne, and abused her power wickedly, using it to further reduce and diminish her city, and avenged herself rampantly, as she wished, upon numerous enemies, or putative enemies, or on anyone she might wish, as the humor might seize her. Muchly was the wealth of Ar destroyed or carried away, to be bestowed abroad, and many were its beauties consigned to foreign collars in the name of decency and justice, to right the wrongs of supposedly guilty Ar. Indeed, it was said that Talena, vain of her beauty, which was considerable, used hypocritical pretexts of state to eliminate many of her actual or alleged rivals. Many women found themselves shorn and shaved, chained, in the holds of slave ships bound for Tyros or Cos whose only crime was their beauty. Hundreds of others were reduced to slavery merely that their wealth might be confiscated by the state. Talena relished not only the powers permitted to her by the occupation forces, exercised at their discretion, and often in accordance with their direction, but filled her coffers in the Central Cylinder with abundant, secret wealth. In this matter she was not alone. Amongst her supporters, and numerous collaborators, battening on the misery of the city, corruption was rampant. The allocation of privileges and favors, franchises and monopolies, proved lucrative. Bribery and theft became ways of life, even amongst the most modest of offices. Mercenaries exacted "taxes" with impunity amongst Merchants. Gangs of youths, flaunting Cosian fashions, roamed the city, looting and vandalizing. Shortages of goods and food became common in the city, except amongst those favored by the state. Fortunes were made in black markets. Some flourished, of course, those with access to the throne, or with access to those who might have such access. The intertwined strands of interest and influence were subtle and widely spread. One of the greatest fortunes amassed in the city was that of a mysterious, shadowy individual supposedly named "Ludmilla," who owned, and, through subordinates, managed, a series of large, ornate slave brothels in the city. These were amongst the few establishments in Ar, in those times, which seemed prosperous and, despite general shortages, were well and reliably supplied, not only with lovely brothel slaves, but even with the choicest of viands and wines. It was later discovered that there was no "Ludmilla," but, rather, that this enterprise was merely one of several instituted and emplaced by the Ubara herself. Further, as a part of the conspiracy mentioned hitherto, it had been deemed necessary to reduce, even decimate, the military power of Ar. Ar must be made weak, vulnerable. Accordingly, much of the might of Ar had been dispatched to the vicinity of the Vosk river, supposedly to counter a massive invasion of Cos and Tyros in this area. Informed that the invasion force had withdrawn into the delta, the forces of Ar, under the orders of conspirators, entered the extensive, treacherous wastes and swamps of the vast delta in pursuit. That was not, of course, as is well understood now, the locus of the invasion. Rather the troops of Cos and Tyros, borne by their lateen-rigged fleets, would be welcomed here in

Brundisium, where, in league with hundreds of mercenary companies, joined here in prearranged rendezvous, they began their march on Ar. Meanwhile, following orders, the forces of Ar, with good heart, penetrated ever more deeply into the delta. The enemy they encountered, of course, was not the expected foe, but the delta itself, with its insects, heat, humidity, uncertain footing, quicksand, tharlarion, and rencers, denizens of the delta, almost invisible, subtle in warfare, masters of the bow and ambush. Few of the men of Ar reached the Tamber Gulf, Thassa, or Port Kar. Most perished in the delta. Some remnants, haggard, exhausted, disheveled, half-starving, ill, harried, pursued, managed to fight their way back to the Vosk, and of these some managed, overland, fugitives amongst swarming enemies, to return to Ar. Some of these veterans of the delta campaign, now embittered, realizing how they had been betrayed, and dismayed at the Ar to which they had returned, formed the nucleus of a resistance, the "Delta Brigade," the natural symbol of which was the letter "Delka," scribbled or scratched secretly, in bold lines, on many a wall or building, which letter, of course, in its shape, resembles a delta, and would recall a particular delta, that of the Vosk. To shorten the story, great Marlenus was recognized, it is said by a slave, in a line of Peasants, delivering suls within the city. This cognizance came to the attention of members of the Delta Brigade, who took in, concealed, and sheltered their Ubar. In their care, days later, it is said that suddenly the long-suppressed memory of great Marlenus again came alive, in a howl of understanding and rage. He sprang to his feet, a larl amongst men. He called for weapons. The Delta Brigade had found their leader. The insurrection was brief, violent, and bloody. The citizens, rallied, armed with whatever they could find, shovels, axes, even stones, and rose *en masse*. Tides of hate, unleashed, irresistible, swept through the streets, through the plazas, into the towers, across the bridges. Oppositions, unprepared, were hasty and ill-organized. Even the camp of Myron, *polemarkos* of Temos, cousin of Lurius of Jad, Ubar of Cos, outside the walls, was overrun. Within the city collaborators, their names posted on the public boards, were hunted down, room to room. In the frenzied vengeance of the mobs hundreds, both men and women, caught, were summarily impaled. Most sought of all was the traitorous Talena herself who could not be found.

"That name, that hated name," said the taverner, "is not to be spoken."

"Talena is avidly sought," said the man in faded blue, in scribal robes.

"Do not name her that," said another man.

"Even slaves no longer bear that name," said another.

The stranger smiled, and quaffed his paga, then put down the goblet on the splintered table.

The collar girl was trembling. She dared to shake her head, negatively, pleading.

"Marlenus of Ar," said the mercenary, "has put a reward of ten thousand tarns of gold on her head."

"Tarn disks of double weight," said another.

"There is not that much gold on Gor," laughed another.

"But yes," chuckled another. "It is the secret wealth of Talena herself, her own illicitly amassed wealth, which is put up to have her returned to Ar."

"Doubtless stripped, and in chains," said a man.

"Doubtless," said another.

"What a vengeance would be enacted upon her," said another.

"She betrayed her Home Stone," said another.

"Woe to the slut," laughed a fellow.

"Thousands before, hundreds even now, of bounty hunters," said a man, "in hundreds of towns and cities, in hundreds of hamlets and villages, seek the former Ubara, Talena of Ar."

"Never Ubara," said a man. "Never true Ubara."

"False Ubara," said another.

"And no longer of Ar," added another.

It was true that Talena was no longer of Ar, as she had betrayed its Home Stone. She was now without a Home Stone, a fugitive, no longer protected by law.

"Seriously, my friend," said the taverner, "do not joke about Talena. If it were even suspected she might be in Brundisium, a thousand tarnsmen of Ar might be aflight within an Ahn."

"Brundisium," said a fellow, "is not prized in the eyes of Ar, for it was here, to our very piers, that came fleets of Cos and Tyros."

"Brundisium is neutral," insisted the fellow in blue.

"We welcomed the foes of Ar," a fellow reminded him.

"We had no choice," said another.

"You were on the streets, waving," said another.

"It will take time for Ar to rebuild her power," said a fellow.

"Meanwhile," said another, "the larls of Thassa have returned to their lairs."

"Their snouts were well burned in the south," said another.

"Girl," said the stranger to the slave.

"Master?" she said.

"I shall not name you Talena," he said.

"Thank you, Master," she whispered. She briefly lost position, half fainting in relief, but she then recovered herself, quickly, and, straightening her back, maintained the beauty of *nadu*. She did keep her head down, perhaps fearing to look into the eyes of masters. It had been said she had not been long in the collar. To be sure, an intelligent woman learns it swiftly, and the more intelligent the more swiftly.

"I did but jest," he said to those about, "that I might sense your views, your moods, concerning Talena, once of Ar."

"May her flesh, bit by bit, be fed to sleen," said a man.

"May she be boiled alive in the oil of tharlarion," said another.

"May she be cast naked, bound, amongst leech plants," said another.

"I have seen Talena," said the stranger.

For a moment the group was silent.

"Of course," said the mercenary. "Thousands, hundreds of thousands, have seen her."

"In Ar," said a man.

"But none have seen her since her disappearance from Ar," said a man.

"I have," said the stranger.

"Where?" asked the taverner.

"—on the ship of Tersites," said the stranger.

"You have a story to tell," said the taverner.

"Yes," said the stranger.

"Put more oil in the lamp," said the taverner to his man, "and raise the wick."

"More paga," said the stranger to the girl, extending the damp, empty goblet to her.

She took the vessel and rose up, backing away, head down, then turning and hurrying to the paga vat.

In a few moments the stranger had renewed his paga, and looked about himself.

"Begin," said the taverner.

But his eyes were upon the girl.

She, perhaps from the silence, perhaps sensing his gaze, lifted her head, but, seeing his eyes upon her, quickly put down her head, again. Some masters do not permit their girls to look into their eyes, but that is rare. Most wish to relish the beauty of the eyes of their slaves, and enjoy reading in them the most delicate nuances of expression, apprehension, fear, hope, desire, expectation, questioning, readiness, eagerness, supplication, love, and such things.

"What lovely hair she has," said the stranger.

It was long, dark, and glossy. Yes, the little beast was nicely pelted. As she had allegedly not been long in the collar, I gathered that it must have been much that way even in her former life. I thought it interesting that a girl who must have once been free would have had such hair. Such hair is much favored in female slaves. It was such as might have been grown to enhance the beauty of a slave, grown to increase her slave beauty, grown to interest men, grown to make her more attractive to masters. I wondered if, in some corner of her mind, she had not, even when free, longed for masters. And she now, perhaps to her consternation, and terror, knelt before them, nude and collared.

"That is, in part, why I purchased her," said the taverner, "in the sales barn at Market of Semris."

Market of Semris is in the vicinity of Brundisium.

"You have sweet thighs," said the stranger to the girl.

"I am pleased, if master is pleased," she said.

He looked at her.

"Forgive me, Master," she said. "A slave is pleased, if master is pleased."

"Do not arouse the slave," whispered the taverner. He then said to the girl, "Keep the palms of your hands down on your thighs."

"Yes, Master," she said.

Sometimes a slave in *nadu* begs, turning her hands about,

placing the back of the hands on the thighs, this exposing the soft, delicate, sensitive palms of her hands to the master. It is a way of supplicating a caress. To be sure, there are many silent ways in which this may be done. The bondage knot, for example, might be looped loosely in her hair. Too, it is a simple matter for the girl to kneel, or belly, and lick and kiss the master's feet, daring to look up now and again in mute petition. Verbally, of course, the master's attention might be variously solicited, from tiny need noises to explicit phrases, such as "I would be reminded of my collar," "I would kiss the whip of my master," "Chain me," "Am I not to be bound tonight, Master," "A slave begs to be caressed," and such. And, of course, certain movements, postures, and such, sometimes subtle, are commonly enough to bring the master to her, rope in hand.

I recalled that the taverner had said that fires had begun to burn in her belly. Those, of course, would be slave fires. Perhaps it seems cruel to light such fires in a woman's belly, which will eventually make her their helpless prisoner, but it is not. First, how can a woman be a true woman whose belly is not periodically, irresistibly, needfully, helplessly aflame, begging for a man's touch. Second, this is not done with free women, of course, but only with slaves, as they are mere beasts, domestic animals, and it much improves them. Who would want a slave in whose belly slave fires did not burn? Such are the stoutest of chains.

"I do not know what we may hear," said a man.

"True," said another.

"Curiosity," said another fellow, quietly, "is not becoming in a *kajira*."

"True," said the taverner. "She need know nothing of these things. I will have her returned to her cage."

"Please, no, Master!" whispered the girl. Then she said, quickly, frightened, "Forgive me, Master."

She had spoken without permission.

"Let her stay," said the stranger."

The lapse was slight, and obviously inadvertent, and had been immediately, fearfully, penitently, corrected. Masters use judgment, and common sense. The breach, so natural and trivial, did not require discipline. It was not as though boldness, or intention, had been involved. The punishment of slaves, as that of other animals, kaiila and such, is used sparingly, and seldom without clear justification. Gratuitous cruelty is frowned upon, and seldom occurs on Gor. To be sure, the whip exists, and the slave knows it will be used upon her if she is not pleasing, and fully pleasing. She is, after all, a slave.

The girl looked up, gratefully. How alive, and inquisitive, the little brutes are in their collars. They want to know everything.

Too, she may have wished, nude and collared, to remain in the presence of the stranger. Certainly, the second time, in delivering paga, she had licked and kissed the cup, before lowering her head and extending it to him, with all the fervor and forward lasciviousness of a helplessly aroused *kajira*, begging to be found worthy of an alcoving. Too, she may have read something in the eyes of the stranger, when he had looked upon her, which shook her to the core. It may have been something simple, such as "I am a master. You are a slave."

"As you wish," said the taverner.

"Of course," said the stranger, "she is to be bound, hand and foot."

The taverner gestured to his man, and he took up the looped binding fiber which the slave had placed on the yellow, carefully folded camisk. In moments, her small wrists, crossed, had been bound behind her and her ankles, crossed, had been fastened together.

Briefly the slave squirmed a little, trying the fiber, and found herself, as she would have expected, the wholly helpless prisoner of its snug coils.

At a gesture from the stranger to the taverner's man the slave, nude, bound, and kneeling, was thrust back a little, a foot or two, rather outside the pool of light, rather into the shadowed darkness, presumably that her presence might be less obtrusive, and that she would better know herself for what she was, a woman and a slave.

"Speak," urged the taverner.

"Speak," said more than one man.

"I sailed on the great ship," said the stranger. "Yea, the ship of Tersites."

Chapter Two

This Occurred Betwixt Cos and Tyros

It was an awesome sight.

One feared it was a ship of no mortal creation, but rather a vessel of Priest-Kings, come from the clouds over the Sardar, gone on air. Yet, as our patrol craft had approached it, and we could more discern its make, it was seen to be clearly formed of wood, carvel-built, six-masted, single-ruddered, massively so, square-sailed.

We detected it first, by the glass of the Builders, from the stem castle, far off, through the fog, not clear, seemingly risen from the sea as might a mountain, as the islands that Thassa sometimes lifts from her bosom, in southern waters, with a roiling of waves, a casting of stones, and smoke and fire, when she pleases.

"It is a fortress, a city!" exclaimed the left helmsman.

"There can be nothing here," said the captain. "These are open waters. Familiar waters. We know them well."

"Take the glass, captain," said the lookout.

"It is an illusion," said the captain, "a lie whispered by the fog, the sea and wind."

"The glass, captain," insisted the lookout.

We were two days out from the port of Telnus, terraced Cos's southern window to the sea, our mother, mighty Thassa, on routine patrol.

We had heard no report, no rumors. Another day, and a junction with the long ships of Tyros, and we would return to Telnus.

No ship, no vessel, might ply these waters without papers, bearing the seal of either Tyros or Cos.

Thus are the farther islands sheltered, protected from illicit trade, and the wealth of Cos and Tyros conserved.

"It is no illusion," said the captain, his eye to the glass.

"What then?" asked his second officer, peering into the fog. The season was nearly over, the time when ships were taken from the water for their wintering, the time when rational mariners withdrew wisely from lashing, gleaming Thassa, leaving her, the mother, to her moods of violence, to her towering, rushing, lifting waves, higher than the masts of round ships, to her bitter storms and cruel ice.

We at the oars, free men all, for our vessel was a long ship, low in the water, knifelike, fit for war, were looking forward to our winter leave, and the paga and girls of the taverns, The Silver Chain, the Beaded Whip, the Pleasure Garden, the Chatka and Curla, the Ubar's Choice, and others.

"It is moving," said the captain. "It is no island, no mountain. It is afloat, moving, slowly, but moving."

"Can we overtake it?" asked the second officer.

"Yes," said the captain.

"Is it wise to do so?" said the second officer.

"I do not know," said the captain.

"There is a chill wind," said the second officer, gathering his cloak about himself.

We, two at an oar, above decks, wore gloves, for the wood was cold.

"Lower the mast," called the captain.

The single yard was lowered, and the storm sail furled. The mast and yard, with its furled sail, were then lashed down, parallel to the deck. On such ships, as you may know, there are various sails, whose use depends on the weather. The mast is lowered when the ship prepares for action. We were lateen-rigged, as is common, this allowing one to sail closer to the wind. In Torvaldsland, and to the north, it is common to use a single rudder, and a single sail, square-rigged.

The captain pointed toward the object in the distance, indistinct in the fog.

The two helmsmen brought us about.

Another gesture from the captain, this to the *keleustes*, increased the beat.

As the mast went down our fellows at the springals lit the bucketed fires in which the oil-soaked wrappings on javelin heads might be ignited.

On the long ship, as opposed to some round ships, one does not stand at the oar. And from the thwart, of course, one cannot, while at the oar, see much over the bulwarks. That is just as well, of course, for the bulwarks provide some protection from arrow fire, certainly from most long ships, which, like us, unlike many round ships, are low in the water. Even galleys with rowing frames have comparable shieldings. In any event, without standing, I could see very little, and one does not stand while at the oar, not on the long ship.

While I was at the oar, it would be well for you to understand, and I would have it understood, that I was not an oarsman, not by choice, not by calling, not by rating. One takes what fee one can when needful. I, once a spear of Cos, even a first spear, leader of nine men, with hundreds of others, after the trouble in Ar, scattered, separated from our commands and units, withdrew to Torcadino, and thence, bribing and spending, and then by recourse to brigandage and banditry, made our way by long marches to the sea, to the small coastal outposts and trading stations maintained by Tabor and Teletus, south of Brundisium, from which, with our last bit of silver, even to the surrender of accouterments and weapons, dispirited, hungry, and ruined, we obtained passage, mostly on fishing craft, little more than refugees, some to Tyros, most to Cos. I went first to Jad, city of my birth, city of great Lurius, our Ubar, where I had been enlisted and trained, but swords were plentiful there, and I was scorned, for my blade, with helmet and gear, was gone, having been bartered, in part, together with my last tarsk, for passage, for life, from the continent, and great Lurius, too, given the cessation of the draining of Ar's wealth, the drying up of that flowing stream of gold, was muchly displeased with the recent events on the continent, and ill-disposed to receive those whom he had once sent to the ships with stirring music and brave banners. Impoverished, weaponless, defeated, despised, and disgraced, those such as I would not be welcomed. We were an embarrassment, visible tokens of a state's shame. I sought fee then in Selnar, and Temos, but was no more fortunate. The defeat in the south, and the indignity of our retreat marked us, clinging to us as a stain. I became an itinerant laborer, concealing that I had once held rank amongst the spears of Cos. I lived as I could, earning what I might, in one town or another, a tarsk here, a tarsk there, and then it came to my attention, from a peddler come north, encountered in a tavern, that openings for oarsmen were being advertised in Telnus. The patrol fleet was being expanded, that the waters between Tyros and Cos might be better secured, better protected against unregulated shipping, this posing an unwelcome, yea, unacceptable, threat to the welfare and profits of our merchantry. And so it came about that I, who had been a spear of Cos, even a first spear, a leader of nine, who had served in the occupation of Ar, who had served even in the Central Cylinder itself, whose wallet had once been heavy with gold, who had walked proudly, who had been feared in the streets, whom none would dare accost, ventured to Telnus, hungry and destitute, seeking so modest a place as one on the thwarts of a patrol ship. Even so, many were the applicants for a single oar. Things were well in Cos for some, but less so for many. Where coin had been abundant, it was now scarce.

"We cannot use you," said the examiner.

"Whom might you use better?" I inquired.

"He," said the examiner, "and he," indicating two fellows.

"I think not," I said.

"Contest?" he asked.

"Yea," I said.

I grappled with each, one after the other, and was twice thrown, and bloodied. I had lost. I lay then on the ground, beaten, in pain, in the bloody mud.

But I heard some men about, striking their left shoulders.

I looked about. I did not see my opponents, who had seemed good fellows, vigorous and brawny, needful of a place, too. They must have gone to the table, to sign the articles, or make their marks upon them.

"You did not do badly," said a voice, by his insignia that of a harbor marshal.

I struggled to my feet.

"You are strong," he said. "When have you last eaten?"

"Two days ago," I said.

"Give him a place," said the marshal.

We plied our levers, at a ten-beat, which strong men can maintain for as much as an Ahn, and continued this beat for something like twenty Ehn, and then the *keleustes*, warned to silence, put aside his hammers. The ship drifted forward a bit, noiselessly, through the fog. Then it rocked in place. One could hear the water lapping against the hull.

There was no command to bring the oars inboard.

The beat need not be rung, of course, but may be called softly, from amidships, if appropriate.

But there was only silence.

Then there was a rift in the fog, like the sudden, whispering drawing aside of a curtain, but briefly.

"Aiii!" cried a man.

We stood then, at the thwarts, and first beheld her.

Then the fog again closed in. I did not think we were more than seventy-five yards from her.

It seemed we were a chip, floating on the sea, off the coast of some ponderous, drifting immensity.

"What is it?" asked a man.

"A ship," said a fellow. "A ship."

"Oars!" called the captain, and we resumed our position.

"Back oar," said the second officer, shuddering.

"No," said the captain. "Stroke!"

"Withdraw," urged the second officer.

"Stroke," called the captain.

We did not know if he were curious, courageous, or mad. I think he was a good officer.

The ship moved a little forward, but there was murmuring behind me and to the side, consternation, and I do not think that every oar was drawn. Had we been a round ship I think the lash would have fallen amongst us.

"If you must," said the second officer, "go closer, look, and then flee, but it is pointless, and none will believe your report."

"Stroke," called the captain.

It is rumored that there were gigantic dragons of the sea,

27

prodigious monsters, lurking beyond the farther islands, aquatic prodigies guarding the end of the world, set there by Priest-Kings, as one might post guard sleen about the perimeter of a camp, but this thing, in the glimpse we had had, was no water-shedding, surfacing monster, toothed and scaled, nothing alive, as least we commonly thought of life, nothing curious, jealous, and predatory.

"Your command will be taken," said the second officer.

"Stroke," called the captain, softly, peering into the fog.

"Desist, Captain, I beg of you," said the second officer.

The captain then was silent, listening.

The patrol ship was not large. She was a light galley, and she, though fitted with ram and shearing blades, was built more for speed and reconnaissance than fencing at sea, the ship the weapon itself. She was only some fifty foot Gorean from stem to stern, some ten feet in her beam. Such ships are less likely to engage a medium- or heavy-class galley than support such larger sisters in their altercations, perhaps hovering about, like a small sleen, awaiting an auspicious moment to take advantage of an otherwise distracted foe. We had only five oars to a side, and a rowing crew of twenty, two to each oar. Our common concern, or prey, were small boats, with a crew of four or five, tiny merchantmen, or smugglers, if you like, hoping to run the blockade to the farther islands. Larger galleys, rogues from the coastal ports, not signatory to the imposed treaties, or, more dangerously, pirates or merchantmen from Port Kar, our enemy, detected, would be reported to Telnus, in theory to be intercepted, if possible, on their return to their home ports. To be sure, interceptions were rare, and it was suspected that this had more to do with understandings and secret fees than faulty intelligence. Many high captains of both Tyros and Cos were wealthy men.

"There," whispered the lookout, suddenly, pointing.

"Ah!" breathed the captain.

The fog had parted, again, and we could see the monstrous structure, now some fifty yards abeam.

Clearly it was a ship. It was wood. It was carvel-built, the mighty planks fitted, not the clinker-construction with overlapping planks. That construction is common with the serpents of the north. It ships more water, but with its elasticity, with its capacity to shift, to twist and bend, it is less likely to break up in a heavy sea. The ship had six masts, apparently fixed, which suggested it was a round ship, which has fixed masts, and often more than one, say, two or three, though never so many as six. The round ship, with its size and weight, though oared, usually by galley slaves, chained to their benches, relies more on its sails than a long ship. Interestingly, though the ship was carvel-built it was square rigged, with tiered sails, on tiered yards. The square sail is an all-purpose sail, whose single canvas may be adjusted to the wind. The mighty structure before us had a blunt, rearing prow. It had no ram, no shearing blades. It would be slow to come about, and a small galley might easily outdistance her, much as a racing kaiila might easily overtake a caravan of bosk-drawn wagons. It was not built for war, but for space and power, for height and storage, perhaps for invulnerability. We did not know what cargo it might carry. In its holds it might carry the stores of a small city. Its maneuverability would be so sluggish that the deft adjustments of shearing blades, responsive to subtleties of the ship's movement, so common in the swift movements of Gorean naval warfare, would be impractical, if not impossible. Too, in such a mountain of wood there would be little use for a ram, as it would be of little use against a swifter, darting foe. To be sure, the ship itself would be formidable. It might plow through piers.

The fog then closed in again.

The great ship had been abeam.

The captain lifted his hand, and then lowered it.

We rocked, gently.

"Back oars," suggested the second officer. "Back oars!"

"No," said the captain.

I sensed he was alarmed. So, too, were we.

It was very quiet.

We were not sure, now, of the position of the great structure, or even if it were moving.

He called for no further stroke.

Then we heard the cry of a Vosk gull. These are large, broad-winged birds, which occasionally fish three and four hundred pasangs from the delta. Smaller gulls nest on the cliffs of both Tyros and Cos.

We did not see the bird.

It was then again quiet, save for the soft sound of water against the hull.

There was then another cry, but it was not the cry of the Vosk gull. It was a wild, shrill, ringing scream, unmistakable.

"That is a tarn!" cried a man.

"Impossible," said the captain.

Even with the fog we could not be so far off our course, or so confused. The tarn, you see, is a land bird, a hook-beaked, vast-winged, gigantic, crested, dreaded, fearsome monster of the skies. Its talons can clasp a kaiila and carry it aloft, to drop it to its death, thence to land and feed on the meat. Its most common prey is the delicate, flocking, single-horned tabuk. A single wrench of that mighty beak could tear the arm from a man. The tarn, you see, never flies from the sight of land. It could not be the cry of a tarn.

Then, again, we heard that shrill scream, as though at dawn, as it might announce itself to the sun, *Tor-tu-Gor*, as it might inform the world of the privacy and sanctity of its nesting site, as it might warn even larls away from its surveyed domain.

The tarn, it is said, is the Ubar of the sky.

So astonishing then that men, so tiny beside its bulk, might saddle and use such monsters as mounts! Such men are called tarnsmen.

"Back oars! Back oars!" cried the second officer, standing wildly at the port rail.

"Back oars!" screamed the captain.

We seized the oars but it was useless. There was no time, no time to even lift the blades from the water.

Emerging from the fog, literally upon us, suddenly visible, was the vast bulk of the great ship.

There was a wrenching of wood and the cries of men, and the stem and stern of the long ship began to rise out of the water, and the planking amidships, shattering, pressed down, sank into the sea, and then the stem, I clinging to it, collapsed back into the water, and doubtless, on the other side, for I could not see, given the obscuring passing of the vast, intrusive bulk, the stern did as well, and Thassa burst up, flooding the thwarts, and then the deck. I stood in a foot or two of cold, swirling water. My station was forward, and I suddenly, unwillingly, realized that I was now clinging to what was only a part of the ship, a recognition I somehow frenziedly fought against acknowledging, not wanting to see it, or understand it, that she had been snapped in two. As the monstrous bow of the great structure continued on its way, placidly, like a force of nature, the remains of the long ship were swept aside. I had heard, above the cries and the breaking wood, from the other side of the passing hull, the sudden ringing of springal boards speeding javelins, doubtless ignited, into the enemy. We were fighting back. But I heard them only once. The decks were awash. Clinging to a remnant of the bulwarks, half in water, I saw the hull of the monster towering above me, fifty feet or more, like a several-storied building of wood, a moving *insula*, wet and glistening, moving. This was some five times the height of a large round ship. In all the world no such a thing had been seen.

Surely this was no human thing, but a creation of the gods of Gor, of the Priest-Kings themselves.

How absurd to have fired flaming javelins at such a vessel. Might that not displease the Priest-Kings, the gods and masters of Gor?

I blinked my eyes, fiercely, to rid them of water. I shook my head, to get my sopped hair behind me. It was cold, clinging to the bit of wreckage. I saw no one about me. I called out, but was not answered.

Then I thought, "No, the Priest-Kings would not build such mortal frames, and, if so, not of wood. Stories had it that they rode within ships, but strange ships, round, flat ships, like disks, disks of metal, which moved like clouds, swift as thought, in silence. Some claimed to have seen them over the palisade of the Sardar. But such stories must be false, as they were denied by Initiates, the white caste, highest and worthiest of all the castes, as they were intermediaries between Priest-Kings and mortals. How wise they were, and how powerful they were, how sacrosanct and holy they were, to have the ear of Priest-Kings, to have at their disposal the prayers, the spells, the rituals, the devotions, and sacrifices by means of which Priest-Kings might be swayed, by means of which their favor might be garnered. It was no wonder that that they were consulted by Ubars bearing baskets of gold, and simple Peasants, with a handful of suls. They were celebrated by cities and villages. They were petitioned by Merchants embarking on bold, uncertain ventures, by gamblers with an interest in the summer tharlarion races. Assassins sought their blessing. Some of the loveliest buildings on Gor were their temples. They lived well. They were frauds, laden with corruption.

I thought I heard the oars of a galley, a light galley, not much different from the patrol ship.

It must be a long ship of Tyros, come early to our rendezvous!

"Ho!" I cried.

"Ho!" I heard, in return, to my elation, some yards away, through the fog.

"Here, here!" I cried. "I am here! Hurry!"

I spat out water, and shook my head. My eyes stung from the water. Water swept over the wreckage, and then drained from it, again and again. I was often immersed. My hands slipped on the bit of railing I held. With my teeth I pulled off the heavy, water-filled oar gloves. Within them my fingers seemed frozen. I thrust the fingers of one hand into my mouth, and then those of my other hand, for a modicum of warmth. It was late in the season, and the waters were cold, and I knew not how long I or another, in the sweep and washing of the water, might be able to cling to so negligible a support. I dug my fingers into the ornate external carving on the wreckage. I was half in the water, half out of the water, on the wet, washed, sloping surface.

"Here, here!" I cried. "I am here!"

I heard some oars being indrawn, through the thole ports.

The sound was close!

"Call out," I heard. "Call out!"

"Here, here!" I cried. The voice I had heard had clearly the accents of Tyros, or Cos, which accents are much the same, many times even indistinguishable.

Then, the fog parting, momentarily, I saw, looming above me, passing, a large, painted eye, black on yellow, that behind the small galley's downward sloping, concave prow, such eyes that she may guard herself and see her way, for as those who follow the sea are well aware, the ship is a living thing, and without eyes how might she see? Without eyes how might she guard herself or hers, how find her way? She is not an object, but a fellow, a colleague, a friend, a companion, a lover, one with whom one shares an endeavor or an adventure, one to whom one entrusts oneself. She stands between you and the deep, cold waters of Thassa. She will not lie to you, or betray you. She will not cheat you or steal from you. She will never forsake you for another. She speaks to you in the creaking of her timbers, in the snapping of her sails, and the cracking of her lines.

Her hull was low in the water, and blue.

"Ho!" I called.

Blue is the common color of Cos.

Odd that a Cosian long ship, another Cosian long ship, would be in these waters. The ship, reassuringly, was not green, for pirates often paint their ships green, that they be the less seen on mighty, rolling Thassa. Many of the vessels of Port Kar, that den of thieves and cutthroats, that scourge of Thassa, were green, almost invisible, under oars, low in the water, the mast down.

"I see you!" called a voice.

Yes, clearly the accent was reassuring!

The galley back-oared on the port side. Her starboard oars were mostly indrawn, or still. The stroke of one of those levers can kill a man.

The hull of the galley was within two or three yards, and a wharfing pole thrust over the bulwarks, toward me. The common galley usually carries three wharfing poles, for pushing away from a wharf, until oars can obtain their purchase. One is usually used at the bow, the second amidships, the last at the stern. They are also used to adjust wharfage, until the lines are snug to the wharf cleats. In battle they help to prevent boardings, keeping another ship at bay until grappling hooks might be dislodged. I seized the pole and pulled myself to an unsteady footing on the wreckage.

"Steady," said a voice.

I was shuddering and freezing, weak with misery and cold.

"Closer," said the voice. "Good, good."

The pole was being drawn inward, I lost my footing and my

feet were in the water. Then to the waist. I clung to the pole. It was being drawn toward the railing, and lifted. I was afraid I could not hold to the pole. I was afraid, half frozen, and numb, that I would lose the pole, and fall back into the water. A hand was outstretched, over the vessel's side, it rocking, toward me.

I grasped it, gratefully, in the seaman's grip, wrist to wrist.

"Hail Cos!" I cried. "Hail mighty Lurius of Jad! Hail Tyros! Hail Chenbar, Ubar of Tyros!"

I was then drawn over the rail, and held in strong arms.

"Hail Cos," I said. "Hail Tyros!"

"Hail Marlenus of Ar," said a voice. "Hail Glorious Ar," said another voice.

"Ar?" I said.

"Strip and bind him," I heard.

I was thrown on my belly to the deck between the thwarts. My wrists were then jerked behind me and my ankles crossed, and I was bound, swiftly, expertly, by two men, hand and foot. My clothing was then cut away and cast over the side.

I lay on the deck between the thwarts, naked, and freezing. I squirmed a bit, fighting the ropes, but my struggles were unavailing. I was prone, between the thwarts, naked and bound, helplessly bound.

I felt a foot on my back. I was pressed down to the deck. "Lie still," said a voice.

I ceased struggling.

The foot was then removed from my back.

"Is he well tied?" asked a voice.

"Yes," said a voice, "he is as helpless as a trussed vulo, or a female slave."

I cried out with rage, and fought the ropes. How furious I was that they had dared to compare my helplessness with that of a bound female slave, a domestic animal, thigh-marked and neck-encircled, a man's purchasable, obedient, whip-fearing work beast and pleasure toy! My efforts were met with laughter. I then lay quietly on the deck, angry and sullen, helpless, as helpless as a trussed vulo, or, I suppose, a female slave.

I was their prisoner.

"Return to the ship," said a man.

Chapter Three

**I Am Interviewed;
What Occurred Prior to My Interview;
I Have Renewed an Acquaintance**

"Keep your head down," said the voice.

I stared at the flooring.

This was now my fourth day on the great ship. I knew, as yet, little about the ship. I did not know her course. I had not been on the main deck. I had been entered into the ship, naked and freezing, my ankles unbound, to permit me to walk, as I could, by means of a side port, of a size and sort with which I was utterly unfamiliar. The galley was nested within the hull itself, which opened to accommodate her, the galley being lifted and swung inboard by means of lines and davits. I suppose this, in its way, is not that much different from the common beaching of Gorean galleys at night, drawn ashore by their crews, as many Gorean seamen do not care to be at sea after the fall of darkness. I would later learn there were six such side ports, three on each side, each accommodating a light galley. In this fashion the light galleys were concealed within the great ship, in such a way that they would not be exposed to missile fire and might be expeditiously launched. For example, in this fashion, the great ship could use them as concealed, surprise weapons, releasing them on a side not visible to an enemy, or, say, applying them at night; similarly, such ships might facilitate reconnoitering, facilitate communication with the shore, provide vessels for obtaining supplies, and such. Indeed, shore-bound intelligence might not realize a mother ship existed, let alone one such as the great ship. There were many applications for such vessels. They could be used for fishing, by line, or net and trident, for boarding, looting, enslaving, and such. Also, they might be launched, if one wished, to dispose of witnesses, a practice favored by some pirates, or, as noted, to pick up survivors, following an action.

Once I had been lifted over the rail of the galley and handed to others, my ankles had been unbound, and I had been blindfolded. I was then led, supported by two fellows, for I could barely walk, through a maze of passages, and then descended for two levels. I heard a variety of accents, several of which I could not place. Several were clearly those of the islands, though some were more akin to those of the continent. I recognized, too, the accents of Ar, as I was familiar with them, from my time in the Ar, during the occupation. I had feared that my captors might have been of cities hostile to Cos and Tyros, but now, as the accents of all, those of the islands and the continent, seemed those of free men, and lacked the softness, deference, and submissiveness of slaves, I gathered that my captors were of diverse origins. I was thus, I supposed, the captive of pirates, for pirate crews are often diversely origined, often recruited from a medley of cast-offs, fugitives, ruffians, murderers, brigands, and such. This surmise, as it turned out, was substantially correct, but was inexact, and over simple. Better put, they were lost men, scattered men, hunted men, men with few resources, outlaws, vagabonds, wanderers, many without a Home Stone, perhaps even having dishonored or betrayed it, rude men, rough men, dangerous men, mercenaries, of a sort, recruited by mysterious leaders, in an obscure cause, which few understood. Why had they not left me to drown? Had they been of vengeful Ar, would they not have cut my throat and put me, bleeding, over the side of the galley? What could they want of me? I could not pretend to be of background, a fellow replete with rich connections, for whom a splendid ransom might be paid. Clearly my hands were roughened from the oar. And, as an oarsman, I would have little if any information pertaining to rich cargoes and secret schedulings. Clerks would know more of that than I. Perhaps they wanted news of the world. Surely it seemed they had their own world, their own city, a floating island of wood. Perhaps they knew as little of the world as the world knew of them. Given the treatment to which I had been subjected, my stripping, and binding, and blindfolding, it seemed clear that I would not be offered the opportunity to sign articles with them, and make one with them, even were I willing, even eager, to do so. And would they not view me as their enemy, for did our ship not fire upon their mountain of wood when it trod, however unwittingly, upon our vessel? I had heard the harsh crackings, marking the launching of sets of javelins, doubtless ignited. We had tried to burn their ship, and how fearsome and dangerous is fire at sea! Too, how could I betray the Home Stone of Jad, or forswear my allegiance to my Ubar, mighty Lurius of Jad? And how could I serve with those of Ar or, say, Port Kar, sworn enemies? Of what value could I be to these men? What might they want of me? Perhaps there were free women on board, and one or another wished to amuse herself with a male silk slave. But I was not such a slave. I heard a metal gate open, and I was conducted within. There was straw underfoot. They sat me down and unbound my hands. Two blankets were pressed to me and I clutched them gratefully. The blindfold was then removed. I was in a small cell, but not the sort of stall, kennel, or cage in which a female slave is kept. In it I might stand upright, and move about. It was not, then, the sort of device, or housing, in which a female slave, designedly, is well apprised of her bondage. Outside the cell, there was a tiny tharlarion-oil lamp, which swung with the motion of the ship. The cell was in some sort of hold, or division of a hold. It was not the only cell in the hold, but it was the only one with an occupant. I wrapped myself in the two blankets and, shivering, burrowed down in the straw.

I had not been killed, as yet, at least. What might they want of me, if anything?

I do not know how long I slept.

I heard no bars, marking the four watches, each of five Ahn, into which the day of a round ship is often divided. A bar signifies the beginning of a watch, struck once, twice for the second Ahn of the watch, and so on. The first watch begins with the commencement of the day's first Ahn, the second with the sixth Ahn, the third with the eleventh Ahn, and the fourth with the sixteenth Ahn. The final division of the fourth watch commences with the twentieth Ahn. Interestingly, at least to those unaccustomed to the routine of the round ship, the bars which do not pertain to one are scarcely noticed, no more than the creaking of timbers, the wash of waves against the hull. One is not likely to much notice, and may easily sleep through, bars which do not pertain to one's watch, but note, and even awaken to, a bar pertinent to one's own watch. The bars are usually unobtrusive. The consistent, repetitive ringing of a bar is a signal of alarm, a sound much dreaded. To be sure, not all round ships regulate their day in this fashion. Some differences occur, port to port, Ubarate to Ubarate. Some round ships do not have recourse to bars, at all, but use clepsydras, sand glasses, and such, to mark watches, and use watch keepers to alert or rouse the pertinent watch. In this way the ship may move in silence. For example, watch bars are not used on a long ship, a ship of war. On such ships bars may, however, serve other purposes, signaling and such. On some ships they time the stroke of oars, but this is more commonly done by mallets on a copper-headed drum, or, if silence is in order, by calling the beat, from amidships. As mentioned, I heard no bars. This suggested to me, but did not prove, that this mysterious, monstrous vessel in which I found myself encelled, despite its size, was not a round ship, or, better, not a round ship as one usually thinks of such ships. At that time I understood neither its purpose nor nature. I did know it was capable of destroying a long ship, riding over it as though it did not even exist.

"Master?" I heard.

I opened my eyes, and rose to a sitting position, cross-legged, in the straw, the blankets down, so that my arms were free. The gate to the cell was open, swung back. I saw nothing beyond it but the wall of the hold, the steps which had led down to this level, the small tharlarion-oil lamp on its chain, moving a bit with the rhythm of the ship. There was no guard behind her, but I did not doubt that one had opened the gate for her, and had then withdrawn. Such as she are not trusted with keys. The gate would lock, if swung shut. It would have been nothing to strike her aside and exit the cell, but there was, in effect, no point in doing so. The vessel at sea, flight would be foolish.

Where would one go? Where would one hide? I would remain where I had been placed, at least for now. I must learn more. I must have more information. Those who had incarcerated me, I realized, assumed my likely judgment in this matter. I found this gratifying. In its way, it said they did not think it likely that I was stupid. In its way, it was a token of respect. I had been given enough time to sleep, to recuperate, to become better aware of my position, and my dependence on the will of others. I might have taken her in hand, but she would have little value as a hostage, as she was an animal, and not one of particular value. Her loss could be replaced indifferently with that of any one of a dozen, or hundred, similar beasts. It would be much like trying to bargain with a verr or vulo in hand. Who would take one seriously?

"Master," she said, seeing my eyes upon her, "may I approach? I bear nourishment."

"Yes," I said.

In her two hands she bore a bowl.

"Broth," she said.

"There," I said, brushing some straw aside, and indicating where she might place the bowl, before me.

She approached, insufficiently humbly I thought.

She bent down.

She started. The bowl had suddenly jerked, and broth had leapt in the bowl, some of it running down the side of the bowl, some spilling to the wood. She looked suddenly frightened. Such as she could be whipped for clumsiness.

"There," I said again, indicating, again, the place before me.

She placed the bowl before me. She now looked down, and to the side, hiding her face from me.

She then rose up, and facing me, for she knew that much, backed away. She seemed eager to withdraw.

"Wait," I said, as one speaks to such as she.

She then stood back from me, facing me, her head down.

I had no interest in punishing her. She was not even mine. I supposed she was part of the ship's furniture, so to speak. I was curious as to why she had started so.

"You know me?" I asked.

"Surely I could not know you," she said.

I looked up at her. Something seemed familiar about her. Was it her voice?

"May I withdraw, Master?" she asked.

"No," I said.

Her body stiffened, but she remained in place.

"Stand as what you are," I said.

"Please, Master!" she protested.

"As what you are," I repeated. "You have been taught, have you not?"

She then stood well, lithe and lissome, supple and graceful, her back straight, her shoulders back, her hip turned.

I examined her lines. I would have guessed a silver tarsk and change.

In such as she slovenly posture is not accepted. Before men such as she must stand well, move well, and such. If they do not the lash will see to their correction.

"Lift you head," I said.

She complied, but with obvious reluctance. Surely she knew that in such as she acquiescence was to be unquestioning and instantaneous.

"Do I not know you?" I asked.

"Surely not, Master," she said.

She must remain before me, of course, as she was, as I had placed her.

She wore a brief ship's tunic, sleeveless, brown, slit at the hips, with a deep neckline, a feature by means of which certain aspects of her value might be the more helpfully assessed.

"Come here," I said to her, "kneel before me."

"Please, Master!" she protested.

"Now," I said.

"Good," I said.

She knelt with her knees closely together, clenched together. The palms of her hands were down, on her thighs.

"Now lean forward."

"Master," she protested.

"Must a command be repeated?" I asked.

"No," she said, frightened. The repetition of a command is often cause for discipline.

She leaned forward, and, as I gestured, even more so, and

I took her chin gently in my hand and then, I, too, leaning forward, lifted her head, and then turned her head from side to side.

I then released her, and sat back.

I laughed, and she drew back, and buried her face in her hands and wept.

"I thought I recognized your voice," I said. "Too, as I recall, you were occasionally careless in your toilette, your veil, more than once, as though inadvertently, being disarranged. You did that to torment us, the lower soldiers, did you not?"

She was silent.

"What do they call you here?" I asked.

"Alcinoë," she said. "I hate the name! I hate it! It is a Cosian name."

"It is a lovely name," I said. "And I am Cosian. My Home Stone is that of Jad."

She before me was the former Lady Flavia of Ar, who had been one of the inner circle of the Ubara, Talena of Ar. I recognized her, from my duties in the Central Cylinder, during the occupation.

"I suspect," I said, "you were on the proscription lists posted in Ar, following the restoration of Marlenus."

The fear in her face confirmed this speculation.

"Do not betray me," she begged.

"I shall have to think about it," I said.

"I was of high caste, of high family, of position and importance, of influence, wealth, and power, and now," she sobbed, "I have this!" Her eyes filled with tears, and she put the fingers of her right hand to the flat, sturdy, metal band which closely encircled her throat.

How lovely such devices are, closely clasping and locked, on the neck of a female! How they enhance a woman's beauty!

What she said was surely true, and she, in the company of the Ubara, Talena of Ar, was an arch collaborator with the occupation forces in Ar. She, and many others like her, both men and women, had been involved in the conspiracy by means of which Ar had fallen, in the opening of Ar's gates, in the razing of her walls, in the machinations by means of which Ar had been subdued and looted for months. She, as others who were confidantes of

41

the Ubara, had become rich in the profiteering attendant on the occupation, as in controlling the supply and distribution of goods, in private marketing, in illicit trade, in the peddling of influence, and the selling of favors. Bribery and corruption had been rampant and those with the ear of the Ubara, those on whom she might choose to smile, prospered, while the common citizenry suffered, struggled to live, knew fear and uncertainty, peril and want, and must endure the contumely and abuse not only of undisciplined, garrisoning soldiers but of wandering bands of uncontrolled, wayward youths who, scorning their own Home Stone, affected the habits, accents, and styles of Ar's masters. Too, Talena, in the name of due tribute, the meting out of justice, the garnerings of recompenses for Ar's alleged crimes, and such, had used her power to bring many of the free women of Ar into the collar, to be transported abroad, to Cos, Tyros, and elsewhere, as slaves. Indeed, the Ubara had used this device to avenge herself on many free women, who might have scorned her during her sequestration under Marlenus, or might merely have been alleged as rivals to the Ubara in the way of beauty. Claudia Tentia Hinrabia, once the daughter of an Administrator of Ar, was one such. She was given as a slave to Myron, the *polemarkos* of Temos, who, behind the throne, was the actual power in Ar. Other beauties of Ar were put in the taverns and brothels, several of which the Ubara owned and managed under the false name of Ludmilla. The Lady Flavia, too, I knew, had, by means of her influence with the Ubara, seen to it that various of her peers, perceived enemies or rivals, were publicly stripped and consigned to the chains of slaves. During the course of the uprising, the restoration, even in the midst of fighting, angry crowds had sought out traitors and collaborators, and brought them, bound and screaming, to improvised impaling spears. Proscription lists were publicly posted, containing the names of many traitors and collaborators yet to be caught and brought to the justice of the spear. I had no doubt but that the name of the Lady Flavia occurred on more than one such list.

"You were close to the Ubara," I said. "Doubtless you know her fate."

"Doubtless there is a reward for her," she said.

"Very much so," I said.

"And you would like to obtain the reward."

"Who would not?" I asked. Actually I thought it highly unlikely that a single individual could bring Talena to Ar. It might require negotiation, and the backing of a city. Otherwise the Ubara, captive, might change hands, from brigand to brigand, a dozen times before being brought before the Ubar's throne.

"May I inquire the extent of the reward?" she asked.

"May I inquire the extent of the reward—what?" I said.

"May I inquire the extent of the reward—*Master*?" she said.

"No," I said.

Her body tightened and a flicker of annoyance flashed upon those somewhat haughty, but exquisite features.

I gathered she did not yet know what she was, except doubtless in some practical or legal sense. It was not yet understood in every fiber of her body, and, helplessly, profoundly, as it would eventually be, in the most remote recesses of her heart. She did not yet think herself, regard herself, recognize herself, know herself, and feel herself, as what she now was, wholly, and truly. She thought of herself as a free woman in a collar, and not yet as a natural, rightful slave, at last appropriately, publicly collared.

"You were close to the Ubara," I said.

"None closer," she said.

"You were her confidante?"

"Yes," she said.

"You were, I gather, the dearest of friends," I said.

"I hated her," she said.

"But doubtless you dissembled friendship, and such," I said.

"I do not know her whereabouts," she said.

"Would you tell me if you knew?" I asked.

"I do not know her whereabouts," she said.

"You do not know her fate?"

"No," she said, "—Master."

I picked up the bowl of broth, and sipped some. It was still warm, and I was grateful for it. I regarded her over the brim of the bowl.

"May I withdraw?" she said.

"No," I said. Such as she does not leave the presence of a free person without permission, either implicit or explicit.

"Tell me the last you know of the Ubara," I said.

I saw she was reluctant to speak. I supposed that she would be one of a small number of individuals, the inner circle, who might have been in the vicinity of the Ubara, prior to her escape, or disappearance. I did not doubt, really, that she was ignorant of the location of the Ubara, as she proclaimed. Had she not been, she might have tried, foolishly, to barter that information for her freedom. So little she knew of the import of her collar! One does not bargain with slaves. In a Gorean court the testimony of slaves is commonly taken under torture. A slave who attempts to bargain is commonly punished, usually with the lash. If a slave possesses information of interest to masters she is expected to communicate it promptly. Failure to do so is cause for discipline. A slave who has had the insolence and temerity to attempt to bargain with masters may hope, after her punishment, which is likely to be severe, that her life may be spared.

"Where did you see her last?" I asked.

"Must I speak?" she asked.

My eyes conveyed my answer.

"You will not believe my words," she said. "I scarce credit them myself, and I saw, or seemed to see, what occurred."

"Continue," I said, taking another sip of the broth.

"It was on the fourth day of the uprising," she said. "Those of Ar had risen, everywhere, it seemed, from doorways and cellars, from within the cylinders and on the bridges, rushing forth, seizing up as weapons things so simple as clubs, poles, staves, and rocks, overwhelming in their numbers even armed men."

We had done our best, of course, we of the occupation, to disarm the populace, pretending this to be in their own best interest, that in this way they would be better protected, that in this way they would be assuring their own safety, security, and welfare. And so might the small, yellow, single-horned tabuk be persuaded to abandon its one weapon, that it might thus be safer amongst prowling sleen. It is important that the subject population be as helpless as possible, that it be unable to defend itself, that those sovereign in the state may thus impose their will, their exactions and abuses, with impunity upon it, having then nothing to fear from the weak, the disarmed, the unprotected, and defenseless. But we had not reckoned with Marlenus of Ar, that he might return. What had been begun by the Delta Brigade, that hated, secret band of subversives, the resistance, implacable to the occupation, came openly alive and flaming with the sudden reappearance of Marlenus of Ar, Ubar of Ubars. It was as though the Delta Brigade had spread an anticipatory terrain of tinder and oil throughout the streets of Ar, into which great Marlenus, come somehow to the city, flung the torch of revolution. His hand seemed visible everywhere. Truly had the banner of Ar been unfurled."

I myself, with my unit, had been withdrawn from the Central Cylinder on the second day of the uprising. It would have been madness to have stayed longer, certainly in the Cylinder, which, given its location, could be easily cut off from reinforcements. We would be besieged in an alien citadel, without support, in the midst of enemies. Who could one trust? We would have been outnumbered by dozens to one, hundreds to one. The camp of the *polemarkos* had already been overrun. Initially it had been surmised the rebellion would be easily suppressed, but soon its extent and power became fearfully obvious. This was no sporadic thing, easily put down with a few blows. This was no simple riot, spontaneous and disorganized, as one protesting the burning of a shop, a scarcity in the markets. Happily the occupation had overseen the dismantling of the walls of Ar. We avoided, as we could, the avenues and boulevards, and sought small streets, away from the shouts of men and the sounds of war, the ferocity of rude battle, and made our way to the *pomerium*, no longer marked by walls and towers. By dusk we were in the countryside. Only later were we to reconstruct what had occurred, the pockets of our resistance, overcome one by one, the decimated retreats, the slaughterings, the terror, the blood, the hunting of traitors and collaborators, the joining of the forces of Ar, maintained during the occupation, to the uprising, the appearance of never-surrendered, concealed weapons, many brought back from the delta, by returning veterans of the Delta Expedition, the contributions of Peasants, masters of the great bow, who had apparently unwittingly sheltered Marlenus prior to the uprising, the numerous proscriptions, the reenthronement of Marlenus, and such.

"You were still in the city, on the fourth day of the rebellion?" I said.

"Yes," she said.

"Why would I not believe what you might say?" I asked.

"It was the fourth day of the uprising," she said. "We had sealed off the upper floors of the Central Cylinder. We were on the roof of the Central Cylinder. Seremides, master of the Taurentians, the palace guard, was in command. There were some forty of us, men and women. Many of the Taurentians had fled, been killed, or captured. Seremides was attempting to negotiate with the rebels. They seemed little interested in his proposals. There were tarns on the roof, by means of which Seremides, and some of his men, might attempt their escape, a hope meager but not forlorn, for the sky is wide and deep. We had been told there would be tarn baskets for the women, but when I emerged on the roof, I saw no such baskets. Seremides had so bespoke himself, it seems, to calm our fears. His power of bargaining, as he saw it, was vested in his control of the Ubara herself. He intended to trade her for the escape of himself and his men. You should have seen the proud Ubara on the roof. Seremides had had her don a slave tunic, and you know what such things are."

"Yes," I said, "I see one."

She perhaps referred to the extraordinary brevity of such a garment, its capacity to cling to a slave's body, its brazen scantiness, its shameful display of the slave's body as that of the animal she is, the lack of a nether closure, that she may know herself at the pleasure of masters, and such.

"And he knelt her, roped, at his thigh, barefoot, with her head down. It much pleased me to see the Ubara on her knees, beside a man, helpless in ropes, her head down, refused permission to raise it, as though a submitted slave."

"Why would he so shame the Ubara," I asked, "remove her robes of state, her veiling, and such?" I asked.

"I think for two reasons," she said. ""First, he wanted it to seem that he understood the uprising, even favored it, even shared its views, and was thus discountenancing the Ubara and her policies, for which he had held a secret animus for months, and, to show his allegiance to the uprising, had taken the tyranness prisoner, and was now willing, for certain considerations, his life, and that of his men, and perhaps a bag of gold, to surrender her, clad and shamed as she was, to the justice of Ar."

She had paused.

"And there was perhaps a second reason," I said.

"I think so," she said. "Are not men beasts?"

"It is true they are men," I said.

Are not women beautiful, and desirable? Who has not seen them in the paga taverns, stripped or silked? Who has not admired them in an exposition cage, on the auction block, under torchlight? Is it not pleasant to see them slave clad and collared, in the parks, on the boulevards, in the markets? Is it not delightful to see them being walked, back-braceleted and leashed, or chained at slave rings, awaiting the return of their masters? What man, truly, does not want to own a beautiful woman, to have her in his collar and at his feet?

"The negotiations, I take it," I said, "did not go well." Certainly, it seemed clear that Talena was not in the custody of the authorities of Ar.

"They might have gone well," she said. "But they did not even begin. Those of Ar did not care to deal. There were mobs in the streets. There was no discipline. They wanted blood."

"Were you not tunicked, knelt, and bound, on the roof?" I asked.

"Certainly not," she said. "I was in my fullness of regalia, in robes, hoods and veils. It was Talena, not I, who was shamefully exhibited, as might have been a slave. Indeed, it was I who found the Ubara cowering in her quarters and led the men to her. It was I who, at the behest of Seremides, cast her the rag of a slave, and bade her don it, and expeditiously, or the men would see to the matter. It gave me pleasure to scorn her pleadings and refuse her piteous supplications for succor. Did she truly think I was her friend? When, to her shame she divested herself of her robes, hoods, veils, and sandals, and was slave clad, I called to the men, 'She is ready. Bring your ropes!' On the roof, we knew the rebels were approaching. We could see rebel tarnsmen in the sky. 'Where is the tarn basket?' I cried to Seremides. 'What is to become of me?' He answered not. I seized his sleeve, but he brushed me aside, and I fell to the flooring of the cylinder's roof.

We could hear the anthem of Ar in the streets below. We knew that rebels within the cylinder would shortly reach the roof. 'Slay the Ubara!' called a man, holding tarn reins, to Seremides. 'Show thus your allegiance to Ar!' Seremides drew his sword. But then the strangeness took place, which I doubt that you will believe."

I addressed myself again to the broth.

"It could only have been the intervention of Priest-Kings," she said.

I did not speak.

"There was a sudden darkness," she said, "as though a dark cloud had suddenly enveloped the cylinder, or its roof. We cried out in consternation. Two of the tarns screamed and one broke away, in flight. 'Where is the Ubara?' cried Seremides. He seemed to be casting about. It could have been a moonless midnight, suddenly precipitated. I felt my robes seized, wildly, and sensed a blade at my cheek. 'I am Flavia!' I cried. 'Flavia!' I was thrust back down. Then there was a sudden blast of light, obliterating the darkness, blinding us, and it seemed, when we could see, that a large metal object, I think thick and circular, was disappearing in the distance."

"And the Ubara?" I asked.

"Gone," she said.

I have attained to the Second Knowledge, but this made little sense to me. It seemed obvious that such an ensuance could be explained, if at all, only in terms of a sky ship, and, such, if it existed, would presumably emanate from the Sardar, allegedly the abode of Priest-Kings. Her story was so untoward and bizarre I thought it not likely she would be lying. If it were a lie, it would be a most improbable lie. Too, such as she could be punished severely for lying. They are not free women, who may lie with impunity. Too, to such an event, there must have been a number of witnesses, not only on the roof, but in the sky, tarnsmen, others in cylinders and on bridges, the crowds in the street below, and such.

"When it became clear that Talena was gone," she said, "Seremides and his men, finding their situation critical, took to desperate flight. I reached for the mounting ladder of Seremides' tarn, but it was jerked away, and, in a moment, I was in the shadow of those great beating wings, the bird lifting itself, scarcely able to keep my footing, my robes and veils whipping about me, and then the monster was in flight, and Seremides, and his men, were streaking away, scattering, pursued by tarnsmen."

"Did Seremides escape?" I asked.

"I do not know," she said.

"How is it that you are here?" I asked. "How did you escape from Ar?"

"I found myself alone on the roof," she said. "The other women, knowing themselves not so highly placed as I, the high confidante of the Ubara, and thus less likely to be borne to safety, and there being no tarn baskets, as noted, had fled the roof, descending into the cylinder to meet whatever fates might be theirs. I resolved to put into action a bold plan, one I had conceived as a last, fearful resort, if all seemed lost, to be executed before the upper levels of the cylinders were attained. I descended to my apartment, but two levels below. I summoned my five sandal slaves, ordered them into an open side compartment, and had them bind, gag, and blindfold one another, I attending to the last. They would not be able to see what I did, nor would they be able to speak, until relieved of their gags. I then went to a small panel in my chamber of couching, slid back the panel, and removed from it a tiny, secret chest, which I feverishly unlocked. Within this chest, as a last, desperate resort, I had placed a slave tunic and collar, the key to which I might conceal in the tunic's hem. I shuddered to even touch such things, the garment tiny and flimsy, the collar light but so imminently practical and efficient, with its tiny, sturdy lock, which went at the back of the neck. I removed the small handful of jewels from my pouch, which treasure I had intended to bear with me in my escape, and concealed them, together with the collar key, within the tunic, in a specially prepared, interior sleeve. I smoothed them about, so their presence would not be evident. I heard pounding at an outer door. I tore away my robes and veils and thrust them beneath the covers of the couch. I dared to look upon myself in the mirror, and I recognized, though not with my customary pleasure and composure, that I was quite beautiful. Momentarily I feared I might never be able to pass as a slave, being far too beautiful."

"Continue," I said.

"In moments I had donned the tunic. I snapped the collar about my neck. I shuddered as I did so. How meaningful must that sound be to a woman who realizes she is now collared, truly. I reassured myself, pressing it with my fingers, against my leg, that the key was at hand, concealed within the tunic. Again I looked into the mirror, and the thought crossed my mind, horrifying me, that I might be found of interest by men. How worthless and disgusting are slaves! How lustful men seek them so! I was profoundly disturbed, terrified, to see my neck in a collar. I seemed transformed, to be something totally other than I had been. How men might see a woman in such a device! I feared I knew! I was terrified, and furious, that I, a free woman, might be seen as a slave, but, at the same time, I was terrified that I might not be seen as a slave, for my life itself might well depend on the success or failure of this deceit. How could I, with my beauty, so far beyond that of a slave, pass as a slave? But I must do my best. Such was my only hope. On the fourth day of the uprising we were well aware of affairs in the streets below, and the proscription lists, and I had learned my name stood high on the lists, not far below those of Talena, Seremides, and others."

"Surely," I said, "you had concealed funds, weightier, more ample treasures, coffers of gold, or such, about the city, to provide you with a larger wherewithal of escape?"

"No," she said. "We did not anticipate the return of Marlenus, the uprising. Too, as it turned out, I would not have been able to reach them, and, had I been able to reach them, it would have been difficult, or impossible, to transport them from the city."

"True," I said.

"Jewels," she said, "must do, what I could easily carry, place in a pouch."

"Or conceal in a tunic," I said.

"Yes," she said.

"So you would escape in the disguise of a slave," I said.

"Yes," she said. "Who would note me? I feared only that my

beauty would betray me, that men, if perceptive, might note that it was far beyond that of a mere slave."

I found her views interesting. One of the highest compliments one can pay a free woman, though perhaps not to her face, is that she is "slave beautiful." Commonly it is only the most beautiful of women who are brought into the collar. After all, one wants to sell them.

"So," she said, "well disguised, and bearing riches, I would make my way to freedom."

"I see," I said.

I wondered if she knew that that ruse, feigning bondage, was not unprecedented amongst free women in straits, for example, in a burning city, being sacked, and such. And I supposed that she did not know that tunics were removed routinely and examined for such articles, jewels, rings, coins, keys, and such, as well as the body of the female.

"The pounding at the door grew more insistent. Too, there was shouting. And I then heard heavy blows against the wood, the striking of some tool."

I supposed this would be siege hammer, or possibly a hand ram, swung by one or more men.

"'Wait, wait, Masters' I cried, using the word 'Masters' as an aspect of my disguise. 'The Mistress is not here!' I said. 'She has fled! I will open the door!' I lifted away the bars, and the door burst inward, striking me to the side. I was bruised. I kept my head down. They must not see how beautiful I was. They must think me a mere slave! 'Whose compartments are these?' demanded a man, with a sharpened half-staff. 'Those of my Mistress, the Lady Flavia of Ar, Master!' I responded. 'Excellent, the slut Flavia!' he cried. 'Where is she?' he demanded. 'I do not know, Master,' I said. 'Fled!' 'She has been proscribed,' he said. 'She no longer has slaves. Report to the vestibule below. You will be reallotted.' 'Yes, Master!' I said. 'What is your name?' demanded another man. 'Publia, Master,' I said. '—if it pleases Master?' he asked. 'Yes,' I said, '—*if it pleases Master.*' 'Publia' is too fine a name for a slave,' said a fellow. 'She is a sandal slave,' said another. 'Consider the length of her tunic, and the fineness of its material.' 'Let her belong to a man,' said another, 'and she will find out what it is to be a slave.' More than one man laughed at this. Some of the men then, after briefly looking about, exited the compartments, to pound on other doors, and some of them began to ascend the stairs, leading to the next level. Of those still in the compartments, I heard one say, 'Ho, what have we here?' 'Tethered verr!' said another. 'Tastas!' said another. 'Trussed vulos!' laughed another. 'Well-prepared puddings,' laughed another, 'ready for delectation!' My prone, or supine, sandal slaves had been discovered, bound hand and foot, gagged and blindfolded. Unnoticed, I slipped through the door. The attention of the brutes, I was sure, as I had some sense of the interests of men, would be occupied for a time with the sandal slaves. How frightful it must be for the slaves, I thought, to find themselves helpless, even blindfolded, in the hands of men. I did not think it likely they could betray me, as they did not know what I had done, or where I might be. I would soon, if all went well, be well away. I had been an excellent Mistress to the slaves, not merely in demanding a meticulous perfection in their many duties as a lady's serving slave, which is to be expected, but in regulating and supervising their behavior, demeanor, speech, posture, and such. I had been much concerned to improve them, for they were, of course, a reflection on me. Accordingly, I rigorously supervised their deportment, and saw to it that they did not stray from the paths of virtue. The standards for a lady's serving slave, you see, are quite high. Such must be refined, dutiful, humble, undefiled, unsullied, and pure. Even to look upon men is forbidden them. Did I not once see Althea, in the market, look over her shoulder, and smile at a handsome drover? I switched her all the way home, across the back of the thighs, and back in the compartments I gave her a whipping she would never forget! Such behavior embarrasses me. Many slaves are hard to tell from a she-sleen in heat. Have I not seen the tears in their eyes, and how they brush against their masters, how they, on their leashes, lift their lips hopefully to his? Who knows what goes on at a slave ring? How tragic I thought, that my lovely sandal slaves might now fall into the hands of men. But I could no longer protect them and preserve their purity. I was not far from the compartments when I heard Althea cry out, as though in joy, 'Masters!' Perhaps she belongs at a man's slave ring, I thought. She could never manage even the secret interior fastenings of my robes of concealment, and a kaiila might have draped my veils more tastefully.

"I descended, level by level. When I reached the vestibule I was horrified to see a number of slaves, doubtless from the lower floors, mostly tower slaves and sandal slaves, naked and on all fours, fastened together, like beads on a string, by a single long rope, successively tied and knotted about the neck of each. 'Take off your tunic,' said a man, 'and go to the end of the rope.' 'Yes, Master,' I said, but, as no one was looking, I went to the end of the line, but then slipped to the side and exited the cylinder. I was outside, on the plaza. I was startled that the fellow who had spoken to me had not been more careful, or more suspicious. It seems he had, without a second thought, taken me as a slave. I found this incomprehensible, and annoying, but I was grateful that he been so negligent, so undiscerning."

"Taking you for a slave," I said, "it never occurred to him that you would not obey."

"But I was a free woman," she said.

"True," I said.

"Why would he suppose that a slave would obey?" she asked.

"Were you more of a slave," I said, "you would understand." The obedience of a slave is to be unquestioning and instantaneous. It does not take an intelligent woman long to learn this, usually no more than a first hesitation, following which they are apprised of their lapse by the switch or lash.

"What would they do with the gathered slaves?" she asked.

"I would suppose," I said, "as confiscated goods, they would become the property of the state, later to be distributed, put on sale or such."

"Suitable for slaves," she said.

"Yes," I said.

"How meaningless and worthless they are," she said.

"They have their uses," I said.

"Though there were many in the streets," she said, "almost no one paid attention to me. It was almost as though I might have been a loose verr."

"Or tarsk," I suggested.

"I made my way through crowds," she said. "There was only one untoward incident. Most unpleasant! Only a hundred yards from the walls, I was accosted by a large female slave. 'High slave!' she sneered. 'Give me your sandals!'"

"You wore sandals?" I said.

"Of course," she said.

I nodded. It was not that unusual for a favored slave, a high slave, a spoiled slave, or such, to be granted sandals.

Most masters, subject, of course, to conditions of weather and terrain, keep their girls barefoot. This is because they like to see the feet of slaves bare, as they like, generally, bareness in slaves. Too, the feet of slaves are often attractive, small, and pretty. Too, of course, being barefoot helps the slaves to keep in mind that they are slaves. The barefootedness of the slave also tends to draw a further distinction between her and the free woman, for the free woman, even of low caste, almost always has footwear of one sort or another, even if it is only a wrapping of cloth. Too, who would put sandals, slippers, or such, on verr, tarsks, kaiila, or such?

"Did your girls have sandals?" I asked.

"Certainly not," she said.

I raised the broth, again, to my lips, surveying her over its brim. She seemed uneasy, my eyes upon her.

"Master?" she said.

She seemed uncertain, as to whether she might continue to speak. I found that encouraging. She was not sure of herself before me. That was appropriate. It seemed clear she wished to speak, but was reluctant to ask permission to do so, for what that might signify, not so much to me, as to her.

I put the bowl to the floor, beside me, with its residue of fluid.

"Master?" she said, again.

I suspected it had been long since anyone had listened to her, long since her hunger, that of a woman, to be heard had been satisfied. To be denied speech is a torment for them. Indeed, the control of their speech, as that of their food, and garmenture, muchly impresses on them what they are. It leaves them in little doubt that they are in a collar. They want so much to speak! I think that we should indulge them in this. Certainly it is another pleasure, that of listening, derivable from them. So put one such as she, a highly intelligent, articulate, aware, sensitive, literate woman, such as obviously belongs in the collar, before you, and listen to her, and with care. She is, of course, to be naked and kneeling, with her hands braceleted or thonged behind her. There is, I assure you, a special flavor or ambiance to such a conversation. Afterwards, when one wishes, one terminates the conversation, and does with her what one wishes.

"Continue," I said.

"This monstrous female," she said, eagerly, gratefully, "perhaps a discipline slave in a pleasure garden, used to keep smaller, more beautiful females in line, or a female draft slave, or a laundress, at best, said, 'Give me your sandals!' 'Never,' cried I, 'slave!' 'Slave?' she said. 'Get out of my way,' I cried, 'slave, or I will have the flesh lashed off your large, ugly bones!' She looked at me, suddenly, warily. 'Is Mistress free?' she asked. 'No,' I said, 'of course not. I am only a poor slave, as yourself.' 'Truly?' she said. 'Certainly,' I said, 'you can see I am tunicked and collared. Now let me pass!' 'You high slaves,' she said, 'think you are better than the rest of us!' 'We are superior,' I informed her. Was that not obvious? 'But we all lick the feet of men!' she said. 'Get out of my way!' I demanded. 'Your sandals!' she said, putting out her hand. 'No!' I said. After all, how could I walk without them? 'You would deny me,' she asked, 'you bauble, you small, well-turned, meaningless morsel of collar meat, you plaything, you caressable little she-urt!' And then she leaped at me and seized me by the hair, and twisted her hands within it, and shook my head, and I screamed with misery, blind with pain. Then she forced me down to my knees, I, actually a free woman, and, without relinquishing her hold on my hair, still hurting me, terribly, went behind me, and jerked my head up. 'I am going to tear the tunic off your little man-pleasing body!' she snarled. 'Please, no, Mistress!' I cried, terrified, in pain, for in my flank there was no iron burn. Lacking that I feared the impaling spear was imminent. 'Mistress, mistress, please, no!' I wept. I was then thrown forward, to my stomach, and, simultaneously, thankfully, she released my hair. I dared not move. I felt my sandals stripped off. When I dared I turned to my side, and looked up, fearfully, and saw her, through tears, standing almost over me. She dangled the sandals from her hand, looked at me, and laughed. She was so large, and strong. I could not have begun to match strength, nor try force, with her. No longer did men, and society, stand behind me. She disappeared in the crowd, and I rose, painfully, to my feet. I pulled down the tunic, for it had come high on my thighs. 'Pretty *kajira*,' laughed a fellow, passing, and made a noise which frightened me. I must remember that I was in a collar! I shuddered, and drew down the tunic even more. My feet were now bare. How strange it seemed for my feet to be bare, to feel grit beneath them, sand, a pebble, the smoothness of street stones. I did not know if I could walk. Could I do more than hobble, painfully? And might this not attract attention, as, say, a crippled kaiila might attract the attention of tawny prairie sleen? Might it suggest that I might be an unshod free woman? But none about seemed to notice me, other, of course, than as a slave might be noticed. More than once I found myself, a free woman, under the appraising glances of men. How slaves are looked upon! I dared not confront them. I dared not reprimand them. I dared not object. I realized, to my astonishment, that despite my remarkable beauty, that of a free woman, I was being seen, and without a second thought, as no more than another slave, perhaps only another 'pretty *kajira*.' This angered me, but at least my disguise was effective.

"I was in the vicinity of the ruins of the walls when I had been halted, abused, and robbed. This was a place of most danger for men patrolled the perimeter of the city, to prevent the flight of those whom the risen, vengeful citizens sought. I thought of trying to hide until darkness, but where would I hide? There was a collar on my neck. And buildings were being searched, room to room. And I feared the perimeter would be illuminated at night, not only by the moons, for two would be full, but by torches and kindled fires. Then, too, I had a sudden, fearsome thought. What if my robes, which I had thrust beneath the covers of my couch, were found, and understood. I had had no time to dispose of them. Even now, perhaps, their scent taken, eager sleen might be straining on their leashes, eyes blazing, salivating in anticipation, their fangs wet, their claws scratching on the stones, pulling their way toward me. And I had no men to protect me! I was as vulnerable as what I was pretending to be, a female slave!"

"Yet you are here," I said, "wherever this may be."

"We are both prisoners," she said.

"I am a prisoner," I said. "You are something other than a prisoner."

"Do not so think of me," she said.

I said nothing.

"Perhaps we can be of assistance to one another," she said.

"You speak as though you might be a free woman," I said.

She regarded me, frightened. I did not give her the "thigh" or "brand" command, but I had little doubt she was now marked. In response to such a command those such as she must kneel on the right knee and extend the left leg gracefully, bared to the hip. The most common marking site on such as she is high on the left thigh, under the hip.

One does not bargain with such as she of course, nor are they permitted to bargain. The very suggestion of such a thing can be cause for discipline. One would not bargain with a verr, kaiila, a tarsk, or such.

"How did you escape from Ar?" I asked.

"I resolved upon, and put into immediate execution, a bold plan," she said. "I walked, as I could, openly, purposefully, to the nearest fellow at the perimeter, one who seemed to be first amongst his fellows. I knelt before him, shamed to do so, but such comported with my deception. 'Master,' I said. 'I and other sandal slaves of the hated Lady Flavia of Ar, traitress to the Home Stone of Ar, have been sent to the perimeter, that we might identify our former mistress, should she attempt to elude the justice of Ar.' 'What is wrong with your feet?' he asked. 'My feet are sore,' I told him. 'I am not used to being barefoot. My sandals were stolen.' 'What is your name?' he asked. 'Publia,' I said, adding, 'if it pleases Master.' 'To whom do you belong?' he asked. 'To the state of Ar,' I told him. 'You are pretty for a sandal slave,' he said. I did not know what to say. My own sandal slaves were lovely. Certainly I had seen men admire them in the markets, and on the boulevards. Then he added, 'You have been complimented.' 'Thank you, Master,' I said. 'Split your knees,' he said. 'Master?' I said. 'You are before a man,' he said, 'split your knees.' 'I am a sandal slave!' I protested. 'Now,' he said. Then he said, 'That is better.' I feared I might die of mortification, to be so before a man. Fortunately, the tunic of a sandal slave, which I had adopted, was ample enough to permit the assumption of such a position without any undue compromising of my modesty. Still, even within the heavy, opaque, shielding of my garmenture, the position was obviously that of a female, recognized as a female, before a man. 'You are no longer a sandal slave,' he said. 'You had best accustom yourself to kneeling so before a man.' 'Yes, Master,' I whispered. I thought of my poor sandal slaves, having fallen into the hands of men, those rude beasts who had entered my compartments. Doubtless they were learning how to kneel so before men. What a pitiable fate had befallen them. I forced from my mind what might be the meaning, the symbolism, of such a position before men. 'How might I be of service to Master?' I asked. He smiled. 'In apprehending the hated traitress, Lady Flavia of Ar!' I said quickly. 'I think,' said he, 'you have already been of much assistance in that respect.' 'Master?' I asked. 'Seize her,' he said. I tried to spring to my feet, but a hand in my hair, twisted, held me on my knees. 'I think,' said he, 'it is you who are the Lady Flavia.' 'No, Master!' I wept. 'Sandal slaves are not sent to the perimeter,' he said. 'A free woman, so disguised, might then be in a position to make away. And not all sandal slaves may be depended upon to identify a former mistress, given the looming of the impaling spear, not even one as imperious and cruel as a Lady Flavia. Too, one does not need spies at the perimeter. All unknowns who try to cross the perimeter are to be detained, to be examined later.' 'I am not the Lady Flavia!' I cried. 'Perhaps not,' he said. 'That may be determined later.' 'Let us lift the tunic,' said a fellow, 'and see if she is marked.' 'No!' I cried. 'No,' said the fellow before whom I was being held. 'That is for a free woman to do. If this is the Lady Flavia, she is still a free woman, and her modesty is to be respected.' 'You made me kneel before you with my knees spread!' I screamed at him. 'You needed not obey, if you were a free woman,' he said, 'but you did obey, and you looked well, with your knees split. Too, it seems reasonably clear that beneath that cumbersome tunic you may have slave curves, which might be of interest on an auction block.' 'Tarsk!' I cried. 'Let us make a determination,' said a fellow. 'Detunick her,' said another. 'No,' I cried, 'my modesty!' 'It is hard to preserve one's modesty,' said a fellow, 'when writhing naked on an impaling spear.' 'I am not the Lady Flavia!' I insisted. 'That will be determined later,' said the fellow before whom I knelt, my hair held. Then he said, 'Bind her, hand and foot.' As might be supposed, I, a possible free woman, possibly even the Lady Flavia of Ar, had, to my misery, become a center of attention. Several of the perimeter guards had gathered about me. I was put to my belly and one man was holding my wrists, crossed, behind me, and another was holding my ankles together, crossed. I felt a cord being put about my ankles, and knotted. But then, suddenly, one of the fellows cried out, alarmed. 'Corso, Corso, mercenaries!' Corso, I gathered, was the fellow to whom I had first presented myself, he whom I took to be in command at this point of the perimeter. It seems that a group of mercenaries, perhaps fifteen or twenty, with some women in tow, roped together by the neck, had determined to take advantage of the distraction my presence had brought about at the perimeter. They were already within fifty yards of the perimeter. I heard the ringing of an alarm bar, the sounding of battle horns. The fellows about me abandoned me, rushing to interpose themselves between the fugitives and the cleared ground outside the perimeter. They were not professional soldiers and I did not think they could stand before well-armed, desperate mercenaries, though they might hold them long enough for more effective troops, summoned by the bar and the horns, to arrive, even tarnsmen flighted from the city. I heard the clash of weapons, and cries of pain. I fought the knots binding my ankles together. In moving a female captive across open country, it is common, when stopping for a repast, or such, to bind her ankles. In this fashion she cannot run and her hands are free to feed herself. One can see, of course, if she tries to untie her ankles. When the repast is done, one can untie her ankles and put her back on a leash or neck rope, her hands perhaps bound behind her. At night, naturally, she may be put to the side, bound hand and foot. Looking up, frenziedly, I saw some other mercenaries, several, rushing toward the perimeter, and, some hundreds of yards away, guardsmen of Ar, regulars, hastening to the perimeter. This was, it seems, a serious attempt to break out of the city, one now involving perhaps more than a hundred men, accompanied by women, mostly stripped, and on ropes. I did not know if the women were free women or slaves. I suspected that many were proscribed free women who had stripped, knelt, and embonded themselves before mercenaries, perhaps only shortly before, that they might be saved, that they might be taken from the city, if only as nude slaves. Fighting was then about me. I could not undo the knots. I took the key to the collar, which I had hidden in my tunic, and, using it as a wedge, and then as a tiny saw, attacked the knots first, and then the cord itself. The cord was not the ropage which might be used to bind a man, but much smaller, and weaker. A strong man might have snapped it in two, but it was quite sufficient, as might have been a lace, to bind a woman, and with perfection. I wept with misery that we could find ourselves so easily, and so helplessly, in the power of men. We belong to them, I thought. Nature has made us theirs! But we have our beauty, our wit, our sensitivity, our intelligence! Have not more men been conquered with a kiss than steel? It is no wonder, I thought, that they make us their slaves! The key's teeth cut, frayed, and severed a bit of the cord, and I whipped it away from my ankles. I crawled away from the city, sometimes covering my head, as men fought about me. More than once I saw the wild, terrified eyes of women, pulling at the ropes on their neck. I concealed myself behind them, and then I rose to my feet, and ran toward the open country. I was not alone, as neck-roped women, and warriors, singly, and in prides, fled the city. There were tarns in the sky and their shadows seemed to race across the grass. More than one mercenary had a crossbow bolt half through his brass-bound shield, formed of layers of bosk hide. The crossbow, even the stirrup variety, loads slowly, and there is little danger from the quarrel if one need only defend oneself from a single direction. Should the tarnsman dismount he fights evenly with his foe, and the more skilled warrior is most likely to survive. I soon realized that the bolts flighted from the crossbows had the mercenaries as targets, and not the women. I realized, again, a difference between ourselves and men. We could be left for later, to be rounded up, like verr or kaiila, and roped at a victor's leisure. We were not contestants; we were loot, prizes.

"'Here, *kajira*, here!' called a mercenary. I fled gratefully to his side. At last I had a man to defend me. I had a champion. I realized then, as I had never before, when I had been sheltered within the arrangements, laws, and customs of a civil order, which I had taken so much for granted, how thin, and possibly transitory, such things were, and what might lie at their elbow, or nigh, on the other side of that lovely curtain, separating comfort and security from the cruelties and hazards of a perilous nature.

"Some think the jungle is faraway, that it is east of Schendi, as distant as the valley of the Ua, but it is not. It is here. It is with us, patient, and waiting. It is as close as the hearts of men.

"'Stop!' I heard, and spun about. A fellow, from Ar, I supposed, had called out. He had not been at the perimeter. I doubt that he thought me free. I think, merely, he wanted to pick up a slave. How fearful, I thought, to be a slave, to be an object, a property, a possession, an animal, something which might be bought and sold, or given away, or, as here, something which might be simply gathered in, simply acquired. Put a rope on her neck and she is yours! But I must not be brought back to Ar! As soon as I was stripped, as I would be, as a slave, my lack of a brand would be obvious, and then there would be inquiries, and the proscription lists would be certain to be examined. I must not be returned to Ar!

"'Begone,' said the mercenary, stepping between me and the fellow. The fellow looked at the mercenary, in his helmet, with his shield, and a spear whose reddened blade had recently drunk the blood of a foe, and then backed away. In a few moments he had disappeared."

I said nothing, but I supposed that the mercenary, before approaching the fellow, would have examined the sky behind him. The woman would not have been aware of this, as she would have been facing her pursuer. Occasionally a warrior on foot and a tarnsman collaborate on a kill. The warrior on foot engages the target, and the tarnsman, unseen, glides in, silently, placing a bolt in the adversary's unprotected back. This act is scorned in the codes, of course, but it is not without precedent in the field. It is common amongst outlaws and rogue tarnsmen.

"'Should you not have killed him?' I asked, frightened. 'I am not a butcher,' he said.

"'Continue to protect me,' I said. 'Turn about,' he said, 'and put your wrists behind you.' 'Master?' I said. 'You are to be braceleted,' he said. 'But then, here, outside the city, in the fields,

I would be utterly helpless,' I said. 'Such as you, pretty *kajira*,' he said, 'are to be utterly helpless.' I trembled, to think myself so much in the power of men, as much as a *kajira*."

I smiled.

"I turned and fled away from him, and I discovered, some hundred yards away, gasping, turning about, my feet now raw, that he had not pursued me. Were such as I so common that we were not worth our pursuit? I was elated to be free of him, but frightened, as well, for who would now protect me? And, oddly, my vanity was offended. Surely I was the most beautiful woman he had ever beheld, and yet he did not pursue me, throw me to the ground and fasten my wrists behind me! Standing in the gentle, green, wind-moved grass, alone, looking about, I saw, here and there, in the fields, small groups, moving away from the city. I could see her towers in the distance. Some of these groups had small strings of stripped, neck-roped women with them. Here and there I saw a tarnsman in the sky, almost certainly one of Ar. I saw no pursuits from the city. I did not know where to go or what to do, and I was suddenly aware that I was hungry. I felt the hem of my tunic, reassuring me of the jewels sewn there, and the small key ensconced in its tiny sleeve."

"You were fortunate to escape Ar," I said.

"I set out in the direction others were moving," she said. "I could not go back to Ar. I thought I might reach Torcadino, from whence I might purchase wagon passage to Brundisium, Besnit, Harfax, or Market of Semris. I would avoid Ko-ro-ba and Thentis as they did not favor those of Ar. Too, one would not seek Port Kar, as it is a den of thieves and cutthroats, and Tharna was out of the question. There is only one free woman in Tharna, Lara, her Tatrix. All others are held in the most severe of bondages. No free woman may even enter the gates of Tharna without being temporarily licensed and placed in the custody of a male. Those of Tharna wear in their belt the two yellow cords, each eighteen inches in length, suitable for binding females, hand and foot."

I knew little of Tharna, but I did know it was a city muchly feared by free women. And yet, interestingly, free women not unoften underwent considerable hardship and peril to enter her gates.

"And I feared, too," she said, "to seek the major islands, for during the occupation many of the women of Ar had been collected and sent there on slave ships."

That was true. In my time in Ar I had seen several coffles of the women of Ar leave the city, to be marched overland to Brundisium, there to be disembarked for Cos or Tyros.

"Perhaps Teletus, Tabor, or Chios, of the farther islands," I suggested.

"I fear the islands," she said.

"There are pirates," I said.

"Yes," she said.

It was not unheard of for women to be seized at sea, to be later disposed of in the markets, sometimes, eventually, as far south as Schendi or Turia.

"Brundisium," she said, "seemed an optimum choice."

"Perhaps," I said.

Brundisium, as many merchant ports, large and small, was in theory neutral. To be sure, it had been the port at which the invasion fleets of Cos and Tyros, unopposed, even welcomed, had made their landfall on the continent, thence to rendezvous with numerous companies of mercenaries, for the march to Ar.

"But I was alone," she said, "a woman, ill-clad, half crippled, and hungry, unfamiliar with the stars, without guidance, only vaguely aware of where Brundisium might be, or how far away she might be."

"Presumably you would need assistance," I said.

"I was well prepared to pay for it," she said. "Night fell. I hobbled on, in the moonlight. Once I stopped, in terror, frozen, for I noted the sinuous passage of a prairie sleen. It passed within a dozen yards of me, rapidly, its snout to the ground."

"It was not on your scent," I said. Sleen can be terribly dangerous to humans, but the human is not its familiar prey. The sleen, in the wild a burrowing, largely nocturnal animal, is a tenacious, obsessive, single-minded hunter, a supreme tracker. On one scent it will often pass by, even ignore, more ample or superior prey.

"When it passed," she said, "I was overjoyed, for I was still alive, but I was then, almost immediately, sick with fear, for such a beast or beasts, I thought, might even now be following my tracks, from Ar, having been given my scent from my discarded robes."

Her apprehension was well-warranted. Indeed, it is not unknown for sleen to have discovered and followed tracks which are several days old.

"I walked much of the night," she said, "keeping to the direction others had taken. The terrain seemed to change, and there were now trees here and there, sometimes groves. Toward morning I could go no further and lay down in the grass, and fell asleep. I awakened late in the afternoon, weak, and starving. I staggered to my feet, and stumbled on. I went almost blindly, putting one foot before the other. As it grew dark I felt a sudden piercing, a fierce, doubled puncturing, in the calf of my right leg and I screamed in pain. I thought 'ost,' but it was the twin, hollow thorns of a leech plant which had struck me. I heard the hideous noise of the pulsating pods sucking blood, pumping it to the roots, and, screaming, I tore the fangs from my leg and fled away, and then stopped, afraid to move, lest there be more such things about, lest I stumble and fall into a writhing patch of such plants. Entangled amongst them, they swarming about me, enwrapping me with their vines and tendrils, it was possible I would not have been able to rise to my feet. I could hear them rustling about, on the sides, like whispers. Then, step by step, with great care, I moved away from the stirring, agitated growths, and continued my journey. My throat, too, was parched. I had been raised in luxury and power. I had wanted for nothing. Never had I been hungry and thirsty like this. Even as a child I had had serving slaves. Now I was alone, my beauty briefly and shamefully garbed, my feet bleeding, blood drying on my right calf, weary, without food or water, without protection, with little idea as to where I might be, what I should do, or where I might go."

I swirled the bit of broth remaining in the metal bowl.

"Then, perhaps near midnight, in the darkness, for clouds obscured the two moons then in the sky, when I thought I could go no further, to my joy, I glimpsed a small light, in the distance. It was, I took it, a small camp. Gratefully, unsteadily, I stumbled toward it. 'Masters!' I called out. The light then disappeared. Surely I had more than enough to hire men, to buy protection, a safe conduct, to Brundisium. 'Masters!' I called out, again. I stumbled in darkness, lamely, toward the point at which I had seen the point of light. 'Masters,' I cried, 'I am a poor starving slave, separated from her master. He will want me returned to him! I am not a runaway! Please be kind to a poor slave. Please help her!' Then I thought myself close to the point at which I had seen the bit of light, but it was dark. It had been here somewhere, surely. Then a powerful hand, from behind, closed itself over my mouth, and my head was pulled back, and I felt the razor's edge of a blade at my throat. 'Make no sound, *kajira*,' I heard, a fierce whisper at my ear, 'and do not struggle.' I could not speak in any event, my mouth held tightly shut, nor would I have dared to resist, or struggle, with the blade at my throat. One swift motion of that blade and my neck would have been half cut through. I sensed two or more men moving about me and he in whose grasp I was. The hand was then slipped from my mouth to my hair, and my head was then held back by the hair, painfully. I winced. The blade was still at my throat. 'Where are the others?' he asked. 'How many are there?' 'I am alone,' I whispered, scarcely daring to speak. He held me thusly for several Ehn. I scarcely dared to breathe, for fear I might cut my own throat. After a time, seven or eight fellows were about. 'We found no one,' said one of them. I almost fainted, as the blade was removed from my throat. 'On all fours, *kajira*,' said the fellow who had held me."

A slave is sometimes put to all fours, that she may move thusly, accompanying masters. In this posture she cannot suddenly run, or dart away. In the situation described the posture was doubtless imposed as a security measure, on an unknown slave, mysteriously arrived from the darkness. In other situations the posture may be imposed upon her as a discipline, to position her for animal usage, to remind her that she is a slave, and so on.

"I resented being on all fours amongst men," she said, "forced to look up at them from such a position, and such. 'Come along, *kajira*,' he said, moving away. I followed him, on all fours. In a few moments the small fire had been rekindled, and I was permitted to kneel, where the firelight played upon me, the men, eleven as I now counted, sitting back from the fire. I could see some small tents, and some paraphernalia of the camp, to my left. I also saw six women, stripped, their hands tied behind them, on a single neck rope, stretched between two stakes, to which each end was fastened. 'I am the slave Publia,' I said, 'separated from my master, Flavius of Brundisium, in the troubles at Ar, seeking to be returned to him.'"

The name Flavius is a common name in the middle latitudes of Gor, at Ar, and elsewhere. I supposed the name had come to her mind, given her name, Flavia, which name, as would be expected, is similarly well known in such areas. It is not unknown, of course, that a slave might strive desperately to be returned to her master. A love unknown to a free woman, in its helplessness, its need, its depth, profundity, beauty, and passion, is often felt by a woman for the man whose collar she wears. Owned, she is his, wholly.

"'What troubles in Ar?' asked a fellow. I was sure the question was not candid, but a test of sorts. The catastrophes in Ar had begun some days ago, hundreds of fugitives from Ar had scattered from the city, presumably most to seek the coast, and eventual security in the islands; and the six women in the camp might well have been from Ar, perhaps proscribed women, begging passage from Ar, even at the cost of the collar. Indeed these fellows in the camp, I supposed, might well have been amongst those who fled from Ar. Who would not know, truly, of the miseries and changes in Ar? But I responded, innocently, as though granting that the question had been asked, as well, in all innocence. 'The uprising,' I said, 'the rebellion, the ending of the occupation, the expulsion of foreign troops from Ar.' 'Who is this Flavius?' asked another. 'A minor Merchant of Brundisium,' I said. I did not wish to claim status for him, as some about the fire might be familiar with the merchantry of the great port.' I knelt with my knees together. Also, it occurred to me that I had not requested permission to speak. Perhaps, I thought, they are permissive with slaves here. But I glanced at the stripped, bound women beyond the firelight and that did not then seem to me likely. 'May I inquire,' I asked, 'what Home Stone Masters revere?' This could, of course, make a great deal of difference in what might then ensue. They looked at one another, and more than one laughed. Although this made me somewhat uneasy, it also reassured me that I was not amongst those who favored either Ar or the island Ubarates. If they were of Ar I might fear being returned to the city with the likelihood of impalement. If they were of the island Ubarates, they would have come, over the time of the occupation and the looting of the city, to think of the women of Ar as suitable only for slaves. 'It seems,' I said, 'that you are independent of fee, and thus open to prospects of considerable gain.' 'Certainly,' said he whom I took to be their leader, he whose knife had been at my throat. 'We may speak freely then,' I said, 'but first, as I have been in the wild for two days, and am weak from hunger, and am exhausted and thirsty, I need food, and drink, bolstering ka-la-na, and rest.' 'Of course,' said the leader, kindly. He nodded to one of his men. He went to the rope of women and put she on the rope nearest to the stake to my right in rope shackles. She would barely be able to stand and move. He then loosened the neck rope from the stake to my right and freed her of its collar-like restraint, after which he refastened it to the stake. He then unbound her hands. She rubbed her wrists, regarding me. The fellow then pointed to me, and said, 'Feed and water her.' I did not care for this way of putting it, as it sounded as though I might be an animal. But I was thirsting and starving. 'Why should I, who was a free woman, wait on a common slave?' demanded the woman. Her hair was then held and she was cuffed brutally, four times. She then, weeping, scarcely able to move for the closely tied rope shackles, hobbled about, to find me food and drink. I took the provender and drink, including ka-la-na, which I doubt she was permitted, from her with the hauteur and disdain of a free woman for the garbages that are slaves. Afterwards I fainted, or fell asleep.

"I awakened several hours later, toward noon, as though I might be in my own compartments, waiting for my girls to open the draperies and bring me steaming black wine and fresh, honeyed pastries, but then, suddenly, flooding back to me were the horrors of the past two days, the roof of the Central Cylinder, my humiliating disguise, the escape, the fields, the sleen, the strike of the leech plant, the knife at my throat, and I opened my eyes on the small camp into which I had stumbled last night, weary, footsore, hungry, thirsting, and miserable. I touched my neck, and felt the collar there, the slave collar. Then I feared the tunic, ample as it might be, might in my sleep have crept up my thighs, and I reached to draw it down, but, even as I thought of this, I became aware of a weight on my left ankle. I sat up, suddenly. I jerked the tunic down, that I might benefit from whatever concession to modesty might be afforded by a slave's garment. Too, I drew my legs back, closely together. There was a rattle of chain. I considered my left ankle. It was clasped by a heavy band of black iron, to the ring of which a chain was attached. This chain ran behind me, where it was padlocked about a tree. I was chained! I, a free woman of Ar, was chained, as might have been a female slave!

"'What is the meaning of this!' I cried, lifting the chain, shaking it."

The left ankle is the common chaining ankle for a woman.

"The leader of the camp approached me. 'Do not be concerned, gentle lady,' said he. 'We did not wish you to be stolen.' 'Stolen?' I asked. 'Certainly,' he said, 'many women have been gagged in the middle of the night, then bound, and carried off.' 'Oh,' I said. 'Such things may be done with women,' he said. 'Free me, now,' I said. 'Certainly,' he said, and shortly thereafter the gross impediment was gone."

"How did you feel, being on a chain, being so subject to male domination?" I asked. "Did you have any surprising feelings?"

"Feelings?" she asked.

"Yes," I said, "any sense of weakness, of openness, of readiness, of hope, of desire, of a yearning to surrender, any inexplicable sense of warmth in your body, any heating or liquidity between your thighs?"

"That is impossible," she said. "I am a free woman."

"I see," I said. "Please, continue."

"They had remained several hours in the camp," she said. "I think, now, that was to allow one of their fellows to reach the Brundisium road, and make inquiries at a road village, in the vicinity of an abandoned inn, the Inn of Ragnar."

"Inquiries?" I said.

"I think so," she said.

"That is a northern name," I said.

"Perhaps," she said.

"When it became clear they were preparing to leave the camp, rather toward the fall of darkness, as though they did not wish to be on the road in daylight, I opportuned the leader for a conference, which petition, it seems, he had anticipated. We withdrew a way from the camp, amongst the trees. When we had gone a little way, he pointed to the ground, and said, 'Kneel there.' 'I do not wish to kneel,' I said. I read his eyes. I knelt. As a man, you probably do not know what it is for a woman to kneel before a man, to be at his feet, to lift your head, to look up at him, or to keep your head down before him, if commanded. It is symbolic of your utter otherness, of your softness before his hardness, your weakness before his strength, your slightness before his might, your beauty and helplessness before his virility and power, your readiness before his command. It is, one fears, as though one were in one's place, before one's master. How, I ask, can a woman so situated, one on her knees, speak to a man?"

"As a woman," I suggested.

"It is a position of petition, or submission, is it not?" she asked.

"Yes," I said.

"I was furious," she said.

"Much depends on the woman," I said. "If one is speaking of slaves, it is appropriate, and prescribed, of course."

"Yes," she said.

"But many women," I said, "long for their masters, beseech the world for the man before whom they might kneel, naked and collared, whose feet they might gratefully kiss. Many women, longing to be subdued, longing to submit, longing to be unqualifiedly possessed, longing to be owned, wholly and absolutely, find their social, biological, and cultural fulfillment in this, in thusly daring to reveal their deepest needs and desires to men. In such things we find not only a loving confession of femininity, but its unapologetic petition and expression. It is not wrong for a woman to reveal her deepest heart and needs. Who but an unhappy, ill-constituted madman or tyrant could find gratification in attempting to legislate the values, loves, lives, and hearts of others?"

"'You may speak,' he said, as though I, a free woman, required such permission. 'I wish passage to Brundisium,' I said, 'and I am prepared to pay for it, as might a Ubara herself. I have riches.' 'You speak as a free woman,' he said. 'I am a free woman,' I said. 'That is fortunate,' he said, 'for were you a slave, and spoke as you do, you would be muchly lashed. The lesson of suitable speech, of deference, and such, for a slave is quickly learned.' 'I lied to you,' I said, 'for such may a free woman do. I am not a slave, and, of course, I have no master, a Flavius or anyone else. I am Publia, a free woman of Ar, not proscribed, but fearful, and thus in flight from the city. I pretended to be a slave, until I might speak privately with you. The myth of Flavius was to dissemble before your men, for why should you share great wealth with them? Rather reserve it, secretly, for yourself. In Brundisium we may pretend you have found a Flavius and have received a reward for my return, commensurate with what a minor Merchant, our alleged Flavius, might afford. Then, you can share a pittance with your men, and reserve the large, unsuspected bounty for yourself.' 'You have holdings, wealth, family, in Brundisium?' he asked. 'Certainly,' I said. I thought that, as things were going well, there would be little need to part with more than the least of the jewels sewn within my tunic. 'The men will wonder at our absence,' he said. 'We must not allow them to grow suspicious.' 'No,' I said. 'We are breaking camp,' he said. 'I want to reach the Brundisium road by dark, and road village of Ragnar, near the old inn.' 'That is on the road to Brundisium, is it not?' I asked. 'Yes,' he said. 'Good', I said. 'You wish to pretend, before the men, to be a slave, do you not?' he inquired. 'Yes,' I said, 'otherwise they may suspect our plan.' 'Then,' said he, 'with all due respect, I think you should accompany us as a slave, bound and leashed.' 'Surely that is not necessary,' I said. 'Am I not yearning to be returned to the arms of my master?' I asked. 'Some of the men,' he said, 'suspect that you are a runaway.' 'I see,' I said."

"You were not curious," I asked, "that an evening stop was scheduled at a road village?"

"Doubtless they had some business there," she said. "I did not inquire."

"Continue," I said.

"My wrists were bound behind me," she said, "and other ropes were looped about my upper body, and tightened. Then I was put on a leash, as though I might be a slave. Thankfully, before the charade of my binding and leashing was accomplished, I had asked for sandals, and had been given them. They doubtless had several pairs, from the women in tow. With the sandals I could keep up with them on the road, without much pain. To be sure, our progress would not be rapid, as our party included its animals, the six slaves, bound, tethered in their rope coffle. Although the switch was occasionally used with them one can do only so much with women and the switch, as, despite their earnestness and fear, they lack the stamina and speed of men. I myself, of course, was not switched. I would not have stood for it. About the eighteenth Ahn we reached the road, and, shortly thereafter, we reached what I took to be the village of Ragnar, no more than some small buildings, mostly dark, some little more than shacks, on both sides of the road. I supposed some of the residents had fields nearby, vineyards, orchards, or such. The village was probably a market at times, for I saw dark stalls, and doubtless, to some extent, it catered, in one way or another, to the traffic on the Brundisium road. There was, for example, from the signs, a wainwright's shop, mostly for repair, I supposed, a Leather Worker's shop, probably for harnesses and traces, a Metal Worker's shop, probably mostly to furnish wagoner's hardware, and such. It must have once had better times, for, I learned, the Inn of Ragnar, for which the village was named, was dilapidated, and closed. Its auxiliary buildings, its stables, its stable yard, and such, like the main building, seemed similarly fallen into a state of forlorn desuetude. Apparently, its well was still in use, as I saw a girl drawing water.

"The leader then conferred briefly with one of his men, he whom I suspected had been absent from the camp earlier, for several hours. I heard the fellow say, 'The twentieth Ahn,' but could make out nothing else. The slaves were then put between two of the small buildings, and the men sat near them, in various attitudes of repose, some fetching food and drink from their packs. To my disgust I saw one of the slaves whimpering for food, and bending forward. A fellow held out a scrap for her, and she bent forward, gratefully, and, hands bound behind her, took it from his hand. The other slaves, too, then, importuned the men for bits of food. Some were fed by hand. At other times scraps were tossed to the ground, which the slaves, sometimes fighting for them, might retrieve as they could, in the moonlight. The leader and I remained standing, outside the group, at the edge of the road. Then he drew on my leash and I followed him, and found myself brought into a small building, one of those few in which a lamp had been burning, visible through the window. It was a Metal Worker's shop, and it was empty. There was a fire in the forge. I thought this strange, for the Ahn. A bell hung at one side of a door, leading through the back, perhaps to the proprietor's private quarters. The leader then removed the leash from my neck. 'Thank you,' I said. I then turned about, that he might undo the ropes that bound me, but he spun me about, rudely, and pointed to the floor, and said, 'Kneel there.' It was a command such that a woman, despite her status, whether slave or free, could not but obey instantly. I was frightened. 'You are from Brundisium?' he asked. 'Yes,' I said. 'Describe its Home Stone,' he said. I was silent. 'You have holdings in Brundisium, treasure, high family,' he said. 'Yes,' I said, 'yes!' 'Then it is clearly in my best interest to hold you for ransom,' he said. 'No!' I cried. 'List your holdings, and the streets,' he said. 'Name your family, its members and their wealth.' 'I lied!' I said. 'I do not have family in Brundisium, but I have great wealth, placed with coin merchants!' 'Name them,' he said. I was again silent, frantic. I twisted in the ropes. Tears burst from my eyes. He then ruthlessly demanded from me information upon information, information which would be common knowledge to anyone from Brundisium, things as obvious as to where lay her Street of Coins, her largest markets, how many gates she had, and such. 'I invested through agents, from Ar!' I cried. 'Name them,' he said. 'It will be easy to examine your claims.' 'I lied!' I wept. 'I lied!' 'And you are a liar from Ar,' he said. 'Do you think I do not know the accents of Ar? You may deny being of Ar but you are belied by the very words in which you enunciate your denial, for they proclaim you of Ar. You are no more from Brundisium than Talena of Ar. Indeed, perhaps you are Talena of Ar.' 'No,' I cried, 'no!' It is strange but one is almost always unaware of one's own accent. Is it not the others who always have an accent? 'No', said he, 'I do not think you are Talena of Ar. I think, rather, you are the Lady Flavia of Ar.'

'No,' I wept. 'No!' 'Stay on your knees, Lady Flavia,' he said. 'I am not Lady Flavia of Ar!' I said. 'But before I return you, naked and bound, to Ar,' he said, 'something is to be done to you. You have been annoying.' He then went behind me and removed my sandals. 'You will not need these any longer,' he said. He put them to the side, on a shelf. 'What are you going to do?' I said. He then went to the cord dangling from the bell which hung near the door leading from the shop, presumably to the private quarters of the Metal Worker. He rang it once, decisively. Shortly thereafter three men emerged from the rear, one the Metal Worker, a brawny fellow in a leather apron, and two others, strapping young men who, I took it, were his sons. The Metal Worker began to stoke the coals at the forge, and thrust two irons into the coals. 'Get up,' said the leader, and I struggled to my feet. The two young men stood behind me. They held my arms. I struggled. I was helpless, in their power. 'What are you going to do?' I cried. He did not respond to me, did not grant me his attention, but addressed himself to the Metal Worker. 'Strip and brand her,' he said.

"In moments I lay supine, head down, ankles elevated, in the rack, my limbs held in the clamps. I wept and squirmed, save that I could not move, in the least, my left thigh. In double clamps, it was held utterly motionless. I looked up at the leader, turning my head to the left. 'Desist!' I wept. 'Desist! I am a free woman!' 'That was determined while you slept,' said the leader. 'You dared to draw back my tunic in my sleep, you dared to examine me?' I cried. He laughed. So, too, did three or four of his men who had now entered the shop. He held the tunic now in his hand. He dangled it. 'And we ascertained,' said he, 'as we had anticipated, further discoveries. What fine lady, such as a Lady Flavia, would flee from Ar without resources?' 'I am not the Lady Flavia!' I cried. He reached into his pouch and drew forth a handful of small objects, which he held where I might see them. They were the jewels I had concealed in the tunic. They sparkled in the light of the lamp. Amongst them was the small key, as well, which fitted my collar lock. I felt sick, helpless, discovered, ruined, and destitute. I no longer had the wealth which I had brought with me, with which I might have hired men and brought myself again to power, and, without the key,

I could not remove the collar. It was now fixed on me with the same understated, flawless efficiency with which it might have encircled the neck of a slave. 'Please, let me go, have mercy!' I begged. Then I shouted, angrily, squirming before him, 'Do not look upon me in that way!' He smiled. 'I am a free woman, a free woman!' I cried. 'Is the iron ready?' asked the leader, of the Metal Worker. I heard an iron moved amongst coals, then lifted from them, and thrust again amidst them. I did not look. 'Nearly,' said the Metal Worker. 'You have everything,' I said to the leader. 'Let me go!' He turned to a sand glass on a nearby shelf. I could not well see it. I remembered someone had spoken of the twentieth Ahn, the fellow whom I thought had earlier absented himself from the camp. 'Let me go!' I begged. 'I will let you kiss me!' 'But you are a free woman,' he reminded me. 'No matter!' I said. To be sure, it is an inestimable privilege, to be permitted to kiss a free woman. 'If you are a free woman,' he said, 'you should not be locked in a shameful collar.' 'No,' I said, 'of course not!' He then turned the collar on my neck, so that the lock was upward, at the front of my throat, inserted the key, moved back the bolt, and removed the collar from me. He then handed the collar, the key left inserted in the lock, to one of the young fellows, one of those I thought likely to be a son of the Metal Worker. The young man looked at the device approvingly. It was, I knew, a quality collar, finely tooled and attractive. I had seen to that in preparing my disguise, which I began on the first day of the uprising, when the outcome was muchly unclear, a rudely armed populace rising against a professional soldiery. It was surely far different from the dark, cheap, plainer, common collars I saw hanging on a projecting spindle at the side of the shop. The leader looked down at me, at my now-bared throat, and, I fear, my lips, and then he looked into my eyes. I realized he wanted me uncollared, the beast, that it might be clearer what he was doing, that he was preparing to kiss a free woman. 'Yes,' I said to him, 'you may kiss me.' 'Your kiss for your freedom?' he asked. 'Yes,' I said, 'yes!' 'I do not bargain,' he said. 'I do not understand,' I said. Then he bent down beside me. As I lay, supine, and backward sloping, my head low, my wrists over my head, behind my head, on each side, in the clamps, my ankles higher, on each side, in their clamps, my left thigh held immobile in its double clamps, he took my hair in his hand. He held my hair, painfully, so that I could not turn my head from him. There was amusement in his eyes. 'No!' I cried. Then his lips were pressed to mine. I was held in place. I could not struggle. For several Ihn I was forced to endure that merciless, shameful contact. Then he drew away from me and gestured to the Metal Worker. I looked up at the leader in consternation, in shock, and reproach. How dared he, and I a free woman! Where were guardsmen that I might summon? Surely that was not such a kiss as might be given to a free woman! Might it not have been more appropriately imposed upon a paga girl or a brothel slut, fastened down for a man's pleasure? But I was strangely, inexplicably, stirred. Unaccountable sensations coursed through me. What might it be, I wondered, to be vulnerably, helplessly, legally, subject to such abuse? What might it be, I wondered, to be in a man's arms, owned by him, to be choiceless, to have no option but to feel and yield. I struggled to put such thoughts from my head, but then I screamed in misery, for the pain had begun.

"I was sobbing wildly, and he placed his hand over my mouth, and I looked up at him, wildly, over his hand, and he removed his hand from my mouth, and said to me, 'Good evening, slave.'

One of the men looked at me, and said, 'A good mark.' I did not even know what mark it was.

I heard the iron immersed in water, and heard the water hiss and boil about the metal.

As I put my head back, sobbing, I felt a cloth measuring tape put about my neck, read, and removed. The Metal Worker then sorted through the encirclements on the projecting spindle, and, a moment later, approached the rack. In another moment, I felt a collar snapped about my neck, and then turned, so that the lock was at the back of my neck. The key was handed to the leader. 'What time is it?' he asked. A fellow, glancing at the sand glass, said, 'A bit past the nineteenth Ahn.' The leader then said, 'Take her out back and tie her to a slave post.'

"I was freed of the rack by the two young men, and, each holding an arm, they assisted me, half carrying me, for I could barely walk, back through the shop, and the private quarters, toward a rear entrance, from which one might approach the stable yard of what had been the Inn of Ragnar. As I passed through the kitchen, we passed a sturdy, stocky woman in rags, clearly of a low-caste aspect, doubtless the companion of the Metal Worker. I was afraid of her because of her overt attitude of contempt and hostility, and, as I was considerably slighter than she, I was sure she could easily subdue me, and hurt me, should it please her. 'Hereafter,' she said, 'do not bring an animal through my kitchen.' As I passed she spat upon me. Behind her was a younger woman, probably her daughter. I think it was she whom I had seen drawing water, earlier. The girl regarded me, curiously. I sensed she might be comparing herself with me, perhaps wondering which of us might bring a higher price in a market.

"Shortly thereafter the two young men brought me to one of several slave posts, thick, sturdy stakes, some four feet high, fixed in the abandoned stable yard behind the closed Inn of Ragnar. I was knelt, my back to the post. My ankles were then crossed and bound behind the post, and fastened to a ring there, and my wrists were crossed and bound, too, behind the post, and fastened to a second ring there. They then withdrew, and I knelt at the post.

"I was helpless and miserable, and in pain, and overcome with the enormity of what had been done with me, and was scarcely able to comprehend the radical transformation which had taken place in my fortunes, from a noble, lofty, exalted, free woman, a legal person, and one of wealth and station, to that of a purchasable object, a vendible beast, an animal, a branded, collared slave, but mostly I was terrified that my identity was suspected, and that I would be returned to Ar, for tortures culminating in the humiliation and agonies of the impaling spear. As Ar might be unable to apprehend Talena, I feared that much of the hatred and rage which would have been levied against the former puppet Ubara might now be visited upon me, not merely as a co-conspirator and abetting traitress, but as one supposedly her dearest friend and colleague, and one certainly, obviously, her highest-placed, best-known, and most-trusted confidante. My affection for the Ubara had, of course, been cunningly feigned, to achieve power and wealth, but this might not be believed, and, even if it were, this pretense might not be seen as redemptive, or counting in my favor. I had, of course, quickly enough, and eagerly enough, agreed that she was to be repudiated, betrayed, and sacrificed for the welfare of our party, that of Seremides and others. Who would not? She was then no longer the key to wealth and power in Ar; indeed, even to have been acknowledged by her, let alone to have been a member of her inner circle, was now a dangerous liability. But this stratagem, to bargain with her for our freedom, even if those of Ar were prepared to bargain, came to naught with her disappearance, her rescue or abduction, from the roof of the Central Cylinder.

"I drew against the cords on my wrists and ankles. I was helpless. I had been tied by men who were obviously no strangers to the tying of slaves. I put my head back, miserably, and felt the metal of the collar rub against the wood. I was collared. My head fell forward, in misery. I was afraid, too, of what I had heard about the twentieth Ahn, which must be nigh. What was to occur then? Clearly it must have to do with me!

"So in the moonlight, in the abandoned stable yard, kneeling, tied to a slave post, I waited."

From what she had told me it seemed clear that some sort of rendezvous was to take place at the village of Ragnar. Leaving a slave bound and alone, of course, is not that unusual. It may be used as a discipline, of course, but that is seldom the case. More often, it is used simply to impress upon her what she is, that she is a slave, subject to the will of her master. Often she does not know how long she is to be left bound, which muchly impresses upon her her helplessness and her dependence on the will of another, this demonstrating for her her vulnerability and utter subjugation. Perhaps he is supping in an adjoining room, and she must wait until she is recollected, or he has time for her. This may also be used as heating technique. Often they will beg to be unbound, rearing and twisting in their cords, that they may be permitted to please their master.

"I lifted my head," she said, "and, looking up, I saw the leader, standing there in the darkness, a few feet from me. 'They should be here soon,' he said. 'They?' I asked. 'They—*Master*,' he said. 'They,' I whispered, obediently, looking up, pulling a little at the cords, and sobbed, '—*Master*.' It was the first time I had truly, appropriately, used that word, not as an ingredient in an imposture, not as an element in a disguise, but in the sense in which it must be truly found on the lips of a slave. 'Search parties emanating from Ar and leagued cities use many such places as the village of Ragnar, scattered over thousands of pasangs,' he said, 'in their endeavors to track and apprehend fugitives. Tarnsmen make wants known at such places, exchange informations, carry intelligences elsewhere, and so on. It was here, earlier today, that we conveyed to an agent of Ar, and he then to his superiors, that we had the Lady Flavia of Ar in custody, and, for a suitable consideration, were prepared to remand her to the proper authorities, here, at the twentieth Ahn.' 'I am not the Lady Flavia of Ar!' I cried. 'Perhaps you are curious,' he said, 'as to why you have been marked and collared. There were two reasons. First, it had come to light that some months ago Talena of Ar, herself, being guilty of a violation of the couching laws of Marlenus of Ar, had been secretly enslaved. Amusing then that it was a mere slave who sat upon the throne of Ar, in imperial regalia. Accordingly it was determined then that the Lady Flavia, if apprehended, should be similarly enslaved, that she should not stand higher than the former Ubara. In no way was she to be deemed superior to Talena. Let the two of them then share the same fate, the collar. The second reason is personal. I found you annoying, and thus, in any event, I would have had you brought under the iron.' 'I am not the Lady Flavia,' I insisted, sobbing. At that point, we heard the hovering beating of a tarn's wings, and, looking up, I saw a tarn, with tarn basket, preparing to alight in the stable yard. I shut my eyes against the dust. 'It seems,' said the leader, 'it is the twentieth Ahn.' 'I am not the Lady Flavia!' I said. 'I am not the Lady Flavia!' The tarn, controlled by a tarnster from the basket, had alit several yards away, across the yard. In the basket there was the tarnster, and a warrior, and, to my surprise, a woman, a slave. The tarnster remained in the basket; the warrior lifted the woman from the basket and set her in the yard, and then leapt from it to the ground. He remained in the vicinity of the basket, and two of the leader's men, not the leader, now come through the back of the Metal Worker's shop, went to join him. At the same time the leader turned about, and, moving measuredly through the darkness, returned to the shop. He would remain indoors, it seemed, waiting for the identification to be confirmed. Perhaps he preferred to come under the purview of Ar as little as possible.

"The slave approached.

"She wore a brief, revealing tunic, cut at the sides, with a disrobing loop. Clearly she had been dressed for the pleasure of men. I was scandalized, but men do with slaves what they please. I surely would never have let my sandal slaves dress so, in a way so exhibiting their beauty, in a way that so blatantly proclaimed their bondage.

"The slave, who seemed marvelously figured, and would doubtless have been of much interest to men, stopped a few feet from me, almost as though startled. Then she seemed to recover herself and approached, and stood before me. I, terribly frightened, put my head down. She took my head in her hands and lifted it, and the moonlight, the clouds separated, fell full upon my face. Tears ran down my cheeks. My head was held still, so that she might examine my face with care.

"'Please, please,' I begged. 'Now, Flavia,' she whispered, 'you are no more than I.' 'Please,' I wept. 'I remember my whipping,' she said. 'Forgive me, Altheia,' I said. 'You were very cruel,' she said. 'Forgive me, Altheia,' I begged. I recalled that when I, in my escape, had been descending the stairs in the cylinder, I had heard her, relieved of her gag, above, seemingly joyfully, gratefully, cry out the word 'Masters!' 'I burned your robes,' she said, 'that they might not give your scent to sleen.' I looked at her, with wonder. 'Do you remember the drover,' she asked, 'at whom I, looking over my shoulder, smiled, and you, in fury, switched me home, and then whipped me?' 'Yes,' I said. He had been a handsome scoundrel, large, well-built, virile, and masterful. 'He recalled me,' she said, 'and searched the public shelves, zealously, and found me, and purchased me. He is now my master. I love him. I am happy.' I said nothing. 'I am a man's slave,' she said. 'Are you a man's slave?' 'No, no,' I said. 'Perhaps you are a man's slave and do not know it,' she said. 'No!' I said. 'You would then be a woman's slave?' she asked. 'No!' I said, frightened. The thought came to me how dreadful that would be. Perhaps I remembered the treatment to which I had subjected my sandal slaves. I did not think it was that unusual.

Whereas free women commonly despise female slaves and treat them with great contempt and harshness, men commonly prize them. Certainly they will pay valuable coin to bring them to the foot of their couch. The relationship between a male master and a female slave is often intimate and loving, though she is never permitted to forget she is only a slave. Too, is it not easier for a woman, in virtue of her sex, to win her way with a male, subject, of course, to the limitations of her collar, to placate him, to evade his whip or switch, to divert his wrath by pleasing him, with her softness, her beauty, her intelligence, her wit, and vulnerability. Many a master, as few a mistress, has been swayed from his purpose by the heartfelt contrition of a naked slave, weeping, covering his feet with her hair and kisses. Better, surely, for a woman to belong to a man than a woman. They see us in terms of desire and pleasure, in terms of love, service, and passion, not in terms of contempt, jealously, and reproach. When a man sees a woman in chains he is likely to exult in her beauty and revel in the mastery; considering how pleasant it would be to own her; when a woman sees a woman in chains, as on a selling shelf, she is likely to feel disgust, anger, hatred, indignation, and rage, and, oddly, envy and jealously. Perhaps she wishes it were she who wore the chains. In any event, a female slave may, and must supply a man with inordinate pleasures; which makes her precious to him, whereas a female slave is likely to fall forever short of the exacting services required by her mistress. 'Perhaps,' said Altheia, 'you have not yet been conquered by a man, have not yet been subdued, have not yet learned to beg for his final, slightest touch, that you might, leaping in your chains, scream your irrevocable submission and surrender to the moons and stars of Gor?' 'Do not betray me,' I begged. 'You are wholly at my mercy, are you not?' she asked. 'Yes,' I said. 'As I was once at yours,' she said. 'Yes,' I said, 'friend Altheia, dear, beloved Altheia.' 'Squirm in your ropes,' she said. I pulled against the cords. 'You are well fastened,' she said. 'Yes, Mistress,' I whispered.

"'Is it she?' called the warrior, at the basket. He had not even bothered to approach. 'Have a lamp brought, Master,' called Altheia. 'A lamp,' said he to one of the leader's men with him, who then went to the Metal Worker's domicile, to fetch a lamp.

'There have been many false alarms,' said Altheia. I did not understand her remark. 'Death by the impaling spear,' she said, 'is a terrible death.' In a few moments a lamp had been fetched from the Metal Worker's domicile and handed to the warrior who had called for it. He then approached, and stood before us. He held the lamp up. 'Is it she?' he asked. Altheia then lifted my head and turned it, carefully, from side to side. 'No,' she said, 'it is not the Lady Flavia.'"

"You realize," I said, "that the slave, in such a situation, given the importance of the matter, might have been slain for such a lie?"

"Truly?" she said.

"Yes," I said. "She would have known that, if not you. You were very fortunate. The slave was very courageous."

"Or foolish," she said.

"Perhaps," I granted her.

"The warrior, an officer, I think, a subcaptain, was furious. 'Another pretense, another attempt at fraud, another attempt to deceive Ar,' he snarled. By now, the leader of the fellows into whose power I had fallen, alerted by one of his men, had emerged into the stable yard. 'What is amiss?' he asked, though he was doubtless well apprised by then of the slave's report. 'This is not the Lady Flavia,' said the officer. 'Surely it is she, I am sure of it!' said the leader. 'Many times, now and heretofore,' said the officer, 'imposters have been presented as Talena or the Lady Flavia, or others.' 'Surely it is she,' said the leader. The officer turned to the slave, lifting the lantern toward me. 'No,' said the slave. 'She is not the Lady Flavia.' 'She is mistaken,' asserted the leader. I kept my head down, trembling. But the officer jerked my head up, and I cried out with pain, and I closed my eyes against the glare of the lamp. 'Consider the exquisite nature of her features,' said the officer. 'Consider her figure. Are those the features and figure of a free woman? Consider the curves, the thighs, waist, and breast, the shoulders. Those are slave curves. Those are auction-block curves!' 'She has the accents of Ar,' said the leader. 'So, too, have thousands of others,' said the officer, angrily. 'You would have me believe this is a free woman?' he asked, thrusting my head back against the slave post. 'This is not a free woman. This is a small, well-curved man's plaything, to be pulled out of a cage for a few tarsks. You would dare to pass off so obvious a slave as the Lady Flavia?' 'It is she,' said the leader, 'she, enslaved!' 'Who are you?' demanded the officer. 'What are you, and your men? What is your relationship to the uprising? What are you doing, at night, on the Brundisium road?' 'At this point the leader shrugged, and stepped back. He had no wish to respond to the officer's questions. Too, he had women nearby, between two buildings, bound and in coffle, and would not be eager to surrender them to another's chains. He and his men did well outnumber the officer and the tarnster but it would be difficult to dispose of them with ease. There were the Metal Worker and his family, and probably others in the village of Ragnar, who would know of them. One could not be sure of killing them all. And the itinerary of the tarnster and the officer was doubtless registered somewhere, and any undue absence would presumably generate a search. There would be inquiries. Too, had he not, already, in his pouch, a wealth of precious stones? 'My apologies,' said the leader. 'We thought the slave once the Lady Flavia.' The word 'once' frightened me. I realized that I was now, in the eyes of the law, no longer the Lady Flavia but an animal that might be named as the free might please. Shortly thereafter the officer and the slave had reentered the tarn basket and the tarnster took the bird to flight, the basket trailing behind on its long harness ropes. I saw its silhouette briefly against the yellow moon. I recalled the authority with which the officer had spoken, and the care, the circumspection, with which the leader had responded. The very word of Ar, I surmised, was once again weighty in moment. I became aware then of the leader looming over me. He was not pleased. I put down my head, quickly. 'Look up,' he said. I did so. 'I am not the Lady Flavia,' I whimpered. 'Take her to a whipping post,' he said, 'and lash her.' Later, as I attempted to comprehend the pain, my back afire, my eyes red from weeping, my wrists bound over my head, the leader's voice was heard, at my ear, but as though from afar. I struggled to understand the words, though he must have been no more than one or two horts from me, whispering. 'You are Flavia,' he said. 'What is your name?' 'Flavia,' I wept, '—*if it pleases Master.*' 'You wished to go to Brundisium,' he said. 'Yes, Master,' I said. 'Well,' said he, 'you will go to Brundisium. You will be taken to Brundisium.' 'Yes, Master,' I said. My arms ached, my wrists tied high, well over my head. My body was stretched. Only my toes were in contact with the ground. In addition my ankles, uncrossed, had been tied to a ring set in the earth beneath the high ring, the over-the-head ring. In this fashion the body is stretched, providing a convenient, practical, exploitable expanse for the whip's work, and the body can recoil and writhe, and pull away from the blows only to the extent that one realizes how little one can succeed in such an endeavor. 'Do you know what will be done with you in Brundisium?' he asked. 'No, Master,' I said. 'You will be sold,' he said. 'Yes, Master,' I said."

I took the last sip of broth, and put the bowl down beside me, at my right knee.

The slave regarded it.

"You were sold in Brundisium," I said.

"Yes," she said.

"Were you auctioned?" I asked.

"No," she said. "I was taken to a slaver's mart."

"What did you bring?" I asked.

"A thousand pieces of gold," she said.

"There will be records," I said, "and they may be checked."

"Forty tarsks," she said.

"Surely not of silver," I said.

"Of copper," she said, angrily.

"Then you did not even bring a single silver tarsk," I said.

"No," she said, angrily.

"Perhaps you now have a better understanding of your worth," I said, "as compared to other women."

"Yes!" she said, angrily.

"Do not be concerned," I said. "You were new to the collar, and untrained."

"I am beautiful," she said, "extremely beautiful!"

"You did not sell for much," I said.

"Beast!" she said.

"What is your brand?" I asked. I could not determine this for her tunic. Too, there was little light in my cell, only that from the small lamp, on its chains, slung from the ceiling outside the bars, moving with the movement of the ship, outside the opened gate.

"The *kef*," she said, angrily.

"There you have it," I said. "The *kef* is for pot girls, for kettle-and-mat girls, for common slaves."

"Even the most beautiful," she snapped, "may wear the *kef*."

I smiled. "That is true," I said. "Men often enjoy putting even the most beautiful in the *kef*, that they may keep in mind that they are only slaves."

"Am I not beautiful?" she asked.

"I would put you in the middle range of slaves," I said. "You would not likely be either the first nor the last put on the block." It is not unusual for slavers to save the best merchandise for late in the sale, when late comers are present, the audience is settled in, interest has been whetted, emotions are running high, purses are most open, and so on. This is not a universal practice, however, as one is likely to make less on early sales. A clever mix of goods is perhaps the most common manner of staging a sale. On the other hand, I think it does not really make much difference, as the merchandise is commonly available for inspection, though through bars, in pre-sale exposition cages. One may then note the goods of interest to one, by their lot numbers, usually inscribed in grease pencil on the left breast, and then wait until they stand in the sawdust, high on the block, exhibited to the house, under torchlight. To be sure, one can be mistaken. Sometimes an item which appears promising in the exposition cage may prove less interesting on the block, and sometimes an item scarcely noticed in the exposition cage will enflame a battle of bids, much to the pleasure and profit of the house. On the other hand, one cannot really measure these matters with scales or marked sticks. Many are the mysteries herein contained. Some men will kill for a woman another might ignore, and some women who might seem to be outstandingly beautiful may not attract much attention. There are doubtless cues, latencies, subtleties, and specificities in such cases which are difficult to identify, let alone quantify. They are, however, undeniably real.

"I am incredibly beautiful!" she insisted.

"You are not a bad-looking slave," I granted her.

"May I withdraw?" she asked.

"How did you come here?" I asked.

"I am not fully sure," she said.

"Who purchased you?" I asked.

"It was done through agents," she said, "but at the behest of strange men, quiet men, sedate men, softly spoken men, men carrying unusual weapons, men with strange eyes."

"I do not understand," I said.

"They are spoken of as Pani," she said.

"Strange eyes?" I said.

"To us," she said.

"Tuchuks?" I asked.

"I do not think so," she said. "There are at least three hundred on board, perhaps many more."

"I was not brought aboard by such," I said.

"There are many others, too," she said, "of Ar, Cos, Tyros, the further islands, even Besnit, Harfax, and Thentis."

It was a pirate crew, mixed, without Home Stones, and such, I had speculated earlier.

"Some fifty such as I," she said, "were exhibited and bought, and, chained, taken by galley north, to the great forests. We were thence marched overland, in coffle, and then, on rafts, floated across the Alexandra. There, in separate groups, unacquainted with one another, we were kept, dieted and exercised, in special palisaded enclaves."

"You were put at the pleasure of men," I said.

"No," she said.

"Interesting," I said.

"This deprivation," she said, "caused much distress to some of our number, who might weep in their kennels, scratch at the logs in the yard, beseech guards for their touch, and roll in the dirt, in frustration."

"In their bellies," I said, "slave fires had been lit."

"Doubtless," she said.

"But not in yours?"

"Certainly not," she said, angrily.

"After months," she said, "we were braceleted, coffled, and hooded, and brought back across the Alexandra on boats. We were then, helplessly, embarked on this great boat. Only once have I been allowed on the top deck. This is a vast, floating thing."

"Who is in charge here," I asked, "and what is the destination of this voyage, and what is its purpose?"

"The Pani," she said, "clearly. It is their vessel. I do not know its destination, perhaps the farther islands, surely not beyond. And I do not know what might be the purpose of the voyage."

"You know little," I said.

"It seems," she said, "that curiosity is not becoming to us."

"Perhaps only the Pani, whoever they might be, know," I said.

"I think so," she said.

"Why do you think that such as you have been cargoed?" I asked.

"We are women," she said. "I suppose we are to be sold."

"Perhaps," I said, "there is a market, somewhere, for women of your appearance, with your sort of eyes."

"Perhaps," she said.

"To be sure," I said, "you might also be distributed as gifts."

"Of course," she said. "We are women."

"Precisely," I said.

"But there are female slaves on the ship which are at the public use of the crew, and private slaves, as well."

"You were brought on board hooded?" I asked.

"Yes," she said. "As might have been verr or tarsks."

"And there are others," I said, "as you, but whom you have not seen."

"That is my surmise," she said. "I think so, from the sound of the coffle chains, the number of boats used, and such."

"Before I was brought on board," I said, "I heard the scream of a tarn, this far from land, in the fog."

"There are tarns on board," she said.

"Many?" I asked.

"Several," she said.

"Why?" I asked.

"I do not know," she said. "Such as we are not privy to the projects of masters."

I regarded her.

She was uneasy. She wished to withdraw.

I continued to regard her.

"Is Master pleased?" she said.

"You are not really bad looking," I said.

"A slave is flattered," she said, bitterly.

"There are many better," I said, "of course."

"Doubtless," she said.

"You might have some possibilities," I said.

"Possibilities?" she said.

"You were very fortunate that you were not betrayed by Altheia," I said.

"She was a fool," she said.

"In similar circumstances," I said, "you would have betrayed her?"

"Certainly," she said. "Instantly, consider the risks."

"I see," I said.

"May I withdraw?" she asked.

"There is, of course, one, I, on board," I said, "who knows you from Ar, and might betray you."

"Do not," she whispered, frightened. "You would not do so!"

"Stand," I said to her, "there."

She complied, and I could then well see her, back a bit, her ankles in the straw.

"I think you still see yourself as a free woman," I said.

"Scarcely," she said, "I have been stripped, braceleted, roped, coffled, chained, trekked, tunicked, marked, collared, lashed, vended, and commanded."

"Even so," I said.

I suspected she did not yet fully understand how her condition, nature, and very being had been radically transformed since Ar, that she was now totally other than she had been. Doubtless she had an intellectual sense of this, who would not, but I suspected that she had not yet acknowledged, manifested, revealed, and liberated the secret slave that was the core of her being.

"Remove your tunic," I said.

"Please," she said.

"Better," I said. "But you are standing as a free woman. Straighten your body, lift your head, turn your hip."

"Please, no!" she said.

"You stood as what you were before," I said. "Do so now, again."

"But I am now naked," she wept.

"Who would buy you as you are?" I asked. "You are before a man, slut."

"Mercy!" she wept.

"Does the Lady Flavia refuse to obey?" I asked. "Good," I said. "That is not bad, Alcinoë, at least for a girl new to the collar."

She wept, but stood well.

"Now turn about," I said, "slowly, and then, again, face me."

"Good," I said.

"Now, clasp your hands behind the back of your neck, put your head back, and turn about, again, again slowly, and then, again, face me. Good. Now you may lower your arms, and regard me, standing well."

She was lovely, in the dim light, standing in the straw, within the cell, the gate open behind her.

"Brush your hair back, with both hands," I said.

Yes, I thought, certainly well worth forty copper tarsks.

"Do you not know how to make a man want you?" I asked.

"No!" she said.

"I am considering putting you through slave paces," I said.

"I do not know such things," she said. "I have not been trained!"

"But you are a slave," I said.

"Yes, yes," she said, "I am a slave!"

I suspected she would respond well, and more quickly than most, to male dominance. Once the collar is on them, it seldom takes much time, some more, some less.

"Often, in Ar," I said, "your veil was loose, disarranged, as though carelessly, before guards and other males."

"You were not to look," she said. "Did I not chide you for your boldness?"

"Poor males," I said, "to be so tormented."

"And surely," she said, "once aware, I hastily restored the propriety of my habiliments."

"You must have been aware," I said, "that men, so provoked, would conjecture your lineaments, beneath those layered, brightly colored robes."

"No!" she said.

"Truly?" I said.

"You had your slaves," she said, angrily, "collared, face-stripped, with ill-concealed limbs. Should that be all you knew? Why should you not have been given a hint, at least, of true beauty, the incomparably superior beauty of a free woman?"

I laughed.

She turned her head away, angrily.

"Forty copper tarsks," I said.

"Beast," she said.

"Now it is you who are in the collar," I said. "Do you truly think you are less beautiful now than then? Indeed, the collar much enhances a woman's beauty."

"May I withdraw?" she asked.

"You were a haughty she-sleen," I said, "a hypocrite, a false friend, greedy, insolent, self-seeking, cowardly, dishonest, cruel, and power hungry."

"May I withdraw?" she said.

"But you did, upon occasion, disarrange your veils," I said.

"To taunt men," she snapped, "to make them miserable, to let them see what they could not have!"

"Most," I said, "might have afforded forty copper tarsks."

"I must return," she said.

"To your kennel?" I inquired.

"To my mat," she said, "to be chained there! Does that please you?"

"It is my impression," I said, "that free women not only despise slaves, but, being women, often envy them. What woman would not wish to be excitingly garbed, to be not only permitted, but to have no choice but to publicly exhibit her beauty? What woman would not wish to escape the inhibitions, the social demands, the conventions and pressures, the robes, veils, and proprieties which so control and confine them? What woman would not wish to realize that she is stunningly attractive to men, that she is the object of mighty male desire? What woman truly believes that she is the same as a man? What woman does not wish to kneel naked, collared, before her master, the joyful, waiting, hopeful instrument and vessel of his pleasure? Surely you have wondered, if only in rage, at the radiance, the joy, the fulfillment, the freedom, the paradoxical happiness, of the female slave."

"Let me go!" she begged.

"So in your supposed carelessness, that having to do with your veiling," I said, "I see more than the cruel delight of an ignoble and petty woman, little more than a she-sleen, protected by the transitory artificiality of station, to torment men. I see, rather, a woman who is displaying herself, as a woman, before men. In your dreams did you not occasionally find yourself back-braceleted and naked in the arms of a master, knowing that he might, if it pleased him, and whether you wished it or not, force upon you uncompromisingly rapturous ecstasies, ecstasies in the throes of which you, at last, will beg to utter the surrender cries of the yielded slave?"

"Please, I beg you," she said, "let me go—*Master!*"

"'Master'?" I said.

"Yes," she said, "Master, Master!"

"Have the slave fires been lit in your belly?" I asked.

"No!" she said.

"But you have begun to sense what it might be to feel them?" I asked.

"No, no," she said. "No! No!" She put her head in her hands, sobbing, and bent over at the waist. "What do you want of me?" she sobbed.

"What do you think a man might want of you?" I asked.

"That?" she said.

"Why not?" I asked.

"I was a free woman!" she said.

"You are no longer a free woman," I said.

"Be merciful," she said. "Dismiss me!"

"Approach, girl," I said.

"'Girl'?" she said.

"Yes, 'Girl'," I said. "Lie here, beside me, girl."

"Never!" she said.

"In disarranging your veils in Ar," I said, "in your time of power, your features, as doubtless you intended, were well bared, though, could you have seen the future, you might have been more careful, more decorous. You are the former Lady Flavia of Ar, and that name, as I understand it, remains high on the proscription lists, perhaps just beneath those of Talena herself, and Seremides."

"Do not betray me!" she pleaded.

"Death by impalement," I said, "is doubtless a most miserable death, and not the swiftest. Indeed, it can take more than an Ahn to descend the spear. And sometimes, suitably braced, increment by transitory increment, the victim given food and water, the execution can take several days, during which time the victim is exposed to the jeers and abuse of the public."

She came and lay down beside me.

"On your back," I said, "and throw your legs apart."

"Excellent," I said.

She stared at the ceiling of the cell.

"You may now beg use," I said.

"I beg use," she whispered.

"Who?" I asked. "The former Lady Flavia of Ar, Alcinoë, some slave?"

"I, the former Lady Flavia of Ar, now Alcinoë, slave, beg use," she said.

"Again, more properly," I said.

"I, the former Lady Flavia of Ar, now Alcinoë, slave, beg use, *Master*," she said.

"Are you ready?" I asked.

"Yes," she said.

"'Yes'?" I said.

"Yes, *Master*," she said.

"Beg to be taught your collar," I said.

"I beg to be taught my collar, Master," she whispered.

A woman is never the same, after having uttered such words.

I noted her body carefully, its tonicity, its readiness. I assessed her breathing, I turned her head to mine, and looked into her eyes. I was pleased. This was clearly a slave ready for use.

I released her head, and lay back in the straw.

Some Ehn passed.

"Master?" she said.

"Yes?" I said.

"I beg," she whispered in the half darkness. "I beg use, Master."

"No," I said.

"What?" she said, turning to me.

"You are dismissed," I told her.

She sprang up in tears and, seizing up her tunic, fled toward the gate.

"Wait!" I said.

She turned, at the gate. "Do not forget this," I said, throwing the metal bowl which had held the broth, ringing, to her feet. She snatched it up, and, tunic clutched in one hand, rushed outside and flung shut the gate of the cell, which action closed and locked the gate. "They are going to kill you!" she cried, from outside, through the bars. "They are going to kill you!" And then she fled up the stairs to a higher deck. I lay down in the straw and was soon asleep.

Chapter Four

I Am Interviewed;
My Fate Is to Be Soon Decided

"Keep your head down," said the voice.

I stared at the flooring.

This was now my fourth day on the great ship. I knew, as yet, little about the ship. I did not know her course. I had not been on the main deck.

If they intended to kill me, I did not understand the delay.

I knelt, head down, naked, bound hand and foot.

"Do you understand my Gorean?" asked one of the men. I had glimpsed them when I was brought before them, my hands bound behind my back, before I was put to my knees, and my ankles lashed together.

"Yes," I said, head down.

There were five men, three were of the sort to which the slave, Alcinoë, had alluded, those whom she had thought had "strange eyes." I had seen such eyes before, sometimes on free men, sometimes on lovely slaves, but rarely. Such eyes are sometimes referred to as Tuchuk eyes. The coloring of the skin was unusual, at least to me. It was darker than that with which I was commonly familiar, but not as dark as the brown of Bazi, nor the deeper, richer browns, even blacks, of Schendi, the Ua Basin, and such. They were, I took it, Pani. Two I took to be chief men, each with a guard or colleague. I would learn that the fellow who had spoken, one of the Pani, lithe, pantherlike, was Lord Nishida. With him was a swordsman, though the sword was of a type with which I was unfamiliar. He was also of the Pani, and his name was Tajima. The other chief man, as I took him to be, was also of the Pani, who, I gathered, were important in this enterprise, whatever might be its purpose. He was heavy, even ponderous, and seemed almost asleep, his eyes half closed, but I sensed in him much danger. He reminded me of a seemingly somnolent larl, pretending to be asleep, lying in the grasses, near a watering hole. Woe to the tabuk which might ignore such a form. The larl does not always move whilst hunting. I knew the man at his side, doubtless a guard. He was Seremides of Ar, who had been the master of the Taurentians, the palace guard, during the brief reign of Talena, false Ubara. I wondered if he knew the former Lady Flavia was on this ship, and I wondered if she knew that Seremides, now calling himself Rutilius of Ar, co-conspirator and traitor, he who had abandoned her on the roof of the Central Cylinder, was also aboard. Each, of course, could identify the other. She would know him by sight, and he, too, I had no doubt, would know her. She, so bold in the presence of common soldiers, would surely, in her vanity, have assured herself that one so important as the master of the Taurentians would be well apprised of her beauty. Might that not be to her advantage? Yet, in his haste to make a swift, unencumbered escape, she had been abandoned, left on the roof of the Central Cylinder. I myself, from what I had seen in the cell, would not have minded owning the former Lady Flavia of Ar, and promptly switch-training her to my tastes, but I suspected that Seremides would dispose of her. Too, of course, I could identify him. He had been the finest sword in the Taurentians, the palace guard, and doubtless one of the finest in Ar. I would learn that he had slain six men to earn his place on this ship. Bladewise I could not hope to stand against him. The larger one of the Pani, the heavier, seemingly somnolent one, was Lord Okimoto. Seremides was his personal guard. The fifth man was not of the Pani. He wore the leather jacket of a tarnsman. He was a large, broad-shouldered, sinewy man, with a wind-burned complexion. His hair was red, of an unusual hue. It suggested Torvaldsland. He was called Tarl Cabot.

"You may lift your head," said my interrogator, he whom I would learn was Lord Nishida.

"Let us cut his throat," said Seremides. "He should never have been brought on board."

That Seremides had spoken seemed to surprise Lord Nishida, who glanced to Lord Okimoto, but Lord Okimoto remained passive, his countenance unreadable. Here, I gathered, Seremides was subordinate to others. It was then unusual, I supposed, that he would have spoken without being recognized, so to speak. I had little doubt he could kill me, and, given his true identity, would wish to do so. This must have prompted his boldness.

"What is your name?" asked Lord Nishida.

"Callias," I said.

"Your hands suggest you are an oarsman," said Lord Nishida.

"I drew oar," I said. "But in better times I was first spear, in a squad of nine."

"In better times?" asked Lord Nishida.

"When Cos, Tyros, and allies ruled in Ar," I said.

"We gather," said Lord Nishida, "that is no longer the case."

I had no idea how much they knew. I had gathered from the former Lady Flavia of Ar that men such as Lord Nishida had purchased slaves in Brundisium, and I supposed they had recruited men and hired ships there, as well, which had then coasted north, to the high forests. Beyond that I knew little. I would learn later that they had found, or built, a ship in the north, a great ship, that on which I now found myself, and had debouched into Thassa from the Alexandra. As it seemed they waited for me to speak, I told them, briefly, of the events in Ar, the return of Marlenus, the fighting, the withdrawal of troops, the proscription lists, the flight of fugitives, and such. I also mentioned the unusual account of the disappearance of the Ubara, which I had had from the former Lady Flavia of Ar, now Alcinoë. It seemed, however, that they were familiar with this. In the end, I suspected I told them little that they did not know. If it were new or important information which they wanted of me I fear they were sorely disappointed. And that, I thought, along with the presence of Seremides, did not augur well for my future.

"Do you have a Home Stone?" asked Lord Nishida.

"Yes," I said. "That of Jad, on Cos."

"I thought he was Cosian," snarled Seremides. "Cosians

cannot be trusted. They are treacherous, and deceitful. Let us kill him."

"Several from Cos are numbered amongst our mercenaries," said Lord Nishida.

Certainly I had heard accents of Cos on the galley which had picked me up.

"What was your ship, and its purpose?" asked Lord Nishida.

"The *Metioche*," I said. "Long ship, light galley, out of Telnus, ten oars, single-masted, guard ship, patrol ship. You destroyed her."

"She pursued us, she crossed our path," said Lord Nishida.

"Too," said Seremides, "we were attacked, flaming javelins launched against us."

Fire at sea, as noted, is a great danger.

"Even an ost," I said, "trodden upon, will strike."

"You pursued us," said Lord Nishida.

"Yes," I admitted.

"An ost," said Lord Nishida, "is not well advised to pursue the great hith, against which its poison is useless."

This is not as surprising as it might seem, as the poison of the ost, as that of many poisonous snakes, is prey-selective, deadly against warm-blooded animals, such as tiny urts, its customary prey, or even larger animals, such as verr and tabuk, but harmless to other snakes, to certain forms of tharlarion, and such.

"It is true," I said.

"He is an enemy," said Seremides, "self-confessed, who pursued and attacked us, a scion of vengeful, hostile Cos. He is dangerous. He may incite mutiny. Kill him, and be done with him."

"Shall we kill you?" asked Lord Nishida.

"That decision is yours," I said.

Lord Okimoto nodded his head. Seremides clenched his fists.

"Why was I picked up?" I asked.

"Is it not obvious?" asked Lord Nishida.

"The fellowship of the sea?" I said.

"If you had been rescued by another," said Lord Nishida, "say, a galley of Tyros, it is our speculation that a dozen ships, within days, in the vicinity of the farther islands, would have sought us, to our inconvenience and distraction."

"Were others of the *Metioche* brought aboard?" I asked.

"No," said Lord Nishida.

"I was the only survivor?" I asked.

"Yes," said Lord Nishida.

I found this hard to believe. I would learn later, however, that there was a simple explanation for this seeming anomaly.

"You are hence to the farther islands?" I asked.

"Beyond them," said Lord Nishida.

"There is nothing beyond them," I said, "only the end of the world."

"If the world had an edge," said Lord Nishida, "would not Thassa have drained away, falling into the void?"

"Perhaps there is a wall," I said.

"Perhaps," he smiled.

"None return from beyond the farther islands," I said.

"You are familiar with the slave, Alcinoë?" asked Lord Nishida.

"Yes," I said. To be sure, I had seen her but once, when she had brought me broth. My food and drink, thereafter, had been attended to by guards.

"She claimed you raped her," said Lord Nishida.

"Was her body examined?" I asked.

"Yes," said Lord Nishida. "Have no fear. She was well lashed."

"Excellent," I said.

"She hates you," said Lord Nishida.

"Excellent," I said. "It is then all the more pleasant to have them crawling to you, the whip borne in their teeth."

"She has been given lower duties," said Lord Nishida. "The scrubbing of decks, naked, and in chains, such things."

"Excellent," I said.

Such things are useful in the training of a slave.

"Our physicians have determined," said Lord Nishida, "that after her sojourn in your cell, she is almost ready to be put on the block."

"Interesting," I said.

"She was recently a free woman," said Lord Nishida.

"Oh?" I said.

"Now, it seems," he said, "she has begun to fear radical

changes in her very being, changes she is not capable of resisting, changes such that a free woman may be replaced by a slave."

"She is a slave," I said.

"To her consternation and terror," said Lord Nishida, "it seems that she has begun to sense what it might be to have slave fires in her belly."

"Interesting," I said.

"They have been lit," said Lord Nishida.

"I scarcely touched her," I said.

"The flames are tiny now," said Lord Nishida, "but they will doubtless grow."

"That is common," I said.

"She will, of course," said Lord Nishida, "fear them, and fight them, with all weapons of her pride and will."

"Of course," I said.

That battle, of course, once the fires have begun, cannot be won. Sooner of later the free woman is transformed into a needful slave, a submitted, begging, belonging of men.

And, interestingly, it is a battle the woman does not want, truly, to win. Indeed her victory as a female lies in her utter and unconditional defeat as a contestant in that unnatural, strange war. She cannot be whole and fulfilled until she is true to the core of her being, that of lying at the feet of her master.

"I have seen this Alcinoë," said Seremides. "She looks well in her collar. Perhaps she might be given to me."

"Perhaps," said Lord Nishida.

That, I thought, would be the end of a slave.

"If," said I, "you feared survivors, who might warn those of Tyros or Cos of your presence, why did you not simply slay me, and cast me over the side of the galley?"

"Do you think we are pirates?" asked Lord Nishida.

"Yes," I said.

To be sure, the vessel itself would seem an impractical corsair, but I knew she sheltered at least one nested galley, which might plausibly exercise the dark vocation of the low, green ships.

"Kill him," said Seremides.

"Are you prepared to deny your Home Stone?" asked Lord Nishida.

"No," I said.

"Kill him," said Seremides.

"Have you anything of interest or importance to impart to us," asked Lord Nishida.

"I fear not," I said.

"No information as to ships and schedules, patrols, or such?"

"Ours," I said, "was the last patrol of the season. Thassa grows cold, and angry. I advise you to turn about and lay to port, if you have a port. This is no time to tempt the indulgence of Priest-Kings, no time to tempt the season, or the patience of Thassa. A galley of Tyros was to rendezvous with us, but that was days ago, and, if you are sailing to the farther islands, much to the east. The absence of the *Metioche*, of course, will be noted, and doubtless galleys will leave Telnus, searching for her, or her wreckage."

"But that, too, will be far to the east," said Lord Nishida.

"Yes," I said.

"He is useless to us," said Seremides. He had slipped his short blade from its sheath. It had been a lovely draw, silent, and smooth. I had not noticed the draw until it was completed, the blade free of its housing. A distraction is involved. One looks to the side and the gaze of others is likely to follow this line, whilst the hand, meanwhile, unnoted, draws the blade. I wondered if Seremides had once trained with the Assassins.

"Return your serpent to its lair," said the tarnsman, not requesting permission to speak. I was reassured that there was no good feeling, obviously, between Seremides and the tarnsman.

Seremides looked to Lord Okimoto, who nodded. The blade snapped back into the sheath, angrily.

"Do you know weapons?" inquired Lord Nishida.

"I was first spear," I said, "of a squad of nine."

"It is my understanding," said Lord Nishida, "that Cos is imperialistic."

"The laws of Cos," I said, "march with the spears of Cos."

"That is a saying, is it not?" asked Lord Nishida.

"Yes," I said.

I would not bend to diminish, nor cloud, the glory of Cos, but I did not regard her as unique amongst the communities of men. Surely violence, aggression, opportunism, territoriality, imperialism, and such, were not her exclusive possessions. Is the way of war not the way of men? Surely her spears were matched ever with spears, her blades with blades. Indeed, how is a state to wax great save by the spear, the blade? If this is the way of Cos, is it not also the way of Ar, Turia, and a hundred other cities? How are trade routes, cities, fields, mines, slaves, and such to be conveniently purchased save by steel? The larl rules his domain; he does not discuss it with the tabuk.

"Tomorrow, friend Callias," said Lord Nishida, "your fate will be decided. Tomorrow, you will live or die."

"My thanks," I said.

"Would you care to have a slave sent to your cell tonight?" asked Lord Nishida.

"No," I said.

"I thought perhaps the girl, Alcinoë," said Lord Nishida.

"No," I said.

"She is pretty, is she not?" said Lord Nishida.

"She is not a bad-looking slave," I said.

"But you do not want her sent to you tonight?" he said.

"No," I said. "I will sleep."

"As you will," said Lord Nishida.

"But I might," I said, "like strong broth."

"It will be so," said Lord Nishida.

Chapter Five

What Occurred on the Main Deck of the Great Ship; Tersites; A Storm Is Imminent

The sixth passage hand was done, the autumnal equinox had been marked in the scribal calendar of Jad, Se'Kara was done, and, as nearly as I could tell, it was the third or fourth day in the seventh passage hand.

It was a bright day.

Had the *Metioche* not crossed paths with the great ship she would now be in her shed in Telnus, in her winter berth, and I, and her crew, cleared and paid by a harbor marshal, wallets bulging with copper, would have gone our ways, some scattering through a hundred towns and villages, others remaining in Telnus, seeking the delights and comforts of the port. For those remaining in Telnus, a refundable fee would have been deducted from our pay, this entitling us to housing in the port dormitory, and the right to a meal, once daily, at the common tables, this an insurance against an empty purse, a hungry stomach, and a lodging on a winter street. This was provided only for state mariners. Private mariners must make do as they can, in the city or outside of it. Some coasting is done but, on the whole, in the off season, the port is quiet. After a lean dark winter spring is welcome. The shed doors are opened, the vessels on their rollers emerge, into the light, as though awakening, and the rigging, refitting, caulking, and painting begins. It is lovely when, later, the ships, wreathed with flowers, to singing and music, are brought to the water. Oil, and wine, and salt are poured into Thassa, the oil to calm her waters, the wine that she may be warmed and pleased, and the salt, in its preciousness, for honor, prestige, life, and hope, and, too, that it may be mixed with her own, that she may accept the ship as one with her, to be sheltered and protected, as sister, as kin. But, woe, I was far from Telnus, and her comforts. Her steep, narrow streets, her lights, her taverns, her slaves, perfumed and painted, their wrists and ankles jangling with bells, with tender lips and well-rounded, warm arms, were far distant.

I looked over the rail.

Thassa was restless.

There were white whispers in the water.

The wind was rising.

This was no time to be abroad on Thassa. Did they know so little of her moods, of her temper?

It was cool on deck, in the open, in the wind, even for the brightness, but I was not uncomfortable. I was dressed warmly, a jacket, cloak, tunic, leggings, soft boots. It was much warmer, of course, below decks, away from the wind. Yet, later, I was sure, the cold, despite the corridors, the braziers, the lamps, would reach even the mysterious labyrinths below.

"As I understand it," said Tarl Cabot, the tarnsman whom I had encountered the preceding day during my interrogation, "you were not armed when found."

"No," I said. "On a Cosian warship only the officers are armed, until an engagement is imminent, and then weapons are distributed."

This arrangement is not that unusual. It adds to the authority of officers, and tends to reduce the likelihood of serious harm amongst the men. It takes time, usually, to beat a fellow bloody and senseless, and he is likely to recover sooner or later, and perhaps put an end to the quarrel over a jug of paga, but an angry word, a swift movement, and a flash of steel, and one may well have lost a shipmate, and eventually, given the friendships and alliances amongst the men, more than one. Those on board a ship constitute a small community, confined within a circumscribed area. A strict discipline must be maintained on board, as in a cage of sleen, lest they tear one another to pieces.

There is nowhere to run. Tempers may flare. Blood may beget blood. I saw that the fellows about, and there were several, were all armed. This confirmed my suspicion that I was in the midst of pirates. In any event, many of these fellows seemed to me dangerous men. This was no common crew. For what purpose, and by what means, might these men have been assembled? I thought again of the cage of sleen. What but the whip and spear might maintain order in such a cage? But, who, too, I asked myself, might disarm such men?

"You know the blade?" asked the tarnsman.

"Passably," I said.

He was a tarnsman. Few men master tarns, few dare their saddles.

"When have you last drawn, fenced, put your skills to the test?" he asked.

"Not since Ar," I said. "Months ago. I sold my blade."

"One does not sell one's blade," he said.

"I needed money," I said.

"One dies first," he said.

"I am not of the warriors," I said.

"But you take fee?" he said.

"Yes," I said.

From his presence at my interview, or interrogation, I took him to be an officer of some sort.

His accent was unusual. I could not place it. Perhaps Harfax.

I did not think he bore me any ill will. Indeed, yesterday, on my behalf, he had stood against Seremides himself. Perhaps he did not know, as I did, the skills of the former captain of the Taurentians. I knew of no blade the equal of his. Something in the eyes or mien of this man suggested he might be other than many here; oddly enough, for the venue, I suspected he might once have been no stranger to honor; such I would not have sensed in Seremides. I wondered if he were once of the warriors, perhaps long ago. Such men may betray the codes, but they are not likely to forget them. It is hard to forget the codes. Is it not a saying of warriors that one does not sell one's blade, that steel is to be prized above gold? And honor above life? How came then such a man here, if he were such a man, on this ship, amidst this unlikely, motley crew? Had he betrayed the codes? But it is difficult to forget the codes. There were always the codes, the codes. I supposed them fools, such men, but there are such men. One mocks them until one needs them. Who else, when one is in mortal jeopardy, would one prefer to have at one's back? They are of the scarlet caste. Such men, at the least, like the Assassins, are likely to kill quickly, and cleanly.

"You inquired, yesterday," he said, "of other survivors, from the *Metioche*. There were several. But none were brought aboard. They were picked up by the private galley of Lord Okimoto, captained at the time by Rutilius of Ar, first in his guard."

"They were slain?" I asked.

"Yes, to a man," he said.

"And thus," I said, "they would not survive, perhaps to enlighten others as to the existence of a great ship, a mysterious, monstrous vessel, unlicensed in our waters."

"Fortunately for yourself," he said, "you were picked up by a second galley, the port-amidships galley, captained by the mercenary, Torgus."

"And now I die?" I asked.

"We shall see," said the tarnsman.

"Hail Rutilius!" we heard. "Rutilius of Ar!"

The men who were crowded about then parted, and stepped back, clearing a space on the deck.

I removed my cloak, setting it aside, on the rail.

The man identified as Rutilius of Ar then stood at the edge of a circle, some feet of cleared space between us. Without taking his eyes off me he unclasped his cloak and handed it to a fellow, a fellow garbed as he was, in the yellow livery of what I would come to recognize as that of Lord Okimoto's retinue. I saw nothing of Lord Okimoto himself. Perhaps the morning's work of Seremides was of little interest to him, the outcome being a foregone conclusion, or perhaps, merely, he did not care to share, or dabble in, the pleasures of his subordinates.

I wondered if Lord Okimoto had instructed Seremides that survivors were to be put to the sword. I rather doubted it. He had not seemed much concerned, in the interrogation, with my fate, one way or another. Quite possibly he had issued no instructions. Quite possibly he had left such matters to the judgment of Seremides, the Seremides I knew.

"Are you ready to die?" asked Seremides.

"I am unarmed," I said.

He slipped the sheath from his left shoulder, and, grasping it, drew his blade, easily, casually. It made no sound, as the sheath was lined. This is not uncommon with the sheath of an Assassin's weapon, this permitting the weapon's noiseless departure. It does, slightly, slow the draw. The sheath with belt he then handed, as he had the cloak, to the fellow with him. When danger is not imminent, the sheath belt is usually worn across the body, as this provides greater security, the weapon then at the left hip. If a locale is deemed dangerous the sheath belt is usually looped over the left shoulder. In this way, the weapon freed, the sheath and belt may be discarded, as it constitutes a graspable encumbrance. The sword was the *gladius*, double-edged, some eighteen inches of steel, long enough to outreach a knife, short enough, light enough, dexterous enough, to work behind the guard of a longer, heavier weapon.

"Five days ago," said Seremides, addressing himself to the seeming rabble about, "without provocation, we were attacked by Cosian pirates, who attempted to burn our ship. We fought. We resisted. We conquered. Then we punished. Those who did not drown were executed, with but one exception, the sleen before you who was mistakenly spared, who should have been bloodied and given to Thassa's hungry children, an offering to her justice, that he not soil our ship with his unclean, impenitent, criminal presence."

"My name is Callias," I said. "My Home Stone is that of Jad, on Cos. Perhaps some of you share her Home Stone with me. I was an oarsman on the Cosian patrol ship, the *Metioche*, out of Telnus. We are not pirates. You were in Cosian waters. We pursued you, investigating. We fired on you in self-defense. If any have been wronged here it is surely we, and not you. I think a mountain has little to fear from a pebble, a draft tharlarion from a stable urt."

Seremides regarded me, measuring me, and smiled.

Some men enjoy killing, and I did not doubt but what one of these was Seremides, formerly first sword amongst the Taurentians. On the other hand, had I been another, and not one who knew him from Ar, I doubt that he would have been much concerned with me, nor would have so zealously set himself to have my blood. I was a witness, as was the slave, Alcinoë, who might identify him as the former captain of the Taurentians, traitor and arch-conspirator, he who had stood high in Ar during the reign of the puppet Ubara, Talena, one of those who, like Talena and the former Lady Flavia of Ar, her confidante, had a price on his head. I recalled how he had so persistently urged my death in the meeting below decks yesterday. He might have killed me then, had it not been for the intervention of the tarnsman, Tarl Cabot. Apparently I constituted a threat to him, at least in his mind, of considerable portent. Were I he I would doubtless have been similarly apprehensive. I looked over the rail, at Thassa, wanting to see her, again, if only for the last time. But she seemed uneasy, cold and dark, and there was a roll of clouds unfurling over her brow in the north.

"I, Rutilius of Ar," said Seremides, "do not countenance an enemy amongst us. Who knows whose throat might be cut in his sleep by this sleen? Will you share water and rations, and loot and slaves, with one who would have delivered you to the teeth of flames or the fangs of sharks? Will we have an enemy, a deadly foe, amongst us?"

It interested me that Seremides seemed to feel it incumbent upon him to justify a projected murder. It had not been that way in Ar. Here it seemed he was not captain, here it seemed a certain wariness might be in order. For that I was grateful. The sword here did not seem to be a law unto itself, or at least his sword. The fellows about, as far as I could see, were not much interested in charges and countercharges, denunciations and defenses, and such, as in seeing what might ensue. I recalled that in Ar, I, and others, in the early morning, had occasionally gathered to watch Seremides make a kill.

"I see no judge here, no court," I said.

"This is the court," said Seremides, "and I am the judge."

"I do not think so," said a polite voice.

I looked to the side, and saw standing there he of the Pani, whom I would learn was Lord Nishida. I did not know how long he had been there, how much he had heard. I did remember that he had said that today was to be the day on which I would live or die.

106

I was pleased to see Lord Nishida present. He wore an oddly cut robe, with short, wide sleeves. In his sash were two swords. This, I sensed, from yesterday, and today, given the deference with which he was regarded, was a person of moment. I knew not how long I might live, so, in this august presence, I pointed to Seremides, and stated, clearly, loudly, and emphatically, "His name is not Rutilius of Ar!"

Seremides instantly rushed at me and I saw the flash of the blade descending but heard a ringing of steel and saw a flash of sparks and another blade had been interposed, that of the tarnsman. Seremides backed away, warily, his weapon poised, the point moving like the head of an excited, coiled ost.

"Many men here," said Lord Nishida, quietly, "are known elsewhere by other names. The guard of Lord Okimoto, as he wills, is Rutilius of Ar amongst us. That is acceptable to us, and is not to be questioned. If you know another name, or another time, or another place, do not speak it. This ship, and our mission, is now our world. What matters elsewhere does not matter here. What matters here does not matter elsewhere."

"I see," I said.

"So," said Lord Nishida, "what is his name?"

I looked at Seremides. "His name," I said, "is Rutilius of Ar."

Seremides smiled.

Could it be, I asked myself, that it does not truly matter to them that Seremides of Ar might be amongst them? But then I thought, perhaps it does not matter, not here. Who would act upon such intelligence? To whom would one remand Seremides of Ar? How would one petition for, or collect, the bounty? Who is there to pay, or act in this matter? Information which might mean wealth and power on the continent, information which might put armies on the march, which might launch ships, which might flight tarn cavalries, would here be without practical consequences. Indeed, here, some might not even know of Seremides of Ar, and of those who knew some might see their fortunes as best linked to his, particularly if, through his agency, Talena might be found. Who would be more likely to know the Ubara, her habits, her hiding places, than Seremides of Ar, from whom she had been stolen on the height of the Central Cylinder months ago? I wondered how he came to be on this ship, and for what reason. I knew the secret of Seremides, but here that knowledge was of little consequence, other than to place my life in jeopardy. Seremides had little to fear from me now. But I had much to fear from him, or from those who might be enleagued with him. Perhaps, I thought, his identity was known to Lord Okimoto, even to Lord Nishida. I did not know. I would be silent. Presumably Seremides knew that the former Lady Flavia of Ar was on board. I recalled that he had asked that she be given to him. I suspected that she did not know he was on board. As a slave, she might have been kept much in ignorance. That is not unusual with slaves. They are slaves. Thus, she might not know that he, unbeknownst to herself, might have seen her, might have looked upon her now-bared face, a face now slave-bare, a face now denied the dignity and modesty of veiling, a face which must now be as exposed to public view as that of any other animal, a face recalled by him from her vanity in Ar. How terrified she might be if she, now as any other slave, a purchasable object, a mere article of property, might be given to him.

"This Cosian sleen," said Seremides to Lord Nishida, while not taking his eyes off me, "is an enemy, to be put to death, one who wished us harm, not to be tolerated amongst us."

"Do you speak on behalf of Lord Okimoto?" inquired Lord Nishida.

"I bespeak on behalf of all," said Seremides.

"Not on my behalf," said Tarl Cabot, quietly.

I was pleased to see that several of the fellows about seemed to take this seriously. The words of the tarnsman, I gathered, were words to which several present might attend.

I would learn later he was a commander amongst them.

"Did you not say, yesterday," asked Seremides, "that today this Cosian sleen was to die?"

"That he was to live, or die," said Lord Nishida.

"That may be easily determined," said Seremides.

"I am unarmed," I said.

"Then kneel down, and lower your head, to be swiftly slain, unarmed. I shall be quick. Or, if unarmed, run, until there is nowhere else to run, and then die. Or seek Thassa. Perhaps you can swim to Cos!"

I recalled the thought of the cage of sleen. Where, within the bars, might a small sleen flee?

"Permit me to perform the execution," said Seremides.

"Execution?" inquired Lord Nishida.

"To put to death this enemy," said Seremides.

"There will be no execution," said Lord Nishida.

"Very well," said Seremides, and turned to me. "Challenge!" he said.

"I am unarmed," I said.

"Arm him!" said Seremides.

"I know your blade," I said. "I am no match for it."

"Arm him!" said Seremides.

"No," I said.

"Challenge! Challenge!" cried Seremides.

"I do not accept your challenge," I said.

The men about reacted to this, looking about, startled. Amongst them, this response was incomprehensible.

Seremides himself seemed startled.

"Cosian," sneered a fellow.

"They are all alike," said another.

"No," said another fellow who, I supposed, was Cosian. Under his reproachful gaze I suffered.

"No place here for such as he," said a man.

"True!" said the fellow I took to be Cosian.

"Craven urt," said another.

"Over the rail with him," said a fellow.

"Kill him," said another, "and be done with it."

I clenched my fists.

"Not at our table will he eat," said a man.

"Let him fear to go on deck after dark," said another.

"Perhaps," said Tarl Cabot, quietly, "you would accept a champion?"

"No!" cried several men, in gray.

Seremides stepped back a pace. Had a sudden flicker of disquiet crossed his features? In any event, for whatever reason, it seemed clear he did not welcome this intrusion. Yet I knew well the former captain of the Taurentians. What had he to fear? City champions had reeled from his blade.

"No," I said, "I will not have another fight for me." The

tarnsman, Tarl Cabot, I gathered, did not know the skills of Seremides. I would not have another die for me. Even were he, somehow, a match for the former Taurentian's skills, it would be wrong of me to accept his intervention. A Merchant, a laborer, a free woman might accept it, but I could not, not in honor. I had served Cos.

"A challenge has been issued," said Seremides. "I do not accept its rejection. That is my right."

"An Assassin's right," I said.

"Prepare to die," said Seremides, "armed or unarmed."

"Hold," said Lord Nishida, lifting his hand, the sleeve falling back about his wrist, as he did so. "Good Callias," said Lord Nishida, "I do not think you are a coward. Why, then, do you refuse to accept the challenge?"

"It is a challenge without honor," I said. "The animosity borne to me by your Rutilius of Ar has nothing to do with Cos and Ar, with politics or war, with defense or security, nor with justice or law. It is personal, and from the past. I know of things of which I gather I am not to speak, and it is because of this that your Rutilius of Ar seeks my blood, that he may have nothing more to fear from me. He knows I am no match for him. Thus, he would conceal a murder beneath a veil of equitable arbitration, of fair contest, mask a murder under the mantle of a duel. If he would kill me let him do so now, publicly, in cold blood, dishonorably cutting down an unarmed man, one who holds him in contempt. So let my death soil him, and cling to him in the eyes of men, marking him, proclaiming him for what he is in fact, a wretch, a dissembler, a fugitive, a criminal, a coward, a butcher."

"I do not know this Cosian," said Seremides. "Nor do I understand him. It seems he has me confused with another. That is neither here nor there. But, if he will not fight, if he is so craven and cowardly, so much a frightened urt, so enamored of his worthless existence, so unwilling to risk it in fair, open combat, that is his choice. Certainly I cannot, in cold blood, slay an unarmed man. Doubtless he understands that, and thus tries to purchase his worthless life, counting on my honor. Such a killing, however in order, he doubtless realizes would not be permitted by my honor, an honor which I hold sacred, and have never betrayed. Too, it would be embarrassing for me to allow the blood of such a piteously craven urt to stain, however briefly, an honorable blade, that of Rutilius of Ar."

Some of the men about smote their left shoulders, in approval.

"Yes, yes," said others.

"Do not go on deck after dark," said a fellow to me.

"But," said Seremides, "if he is to crawl amongst us, as the slithering ost, unnoticed but deadly, tiny and poisonous, must he not in some way purchase his passage?"

"Yes," said more than one man.

"That was my intention," said Lord Nishida.

"I have no money," I said.

"One purchases one's passage with steel," said Seremides. "I earned my berth by slaying six men."

"True," said a fellow, "six."

"Passage is dear on this vessel," said a fellow, "not free."

"The Cosian has proved he is afraid to fight," said another.

"At the ringing of steel, the laughter of blades, he would hide," said another.

"Over the rail with him," said another.

"Berths are limited, Cosian," said Seremides. "They are to be earned, and in such a way that the best occupy them. Let the slow and clumsy perish, let the swift and skillful live. Let the weak die, let the strong survive. It is the way of nature, that of the tarn, of the sleen and larl. If one is added, let one be subtracted."

I shrugged. "Give me a blade," I said.

"Excellent," said Lord Nishida. "It is as I and Tarl Cabot, tarnsman, intended."

I had thought the tarnsman bore me no ill will. Now I was to be matched, to the death.

A blade was brought, nicely balanced. It was a not unfamiliar sensation, having such an instrument of war again in my grasp. Surely I preferred it to the oar. I touched the blade to my sleeve, and saw the threads part. I looked about. One or two men looked uneasy. One stepped back. I smiled. I was now, again, a man among men.

The tarnsman smiled.

"Bring the thief and wretch, Philoctetes, from his cell," said Lord Nishida. "He has fed enough."

The cloaks of some of the men moved in the wind. The yards above, carrying their large square sails, creaked, turning, as the sails took the rising wind, moving from a gray north.

In a few moments the prisoner was on deck, and given a weapon, rather as mine. We stood a few feet from one another. He was in a ragged blue tunic. He stood unsteadily.

"My dear Callias," said Lord Nishida, "you behold before you a trustless rogue, Philoctetes, a miscreant and felon, a liar, a cheater at stones, one who robs men at night, who steals food, obtaining extra rations for himself, a villain who would cut a throat for a copper tarsk."

"I trust that he is skilled," I said.

"Enough," said Lord Nishida. "He may not have the skills of one who stood first spear, but we deem his skills adequate for our purposes, that of adjudicating a war right to a berth. I advise you not to take him casually. A lucky stroke might fetch him freedom."

I moved the blade about.

It had been long since I had held such a weapon.

Lord Nishida, the tarnsman, and others, moved back, further enlarging the space at our disposal. The boards of the deck were white, and closely fitted, stone cleaned.

Philoctetes seemed unsteady.

"Has he been fed," I asked.

"Yes," said Lord Nishida.

I faced Philoctetes. "Are you ready?" I asked.

"Yes," he said.

"You wear the blue of Cos," I said.

"It is my right," he said.

"You are Cosian?" I said.

He shrugged.

"My Home Stone," I said, "is that of Jad."

He regarded me. "That, too," he said, "is mine."

"You must," said Lord Nishida, addressing me, "be prepared to forswear your Home Stone."

"One of us is to die?" I asked.

"Yes," said Lord Nishida.

"Have you forsworn the Home Stone?" I asked Philoctetes.

"No," he said.

"Then," said I, "stand at my back and we will die together."

"You are serious?" he asked.

"Yes," I said, turning my back to him, facing those about, my sword ready. I saw several of the men about look at one another, and then draw their weapons.

"You are Callias?" asked Philoctetes.

"Yes," I said, puzzled. I could not see him behind me. I did not sense him at my back.

It occurred to me, suddenly, that the back of my neck was open to his blade.

"Hail, Callias!" I heard, from Philoctetes. "Hail, Callias!" cried men about, and the swords which had been drawn were lifted, in salute. I spun about and saw that Philoctetes did not now seem as he had before. He stood straight, and powerful, solid on his feet. He had wiped something from his face, a pale salve or such, and it seemed ruddier now. The blade he had returned to a fellow behind him. "Hail Cos," he said, and we embraced.

"Excellent," said Lord Nishida. "It came about as I had expected."

"I could not kill one whose Home Stone I shared," I said.

"We thought not," said Lord Nishida.

"I did not forswear my Home Stone," I said.

"From yesterday," said Lord Nishida, "we did not think you would, but we did not know."

"Philoctetes played his role well," observed Tarl Cabot.

"What if I had forsworn my Home Stone?" I asked.

"That would have been a great disappointment," said Lord Nishida. "Our journey is long and dangerous, and we will have need of men who will not forswear their Home Stones."

"What if I had fought?" I asked.

"You would not have fought," said Lord Nishida, touching the unusual, curved hilt of one of the swords in his sash, "for I would have cut off your head, before the blades could touch."

"Welcome," said Tarl Cabot, "to the ship's company."

I looked about, but Seremides had left the deck.

I heard the snapping of canvas overhead.

The men about had sheathed their weapons, and were going

their ways when, turning about, a cry of wonder escaped them. I looked forward, to the stem castle, to discern the reason for their awe. There, on the stem castle, behind its aft rail, a small figure, bent and twisted, stood, in cloak and mariner's cap, looking to windward, to the north.

"Tersites!" cried men.

"He is dead!" exclaimed others.

"We witnessed his burning," said another.

"I was at the pyre," said another.

"I have heard of him," I said. This was true. Legends of the mad, half-blind shipwright, Tersites, I did not doubt, had reached even the farther islands. Until now I did not realize he was a real person. From the outcry I gathered that many had not realized he was aboard.

"I saw him burned," whispered a man.

"No," said Tarl Cabot.

"You knew he was alive?" said Lord Nishida.

"I examined bones, found amongst the ashes of the pyre," said Tarl Cabot. "They were the bones of a tarsk."

"It was better," said Lord Nishida, "that he be thought dead, that such a word be carried south, that the apprehension of enemies be assuaged, that none might seek his secrets, that his plans would be thought lost forever, that no ship such as this could be built, or, if built, duplicated."

"Yet," said Cabot, "we were attacked, at the mouth of the Alexandra."

"The concealment of the northern forests proved insufficient," said Lord Nishida.

"Surely you will explain to me one day the nature of our enterprise," said Tarl Cabot.

"It has to do with Priest-Kings and Others," said Lord Nishida. "It is, I take it, a wager of sorts."

"And what hangs upon the outcome of this wager?" asked Tarl Cabot.

"I think," said Lord Nishida, "the fate of two worlds."

"Callias," said Philoctetes, "a storm is near. Come below. Leave the taking in of sail, the governance of the ship, to mariners."

"It is too late in the season to be abroad on Thassa," I said.

"I agree," said Philoctetes.

114

"I trust that oil was poured into the sea, and wine, and salt," I said.

"No," said Philoctetes. "They were not. Come below. A storm is upon us."

I fetched my cloak, and accompanied Philoctetes below.

Chapter Six

The Farther Islands Fall Astern

"There," said Tarl Cabot, "do you see them, the three of them, the farther islands, Chios, Daphna, Thera?"

They were dim, in the distance, in the snow, but one could make them out. I had never been this far west of Cos and Tyros, but the merchantry of the major island Ubarates, including Cos, of course, traded here, and rogue ships, from Port Kar and Brundisium, did as well. Indeed, the major reason for the western patrols, as that of the *Metioche*, was to police these routes, limiting them to licensed traffic.

It was the second week past the eighth passage hand.

"Yes," I said. "I see them."

In an Ahn, they would be astern.

At Cabot's thigh knelt a slave, well-bundled.

She did not seem agitated. Did she not understand we would soon be west of the farther islands?

When she had heeled her master to the rail, where he had joined me, I had examined her, as men will a slave, insofar as was possible, given her furs. She had lowered her eyes, that they not meet without permission those of a free man. Then she had knelt. I supposed she would be excellent, stripped to her neck-encirclement. Certainly her features were exquisite, and the furs, as they were cunningly wrapped and fastened, the clever she-sleen, suggested, as much as concealed, the delights at the disposal of her master. Slaves often garb and present themselves in such a way that others may envy their master for their possession.

She was quite lovely. I thought she would bring good coin off the block.

She did not meet my eyes. She was, after all, her master's property, not mine. Even the casual glance of a slave might enflame a fellow. A slave who is careless with her glances, her smiles, might be beaten.

If I owned Alcinoë, and she smiled at another fellow, I thought I would give her a good switching.

It would teach her a lesson.

It would do her good.

I regarded Tarl Cabot's slave.

I was pleased.

She had about her the look of a woman who is well owned, well mastered.

Commonly a slave rejoices that she is owned. It reassures her and fulfills her. She has come to understand that her sex is rightfully the property of men, and that, in her collar, the tensions and wars are over. She kneels in her place, where she wishes to be, at her master's feet.

One is familiar with the haughtiness, the arrogance, the pride, of the typical free woman, defended by guardsmen, ringed by the walls of her city, well-veiled, well-robed, secure in her status, unassailable in station, ensconced in society's regard, but there is another pride, too, little spoken of, which is, perhaps surprisingly, that of the slave. Even when she kneels before the free woman, in her mockery of a garment, fastened in a collar, her lovely hair in the dirt before the free woman's slippers, she knows herself special, and prized, in a way the free woman is not. She realizes that she, amongst many women, is the one who has been found "slave desirable," the one whom men will put in a collar, the one who will wear a collar. She revels in the fact that she has been found worthy of being owned. She is proud to be owned. This is a mark of quality, a badge of excellence. She is a prize amongst women, so desirable that men will be satisfied with nothing less than owning her. She is that desirable. She knows that she is the most coveted, the most lusted-for, the most delectable, exciting, and sought of women, the female slave. How could she not feel superior, in her sex, as a female, to the free woman in her vain, shallow trappings of dignity and station? Many have been free women, and they know the grief, the sorrow, the frustration, the misery, and loneliness, so often concealed within those cumbersome, ornate robes. The free woman often hates the slave; the slave, often, feels not only fear of, but also pity for, the free woman. So one might then contrast two prides, that of the scornful free woman, richly robed, elevated in society, switch in hand, and that of the timid, frightened creature, perhaps in a rag, a collared animal, who kneels before her. The free woman has pride in her status, the slave in her sex, in her holistic fulfilled womanhood.

One might also note the gratitude of the slave. She loves and serves, and is grateful to have been granted this privilege. It is not unknown for even free women to kneel before a man, press their lips to his boots, and beg him for his collar, that they may belong to him, as his slave. The depth of this need, of this desire, and the profundity of this love, the wholeness of it, the desire to give oneself, to surrender oneself, wholly, to another, is one of the mysterious recurrent songs of nature, its origins perhaps lost or obscure, but its strains familiar amongst her survivors. So she rejoices that she is owned, for she has now at last what she has long longed for, a master. She is a slave at his feet, doubtless stripped and collared, to be treated as he wills. To what less could she be so helplessly responsive?

He is male, and she female, he master, she slave.

How beautiful are women!

Only in the collar can they find themselves.

"You have a lovely slave," I said to him.

"I call her 'Cecily'," he said.

"That is a strange name," I said.

"She is a barbarian," he said.

That, I supposed, explained her lack of agitation. She did not realize the import of being beyond the farther islands.

The girls of Gorean origin were being kept chained below decks, some hooded, and sedated. One could not blame a girl for being uneasy if she were being drawn, say, wrists bound behind her, naked, on a tether, into a larl's den.

"Is she any good?" I asked.

She thrust her cheek against her master's thigh. Clearly she was ready. It is pleasant, I thought, what men can do with slaves.

"A touch," said Cabot, "and she juices and steams."

"She is hot-thighed, then?" I asked.

"Yes," said Cabot, "helplessly so."

"Then she is broken in, nicely?"

"Yes," said Cabot.

I thought of Alcinoë.

"I have heard," I said, "that barbarians are good."

"Any woman is good," said Cabot, "once she is broken to the collar."

Again I thought of Alcinoë. How pleasant it might be, she now a slave, to break her to the collar, to have crawling to my feet, begging a caress.

"Barbarians sell well," I said. I wondered what Alcinoë might bring.

"Few are left long on the chain," he granted me.

"It is said they lick the whip quickly," I said.

"It has to do with their background," he said. "Where they are from they are commonly denied their needs, to be owned and mastered. On Gor they find themselves at last in their place, at the feet of men. Many are astonished at the fulfillments attendant on the summoning forth, the commanding forth, of their deepest and most precious selves. They find happiness, and fulfillments, which they scarcely knew might exist, but had only dimly sensed, in their most secret dreams. On Gor, they find themselves choiceless, given no choice but to be what they truly are, and want to be, not pretend males, not sexless cogs in a societal mechanism, not pretenders and haters, but what they truly are, actually are, and want to be, most profoundly, women. Where they come from they are taught to repudiate nature, to replace her with conventions and principles alien to their deepest needs and feelings. They are taught to revere frigidity, like a free woman, to praise inertness as dignity, to fear the raptures of uncompromised submission. Denied themselves, denied masters, they writhe in frustration, and, hating themselves, and their imprisonment, they think they hate men. Taught to deny their sex, starved for sex, they find themselves then on Gor, in collars, at the feet of men who will have whatever they want from them, and what they want, too, in their hearts, to be had from them. Their exile from their own bodies and needs is at last over. It is as though, at last, starving and thirsting, they were permitted food, though from the hand of a man, and granted water, though from a pan at his feet. Often the happiest moment in the life of one of them, to that point, is when the auctioneer closes his hand, and they realize that, exposed and desired, exhibited and bid upon, they have been sold. No longer are they alone; at last they are possessed; at last they are owned. At last they have a reality and an identity. At last they belong. Indeed, they are now, literally, a belonging, a property of their master. And do they even know, out there in the darkness of the crowd, who has bought them?"

"What is this strange place from which these creatures derive," I asked, "to what country might such pathetic, deprived creatures be indigenous?"

"It is called Earth," he said.

"Why did you join me at the rail?" I asked.

"I thought," said he, "you might be considering Thassa, that you might be thinking of reaching Chios."

"The waters are cold," I said. "I might die before I could reach her."

"Perhaps," he said. "But if you are a strong swimmer, I think you might have reached shore."

"I think so, too," I said.

"You were considering the matter," he said.

"Yes," I said.

"But you did not leave us," he observed.

"No," I said. "I thought I would stay."

"Yesterday," he said, "a galley was commandeered, seized and launched, and seventy men, pursued, beached on Thera, fleeing inland. Two other galleys followed, she was recovered, and brought back. Some others went over the rail, seeking Daphna."

"Many desertions," I said.

"Yes," he said.

"It seems not everyone wishes to go beyond the farther islands," I said.

"It seems not," he said.

We stood there at the rail for a time, in the falling snow. Then we could no longer see the islands.

Before us was darkness and snow, and the surging of Thassa.

"You, however," said he, "have remained with us."

"Yes," I said.

"Why?" he asked.

"I thought I might like to see what lies at the end of the world," I said.

Chapter Seven

We Man the Pumps;
There Is Unease Amongst the Men;
We Are Spoken to by Tyrtaios

My ankles were in freezing water. My back and arms ached. Twelve of us, in this shift, manned the pumps.

Nine storms we had endured since I had been taken aboard.

Thassa grew more cruel each day. Few dared to go on deck. Some had been washed away. Men clung to ropes, crossing the deck, leaning into the wind. The tarns had not been flown in six days. Some had died. When the tarn cannot fly, it dies.

The unusual men, the Pani, spoke little, lest it be amongst themselves. But amongst ourselves, the others, there were murmurs of discontent, these subsiding in the presence of officers.

Occasionally, one heard the howling of a sleen, restless in its cage.

Too, off certain corridors, from behind heavy wooden doors, each with its tiny, sliding, rectangular viewing panel, one could hear the lamentations, the weepings, of female slaves. It had been clear to me, almost from the beginning, that there were female slaves on board. One, the slave girl, Alcinoë, once the high lady, Flavia of Ar, confidante even of the former Ubara, Talena, had been sent to me in my cell, barefoot and tunicked, to humbly serve me, to bring me, in her abject servitude, a free man, now unspeakably above her, she now less than the dust beneath his feet, a bowl of broth. Others, in groups, in good weather, had been exercised on the open deck, performing their movements in unison, to the cries of their keeper, sometimes, shuddering, to the snapping of his whip. From their reactions I gathered some had felt it. Certain slaves interestingly, were brought into public view only when hooded. I thought them to be perhaps high slaves, perhaps of such beauty that, should it be bared, men might be driven wild with the need to seize and possess them. Might they not have divided the crew into warring factions? Some slaves were private slaves, owned by one fellow or another. I envied them having such a soft, delicious object chained to their bunk, to be enjoyed as, and when, one pleased. One such was the lovely Cecily, girl of the commander, Cabot; another was called Jane, the slave of his friend, Pertinax. I did not understand the name 'Jane', a lovely but unusual name, which I took to be a barbarian name. Her accent was of Ar, and I did not inquire further. This Pertinax would often scrutinize the slaves being exercised, as though he might have an eye for one. But it seems he did not discern her. Perhaps she was one of the hooded slaves, or amongst those not brought to the open deck. The slaves, I gathered, had been, on the whole, purchased here and there by the Pani, over several months, perhaps for the contentment of themselves and others, perhaps as trading goods, perhaps as merchandise, to be eventually sold in one market or another. It is not unusual, on large ships, round ships, and longer voyages, for slave girls to be brought aboard. Gorean men relish slave meat and do not like to be long without it. By the time the women have learned their collar, of course, they, too, need men. It can be pleasant to torment a hot, begging slave. Free women, on the other hand, unless passengers on particular ships plying established routes, are seldom aboard Gorean vessels. Many Gorean mariners fear to travel with a free woman on board, regarding such as harbingers of ill fortune. Whereas this trepidation is often unwarranted, their reluctance cannot be dismissed as simple superstition. There have been many instances in which the presence of such a female, aloof and inaccessible, arrogant and troublesome, has produced dissension. Too many such women, too, on long voyages, perhaps in their boredom, are careless in their veiling, and enjoy exploiting the provocations, the tauntings, of their sex, casting an alluring eye here, dropping a piquant word there, amusing themselves with the igniting of fires they have no intention of extinguishing. Are they unaware of the turning of a hip, or the hithering sway manifested so subtly in their departure? Gorean men are no strangers to the secrets beneath those cumbersome robes, secrets which the free woman seems to be seeking to share. Is it so delightful, really, to encourage and then scorn, to invite and then rebuke, to tempt and then denounce? Is it in their best interest, really, to practice so petty a power? Surely they must understand the danger of proffering goods they have no intention of selling. Surely they must understand they tread a narrow bridge. Surely better to attend to the curfews and avoid the byways of darkness. What wise woman would let the door of a paga tavern close behind her, unless she wished to find herself within? Gorean men are not long-suffering, nor are they patient. It is not unusual for a lofty free woman, enrobed and veiled, to embark on a voyage, at the end of which she is led down the gangplank, stripped and shackled, on a chain, to be conducted to a convenient market. They now belong to the sex they professed to despise. They will now live to serve and satisfy men. But did they not court the collar? Do they not now find their fulfillment in the chains they wished to wear? But women, free or slave, are seldom allowed on the long ships, the ships of war. On such ships, such as the *Metioche*, duty is paramount and discipline is strict. On such a ship, women have no place; distraction is unacceptable; too, such women would be encumbrances, would be in the way, should an engagement ensue. Lastly, the female slave is property, and such ships seldom carry cargo. Too, such ships may enter battle, and the female slave, who surely has her value, such as it is, no more than other goods is to be put at risk. Needless to say, at the voyages' end, such mariners, starved for the scent of perfume and the clasp of warm arms, are likely to lose little time in seeking the comforts of the taverns. Girls are often sent to the wharves, when ships are due, in camisks adorned with advertising, to solicit patronage for their masters' establishments.

I heard, again, the howling of a sleen. I had not seen it, but, from the sound, I supposed it must be a large brute. It carried from deck to deck.

I did not understand how such a beast might be on board.

There were two major keeping areas, for female slaves, off two long corridors, one on the Venna deck, and one lower, on the Kasra deck, these two corridors, as others, apart from them, leading fore and aft, the length of the vessel. Lately, given the miseries of the weather, the constant rolling and pitching motion of the ship, the distance from shore, the uncertainty of the voyage, their terror at realizing themselves now being taken beyond the farther islands, and fearing perhaps to plunge any moment from the edge of the world, one might hear, as mentioned, from behind the thick doors, the lamentations, the weepings, of female slaves. One could listen, too, for the rustle of chains, as they might move about, or thrash on the straw in their misery. One may silence slaves by going amongst them with a whip, but, compassionately, it had not been done. They were not, after all, males, sturdy quarry slaves, hardened oar slaves, and such, but females, mere females, miserable and pathetic, soft and small, helpless in their collars and shackles, only frightened slave-block goods, so desirably and wonderfully different from men. How inordinately precious and desirable they are!

How inevitable it is to relish them, and strive to possess them!

How comprehensible that they should be sought and secured, roped and chained, that they should be bought and sold, that they should be branded and collared, that there be no mistaking them; how natural and perfect that they should be owned and mastered.

It is what they are for.

Nature has designed their soft lips to be pressed to the feet of men.

Tersites, master of the ship, and master shipwright, to whose specifications the great ship had been built, had refused to pour oil, and wine, and salt into the sea. A mariner had attempted to do so, in the wind and rain, in darkness, after the twentieth Ahn, but was apprehended by the deck patrol, and, by order of Tersites himself, was put under the lash, the snake, twelve strokes. The fellow was strong, and survived.

As I worked at the pump, my thoughts strayed to the slave, Alcinoë. I had not seen her since she had served me. I recalled she had claimed to have been raped by me, which allegation

was demonstrably false, as proven by her body. I had learned
she had been lashed for that indiscretion. A whipping would
do her good. She must learn that a slave girl is not permitted to
lie. A free woman may lie, but not the female slave. I wondered
why she had made her allegation. Perhaps she, still incognizant
of the nature of her condition, that of slave, had thought that I
would be slain upon her assertion, and thus that she would have
nothing to fear from me, that I might reveal her identity, as the
former Lady Flavia. Whereas one speaks commonly of "slave
rape," that usually means little more than using them as one
wishes, unilaterally, peremptorily, forcibly, and such. Technically,
it is not clear that one can rape a slave, any more than one could
rape a verr or tarsk. In a legal sense, a slave cannot be raped, no
more than any other domestic animal. On the other hand, there
might well be social, legal, and economic consequences if, say,
A was to use the slave of B without B's authorization. To be sure,
unless honor is thought to be involved, which may lead to blood
and death, such matters are usually resolved amicably, perhaps
by an apology and the payment of a use coin, A's putting one of
his slaves, B's choice, at the disposal of B, or such. The rape of a
free woman with whom one shares a Home Stone, on the other
hand, is a very serious offense. Fellows have been tortured, and
publicly impaled, for that sort of thing. I wondered if Alcinoë
had wanted me to put her to use, but was angered, even insulted,
that I had not done so, and so pretended, perhaps in her vanity,
that she had been put to use, as would have befitted the branded,
female occupant of a slave collar. Perhaps she merely wished to
have me beaten, as a presumptuous prisoner, availing himself
of a cell slave, but had misjudged the matter, and found that it
was she herself who was fastened in place for the lash's kiss. I
would not have minded, of course, putting her to my purposes,
and had mulled over the thought often enough in Ar, and since
Ar, after she had, more than once, lowered her veil before me,
almost as though insolently daring me to take her in my arms,
which might have been a serious and dangerous business in
that time and place. Why had she lowered her veil before me?
Merely to torment me? Probably. But it was hard to say. I did not
doubt, incidentally, that she had been similarly careless with
higher officers, and certainly with Seremides. It was clear that

he would be able to recognize her. Might that not instill terror in that now-collared, lovely thing? Why had she behaved in so perilously compromising a fashion? Was she perhaps so vain of her beauty that she could not resist its display? After all, what beautiful woman does not wish to be recognized as beautiful? But it seems she was bold, or unwise, indeed, unless, perhaps, she longed to feel on her small limbs the weight of chains, and on her neck the clasp of the proprietary collar.

On the Kasra deck, the rectangular viewing plate was easily slid back. I had occasionally, as had others, slipped it to the side, and gazed within, examining the occupants of the keeping chamber. Each girl was stripped, but had been given a heavy blanket, which most, in the straw and cold, shivering and shuddering, held about themselves. Many were the shallow pans about, and buckets, utilized by the frightened, miserable, retching slaves. Even seasoned mariners could scarcely walk the corridors without reeling, without bracing themselves against the walls. When the panel slid back, though the noise was tiny, many of the girls would cry out, piteously, kneeling, holding out their small hands toward the door, some rising and running to the end of their ankle chain, begging to be taken elsewhere, anywhere, to be released from the stale air, the confinement, and stench. There must have been better than a hundred slaves crowded in that small, cramped area. In my various observations, I did not see Alcinoë. If she were there, it seemed she might be placed toward the back of the area, or to the side, where it would be difficult to see her. Accordingly, I surmised that she might be in the keeping area above, that on the Venna deck. I did not know. It would turn out she was indeed housed in the Kasra area, but it was difficult to make determinations, given the paucity of light, from some two lamps, in that area. The rectangular, sliding panel on the Venna keeping area, above, which opened from the narrow, third port corridor, was fastened shut. It could be opened only by forcing it, and I speculated that that would be dangerous to do. The contents of the keeping area on the Venna deck were apparently not to be looked upon with impunity. I did not know why that would be, unless they were unusually beautiful, or some of them, at least, were in some way special, perhaps being reserved for particular masters at the voyage's end. Perhaps she for whom it seemed that the commander's friend, Pertinax, might be alert was confined within, on her chain. Too, I suspected that, for whatever reason, Alcinoë might now be amongst the Kasra area's occupants. Did someone realize her possible political importance? Seremides, perhaps? Or was she confined this deeply within the ship because she had incurred the displeasure of masters, having been apprehended in a lie? She had, it seems, been discovered to be lash-worthy, and had been put under the lash. Perhaps her wearing her chain here, then, was an additional punishment. Surely she was learning what it was to be a slave, and be at the mercy of men. Having seen many women exhibited, on the public shelves, in the exposition cages, on the block itself, it did not seem likely to me that the women of the Venna keeping area would be more beautiful, or really that much more beautiful, than those I had seen in the Kasra holding area, those heeling private masters about, those exercising on the deck, and such. I thought the Pani, whom I took it were responsible for the purchases, had shown excellent judgment. Although many of the slaves were now filthy, and ill, and frightened, I had no doubt that, scrubbed and groomed, they would prove to be excellent merchandise. Certainly I had seen worse sold even in the Curulean, in Ar.

Some of the women, from the Kasra area, had, in former weeks, been put in the public pleasure chambers, chained beside their mats, for the use of the crew, but this availability had, at least for the time, been discontinued. This had much to do with the discontentments of Thassa, with the wind and weather, the towering waves, the plunging about of the ship, and the water she was taking in, some from opening seams, at different levels, forced inside, some draining down to the lower decks, when a hatch must need be opened, and then forced shut. One hatch had been snapped away, and washed overboard, the upper deck awash. That accident alone had brought water to a dozen companionways. When I had slid back the plate on the observation panel of the Kasra keeping area, particularly of late, a number of its occupants, those who could stand, and not merely roll miserably about in the soiled straw, had not only flung aside their blankets and hurried forward, until stopped by their ankle chains, holding out their hands to me, begging to be freed of their chains and their wretched housing, but writhed and exhibited their charms, and bucked and swayed before me, hopefully, desperately, piteously, that I might be moved to call for them, and take them from their chains and current keeping area. I did not blame them for wishing to be relieved of the miseries of their chain and housing, and at almost any price, but, too, I had seen such behavior even in calmer weather, when Thassa was pleased to be serene, or seemingly so, perhaps meanwhile planning her next onslaught on men so foolish as to breast her waves in seasons unwise, if not forbidden. Several of the slaves, you see, could not but help, now, to belong in their collars. In their bellies the slave fires, so resisted by, and so scorned by, free women, had been callously and mercilessly ignited by heartless masters. They now belonged to men, and needed men. The victim of such fires will crawl naked to the feet of even a hated master, begging him piteously and desperately for his least caress.

I snapped shut the observation panel, and heard cries of misery.

The free woman has much to bargain with, her wealth, her position, her caste, her possessions, but once enslaved what has she but her beauty, and that does not even belong to her. She is helpless, and cannot bargain. Even to suggest such a thing is to invite the lash. Her beauty, like the whole of her, is the property of her master. And it, like the whole of her, may be easily ignored, or scorned.

Is not the most helpless of women the slave girl?

Slave girls often find themselves confined, or chained or roped, bound in one fashion or another. Such things, of course, are not necessary, but are imposed upon them, that they may better understand themselves as slaves. The total and irrevocable bond, of course, is that they are slave, only slave. This is clear in a hundred ways, from their brand, their collar, their clothing, if permitted clothing, their behaviors, their demeanors, their diction, their deference, their expressions, their place in society, and, once they are broken to the collar, their softness, their radical femininity, their insistent and irresistible feminine needs, their piteous and helpless need to surrender to a master, their desire to serve and love, and so on, but, still, all in all, there is a role for the bracelet, the shackle, the chain, the thong, the lace, the rope, and such, which not only impresses upon them their bondage, but arouses them, bringing them to slave heat. It is a rare slave who does not sometimes kneel before her master, and whimper, "Your slave, my Master, would be chained. Please, my Master, chain your slave."

It is a common belief amongst Goreans, though seldom voiced in the presence of free women, that men are masters and women slaves. As it is said, all women are slaves, only some are in collars, and some are not. Thus, it is thought that women are the properties of men, that women are property, even free women. They have yet, of course, to be claimed, and meet their master. It is a rare Gorean who does not speculate what even a free woman, bundled in her stiff, ornate robes, concealed within her layers of veils, would look like, stripped, collared, and at his feet, perhaps on all fours, looking up at him, frightened, the whip or switch between her teeth, hoping it will not be used upon her. It is only in the mastery that the male achieves his full manhood, and it is only at his feet that the female finds the fulfillment of her womanhood, in surrender, in submission, in service, in love. The answer to an unhappy, dissatisfied woman is a master, whom she must hope to please, lest she be lashed.

Many were the murmurs against Tersites. Why had he not performed, or had performed, the simple ceremony of pacifying Thassa, of seeking to smooth her waves with a bit of oil, of mingling man's salt with hers, to plead kinship, friendship, even alliance, of giving her some wine, that she might be warmed, and pleased? Would it not have been acceptable to mollify Thassa? Why not? Would it have cost so much? Might she not be insulted at such an omission, such an oversight, even such an insolence? Would she not remember such a slight, and bide her time, gathering her clouds and winds, waiting until one was far at sea, far from shore, alone? Had not hundreds of ships and thousands of men departed from one port or another, never to be seen again? It was not for no reason that most Gorean mariners seldom ventured from the sight of shore, even beaching their ships at night.

"Let Thassa rage," had cried Tersites. "Let her do what she

can, and be mocked by my work. Let lesser men grovel to her might, crave her indulgence, beg her favors! I fear her not! No oil, no salt, no wine for her! Let cowards proffer such gifts, such petitionary offerings! I do not! The stoutness of my timbers defies her. Let her seethe and hiss, unflattered, and uncourted, and whistle and roar, snarl and growl, and lift and fall, and pitch, and howl and tower, and squirm and buck as she will, she will not say no to my will, nor stay the passage of my ship. Fierce, green Thassa has met her match in my ship, met her master! Tersites teaches men how to sail in all seasons and weathers! Tersites goes where he wills; he asks no permissions, solicits no favors, dreads no threats, and fears no rebuke. Let Thassa shrink and tremble before Tersites and his mighty ship! He subdues her! He humbles her! He breaks her to the yoke of his will! Yea, I, Tersites, whom men scorned, whom men ridiculed and banished, whom men despised and mocked for years, now, first of all men, at last, mighty and glorious, conquer dreaded Thassa. I dare you, violent Thassa, to do your worst. Tersites and his ship invites your enmity, that men may marvel that so mighty a foe he has reduced to such futility. My ship cleaves your waves, braves your winds, and scorns your storms! We tread upon you, mighty Thassa, passing as we will and please! Do your worst, mighty Thassa! You are mocked! You are scorned!"

Dusk came early, and it seemed the cold never left.

Sometimes the waves struck the hull like hammers, and we feared, within those ribs of wood, that the sea might burst in upon us.

It was now the fifth week following the Eighth Passage Hand. Tomorrow would be the first day of the Ninth Passage Hand, at the end of which is the winter solstice, and the first day of Se'var-Lar-Torvis, the month of the Second Turning of *Tor-tu-Gor*, Light-upon-the-Home-Stone.

"Do not slacken!" called a fellow, Torgus, from the steps of the companionway, behind us, and to our right.

He was of the tarn cavalry.

He had his marked pole, testing the water. He seemed satisfied, the water had not inched higher in the last Ahn.

"Good fellows!" he called.

The ship was six-masted, square-rigged, seven decked, carvel-built, and single-ruddered, not guided by a steering board, or the double rudders of the typical Gorean ship. The nested galleys, on the other hand, were typical of most Gorean vessels, long or round ships, oar-banked, double ruddered, single-masted, and lateen-rigged. The long ships are commonly open to the weather, like the dragons of Torvaldsland, and the round ships, larger and slower, are commonly decked, this to shelter passengers, if there be passengers, and protect cargo.

The fellow, Torgus, turned about and, with his pole, ascended the steps.

We were not the only pumping crew at work, as there were several others, I knew not how many, these engaged elsewhere.

We had three pumps, in the forward port hold, and four men were at the handles of each, two men to a side.

One fellow, Tyrtaios, lean and hard, a snake I thought in a warrior's body, left his pump and waded to where I worked. "Take my place," said he to Durbar, who worked beside me. Durbar did as he was told. I had observed this fellow Tyrtaios in the hold, under the single swinging lamp, on its chains, which supplied the feeble light within which we worked, which cast wild shadows about, which seemed like the flutterings of frightened jards. Tyrtaios had worked at the other two pumps, as well. Several days ago, an altercation had taken place between this Tyrtaios and a man named Decius, with respect to a bench-place in the mess. A day later Decius was gone. We supposed he had been washed overboard whilst making his way to the helm deck. Durbar, not speaking, took the place at the second pump, that place vacated by Tyrtaios.

For several Ehn we continued to man the pump, in silence, and then Tyrtaios spoke to us, the other three at the pump.

"We are moving north," he said.

"West," said Andronicus, once of Tabor, once of the Scribes. Andronicus was no stranger to the Second Knowledge. He could read.

"No longer, for days, even before the storm," said Tyrtaios.

"Our course is west," said Andronicus.

"We are not on course," said Tyrtaios. "I was to the helm deck. Half blinded by water I saw briefly, clouds apart in the wind, the star of Hesius. It was at the bow. Four times later, too, on different days, the star of Hesius lay before us. Two helmsmen confirmed this."

"We have been blown off course," I said, levering the pump.

"Tersites is taking us north," he said. "The wind is his ally."

"Why so?" I asked.

"If we are going north," said Andronicus, "and by intent, Tersites plans to shorten the voyage, by the northern circle."

"I do not understand," said Thoas, across from Tyrtaios.

"Gor," said Andronicus, "is like a ball, and one may shorten distances by curving to the north and then curving back to the south.

"He has gone too far north," said Tyrtaios.

"Perhaps," said Andronicus.

"The wind," I said. "We fly before it."

"Ice has been seen in the water," said Tyrtaios, "ice the size of galleys."

"Then we are too far north," said Andronicus.

"The wind," I said.

"Tersites," said Tyrtaios, "is mad. That is well-known. He will kill us all."

"What is to be done?" asked Thoas.

"We must turn back," said Tyrtaios.

"It is true," said Andronicus, "that the ship may break apart."

"There may be little time," said Tyrtaios.

"There is, too, the brink, the falling away place, where the world ends," said Thoas.

"And before the next watch," whispered Tyrtaios, "we may fall from the world, to fall forever."

I did not think Tyrtaios believed what he said, but many amongst the crew might.

"No," said Andronicus. "Gor is like a ball. There is no edge."

"You do not know that, wise one," said Thoas. "You have not been there. Perhaps your scrolls, what you read, are false."

"There is much evidence," said Andronicus.

"Use your eyes," said Thoas. "The world is flat, as may be easily seen, and, if so, it must end somewhere."

Andronicus was silent, which silence Thoas apparently took as having had his point conceded.

"But Thassa must have an edge," said Tyrtaios.

"Of course," said Andronicus.

"None have returned from beyond the farther islands," said a fellow at the nearest pump.

"And we are beyond the farthest islands," said the fellow beside him.

"Lower your voices," whispered Tyrtaios, looking about.

The two returned to their work.

"We must be the first," said Tyrtaios to us, in a whisper.

"And how may that be done?" asked Thoas, apprehensively.

"We must urge Tersites to turn back," said Tyrtaios.

"He will never do so," said Andronicus. "He is at war with Thassa."

"We must force him to turn back," said Tyrtaios. "He cannot man the ship without us."

"There are the Pani," I said, "the soldiers of Lords Nishida and Okimoto."

"They must join us," said Tyrtaios.

"I think that is unlikely," said Andronicus.

"We outnumber them," said Tyrtaios.

"Tersites will never turn back," said Andronicus.

"Then," said Tyrtaios, "it may be necessary to seize the ship."

"I signed articles, long ago," said Andronicus.

"Not to go to our deaths," said Tyrtaios.

We continued to work the pump.

"Many are of my mind," whispered Tyrtaios.

"Some are not," said Andronicus.

"What if I told you, if we return to the continent," whispered Tyrtaios, "that riches would await us all?"

"We have nothing but our fee," said Thoas. "Of what do you speak?"

"I speak no further," smiled Tyrtaios. "But there would be wealth enough for all, great wealth."

I did not understand his words.

I knew there was a pretty price on the pretty head of the slave, Alcinoë, once the Lady Flavia of Ar, once confidante of the former Ubara, Talena, but it was scarcely enough to enrich several hundred men, mariners and soldiers, Pani, and others.

"Division at sea," said Andronicus, "as fire at sea, is a hazard no rational man will countenance."

"Surely," said Tyrtaios, "the rational man weighs risk against gain, and recognizes that even considerable risk is more than outweighed by the prospect of prodigious gain."

"I signed articles," said Andronicus.

"I hear steps on the companionway," I said.

We fell silent.

It was the fellow, Torgus, come again, with his pole.

He stood on the first step of the companionway, and carefully lowered the butt of the stick to the deck, under the water. "Good fellows!" he called. "Good fellows! The water is down. A hort! Your relief is at hand. Go to the mess, and get paga."

As we ascended the companionway others passed us, on the way down, to tend to the pumps. I saw again, amongst them, as I had on former days, Tarl Cabot, himself, commander of the tarn cavalry, and his friend, Pertinax. "Well done, fellows," said Tarl Cabot to us, as we passed. How odd, I thought, that officers, these two, would take their turn at the pumps. Did they not understand their station? Had they so little dignity? How could they expect to keep the respect of their men, if they so lowered themselves, if they so demeaned themselves, if they so compromised their position? But, too, I thought, would men not die for such officers?

I saw Tyrtaios wait on the steps, for Andronicus to pass him, and he would then be behind him.

This clearly made Andronicus uneasy, but he continued on.

At the next level, when we reached it, Tyrtaios, then waiting, spoke to me. "Do not forget what I have said," he said.

"I will not," I assured him.

I heard a passing mariner say to his fellow, "The weather is clearing."

I took the blanket handed me at the door to the mess. I dried my feet and legs, and shivered, and stepped inside. I could smell fresh Sa-Tarna bread, roast bosk. My body ached, I was weary. I was looking forward to food, and hot paga.

Chapter Eight

The Ice;
I Hold Converse with a Slave;
Rations Grow Short;
I Consider the Matter of Seremides

The day was dim and cold.

It must be near noon, but it seemed more like dawn. *Tor-tu-Gor*, Light-upon-the-Home-Stone, was low, lying almost upon the gray horizon.

The ship was not moving.

It was quiet, except for the men below, outside, moving on the ice about us, with their staves, posts, and axes, striking at the ice. Even on deck one could hear the crunch of their boots on the ice below, the striking of the posts downward, each handled by two men, on the ice, the sharp crack of the Torvaldslander axes striking on the horizontal, encroaching wall that seemed about to encircle the mighty ship. Sound carried clearly. One could hear conversations yards below.

"We are in the grasp of Thassa," said Philoctetes to me.

"She will have her way," said a fellow.

On the stem castle, one could see the small, misshapen figure of Tersites, hidden in furs, pacing from side to side, sometimes howling in rage, sometimes pausing to shake small, gnarled fists at the thick, white expanse, like rock, that stretched about us.

"This voyage was madness," said a man.

"Curse Tersites, curse this ship, curse the Pani!" hissed a man.

I had heard no more of sedition from Tyrtaios, who was of the retinue of Lord Nishida. If he harbored thoughts of insubordination, even mutiny, he did not now speak them. They lay dormant, if seething, within the walls of his own dark, coiled, serpentine heart. There is a time to strike, a time to wait. What point to seize a ship, to risk one's life, when the prize, even if won, would be without profit? Only a fool would hope to steal a wagon without wheels, a kaiila which cannot be untethered, a girl whose chain he cannot loosen, a treasure which cannot be carried away.

"Away!" called a man, standing at the rail.

One of the great saws, heavy, eleven feet in length, with gigantic metal teeth, fashioned from iron timber braces, by the ship's Metal Workers, on its rope, was lowered over the side, to the men below. There it would be weighted, its back rings fitted with draw chains, and the whole fixed in its pulleyed frame, to be dropped and raised, again and again, and, by means of the draw chains, pulled against the ice.

I had wondered, from time to time, of the hints of Tyrtaios, those of untold wealth for all. Surely that lacked all foundation in fact, and who, save the simplest and most gullible, might be deceived by so obvious and meretricious an enticement, so transparent a fabrication? And yet, I wondered, why would one of the seeming astuteness of Tyrtaios put himself so at risk, as he would be when the vacuity of his promise became manifest, as it must, in time? He, I thought, must be as mad as Tersites himself.

In my turn, I helped draw the used ax, that which had just been replaced, freed of its weight and chains, to the open deck. Its teeth would be sharpened, and then, again, within two Ahn, it would be put to work below.

The days were short, the nights long. In the land of the Red Hunters, farther north, north even of Torvaldsland, it was said that night would reign unremitting for weeks, from passage hand to passage hand, and to passage hand again, as in their summer, oddly, *Tor-tu-Gor* would never set. Yet even in their night, interestingly, one might see, from the light of moons, from that of stars, and, sometimes, it was said, from mysterious, shifting curtains of light, these many things reflected from the bleakness of the silent, frozen sea.

The mighty ship had been seized by Thassa, in her fists of ice, better than thirty days ago. The ice had formed about her, and lifted her, mighty as she was, from the surface of the sea, aslant, and crooked, yards toward the sky. This had proved fortunate for, as later became clear, the massive press of ice on each side might snap apart even timbers as fearsome as those of the great ship of Tersites, might break them apart as easily as a child might snap the twigs of a play fortress. Thassa had reserves on which she might draw, the vast pressures of her solidifying surface. Twenty days ago the ice had shifted, with a great, splitting roar, and our great, weighty bulk had slid downward, deeper into the ice, then through the ice, and righted itself. We rejoiced that there was again water beneath our keel, and that we might again negotiate a righted deck, but, by morning, as the ice closed in, almost invisibly forming, Ehn by Ehn, hort by half-hort, our joy turned to terror, for one could remark the groaning of timbers, the cracking of stressed beams. "Do nothing!" had cried Tersites. "The ship is strong! She will neither bend nor break. Mightier than Thassa is she, my ship, always, in every way, do nothing!" But the ice, like the forge pliers of a Metal Worker, slowly, little by little, began to close on the wood. "Do nothing!" cried Tersites. But now none heeded him. Aëtius, his confidante and loyal apprentice, in whose management was the day-to-day handling of the ship, dared to countermand his orders, this with the support of Lords Nishida and Okimoto, and the counsel of Tarl Cabot, admiral in Port Kar, member of the council of captains, and the war with ice had begun, to keep it at bay, by whatever means necessary. Accordingly, some feet of ice, with great travail, had been cleared about the hull of the great ship, and, by day, and under torches at night, flickering weirdly on the ice, men, in shifts, struck, hacked, and sawed away at the foe, the silent, ever-forming, encroaching ice.

Some men had been lost in this battle with Thassa, men who, for the most part, had been careless, and lost their footing, or beneath whose weight an unexpected edge of thinner ice had given way. Some had been caught under the ice. Most had died from the cold. In such water a man would die within Ihn. The first who had been lost in such a way was Andronicus. I had served at the pumps with him, in the forward port hold. He had been lost at night. Tyrtaios, in his vicinity, had been unable to save him.

I looked over the rail, at the gray sky, the dim globe of *Tor-tu-Gor*, at the horizon, the flat, white, frozen desert about.

It seemed not unlikely that the voyage of the great ship had now come to her final port, one of Thassa's choosing.

"Days pass," said a man, wearily.

"It is endless," said another.

"Thassa is mistress," said a man.

"It is hopeless," said another.

"Be silent," said another, "or you will be stripped and lashed, and then thrown bound to the ice."

It was true that the soldiers, or *ashigaru*, as they were called, of Lord Okimoto were amongst us.

How can one maintain morale, when all is lost?

At least some tarns were aflight.

One even now struck the deck, its wings snapping, soon to be led below.

Its rider, now dismounting, was one of the Pani, a man called Tajima, who was of the retinue of Lord Nishida, but serving in the cavalry.

Even from the height of tarn flight there was seen no break in the ice. It was everywhere about us, perhaps for hundreds of pasangs.

I was pleased to see a tarn return. Several had not. They were, after all, in a way, the eyes of the ship. It was from such saddles that one might see afar. Tersites, in his arrogance, his pride, and waywardness, had not deigned to give his vessel eyes. How then could she see her way? Is it not perilous enough to go forth upon Thassa at all, even in full cognizance, even when assured of her smiles and charms, without venturing upon her in forbidden seasons, blind? It was not known why several tarns had not returned to the ship. One suspects they had been flighted east or south, obedient to the reins of deserters, understandably loathe to die on the ice. But there were other thoughts, too. Perhaps the tarns themselves, now unhobbled, unwilling to return to the imprisonment of the cramped cots below, where they had seen their fellows die, now drunk with their sudden freedom, in the cold, fine, piercing air, exhilarated, and exultant, had chosen to reclaim for themselves their rightful realm, the deep, broad, high country of the sky. The tarn is a dangerous bird, half wild even when domesticated. It would be an easy thing to resist the reins, and turn upon a rider. And even an obedient tarn must eat, after a time. And then, presumably, one must die, tarn or rider. And if the rider survive, how will he live, afoot, alone, in the cold, in the long night?

But the man Tajima had returned.

I suspected he was an able rider.

Because of the risks few tarns were now flighted.

And tarns who cannot fly will, after a time, die.

I could see, some hundred yards off, dark on the ice, the bodies of two sea sleen. There must be a breathing hole there. When approached, they would disappear beneath the ice, for it was they who were being approached. On the other hand, some, seen first beneath the surface, a detectable, sinuous, twisting, moving body, a foot or two below, would suddenly emerge, beside the ship, snouts raised above the surface, with an explosive exhalation of breath, and then a drawing inward of air, these come to open water about the ship, to breathe. It was they who approached. It was eerie to look into the large, round, dark eyes of a sea sleen, peering at one from the icy water. The sea sleen will attack a human in the water, which it will see as food, but it is unlikely to attack one on the ice. Its usual prey is parsit fish, or grunt. In the case of the northern shark it is both prey and predator. Some sea sleen hunt in packs, and these will attack other sea mammals, even large sea mammals, such as whales, which they will attack in swarms, in a churning, bloody frenzy. We were instructed to stand in truce with these marine predators. If one came on the ice, we would push it back in the water with poles. One caught at a pole and snapped it apart with one swift, wrenching closure of its wide, double-fanged jaws, like a toothed trap door set low in that broad, viperlike head. In time one might need them for food. Thus, one welcomed them to come to the side of the ship, to breathe. To be sure, the sea sleen, like its confreres on land, is an intelligent animal, and we did not think it unlikely that it might prove quite dangerous if it were attacked, or thought it necessary to protect a breathing hole. Certainly one did not wish to risk a body, slipped from the ice, being dragged under the water and the hull before we might hurry it back to the ice, and break the stiff, frozen furs from its shuddering body. After the loss of the second man at the hull, the workers on the ice, most of them, those working close to the water, tied themselves together, that the error of a lost footing might not invariably prove fatal. In the water, it can be difficult, hands slipping, no purchase gained, to draw oneself back on the ice. One can die at the edge of the ice, scratching at it, treading water. One does not have long to live in such water. With the rope, on the other hand, one can be extracted from the water swiftly. So simple an expedience had saved more than one life. It was unfortunate that this safety practice had not been in place in the time of Andronicus. To be sure, some men would not avail themselves of the rope, and some, for ease of movement, or comfort, would sever the safety rope themselves. Andronicus, for all we know, might have been one such, so unwise. It was hard to say. And if such were the case, then, even as before, it would have been understandable that Tyrtaios, despite his best efforts, might have been unable to save him.

Of late, in the cold, and half darkness, some of the girls, lesser girls, I took it, from the Kasra keeping area, as well as several from the higher area, the Venna area, warm-shod and well furred, had been released to serve about the ship. Muchly were they pleased, these fortunate ones, to be relieved of the ankle chain, and be loosed from the dank, straw-strewn keeping areas, to which they would be later returned, to be again chained in their places. Many were the small services which these more fortunate ones might perform. Some, like the women of the Red Hunters, repairing rent garments with thong and awl, or, with their lips, teeth, and tongue, softening leather, and attending to stiffened garments, melting and biting the ice away from the fur; and many others would attend to the small, common domestic pursuits of the female slave, the dusting and cleaning of quarters, the making of bunks, the polishing of leather, the shining of the metal fittings of accouterments, laundering, ironing, sorting and folding clothing, sweeping, mopping, scrubbing, waiting upon the long tables, serving menially in the kitchens, as scullions, and such. And others served here and there about the ship in yet other ways, ways similarly appropriate for slaves, carrying messages, running errands, bringing food and black wine, not paga, to the men, both those on deck and those on the ice below, being lowered on a stirrup rope, to be drawn from the side of the ship to the ice by hooked poles, and such. Some of the women, doubtless those once of high caste, and not yet fully aware of their condition, that they were now no more than collared slaves, might, while grateful for their temporary release from the keeping areas and the greater latitudes of movement now permitted them, resent, or attempt to resent, the fact that they now found themselves put to such small, various, repetitive, servile, homely pursuits, perhaps finding in them a pretext for disgruntlement or humiliation. But soon, were their reservations noted by masters, they would address themselves eagerly, diligently, and thankfully to such pursuits, certainly after, say, having been fastened, small wrists tied high over their head, at a whipping ring. They now understood that such tasks were right for them, as they were slaves, and they were grateful to be permitted to live, to perform them. But most of the slaves, by far the greater number, being well apprised by now of the meaning and import of their neck encirclements, and radiant with collar joy, knowing they had irrevocably lost the battle with men which they had never, truly, desired to win, addressed themselves with a light heart and willing hand to such tasks, suitably enforced upon them as what they were now, owned, subdued females, and would hum and sing at their work. As slaves, they knew themselves set appropriately to the tasks and duties of slaves, this confirming upon them what they were, and desired to be, females who had no choice but to serve and please, even to the severities of the whip and chain, females joyful to be true females, females desiring to be owned by men, females wanting to be possessed by masters. In such things can one not hear the crackle of the fire at the mouth of the cave, the drums in the forest, sense the feeling of one's wrists drawn behind one, and thonged together, snugly, and then the being seized in the mighty arms of hunters and warriors, whose they are, and who will do with them as they will?

It was the second day of the Eleventh Passage Hand.

"Hold, slave!" I snapped.

There was no confusing of men with women.

Even within the bundling of the furs heaped upon them their bodies could not be concealed, the figure, the slightness, and movements, no more than those of free women could be entirely concealed within the layers of their fanciful, absurd robes. What male does not sense the vulnerable, inviting nakedness of a slave within a woman's assorted garmentures, no matter how contrived and pretentious?

And do not even free women sense that men see them thusly, see them exposed beneath their robes, see them as they would be without them, as they might be, say, were they commanded to put them aside, or as they might be, say, were they torn away? When they sense themselves under the scrutiny of men, do they not turn nicely, and stand well, and pose, and display themselves as the goods they know themselves to be? Surely they are aware, in some way, that they are slaves, and belong to men. What do they need then, but the chain, the block, the auctioneer's cry?

She turned about, frightened, the vessel of steaming black wine, wrapped in its thick cloths, from the wool of the bounding hurt, held in two hands.

Yes, it was she, at last!

What could be special about her, only a slave?

Doubtless only the gold she might bring, were I to cast her to her knees, shackled and naked, before Marlenus of Ar.

"You," she might have said, but it was only her lips that formed the word.

I was annoyed. I pointed to the deck, sternly.

Did she not know she was in the presence of a free man?

Swiftly she fell to her knees, and put her head down.

"First obeisance position," I said.

She put the black wine to the side on the deck, and put her head to the boards, before me, her hands beside the sides of her head.

I let her remain in that attitude for a time, for better than an Ehn, that she might well understand herself in first obeisance position before a man, and then I knelt before her and pulled her head up, and brushed back the hood of her furs.

"Yes, it is you," I observed.

"Yes!"

She was even more beautiful than I had remembered.

I thrust her head back, so that she was looking up, and felt about her throat, under the fur.

She was nicely collared.

"A ship's collar?" I asked.

"Yes!" she whispered.

"Yes?" I said.

"Yes, Master!" she said.

I was pleased she had not yet been claimed or assigned.

Might she not have been uneasy, could she have sensed my pleasure, my satisfaction, in having made this determination?

To be sure, almost all the slaves on board wore the ship's collar, were ship slaves.

"You are still Alcinoë?" I asked.

"That is what they call me," she said.

"Then that is your name," I said.

"Yes, Master."

"What is your name?" I asked.

"Alcinoë," she said, "—Master."

"Do not forget it," I said.

"No, Master," she said.

I moved about her a bit, and, with my two hands, felt beneath the furring wrapped about her left ankle.

A metal band had been hammered shut there, and, now flat against the band, in its welded staple, was a smaller ring, to which a chain might be attached, or through which a chain might be run, one by means of which several girls might be secured.

In the keeping areas the girls were commonly kept chained.

"I have not seen you about," I said.

"It is hard to exceed the length of our chain," she said.

I twisted my hand in her hair, held her, and cuffed her twice, sharply.

She looked at me, my hand tight in her hair, startled, disbelievingly. Tears sprang to her eyes. Her lip trembled. Did she truly think she might play with a free man? Did she truly think she might speak as a free woman? Did she not know she was a slave? Did she truly think that I, or any free man, would not put her to discipline?

Let her learn differently.

Sometimes a master will allow his girl a bit of slack on her leash, so to speak, which is sometimes pleasant, but that only makes it all the more sweeter to bring her again to her knees before him, his slave.

"It is appropriate that you be chained, is it not?" I asked.

"Yes, Master," she said.

"Why?" I asked.

"Because I am a slave, Master," she said.

I stood up, before her, and regarded her.

"Keep your back straight," I said.

She straightened her back, and looked straight ahead.

"I have not seen you since the cell," I said.

"Nor I you," she said.

"It is my understanding that you claimed I had put you to use," I said.

"Doubtless Master knows the story," she said.

"Perhaps," I said.

She dared to look up, frightened.

"Please do not have me whipped," she said.

I supposed that I, as the putatively offended party, might suggest a repetition of her punishment, for my own satisfaction, the first having been administered merely because she had been caught in a lie.

It is interesting how a slave who has felt the whip so fears it. They will go to great lengths to avoid its kiss.

To it they know themselves subject.

Like most men, most masters, I thought that the whip, if applied, should be applied judiciously, and, preferably, not at all.

It is, after all, primarily an instrument of correction.

And, hopefully, correction will not be necessary.

What one looks for from a slave is service, and inexpressible, inordinate pleasure. Why else would one put them in collars, buy them, and own them, and master them?

To be sure, if they are not fully pleasing, they must expect to be punished, and well. They are, after all, slaves.

Too, interestingly, a slave may sometimes desire to be

whipped, perhaps to reassure her of her master's attention, that she is still important to him, that he regards her as still his slave, that he regards her as still worth whipping, and perhaps, sometimes, she simply desires to be whipped, to be reminded that she is a slave. To the slave her bondage is inexpressibly precious. And surely little could better convince a slave of her bondage than finding herself being whipped as the slave she is.

"Where are you housed?" I asked.

"In the Kasra area," she said.

It was then further confirmed, as I had earlier conjectured. She was neither claimed nor assigned.

She was a simple ship's slave.

"Please do not have me whipped," she said.

The whip hurts; a slave will commonly do much to avoid it. Certainly they are seldom in doubt as to their bondage. They know themselves subject to it. It is often most effective when merely dangling inert upon its peg. It is sometimes put to the lips of a kneeling slave, that she may lick and kiss it, in trepidation and reverence. It is a symbol of the mastery. When a slave is found errant, she is sometimes required, kneeling, to beg for its attention. Sometimes, after having received its attention, she is required to kiss and thank it. "Thank you, dear whip. I shall try to amend my ways. I shall strive to become a better slave."

"How long have you served about the ship?"

The ship was large, and one had varied duties, here and there.

"This is the third day," she said, adding, "—Master."

"Why did you claim I had put you to use?" I asked.

"I do not know, Master," she wept. "I was angry, I was frustrated, I felt rejected, I felt insulted. I am sorry. I am sorry! Please do not have me whipped, again. It hurts. It hurts, so!"

"You were punished," I said, putting the matter aside.

"I was in a collar," she said. "I was alone with you! I could not have prevented you. I could not have resisted. Why did you not put me to use?"

"I was not pleased to do so," I said.

"I see," she said.

"Why did you, in Ar," I asked, "a great lady, lower your veil before a common soldier?"

"I do not know," she said.

"Perhaps to torment me?" I suggested.

"Perhaps," she said. "I do not know."

"Perhaps," I said, "it was the act of a slave, one who desires to be taken in hand, and braceleted."

"Surely not!" she said.

"I can understand such things," I said, "before high officers, before men who determine the opening and closings of gates, men who hold the keys to cellars of gold, to the trove of Merchants, men who command armies, who grasp the reins of power, whose word will launch fleets, but not before common soldiers."

She put her head down.

Beside her the vessel of black wine no longer steamed.

"Slave?" I said.

"Few men know," she said, "the secrets even free women confide to the silence and secrecy of their pillows."

"But it was surely foolish," I said.

"I did not expect to be a fugitive," she said. "I thought the power of Talena in Ar was secure. Ar was beaten and downtrodden, confused and set against herself, cleverly divided so that she would be helpless before her foes. We did not anticipate the return of the great Marlenus."

"Most who could recognize you," I said, "might be unwise to return to Ar, having prices on their own heads, as Seremides."

"They might well win their own amnesty," she said, "were they to deliver a fugitive more sought than themselves. Such things are negotiable, through intermediaries."

"Seremides," I said, "is on board."

"No!" she said.

"Under the name Rutilius of Ar," I said.

"He must never see me!" she whispered. "He must never know I am on board!"

"Who?" I asked.

"I," she said, "of course, the Lady Flavia!"

"The Lady Flavia," I said, "is not on board."

She looked up at me.

"A slave, Alcinoë, is on board," I said.

"As you wish," she said.

"Do you enjoy having this conversation on your knees?" I asked.

"It is appropriate, is it not," she asked, "as I am a slave, before a free man."

"Yes," I said.

"I see," she said.

"I am permitting you to keep your knees closed," I said.

"Master is kind," she said. "What if I should wish to open them, before you?" she asked.

"Do not do so," I said.

"I see," she said.

I recalled that she had claimed that I had raped her.

"Seremides," I said, "knows you are on board."

"No!" she cried, in misery. "Surely you did not tell him!"

"Stay on your knees," I warned her.

"No," I said, "I did not tell him. Why should I tell him? Better, surely, that it be I alone who should bring you before Marlenus."

"You would bring me before Marlenus?" she said.

"Who would not?" I asked.

"Might I not prove a pleasing slave, Master?" she asked, tears in her eyes.

"One does not know," I said.

"Alcinoë would do much to please her master," she whispered.

"Speak louder, slave," I said.

"Alcinoë would do much to please her master," she said.

"That is only fitting for a slave," I said.

"Yes, Master," she said.

"For the bounty on your head, pretty *kajira*," I said, "one might purchase a galley, and a dozen slaves whose beauty would shame yours, as yours, such as it is, might shame that of tarsk sow."

"Surely not!" she said. Well had I stung the beauty's vanity.

"Well, perhaps," I said, "as much as yours would be beyond that of a typical copper-tarsk girl, a pot girl, a kettle-and-mat girl."

"I thought my beauty too great for that of a female slave," she said.

"But now," I said, "you are more familiar with that of female slaves."

"But I am beautiful!" she wept.

"I doubt that you would bring gold off the block," I said, "but I think you would bring silver."

"Surely I am beautiful!" she said.

"Yes," I said, "you are beautiful, you are a lovely slave."

"Am I not attractive?" she asked.

I did not tell her of the nights I had dreamed of having her, collared, in my arms.

"I have had better chained at my slave ring," I said.

"You have had others chained at your ring?"

"Now and then," I said.

"And how would you chain me," she asked, "by throat or ankle?"

"As it might please me, on one night or another," I said.

"And such is the master," she said.

"Yes," I said.

"I have never been at the foot of a man's couch," she said.

"In the beginning," I said, "you would be slept on the flooring itself, or a mat."

"Not on furs?"

"No," I said.

"I would be slept as a low slave?"

"Of course."

"Do you find me attractive?" she asked.

"Few slaves are without interest," I said.

"I would like to be attractive to you," she said.

"More attractive than a sack of gold?"

"I would scarcely dare hope so much," she said.

"Master," she said.

"Yes," I said.

"If you did not know who I was, and you saw me on the block, naked, exhibited, posed, fearing the whip, writhing on command, might you not find me of interest, and bid for me, and hope to take me home—I, only a slave, on your chain?"

I recalled that she had lowered her veil before me, in Ar, I, only a common soldier, and more than once. However far above me she was then, I was now thousands of times higher than she, for she was now slave.

"Perhaps," I said, "provided I could get you cheaply enough."

"Perhaps," she said, "Seremides does not really know I am on board."

"He knows," I said.

"How do you know Seremides knows I am on board?" she asked.

"Some days after having been brought on board," I said, "I was interrogated by ship's officers. Seremides was amongst them. Your name, Alcinoë, came up, given the contretemps of the cell. Seremides mentioned that he had seen you, and that you looked well in your collar."

"Do I look well in my collar?" she asked, bitterly.

"What woman does not?" I asked.

"Of course," she said. "We are females, the properties of men."

"He suggested," I said, "that you be given to him."

"I see," she said, shuddering.

"But, it seems," I said, "that his request has not been granted, at least as yet."

"He refused to abet my escape from Ar," she said. "The mounting ladder was jerked away from me. I was left behind, abandoned."

"Now, of course," I said, "things are different. Now, a sack of gold might be tied about your neck, as you might be led, naked and bound, leashed, to the impaling pole, the sack to be cut from your neck and given to Seremides, as you are lifted, striving not to move, into public view."

"We are likely to die here, in the ice," she said.

"It seems so," I granted her.

It was feared that some men might leave the ship, to try to cross the ice east, in the half darkness, perhaps to Torvaldsland. Pani had been set about, to guard the bulwarks, and, on the ice, to supervise the work about the ship. This venture, whispered about, to leave the ship, seemed to me madness. We were hundreds of pasangs from land, and who knew how far the ice might last, but, it seemed, even so woeful and improbable a scheme might have some appeal to forlorn, desperate minds, minds half crazed by the imprisonment of the ship, the silence, the darkness, the cold, the endless labor at the ice, the growing shortage of rations.

"I wonder where Seremides saw me," she said.

"It could have been anywhere," I said, "perhaps when you were unhooded, after boarding, perhaps while you were awaiting a chain assignment, in a companionway, in a corridor, on one deck or another, perhaps when you slept, in the Kasra holding area, to which he, as a high officer, might have had access."

"Few, if any, men are allowed there," she said. "We are managed by first girls, large tharlarion-like women, female whip slaves."

"Interesting," I said. I supposed it made sense that free men, on the whole, would not be allowed to walk about amongst chained slaves.

After all, should one not pay for them?

"Sometimes," she said, "girls moaning and needing men would be switched to silence. When free I despised the needs of slave girls, but then I did not understand how they felt, how helpless they were in the throes of their needs; I did not understand what was going on in their bodies, that made them cry out, and whimper, and scratch at the boards, and moan; I did not understand what men had done to them, to so ignite their needs, to make them so piteously the prisoners of their own bodies, of what they were, the helpless victim, captive, and slave of their own womanhood."

"One cannot ignite needs which are not there to be ignited," I said. "What men have done is simply to free the secret slave in the heart of every woman, she longing for the sunlight of submission and fulfillment."

"Four times," she said, "I was awakened from my sleep, the switch flashing upon me. 'Stop thrashing in your chains, slut,' I was told. Had I been doing so? I did not know."

"Presumably you were doing so," I said.

"The switch stung," she said.

"That is its purpose," I said.

I recalled having learned, during my interrogation, that physicians had determined that the slave, Alcinoë, after her time with me in the cell, was almost ready to be put on the block. Apparently she had begun to sense, or fear, the beginning of involuntary, radical changes in her body, incipient glimmerings heralding the onslaught of needs which would inevitably put her vulnerably at the feet of men, the fires which, in a woman's belly, mark her, more than a brand and collar, a man's slave.

"In any event," I said, "he saw you, and I am sure he recognized you."

"I did not see him," she said.

"It is enough that he saw you," I said.

"Are you sure," she said, "that he saw me?"

"Yes," I said. "Do not any longer think of yourself as concealed, as inaccessible, as a free woman. You are now an animal. Your features must be as brazenly exposed as those of any other animal, a kaiila, verr, or tarsk. Anyone, as upon them, may look upon you, and boldly."

Tears sprang anew to her eyes.

"Is this truly surprising?" I asked. "Did you not see many slaves in Ar? Do you still think of yourself as free? What of your own girls? What if one had dared to veil herself, even in play?"

"I would have lashed her," she said.

"You are surely well aware," I said, "that as a slave, an animal, you may or may not be clothed. You are surely aware of such things. Your garmenture, if any, will be decided by those who own you. Your features, and, if owners wish it, your body, will be denied the least protection."

"Yes," she wept, "yes!"

"Keep the palms of your hands down on your thighs," I said.

"Yes, Master," she said.

"And keep in mind that your features," I said, "if not your body, must be regularly and fully exposed. Free women will insist on that. Your features, at all times, must be denied even the least thread of the most diaphanous veiling."

"How easy then," she said, in misery, "I all unknowing, for him to see me, and identify me!"

"For him," I said, "or anyone."

"Even a common soldier," she said.

"Yes," I said, "even a common soldier."

"And anyone might bring me to Ar," she said.

"Yes," I said, "even a common soldier."

"Such as you," she said.

"Yes," I said.

"How helpless we are," she said, looking up, "we, so exposed, our lips, our features, our smallest expressions, naked, bared to the view of anyone!"

I was muchly pleased that slaves were denied veiling.

How beautiful and distraught she looked!

How this puts them so much the more where they belong, in our power!

"You may not hide yourselves," I said.

Her eyes were bright with tears, some coursed down her cheeks, running under the fur.

"You are a slave," I said.

"Yes," she said, "I am a slave!"

Denial of the veil is one of the things, as noted, insisted upon by free women for the slave, this marking another dramatic difference between them, at least between those of high caste and the slave. Low-caste women, in their work, not unoften do without veiling. Good-looking girls of low-caste sometimes go about unveiled deliberately, hoping that they may catch the eye of a slaver, and perhaps be sold into a high household, or come into the chains of a handsome, well-to-do master. One of the most delightful vengeances of a free woman upon a rival is to have her rival reduced to slavery, and then have her at her feet, tunicked, and face-stripped, as a serving slave, perhaps to be later sold, out of the city. One of the most interesting things about barbarian slaves, which may surprise many, is that few seem to understand, at least at first, the shame that is done to them by denying them the veil. They seem more concerned with the baring of their bodies, which is suitable for slaves. But such are shameless and suitably enslaved. Are they not already half-slave, even before being fitted with the collar? They only become sensitive to such matters when, later, they become aware of the meaning of their bared faces. But, after a time, even Gorean women, as well as barbarians, in bondage, think little of their lack of veiling, at least when not in the presence of a free woman, particularly of high caste. Then they are often forced to feel their shame keenly. Commonly though, they, and barbarians, as well, come to revel in the lack of veiling, and, indeed, in the shame of their commonly brief and revealing garmenture, if allowed garmenture, become insolent in their shameful pride, so deplored by free women, of revealing their beauty, of both face and body, to the eyes of men.

One might note in passing how the slave tunic, or the scandalous camisk or ta-teera, are viewed by free women, slaves, and masters. The free woman regards such garments as a degradation, an unspeakable humiliation, a badge of shame, fit for natural slaves, say, women of alien or enemy cities. But, too, they often seethe with envy that it is not they who are exposed so blatantly, and desirably, to the eyes of males. Might they not, too, be so attractive, were they so excitingly clad, so invitingly bared? And how angry they are that men, who should be above such things, look with such obvious favor on mere slaves! The slave, of course, may at first be miserably shamed to be so garmented, to be put in such a garment, but, soon, she comes to exult in its attractiveness, its brevity and lightness, and the freedom it affords, not only of movement, but more significantly, its gift of psychological, emotional, and intellectual freedom. Too, of course, such a garmenture is sexually arousing, and frees the slave to be the warm, arousable, appetitious, excitable, needful, sexual animal, the slave, she has always longed to be. And as for the views of men with respect to such garmentures, one supposes they need no elaboration. By means of such garments, women, the most desirable properties a man may own, are dressed for his taste, delectation, and pleasure. Were it not for the security of their Home Stones, one supposes there would be few free women in a Gorean city. One wonders sometimes if they understand that the freedom which, in their arrogance, they take so much for granted is tenuous and fragile, a revocable gift of men. Let them think of Tharna, and tremble, or, if they wish, present themselves naked before her gates, petitioning entrance.

"Why is Seremides on board?" she asked.

"There is a price on his head," I said. "Perhaps, then, to flee."

"Perhaps," she said, "but one could flee anywhere, to Torvaldsland, to the deeper recesses of the formidable Voltai, to the vast Barrens, to the long Valley of the Ua, anywhere. Here, he is trapped, on a ship."

"Perhaps," I said, "he hopes to recoup his fortunes, at the World's End."

"Perhaps," she said.

"Perhaps," I said, "he knew you to be on board, and has in mind your apprehension, and eventual remanding to Ar."

"Surely that venture," she said, "would be fraught with peril. The price on his head, I suspect, is greater than that on mine."

"I agree that is likely," I said. He had been, of course, the captain of the Taurentians, and had been close to Myron, the *polemarkos* of Temos, commander of the occupation forces in Ar.

"Still," I said, "do not underestimate your value in Ar."

"To another," she said, "but I think not to Seremides."

"He might negotiate, anonymously, through others," I said. I did not doubt that he had cohorts on board, if not brought with him, then later recruited.

"Perhaps," she said.

"You do not think he seeks you?"

"I think," she said, "he is after greater game."

"What, then?" I asked.

"I am not sure," she said. "I do not know."

"In any event," I said, "a slave is far from Ar."

"Yes," she said, "a slave is far from Ar."

"Return to first obeisance position," I said.

"Surely not!" she said.

"Now," I said. "Good."

"Now," I said, "to second obeisance position."

"Please," she protested, her head to the deck.

"Must a command be repeated?" I inquired.

"No!" she said.

The repetition of a command is often a cause for discipline, and she was well aware of what that might involve.

She was now on her belly before me, her hands at the sides of her head.

"Lips to boots," I said.

She pressed her lips to my boots, left and right, kissing them, and licking at them.

I let her continue to do this for a time.

It is pleasant for a man to have a beautiful woman, for she was beautiful, so at his feet, so at his mercy.

I noted a particular movement in her body, one I had seen before in a slave. I smiled. She was beginning to understand what it might be, to be a slave. Already, I suspected, she had begun to hope, forlornly, that I might be pleased to attend to her, as one who, in his lenience or indulgence, might attend to a slave.

"Enough," I said. "Position."

She knelt then before me, as before, back on her heels, head up, back straight, the palms of her hands down on her thighs.

"You wear your furs well," I said.

"Thank you, Master," she said.

"To be sure," I said, "I would prefer you in a tunic, or less."

"May a slave not open her knees before Master?" she said.

"Do you wish to do so?" I asked.

"I think so," she whispered.

"No," I said.

"I see," she said.

"Is a slave white silk or red silk?" I asked.

"Must a slave respond?" she asked.

"Of course," I said.

"A slave is white silk," she said.

"That is unusual," I said.

"For a slave," she said.

"You are a slave," I said.

"Yes, Master," she said, "I am a slave."

"It seems, slave," I said, "you have let the black wine grow cold."

"Master?" she said.

"Thus, you are remiss," I said.

"I have been detained!" she said, frightened.

"You are remiss," I said.

"Yes," she said, "I am remiss."

"Then, rise," I said, "hurry to the kitchens, to heat the wine, or replenish your vessel."

"Yes, Master," she said.

She retrieved the vessel, wrapped in its cloths.

"And hurry," I said, "run, run!"

"I was the Lady Flavia of Ar!" she said.

"Hurry," I said, "run, run!"

She turned about, in misery, and, holding the vessel in its cloths, hurried away. She stopped once, to look over her shoulder, and then, frightened, disappeared through the second hatchway amidships, that between the second and third masts.

I feared for her safety, and that of all of us.

Night was falling. On the ice below the work lamps, on their tripods, had been lit. Pani, with bows and glaves, patrolled the perimeter below.

They had earlier stopped two men, set to trek the ice. One had been killed, the other flogged.

Rations were growing short.

I thought of the slave, Alcinoë. Off the block, sold for her simple quality as a female, she might bring one or two silver tarsks. In the south, delivered to the justice of Ar, she might bring a double handful of golden tarn disks. What a fool one would be, not to advantage oneself of such an opportunity. On the other hand, she was pretty, and might make a good slave.

It was hard to tell about such things.

Reasonably clearly, she was already beginning to sense what it might be to be a slave.

That was promising.

I wondered if, in the darkness of the Kasra keeping area, she might have pressed her fingers to her lips, and then softly to her collar.

I recalled she had been switched awake four times.

Presumably she had been thrashing in her chains.

She is coming along nicely, I thought, even predictably.

What woman can be truly fulfilled, who is not a slave, who does not know herself owned, who does not know herself the absolute property of a master, a master whom she knows she must serve with perfection, a master whom she knows, to her joy, will have the wholeness of her womanhood from her?

The watch was called, and I would go below.

I wondered why Seremides was on board. It might have been simply his intention to flee. Who, after all, would think to seek him beyond the farther islands? Or perhaps he wished to seek a fortune in a new, untried venue, a fortune, like many, obtainable by sword skill? Perhaps, on the other hand, he sought the former Lady Flavia of Ar. The reward for her return to Ar was far from negligible. Might it not purchase a galley, and several slaves, of high quality? But she had thought he was after greater game, of some sort. But what might that be? Also, as she could recognize him, her death might be worth far more to him than the gold her delivery to Ar might bring. To be sure, I, too, might recognize him. I had taken care to avoid being alone with him. Clearly I constituted a danger to him, and, as a free man, one far more dangerous than that posed by a slave. I had little doubt he would eventually seek his opportunity, perhaps a thrust in the darkness, a feigned misstep at the ice, the provoking of a quarrel, or such.

I saw two or three men emerge onto the darkening deck. I thought little of it at the time.

Chapter Nine

The Mutiny

I awakened to the screaming of tarns and the beating of the ship's great alarm bar, over and over, incessantly, deafeningly.

"Deck, deck, deck!" I heard.

Outside our crew area, one of several, I could hear feet running in the corridor, others climbing the stairs in the nearest companionway.

"Beware," called Philoctetes. "There is swordplay."

We could hear the ringing of steel.

It was past the twentieth Ahn.

"Lamps have been shattered!" I heard. "Put out the fires."

We tumbled from our quarters, casting our furs about us. Most of us had been disarmed, a concomitance of the weeks of short days and cold, the length of our seizure by the ice, the reduction in rations, the deterioration of morale, the growing fear, the gradually increasing sense of desperation and hopelessness, the surliness of many, but there are always hidden weapons.

"We are under attack!" I heard.

"No, no!" I heard.

"What is going on?" called a fellow.

"Lamps have been shattered!" I heard.

In our quarters we looked wildly to one another. Muchly did we fear fire.

"No!" I heard. "No! To the weapon room!"

The Pani were still armed, and officers, and various guardsmen.

Philoctetes opened the door to the corridor, cautiously, and peered out. It was apparently then empty. We followed him into the corridor. Some tharlarion oil from a lamp, like spread grease, was burning on the flooring. The lamp itself was still on its chains. It was not difficult to smother the flames, with furs, or stamp them out. The most serious fires on a ship are likely to originate in the kitchens. It did not seem likely anyone was trying to fire the ship. Most likely the lamp, in the low-ceilinged passageway, had been jostled in the passage of armed, rushing men. We encountered no shattered lamps, nor any indications of arson.

We could hear, above us, however, the sound of steel, the cries of men.

There must be fighting in corridors, or elsewhere.

We also heard the grating of the large tarn hatch, amidships, being rolled back. This is done with a double windlass. It takes several men to move the hatch.

When the ship had debouched from the Alexandra, and entered Thassa, I had been told there were something like two hundred tarns aboard. They were housed in three large areas, each occupying a substantial portion of its own deck. The highest area was on the first deck below the open deck. The other two areas, by ramps, led to the highest area, it alone having the sky accessible, once the great hatch was rolled back. As the tarn is a large, dangerous, aggressive bird, and territorial in the wild, many of the ship tarns had separate stalls, or cages; others were chained apart, by the left foot; some others, crowded together, literally had their wings bound, their beaks strapped shut, save for feeding.

Restless, and many long unflighted, it was unusually dangerous to be amongst them. Few but tarnsmen or tarnkeepers would approach them, and then with great caution.

"Let us to the weapon room," said a fellow.

There, one supposed, arms might be issued to us, were they deemed in order. As it turned out, however, the weapon room had been stormed earlier by a number of disaffected crew members, in effect, mutineers, who were intent on freeing tarns, and risking a flight which might lead to land, a flight presumably to the east, where lay Torvaldsland.

I knew little of tarns, the control of such monsters, their dispositions and habits, their ranges of flight, and such, but it seemed improbable, given our conjectured position, so far west of even the farther islands, that one might reach land, say, Torvaldsland, before the tarn might, even with the might of its legendary stamina, fall to the ice, in the dimness or darkness, unable to continue on, to die of cold and exhaustion, or, starving, turn on its rider. If landfall were practical from our current position surely our outriders and scouts would have discovered this, returned, reported it, brought back much needed supplies, and such. But it was true some deserters had, in the past weeks, now and then, flighted a tarn away, over the ice, into the gray sky, and had not returned. Who knew that some of them might not have reached land. Twice, riderless tarns had returned to the ship, their harnessing torn apart or missing, their beaks red with frozen blood. They flew at those who would have led them below. They were killed.

In our small quarters there were some forty fellows, mostly of Cos, Tyros, or the smaller islands. We did not mix well with the fellows from the continent.

I would conjecture there were some five hundred of the unusual men, the Pani, on board, divided amongst the commands of Lords Nishida and Okimoto, some two hundred and fifty each. And of others, mariners, soldiers, artisans, and such, perhaps two thousand, these recruited variously, many, particularly the mercenaries, in Brundisium, often fugitives from the restoration in Ar. I was not clear on the purpose of the voyage, but it doubtless had to do with war, for our ship, despite what might be the views of its shipwright, Tersites, was serving essentially as a transport, one undertaking an unprecedented voyage, whose intended destination seemed likely to be known only to the Pani. The male Pani, for example, were uniformly warriors. This I found significant. There were a handful of Pani females aboard, but I saw little of them. They were spoken of as contract women. I did not understand their status. It did not seem they were slaves. The other men aboard, other than the Pani, or at least the overwhelming majority of us, as were the Pani, were men accustomed to weaponry and the arbitrations of force. The ship, then, as noted, was essentially a transport, conveying a small army to foreign fields. The slaves on board, perhaps some two hundred in number, would have their various purposes, serving in various ways. Too, of course, such women are a form of wealth, as they may be sold, traded, bartered, given as gifts, and such. I did not doubt but what such goods would figure in the plans of the Pani. Of tarns, I had been told, as mentioned, that there had been something in the neighborhood of two hundred on board when the ship of Tersites had entered Thassa from the Alexandra. A tarn cavalry was clearly intended, which was, I suspected, intended to be a decisive arm in some projected campaign. I gathered that tarns might be unknown at the World's End; else why would they be aboard? The Pani seemed to have no shortage of resources, given their financing of the ship of Tersites, the hiring of hundreds of mercenaries, the purchasing of slaves, and such. Thus, if tarns were common at the World's End it would be more expeditious to obtain them there. If they were not known at the World's End, then their judicious application in battle, reconnaissance, raids, and such, might indeed prove formidable. Even their appearance might inspire awe, even terror. To be sure, there were no longer some two hundred tarns on board. Some had been flighted, and had not returned; some had died; two had been killed. There was secrecy with respect to the figures involved, as would be expected, as with the number of catapults, and such, but rumors suggested a current count of something like one hundred and seventy healthy tarns on board. We knew of three weapon rooms, but suspected there were others. One aspect, at least, of the naval power of the ship of Tersites was clear. She nested six galleys. The tarnsman, Tarl Cabot, was apparently the commander of the tarn cavalry. Several times, in better weather, he had had it aloft, in training exercises. It is impressive to see such mighty beasts in flight, the stroke of the wings to the beating of the tarn drum, the wheelings and maneuvers, in unison, to the signals of banners and trumpets.

"Follow me," said Philoctetes, who was first in our small company. We followed him up the companionway to the next deck, and then to the next. Unarmed, I was uneasy. We could hear the ringing of steel here and there. Who greets a larl without a spear in one's grasp? Of the three weapon rooms we knew about, two were forward, and one amidships. Ours was amidships. It was on the deck now above us. The tarn areas were also amidships, consuming most of three decks. As noted, the highest area was on the first deck below the open deck, the lower two areas having access to it by ramps. As noted, only the highest area would open to the sky, once the great hatch was rolled back. We were now, on the companionway, moving past the highest of the two lower tarn areas. Most of the cries, the noise, the screaming of tarns, came from above, the first tarn area, that which might be opened to the sky.

I heard the snap of a bowstring above, and a fellow, on the flooring above, dark, briefly outlined in the light of a tharlarion-oil lamp, turned about, slowly, and then tumbled part way down the companionway, toward us, some five stairs. Philoctetes pulled him aside, and looked up. He then thrust the body down, past us. The arrow had been broken in the fellow's fall, against the stairs.

"It is a Pani arrow," said a fellow.

The Pani arrow is long, rather like that of the peasant bow, but the Pani bow is unlike the peasant bow, as it is longer, and lighter. Both bows are different from the short, stout Tuchuk bow, or saddle bow, which, I had learned, had been introduced by the tarnsman, Tarl Cabot, into the weaponry of the tarn cavalry. In the corridor above, the Pani bow must have been used diagonally, given the low ceiling of the corridor. The ideal weapon in closed spaces would be the crossbow, not only because of its size and maneuverability, but, even more, because the bolt or quarrel may wait patiently in the guide, the cable back, ready to spring forth instantly, at the press of a finger on the trigger. It takes a moment, of course, to draw a bow, and it requires strength to keep the bow drawn. The Pani bow, the peasant bow, and the saddle bow, of course, and such bows, have a rapidity of fire which far exceeds that of even the stirruped crossbow.

At the foot of the companionway two men, in the dim light, turned the body.

"I do not know him," said a fellow.

"He has a blade," said a man, gratefully.

One of our men, finger by finger, pried loose the blade from the clenched hand.

"Now we have one sword," said a man.

163

"Leave it," said Philoctetes. "Armed, you may be mistaken for a mutineer."

"You would have us defenseless?" asked a man.

"Wait," said Philoctetes, "until all are armed."

"Not I," said a man, Aristodemus of Tyros.

"Give it to him," said a fellow. The blade was surrendered to him. We took him to be first sword amongst us.

"Conceal it," advised Philoctetes.

Aristodemus placed the blade within his furs.

Standing on the stairs, Philoctetes called out, "Friend! Friend!"

"Beware!" I called to him.

He then, cautiously, ascended two or three more steps. "Friend!" he called, again, not showing himself. "Friend!"

He then, from the stairs, peered into the corridor. Then he turned back to us. "I see no one," he said.

"There are doors," I said, "corners, where the passageways intersect."

The arrow had been sped from somewhere.

"Stay back," said Philoctetes, and he ascended to the corridor, his hands held over his head.

I would have given much for even a buckler.

Philoctetes lowered his hands, and turned to his left.

The archer, it seemed, had gone.

In a moment we had followed him, and crowded behind him. We saw that the weapon room had been broken into. Most of the weaponry, spears, swords, crossbows, longbows, javelins, glaves, maces, axes, Anango darts, gauntlet hatchets, edged battle weights, bladed chains, and such, was gone. Some of the bows and spears, ax hafts, and such, had been broken, or splintered. I suspected that much of what had not been seized, might have been carried to the open deck, and cast overboard, that it not be available to others. At that time we did not know the numbers of the mutineers. Their attacks, however, seemed to have been organized, and coordinated. I wondered if Tyrtaios or Seremides was involved. It seemed unlikely, for both men were astute. There would be little point in seizing the ship, given her present straits, and, if their hope was an escape, however improbable of success such an effort might be, they would presumably be content to seize one or two tarns and flee, following in the wake of earlier deserters. Three men were dead in the corridor; one was of the Pani, probably the room guard, posted outside the door, and two others, who may have fallen to his swift, small sword, each, apparently, by a single stroke. He of the Pani, in any event, whether offered terms or not, had obviously refused to surrender the weapons in his charge, preferring rather to die in their defense. I would later learn that this standing at one's post, this adherence to duty, was typical of the Pani.

"We are unarmed," said a fellow. "There is nothing we can do, one way or the other. Let us return to our quarters and abide the outcome."

"We might side with the winning party," said a fellow.

"There is no winning party," said another. "This is not about the ship. This is about flight."

"There is no escape from the ice, unless it be by tarn," said a man.

"Perhaps we can secure a tarn!" cried a fellow. "There is fighting, confusion!"

"To the high cot!" cried a man.

"The first tarn hold!" cried another.

"Yes!" cried another.

"Hold!" said Philoctetes. "It is madness!"

"We are unarmed, we pose no threat, none will fire upon us, none will cut us down," said a man.

"If you interfere, you will be deemed a threat," said Philoctetes. "You would deal with desperate men, of either side, who will strike without hesitation or compunction."

"To the cots! To the tarn holds!" insisted a man.

"To the high cot!" said another. "The first tarn hold! Only it opens to the sky!"

"That is where the fighting will be!" said a man.

"Traps will be sealed on the others!" said a man.

"Do not let others seize our only chance to live!" cried a man.

"Are we cowards?" shouted a fellow.

"To the tarn hold!" screamed a man.

"The first, the first!" screamed a man.

"I have a sword," said Aristodemus, he of Tyros.

"Follow Aristodemus!" said a fellow.

"Follow me!" cried Aristodemus, brandishing the sword, now removed from the concealment of his furs.

"To the high cots!" cried a man.

"To the first tarn hold!" shouted a second.

"Wait!" begged Philoctetes, but he was pushed aside, fell, and men rushed past him.

I crouched beside Philoctetes. He held his arm, which was, as it turned out, broken. We were then alone in the corridor. He looked after the departing men. "Fools," he hissed, "fools!"

There were footsteps in the corridor and some seven or eight Pani, with their odd, long-handled, curved blades removed from their sashes, hurried past us.

"Go with them," said Philoctetes. "The tarns, the ship, must be saved."

"You came to the weapon room," I said. "It was your intention to stand with the ship."

"Yes," he said, "for Cos, for honor!"

I looked to the body of the slain Pani some feet from us, sprawled across the doorway. It had been half hacked to pieces, probably in the frustration and rage of those desperate men in whose way he had so resolutely stood.

"For Cos then," I said, "for honor!"

I then sprang from the side of Philoctetes and hurried after the Pani.

The keeping areas for tarns on the ship of Tersites are large, though small enough, considering the monsters they must house. Some spoke of them as tarn holds, though they were not holds as one would usually think of such places. Some spoke of them, as well, as the "cots," though they bore little resemblance to the common tarn cots, if only because of their vast dimensions, even to those which might be maintained by professional tarnsters in the high cities, specializing in freight and haulage. The great ship itself, made possible by Tur wood and bracing, would be something like a hundred and ten yards from stem to stern, and, abeam, some forty yards. It had nine decks. The tarn areas occupied almost the whole of three decks, as noted, each being some seventy yards in length and some thirty yards in width. Unlike many of the tarn cots in the cities, which are lofty and allow room for perches at various heights, the ceilings of these areas were not more than five yards in height. This, despite the width and length of each, gave each an enclosing, cramped aspect. There were three rows of wooden-barred cages, or stalls, in each area, each extending for much of the length of the cot area, these three rows being separated by two aisles. An open space was provided fore and aft in each cot area, in which some birds were chained in place, and others, in effect, bound, wings pinioned by ropes, beaks strapped shut, save for feeding. In these areas, also, might be stored tackle, saddles, straps, reins, and such. The birds were usually saddled and mounted in a narrow, shuttered area, and then led to one ramp or another, the first two ramps each leading to a higher deck, the last to the open deck itself, whence the bird might take flight. Whereas the tarn, in virtue of its strength, can take flight directly, interestingly, almost vertically, from a horizontal surface, they would usually, on the ship, as from a cliff, launch themselves through an arranged opening in the bulwarks, spread their wings, catch the air, and then strike their way upward.

The Pani moved swiftly through the corridor, single file, in a smooth, shuffling gait, almost in cadence. The narrowness of the corridors, which one or two men might plausibly defend, and the lowness of the ceiling, and the dangling lamps, discouraged a more frenetic, disorderly passage. I recalled the spilled oil, flaming, outside our own quarters, which we had quickly extinguished.

By the side passages, and companionways, and our progress, I took it we had ascended higher than the two lower levels of the housing area for tarns, and were near the upper deck, or open deck. The two lower areas had large traps, which must be raised, the first to provide its ramp's access to the second level, and that of the second level to provide its ramp's access to the highest level, the ramp of which led, once the great hatch, some yards square, was rolled back, to the open deck. It was there the serious fighting, after that in the corridors and companionways, would take place. There would be the tarns most sought, those which might be most swiftly brought to flight.

There were, naturally, several entryways, for men, supplies, feed, and such, both on the port and starboard side of the ship, at the various levels, to the tarn areas. The Pani had, however, judiciously ignored the entryways to the lower levels. They followed the sounds of war, and sought their source.

There were bodies in the corridor, some living.

We threaded our way amongst them.

The sound of steel on steel was now bright and sharp. I was very conscious I had no weapon. I heard the wild, shrill scream of a tarn. I heard the splintering wood, the cries of men, the snap of a bowstring.

We had come to an opened door. Near it, cut down, were two Pani. Through this door, I took it, and perhaps others, the mutineers had entered the high tarn deck. The great hatch is so arranged that it may be moved by means of either, or both, of two windlasses, one inside the tarn area, the other accessible from the main deck. I suddenly shuddered, realizing the plan of the men I followed. In the light of the nearby lamp, hung from the low ceiling of the corridor, I noted that more than one of the Pani was either wounded, or his garments had been slashed. Thus, these men had been in the fight earlier. They had now come about the ship, and were intending to take the mutineers from behind. Surprise would be with them for only a moment, but I had little doubt that it would be a moment of which the most would be made. I was still not clear on the number of mutineers. I did know, now, there were eight Pani at the door, and one unarmed Cosian. Perhaps, I thought, they, in so small a number, will merely attempt to hold the door, to prevent mutineers, should things turn against them, from withdrawing through it, perhaps to discard weapons somewhere, and thence to lose themselves amongst hundreds of others, innocent others not involved in their cause. I was wrong. The Pani, silently, swiftly, their long-hilted, tasseled swords grasped in two hands, fell upon armed men from behind. I think they slew twice their number before men became aware of their presence, and turned to face them. Then the battle near the door began. I stood in the doorway, half crouched down. In the melee, farther on, the mixing was such that I could not tell, except for the occasional Pani, who might be mutinous and who not. Certainly men fought men, and who knew who might be of which party. I saw disruption, confusion, blood, carnage, and death, both of men and beasts. The hatch had been rolled back. The main deck, or most of it, I took it, was in the hands of mutineers, as many ran down the ramp, to try to free a tarn, sometimes to fight with others for the bird. Some tarns, their doors opened to fetch them forth, tried to fly, and dashed themselves against the ceiling, or the stalls, or cages, opposite their own. In the narrowness of the aisles some had broken a wing and, with beak and long, curved, vicious talons, as thick as a man's wrist, in their confusion, rage, and pain, attacked anything within reach, the thick wooden bars of cages, one another, the bodies of men. I saw a head torn off, and, more than once, a body held down, grasped in talons, being torn apart, being eaten. Several tarns, sensing the sky, the hatch now open to the far, bright stars, with a great snap of their wings, sometimes dragging saddle and harnessing behind them, disappeared into the cold night. Others, trying to escape, were killed. I saw one man clinging to a saddle girth carried out, and away, and thence, losing his grip, fall screaming to the ice below. Some fighting was taking place on the open deck. Some were forced over the bulwarks. Below, clearly enough, in the interstices of combat, men backed away from one another to look wildly about, struggling to regain their breath. In the stillness and frigidity of the air, I could hear the churning of water and the snorting of sea sleen below. Some men, mutineers doubtless, despairing of success, began to move from stall to stall, cutting the throats of tarns. If they could not escape, it seemed that they would have it that none might do so. I saw Tarl Cabot, and his confrere, Pertinax, and the fellow, Tajima, a fine rider, fighting, to protect tarns. Men drew away from Cabot. Few, it seemed, cared to cross steel with him. One thrust at him with a spear, doubtless stolen from a weapon room, but he caught the weapon and jerked its wielder forward, startled, wide-eyed, onto the sharp blade of the small swift sword, the warrior's *gladius*. Almost in the same moment he freed the blade, and parried a thrust, the last his now-backward-reeling foe would make. I think some mutineers did mount tarns, and manage to leave the ship. The count was not clear. I saw one of the Pani directing his bow toward me. "No!" cried Cabot, touching the fellow's arm. "Callias!" he called to me, remembering my name. "To us, to us!" he called, his reddish hair wild under his talmit.

Those helmeted were largely mutineers, who had prepared for this hour. I edged about cages, trying to reach the tarnsman. In doing so, I became aware, as I never had been, of the size, the power, and awesomeness of the tarn, for I came within feet of one, whose head, far above mine, with its bright, glistening, dark eyes, was moving, alertly, from one side to the other, as though more puzzled, or curious, than anything else. How tiny a man is on the back of such a beast! What sort of men, I wondered, might once have caught, tamed, and trained such monsters! Indeed, what men, even today, I wondered, would have the courage to come within yards of such a monster, let alone command it from a saddle!

Cabot bent down and retrieved a blade. He cast it toward me, and, a foot or two from me, almost within my reach, it sank into one of the broad, rounded wooden, postlike bars, some five horts thick, of a tarn cage. I drew it free, with a sudden sense of exhilaration. Such a blade, though short, could reach the heart of even a larl. It bore the ship's mark, the Tau, for the ship of Tersites. I had little doubt it had been removed, stolen, from a weapon room, perhaps from the very one we had found ransacked, and nearly emptied, save for destroyed arms.

I brandished it, sensing the heft, the weight, the balance. Yes, I thought, yes! It was the sort of blade to which one might grow accustomed, the sort of blade to which one might entrust one's life, placing its sharp, narrow wall of agile metal between oneself and death.

Cabot grinned. "See that you use it honestly!" he called.

He had armed me.

For such an officer one would die.

I worked my way to his side.

I fenced away an antagonist, and then another. I did not see the foeman moving to my right, but I did see him fall. I owed my life to Tarl Cabot. Even in the test of combat one should be as acutely aware as one is keenly alive. Surely the foe most dangerous is he who is likely to be the least noticed.

Near the ramp, on its left, I saw Seremides fell a man. I was familiar with his skill from Ar. Few could match him. Seremides then was loyal, or not ready, now, to show himself disloyal. I saw him disable another man, and then twice slash his face, once on each side, and then his blade, swift as a striking ost, entered the throat and withdrew, only a hort, but enough. I had seen him do such things in Ar. He was fond of such death play. He was vain, and enjoyed such flourishes. Eleven times I, and others, had been invited, in the dawn, in the square before the Central Cylinder, or in one park or another, to witness his games. Often his victim, provoked to accept a challenge, would have been guilty of little more than entering a portal before him, or brushing against him in a theater or market. Seremides had his likes and dislikes, however they might be founded, and it was better not to be disliked. He could bide his time, with the patience of a concealed sleen, in ambush, waiting for his opportunity, even an opinion to be expressed, whatever it might be, and would then contradict it, and then heat the matter with aspersions and derogations to the point of martial arbitration. The opinion was immaterial; paramount would be the quarrel, the pretext, that being the quarry sought, the quarrel, always the quarrel. Wise men attended his words, intently, and graciously, spoke little in his presence, and would forbear to disagree. One tried to please him. He enjoyed killing. He was of the retinue of Lord Okimoto.

I was pleased to see him in the high tarn hold, though I would have been better pleased to see him amongst the mutineers. I had feared he might by now have departed the ship, in tarnflight, the slave, Alcinoë, bound belly up across his saddle, in some desperate attempt to reach Ar. But such an effort would be irrational, and would presumably conclude not with a sack of gold, but with the death of both on the ice. Too, he would have had to break into the Kasra area, no simple task, and even were he successful in accomplishing this, she, as the other slaves, would still be on her chain. No, this was not the time to think of bringing a slave to Ar. Not the time for either of us. And why should it be he, and not I, who would place the fugitive before Marlenus? The bounty on the high-born, beautiful, officious slut, now collared, was high. Why should the gold be his and not mine? She was a traitress, a conspirator, a criminal, a profiteer, a betrayer of her Home Stone, once even the confidante of the arch traitress herself, Talena, of Ar. Surely she should be returned to the justice of Ar. I wondered if she might make a good slave.

She was attractive. It might be pleasant to have her at one's feet, her lips pressed fervently, hopefully, to them. If she were not pleasing, or if one tired of her, one could always return her to Ar. She was highly intelligent. Such things would be easy for her to understand. It might be pleasant to have her under one's whip, if only for a time. Why could I not forget her? Had I not, even from Ar, dreamed of her small wrists fastened behind her, in my bracelets? The bounty might win me a dozen slaves, even more beautiful than she, perhaps even a galley, but would these, together, the gold washed with blood, be of greater value to me than a single slave whom one might master with severity, but for whom one would die?

"Beware!" cried Cabot, angrily. I fended the blow. I thrust. The fellow stumbled back, bleeding.

Beside Seremides, near the ramp, was Tyrtaios, who was of the retinue of Lord Nishida.

The tarn in the cage behind me screamed, and for a moment I could not hear.

I saw more Pani entering the area, from side doors. Lower portions of the ship, I supposed, had been secured. Many men, I conjectured, had been sealed in their quarters, or warned to remain within.

It seemed clear to me that the tide of war on this strange field, a lower deck on a great ship, was not favoring the mutineers. I conjectured their numbers might have been as few as two to three hundred. Certainly they had not hoped to stand against united Pani, loyal to their lords, and better than a thousand men who might have been armed and brought into the fray from below. No, they would have hoped to strike swiftly, seize the mounts, and then, before resistance could be mustered, make good their escape. But the ship was locked in Thassa's ice. Escape even under ideal conditions, given our presumed location, would have been unlikely. And, in any event, there were fewer tarns than mutineers, even from the beginning, and certainly after the killings, the slaughter, the injuring of birds, and the escape of several. Mutineers, I later learned, had been killing one another to attain the saddle of a tarn, many presumably having hoped to buy that place with steel, when, unfortunately for them, the ship's loyalist forces, Pani and others, rallied and came to the first tarn hold.

"In, in, in!" cried a tarnkeeper, swinging open one of the large, wood-barred gates of a cage. Another, before one of the monsters, was shouting and raising his arms. Tarns, like larls and sleen, tend to find noise and violent motions disconcerting. Larls have been known to withdraw before a shouting child beating on a pan with a metal spoon. One of the monsters backed into the cage, beak snapping with menace, and the tarnkeeper at the gate swung it shut, hooking the latch in place. I saw another tarn down the aisle being similarly housed.

A fellow ran past. I did not know if he were a mutineer or not. I did not strike at him.

"Throw down your arms!" cried Cabot to mutineers. "Throw down your arms!"

Some did, and were hastily bound by Pani, neck to neck, hands behind their backs.

A number of mutineers, however, desperately, fighting, were backing up the ramp toward the open deck. That deck, at least amidships and forward, I gathered, had been largely, most of the time, in the hands of the mutineers. The hatch windlass on the open deck, it seems, had been that used in rolling back the hatch. Many mutineers had come down the ramp from the open deck.

Some of the mutineers on the ramp, those a little behind the points of engagement, turned about, and fled up the ramp. Many of these were felled on the ramp by Pani bows, now with clear targets. Several arrows were lodged in the ramp itself.

Behind me I heard a man weeping, a tarnkeeper. He held the gigantic, limp head of one of the monsters to his breast.

We heard a grating noise. Several mutineers were on the open deck. They were trying to close the hatch.

"Ropes!" I heard, from above. "Food!"

"Do not close the hatch!" screamed mutineers still on the ramp.

It rumbled shut.

"Sleen, sleen!" cried abandoned mutineers.

Our men drew back. The Pani archers, in lines, set arrows to the strings of their bows.

"Throw down your weapons!" cried Cabot to the men on the ramp.

They cast them away, clattering, rolling and sliding, down the ramp.

"No!" cried Cabot.

The lines of Pani archers loosed their arrows.

I think there were none on the ramp, who were not transfixed with two or three arrows.

"Stop!" cried Cabot, to Pani ascending the ramp, cutting throats. "Stop!"

Seremides, at the foot of the ramp, lifted his sword in salute to Lord Okimoto.

He had come now to the first tarn hold.

His hands were folded within the wide sleeves of his garment. "Those who are disloyal must die," he said.

Cabot ran to the ramp, climbed it two thirds of the way, and interposed himself between stricken mutineers and two of the Pani, who bore red knives. They stepped back, and two others rushed forward, their curved blades lifted, grasped in two hands. The eyes of Seremides, at the side of the ramp, blazed with delight. But the man Tajima who had followed Cabot on the ramp had placed himself between Cabot, who, crouched down, was on guard, and the two Pani. "Stop!" he cried. "Stop, in the name of Lord Nishida!" The two Pani stepped away, each to a side, their blades respectfully lowered. This cleared an opening to the bottom of the ramp, where stood the placid Lord Okimoto.

"Is the honorable Tajima, swordsman," asked Lord Okimoto, politely, "authorized to speak for Lord Nishida?"

"I speak as he would speak," said Tajima.

"Does the honorable Tajima, swordsman," asked Lord Okimoto, "hold a blade, unhoused, in my presence?"

"No, my lord!" said Tajima. He bowed, and swiftly replaced the blade in his sash.

At that point the large hatch above began to move once more, slowly, rumbling, this time opening, revealing the sky.

We heard no sounds of fighting on the deck. I took it the deck was cleared.

Cabot remained on guard.

Several Pani, behind Lord Okimoto, put arrows to the strings of their bows.

"Is the honorable Tajima, swordsman," asked Lord Okimoto, once more, politely, "authorized to speak for Lord Nishida?"

"I am authorized to speak for Lord Nishida," said a voice from the deck, at the top of the ramp.

I looked up. The figure was in battle gear, and it removed from its head a large, winged helmet.

"Ah," said Lord Okimoto, politely, "Lord Nishida."

"What is going on?" inquired Lord Nishida.

"I am first, am I not?" inquired Lord Okimoto.

"Of course," said Lord Nishida, bowing his head briefly, acknowledging the priority of his colleague. It was my understanding that each lord had something like two hundred and fifty Pani in his command, that those of Lord Nishida had been housed at a place called Tarn Camp, north of the Alexandra, some pasangs from its headwaters, and that those of Lord Okimoto had been housed differently, but in the vicinity, somewhere south of the Alexandra. The two complements had joined forces before the great ship began its journey downriver. I did not doubt, however, that they had been in close communication during the building of the great ship. Most, but not all, of those who were not Pani had been with Lord Nishida at Tarn Camp. Many had been recruited in Brundisium, and, over months, in larger and smaller numbers, in larger and smaller ships, had coasted north, thence at one rendezvous or another, to move overland, east to Tarn Camp. They were a motley lot, mostly mercenaries, several from the free companies, many once of the occupation forces in Ar. But amongst them as well were landless men, younger sons, men without Home Stones, bandits, pirates, adventurers, soldiers of fortune, thieves, fugitives, wanted men, cutthroats, fugitives from Ar, such as Seremides, and others. The Pani had apparently much gold to invest in recruitment, and had not been sparing or particular in its distribution. I sensed that it had been only after the great ship had been at sea for a time that the risks involved in assembling such men were better understood. The Pani, I suspected, perhaps because of their cultural background, in which certain values might be presupposed and never questioned, might have underestimated the dangers involved. Perhaps, too, given the exigencies of their task, whatever it might be, and its urgency and prospects, whatever they might be, they had been concerned to move as swiftly as would prove practical. Perhaps they felt they had had little time in which to be particular. Their final intention, in any case, I suspected, was to put together a formidable force as quickly as possible, a force of skilled and dangerous men, men free of certain indigenous and traditional loyalties, which, disciplined, and closely managed, might in unfamiliar, remote venues be well applied to the business of war.

"Disloyalty," said Lord Okimoto, "is to be punished by death. It is our way. Those beneath you, on the slanted surface, were disloyal, and several behind me, now suitably subdued and tethered, were disloyal, as well."

The mutineers who had, at Cabot's word, discarded their weapons, and were now kneeling, bound and neck-roped, Pani about with drawn blades, looked at one another in apprehension, and surely to Cabot, as well.

"I see Tarl Cabot, tarnsman," said Lord Nishida. "I would hear him speak."

"His blade is unhoused," said Lord Okimoto.

Cabot sheathed the *gladius*.

"Lords Okimoto and Nishida," said Cabot, evenly. "Mutiny is done. Weapons were surrendered freely. Men have placed their lives and trust in your hands. Otherwise they would have died with weapons in hand. Men do not surrender to be slaughtered. That is not our way."

"One wonders, Lord Nishida," said Lord Okimoto, "if Tarl Cabot, tarnsman, is loyal."

"He and others fought with us!" exclaimed Tajima.

Lord Okimoto looked at Tajima, with surprise.

"Forgive me, lord," said Tajima, lowering his head. He had not been invited to speak.

"Where is Nodachi?" asked Lord Okimoto.

"He is on the deck, he meditates, he slew seven," said Lord Nishida.

I did not know of whom they spoke, but I gathered his opinion might have been valued.

"Lords Okimoto and Nishida," said Tarl Cabot. "Men did not wish to die. They fear the ice. They are hungry. They sought escape. They were desperate, crazed, not thinking."

"The attack was well planned, well organized, well coordinated," said Seremides. "That is not the way of crazed, unthinking men."

"My esteemed colleague, the noble Rutilius of Ar," said Cabot, "is well aware that a handful of uncrazed, thinking conspirators, men of malice and cunning, may organize, coordinate, and direct, the actions of others, men on the brink of despair and panic. It is my suspicion that this act was an attempt to conserve rations, to prolong the life of some by ending that of others, perhaps an attempt, even, to thin your forces, so as, eventually, to seize the ship."

"Absurd!" cried Seremides.

"It is not clear, of course," said Tarl Cabot, "who it might be who organized and arranged this mutiny."

"It seems they are slain by now," said Seremides.

"Perhaps, perhaps not," said Tarl Cabot.

"I was unaware," said Lord Okimoto, "that Tarl Cabot, tarnsman, had requested permission to speak."

"I speak as I will," said Cabot. "It is the way of my caste."

"He is of the scarlet caste," explained Lord Nishida.

"Ah," said Lord Okimoto.

"Lords," said Cabot, "I do not know our destination, nor your purpose, but the destination seems remote, and the purpose important. I think then that practicality, if not mercy, if not honor, should urge lenience in this matter."

"May I speak?" asked Tajima.

Lord Nishida, with a slight motion of his head, granted this permission.

"Many months ago," said Tajima, "we had been sorely defeated, and driven to the edge of the sea. Surely there are those of us here who remember that well. It was the fall of night that saved the few of us, no more than seven hundred, not even that, from the thousands with which we had begun. Never had there been such a battle. We were weary, and far outnumbered. Many were wounded, sick, and hungry. We waited for the morning, on the beach, to die. Then, by the will of whatever

177

gods there be, by whatever names be theirs, we found ourselves, and gold, on a far shore. Now we would return. Those arrayed against us are many and formidable. I do not think we can spare one tarnsman, one spearman, one swordsman, one archer. I, too, speak for lenience."

"There has been disloyalty," said Lord Okimoto.

"I speak for lenience," said Lord Nishida.

Suddenly many eyes turned toward the top of the ramp, to the open deck, where, now beside Lord Nishida, there stood a silent figure, clearly of the Pani. He wore a short robe, with wide sleeves. He was of medium height, but square in the shoulders. His ankles and wrists were thick. His hair was bound back. He carried a sword, which seemed almost a part of his hand. He was one of those who would not sleep lest such a blade lay at his side. His face was broad, his eyes bright. I could read no expression on his face, no more than upon a rock.

"Have you heard?" inquired Lord Okimoto of the figure.

It nodded, quickly, abruptly, and then, again, it was still, as still as if it might have been formed of rock, or carved of wood.

"It is Nodachi," said one of the Pani.

I gathered from his observation, that it was not usual for this individual to be about, amongst them.

"What shall it be, honorable one?" asked Lord Okimoto.

The figure thrust his sword beneath his sash, and turned away.

"It is lenience," said Lord Nishida.

"What does it matter," cried Seremides. "We shall die on the ice anyway!"

The mutineers who had been on the ramp did not survive. There was not one who had not been struck by at least two arrows. It is not well to be the target of a Pani marksman. Cabot's interposition, at the risk of his own life, had won at best a few moments more of life for those he had sought to protect. The tethered mutineers, some sixty or so, were taken below, in the custody of Pani, and put in chains.

"Those of the cavalry," called Cabot, "return to your quarters."

There were probably some twenty or thirty fellows there who were in his command.

Other officers, too, dismissed men.

Pani, too, began to file from the tarn hold. Lord Okimoto and Seremides had already departed.

I had understood little or nothing of that of which Tajima, the rider, had spoken, that about night, a battle, the waiting at the beach, and such. I did understand, and well, his concern to conserve men. In battle each man on one's side is precious. Who, when the enemy appears at the horizon, would be willing to spare even a single slinger, in rags, with his sack of absurdly engraved lead pellets, let alone a spearman, or swordsman?

Cabot climbed up the ramp, to the open deck.

The fellow, Nodachi, was gone.

Hundreds of fellows were still below, either sealed in their quarters, or remaining there, given the instructions of Pani corridor guards. Many of these fellows would probably not even know, until later, what had been going on.

I trusted that Philoctetes had sought the care of a physician.

"Lord Nishida," said Cabot, respectfully.

"I would have regretted losing the commander of the tarn cavalry," said Lord Nishida.

Cabot smiled. "I, too," he said.

"There was war here, on the deck," said Lord Nishida.

"Clearly," said Cabot, looking about.

The battle on the open deck had surged back and forth, for more than an Ahn, but then, obviously, in the end, the ship's forces had triumphed.

"There were mutineers who fled to the deck, late in the war below," said Cabot.

"Many had seized food, and there were ropes," said Lord Nishida. "They went over the side, to the ice. Some fell to the water. There were sea sleen at the ice. Many succumbed. But most made it to the ice."

"They hope to reach land, over the ice," said Cabot.

"They will die on the ice," said Lord Nishida.

"I fear few knew of the Stream of Torvald," said Cabot.

"The Stream of Torvald?" asked Lord Nishida, curious.

"Yes," said Cabot, "it is a warm current, a river in the sea, so to speak, pasangs wide, which keeps Torvaldsland from being ice locked in the winter."

I shuddered. The ice, then, even in winter, would not reach Torvaldsland.

"I must attend to things below," said Lord Nishida.

"Callias fought with us, and well," said Cabot, indicating me.

"Of course," said Lord Nishida. "He has, as I recall, what you speak of as a Home Stone."

"Yes," said Cabot, "he has a Home Stone."

Cabot then took his leave and Lord Nishida went down the ramp to the tarn hold.

I followed him, as I thought to return to my quarters.

I stopped to examine one body. It was that of Aristodemus, he of Tyros. He had fought with the mutineers.

Lord Nishida stopped to regard two trussed mutineers. They were in the keeping of tarnkeepers.

"Why are these men not below, with the others?" he asked.

"He, and he," cried a tarn keeper, "killed tarns."

"I see," said Lord Nishida.

There was then a shrill scream, of a raging tarn, angry and wild, in a nearby cage.

"Free them," said Lord Nishida.

The tarnkeepers did this, with much reluctance.

The mutineers regarded one another with triumph.

"Now," said Lord Nishida, "cut away their clothing, bloody them a little, and put them in the cage with the bird."

"No!" cried the mutineers. "No!"

Eager tarnkeepers rushed upon them.

I exited the tarn hold through the same door through which the eight Pani and I had entered it earlier. Outside in the corridor, I heard hideous screams behind me.

I returned to my quarters.

Chapter Ten

After the Mutiny

I lay in my bunk, weak with hunger.

From day to day, usually at night, one fellow or another had left the ship, following in the wake of mutineers, from weeks ago, descending to the ice.

But few now would essay the ice, if only from weakness.

Pani no longer policed the work areas. There seemed little point in it now, now that all, in a few days at most, would be lost.

It was all we could do, in the last few days, to keep the ice from crushing the ship.

And it is all pointless, I thought. What does it matter now? Thassa, like the ice itself, was patient. Some men had cut their own throats.

I wondered if they were still feeding the slaves in the Kasra and Venna keeping areas. I supposed so. Men are fond of their animals, verr, kaiila, slaves. Cabot, I knew, shared his own meager rations, now reduced to meal, with a sleen. The name of the sleen was Ramar. It was lame.

It was two Ahn until my watch.

I lay in the bunk, worn, and, I thought, half mad. I was literally afraid I was losing my mind. Yesterday, half delirious, I had had the absurd notion that the work had been less arduous.

The watches, I had later learned, had been shortened.

It was now late in the Waiting Hand.

During the Waiting Hand, in Cos, as elsewhere, surely in Ar, I do not know how it is in Brundisium, one does little. It is a time, in effect, of fear, misery, despair, and mourning. The shops are closed. The streets are empty. Many doors and windows are sealed with pitch, to prevent the entrance of ill luck. Too, commonly wreaths of laurel or veminium have been nailed to the door. Ill luck, as is known, cares little for either. One remains indoors, one eats little, one seldom speaks. One waits, for this is a time of terror, to see if the world will end, or begin once more. It is the year's end. Some cities have been attacked during the Waiting Hand, sacked, and burned, citizenries refusing to leave their homes, refusing to take up arms, at such a fearful, inauspicious time. It is doubtless all madness, and groundless, but still few will willingly go abroad at such a time. Even the higher castes are uneasy at such a time.

Yea, it is a miserable time, the Waiting Hand, but I tell you nothing.

I lay in my bunk, hungry, and weak.

I hoped I could respond when my watch was called. Some men, good men, could not.

I had made my way at times past the Kasra and Venna areas. Few were the sounds that now emanated from those places. Within those holding areas I had little doubt that the large women, the whip slaves, muscular, freakish, and mannish, with their switches, thinking themselves the truest of women, perhaps because they were the most like men, would take the largest and best portions of food for themselves. How they would abuse the smaller, beautiful, more feminine women in their power! It was interesting how some women, such large, gross, misshapen, unhappy women, could hate other women, smaller, lovelier women, clearly, fittingly, and appropriately the slaves of men. Did they envy them? It was hard to say. Certainly slaves feared them, even as they did free women, who despised them for their weakness, needs, and bondage. But such gross women, slaves, would kneel, tremble, and grovel, no differently from their smaller, fairer sisters, before a free woman. It was no wonder then that lovely slaves looked to the protection of males from such gross brutes, and free women. What hope had they for safety, understanding, and compassion, and happiness, save from males who would relish their beauty and master it, uncompromisingly, putting it to the purposes for which the slaves knew it had been formed by nature. To be sure, I had seen such gross slaves occasionally taken in hand by a man, to whom, and before whom, they were as small, weak, and helpless as the lovelier slaves had been to them, and before them. Such gross women, sold perhaps for a pittance, and taught the meaning of their sex, if only by the whip, discovered the femininity they had thought nonexistent, and had professed to despise in their smaller sisters. They, too, suitably mastered, as women may be, soon learned themselves, and love. One need not be a gold-piece girl or a silver-piece girl to be fulfilled in bondage. Now they know themselves, and gratefully, and humbly, as mastered females, as only another sister in bondage.

I thought of Jad, her opulent streets, of the countryside, of the terraces of Cos, of her grapes, fresh, sweet, and full, of Ar, of glorious, imperial Ar, with its countless towers and its wide boulevards, of the occupation, of my squad, of the rising in the city, the flight to return, the welcome we did not receive, the poverty, the casting about, of Telnus, her taverns, her harbor, and shipping, of the *Metioche*, and of the great ship of Tersites. And I thought of a slave in my collar, at my feet, looking up at me, knowing that she was mine. I wondered if I should permit her clothing.

It is interesting how the body of a woman in bondage increases in sensitivity. Part of this is doubtless due to the fact that she is likely, if clothed, to be lightly clothed, in, say, a tunic or camisk. Thus she is likely to be very aware of a gentle movement of air upon her body, of the stirring of a bit of silk, or rep-cloth, against her thighs, of a wisp of hair against her forehead, of the feel of a mat or the knap of a rug, or the smoothness of tiles, beneath her bared feet. But I think that only a small part of this increase in sensitivity is due to garmenture. Most, and by far the greater portion of this awareness, seems clearly consequent upon her condition itself, that she is owned, that she is bond. This brings her alive in ways incomprehensible to the free woman. Hearing the step of her master on the stairs, or beyond the door, she may suddenly become aware of the exact feeling of the collar on her neck, his collar, which she cannot remove, a sensation of which she had been heretofore totally oblivious. And perhaps she hopes he will chain her helplessly on the furs at the foot of his couch, and then, with merciless sensitivity, with a master's ruthlessness and gentleness, with severity and kindliness, remind her that she is a slave, only that, forcing her to endure, for Ahn, at his pleasure, perhaps for a morning or afternoon, or a day, the ecstasies of slave orgasm after slave orgasm. Certainly her senses, too, become alive, as they were not prior to her embondment. She discovers, now a half-naked slave, an animal, a new and rich world, one filled with fresh and remarkable sounds, scents, sights, touches, and tastes. Surely this world was there before. But before she was not owned, was not in her place in nature, as a female, was not before in a man's collar. Why is it she was never aware of this glory before? Surely wind had always whispered in the tall green grass, and stirred the shimmering leaves of the Tur tree. And in the public garden she only now becomes aware, following her master, heeling him, that the rich sequence of blossoms is not only arranged like music, with its color, tint into tint, shade into shade, tone into tone, to dramatically enhance the delight of a walk, but there is another music, as well, a planned melody of scent. Much thought, much art, much arrangement, much planning, goes into a park, a garden. And how beautiful are the towers against the evening, stormy sky, the light of *Tor-tu-Gor* half hidden in the dark clouds. Did she never notice before the stateliness of a kaiila's gait, that sinuous movement of a sleen's spine, as it moves, avoiding open spaces, the tidelike mightiness of a tarn's wing, as it preens. And the world becomes so rich, too, to the touch, to the fingertips, the feet, the lips, the body. What do free women know of the weight of chains, and their sound, of the feel of one's limbs bound back, coarsely, with rough rope, of one's wrists thonged quickly, snugly, behind one's back, of the clasp of slave bracelets, of the feel of the floor on one's bared knees, of the feel of the whip to one's lips and tongue, as one performs whip-love before the master, rendering to a symbol of his mastery its due reverence and homage? And, of course, there is, too, taste, that of the bit forced back, between her teeth, and fastened there, of the gag, the disgusting horror of slave wine, the delicious releaser, inspiring terror, the taste of simple, plain food, perhaps from a pan on the floor, when one is hungry, its quantity well monitored, the spoonful of ka-la-na for which she has begged, the joy of savoring a tiny, hard candy thrown to her, or fed to her by hand, for which she has waited long. The slave girl knows many small, homely joys, and appreciates them, and treasures them, in ways the haughty free woman, secure in station and status, can only mock. But let her wear the collar and she will soon become aware of the preciousness of tiny things, wondrous, marvelous tiny things, longed for and hoped for, things which she might, hitherto, have held in disdain or contempt. It is little wonder that the female slave, owned, and mastered, is alive in a thousand ways undivulged to her free sister.

I thought of a particular slave. If I owned her, I thought I would keep the name Alcinoë upon her. It is a nice name. Too, I thought it appropriate, as the women of Ar, or the most beautiful of them, at least, are worthy only to be the slaves of such men as those of Cos.

To be sure, she would be worth much in Ar. I wondered if she would be worth more at the foot of a man's couch.

I supposed that would depend on the man.

I would have to give the matter some thought.

I then, weak, and miserable, fell asleep.

I awakened to a gigantic crashing noise, deafening, almost like dry thunder, and thought the ship was done. Thassa had claimed her. She had lifted her and broken her apart in her mighty fist. Surely, any moment now the great vessel would settle, water pouring in through broken timbers. Then, too, I was suddenly terrified, because the sand glass had emptied. I had missed my watch! I had not been summoned. One can be flogged, with the snake, under which men have died, if a watch is missed. Men have been cast overboard for such an omission. But no one had come for me, calling out, shaking me, pounding on the door. Had there been more desertions? Had the last watch, mad with hunger, sought the ice? Then I heard much shouting. I could make little out of it, and, as I tried to piece together the shreds of my confusion, my fear, the noise about, it became clear to me that the shouting was a shouting of joy, and I heard hundreds of feet hurrying down the low corridor and up companionways. From somewhere I heard a number of voices raised in an anthem of Ar, and, but moments later, I heard its answer, a lusty song of Cos. I fled from my quarters, half-clad in furs, and hurried up the nearest companionway, and the next, continuing until I reached the open deck, and saw hundreds of men, many gathered near the bow. I climbed a bit up the forward mast, and was not alone, for some clung to it before me. On the deck, men were pointing forward. Before the ship, as far as I could see, the ice had broken.

The Waiting Hand was done.

Today, I realized, was the first day of En'Kara, the first day of En'Kara-Lar-Torvis, the Vernal Equinox, the first day of Spring.

The world would begin again.

Too, in the distance, I could see a spume over the water, like a thread of vertical fog, like a line, then drifting apart, like a cloud, where a whale had emerged. And then another. The Red Hunters, I had heard, hunt such beasts in skin boats. On both port and starboard, I heard, too, the opening of the galley nests, and the extension and rattling of davits. Galleys would be lowered to the ice, and slid toward the open water. In a few Ehn I saw the first galley, to shouts of gladness, slip into the open water. Many soldiers were on board, with ropes fastened to spears.

On the stem castle I saw the small, crooked, frenetic figure of Tersites dancing, lifting his hands to *Tor-tu-Gor*, and going to the rail, from time to time, to shake his fists down at Thassa.

I did not think that was wise.

Eyes had not even been painted on the ship.

Suitable ceremonies had not been performed.

But even Thassa, it seems, could not alter the orbit of a world.

The Waiting Hand was done.

The world would begin again.

Chapter Eleven

Parsit

"Look," said Cabot, pointing abeam. "Four of them!" He handed me the Builder's glass.

I was familiar with this instrument because I was one of several regularly sent aloft, to the platform and ring, that the horizon might be scanned, that large sea life might be noted, that land or a ship might be sighted. To be sure, we had seen no land since the farther islands, and the last of those, Chios. And how might one expect to see a sail this far at sea, for we had come farther than any vessel had formerly come, at least to our knowledge. To be sure, many ships had ventured beyond the farther islands. It was only that none, at least to our knowledge, had returned. Were there ships at World's End? The Pani had insisted that regular watches be kept, from the platform and ring, even at night. Perhaps there were ships then, which might come forth, from the World's End?

"Tharlarion," I said. We had seen such things before. But they were unusual tharlarion, unlike those with which I had hitherto been familiar, prior to the last few weeks.

"They approach," said Cabot.

I had never seen them come this close. I think they followed the ship for garbage, usually a half pasang behind, in the great ship's wake.

They had learned no fear of us.

And we, as it happened, had learned no fear of them.

Never had they been this close.

"Look," said Cabot, pointing down.

There was a shimmering in the water, like fluttering candles.

"Parsit fish," I said. It was a large school. The passage of the ship had divided the school, and its motion had drawn several to the surface. Schooling protects fish. It is difficult for a predator to single out prey. One target replaces another. They flash in and out; they appear here and, in a flicker, there. Who could concentrate on a single flake of snow in a blizzard, a particular grain of sand in a Tahari wind? The predator is distracted, and confused. It flies at the mass but how shall it snap shut its jaws on the single victim it might manage, which it can scarcely note for less than a tenth of an Ihn, before another appears, and another. It will lunge into the mass, to break it apart, that single victims may be separated and tracked, but the schooling instinct, like that of flocking birds, swiftly returns the fish to the group. The school, of course, may be, and is, preyed upon. But the matter, as there are many fish that school, seems to be one of averages. One supposes that the school must increase the likelihood of the survival of any given fish. To be sure, the school is vulnerable to the nets of men. In such a case, the school, so obvious and visible, so large and slow moving, becomes a most perilous habitat.

"Parsit! Parsit!" cried several men, rushing to the bulwarks. Some mariner's caps were flung in the air.

Many times we had launched the nested galleys, though not of late, in pairs, nets strung between them. Our concern was less with food than fresh water. He who drinks the water of Thassa, with its salt from a thousand rivers, from the Alexandra, to the Vosk, to the Kamba and Nyoka, soon dies, of misery and madness. Still, there was little danger at present, for the great casks, taller and wider than a standing man, were scarcely tapped. And spread sails, formed into great basins, given the frequency of spring rains, had supplied more than enough water for tarns and slaves.

Several of the men were striking their left shoulders with the palm of their right hand. Others were cheering.

Their elation had not to do, however, with the possibility of augmenting the ship's larder, but with something, at least at the time, of much greater interest.

We were joined at the rail by Lord Nishida.

"The men are pleased," said Lord Nishida.

"They see Parsit," said Cabot.

The Parsit, as many similar fish, require vegetation, and vegetation requires light, and thus, typically, such fish school off banks, in shallower water, where light can reach plants tenaciously rooted, say, some dozens of yards below in the sea floor. The banks are usually within two or three hundred pasangs of land masses. Thus the jubilation of the men.

"We are near land," said a man.

"It is too soon," said Lord Nishida, quietly.

Aëtius, second to Tersites himself, bespoke himself, to Lord Nishida, politely, "You think they are open-water Parsit?"

Strictly there are no "open-water Parsit," that is, Parsit who would inhabit the liquid desert of a sea untenanted by a suitable food source, but the expression is often used of migratory Parsit. Great schools of migratory Parsit migrate seasonally, moving from the austral summer to the northern summer, as some birds, thus availing themselves of seasonal efflorescences of plant life. They fatten before each migration and, thousands of pasangs later, arrive, like migratory birds, lean and hungry, at familiar banks, thousands of pasangs from each other, where they are welcomed, again, with abundances of food. In this season they would be moving northward.

"Tarl Cabot, tarnsman?" inquired Lord Nishida.

"No," said Cabot. "I do not see them as open-water Parsit. They were not moving north."

"They are localized Parsit then, indigenous," said Aëtius, pleased.

"I think so," said Cabot.

Men were cheering, near the rail, pounding on one another, clasping one another in joy.

"Then," said Aëtius, pleased, "we are near land!"

To be sure, it might yet be hundreds of pasangs distant. Much depended on the flooring of the sea.

"It is too soon," said Lord Nishida.

If Lord Nishida was correct, I feared there would be, as days wore on, ugliness amongst the men.

"Clearly," said Aëtius, his hands clasped on the rail, "they are Parsit."

"We know clearly," said Cabot, "only that there must be a food source somewhere about."

"I do not understand," I said.

"Tarl Cabot, tarnsman," said Lord Nishida, "I would speak with you, privately."

Tarl Cabot then followed Lord Nishida to the privacy of the stem-castle deck.

We had seen little of Tersites for several days.

"Aii!" cried a fellow, near me, pointing.

I gasped, and clung to the rail, looking down to the water.

The gigantic body rolled in the waves, almost at the side of the ship, the water washing over the glistening body. I saw the huge paddlelike appendages of the creature, briefly, and then they were again concealed in the dark waters of Thassa. A tiny head, small when taken in proportion to the whole, surmounting a long, sinuous neck, was raised from the water. The head was triangular, and the jaw, which it opened, revealed a dark tongue, and several rows of tiny teeth. Two round eyes regarded us for a moment, and then the head, on its long neck, disappeared beneath the waves, and the body, too, though I could see it for a few moments. The ship, great as it was, was jarred, as the creature must have brushed against it.

I had never seen tharlarion of this sort before the voyage, and never until now had I seen one this close. It was the size of a small galley. For all its bulk it, buoyed by the water, had moved with grace. It had come for the Parsit, whose school had been disrupted by the passage of the great ship.

Chapter Twelve

I Am Set Upon;
The Deck Watch;
A Light

It was night.

It was cold.

The rain was fitful, I could see the Prison Moon.

I was on the platform, within the ring, that on the forward mast, or foremast.

Far below, on the deck, dimly, I could see the small, tunicked figure, still bound to the second mast, her hands fastened above her head, five strands of rope about her belly, pulling her back, tightly, against the wood. A free man had found her displeasing. She would doubtless soon learn to be more pleasing. It is what she is for.

On the deck, during the day, the weather was warm enough, certainly. To our pleasure, the slaves had been returned to their tunics. It is extremely pleasant to see a barefoot slave, in a tunic or less. On the platform, however, within the ring, it can be quite chilly, even when it is warm below. And now, at night, it was indeed unpleasant. Within my cloak I shivered. Should the rain continue, the cloak would be soaked. Miserable, too, I thought, would be the small thing bound below. Her head was down. The tiny tunic, of rep cloth, clung about her. She would learn to be a better slave.

As I suppose I have made clear, I am not by caste of the Mariners. It is one thing to draw an oar, and do one thing or another about a ship, even to be of its fighting complement, and quite another to read the weather, and water, and the stars, to plot courses, to keep a steady helm in a hard sea, to manage lines and rigging, and such. There were, of course, things I could do, such as keep a high watch, as I was now doing. The platform and ring, and each mast had such an arrangement, are near the summit of the mast, and encircle it, allowing the lookout to move about the mast. In this fashion, if it desired, there may be more than one lookout on each platform, within each ring. To be sure, usually only one ring and platform was manned, and that by a single lookout, commonly, as tonight, that of the foremast. It is different, of course, if one is in dangerous waters, fears an attack, or such.

I clung to the ring, which was cold, and wet, that I might be steadied. The motion of the ship, whether its side to side rolling, or yaw, or its plunging, the lifting and falling of the bow, its pitch, is exaggerated at the height of the mast. It takes time for one of the land, say, an infantryman like myself, to accustom himself to the sea, but I had managed this well enough, quickly enough, after two or three days in the *Metioche*, but this had little prepared me for the high watch here, with the distance and violence of the mast's motion. Such, for a time, can disconcert and sicken even a seasoned mariner. Perhaps that is why the high watches are usually restricted to selected crewmen, who manage the watch regularly. I was now, with several others, frequently assigned such a watch. In the beginning it is well not to look down, or at the water, to the side. It helps to keep one's view away from the ship, and to the horizon, which, in any event, is where it should be, anyway. After two or three days of the high watch one's body, one's belly, one's sense of balance, and such, are likely to adjust to the motion. Some adapt more quickly than others, of course, and it is from these that the high watches are usually drawn. Some men, interestingly, find themselves unable, apparently indefinitely, or, at least, within a reasonable time, to make the pertinent accommodations. To be sure, in fair weather a high watch is not all that different from a deck watch, or a stem- or stern-castle watch. After the first few days I was no longer bothered by the high watch, and, given a decency of weather, had begun to enjoy it. You are away from things, and seem closer to the wind, the clouds, and sunlight, and, all about, for pasangs, stretches the vast, encompassing ambiguity of Thassa, subtle and minacious, welcoming and threatening, benignant and perilous, restless, sparkling, and dangerous, green, vast, intriguing, beckoning Thassa. It is easy to see how she calls to men, she is so alluring and beautiful, and it is easy, as well, to see how, with her might and whims, her moods and power, she may inspire fear in the stoutest of hearts. Be warned, for the wine of Thassa is a heady wine. She may send you gentle winds and shelter you in her great arms, bearing you up, or should she please, break you and draw you down, destroying you, to mysterious, unsounded deeps. In her cups you may find many things, the unalienable riches of moonlight on water, her whispering in long nights, against the hull, her unforgettable glory in the morning, the brightness of her noontide, the transformations of her sunset and dusk, her access to far shores, the sublime darkness of her anger, the lashing and howling of her winds, the force and authority of her waves, like pitching mountains. She is the love of the Caste of Mariners. She is a heady wine. Her name is Thassa.

The wind changed.

The rain became heavier.

The glass of the Builders was on its strap, across my chest. As most of the lookouts, I had fastened a safety rope about my waist. One can lose one's footing, particularly in heavy weather, or when the platform is iced, and slip between the platform and the ring, which is waist high.

I felt the first rattle of hail.

We had had two hail storms of great severity when farther north, storms such as those which, in the Barrens, north and east of the Voltai, sometimes decimate flocks of migrating birds, striking them from the sky, flocks which, obedient to their hereditary imperatives, refuse to land and seek shelter. Sails had been quickly reefed, lest, by a rare, larger stone, they might be cut. Hundreds of tiny impressions marked the deck. In places a larger stone had splintered a plank, or gouged a railing. Some stones were the size of a man's fist. All hands had soon been ordered below deck. The tarns had been much agitated by the pounding on the deck above them. There was little to fear now, however, as storms of that severity seldom, if ever, occur at this latitude. Still I backed against the mast, and drew the hood of my cloak over my head.

The hail picked up a little.

It was not a serious hail, but it would keep the deck largely untenanted.

I now suspect that had much to do with what occurred.

I looked back, below, to see the slave, punishment-bound, at the second mast. Her feet were bare, as is common with a slave in good weather. Free women feel that a slave, as she is an animal, should not be shod, no more than a verr or kaiila, but such things are, of course, up to the master. Some slaves, high slaves, may have sandals, even slippers, set with precious stones, but a free woman is likely to order them to remove such presumptuous footwear in their presence, and sometimes to bring them to them, dangling from their mouths, humbly, head down, on all fours, rather as a pet sleen or slave might bring footwear to her master. Little love is lost between the free woman and the slave. Interestingly, the female slave is honored to bring footwear in her teeth, head down, humbly, on all fours, to her master, as the animal she knows herself to be. "I am yours, your beast, Master. May I be found pleasing." She is then likely to kiss his feet, place them carefully within the sandals, and tie them for him, following which she is likely to again kiss his feet, back a bit away, and then kneel before him, head down. She is his slave. He is her master. It is quite different, of course, before another woman. What right has one woman, only herself a woman, to so shame, crush, and mortify another woman? This is not the natural relationship of a woman to a man, but a cruelly humiliating, unjustified, unnatural travesty of a biologically ordained rightness. Are they not both females, both fittingly the possessions of men, merely that one is collared and one not? Why does the free woman so hate the slave? Does she envy the trembling slave that lovely band fastened about her throat, proclaiming her beauty and desirability? Does she envy her her happiness, her contentment, her fulfillment, her master? "Would you be so different from me, proud mistress," might wonder the slave, "were you tunicked, as I, and your neck encircled, as mine, in a similar claiming device?"

The deck was wet, and cold.

Below, her hair was dark, and long, and, now wet, was much about her face. Sometimes she had lifted her head, her face white and rain-streaked, to look up at me, but I had paid her little attention, and she would soon put her head down, again. Her figure, always of interest, had been improved, I thought, since the beginning of the voyage. This had to do with the regimes of diet and exercise imposed upon her. One may do much what one wants with animals, to improve them. As her vitality and health improved she, well-collared, now a mere pleasure animal, like her sisters, would twist ever more helplessly in her bonds. Slavery much increases the sexual appetites and needs of a female, until they can become almost unbearable.

I looked about, though with the clouds, the darkness, the rain, the spattering of hail, there was not much to see.

The deck was now muchly deserted, given the darkness and weather, save for the helmsman, the stem-castle watch, the slave, and two men maintaining the deck watch. The first deck watch had been relieved; the second was now on duty. I would later learn its nature.

I had come to enjoy, and look forward, to the high watches. Solitude on a ship is rare, and the high watch afforded one of the few opportunities on a ship, say, a round ship, and certainly on the ship of Tersites, to be alone. And, when one is alone, one thinks. It was clear to me that Seremides, serving in the retinue of Lord Okimoto, as a bodyguard, viewed me as a threat, as I could recognize him from Ar. Some of those closest to him, and, I feared, in desperate league with him, such as Tyrtaios, in the service of Lord Nishida, might know him only as a master swordsman, Rutilius of Ar. I did not know. I would later learn of five originally suspect men, not of the Pani, armsmen, originally with Lord Nishida, of which number Tyrtaios was but one, the others being Quintus, Telarion, Fabius, and Lykourgos. Two, however, Quintus and Lykourgos, had somehow perished in the great forest, during the march from Tarncamp to the Alexandra. I had no reason to believe, however, that this had anything to do with Seremides. Certainly I had heard of no altercations with him. I knew little or nothing of Telarion and Fabius. I felt I knew much of Tyrtaios.

Every once in a while I glanced back, and down, at the bound slave. Her name was Alcinoë. Originally, she had been from Ar. She still had something to learn about her collar. That was why she was bound as she was. Sometimes it takes a little time for a woman to realize that she is now only a slave. But in time they understand this quite well, at a man's feet.

I was careful not to be alone with Seremides, and refrained from entering into converse with him, even when he seemed the most congenial. I had seen in Ar, more than once, how the most seemingly innocent discourse could be suddenly, cleverly, twisted into a provocative quarrel, and an exchange of insults, leading to swords, commonly in a park or in the Plaza of Tarns, at dawn, when few were about. One advantage of the high watches, as opposed to deck watches, corridor duty, stores guarding, work in the sail room, and such, is that it is difficult to be approached. Indeed, I had been suggested to Aëtius for the high watches by the tarnsman, Tarl Cabot. Interestingly, beyond this, he had often kept me near him, as though I might be a guardsman. In such times, of course, I was armed. In any event, I suspected that the fact that I was still alive might be due in no small part to the tarnsman, Tarl Cabot. His sword, it seemed, stood between Seremides and Callias. But, too, I thought, and shivered, perhaps more was involved, more than I had suspected? Might it not be I, Callias, who would serve to lure Seremides in? Clearly there was bad blood between the tarnsman and Seremides. Might there not be then some trap I did not understand, in which I might be the bait?

How astonished I had been when it had become clear to me that the tarnsman, Tarl Cabot, did not fear Seremides, but, on the contrary, appeared ready to welcome an opportunity to match steel with him, and how more astonished I had been to note that Seremides was clearly reluctant to accept such a match. What sort of man might be the tarnsman, Tarl Cabot? But even the finest steel is of little avail against poison, against an Anango dart at the base of the skull, against a knife in the back.

I looked down, and back, again.

It is pleasant to look upon a slave, particularly a beautiful, well-formed slave. I wondered how she might perform on the block. They are encouraged to do well. It is not pleasant to be returned to the cage, unsold.

How desperately they strive to please the auctioneer, to present themselves as superb merchandise, as goods well worth bringing home! How they strive to win a buyer!

It is not pleasant to be returned to the cage, unsold.

Too, if they sell for more money, they are likely to have a better-fixed master, a prettier collar, a better kennel, a better diet, an easier life, perhaps even sandals.

In any event, it is not well to be returned the cage unsold. That can be distinctly unpleasant.

It was the third month, the first week past the second passage hand. This is the month which in Ar is called Camerius. In other places it has other names, in Cos the month of Lurius, named for our great Ubar, whose palaces and fortresses are in Jad. In Ko-ro-ba, it is spoken of as Selnar. I do not know how it is spoken of amongst you, in Brundisium. Ah, the month of Policrates! Very well, let it be so. In any event, it was the third month.

Our course from the ice had been south and west.

There were few on deck, from the Ahn, somewhat past the Eighteenth, from the bars, and from the miseries of the weather.

While we were at table, the girls, as expected, had served. They had been clad in modest tunics. This was no Ubar's victory feast, in which the daughters of the conquered, still free, must serve naked. Some decorum must be preserved, if only for the sake of the ship's discipline. Paga slaves, house slaves, pleasure slaves, and such, serve one way at the low tables common in households, inns, taverns, and such, and rather differently at the ship's tables, which are higher, and which are, as are the benches, fastened in place, this to prevent shifting in rough seas. The benches anchor one in place, so to speak, as sitting cross-legged at the low tables would not. Too, one may hold to the table itself, which is, incidentally, bordered by a slightly raised rim, or sometimes by a small railing, this helping to keep things in place. Goblets are weighted, for steadiness, and plates are flat-bottomed, and square, to minimize movement, by maximizing the amount of surface area in contact with the table.

It was much darker now.

The night was now moonless.

Even the Prison Moon was no longer visible.

I did not know why it was called the Prison Moon. It had a grayish look at dawn and dusk, almost, interestingly, as though it might be a sphere of metal, and not a natural moon.

Such illusions are interesting.

One could no longer make out the horizon. One would sense it, of course, rather than see it. One knew where its line would be from the platform and ring, rather as one knew a different horizon from the deck, and another from the stem castle.

There was some light on deck, of course.

A lantern was mounted near the helmsman, and another on the stem castle. Given the darkness, the lanterns seemed bright. In daylight, of course, it would be difficult to know if they were lit or not.

Thassa seemed quiet. My watch would be over at the second Ahn.

There were few on deck.

It was now very difficult to make out the slave below.

Given the height of the tables the girls serve while on their feet. Some similarities, of course, obtain. Service is to be deferent, and, for the most part, silent. If a slave speaks, she is expected to speak as a slave, not a free woman. It is, after all, a privilege for a slave to be allowed to speak in the presence of a free man. They are not free women. Free woman may do much what they please. Slaves may not. Commonly the eyes of the slave, she serving in general, as at the long tables, will not meet those of a free man. She will commonly serve head down, and will keep two hands on the goblet or plate until it is placed softly, gently, carefully, deferently, before the free person.

The girl, Alcinoë, and three others, had been assigned to our table.

Today she had dared to place a goblet before me held with one hand. The two-handed grasp is much more aesthetic; it suggests deference; it frames her body, and it brings her wrists together, as though they might be chained. It is prescribed in slave serving. It makes it impractical, too, of course, to hold a dagger, say, behind one's back. Similarly, the scantiness of common slave garb, though its principal purpose is to display the slave's beauty, has the additional advantage that it tends to render the concealment of a weapon impractical. Such small customs have, interestingly, historically, foiled a number of assassination attempts, in which a free woman, disguised as a slave, sought to obtain a proximity to, say, a general or Ubar, sufficient to bring a weapon into play. The would-be assassin, perhaps discovering that she must keep both hands on, or, more likely, unwilling to keep both hands on, say, a vessel is reluctant, hesitant, or disconcerted. This noticed, she is examined. Discovered to lack a brand, that omission is soon rectified, and she is sent to a market. Naturally, puzzled, and somewhat irritated, I turned about to regard the slave who had dared to serve improperly, and she had dared to meet my eyes, angrily, and then look haughtily away. I did not understand this behavior. Surely she knew better. Perhaps she was uninformed. Perhaps she was unpopular with the large women, her keepers, in the Kasra area, and they had neglected to enlighten her on the proper protocol, the proper etiquette, of serving? Perhaps they wanted her sent back to them, weeping, hands thronged behind her back, running, a punishment tag wired to her collar. The punishments are up to the keepers, and may be various, ranging from whippings and switchings, to a reduction in rations, to unpleasant ties, of which there are a great number. Slaves are kept well in line, and it is not difficult to do. I chose, unwisely, to ignore this breach of decorum. That is usually a mistake, as it may encourage an animal to take similar, or further, liberties. The leash on a slave, so to speak, is to be tight, and short. She must never be allowed to forget that she is a slave, only a slave. I do not know why I did not act. Perhaps I was puzzled. I did not even understand it. She had not behaved so with the other fellows at the table. Was I somehow special? I did know her as the former Lady Flavia of Ar. But it seems that that might have encouraged not liberties on her part, but a zealous circumspection in such matters, a particular desire to please. Did she think it demeaning, rather than utterly appropriate, that she should be serving men? Did she still think of herself as she had in Ar, a woman of power and station, far superior to, say, a mere guard, a soldier, she still a fine lady who was now, inexplicably and unconscionably, set to menial, shameful tasks, fit only for a slave? In our mess, of some one hundred and sixty men, mostly armsmen, at four long tables, some twenty to a side, sixteen slaves served.

Wedges of Sa-Tarna bread were next distributed, and a half larma to each man, useful in prolonged voyages, a precaution against weakness and bleeding. The bread was placed not at my right hand, but insolently before me, half torn. The larma half was small, dry, and withered; it had been crushed, perhaps yesterday, voiding it of most juice. There was little but rind left. It may have been retrieved from garbage. I did not care for the slave's games, nor her expressions. I wondered if others, my fellows, or the other slaves, took notice of these tiny things. Perhaps not. Alcinoë, of course, was a ship slave. I did not own her. To be sure, I did have the rights of a free man, and of a member of the ship's company. Slowly, within me, anger began to seethe, like the boiling mead, honeyed, bubbling, and fermented, sometimes prepared in the north, in the "country of dragons," the camps and villages above Kassau. Next, the square trenchers were to be filled at the serving table, and brought to us. I saw the slave who, in turn, would have brought my trencher, but Alcinoë thrust herself before her, had the trencher filled, and then approached. Apparently she intended to serve me herself. She moved her hips nicely. Perhaps she had learned something of her collar. I considered her squirming and begging in my arms. It is easy enough to do that with a slave. But her head was up, and her expression was distinctly unpleasant, even disdainful. Did she not know that such an attitude might be a cause for discipline? I supposed not. She struck the trencher down before me, insolently, with a crack, and gruel and strips of roast tarsk spilled upon the table. Men, surprised, looked about. I saw two of the other slaves pale. I gathered then they were not unaware of the sport, or provocations, of the haughty Alcinoë. She turned arrogantly about, but cried out, dragged backward, off balance, half falling, my hand in her hair. I then turned her about, and flung her, hands forward, to the table. I then kicked her legs backward, and she was leaning forward, awkwardly, her hands braced on the table. "Remain as you are," I said. Two of the other slaves laughed delightedly, amused at the discomfiture of the hitherto arrogant Alcinoë. So, I thought to myself, they well knew what had been going on. "Switch!"

I called, and one of the amused slaves darted to a peg on the wall, retrieved the slender, supple implement, and hurried to me, where she knelt, and, head down between her extended arms, lifted the device to me. "What are you going to do," asked Alcinoë, frightened, uncertainly, and had the presence of mind to add, a moment later, "—Master!" I then switched the back of her thighs, with several stinging strokes, and she began to cry. But she dared not move. I then handed the switch back to the pleased slave who had brought it to me, and she returned it promptly to its peg. "More Sa-Tarna!" called a man, and the girls began, again, with the exception of the chastened Alcinoë, to serve. Conversation resumed about the board. Nothing of importance had occurred. "Kneel down, under the table, at my left knee," I said to Alcinoë. She obeyed. She could not kneel straightly, given the height of the table. Bent over, she turned her head, and looked up at me. It was hard to read the expression in her eyes. It was something like astonishment, fear, and wonder, and perhaps something else. Paga was brought to me, and more bread, and a good larma, and another trencher, steaming and well-filled. She knelt docilely under the table, at my knee. The back of her thighs must have stung. There were tear stains on her cheeks. I took my time with the meal. I had little to do for another Ahn, when it would be my watch. "May I speak, Master?" she asked. "No," I told her. Later, I took some Sa-Tarna from the table. "Open your mouth," I told her. She looked up at me in wonder, and obeyed. I thrust the Sa-Tarna into her mouth. "Feed," I said. Her mouth must have been dry. It took her some Ehn, partly choking, to down the bread. She had now been fed by hand, by my hand. Commonly this is done only between a master and his slave. She began to tremble. I took a final Paga, and nursed it. When I was finished I took her by the hair and pulled her from beneath the table, and held her, bent over, in common slave-leading position, at my left hip, and left the table. Shortly thereafter, after ascending several companionways, she at my hip, I arrived on the open deck. I put her before the second mast, and tied her hands before her. "You are tying me," she whispered. I did not punish her for speaking without permission. I did not understand the awe, the gratitude, in her voice. I then lifted her hands up, crossed, and tied them over her head. Then, with several coils of ship's rope, about her belly, I bound her back against the mast. "You have tied me, Master," she whispered, squirming a little, helpless. Interestingly, she did not seem distraught, but, if anything, reassured. "Thank you for tying me, Master," she said. "Master," she said. "Yes?" I said. "I have always wanted to be tied by you," she said, "even in Ar. I wanted you, even in Ar, to take me in hand and bind me, to make me helpless." I glanced up at the foremast. "I must soon to my watch," I said. I turned away. "Master!" she called. I turned about. "I am helpless, Master," she said. "Will you not press your lips upon mine?" "Do you beg it?" I asked. She hesitated, and then she said, softly, piteously, "Yes, Master." She leaned a little forward, closed her eyes, and pursed her lips. When she opened her eyes, I suspect I was already climbing the ratlines, ascending the foremast, to the ring and platform. I heard her cry out, "I hate you! I hate you!" "Do you wish to have a punishment tag wired to your collar?" I called to her. "No, Master!" she cried, frightened. "No, no, Master!" As I climbed further, I stopped, to look back at her. She was thrashing in the ropes. I had seen slaves in such a plight before. A touch can make them scream. The physicians had been right about her, and that had been long ago. She was a slave, ready to be harvested. The fellow whom I was relieving was now muchly beside me, descending the lines. "What is that?" he asked. "A slave," I said, clinging to the lines beside him. "The weather tonight is likely to be nasty," he had said. "Excellent," I had said.

My watch would be over at the second Ahn.

The deck seemed muchly deserted. There would be the helmsman, and a bound slave, the stem-castle watch, and the deck watch, which was by two men, whose names I would soon discover.

There was another spattering of hail.

I heard a creaking, a straining, of the ratlines, to my right.

I doubted it was my relief. It was not yet the first Ahn.

I was unarmed.

"Who is there?" I called.

"Your relief," I heard.

"Aeacus?" I called.

"No," said the voice, "Leros."

The voice was then closer.

Aeacus, of course, was not my anticipated relief. That had been a test on my part. I then realized that whoever was approaching had access, or his informant had access, to the watch order.

"Good," I said.

But the voice was not that of Leros.

"The sign, the word," I said, "friend Leros."

"That is not necessary," said the voice.

"It is required," I said. "The tarn is angry."

"The sleen is pleased," said the voice, nearer now, in the darkness.

So, I thought, he who approached, or his informant, had not only access to the watch order, but to signs and countersigns, as well. Such are changed daily, sometimes more often. It might seem that such things, on the ship, in its isolation, would be pointless, but it was deemed not so. Since the mutiny the high military authorities on board, Lords Okimoto and Nishida, of the Pani, of whom I took Lord Okimoto to have priority, had increased security considerably. Passwords, and such, of course, are familiar in martial environments, at any time, but particularly at night in the field, in darkness, and so on. They can be used at gates, fords, bridges, and such. Where large numbers of men are involved they are particularly important, as one is not likely to know everyone. Access to storerooms and weapons rooms is often by sign and countersign. Even one well known, even a friend, after all, may not have authorization to enter or pass. It is not unknown for such signals to be used even in single holdings, if large enough; indeed, such holdings are sometimes labyrinthine. We used them, for example, in the Central Cylinder, in Ar, during the occupation.

I sensed a hand might have reached up, to the platform.

"May I ascend?" asked the voice.

It was not the voice of Leros.

"Certainly," I said.

There is a moment when one climbs to the platform, if it is occupied, in which one is quite vulnerable.

As the voice had spoken clearly, there was no knife clenched between the teeth. The weapon then would have to be retrieved before it could be used, say, from a neck cord, a shoulder sheath, or such.

I could understand trepidation on the part of the climber, but only if he were uncertain of me, or thought me uncertain of him. Leros would never have asked such a question. It would not have occurred to him to do so. The mistake was tiny, but it was enough to assure his death.

By the time the stranger had got his feet under him and was able to stand, the knife would be in his hand.

"Give me your hand," he said.

In this way I would be well located, well held.

He must have been reaching out, over the platform.

"Take instead," I said, "my foot."

"What?" he said.

I, clinging to the ring, with all the force in me, kicked out into the darkness.

I heard bone and face crack beneath my boot, and a weird cry, and heard the body strike the ratlines at least twice, before there was a splash below. At almost the same time I could sense vibrations in the ratlines and I knew there was another climber.

"Who is there?" I called.

There was no answer, which told me what I wanted to know. The knife would be clenched between the teeth.

"Man overboard!" I cried, loudly, down to the stem-castle watch, and then back to the helmsman.

He began to put about.

The more men I could bring to the deck the better.

I did not understand why the deck watch did not immediately sound the alarm bar.

I wrapped my cloak about my left arm.

I sensed the knife slash widely, wildly, almost at my ankles. I stumbled backward. A form lunged under the ring to the surface. I threw myself forward, against it. I felt the blade cut through the cloak, but then it was tangled in it, and I lifted my arm pushing the knife hand to the side, and clasped the wrist, and pressed the form to the side, and we grappled in the darkness. I clung to the knife wrist, with an oarsman's grasp. A hand tore at my hair, pulling my head back, and then scratched across my face. I put my head down, and seized the body with my right arm, so his hand could not reach me, and thrust the body back, toward the ring, and pinned it against the ring, and pressed it back, and back. I heard the spinal column snap, and thrust the form over the ring, and, a long moment later, heard it strike the deck below. I could not understand why the alarm bar had not rung. I staggered back, panting, against the mast. The mast swung with the rolling of the ship, a surprising swell, perhaps from the helmsman's work.

Almost at the same instant I sensed something pass my head, like a sudden, fierce whisper in the air.

I instantly threw myself to the platform, within the ring.

No bird so flies, not so swift, not so straight, so piercing the wind.

An instant after something new struck the mast, ringing on a metal brace, and caromed far off, over the side, abeam.

I would later discover a gouge on the brace, rather where my head, a moment before, might have stood.

Why did the alarm bar not ring?

To my relief I saw several men begin to emerge from the hatches, doubtless responsive to the ship's change of motion. Some carried lamps, others lanterns.

It was then the alarm bar began to ring.

In the light of a lantern, below, some men crowding about, I could see the body on the deck.

I saw Tyrtaios pounding on the alarm bar.

"Ho," called a voice from below, carrying upward, "noble Callias, do you do well?"

"Yes," I called down.

"Praise the Priest-Kings," said the voice.

It was Seremides.

Neither he nor Tyrtaios were armed with a crossbow. Such weapons had been perhaps cast overboard.

It was then I understood that Seremides and Tyrtaios were the deck watch.

"Launch a galley!" I called. "One is overboard!" I pointed ahead, the ship now brought about, to where I thought the first assailant had struck the water.

Within the Ahn, by one of two galleys, lanterns suspended on poles over the water, part of the body had been recovered.

As I had heard no cry after the first moment of the descent, I suspected he had been dead when he had entered the water, perhaps from a broken neck. We were not clear, at that time, what had fed on the body.

Tyrtaios, below, charged that I had gratuitously killed my relief, but he was cautioned to silence by Seremides, who perhaps feared an inquiry.

By that time Leros had come to the open deck, and it was clear that neither assailant was my relief.

Below I saw the unmistakable figure of the tarnsman, Tarl Cabot.

Seremides drew away from him.

Lords Okimoto and Nishida appeared on deck.

Leros was sent aloft early, that I might be questioned. I knew neither assailant; they turned out to be two men of Lord Nishida's retinue, neither of the Pani, Fabius and Telarion. I did not even know them. Later Tarl Cabot spoke to me. "There were five," he said to me, "whom Lord Nishida suspected, and wished to keep close to him, convinced that one at least was a spy and one, perhaps the same, secretly of the Assassins. Two were slain in the northern forest, on the march to the Alexandra, by name Quintus and Lykourgos, and now two others, Fabius and Telarion, are gone."

"There is a fifth," I said.

"Yes," said Cabot.

"Tyrtaios," I said. I knew he was of the retinue of Lord Nishida.

"Yes," said Cabot.

"You think he is a spy, or an Assassin?" I said.

"Quite possibly," said Cabot.

"Why?" I asked.

"Perhaps I think he would look well in black," said Cabot.

I did not respond.

"I examined his quarters," said Cabot. "I discovered a small brush, and a tiny vial of black paint."

"To paint the dagger," I said.

"It would seem so," he said.

"Then," said I, "he is of the Assassins."

"It would seem so," said Cabot.

"You have informed Lord Nishida," I said.

"Yes," said Cabot.

"Surely, then, he will dismiss him," I said.

"I think not," said Cabot.

"Why not?" I asked.

"That is known only to Lord Nishida," said Cabot.

"Perhaps he has need of an Assassin?"

"Perhaps," said Cabot.

"Tyrtaios is interested in taking the ship," I said.

"He will not move until it is practical," said Cabot.

"Tyrtaios is dangerous," I said.

"Yes," said Cabot.

"He should be done away with," I said.

"I do not think so," said Cabot.

"Why not?" I said.

"At our destination," said Cabot, "we may need every sword."

At this point, Seremides approached, Tyrtaios at his back.

"I am pleased to see that you do well, noble Callias," said Seremides. "We had feared you might have been injured. We cannot understand the apparent attack upon you, of which you have informed us."

"I cannot account for it myself, noble Rutilius," I said. "I did not know the men."

"It is perhaps then a mistake of some sort, that they thought you another, an enemy, or such?"

"I think so," I said, "noble Rutilius."

"A most tragic misunderstanding," said Seremides.

"Yes," I said.

"At least, you are well, unhurt, and safe," he said. "That is what is most important."

"My thanks," I said, "noble Rutilius."

He, with Tyrtaios, withdrew.

"I knew not," said Cabot, "the noble Rutilius of Ar was so solicitous of your welfare."

"His name is not Rutilius," I said.

"I know," said the tarnsman.

"There were, I think," I said, "quarrels, too. One struck a mast brace."

"I am not surprised," he said.

"Forgive me," I said, "but I think I shall look in upon a slave."

"Certainly," said the tarnsman.

The slut had not cried out, had not attempted to warn me. So now let her find herself shuddering in abject terror beneath the stern gaze of Callias, Callias before her, a Callias very much alive.

To be sure, I could well understand why the bound slave would not have attempted to warn me of danger, even were she aware of it.

I knew, after all, her former identity.

I turned my attention to the second mast, and approached it, the tarnsman with me.

I expected to find her white with terror, as she must now realize I was still alive. To be sure, it is a rare slave who will meddle in the matters of masters. It is hers, is it not, as an animal, to await the outcome, and learn her disposition? To meddle may be to invite death. Is it not better for a slave to see little and know even less? As it is said, curiosity is not becoming in a *kajira*.

I was then before the slave.

"Interesting," said the tarnsman.

The figure which earlier had been barely discernible from the platform and ring, and had been relatively still, for so long, was now struggling. I was much surprised. A lantern was lifted by a fellow. I could no longer detect her long, dark hair, where it had fallen loosely about her white tunic. Her head had been covered, wrapped about or hooded, with some light material, cloth, or canvas. She made tiny, futile noises, scarcely audible a yard or two from the mast. I unknotted the cord holding the sacking over her head, and thrust it up enough to see her mouth, only that. The packing had been thrust deep in her mouth, and bound in place, tightly, behind the back of her neck. I jerked the sacking, which was of canvas, back down, over her head.

She whimpered piteously, beggingly. Even when a woman is gagged, one can easily read such sounds.

"Are you going to leave her like that?" asked the tarnsman.

"She is a slave," I said.

"Unhood her, ungag her," said the tarnsman. "She may have seen something."

I complied, and the girl turned her head aside, and blinked

against the lantern. Then, she turned to face me, and lifted her head, her eyes half shut. "Oh, Master!" she breathed.

Her exclamation seemed one of unspeakable relief, of joy, of gratitude. It was almost as though the collar on her neck might not have been a public collar, say, that of the ship of Tersites, but, rather, a private collar, say, that of Callias of Jad.

I did not understand this.

The tarnsman seized her chin in his right hand, and lifted and turned it, so that she must look upon him. I gather the grip was painful.

"Speak," he snarled. "What occurred here? Who was about? How did it happen? Speak, female, speak, woman!"

I was startled that he has spoken to her in terms of her sex, simply, regardless of her condition, that she was so obviously bond. It was clearly the voice of one of the master sex addressing one of the slave sex, bluntly, directly, intending to be told the truth. I suspected, this unsettling me, he would have spoken identically even were she free. It seemed incomprehensible to me, of course, that a free woman, for example, might be so addressed. But what was a free woman but a slave without a master? How stood the conventions of society, the habits, rules, customs, and such, against the biological facts of an uncontaminated nature? Surely he spoke to her in a way that went far beyond the trivia of tunics and collars, brands and chains. What do they do, such things, the collar, bracelets, and such, other than confirm her womanhood upon a female? To be sure, slaves, as free woman are not, are well advised to answer quickly and truthfully any queries of a free man. There are many ways to encourage speech in a reluctant slave. Indeed, as you know, in a court of law, the testimony of slaves is commonly taken under torture.

I saw that she was terrified of the tarnsman.

"Speak," I said to her, *"kajira."*

She cast me a grateful glance, grateful that I understood her helplessness, and terror, and that she was only a slave.

I was therein pleased, for it betokened to me that she before me now well understood her condition, that she was truly a slave, and only a slave.

This is a moment of truth, of understanding and insight, of submission, which few women in a collar ever forget.

"I saw nothing! I know nothing, Master!" she said. "It was dark. My head was down, my eyes were closed. They approached silently. I was suddenly started. I heard a tiny noise. My head was yanked up, by the hair. It hurt so! I saw two men! One from each side! Masked! I opened my mouth to scream, and a fistful of wadding was thrust into it, and I could scarcely whimper. This was secured in place, and something was pulled over my head, like a sack, and I could not see, and I felt a cord knotted at my throat, this securing the covering in place. I struggled. I was frantic. I was helpless. I could see nothing. I could not speak. I did not know what was transpiring. I know nothing, nothing, Masters! That is the truth, Masters! Be merciful to a slave! She is collared, she dares not lie, Masters!"

I looked to the tarnsman. "It is possible," I said to the tarnsman, "that the slut knows nothing."

"'Slut', Master?" asked the slave.

"Yes," I said.

"Yes, Master," she said.

"It is possible," said the tarnsman, "and likely. It is likely that these men would wish no witnesses to their act, even if the act were such that it might be condoned, or even hoped for, by the slave."

"Oh, no, Master!" said the slave.

"Blackmail, amongst confederates, or conspirators," said the tarnsman, "is always a possibility. Thus the fewer that witness a deed the better. That the slave was not slain may indicate that they find her of interest, presumably slave interest. That is understandable. She is not a poor piece of meat. I think she might sell well."

The slave looked at him, startled, gratefully. Once she had regarded herself as too beautiful to be a slave; then she had come to realize that her beauty, while not negligible, was far exceeded by many slaves. This can be a very sobering experience for a woman, even one of great attractiveness, finding that her beauty, perhaps quite extraordinary for a free woman, may be quite average for a slave. For the first time she finds herself placed amongst, and ranked amongst, women of great interest to men, women even selected with this in mind. In so chastening a situation the female's original complacency and arrogance is likely to be replaced by a hope that men, or some men, might find her at least similarly pleasing. Certainly she will try to be so. It might also be recalled that the slave had become even more beautiful after her collaring. This commonly occurs, and, doubtless, a number of reasons are involved, ranging from the physiological to the psychological, from the physical to the emotional.

"That it was done easily and efficiently," said the tarnsman, "her neutralization, her removal from the game, from the board, so to speak, the straightforward gagging and hooding, suggests that they are proficient in such things, are perhaps slavers or raiders, or others, accustomed to the acquisition and management of women. This gives us some information. Also, that there were clearly two men involved is worth noting."

I nodded.

"Do you know more, slave?" asked the tarnsman.

"No, Master," she said.

"She is perhaps lying," I said.

"No, no, Master!" said the slave.

"It is strange, is it not," I said, "that the deck watch failed to note such intruders, and that the alarm bar did not ring until men were pouring onto the deck?"

"Do you think it strange?" asked the tarnsman.

I considered the deck watch.

"No," I said.

"Nor I," said he.

I undid the ropes which held the small wrists of the slave above her head, and then freed her of the belly ropes.

The hail had stopped, but the air was still moist.

Leros had now been on the platform and ring for several Ehn. He had had his cloak bundled on his back.

When freed, the slave, not dismissed, and in the presence of free men, went to her knees.

Her head was down.

This was appropriate.

Many are the beautiful symbolisms between masters and slaves.

How natural are such things.

And how perfectly they reflect categorical relationships, and absolute realities.

"Your tunic is soaked," I said, "and your hair is bedraggled."

"A slave fears she is not pleasing to masters," she said.

"You are suitable on your knees, with your head down," I said.

"May I lower it further, Master?" she asked.

"I do not understand," I said.

I felt her lips on my boots.

"I am sorry if I displeased Master," she said.

I was silent.

She, this woman, was at my feet. I recalled her from Ar. She, this slave, was at my feet. I recalled her from Ar.

"Thank you for punishing me, Master," she said.

"It is nothing," I said.

"It is late," said Tarl Cabot. "She is to be returned to the Kasra area, is she not?"

"Yes," I said.

"She was displeasing," said the tarnsman.

"Yes," I said.

"Shall I have a punishment tag brought," asked the tarnsman, "and a thong?"

The punishment tag, as noted earlier, would be wired to the slave's collar, her hands would be tied behind her back, and she must hurry to her keeping area, where discipline would be meted out by her keepers, the large women.

"What do you think, slave?" I asked her.

I recalled her former terror that this might be done to her. I gathered it was very unpleasant for a lovely slave, a slave such as she, well-curved and delicious, a man-pleasing slave, the sort that men wish to buy, the sort that men wish to own, the sort that men find attractive, and care for, an exquisite, feminine slave, to find herself at the mercy of the ill-tempered, hating, envious, jealous, unhappy, gross brutes likely to be found in charge of a keeping area.

"It will be done with me as masters please," whispered the slave, head down, at my feet.

"It will be done with you as masters please," I assured her, "have no fear, slave, but what would you like?"

212

"That it may be done with me as masters please," she said. This answer pleased me.

"You have come far in bondage," I said.

"It is my hope to please my masters," she said.

"You have been punished enough," I said. "You may go."

"Keep me," she said. "I beg to please you!"

"Please me?" I said.

"Yes!" she said.

"How?" I asked. "In what way?"

"As a slave," she said. "As the slave I am!"

"Do you know what you are saying?" I asked.

"Oh, yes, Master!"

"Speak," I said.

"I beg attention," she said.

"Attention?" I said. After all, why make things easy for a slave, particularly such a slave.

"You would make me speak, of these things, I, knowing who I once was?"

"Of course," I said.

"Seize me, take me!" she wept, lifting her face to mine. "Put me to use! I beg it! Employ me as a means to your pleasure, a mere means! I ask nothing else, or further! I am collared! Behold me! I am a needful slave! Be kind! I beg! Put me to your pleasure! What am I for if not to please you? Put me to your pleasure, Master! Use me! I beg it!"

"And it was so," I asked, "even from Ar?"

"Yes, Master," she wept, putting her head down. "Even from Ar!"

I found this answer of interest.

"The deck is hard, cold, and wet," said the tarnsman. "There is a large coil of rope nearby."

The lantern was lifted a little higher, better illuminating what knelt at my feet, head down.

She did not now dare, her confession uttered, to raise her face to mine.

"Your use has not been given to me, slave girl," I said.

"But you have tied me," she said.

"As might any man," I said.

She put her hands on my legs and looked up at me. I saw in the light of the lantern that her face was streaked with tears.

"Might not a slave find favor with Master?" she asked.

"Go," I said.

"Master!" she begged.

"Must a command be repeated?" I inquired.

"No, Master," she said, quickly. She then pressed her lips again, fervently, to my boots, and then rose to her feet, backed away, head down, and then turned and ran, weeping, from the lantern light, disappearing in the darkness.

"You well know how to handle a slave," said the tarnsman.

I did not respond.

"The slut was quite ready," said the tarnsman.

It is interesting to see how helpless slaves can be, like a blanket of heat and need. Much, I supposed had to do with the collar, with slavery itself.

Odd, I thought, how bondage can free them.

It is no wonder men put them in collars.

They belong in a collar. They want them. In the precincts of the collar they find themselves, fulfill themselves, and are whole.

"Her use is not mine," I said.

I looked at the large coil of rope to the side.

"To be sure," said the tarnsman, "it is scarcely the furs of love, spread on the floor at the foot of a master's couch."

As is well known, it is a mark of great favor for a slave to be permitted on the couch of a master.

If I owned the lovely Alcinoë, I doubted she would soon be there. Such a mark of favor is not easily purchased.

"She is a ship slave," I said. "I do not own her."

"It would be dangerous, as well," he said, "for he who calls himself Rutilius of Ar finds her of interest."

I had gathered that from long ago.

"I wonder what is his interest in her," said the tarnsman.

"She is not without slave interest," I said.

"She has grown in beauty," said the tarnsman.

"That is common in the collar," I said.

"True," he said.

"It seems she has become a helplessly hot little slut," he said.

"That, too, is common in the collar," I said.

"True," he said.

"If she were a free woman," said the tarnsman, "I suspect she would purchase a collar, and kneel before you, begging you to make her your slave."

I was silent.

Few free women can so conquer their pride. Slaves, on the other hand, are not permitted pride.

That is one of the attractions of a slave.

Free women often fear to be in a man's arms, fearing what will become of them. Perhaps few understand the meaning of their restlessness, their irritations, their distractions, their turnings and thrashings in the night, or perhaps, somehow, they understand them only too well.

Many pillows have been dampened with the tears of free women.

Do they know the source of their tears?

Perhaps.

Many are the cultural expectations imposed upon the free woman. Is she not more of a slave than a slave? Abundant are her limitations; narrow are the corridors permitted for her movements; stout are the bonds of convention wherein she is bound. Can she fail to sense the invisible ties which bind her? How natural, then, imbued by unquestioned prescription and expectation, for her to justify the walls within which she is imprisoned. How natural then her pride, her aloofness, her struggle to maintain the pretenses demanded of her. What is her will compared to the weight of society? Too, is it not easy to make a virtue of necessity, that ice should commend cold, and the stone its lack of feeling? How natural then that she should, with all innocence and conviction, often with a raging earnestness, praise the treachery which has been done to her, and struggle to betray herself, to deny herself to herself. How natural then that she should compete with her sisters in her imperviousness to desire, in her frigidity and inertness, in her estrangement from herself. How glorious is the free woman! She possesses a Home Stone, as a slave may not. But she is a woman, still, and that, however denied, is adamant. It continues to exist. Its hereditary coils reign in each living particle of her body. Truth, primitive and antique, remains true. Her nature is with her, for it is herself. Does she suspect at times that there is a slave masquerading within her robes? Does she not, at times, hear the whimpers, the cries, of the slave within her? Does she not long, at times, for the collar of a master, for the weight of his chains? Does she not know in her heart that she is his rightful slave?

"You did not call for the punishment tag," said the tarnsman, "or the thong."

"No," I said.

I did not care for the large women. I thought discipline, if required, was best administered to a slave by a male. That is the natural way, and is far more meaningful to the slave. She is, after all, his. And he is, after all, her master.

Too, I thought the slave had been sufficiently punished.

I glanced upward to the platform and ring, on the foremast, where Leros now stood his watch. The light of the lantern carried only partway on the mast. I shuddered.

"I would be armed," I said.

"You are not an officer," he said, "and not all officers are armed."

"I would be armed," I said.

"Then so, too," said he, "would a thousand others."

"The platform and ring," I said, "is muchly open. It is an insecure, fragile fortress."

"Less insecure, less fragile, I fear," said he, "than a hundred others, remote passageways, darkened corners, blind turnings."

"Had I used the slave, and Rutilius heard of it," I said, "he might have sought me out, openly, in rage."

"Quite possibly," said the tarnsman.

"And you would have been near?" I said.

"Possibly," he said.

"I am bait?" I asked.

"Possibly," he said.

"His name," I said, "is not Rutilius. He is Seremides, former master of the Taurentians."

"I know," said the tarnsman. "I know him from Ar."

"What is the bad blood between you?" I asked.

"It is not important," he said. "It has to do with a woman."

"What woman?" I asked.

"Talena, Talena of Ar," he said.

"The Ubara!" I exclaimed.

"Once," he said.

"Why is he here, on the ship?" I asked.

"I gather he thinks I know her whereabouts," said the tarnsman, "that he might somehow find her through me."

"For the bounty?" I said.

"Of course," said the tarnsman. "And an amnesty for himself, for bringing her to Ar."

"There would be riches and freedom for him," I said, "and great jubilation in Ar, when she was publicly impaled."

"It would be holiday," he said.

"Do you know where she is?" I asked.

"No," he said. "But I suspect Seremides does not believe me. I am, in a way, much pleased that he is on the ship, as here I may kill him, and, at the least, he will be unable to pursue and capture Talena, for the bounty."

"You know the Ubara?" I asked.

"Yes," he said.

"You could recognize her?"

"Yes."

"Doubtless," I said, "you would like to capture her and bring her shackled to the justice of Ar."

The reward for her return to Ar was considerable, amounting to a dozen wealths, which might purchase a city or hire a hundred free companies.

"No," he said, "I would have other plans for Talena."

I shuddered at the tone of his voice.

I myself could recognize the Ubara, of course, but I did not think it judicious to bring this to the attention of the tarnsman.

"Where might be Talena?" I wondered.

"I do not know," said the tarnsman.

"We have been long at sea," I said. "By now any of a thousand hunters might have apprehended the Ubara. She may have perished naked and screaming months ago in Ar."

"I think not," said the tarnsman.

"Why do you think not?" I asked.

"It is late," he said.

"I wish you well," I said.

"Beware of Seremides," said the tarnsman.

"I shall," I said. "I wish you well."

We turned about, to leave the open deck.

I doubted that I was the less in danger from Seremides, for having forgone the use of a slave. It might have been pleasant to fling her upon the coil of rope, head down, and thrust up her tunic, but one must concern oneself with discipline, and the ship. Too, her use was not mine.

Such things concern some men.

Not every man will untether another's kaiila.

We had scarcely moved toward the port companionway leading under the stem castle when our progress was suddenly arrested by a cry from the height of the foremast.

"Ho!" cried Leros from above. "Ho! A light, a light! Ahead, ahead, a light!"

The bar sounded, struck twice.

Cabot and I hurried, followed by his lantern bearer, along the narrow port passageway about the stem castle, and stood at the bow. We heard others climb the steps to the stem-castle deck. We heard others hurrying about the starboard passageway about the stem castle, and were soon joined at the bow.

"Ahead, dead ahead!" called Leros, from above, his voice seemingly far away.

"There!" said Cabot, pointing.

Twice more the bar rang.

We could see the light now, even from the deck level.

"It is a ship!" cried a man.

"No!" said Lord Nishida, suddenly beside us. "It is too soon, too soon!"

At the same time, with a shift of the moist wind, a heavy, sweet odor emerged from the darkness.

"Turn about! Turn about!" cried Lord Nishida.

By now, given the ringing of the bar, one supposed that Aëtius, and perhaps even Tersites, and the major officers quartered astern, closest to the helmsman, had come to the command deck, the stern-castle deck, whence orders might be most conveniently and immediately conveyed to the helmdeck, some feet below.

Lord Nishida turned about and began to hurry aft. Cabot and I, and the lantern bearer, followed him. We pressed our way through excited and curious men, in their crowds, come from below decks, rushed forward.

Save for the lanterns rushing about the deck, it was dark.

The odor became more pervasive.

I heard something brush the side of the hull.

In a few Ehn Lord Nishida was at the foot of the helm deck. There were dark figures on the stern-castle.

"Put about!" cried Lord Nishida to the stern-castle deck. "Put about! Put about!"

From the darkness above came the shrill voice of Tersites. "Forward!" it cried. "Forward!"

"Fools! Fools!" cried Lord Nishida.

He clambered to the helm deck and began to fight the helmsman for the helm.

Two mariners pulled him from the helm.

"Forward!" cried Tersites.

The wind turned, and was fair, swelling the mighty sails, and the great ship, like an unleashed sleen, leaped forward.

It was an Ahn later that the sails fell slack, and the ship ceased to move.

Once again the heavy, sweet odor was pervasive.

One could now, in the light of the dawn, see the color about, yellow and purple, the myriads of blossoms, many a foot in width, opening to the morning sun.

I now heard the voice of Aëtius, above, frantic with concern.

"Put about! Put about!" he called to the helmsman.

"No!" screamed Tersites.

"We must put about, dear master!" cried Aëtius.

"Never!" said Tersites.

"Take him below!" cried Aëtius.

A mariner took the shipwright by the arm, and conducted him, that small, misshapen figure, protesting, struggling, from the stern-castle deck.

"Put about!" called Aëtius, to the helmsman.

"I cannot!" he said. "I cannot!"

Chapter Thirteen

We Board an Unusual Ship;
The Mystery of the Parsit Is Solved;
There Is Evidence Our
Presence Has Been Noted

I looked about.

"It is an odd ship," I said to Tarl Cabot.

We had clambered aboard the vessel, from a small ship's boat, cutting through the masses of snarled, ropelike, blossomed vines which encircled it, covering it, almost obscuring it. It was one of several such derelicts we had noted, resting variously in the sea, a pasang or two apart. We did not know how many such vessels might lie trapped in this place, in this welter of tangled, blossoming growth which stretched far about us. At first, from several hundred yards away, we had thought them only inexplicable mounds in the sea, hills of flowers uncannily forced upward by the riot of growth, vines upon vines. Then we learned the tendrils had clasped and climbed, and covered the works of men. The odor of these enormous fields of growth, alive, rocking and swaying in the sea, with their ubiquitous, massive blossoms, yellow, and purple, which had struck me one night some weeks ago as so pervasive, striking, and unpleasant, was doubtless as physically present as ever, but, interestingly, one now scarcely noticed it, excepting with an effort of attention. The odor, in time, became a lulling odor, and, no longer noted, but invariably present, tended to produce a sense of lethargy.

"Not really," said Cabot. "It is only different."

It had a high stem-castle, and two fixed masts. It was a round ship, of sorts, a vessel not made for war. Surely there was no ram, no shearing blades, no sockets for fixing catapults or springals. It would move solely under sail. There were no oar decks. It was somewhat larger than a medium galley. What most struck me was the battening, the sail-reinforcing ribbing, to which clung the shreds of matting.

"I wonder how long it has it been here," I said.

"It is hard to say," said Cabot. "A hundred years, perhaps two hundred."

"That is long," I said.

"The hull," he said, "is bored by ship worms, and rotted. The deck is split and the boards shrunk. Were it not for the clasp of the foliage, suspending her, she may have disappeared long ago."

He punched downward with the heel of his sea boot and the board broke under the blow, revealing a brown, spongelike mass of fiber.

This was the first time I had been on one of the derelicts, but they were not unknown to many of our armsmen and mariners who had boarded them to loot the cabins and the dozens of small holds, or compartments, in each, which, at one time, though now half flooded, may have been watertight. The sea chests of many of our fellows were now heavy with pierced coins, pearls, and precious stones.

Few skeletons had been found on the derelicts, which suggested that men, perhaps in madness or desperation, had somehow fled these strange fields or perished in the sea.

The strange ships were flat-bottomed, and so could navigate rivers, perhaps by poling or towing, and shallow waters, as well as the sea. Several, on the other hand, possessed daggerboards, which, by means of a slot in the hull, might be raised or lowered, these, when lowered, providing greater stability in open water. But all, however fitted, had been arrested here, tangled in the growth.

One could almost walk upon the vines, but one could draw a small ship's boat, or raft, through them, hoping eventually to reach free water.

The mystery of the parsit was solved, of course, as this wilderness of efflorescent plant life in the sea, floating like a vast park of life, drew myriads of small creatures, and these would draw the parsit, and the parsit would draw the shark, the grunt, and the unusual tharlarion.

So there was no reason to believe that we were near shore.

This growth, called the Vine Sea, is unanchored.

Lord Nishida's and Lord Okimoto's course, given to Aëtius and Tersites, had intended to skirt the Vine Sea by a hundred pasangs, but the Vine Sea moves, obedient to wind and current, and it was apparently far beyond its usual haunts. Lord Nishida's distress, weeks ago, at night, was occasioned by the perfume of the Vine Sea, which informed him that the ship had come upon it, he recognizing the full horror of its hazard. The obstinacy of Tersites, a fair wind, and a fortuitous canal opening in the vines had allowed the ship to proceed too far, in the darkness, and then, the wind failing, the Vine Sea had closed about her, tendrils reaching to her timbers. Men on ropes, in shifts, for days now, had scraped and tore away the tendrils which had begun to clutch at the hull, and sought to climb it, as Tur-Pah the Tur tree.

I brushed away insects, hovering about.

So the mystery of the parsit had been solved.

Most of us took it as well that the mystery of the light, that which Leros had first seen, from the platform and ring, was solved. That was seemingly solved on the second night. What had seemed a single blaze in the darkness, far off, was now attributed to the luminescence of a gigantic swarm of lamp flies, in their hundreds of thousands, of which swarms, we later learned, here in the Vine Sea, there were several. This sort of thing usually occurs when a ship is offshore, say a pasang or so, and in the vicinity of Bazi or Schendi.

I did not know why Tarl Cabot had come to this ship, as there were others. Why this ship and not another? I did know that he and Lord Nishida had surveyed it, from a ship's boat, this morning, as they had others, on other mornings, with the glass of the Builders.

What was special about this ship?

Certainly it had already been looted, its four cabins and its many smaller holds, or compartments.

Aëtius had kept Tersites sequestered in his cabin, fearing to let him be seen on deck. The crew, and the armsmen, might kill him. Always were they uneasy in the presence of the shipwright, fearing his eccentricities, the strangeness of his mind, the unpredictable and erratic exercises of his power, his officious negligence and scorn of customary precautions and ceremonies, his omission of traditional offerings, placations, and petitions, his pride, his insolence, his defiance, his seemingly gratuitous challenge to mighty Thassa, a challenge, as it were, to war, pitting his ship, a splendid artifact, but no more, against vast, deep, surgent, capricious, mighty Thassa. It was clearly his command which had sped the great ship forward in the darkness, despite the warnings of Lord Nishida, with the consequence that she was now trapped, mired in growth, bound fast in thick, living cordage, bound in the garden of the Vine Sea, surely one of the most dangerous and beautiful of Thassa's gardens. Of what value were riches if one could not spend them, and one were to die in place, amidst heaps of treasure, the richest and poorest of men.

Cabot, carefully, began to climb one of the ship's two masts. It was some forty feet in height, and surmounted by what I took, despite its unusual appearance, bowl-like, but with a grated cover, to be a ship's lamp or lantern.

He soon attained the summit of the mast.

He was grinning. He gestured to me. "Come up!" he said.

I slowly made my way up the mast, hort by hort, and was then beside the tarnsman.

"Here," he said, "are no lamp flies." He rubbed his hand about the grating of the lamp, or lantern. His hand was dark with soot. He thrust up the grating on its hinge, and, clinging to the mast with one hand, wiped his other hand within the bowl, and his hand, withdrawn, was moist, and glistened where soot had been rubbed away. He held his hand out to me. I could smell oil, probably from tharlarion.

"It is fresh," I said.

"Fresh enough," he smiled.

"But the ship, I thought," I said, "was a century or more old."

"It is," he said, "at least."

"But this lamp," I said, "has been fired, surely within the year."

"When, do you think?" he asked.

"When Leros held the high watch," I said.

"Yes," he said. He then closed the hinged, gratelike lid on the lamp, and began to descend the mast. And I followed him.

We were soon again on the deck of the strange ship. Our small ship's boat, with four oarsmen, was tied alongside.

I looked at the tarnsman.

"Lord Nishida was right," he said.

"I do not understand," I said.

I knew that the tarnsman and Lord Nishida had scouted several derelicts, surveying them with the glass of the Builders.

"Lord Nishida," he said, "has lost the element of surprise."

"I do not understand," I said.

"We are expected," said Tarl Cabot. "The lamp was set as a beacon, to lure us into the Vine Sea, where doubtless it is hoped we will die."

"This is the end," I said. "None escape from here. Note the derelicts. Many brave ships with their crews have perished in this place. There is no escape, there is no wind."

"Yet," said Cabot, "the beacon was lit, and those who set the trap are gone. There is thus an exit from this place."

"Perhaps with small boats, with rafts, or such," I said, "but then one is defenseless on Thassa, perhaps a thousand pasangs from land, perhaps more."

I supposed, if Lord Nishida and the tarnsman were right, that a mother ship at the edge of the Vine Sea might have dispatched a small party to the derelict. What puzzled me was that such a ship had not been seen, even from the high watch. Perhaps, unlit, it had approached at night and set a small crew about the business of the lamp. Or perhaps we had enemies amongst us, forewarned, from months ago, even from Brundisium, or the northern forests, who would fail to report such a sighting. Had helmsmen failed to keep the charted course? The Vine Sea moves, like a vast garden in the sea, but perhaps it had not moved as much as had been thought.

"Think, Callias," said Cabot. "Few bodies, on any derelict, have been found."

"Most would have sought some sort of flight from the Vine Sea," I said.

"I think so," he said, "and certainly as supplies of fresh water grew scarce."

"Much treasure was left behind," I said.

"Perhaps," said he, "much was taken, as well."

"Would men not return for the rest?" I asked.

"It seems likely they failed to reach land," he said.

"Then," I said, "the Vine Sea is victorious, in the end."

"The lighters of the beacon have come and gone," he said.

"Why would they not loot the derelicts?" I asked.

"Perhaps," said he, "some things interest them more, and, too, there is little hurry about such matters."

"I do not understand," I said.

"Our mariners, and armsmen," he said, "have spent days here, accumulating treasure."

"So?" I said.

"Would it not cost blood to deny them their gold?" asked Cabot.

I remembered the mutiny.

"I think so," I said.

"Lord Nishida thinks we are being held in place," he said, "whilst a fleet is moving toward us."

"There is no escape from here," I said, and I swept my hand toward the horizon.

"Clearly some have failed to escape," said Cabot.

"There is no hope," I said.

"Consider the derelicts you have seen," said Cabot. "None is larger than a medium-class galley, and none is oared."

"True," I said. It seemed so to me, at any rate, from what I had seen.

"And the ships are merchant ships, apparently, and, one supposes, would be crewed accordingly, with complements sufficient to the vessel, and perhaps little beyond that."

"So?" I said.

"I see no large ships here," said Cabot. "A large ship, with many in the crew, could work the vines, even over days, or weeks, cutting a path. Too, a large ship, with the force of the wind in her sails, might tear herself loose."

"I find that hard to believe," I said.

"A fresh wind," he said, "might clear the air."

I noted, again, the perfume of the garden, so sweet, pervasive, and heavy. I wondered if it did not have its role to play in this strange place. I could see two other derelicts from where I stood, smothered in flowers. "The flowers are beautiful," I said.

"And perhaps deadly," said Cabot.

"A slow poison?" I said.

"Let us hope not," he said.

Two men had thrown themselves from the bulwarks of the great ship, screaming, into the vines below.

Men had looted one another's sea chests openly, and then died in the corridors and companionways.

Two warriors of the Pani, which groups had not participated in the looting, had slain one another, which, given the custom of their discipline, was unthinkable.

"We cannot wait here indefinitely," said Cabot.

"We must try to break free?" I said.

"Why has it not been attempted?" asked Cabot.

"The looting, the danger?" I said.

"The looting was done, days ago," said Cabot, "at least of the ships conveniently accessible."

"The flowers?" I said.

"I think so," said Cabot.

"They are beautiful," I said.

"Yes," said Cabot. "They are beautiful." He then went to the rail, and lowered himself to the waiting ship's boat, and I followed him.

Chapter Fourteen

The Tharlarion;
Two Galleys Are Lost;
I Find Myself Alone with Seremides

Oars snapped, and the small galley, the large glistening body rising under it, tipped fearfully to port.

She was one of the six nested galleys, normally housed in the hull of the great ship.

Water poured over the bulwarks. I stood at the oar which I shared with a fellow from Turmus, Licinius Lysias.

The large body, rolling beside us in the water, was almost as large as the galley itself. It turned away from us suddenly, its arched spine high above the water, and buffeted the galley which lay to starboard. There a fellow, cursing, jabbed down at it with a spear. There was a snort of pain and the large form was gone. The blade of the spear was awash with blood.

That would bring the sharks lurking beneath the vines, which extended some yard or two beneath the water.

Our galley, and the other, rocked back to an even keel.

All six galleys were forward of the great ship, like a mountain behind us. From each galley there looped two stout ropes back to the ship.

Before us was a cloud of small ship's boats, filled with oarsmen and armsmen, attacking the vines.

The sails of the great ship behind us hung loose, scarcely stirring.

Looking back I could see a tarn against the bright sky.

Eleven days now we had been at the oars.

With tarns we were muchly advantaged. Without them small boats would have had to scout the Vine Sea to find its nearest edge. It had not been visible from the foremast. Oddly enough we had had a considerable change in course, in seeking open water. Some said that the Vine Sea had shifted in its restlessness, extending its blossomed tentacles, and that what had been nearest was no longer nearest, and that a new tortuous route must be now devised before one might reach the open sea, but others said that sails had been seen afar, and it was that, and that alone, which had dictated our new course.

Two spare oars were set in place to starboard, and we transferred two oars, as well, from port to starboard, one of which was manned by myself and Licinius Lysias. I could see the galley to starboard, some yards away. It was captained by Seremides. I recalled my mates of the *Metioche*. He had returned none to the great ship. Our galley was captained by the warrior Pertinax, a friend, it seemed, of the commander of the tarn cavalry, Tarl Cabot. This Pertinax, with some others, was a student of the taciturn swordsman, Nodachi, of whom I knew little. I had seen him at the time of the mutiny. I had also seen him at times on the open deck, sitting cross-legged, immobile, staring forward, for long periods, an Ahn or two at a time. And then, sometimes, he would rise to his feet, remove his two curved blades from his sash, and engage unseen opponents. I thought him insane, but I would not have cared to meet him in the business of war.

"Pull, pull!" screamed Seremides, and I saw his knotted rope fall, again and again, amongst his oarsmen. I did not care for this. How was it that they did not rise up, did not object? They were not slaves, chained to their benches. They were free men. Why did they not rise up and attack him? Because, I supposed, he was Seremides. He may have wanted to be attacked, for it was long since his sword had tasted blood. It may have been thirsty for that sudden, bright, exhilarating draught. The thick ropes jerked tight, leading back to the great ship. He should coordinate his efforts with the draw of the companion galley, ours. Was he so importunate and impatient, or was he, rather, anxious to intimidate our captain, Pertinax, the friend of Tarl Cabot? Certainly there were few whom the sword of Seremides, former master of the Taurentians, could not render diffident and complaisant. All feared him, save perhaps Tarl Cabot. Seremides had requisitioned me for his crew, but Cabot had assigned me to that of his friend, Pertinax. Again and again, to my right, across the yards between the galleys, the rope fell. I am not sure that I would have accepted the blows of Seremides. And that, I supposed, was why he had requested that I be assigned to him, that I might rise up, attack him, and then be slain for insubordination. Well would he have been within the rights of his captaincy. Discipline demands that one endure and obey, but it is not always easy to do. I supposed I would have accepted the blows. Yes, I would have accepted the blows. I guessed that Seremides, who knew my fear of him, knew that, but, still, he would have derived some satisfaction in their administration. He had little to fear, given his sword, and his standing with Lord Okimoto.

Amongst the slashed, trailing vines between the galleys, sometimes entangling the oars, I saw, occasionally, the dorsal fin of a shark, briefly emergent, then whipping again beneath the water. Usually the fin disappears gracefully, slipping from sight, but the creature was excited. I recalled the tharlarion, struck earlier. There would linger ribbons of blood in the water. The shark of the Vine Sea, though nine-gilled like his cousins of the shorelines and tropics, is sinuous and eel-like, which, I suppose, facilitates its movements amongst the vines. Suddenly, ahead, some twenty yards, between the galleys and the numbers of ship's boats, the gigantic body of the wounded tharlarion emerged, its vast body, neck, head, and wide paddlelike appendages running with water, bright in the sunlight. It bellowed with pain, and dived again. "Back oars!" cried Pertinax. We rocked in place. The galley of Seremides, too, paused. The waters seemed placid. The other galleys, too, farther to starboard, must have held their position, as the great ship behind us neither moved, nor was drawn to the side. "Oars inboard!" called Pertinax. We drew the large levers inward. This is sometimes done in battle, when shearing is imminent. It takes no more than four or five Ihn. The ropes leading back to the great ship, no longer taut, slipped into the water. The oars on the galley commanded by Seremides were similarly retracted. I wondered what horrors might be being enacted in the depths. Many blossoms floated on the surface, amongst the vines. The sea tharlarion, in its varieties, not other than its brethren of the land, breathes air. Like the sea sleen, on the other hand, it can remain submerged for several Ehn, whilst fishing. I stood by the bulwarks and looked down. I could see no shimmer of parsit near the surface. They had departed the area. The sunlight glistened on the water, amongst the streamers of cut vines, the floating blossoms. Four or five Ehn passed. By now I supposed the tharlarion, and its relentless pursuer, or pursuers, might be a pasang or more distant. Still I had seen no parsit beneath the water. "Out oars!" cried Seremides. "Wait!" called Pertinax. "Wait!" "Out oars!" cried Seremides, angrily, and, his rope falling amongst his oarsmen, the oars of his galley slid outward. We grasped our oars. "Hold!" said Pertinax. "Pull!" called Seremides, to starboard. "Wait!" Pertinax warned us. "Pull, pull!" said Seremides, and the ropes attached to his galley, leading back to the great ship, lifted, dripping, from the water. "Stop!" called Pertinax. "Move, fool!" called Seremides. "Move, slackard!" "Keep your distance!" cried Pertinax. Seremides' galley began to move toward ours. "To port!" he called to us. "Out oars! Row! Move!" The galley of Seremides kept its original heading, dictated by its towing ropes, while we were still, towing ropes slack, now almost across his bow, rocking in the water. "Poles!" cried Pertinax, and men seized up the launching poles, used in thrusting a galley from a wharf, cushioning her approach to a wharf, holding her away from rocks, or such. It is customary that there be three such poles, as you of the port know, one for the bow, one amidships, one aft. "Back oars!" cried Seremides, alarmed. The two galleys grated against one another. I heard oars splinter. Our oaring was inboard. "Fool, fool!" screamed Seremides to Pertinax. Pertinax's face went white and I saw his hand move to the hilt of his sword. But already the blade of Seremides was free of its sheath, and, his eyes alight with eagerness, he leaped aboard our galley. I rose at the bench and cried, though it might be insubordination, to Pertinax, "Do not unsheathe your blade!" He slammed the blade, half free, back in its sheath, looked at Seremides before him, unflinching, and said, "Welcome aboard, noble Rutilius."

Seremides cried out with rage, looked about himself, saw that he might have to deal with twenty angry, violent men who would stand with their captain, and returned his weapon to its housing. "I see," said he, "barbarian, that you are not only a fool and a slackard, but a coward, as well."

"Barbarian I may be," said Pertinax, "but I am neither fool nor slackard, and I trust, not a coward."

"Tell your men to hold, to remain in place," said Seremides, "and we will make test of the matter."

Several others, as well as I, had risen from the benches.

"Hold!" said Pertinax.

"No!" cried more than one.

The hand of Pertinax went to his weapon.

Seremides grinned, stepped back, drew his blade, and set himself, easily, his body swaying a little, with the movement of the vessel. His galley scraped a little against ours. I saw no love for him across the rail.

I sensed a rising under my feet, something stirring, something approaching, from far below, water moving away from it. I do not think that either Seremides or Pertinax noted this.

"Defend yourself," said Seremides. I had heard those words, sensed the eagerness in the voice before, more than a dozen times, in the early morning, in the dampness and cold, in a park, or in the Plaza of Tarns, long ago, in Ar. I sensed that the whole rationality of Seremides was now focused narrowly, exultantly, on the victim before him, that the ship, its discipline, Tarl Cabot, Lords Nishida and Okimoto, the apprehension of the former Lady Flavia of Ar, or even of the former Ubara, Talena, was as though they were not. I thought of the sleen whose hunt is done, who has the tabuk or verr cornered before him. What command could stay him, what consideration could distract him, what give pause to so single-minded and formidable a force of nature?

The blade of Pertinax was but half drawn when both galleys burst apart, leaping from one another, the gigantic body of the tharlarion rising between them, springing forty feet or more from the water, expelling a snorting burst of air, several of the eel-like sharks fastened in its flanks; it seemed oddly still for a moment, upright, at the height of its leap, and then fell back in the water, drenching us, half filling the galleys with water; I pulled rent vines from about me; blossoms were at my knees in the water. I felt a descent as of heated fog, and realized it was the air the creature had expelled, settling cloudlike about us. The thing had returned. How could that be? Surely it was a coincidence, that the great beast, lacerated, in its agony, running blood, had come back to this place. The long neck, yards in length, snakelike, lifted, and the small head swayed about, as though searching, with the single eye left. It had returned to the place where it had been first hurt. I could see the tails of sharks whipping against the water, trying to drive their jaws deeper into the beast's flesh. Other fins were approaching, knifing through the blossoms. I heard a man scream on the galley of Seremides, and he poked upward with his spear. The small head on the great body, with its triangular jaws, with its rows of tiny, fine teeth, reached down, almost gracefully, and lifted the screaming fellow yards into the air. It then threw its gigantic, massive, glistening body, sharks clinging to it, over the gunwales of the galley of Seremides, pressing it under the waves, men leaping into the sea on either side. It then, dragging its burden of sharks, its victim still struggling in its jaws, dove, and the snap of that great tail, striking upward, tipped us, and then, striking downward, propelling that enormous bulk, clove our galley, and we were plunged into the water. The sea about us was red, and I spit out water. Within it was the taste of blood. I saw a fellow two yards away drawn beneath the water. "Ho!" I heard. "Ho!" The small ship's boats had put about and were returning. The other galleys, too, loosing their towing ropes, would be soon at our side. I pulled myself half onto a nest of vines, half in the water, half not. A splintered oar floated past. "Here!" I heard. Men were being drawn into small boats. But they would be soon swamped. They clung to the gunwales of the ship's boats, and armsmen and oarsmen struck down with tools and oars, to protect those in the water. I heard an oar count being called, over the water, and one of the towing galleys was near. I could see it in a bit then, with ship's boats clustered about it, men being drawn aboard, from the boats, from the water. A dorsal fin moved smoothly by. I remained as still as possible. I was not bloodied. If one moves, one should move as smoothly as possible, not awkwardly, not hastily, not erratically, not as though one might be injured, or helpless.

Men swam toward the small boats, the nearest galley.

I saw more than one drawn beneath the surface. Fins were everywhere. I felt the mat of vines to which I clung turn, and begin to drift. The wreckage of the galley of Seremides seemed farther away now. I saw no sign of the galley of Pertinax. Soon, as I lay, I could no longer see the small boats, or any galleys. There is restlessness in the Vine Sea, as in any sea, and swells, and local currents, and the sea itself, tangled and beautiful, oppressive, and terrible, despite its vastness, moves from time to time, seasonably, predictably, even hundreds of pasangs, as might any object, large or small, afloat on Thassa, with her hundred moods and thousand currents.

I think most of my fellows had sought the small boats.

As noted, I could not now see them, as I was positioned, but I knew they were there. I could hear men in the distance. Were I able to stand I had little doubt I could see them, and certainly one or more galleys. Even as I lay still in my bed of vines and blossoms I could, turning my head, see the great ship, in the distance.

It was now quiet about me, save for the lapping of the water.

There seemed none about.

I was much alone.

I was not afraid of being left, or abandoned. I was afraid, rather, of what I knew was in the water.

"Ho, Callias!" I heard.

"Tal, Durbar!" I called.

I remembered him from the pumps, when, during the time of the great storms they had been manned twenty Ahn a day.

He was better situated than I, for he crouched on two nailed beams, which must have been from the hull of one of the two destroyed galleys.

He was some forty feet away.

There was other wreckage about.

Needless to say, I was much pleased to see him.

"You are in danger!" he called.

I considered swimming to join him.

A blossom floated by.

A fin glided past.

"Perhaps less here than there!" I said.

I was not eager to negotiate the water between us.

"As you will!" he said.

But I saw a swimmer clamber to his makeshift vessel. One end of the beams descended beneath the waves, under the weight of the newcomer. I did not think they would well bear the weight of two. Durbar turned about, cried once, and reeled from the beams, plunging into the water, his jacket red. Across the space between us I saw Seremides, his eyes on me. He did not have his sword, but there was a knife in his hand. He stood unsteadily on the narrow wreckage.

In the water Durbar, the water red about him, gasping, confused, extended his hand to Seremides, who did not accept his hand, perhaps fearing the loss of balance, but motioned him closer. When Durbar got his hands upon the beams Seremides kicked out, viciously, and Durbar, I think his neck was broken, slipped away, beneath the water.

Seremides stood on the beams, regarding me.

"Noble Callias," said he, affably. "Approach."

I remained where I was, and looked about. I saw no one near.

"That is an order!" said Seremides.

"Deliver it to another," I said.

Seremides looked about, and then put the knife in his belt, and then, kneeling on the beams, pulled at some floating vinage, and his narrow vessel inched toward me. He tried to urge it toward me, too, with his body. He dipped his right arm into the water, and pushed back, against the water. Again his tiny bark approached me, a little. It was heavy, and not easily moved. I did not think he would risk throwing the knife. I suspected the turning currents, the natural eddies amongst the vines, might bring us together, sooner or later. It would be a matter of time.

I wondered how many men, if about, would welcome this opportunity to do away with Seremides.

But we seemed much alone.

The nearest galley, I conjectured, from the faint sounds I heard, men calling out, was two hundred yards distant. It would probably be encircled by small boats.

Much vinage was now about, as it had drifted back, tending

to close the road which had been cut through it. Such things shift in the currents, closing gaps, being arrested only against more of its kind.

Seremides stood up and looked about.

Apparently he saw no one, at least nearby.

He then, eyes glinting, once more kneeling down, tried more earnestly, even rashly, even heedlessly, to force his way toward me.

I took it he wanted to reach me before others might note our position.

I did not think it wise for Seremides to splash at the side of his support.

There was still blood in the water, from the tharlarion, from some fellows taken by sharks, and, now, from Durbar.

Too, I had seen a fin glide by, but a moment ago.

Perhaps he, then in the water, had seen it, too.

The possible danger of his activity must have occurred to him, as he soon ceased to propel his craft in that perilous fashion.

The splashing, of course, had occurred.

Hopefully, it had been unnoted.

An occasional swell, lifting the circumambient vines and blossoms, moved his small vessel, and the raft of vinage to which I clung.

"Ho!" I called, half in water, half prostrate amongst the vines, unable to stand. "Help! Help!"

But none heard me.

"Swim to me," coaxed Seremides. "Join me. It will be safe. I will not hurt you."

We were now some ten or fifteen feet apart.

I felt something long, seven or eight feet in length, and rough, like a rasp, pass, moving beneath the water, against my leg.

I clutched the vinage.

"So," smiled Seremides, "you are frightened."

He removed his knife from his belt.

I did not think, again, he would risk throwing it.

He stood, unsteadily, on his support.

"The sea is my ally," he said. "It will soon enable me to greet you."

I said nothing. There seemed no one about.

His small bark drifted nearer, as did a number of vines and blossoms. So, too, it must have, Ehn earlier, when bearing Durbar.

"I have waited long for this," said he, "noble Callias."

There was then a swell of water, and I saw it lift his vessel two or three feet, and he cried out in triumph and I knew that, in its descent, sliding down the slope of that swell, it would be upon me, and I plunged beneath the water, dragged myself down, beneath the vines, swam what I could, some yards, and then, gasping, shaking my head, I emerged amongst clustered vines, some wrapped about my body, and legs, snakelike.

But I saw nothing of Seremides.

I was terrified to be in the water, as I knew what was there.

I knew he must be in the water, but I feared him the least of what might be about.

I forced myself down again and, as I could, circled back, and, after twice emerging amongst the vines, came to some open water, and felt wood, and drew myself, panting, wiping my eyes, onto the two fastened beams which had borne, in turn, Durbar, and Seremides, and now bore me.

I saw nothing of Seremides.

I stood, unsteadily, on the beams.

I could then see two of the four intact galleys in the distance and, several hundred yards away, the great ship itself.

I cried out and waved, but did not know if my presence was noted.

I was not overly concerned about being picked up, as I was sure the great ship was far from clear of the Vine Sea, and I had little doubt that there would be a thorough search for survivors, perhaps extended over two or three days. I had gathered that every man was valued, if only as a tool or beast of sorts, by the Pani, and I was sure that I could count on the patience, and diligence, of Tarl Cabot, and several others. I took them as good officers and honorable men. They would seek the best accounting possible.

"Help!" I heard. "Help!" The cry was weak, and yards away. At first I could not locate its source, but then I saw a hand lifted over the vines, and a head, lifted, briefly, which then slipped again from sight. Something was struggling, tangled in the vines. I did not know if the two beams on which I stood had moved muchly or not. I knew I was now in relatively open water, which suggested it was part of the road cut by the ship's boats through the vines, though it was much narrower now than hitherto, given the eddies, and the drifting of the vegetation.

"Help!" I heard, and saw the head of Seremides emerge from the vines. "I am caught!" he cried. An arm flailed about, grasping at vines. It was possible he could be pulled under, as the vines beneath the surface shifted in the currents. In any event, it seemed he was tangled in the ropelike growth, and, apparently, could neither dive beneath it, should he wish to do so, nor swim through it.

"Help!" called Seremides. "Help!" He held out a hand to me, tangled in vines.

I stood unsteadily on the beams.

"All is forgiven!" cried Seremides. "I pledge friendship! I have power! I can do much for you! Help me! I will reward you! I will secure you promotion! When the ship is ours you will stand high! Gold, women! I will see that she who was once Flavia of Ar is given to you! Would she not be pleasing in your collar? When the voyage is done, take her to Ar for the bounty!"

"Pull yourself out, by the vines," I said.

I was not anxious to approach him, and much vinage lay between us.

"I cannot!" he said. "By the Priest-Kings, by the Home Stone of Cos, save me!"

I crouched on my small craft and caught at vines, trying to pull the two nailed beams toward him.

"You agree!" he cried.

"I agree to nothing," I said.

"Hurry!" he cried. "Hurry!"

My makeshift bark caught in the vines. I was then some twenty feet from him. I could make no further progress.

"It is safe," he said. "Crawl on the vines. Draw me free!"

As the vines were thick there, it was possible, on one's belly, half in the water, half out, to reach him.

He was an officer of the ship.

He stood high.

He was much my superior.

In the swell he must have lost his footing and plunged into the foliage, submerged, swam, came to the surface, and found himself feet away from the beams, snagged in the coiling vines.

"Help!" he said, reaching out.

I lowered myself from the nailed beams, and, half swimming, half crawling, muchly supported by the dense growth, came nigh.

"Closer!" he said.

I moved closer.

"Give me your hand!" he said, reaching out.

I extended my hand, but suddenly drew it back.

In a flash of thought I recalled Seremides, from a dozen times and places, images rushing upon me, a goblet lifted, a door opened, a hand gesturing, a pen in hand, signing an order, a sword, reddened, held over an adversary's throat in the early morning.

"Your hand!" he demanded, angrily.

The hand extended to me, that it might grasp mine was his left hand. His right hand was under the water.

Seremides, former master of the Taurentians, was right-handed.

"Die, Sleen!" he cried, tearing himself upward, out of the vines, the right hand dripping with water, the sun flashing on the wet blade in its grasp.

I had not given him my hand. I had kept back, a little. That meant he must close the gap between us, must move toward me, and this, in the water, given the absence of footing, the presence of the foliage, could not be easily done. He was trying to scramble toward me, half in water, half out, over the raft of vegetation. The knife struck out at me twice, three times. I backed away as I could, slipping, half sinking through the vines, while he, similarly hampered, cursing, pursued me, foot by foot. I, backing away, suddenly slipped downward, through a gap in the vinage, and felt circles of vines about my legs and lower body, through which I had plunged. I was enmeshed. I reached about. I could obtain no purchase. I was held in place. "Noble Callias!" grinned Seremides, moving a hort closer. My only chance would be to grasp his knife wrist, and I thought there was little chance of that. Seremides would not be so foolish as to make a long strike, which might be blocked or intercepted. He would prepare carefully for the kill, feinting, darting, keeping the blade forward of my grasp, but slashing, striking, again and again, at the hand, from which he might sever fingers, or slash a wrist, disabling the hand. I would then, eventually, be as helpless as if bound. I did not think he would finish me quickly. I had seen him finish more than one man slowly, pleasantly. Some had begged to be done with.

"Ho!" we heard. "Is anyone there?"

Seremides turned white.

It must be a search party, in a small boat.

"Yes!" I called, loudly. "Here! Here!"

"Sleen!" hissed Seremides, and, his leisure vanished, he lunged forward, desperately, but the blow was short. He crawled closer and struck again. There was no leverage, no footing. He struck again. I reached for his wrist, but missed it. He struck again, and I managed to grasp his wrist, with two hands, and we turned in the water amidst the vines, struggling, thrashing about. "Here! Here!" I screamed, for there were men somewhere about. I suddenly sensed the blade was no longer in his right hand, and swept backward, water in my eyes, fending myself as I could. The knife cut through my tunic ripping it across the chest. I had not even seen it. Then I saw the knife was again in his right hand. I was then muchly on my back, where I had thrown myself backward, and my arms were tangled in the vines. I saw the glint of delight in his eyes, and saw the knife raised. I could not free my arms, either to block or intercept the blow. In a moment I might work myself free but the moment was not mine. In that moment a tethered tarsk could not have been more helpless. "Now, Sleen!" he whispered.

I saw the sky, a bright blue in the spring afternoon.

"Aiiii!" I heard, a sudden, startled, weird, hideous cry, and the knife arm, and the head, and the torso of Seremides suddenly disappeared beneath the water, which churned, rocking the mat of vines, lifting and scattering the broad blue and yellow blossoms amongst the foliage.

"Where are you?" called a voice.

"Here, here!" I said.

I was not thinking clearly.

It was a moment before I understood what had happened.

I saw Seremides emerge then from amidst the vines and blossoms. He was alive. He was some eleven feet away. He no longer held the knife. He grasped at the vines. I had never seen the eyes of a man look so. I had never seen such an expression on a human face, one of such horror.

"Callias!" he whispered, holding out a hand to me.

I made my way to him, a bit before he lost consciousness. I turned him on his back, and drew him through the water, and over the vines, to where I had departed the small vessel of nailed beams. Behind us there was a trail of blood, in the water, over the vines.

I drew him onto the makeshift vessel.

The shark had taken the left leg, from above the knee.

I heard the dip of oars in the water.

"Here!" I called, standing up, lifting my hand.

In moments I, and two oarsmen, had put Seremides in the ship's boat.

"You have saved the life of Rutilius of Ar, well done," said the rudderman.

"He is a high officer," observed one of the oarsmen.

"You will be commended for this," said another.

"Why did you not let him die?" asked an armsman.

"He will bleed to death," said another armsman.

I tore away part of my tunic and thrust it against the part of the leg left.

"Let him die," said a fellow.

"Put him overboard, kill him," suggested an oarsman.

"Have you twine, rope, a belt?" I asked.

"Use this," said the rudderman, tossing me a length of knotted rope, which bore some reddish stains.

"We found it floating nearby," said an armsman.

I fastened the rope about the stump of the leg, and tightened it. The blood slowed, and then stopped.

"He needs care," I said, "the attention of physicians."

"Back to the ship," said the rudderman.

"There is no hurry," said an armsman.

"He is going to die," said an oarsman, looking at the prostrate figure between the thwarts.

"No," I said, "he is Seremides, he is strong."

"He will wish he was dead," said an oarsman.

"He is an officer," said an armsman.

"No longer," said another armsman. "There are no crippled officers."

We began to make our way, largely through open water, to the great ship.

Seremides opened his eyes. They did not seem the eyes of the Seremides I knew. He looked up at me. "Do not hurt me," he said.

Chapter Fifteen

Seremides;
The Slave, Alcinoë

"Turgus commands a galley!" said the fellow to Seremides.

"Let me alone," said Seremides.

Seremides supported himself with a narrow, sticklike crutch, perhaps a hort in width, at the top of which, fitted over the shaft, was a small, rounded crosspiece. This was under his arm, tight against his body. Lord Okimoto had found Seremides of use earlier in the voyage; his sword had been formidable, and he had muchly facilitated Lord Okimoto's contacts with those of us not of the Pani. He was, in a way, a liaison between Lord Okimoto's group and the mariners and armsmen not of the Pani. As we feared Seremides, so, too, we were concerned to be found pleasing by Lord Okimoto. Tyrtaios, who was of the retinue of Lord Nishida, had a somewhat similar role, but, if he were latently more dangerous than Seremides, he did not have the temper, and the character of Seremides, which had much to do with intimidation, humiliation, and the drawing of blood. If Seremides disliked you, or was thinking of killing you, it was reasonably clear; indeed, it pleased him that you might suspect such things; but with Tyrtaios, one could not be sure. One did not know. In its way, this rendered Tyrtaios more frightening. His view was long; he was patient; he seldom acted on the moment, but each action, one suspected, rather like the carving of a bow or the sharpening of a knife, had its contribution to some end in view. Seremides no longer wore the yellow livery of Lord Okimoto, for Lord Okimoto had dismissed him from his service. Seremides, now, had no master, and no men. He wore a short, brown, ragged tunic, a cast-off. Tyrtaios, who had been of the retinue of Lord Nishida, had now been requisitioned by Lord Okimoto to fulfill the role which had been that of Seremides. Accordingly, Tyrtaios was now of the retinue of Lord Okimoto, and no longer of that of Lord Nishida. There remained four nested galleys. Tyrtaios' place with Lord Nishida had been taken by Turgus, an officer in the tarn cavalry, who had been given the command of one of the four remaining nested galleys. When called to flight, Turgus' galley was to fall to Pertinax, and if the entire cavalry were put aflight, I was pleased that the galley's command would fall to Philoctetes, a mariner of Cos, for whom I would be eager to draw oar.

We were now beyond the Vine Sea.

It had taken days to effect our escape, against the thickets of vines, and the renewal of growth.

Our tarn scouts had been invaluable, apprising us of the movements of that frightful garden in the sea, the circumambient, encroaching barricades of which might shift radically in days. That border which might lie within a dozen pasangs on one day might, as one sought it, given the shifts in wind and current, lie twenty or thirty pasangs away the next, and what had been further might now be nearer. The ropes of vines which entangled so many ships might extend their snares, as they would, but the great movements had their rhythms, and these, with tarns, could be tracked. Thus our sea road might be cut in a direction which seemed hopeless on a given day, given the tentacles of the garden, but, given the movements of the sea, might beckon on the next. The border, so to speak, as far off as it might be in any case, tended to move, and with some periodicity; it was thus sometimes closer, sometimes farther away. Charts, prepared on the basis of the reconnaissances of the tarn scouts, plotted these movements, and we moved toward the border, or edge, which, on the whole, was often closer than farther.

Even so it seemed unlikely we could have freed the great ship, as opposed to small boats, if we had not had an enormous complement of men, a small army, to work at the vines in our path, and cut them away from the ship. After the losses of the mutiny we fortunately had still better than two thousand men who might be applied to the work, some four hundred and fifty Pani, distributed between the commands of Lords Nishida and Okimoto, and some seventeen hundred mariners and armsmen, mostly armsmen.

If it were not for the tarn scouts and the complement of men at our disposal, it seems unlikely we could have effected the release of the great ship. On the final day, we heard the cry from the foremast, "The sea! The sea!" There was much cheering, from the small boats, from the towing galleys. We redoubled our efforts. Toward noon we saw tarnsmen returning to the great ship, hastily, almost frantically. There seemed agitation about. The grasping arms of the Vine Sea, from the north and the south, were drifting toward us. It had taken us longer than anticipated to reach this point. I remembered the signal, the beacon. Lord Nishida, I recalled, had feared the imminence of an enemy. It was at this point that I was suddenly aware of the movement of wind. "Ho!" cried men. The expansive blanket of odor, of the blossoms of the Vine Sea, with their clouds of insects, surely pervasive, yet seldom noticed for days, seemed suddenly rent. Briefly I drew in the first breath of the free air of Thassa which I had drawn since the night at the edge of the Vine Sea. Licinius Lysias, who had survived the sinking of the galleys of Seremides and Pertinax, rose at the bench, and pointed backward, toward the great ship. "See?" he cried. "Yes!" I said. The huge sails which had for so long lain slack from their yards, stirred. "Wind!" cried men about us. What a beautiful sight it was, to see the shaking, and then the lifting, and swelling, of those vast breadths of canvas. "Cast off the tow ropes!" we heard. The great ship was moving, like a mountain at sea. We went hard to port. The galleys, and the small boats, scattered, some being dragged over the vines. The great ship approached. Then it was abeam, and then off the bow. One of the small boats, tardy, caught in the vines, was crushed, and men leapt to the water, to be drawn aboard others of the cutting boats. The single, gigantic rudder of the ship of Tersites, was swathed with vines, but the wind drove her ahead. We saw yards of vines being torn from the sea. By evening the great ship was free of the Vine Sea and, sails furled, and sea hooks cast, she waited, a pasang west of the vines, the odor, and insects, while the numbers of ship's boats, and the four galleys, rejoined her. By nightfall the small boats were tiered in the galley holds, and the galleys themselves, scraped clean of vines and clinging blossoms, were nested. The wind shifted to the south, and we could no longer smell the Vine Sea. Rather we felt the sharp, salted air of bright, vast, green Thassa, fresh and clean, once more in our nostrils, in our lungs, and blood. We were again alive. Behind us was the Vine Sea.

The summer solstice had now occurred.

It was the third week in the month of En'Var.

"Perhaps you remember me?" said one of the four fellows gathered about an uneasy Seremides on the open deck.

"No," said Seremides, "no!"

"You are lying," said the fellow, Tereus.

"No," said Seremides, trying to turn away, but he was held in place.

Seremides was no longer armed, for he was no longer an officer. He did small things about the ship, in the pantries and kitchens.

"I am Tereus," said the man. "I sat third oar on your galley. My back wears still the welts of your rope."

"I was there, too," said another man, Aeson.

"And I," said the third, Thoas.

"And I," said the fourth, Andros.

"I do not know you!" said Seremides. "I know none of you!"

Some slave girls had gathered about.

Surely they had business elsewhere.

I was nearby.

Tereus kicked the crutch out from under Seremides and he fell sprawling to the deck, and could not regain his balance.

There was laughter from the girls.

Seremides reached for the crutch, but Tereus kicked it away from him. He tried to crawl toward the crutch but was kicked back, and then, the four of them, with belts, and ropes, apparently brought for the purpose, began to belabor him, fiercely, he at their feet, and Seremides began to whimper, and moan, and he folded his body on the deck, drawing up his knees, and covered his head, and, under their repeated blows, began to shake and shudder. His body trembled, as if chilled. I saw blood through the back of his tunic. "Go away!" he begged. "Leave me alone! Leave me alone! Do not hurt me! Do not hurt me! Please, stop! Please, mercy!"

Some of the slave girls, there were six of them, clapped their hands with pleasure.

"Mighty Rutilius begs for mercy," said Tereus.

"Rutilius, the scullion, weeps!" laughed Aeson, and Thoas and Andros joined in the merriment.

Muchly, too, were the slaves pleased.

How pleasant to see the once formidable Rutilius so discomfited.

Tereus, and his cohorts, resumed their beating.

"For the sake of the Priest-Kings," I cried, at last, "it is enough."

They looked up, desisting.

There were four of them.

"Be done with it," I said.

"Perhaps you would like some of the same," said Thoas, swinging his looped belt. He was sweating.

"It was you," said Aeson, "who brought this wretch back."

"Why," said Tereus, "did you not leave him for the sharks?"

"He has been beaten enough," I told them. "If you would beat someone find a whole man."

"You are a whole man," said Tereus.

"Better," said Andros, "you had left him in the sea."

I shrugged.

"I advise you, dear Rutilius," said Tereus, "not to be on the open deck after dark."

Thoas delivered another kick, from which the bent, cringing, knotted body of Seremides recoiled. "Seek Thassa, sleen," he said.

"It is enough," I said to the men.

"Do you seek to interfere?" asked Tereus.

"It is enough," I told him.

Tereus looked at me, and he, and his fellows, lifted their belts and ropes, and I prepared to defend myself.

But Tereus looked behind me.

"Yes," he said, then, satisfied, contemptuously, "it is enough."

The four then turned about and left. This had occurred in the vicinity of the second mast.

I sensed someone behind me, and I turned. The strange warrior, Nodachi, stood there.

Then he left.

I did not know how long he had been present.

The body of Seremides shook with tears.

"Stop it," I said. "You are a man."

Whereas Warriors, or men, might weep, as under the snake, which would draw tears from rocks, or weep as might larls in raging grief, if a city falls, a fellow is slain, or a Home Stone dishonored, this was unseemly. Did those on his galley, whom Seremides had so roundly abused, carry on so?

"Do not hurt me," said Seremides.

Seremides, unarmed, no longer whole, clad in a cast-off tunic, cringing, might have been the sorriest beggar in the Metellan district, in Ar. So the dreaded master of the elite Taurentians had come to this?

I wondered if he would be any longer regarded as worth the impaling spear in Ar. Would it not embarrass the city to publicly expose so abominable and craven a wretch upon her lofty walls? Surely better the bow string in the darkness of a prison's cellar.

"Hail, Rutilius, mighty master!" laughed Iole, first amongst the lingering slaves.

There was laughter from the girls.

The body of Seremides shook with weeping.

"You are a man," I said to Seremides. "Be silent."

"He is no longer a man!" scoffed Iole.

I wondered if this were so.

"Hail, Rutilius!" laughed another of the girls, Pyrrha.

I regarded the girls, angrily, and they instantly became subdued.

"Who amongst you dares to so speak the name of a free man?" I asked.

"None, Master," whispered Iole, quickly.

"You are in the presence of a free man," I informed them.

"Master?" said Thetis.

"First obeisance position!" I snapped.

Moaning, frightened, the six girls went instantly to first obeisance position, kneeling, their heads to the deck, the palms of their hands beside their head. I let them remain that way for a time, waiting to learn their fate.

"May I speak, Master?" whispered Iole.

I went to her and pulled her head up, by the hair. She tried to turn her head away, and down, but, by the hair, I, crouching, held it so that she must look at me. Her eyes were bright with fear, and tears.

"Yes," I said.

"Forgive us, Master," she said, "if we have been displeasing."

"You have not been fully pleasing," I said.

"Forgive us, Master!" begged Iole.

"Yes, Master," said the others.

It is the duty of a slave to be fully pleasing, to the best of her ability, and it is for the master to judge of her ability.

"Be as you were," I told Iole, releasing her, and she resumed first obeisance position. She trembled.

"It is no wonder we put you in collars," I said.

"Yes, Master," she whispered.

"I have a mind," I said, "to send for punishment tags, wire them to your collars, and send you running, hands thonged behind you, to your keeping areas."

In such a case the girl is expected to beg her keepers for discipline, that she may be improved. If she does not, the punishment is doubled, or trebled.

"Please, do not, Master," begged Iole. "We are contrite!"

"Up," I said, "go, be about your work."

The six slaves sprang gratefully to their feet and fled from the open deck.

Tereus, and his fellows, had been neither reprimanded, nor punished. Why then should the lash be put to the vulnerable, bared backs and legs of slaves? Their guilt, if guilt it was, was less.

I recalled them.

How delightful they were, in their tiny tunics. How pleased I was that there were two sexes, and one that of the female. How utterly beautiful, and fascinating, is the human female, so utterly different from the male, such a delicious and perfect complement to him, and his needs, as he to her, and his to hers.

They make lovely slaves. And that, of course, is what they should be. Women require masters, as men require slaves.

Women are lost without a master, and men forlorn without a slave.

It is the truth of nature.

I turned to face Seremides, crouching on the deck.

"You have not been under the snake," I said.

He put his head down.

"Perhaps you should be put in a collar, and given to girls for their play," I said.

"Do not hurt me," he whispered.

"Where has Seremides gone?" I asked.

He looked about, frightened, for I had used his true name, and had spoken it aloud. Then he said, "I am he."

"Perhaps you were always thus," I said. "But before we could not see it. Before it was well concealed."

"I was feared," he said, tears in his eyes.

"Now," I said, "you are the sport of slave girls."

"Tyrtaios," he said, suddenly, looking beyond me.

I had not noted the approach of Lord Okimoto's new high officer.

"Tyrtaios," said Seremides, plaintively, and put his hand out to him. "Tyrtaios, will you not help me? Have we not plans? Are we not equals? Are we not to share in all things? Are we not friends, allies?"

Tyrtaios continued on his way.

"I fear," I said, "your succor, your allegiance, all that you could supply of profit or value to another, is now naught."

As Tyrtaios made his way forward, he passed a slave girl, making her way aft, a small sa-tarna pannier on her back. The officers, as the men, eat in shifts, during designated watches, but the officers and the men do not eat together. The officers' cabins are aft, some in the stern-castle itself.

Now that we were free of the Vine Sea, Tersites was occasionally seen, on the stern-castle deck. Aëtius, however, discouraged his presence amongst the men.

When the girl had passed Tyrtaios she had averted her eyes and lowered her head, deferently, as befitted her status, slave. If he had addressed her, or placed himself before her, she would have knelt. The entire mien of the slave, behaviorally and verbally, is to make clear to herself and others her truth, that she is only a slave. She is to be docile, complaisant, submissive, and beautiful. A free woman may speak and behave as she wishes, a slave may not. When a free woman stands proudly she may do so as she wishes, independently, regally, even defiantly. When a slave stands proudly it is commonly to display her beauty before free men.

"Girl!" I said.

Frightened, the slave turned, catching sight of me, I think for the first time, and probably, too, the fallen Seremides.

I motioned her to me.

She seemed startled, and grateful, almost pathetically so, that I had deigned to note her. Ship slaves, in any event, aside from my personal knowledge of the slave, are often starved for attention, that of masters. It is very different from a private slave, who is likely to live a life closely intertwined with that of her master, one in which she is no stranger to his table and his furs, one in which she is frequently well apprised of the warmth of his arms and the weight of his chains. She is worked and used, prized and celebrated, day in and day out. She is his, in the fullest sense, desired, owned, and mastered. How could she respect a man who does not so desire her that he will be satisfied with nothing less than the owning of her? Is she truly so little thought of that he will not make her his, that he will not collar her? I had given the slave no notice, in weeks. But, too, aside from her delight at being recognized, and summoned, she seemed uneasy, even frightened, perhaps because the sa-tarna in the small pannier on her back might be warm, wrapped in napkins, and bound for an officers' mess.

She suddenly caught sight of Seremides, helpless on the deck, unable to rise. I did not know if she had heard of his fate or not, but, I think, clearly, this was the first time she had seen him, since the Vine Sea. I was curious to see how she might act. I remembered her from Ar. I could well anticipate her relief, perhaps delight, to find the man she most feared so reduced, so miserable, so helpless.

Might she not shriek with triumph, and pour upon him with impunity her scorn?

But she seemed startled, uncertain, almost frightened.

"You know this man?" I asked her.

I was not sure she even recognized the handsome, proud, temperamental, dangerous Seremides in this cringing, abject creature half lying before her on the deck.

"Yes," she whispered, "—Master."

I thought she would have little to fear from him now. Certainly I had been freer on the ship since the Vine Sea. Indeed, it now seemed the crippled Seremides avoided me. Did he fear I might kill him?

The slave regarded the creature before her.

There was little chance now he would bring her to Ar, and arrange her delivery to Marlenus.

Too, there was little chance now, as far as I knew, that he could locate Talena, and bring her to Ar, thereby winning not only her bounty but his own amnesty.

"You are smiling!" cried Seremides.

"No, Master!" she said, and knelt.

If anything, I saw horror, and pity, in the frightened eyes of the slave.

"Girl," I said.

She looked at me. I pointed to the crutch which had been kicked across the deck, out of the reach of Seremides. Left alone, I had little doubt he could drag himself to it, and, with it, perhaps clinging to the rail, rise to his feet.

Alcinoë rose, fetched the crutch, and returned to a place before Seremides, where she knelt and, head down, between her arms, lifted the crutch to him.

He seized the crutch.

I feared he would use it to strike the girl. He was still a strong man, and a harsh blow, as she knelt, might break her arm or shatter an elbow.

I held the crutch, and Seremides could not use it. I felt the wood move in my hand, as he tried to free it, but he could not do so.

"If you wish, *kajira*," I said to the girl, "you may abuse him, scorn him, taunt him, beat him, speak to him and treat him however you may wish."

She shook her head. "No, Master," she said.

"You do not desire to do so?" I asked.

"I may not," she said.

"You do not desire to do so?" I asked.

"No, Master," she said.

I was pleased at this answer.

"Be about your business, *kajira*," I said.

She rose up, backed away a little, and then hurried aft. I could see the white napkins in which the sa-tarna loaves were wrapped, through the wicker of the pannier.

"Sleen," said Seremides, "you wanted her to abuse me!"

"No," I said.

"You would have permitted it!" he said, angrily.

"No," I said.

"You could have left me amongst the vines," he said.

"Yes," I said.

"Why did you not let me die?" asked Seremides.

"You are of the ship," I said.

I then left him, to hoist himself, by means of the crutch, to his feet. I gave him no help. I had no wish to demean him.

"Callias," said Tarl Cabot, who came from forward.

"Commander," I said.

"I want you on the foremast, every third watch," he said.

"As you wish," I said.

"We need good eyes, and alert fellows aloft," he said.

"I will do my best, commander," I said.

"Good," he said. "I am informed by Lord Nishida that these are dangerous waters."

I remembered the beacon.

"Yes, commander," I said.

Chapter Sixteen

The Warning Ship;
The Small Boats;
Assassins;
The Fleet of Lord Yamada

I let the glass of the Builders, in its sling, drop to my hip. "Ho!" I called down to the deck. "Ship! Ship, to the bow, starboard!"

Those on deck rushed to the starboard rail. I saw men moving about, too, on both the stem and stern castles. Officers were emerging from below decks, men, too. The bar, under its hammer, rang alert.

We had seen little that seemed dangerous in the last several days, despite the fears of Lord Nishida. Oddly, however, once or twice, we had noted a dark cloud in the sky, from which a dust of ash had coated sails and fallen to the deck. At the same time, the wind, fitfully, had seemed acrid, and breathing had been unpleasant.

Now, however, the sky was blue, the clouds white, the air clear. Thassa was serene, the wind gentle.

Orders had been issued from the stern castle, for the great ship heaved to. Shortly thereafter one of the nested galleys was being lowered to the water. An Ahn later I reported the galley had hoisted the green pennon.

The ship that I had seen was much like those lost amongst the serpentine entanglements of the Vine Sea.

It held no steady course, and was, as far as we could tell, until investigated, adrift.

The hoisting of the green pennon had been premature, a mistake that would not be repeated.

We would lose, in consequence, one of our four remaining galleys.

By the time the great ship drew near the drifting vessel, my watch was done, but I remained on deck. The galley was drawn up alongside the apparent derelict. From the starboard rail, given the height of the ship of Tersites, we could look down on both our galley and, higher, the deck of the seemingly unmanned ship.

"I do not like it," said Tarl Cabot to Pertinax, the two of them some few feet from me.

"It is ugly," said Pertinax.

The encountered ship had two masts, but it bore no sails. From each of the two yards there hung several bound bodies, suspended by the feet, whose throats, it seemed, from the condition of the deck below, had been cut, perhaps a moment before they were emplaced, dying. Similarly, several others were nailed, by hands and feet, to the masts, the deck, and bulwarks.

"Yes," said Cabot to Pertinax, "ugly, indeed, but that is done. What I do not like, now, is what is not done."

"I do not understand," said Pertinax.

"I am not sure," said Cabot. "It may be nothing." He looked about, and saw me. "Callias," he said, "summon Lord Nishida."

"That will not be necessary," said Lord Okimoto, who was nearby, Tyrtaios at his side.

"Lord?" said Cabot.

"Speak to the commander," said Lord Okimoto to Tyrtaios.

"I am informed, commander, by Lord Okimoto," said Tyrtaios, "that the ship, as seems obvious, is a warning ship, and that it is perhaps one of several. Further, you may have noted the scrolls which were hung amongst the bodies, and from the yards. They are identical. Some have been brought aboard. I cannot read the writing as it is in a strange script, but the message is in Gorean, and has been conveyed to me by his Excellency, Lord Okimoto. The scrolls allege that the bodies on the ship are those of criminals, men who were enemies of the *shogun*, men who conspired against him, who dared oppose his will, whose loyalty was suspect, who failed to pay their taxes, who tried to hide food, who failed to speak of him with sufficient reverence, such things."

"I see," said Cabot. "And who is this *shogun*?"

"The great lord, Yamada, our enemy," said Lord Okimoto.

"I am uneasy," said Cabot.

"You may speak to Tyrtaios," said Lord Okimoto.

"I would consult with Lord Nishida," said Cabot to Tyrtaios.

Tyrtaios looked to Lord Okimoto. "Of course," said Lord Okimoto. He then turned about, and left, and, in a moment, was followed by Tyrtaios, who, I suspected, did not care to follow any man.

"There is danger here," said Cabot to me.

I recalled the beacon.

Cabot looked over the rail, at the presumed derelict. "Was the ship examined?" he asked.

"Yes," I said. "Men went below decks. Else the green pennon would not have been flown."

"Were any of the Pani?" asked Cabot.

"No," I said. The launched galley had been manned by mariners, oared by armsmen.

"Summon Lord Nishida," said Cabot to me.

"Lord Okimoto will not be pleased," I said.

"Summon him," said Cabot.

I turned about and hurried aft, below decks, where I found Lord Nishida, in his cabin, in meditation.

"Lord," I said, softly, for he seemed utterly still, sitting on a woven mat, with his legs crossed.

Two contract women, as they are called, Sumomo and Hana, knelt nearby.

Though he had been absolutely still, at this tiny sound, my voice, he lifted his head, instantly alert.

"The commander of the tarn cavalry would speak with you," I said. "We have come upon a ship, a strange ship, adrift, filled with bodies and scrolls."

"Why was I not informed?" he asked.

I looked to the two women in the background, kneeling. The woman, Hana, looked at Sumomo, frightened. "Lord Nishida," said Sumomo, "was in meditation."

"Men have been about," I said, "there has been noise, shouting, the bar was hammered, to signal an alert."

"Lord Nishida was in meditation," said Sumomo.

"I feared this," said Lord Nishida, winding his sash about his widely sleeved robe, and thrusting two swords, both curved, a longer and a shorter, within the sash.

In an Ehn he was on the open deck, hurrying to the starboard rail, where he stood beside Cabot, his hands on the rail, looking over, past the galley, to the deck of the seeming derelict.

"The demon, Yamada," he hissed.

"It is a warning ship, it seems," said Cabot.

"I fear it is more than that," said Lord Nishida. "Who has boarded that ship?"

"Mariners, armsmen," said Cabot.

"None of my men, none of the men of Lord Okimoto?" said Lord Nishida.

"I do not think so," said Cabot.

"Have you heard or seen anything unusual," asked Lord Nishida, "a whistle, a flash of fire?"

"No," said Cabot.

"There may be time," said Lord Nishida. "Do not strike the bar. Call softly. Recall the galley, the men, instantly."

"I do not understand," said Pertinax.

"They are waiting for the others," said Lord Nishida.

At that moment there was a long whistle, and I picked out a shaft, an ascending arrow, fired from somewhere on the ship below. It reached the zenith of its flight, turned in the air, scarcely visible, and then, with a different whistling pitch, descended. Almost at the same time, another arrow, trailing a spume of smoke, ascended from the ship, paused at the height of its trajectory and then, trailing its tail of smoke, descended, falling into the water.

While this was going on Lord Nishida cried to the deck watch, "The bar, the bar, strike it, strike it."

Below, as though from nowhere, large numbers of men, of the Pani sort, emerged wildly from hatches, screaming, wielding weapons, swarming over the deck.

The bar began to sound, hammered again and again.

Weapons would be issued.

The boarding party below had been armed, of course, but on the great ship itself, on deck, few were armed, only the officers, some guards, and the deck watch. Our first defense, of course, was the ship itself, its height.

To my dismay I saw the boarding party, surprised and outnumbered by dozens to one, swept aside in bloody rout. A hundred Pani must have leapt into the galley, which rocked and almost capsized.

The enemy, I gathered, had not expected a vessel the size of the ship of Tersites, and many stood confused below, crying out, and shaking their weapons. This was no ascent of a few feet, to the deck of a common round ship, or that of the batten-sailed ships of the sort with which we had familiarized ourselves in the Vine Sea.

Some grapnels, on knotted rope, were slung upward from the galley, but fell short.

I heard weapons being spilled on the deck, brought from below, and men seized up blades, spears, axes, and pikes. And armed men, in their dozens, were pouring onto the deck, having armed themselves below in the weapon rooms.

I saw fires lit on the ship which had seemed deserted, save for the dead, when we had come upon it.

Fire, if it can but obtain its hold, may climb to the clouds.

The Pani below had set fire to our galley and were trying to thrust it against our hull. Those who had boarded it but moments ago leapt into the water or perished in the flames.

"Bring water from port!" screamed Aëtius from the stern-castle deck. "Protect my ship! Save my ship!" screamed Tersites, from beside him.

Buckets, on ropes, were thrown to port, to draw water, to fight flames.

Our galley burned beside our hull, on the starboard side.

The Pani who had surprised our boarding crew had apparently been concealed below, under the compartments. Our Pani might have suspected this, but the boarding crew, being less familiar with the draft and construction of such ships, had not.

"To port, to port!" cried Aëtius to the helm deck.

The great ship, sails unfurled to the wind, rudder turned, moved to port, away from the derelict, and our burning galley.

Many men were now armed.

But there seemed little need, now, of the sword, the spear.

"Take in all weapons!" called Aëtius from the stern castle, to the deck watch. "Turn in all weapons." Aëtius, since the mutiny, was zealous to keep the crew unarmed.

"No!" called Tyrtaios. "No, by order of his Excellency, Lord Okimoto!"

Weapons had been issued, as noted, in the general alarm. I was not sure it would be easy to retrieve them from men such as manned the great ship.

Why, I wondered, would Lord Okimoto wish to have the men retain arms. It now seemed clear, as it had not before, that there was little danger of being boarded, that the enemy had not the engines by means of which that might be effected.

Then I shuddered, suspecting the purpose of the Pani lord. The ship, the danger of fire now muchly averted, was to return to the derelict, and men were to descend to the derelict, and eliminate any who might live to tell of the great ship, its nature, its men, its course. I shuddered, remembering the fate of the *Metioche*. Too, I suspected that the Pani on board would not be likely to accommodate themselves to the housing of Pani prisoners, who might be as uncompromising, resolute, and irreconcilable as they themselves, as fanatically dedicated to their leaders as ours were to theirs, Lords Nishida and Okimoto.

In retrospect, it seems likely to me that the enemy anticipated a dalliance on the part of the great ship, a lingering to avenge a boarding party, a lingering to exterminate survivors.

In any event, hardly had Tyrtaios conveyed the order of Lord Okimoto, than we heard the high watch, from the platform and ring, high above, cry out, "Beware! There are a hundred ships! We are surrounded!"

I had no doubt the ship we had encountered was a warning ship, and an ambush ship, but, too, it seems, it had served another purpose, that of a trap, a distraction, a bait, of sorts.

The alarm bar continued to sound.

There were no hundred ships, but there were a great many. They were small, and oared.

They reminded me of a swarm of insects, as in the Vine Sea. They were low ships, green, partly covered, some two hundred yards away.

"The glass, a glass!" cried Tarl Cabot, and a glass of the Builders was thrust into his hand.

Buckets of sea water were still being spilled over the starboard side of the great ship, where small, scattered red plants of fire sought to grow.

In a moment Tarl Cabot lowered the glass of the Builders.

He sought out Lord Nishida. "There will be fire, there will be boarders!" he said.

"How can it be?" inquired Lord Nishida.

The small ships were approaching rapidly. Such an oar count can be maintained only for a short time.

"Marshall two hundred armsmen," said Lord Okimoto to Lord Nishida.

"To what end?" asked Lord Nishida.

"We have lost a galley," said Lord Okimoto. "The demon Yamada has violated the truce of the warning ship, which should be but a warning."

"Small ships approach," said Lord Nishida.

"We will launch the galleys, and deal with them later," said Lord Okimoto.

"We have little room for prisoners, lord," said Tyrtaios.

"There will be no prisoners," said Lord Okimoto.

"Excellent," said Tyrtaios.

A cloud of the small ships clung now about the hull of the great ship.

"To starboard," called Lord Okimoto. "Come against the warning ship!"

We were some fifty yards from the warning ship.

"Beware the small ships, lord!" exclaimed Cabot. "They are all about!"

"Does the larl fear urts?" inquired Lord Okimoto.

"A thousand urts may easily kill the larl," said Cabot.

"I find the apprehension of a warrior surprising," said Lord Okimoto. "The small ships may be dealt with at our convenience. They are harmless. They cannot reach us."

"They are not harmless," said Cabot.

"They cannot reach us," said Lord Okimoto, quietly, patiently. He then turned to Tyrtaios. "To starboard," he said. "We shall come against the ship of deceit. We shall administer a rebuke to the demon, Lord Yamada."

"Yes, lord," said Tyrtaios.

"Have boarding nets prepared," said Lord Okimoto. "Form boarding parties. The nets will be cast at my word."

By means of such nets dozens of men might simultaneously descend the side of the ship.

"Prepare, rather, to repel boarders!" said Cabot.

"You are mad," said Lord Okimoto.

At that point a grapnel, attached to a length of chain, and that to a course of knotted rope, looped over the rail, struck the deck, scraped back across the deck, and was caught against the rail.

I wondered at the arm which might have flung such a device so high, so far.

I saw the grapnel jerk against the rail, and twist in stress, and knew one or more men were climbing the rope.

"There will be others!" cried Cabot.

"Do not let them anchor!" cried Cabot. "Throw them over the side. Cut the ropes, behind the chain!"

He had hardly spoken when two, and then ten or more, such devices dropped to the deck.

Men hurled some back over the side, before they could catch. The knife, the sword, slashed at the ropes of others. Many, however, given the swiftness with which they were drawn back, caught against the rail. Once this was done, they were difficult to dislodge, for the stress on the device, and the chain.

I saw one of the enemy Pani put an arm over the rail and he dropped back, headless, and fell into the sea. Nodachi drew back, readying himself for another stroke.

I retrieved a sword from the deck, and went to the side.

I also heard a striking at the sides of the great ship, like a rain of wood, and smelled burning pitch.

Each of the small boats, as far as I could tell, was similarly equipped. Each grapnel, with its rope and chain, was launched from a small engine, a tiny catapult, mounted between the benches. And behind the catapult was a vat, filled, from the odor, with burning pitch. Archers were dipping arrows, whose shaft, behind the point, was wrapped in cloth, which cloth was then saturated with flaming pitch, which arrows, one after another, were then being fired into the hull.

This, doubtless, was what had been determined earlier by Cabot, with the glass of the Builders.

One could not well cut the chain behind the grapnels, but axes cut at the rails, and several of the grapnels, given the stress of climbers, broke loose.

We heard men plunge back, into the sea, or onto the small boats at our hull.

I heard more striking of arrows into the hull.

I saw more than one man, trying to free the hold of a grapnel, felled by a long arrow, fired from one of the small boats.

Some enemy Pani did attain the deck, mostly forward, on the port side. They were met by our Pani and armsmen.

I saw no mercy shown, on either side.

Meanwhile, in accord with the instructions of Lord Okimoto, the great ship had come about, toward the warning ship, and there was a rending crash, as the great ship crushed the smoldering remains of our galley, almost at water level, and eight or ten of the small boats, caught between the grinding hull of the great ship and the drifting warning ship, with its dozens of armed Pani on its deck, and its grisly cargo of death. Indeed, the warning ship itself was partly afire, on its starboard side, where the flaming mast of the galley, with its lateen sail, had collapsed against its aft bulwarks.

"Draw away!" urged Lord Nishida.

Lord Okimoto issued orders to Tyrtaios.

Tyrtaios called out, to the lines of men about him, "Boarding nets!" he cried.

These nets were cast.

The Pani below, not uneagerly, readied themselves.

"Prepare to board!" called Tyrtaios.

I doubted that Tyrtaios, under the circumstances, thought it well advised, given fire and our own troubles, to board the warning ship, but he failed to demur. I did not think he was ignorant, or a sycophant; I thought it rather that he was concerned to ascend in the favor of Lord Okimoto, steadily, relentlessly, for his own purposes. Lord Okimoto, on the other hand, was well aware of the sizable complement of fighting men on board, a small army, who would, in any likely contest, as on an open field, far outnumber the enemy Pani in the small boats and on the warning ship, perhaps by as many as four or five to one; and was, accordingly, prepared to expend his men liberally, using his superior numbers to sweep aside opposition. I wondered, too, if his apparent hatred for this Lord Yamada, and his indignation, certainly not misplaced, at the misuse of a warning ship, might not have colored, if not obscured, his judgment.

The greatest danger, of course, was fire.

If the enemy had any idea of the men on the great ship they would not expect to take the ship by arms. On the other hand, and the thought alarmed me, the boarding might well serve to distract from, and delay attention to, what might be the latent but paramount intention of the attack, the destruction of the great ship by fire. Is not the name of war deception?

The nets had been cast.

Armsmen swarmed over the side.

To be sure, nets, like roads, may be traveled in more than one direction.

"Recall the men!" said Lord Nishida to Lord Okimoto.

"Enemies yet live," said Lord Okimoto, peering toward the deck of the warning ship, where men fought, under swaying bodies suspended from the yards, amongst bodies nailed in place.

I looked, too, and our fellows, I was pleased to see, accredited themselves well. Those whom the Pani had recruited were on the whole large, strong, agile, skilled men, many from the free companies, many from the occupation forces fugitive from Ar, and many, I fear, from amongst brigands and renegades. They had recruited less for honor and loyalty, I feared, than for the capacity to endure hardship, march, and kill. And the Pani who served Lords Nishida and Okimoto, I gathered, though perhaps on the whole of a nobler breed, were likely to be extremely dangerous men, winnowed by years of conflict, men largely the survivors of lengthy, bloody wars.

"The warning ship is afire!" said Lord Nishida. "It is done! Recall the men!"

"No," said Lord Okimoto.

"This shall be called to the attention of Lord Temmu," said Lord Nishida.

I had no idea, at the time, who this Lord Temmu might be. I would learn later it was the name of the high lord, or *shogun*, to whom Lords Nishida and Okimoto were pledged.

"You dare not!" said Lord Okimoto. It was the first time I had seen the equanimity of this Pani nobleman jarred.

Lord Nishida did not speak.

"I am senior, I am first," said Lord Okimoto.

"Though it means the knife," said Lord Nishida.

I understood little of this conversation.

I looked about, sword in hand.

Tarl Cabot was forward, on the port side, with his friend, Pertinax, and the Pani tarnsman, Tajima, fighting with our Pani against boarders, who were heaviest in that quarter. I thought to join them, and moved a bit toward them, but then hesitated, curious.

I saw two Pani whom I did not recognize from the ship, though both wore yellow, the color of the livery of Lord Okimoto's men. I did not know them, but they must be ours, I thought. Our Pani kept much to themselves. What struck me as odd was not that they had not joined in the fighting for us, but, rather, slipped through the engaged men, looking about, across the largely open deck. At almost the same instant, it seemed they had descried their objective, for each, with both hands on a long handled sword, uttering no sound, ran toward us. I was some seven or eight feet behind Lords Nishida and Okimoto, for I had already moved toward the fighting at the forward port quarter.

As the first fellow passed me, I cut to my left, and hit the side of his neck, and his body, the head half gone, spun to the side, momentarily interfering with the progress of his fellow, a pace or two behind him. Tyrtaios, alerted by the sounds, turned and blocked a blow that would have cleft the head of Lord Okimoto. At the same time I, behind the fellow, seized the opportunity, and cut apart the spinal column at the base of his skull. This had all happened very quickly, and I think that Tyrtaios was as startled as I. Both of us had reacted instinctively.

The two Pani, in yellow livery, were on the deck then, the planks run with blood, at our feet.

"Assassins," said Lord Nishida.

We heard a cry, from the port side. The last boarder there had been thrust back, over the rail.

The Pani who had been engaged there, with the exception of some two or three left guard at the rail, now rushed elsewhere.

I gave little for the chances of any remaining boarders.

Most perished, but several, who had time to turn their back, threw themselves over the rail, back to the water, presumably to be picked up by the small boats still about.

I was startled to see Seremides, hobbling on his crutch, near the forward port rail, where fighting had taken place. He held a sword, doubtless taken from the weaponry earlier spilled upon the deck. The sword was bloodied. As few could not, by simple movement, a subtle alteration of position, a simple variance of attack, quickly dispatch a foe so handicapped, I thought Seremides must be a fellow of great courage, to have dragged himself to the deck, and worked his way, painfully, awkwardly, his body suspended on his crutch, step by step, toward the fighting. I had thought he would have cowered below decks, perhaps in a kitchen, or in the darkness of a storeroom. But he had not. He had come to the open deck, and found a weapon. He was, it seemed, of the ship. He might no longer wear the yellow livery of Lord Okimoto's retinue, but now, it seemed, he had made it clear, and to all, that he was such as had worn it well.

I could smell smoke.

"Recall the men, lord," said Lord Nishida. "We must attend to the ship."

"We must not leave a living enemy behind us," said Lord Okimoto.

Tarl Cabot, wiping an arm across his eyes, his sword bloody, approached us. He looked about. "The deck is clear," he said.

"I fear the loss of the ship," said Lord Nishida.

"No enemies are to be left behind us," said Lord Okimoto.

"The main timbers of the ship," said Tarl Cabot, "are Tur

wood. It burns longer than softer wood, such as that of needle trees, but it is harder to ignite."

"Surely there is danger," said Lord Nishida.

"Certainly," said Cabot.

"We have time to exterminate the vermin about," said Lord Okimoto.

"No," said Cabot.

"I do not understand," said Lord Okimoto, politely.

"We do not have the time," said Cabot.

"It is true," said Lord Okimoto, "the small boats will scatter, and the matter will be difficult."

"I fear," said Lord Nishida, "the difficulty the commander has in mind is quite different."

"You may speak," said Lord Okimoto.

"I take it," said Cabot, "that we are not, as far as you know, near to land."

"No," said Lord Nishida, "we are only days from the Vine Sea."

"The small boats are not seagoing vessels, certainly not in their numbers, no more than our ship's boats."

"Ah!" said Lord Okimoto.

At this moment there was a cry from the platform and ring, high above us. "Sails, ho! Ships! Ships!"

"How many?" called Cabot.

Aeacus, who was above, scanned the horizon with the Builder's glass.

"Ten, twelve!" he called down to the deck.

"It is the fleet of Lord Yamada," said Lord Okimoto.

"I feared so," said Lord Nishida.

"They will be warships," said Lord Okimoto. "We cannot match them, ship to ship."

"No," said Lord Nishida.

Lord Okimoto turned to Tyrtaios, regretfully. "Inform the deck watch," he said. "Sound the recall."

"No!" said Cabot.

"No?" said Lord Nishida.

"Not yet!" he said. "Tajima!" he called.

"Captain san," said Tajima.

Cabot then spoke hurriedly to Tajima, the tarnsman, in a language I did not recognize. It was not Gorean. And Tajima, to my astonishment, responded in what I took to be the same language.

Within a handful of Ehn forty riders of the tarn cavalry were at the rail, each armed with the small Tuchuk bow, used by the tarn cavalry, a weapon of considerable power, which may be swept easily from one side of a saddle to the other.

"Now," said Cabot, "sound the recall."

The ship's bar rang the recall.

Our men backed to the moving hull of the great ship, turning, grasping the rope rungs of the boarding nets. The enemy rushed forward, but only some yards, before turning back, stumbling over falling bodies, riddled by arrows.

The retreat of our armsmen had been satisfactorily covered.

"Hard to port! All canvas!" called Aëtius from the stern castle.

Some of the enemy managed to reach the nets, as well, and began to climb, but, after a few yards, they dropped back in the water and swam to the wreckage of the galley, and that of some small boats, from which they were drawn to the deck of the warning ship, now falling back.

"It is regrettable," said Lord Okimoto, "that we have left living enemies behind us."

"It is the fortunes of war," said Lord Nishida.

"Our presence is now known," said Lord Okimoto.

"It was known before," said Lord Nishida.

"But," said Lord Okimoto, "perhaps not its nature, the ship, our numbers."

"No," said Lord Nishida.

"The enemy now knows much," said Lord Okimoto.

"But our greatest secret may not be known," said Lord Nishida.

"At least," said Lord Okimoto, "its size, its appearance, its stamina, its range of flight, its terribleness."

"They will think we have enlisted dragons," said Lord Nishida.

I took them to be speaking of tarns.

The deck watch set men to the ropes and buckets, and, as the great ship, its sails filled, took its way west, streaming water ran with the wind across her sides. Most of what might have been hundreds of small fires had died out of their own accord against the Tur wood. The greatest marking, if not damage, had been done forward on the starboard side, where the flaming galley had been moved against the hull. Over the next four days, men, with small files and vessels of caulking, were fastened in the boarding nets, which were moved from port to starboard, and along the hull, and these fellows cleaned and repaired the timbers, removing hundreds of blackened arrow shafts, and sealing fissures and clefts in the wood. The arrow points, worked free, were saved, in small bags, worn at the belt.

The pursuing fleet of Lord Yamada had soon fallen behind. The ship of Tersites was no warship, no agile, many-oared knife in the water. But she had good lines, six masts, and an enormous spread of canvas. I thought there was little at sea that could overtake her with a fair wind. Tersites, with his small, crooked body, may have been half-blind and more than half-mad, but he had built a ship which, I think, will be remembered in a hundred songs.

Our losses had not been considerable.

Amongst those who were lost were two oarsmen, Thoas and Andros. They had been struck from behind.

I will report one part of a conversation heard the evening of the day of the altercation in the vicinity of the warning ship, which altercation took place on the second day of the second week past the fourth passage hand, as it has some bearing on what occurred later.

"What course has been given to Aëtius," inquired Lord Nishida.

"We are continuing on, directly," replied Lord Okimoto.

"You know our location," said Lord Nishida. "Surely it is time to veer north. You know what lies ahead."

"We shall move north later," said Lord Okimoto.

"You know the season," said Lord Nishida, "and what lies ahead."

"Yes," said Lord Okimoto.

"Why then do you continue on?" inquired Lord Nishida.

"Because," said he, "I think the fleet of Lord Yamada will fear to follow."

Chapter Seventeen

The Floating Stones;
Unusual Precautions Are Taken;
I Converse with Tarl Cabot

Many of the crew, and certainly myself, were fascinated by the floating stones which appeared occasionally in the water, as we sailed west. More than one had been drawn aboard. They were rock, but light. One could crumble it in the hands, crush it against the deck. When we broke such stones open, we found the interior spongy, and porous, riddled with tiny apertures. We did not know the origin of these anomalous substances. If any knew, the information was withheld from us. Through familiarity, we soon lost interest in these strange stones, which, as we moved on, were occasionally encountered in drifts or shoals.

Oddly enough, by command of Lords Okimoto and Nishida, ropes were strung about the open deck, this though the weather was clear. Two days after this it was ordered, despite the heat of the day, that hatches were to be secured, save when used for ingress or egress. A day after that, access to the open deck was primarily restricted to officers and the duty crew. It was close below decks. There was much grumbling amongst the men. It was doubtless particularly unpleasant for the some two hundred *kajirae* aboard, intended for gifts, eventual sale, trade goods, and such, on their chains in the keeping areas. Often, in good weather, in the groups into which they were divided in the Kasra and Venna keeping areas, they would be brought to the open deck for an airing and exercise. At such times they were not chained, or even roped. To where might they run? Off-duty crew members might gather about while the girls, in one group or another, were brought to the deck. And much was the good-natured raillery, suggestions, observations, evaluations, hootings, whistles, jokes, gestures, and such, to which the lovely properties were subjected. Sometimes they clung together, frightened, as men closed in about them, but they soon realized it was forbidden to touch them, and then several of them dared to torment the men, with the movements, the posings, the expressions, and gestures of slaves. But did they not know they might be noted, and marked, well remembered by one fellow or another when, obedient to the snap of the whip, they might ascend the auction block? One fellow could not resist such provocation and seized a blond *kajira*, crushing her to him and raping her lips with the kiss of the master. He was flogged and she put under the five-stranded slave whip. He grinned under the lash but she wept, but I think, too, she would not forget that kiss. Did she not, later, often enough, when possible, place herself within his purview? Surely he marked her, and might keep her in mind. Perhaps she dreamed of being led to his quarters, bound, on his chain. I used to watch, when convenient, the second group from the Kasra keeping area, for in it was a slave, a ship slave, whom I thought might one day prove to be not without some interest. She had streaming dark hair, lovely flanks, an exquisite figure, and an inviting love cradle. Her face, so vulnerable so delicate, so beautiful, now that she was in bondage, might have made a bronze mirror cry out with pleasure. Her name was Alcinoë. I had thought she had behaved well when confronted with the horror of Seremides, but, of late, it seemed she had tried to carry herself as a free woman, that is, as much as possible when one knows there is a collar on one's neck. I gathered she was pretending not to notice me, or the others. She affected a haughty, supercilious expression, and, once, when she looked at me, she looked away, her lip curling, as though in contempt. This amused me. Did the slut not know she was marked, incisively, unmistakably, and quite nicely; did she think she could slip a collar? I recalled her insolence in the place of dining. Did she not recall her punishment, at the mast, nor my lenience in not running her back to the Kasra keeping area, hands thonged behind her, a punishment tag wired to her collar? I recalled how she had begged, kneeling, at my feet, as a slave, plaintively, the attentions of a master, which attentions had been denied her. Was she now concerned to pretend that that had never happened, or that it had been of negligible consequence? Did she dare now attempt to assume the airs, the attitude, of a free woman? Did she not know that at a mere snapping of fingers she must tear away her tunic and prostrate herself?

I was not the only fellow, of course, as you may have gathered, who enjoyed seeing *kajirae* brought to the deck, and exercised. They are so beautiful! It was delightful to see them, too, in their free Ehn on deck, hurry to the rail, throw back their heads, and drink in the keen, rushing fresh air of vast, glorious Thassa.

I did not know how much they knew of our venture, of the course, of the incidents at the warning ship, and such.

Did they know that war had been done on this very deck, now sanded and smoothed clean?

Did they know of the fleet of Lord Yamada?

Did they understand that these waters, so glasslike, so serene, might be fraught with peril?

I supposed not.

Would one explain such things to verr or kaiila?

Curiosity is not becoming in a *kajira*.

I have upon occasion mentioned an officer named Pertinax, a friend, it seems, of Tarl Cabot, the commander, or captain, of the tarn cavalry. He had been, for example, this Pertinax, captain on one of the galleys lost in the Vine Sea, that on which I had shared an oar with Licinius Lysias, the fellow from Turmus. In any event, when the first group of the Venna keeping area was brought for its airing and exercise to the open deck, this Pertinax was usually about, interestingly, seemingly preoccupied with one duty or another. It was not difficult, after a time or two, to detect that his presence at such times was not likely to be a matter of coincidence. It seemed clear, after a bit, that the object of his attention was a particular slave, a blue-eyed, blond-haired barbarian named Saru. Her hair was only half-grown, and thus I supposed she was either a recent slave, for some barbarian females come from the barbarian lands with their hair short, or that it had been shaved once or twice, perhaps as a punishment, or for use as catapult cordage, for female hair is much desired for that purpose. In any event, his interest was clearly justified, as she was a nicely formed, even luscious, bit of collar-meat. Barbarians, incidentally, are often of high quality, perhaps because of the time and cost of their acquisition and transportation. For this reason, if no other, they are likely to be selected with great care. It is not as though a city fell, and its women, naked, chained together, in lines a pasang or more in length, were marched away between the lines of victors, now their masters, to new walls, within which they would wear collars. It is rather as though they were fruit in an orchard, to be scouted with circumspection, and only then, after careful consideration, the choicest of the choice, selected for the delectation of foreign tables. This sort of selection is apparently not as difficult as it might seem, for, at least according to my understanding, many women in barbarian lands, even free women, do not dress their faces, but leave them naked, as naked as those of slaves; that it is not unusual for their calves and ankles to be discernible; that their small hands are often ungloved, and such. Is it not obvious that such women are slave stock, that they are suitably embonded, that they are by nature the rightful properties of masters? Surely they must long for the collar, and their fair limbs for the shackles, and the weight of chains, else they would not so blatantly invite them. Too, interestingly, in the barbarian lands, it seems that many women are distressed and forlorn, many not knowing why, denied the rights of their nature, forbidden the fulfillments of their ownership and submission, forbidden the joys of the surrendered, yielding slave. On Gor they come home to themselves, and their sex, and find the fulfillments denied to them in their own countries. Not only is the barbarian slave often intelligent and beautiful, such things involved in their selection, but, commonly, as well, she is hot, devoted, and dutiful. Embonded, she finds her freedom; enslaved, she is most content. In any event, whatever may be the reason, or reasons, such women tend, almost invariably, to do well on the block. They are prize stock. Men bid heatedly for them. This is perhaps one reason they tend to be resented, if not despised and hated, by their Gorean collar sisters, and, certainly, by free women. It is probably not pleasant to be a barbarian slave amongst Gorean women, either slave or free. Men, of course, like them.

I did not know if the slave, Saru, knew herself observed, for when she would turn, Pertinax would usually be otherwise occupied. To be sure, I would suppose it was suspected. When a slave knows herself observed, other than casually, she may well suppose the fellow is considering her against his resources. I did see the slave, once, seeing his eyes upon her, cry out, softly, and extend her hands to him, but he looked away, paying her no attention. As they were both barbarians I wondered if they had known one another in the barbarian lands. If so, that might well be forgotten. A mighty chasm now separated them, unbridgeable, save by the chain or whip. He was a man, and an officer, she a woman, and a slave. I was interested in this matter, and had made some inquiries. She was not a ship slave, but the property of Lord Nishida himself. She was apparently being groomed to be a gift for the *shogun*, Temmu. Her eye color and hair color were unusual, I gathered, in the lands of the Pani. Doubtless that would add something to her interest, or value. Lord Nishida had two contract women, as the expression is, at his disposal, Sumomo and Hana. These women, I gathered, were not slaves. Certainly they were not collared. On the other hand their contracts could be bought and sold, and the women would accompany the contracts, which did not, to me, seem all that different from being slaves. To be sure, they had a higher status, and were presumably respected and treated with courtesy. The Pani did, of course, keep slaves, as the gifting of Saru would make clear, as well as the likely disposition, sale or such, if land were ever reached, of the lovely beasts normally housed in the Kasra and Venna keeping areas. Saru's outburst, and appeal, for the attention of Pertinax, brought her two strokes of her trainer's switch, and she shrank down to the deck, covering her head. The switch was lifted, but did not fall a third time. Pertinax noted the punishment of the slave, and smiled, as she lifted her head to him in horror. Then he turned away. The strokes had been well deserved. A slave should know better.

She put down her head again, trembling.

She then understood that he approved of her punishment, that he recognized its suitability, and that, in similar circumstances, she would receive no less at his hands. She realized then that she was a slave, and even at his hands, should he one day own her, would be treated as what she was, a slave, and nothing more, as was appropriate.

When a barbarian male recovers his manhood, it is not likely to be relinquished.

I was concerned, however, at the interest taken in the blond slave by Pertinax, for she belonged, as I had learned, to Lord Nishida. It can be quite dangerous for one fellow to take too great an interest in the slave of another. A subtle line exists in such matters. Many masters, in their pride and vanity, and as evidence of their wealth, good fortune, or taste, enjoy displaying their slaves, much as owners of various goods, of various sorts, enjoy displaying other sorts of properties, statuary, rare coins, artworks, fountains, veminium gardens, classical czehars, early editions of famous scrolls, antique kaissa sets, and such. For example, it is not unusual to see masters in the parks, in the plazas, and on the boulevards leading, or being preceded by, a leashed slave, often with her small hands braceleted behind her. The back-braceleting of slaves is quite common, for it draws the arms back, this accentuating the beauty of her breasts, and proclaiming her vulnerability. These masters usually relish the admiring glances cast upon their properties, the compliments received, and so on. This is not unusual. The case is similar with other animals, prize sleen, silken-coated kaiila, even saddle tharlarion. To the male, of course, the female slave is of particular interest. Thusly, in the case of the female slave, the natural possessiveness, the easily aroused suspicion and jealousy, of an owner is particularly engaged. It is one thing, for example, to welcome attention bestowed on a prize kaiila and even another's envy of one's possession of so splendid an animal, and quite another to suspect that the other may have designs upon the beast. Slave theft, as other forms of theft, is not unknown. To keep a slave chained at night then is not simply to keep her in place, to help her keep in mind that she is a slave, and to have her conveniently at hand if she might be desired, but, as well, to guard against the work of slave thieves. It is easy to surprise, gag, turn, and bind a woman, but it is quite another to free her from a chain. So slaves are often chained at night, even in public barns. Consequently, almost all slave theft, as opposed to the theft of other valuables, takes place during the Ahn of day. Another discouragement of slave theft, aside from commonalities of Home Stone, and such, is that slaves, particularly in the high cities, tend to be abundant, and cheap. Why risk the theft of a slave when one might purchase one, perhaps better, at the local auction house? Prices are sometimes depressed, too, particularly in the fall and winter. To be sure, some slaves are extremely desirable, and those tend to be the most carefully supervised, guarded, and watched.

I wondered if Lord Nishida knew of Pertinax's interest in the slave in question. I hoped not. On the other hand, as I understood it, Lord Nishida had no great personal interest in the slave, other than her political value, as a gift to a greater lord. Indeed, I was given to understand that he had, at least originally, reservations concerning the personality and character of the slave. Given the length of her hair, then, it might have been, once or more, shaved, perhaps as an indication of his encouragement that she hasten to improve herself. And, in any event, the hair might be used for catapult cordage. Indeed, in one of the storerooms, there were rolls of woven female hair, ready for cutting and fastening in the engines. Some was blond, and perhaps some of that had been harvested from the slave. The female slave who is a female, and the most female of all females, is often a vain creature, and will do much to avoid her shearing. The mere threat of shearing often does much to improve a girl. Female hair, incidentally, is much stronger, and more pliant, than common cordage. Too, it is weather resistant, as common cordage is not. Thus it is preferred on the walls of cities, at bridgeheads, in the fields, on the decks of warships, and such.

If Lord Nishida knew of the interest of Pertinax in his slave, he had not, at least as yet, as far as I knew, brought his disapproval, doubtless subtly, to the attention of Tarl Cabot, the commander of the tarn cavalry, who then, presumably, as Pertinax's friend, and commanding officer, would advise him of his possible indiscretion. Lord Nishida, of course, as I read him, was a highly intelligent, patient, rational man. He would doubtless proceed indirectly, and politely. If the girl was the property of Lord Okimoto, the matter might proceed differently. His Pani would be likely to set upon Pertinax, strip him, tie his feet together, and cast him, on a rope, over the stern, for the few sharks which tend, even in the open sea, to follow a ship, for the garbage. In any event, I thought Pertinax would be well advised to forget the slave. Surely there were many others he might consider with less risk, and several of these others, at least in my view, would bring a higher price off the block than the blonde, not that there was anything in particular wrong with her.

I will mention one anomaly, however, something that did not seem to fit into the common routines and practices of slave management on the great ship. It had to do with a particular group of slaves, from the Venna keeping area, where higher slaves were commonly housed. The anomaly was that this group was always brought to the deck hooded. The hoods were common slave hoods, opaque, enclosing the head completely, and fastened about the neck with a buckled strap, except that each buckle, once fastened, was secured in place by a small padlock, joining the buckle and a deep-sewn collar ring. The hood, thus, could not be casually removed. I did not understand the necessity, or advisability, of the hooding. It was explained to me that the slaves were of such beauty that hooding was a precaution against loosening the larls of desire amongst the crew, even the Pani, with the result of anticipated bloodshed, but I found this hard to believe. Whereas many women are beautiful, and many more beautiful than others, I doubted that amongst truly beautiful women there was that much difference. I was familiar with the markets in Jad, in Temos, in Brundisium, and Ar, and had seen enough beautiful slaves, indeed, women who had brought gold from buyers, rather than silver, to know that amongst beautiful women extraordinary differences, at least of figure and features, did not exist. Differences in price would be more commonly a function of origin, education, intelligence, training, and such things, than beauty. For example, a woman of high-caste origin would be likely to sell for more than a similar girl of a humbler origin. This was not to deny that the hooded slaves were doubtless beautiful, and, certainly, as they were tunicked, there was no doubt about the attractiveness of their figures. Indeed, most seemed at, or near, ideal block measurements, those measurements sought by professional slavers before bringing their merchandise to the large, sawdust-covered pedestal from which they would be vended. The thought crossed my mind that perhaps the hoods were emplaced to conceal the identity of the slaves, but there seemed no point to this as there would be few on the ship, or, presumably, at its destination, to whom their identity would be of any interest. As it is said, the identity of a slave is given to her by the collar. In this sense, there is only one identity for a slave, that she is a slave. The hoods would not be worn, of course, in the privacy of the Venna area itself. Perhaps that was why the observation panel in the door of the Venna area was fastened shut, and could not be slid aside, as that of the Kasra area, below. They would be hooded before leaving the area, and unhooded after their return to the area. It might also be noted that this group, when brought through the corridors and up the companionways to the open deck was in belly coffle. In this way, a single rope, tied snugly about their bellies, held them together, a rope which, given the delight of their figures, even though their hands were free, could not be slipped. All in all, I did not understand the nature of the group, or the reasoning behind the hooding. The belly coffle, of course, given the hooding, was a sensible arrangement. It tended to keep the girls together, and would reduce the likelihood of accidents. In their exercising, the two free ends of the rope were usually fastened about masts, commonly the third and fourth mast. The deck of a ship, the structures and paraphernalia about, the footing often uncertain, sometimes difficult, is a venue no rational person would choose to traverse blindly. Even were one not hooded, the open deck might be dangerous; the great ship, after all, despite its breadth, was a narrow, moving platform, little more than a pitching twig, so to speak, in the midst of a wide, deep, capricious sea.

As mentioned, of late, ropes had been strung about the deck, rather in the fashion that such ropes are used in rough seas. This seemed puzzling to me, as the weather was clear. I have also mentioned the closure of hatches, and the restriction of the open deck primarily to officers and the duty crew. All of this, given the weather, made no sense to me. As I was soon to relieve Aeacus at the foremast's platform and ring, I felt entitled to come early to the open deck. As mentioned, it was close below decks.

I looked about.

Tarl Cabot was at the bow, below the stem castle, scanning the horizon with a Builder's glass. There were some dark clouds, or what I took to be dark clouds, on the horizon, both to the north and south. As I had frequently served with the commander, largely at his assignment, prior to the fate of Seremides, whom I no longer regarded as a threat, I decided to stand near to him, at the rail. As it did not seem appropriate that I address him, I remained silent, hoping he might recognize me. He looked about, and smiled. "Tal, Callias," he said. I gathered I had been less subtle than I had intended, but he did not seem offended. "Tal, Commander," I said. He understood, I suppose, that I hoped to speak with him. He made things easy. It was his way.

He handed me the glass. "What do you see?" he asked. "I see little," I said, "three dark clouds, one to starboard, two to port."

It pleased me that he had asked my opinion.

"Rain?" he inquired.

"I see no curtain of darkness beneath the clouds, and thus it is not rain," I said, "but doubtless they are rain clouds."

"Do you anticipate a storm?" he asked.

"I think not, from the sky," I said. Surely that was evident.

"You think they are rain clouds?" he said.

"Certainly," I said.

"I am told," he said, "by Lord Nishida that they are not clouds."

"What then?" I asked.

"Smoke?" he said.

"Impossible," I said. "There is nothing to burn, there is only the sea."

"I am told," he said, "that such things are not smoke."

"Clouds, then," I said.

"No," he said, taking back the glass. "Ash," he said.

I recalled the coating on the sails some days earlier, the staining on the canvas, the granular, sootlike darkness on the deck, the brief sense of something stifling about, how, for a moment or two, it had been hard to breathe.

"There was ash before," I said.

"What might be its source?" he asked.

"I know not," I said. "I am afraid. Perhaps from the Sardar, a sign of the displeasure of Priest-Kings."

"The Sardar is far," he said.

"True," I said.

"No natural origin?" he said.

"No," I said, "there is nothing to burn in the water."

"Do you know the name of these waters?" he asked.

"No," I said.

"There are various names," he said, "the Raging Sea, the Sea of Fire."

"The sea is calm," I said. "Thassa sleeps."

"She may awaken," said Cabot.

"I understand little of what is occurring," I said. "Why, in a gentle sea, are the storm ropes strung, why must the hatches, in warm weather, remain closed, why are few now allowed on deck?"

"I too know very little about these things," said Cabot.

"At least," I said, "we are no longer pursued by the fleet of Lord Yamada." This seemed clear, from the reports of the mizzenmast watch.

"Why?" asked Cabot.

"I do not know," I said. "Perhaps they cannot match our speed."

"Surely," he said, "you note we have spread no more than a fifth of our canvas, and are moving slowly."

"True," I said.

"Why?" he asked.

"I do not know," I said.

"We are proceeding with caution," he said.

"Why?" I asked.

"I do not know," he said.

"The sea is calm, the sky clear," I said.

"There is ash in the distance," he said.

"It is far away," I said.

"True," he said.

"I see no danger," I said.

"Nor I," he said.

The bar sounded.

"The watch turns," I said. "I must relieve Aeacus."

"Do not neglect to fasten the safety rope," said Cabot.

"The sea is calm," I said, "unusually so."

"Do it," he said.

"Yes, commander," I said.

To be sure, this was a matter of routine with me.

"Following the recall," he said, "a count of weapons was made."

"Yes?" I said.

"Several are missing," he said.

I nodded. I was not surprised.

"Callias," he said.

"Commander?" I said.

"If you were the admiral of the fleet of Lord Yamada," said Cabot, "and you outnumbered your enemy ten or more to one, would you not press on, hoping to bring about an engagement, even if weeks later?"

"Yes," I said, "I would press on."

"And yet the fleet soon desisted in its pursuit."

"Yes," I said.

"Why?" he asked.

"I do not know," I said.

"I fear," he said, "we will soon learn."

I then ascended the ratlines, to relieve Aeacus.

Chapter Eighteen

I Converse with a Slave

"Doubtless you are pleased to see me so?" she said.

I pointed to the deck and she knelt, angrily, before me.

"Head down," I said.

She put her head down.

"Yes," I said, "I like to see you as you are."

She was in a light, brown, soiled work tunic, of simple rep-cloth, little more than a rag, which clung about her beauty.

The light yoke was still across her shoulders, and, suspended from it, on two short chains, each culminating in a hook, were two pails. As she knelt, the pails could rest on the deck.

I had accosted her from behind, as she had approached the rail, with her burden. "Slave," I had said, sharply.

"Master!" she said, the instantaneous, unthinking response of a collar girl. That pleased me.

"Turn about," I had said.

She complied, the pails swinging on their short chains.

"Stand straightly," I said. She was not a free woman. Did she not know she was a slave before a free man?

I walked about her.

She knew herself considered.

It is common to so scrutinize slaves.

They are familiar with this sort of thing from the first chain that is put on them.

"You recognized my voice," I said.

"Yes," she said, bitterly.

I approached her, with master closeness.

This did not please her.

"Lift your chin," I said.

I then adjusted her collar. I lifted it up, against the bottom of her chin, and then put it back, and pulled it a bit, straightening it, against the back of her neck. She was thus reminded that she wore it.

"You may lower your chin," I said.

She regarded me, her eyes flashing with fury.

I smiled, amused, and this further enflamed the small, lovely property.

A slave is permitted the pride of a slave, of course, but not that of a free woman. She is not a free woman. In her, such pride is a travesty, a joke. Its may also be a cause for discipline.

I wondered if she still thought of herself as a free woman, or was trying to think of herself as a free woman.

I did not think she would be successful.

I stepped back, regarding her.

The tunic she wore was fetching, if only because there was so little to it. It was high on her thighs, especially the left thigh, for her brand was evident. The hems were ragged. In places it was rent. It was muchly stained and soiled. In front it was torn to her belly.

It was then she had said, "Doubtless you are pleased to see me so," and I had pointed to the deck, and knelt her, head down.

"Yes," I had said, "I like to see you as you are."

She trembled in rage before me, but dared not raise her head.

"When," I said, "you were the Lady Flavia of Ar, high in the city, confidante of the Ubara herself, I would suppose you did not anticipate that you would one day kneel collared before one who was once a mere guard."

"No," she said.

"'No'?" I said.

"No," she said, "—Master."

"I note," I said, "that you bear wastes."

She was silent.

These are borne to the rail, where they are emptied, following which the pails, seriatim, on a long rope, are rinsed in the sea, thereafter to be returned to the chain hooks on the yoke.

"Only the lowest of slaves are put to such labors," I said.

"Some are so punished," she said.

"Are you being punished?" I asked.

"No," she said.

"Then you are amongst the lowest of slaves," I said.

"Or deemed so," she said, keeping her head down.

"You are of the Kasra keeping area," I said.

"Yes," she said.

"From what area are the wastes?" I inquired.

"From the Venna area," she said.

"Then," I said, "the girls of the Kasra area dispose not only of their own wastes, but those from the Venna area, as well."

"Yes," she said. "There the wastes are placed outside the heavy door. We do not enter that area."

"Did you know," I asked, "that the higher slaves are housed in the Venna area, and the lower in the Kasra area?"

"May I look up?" she asked.

"Yes," I said.

"No," she said, "I did not know that."

"Doubtless there are exceptions," I said.

"I trust so," she said.

"One would certainly not wish for a higher slave to dispose of her own wastes," I said.

"One supposes not," she said.

"That would be deplorable," I said.

"Doubtless," she said.

"Would you like to be moved to the Venna area?" I asked.

"Certainly," she said.

"Its deck is higher, its air is better," I said.

"How might this be arranged?" she asked.

"I need only broadcast the matter of your former identity, your fugitive status, the bounty involved, and such."

She looked up in terror. Then she looked about, frightened. We were much alone. From some yards away she would appear to be no more than an accosted work slave. "Please do not, Master!" she begged.

"The Kasra area now seems more attractive," I speculated.

"I do not want to be impaled," she whispered.

"You are in little danger of that," I said. "You are far at sea, in waters scarcely suspected, even by those of the far islands. Who here could bring you to Ar? How could it be done? Her walls are thousands of pasangs away."

"Eventually," she said, "—if we were to return."

I was not at all sure we would return. Who knew the mysteries at the World's End?

"Then, certainly," I said.

"Master is free," she said. "He is a man, he is strong, he is a warrior. I am small, weak, helpless, a woman, and a slave. He could easily bring me to Ar."

"Yes," I said.

"Would Master bring me to Ar?" she asked.

"You are no Talena, no false Ubara, no unmatched prize," I said, "but the bounty on you, even so, is not negligible. It might purchase a galley, several slaves."

"Some slaves," she said, "have been exchanged for a city. Might one not be worth a galley, and might not one slave be worth several slaves?"

"It would depend on the slave," I said.

"Buy Alcinoë!" she said.

"Only a slave begs to be purchased," I said.

"I am a slave!" she said.

"You were always a slave," I said, "even in Ar."

"Yes," she said, defiantly, "I was always a slave, even in Ar!"

"And now," I said, "you are where you belong, in a collar!"

"Yes, Master!" she said.

"You are not for sale," I said.

"If I were for sale," she said, "would you bid for me?"

"I would think about it," I said.

She pressed her lips to my boots. "I would be a slave of slaves to you!" she said. "Even in Ar I dreamed of myself, collared, in your arms!"

"It is interesting," I said, "to have the former Lady Flavia of Ar so before me."

"She is at your feet," she said, "now no more than a pathetic, petitioning slave."

"Perhaps she wishes her former identity kept secret," I said.

"Tell no one," she begged.

"I do not need to," I said.

"Master?" she said, looking up.

"You are clever," I said.

"I would give myself to you!" she said.

"You need not," I said. "If I buy you, you are mine."

"Master?"

"Does the tarsk give herself to the tarsk buyer?"

"Even from Ar I have loved you!" she said.

"As a free woman?" I asked.

"No," she said, angrily, bitterly, tears in her eyes, "as a conquered, abject slave her master!"

"I have little to fear from you," I said.

"I do not understand," she said.

"Were I to spare you from the impaling spear," I said, "and it were we alone, only we, who knew your identity, might I not expect a knife in the night, poison in the proffered goblet of paga?"

"No!" she said. "From the moment I first saw you I sensed you were my master. I fought this, I amused myself with you, I tormented you, but I wanted you to tear my veils and robes from me, to cast me to your feet, to lock me in your collar!"

"Interesting," I said.

"I wanted to be owned," she said, "to be a possession, and yours!"

"It is hard to know if you are more clever or more beautiful," I said, "but I think you are not as clever as you think."

"Master?"

"Your secret is not ours alone," I said.

"Seremides knows," she said, "but is helpless, not to be feared, ruined!"

"Even before the Vine Sea," I said, "he knew he could not bring you alone to Ar, for the price on his own head. He could accomplish such a thing only in the case of Talena, whose capture and delivery would guarantee his own amnesty. Accordingly he would require confederates."

"He may not, as yet, have enlisted them!" she said.

"It is my speculation that Tyrtaios knows," I said, "and perhaps certain others of their circle."

"Surely not!" she said, alarmed.

"There are possibly others, from Ar, or elsewhere, who may know, or suspect, as well," I said. "Seremides' interest in you has been long noted, even from early in the voyage, by several, for example by Lords Nishida and Okimoto, and the tarnsman, Cabot. They may not know your identity, but they surely suspect something of the sort, a fugitive status, a possible bounty, and such, and after suitable inquiries might well discover your former identity. Indeed, they need only see that you are delivered to Ar, where your identity, as that of various other fugitives, would be soon determined."

"I am lost!" she moaned. "Protect me!"

"Perhaps it will be I," I said, "rather, who would bring you to Ar."

"Yes," she whispered, "perhaps it will be you."

"You have little to fear at present," I said. "Indeed, I suspect that none of us will live to see Ar."

"Would you truly bring me to Ar?" she asked.

"I do not think so," I said.

"Why?" she asked.

"I do not like gold which is washed in blood," I said.

"Is there no other reason?" she asked.

"Your figure," I said, "is not without interest."

"My figure?" she said.

"Yes," I said.

"Ela!" she wept. "I am unworthy to be a free woman. I desire to be naked, and lusted for. I desire to be collared, and lavish kisses upon the feet of a master! I desire to love and serve, wholly, unstintingly, selflessly, as a slave!"

"You have work to do," I said.

"If others know my identity," she said, "why have I not been moved to the Venna keeping area?"

"If it were up to me," I said, "I would keep you where you are, in the Kasra area, with low slaves, that you might the sooner learn your collar."

"I assure Master," she said, "I am well learning it."

"And," I said, "those who know your identity, or suspect an identity of some interest, would not be eager to share that information. Let her stay then in the Kasra keeping area. There is less risk then of another suspecting something, and bringing her stripped and shackled before the throne of Marlenus."

"I love you, Master," she whispered. "Do you not love me, a little?"

I laughed at the absurdity of the question. "Love," I asked, "love—for a slave?"

"Forgive me, Master," she said.

"Be about your work," I said.

She struggled to her feet, in the yoke, with its suspended buckets, and turned about, toward the rail.

I could not resist administering a sharp, stinging slap, below the small of the back.

She cried out and stumbled forward, almost spilling some of her noisome burden. Fortunately none was lost. She turned about, to look at me, more startled than reproachful, and I pointed to the rail, and she turned about again, and went to it, to empty the pails. I thought she walked nicely. As she had suggested, she was well learning her collar. Fortunately there was no free woman present, or her beating might have been ordered.

"That slave," said a fellow, passing by, "is well formed."

"Many are," I said.

I wondered if I might possibly care for a slave, one such as Alcinoë. I dismissed the thought as absurd. How soon they might attempt to exploit such a weakness. Let them remember what they are, slaves, and no more. Let them kneel, the whip held before them. Let them lick and kiss it, in all trepidation and deference, and hope that it will not be used upon them.

Chapter Nineteen

The Great Ship Is Tested;
I Have Beheld the Formation of Islands

"Ho, watch," called Tarl Cabot, from far below, on the deck.

I spun the Builder's glass in a circle, examining the same horizon, as ever.

"Nothing, commander," I called down, to the deck.

He then was making his way aft, perhaps to his quarters.

I was at my regular watch, at the platform and ring, on the foremast. The weather was warm, and the sea tranquil. I could not remember several successive days in which our progress had been as uneventful. I had seen little to justify the ominous nomenclature confided to me by Tarl Cabot, that this was the Raging Sea, the Sea of Fire, or such. We continued to encounter, ever more frequently, the porous, floating rocks. Too, there was often one or more of the mysterious clouds, or volumes of ash, or whatever they might be, on the horizon. The storm ropes remained in place, the hatches were kept closed, save for ingress and egress, and few were allowed on deck, other than officers, who were not about the business of the ship. There had been fights below decks, particularly amongst the armsmen, who chafed at their confinement. It was hot below decks, and the air grew foul. Men grew ugly. It must be miserable, I supposed, in the Kasra and Venna keeping areas, as well, the penned beasts sweating on their mats, in their chains. Girls now, I understood, vied to carry wastes, that they might, even in so humble and homely an activity, feel the fresh wind of Thassa tug at their tunics and sweep through their hair. The hatches and portals to the open deck were now guarded, from within, by Pani swordsmen. More than one man had died under their swords.

My conversation with Tarl Cabot, alluded to earlier, having to do with the fleet of Lord Yamada, and such, had occurred on the third day of the fifth week past the fourth passage hand. It was now four days later, the second day of the fifth passage hand.

I saw four slaves, below, with their yokes, emerging from a hatch, closed behind them, bringing wastes to the rail. One was the slave, Alcinoë. As far as I knew, she was still white silk. If there were others, I supposed them to be mostly in the Venna keeping area. Some men will pay more for a white-silk girl. Needless to say, white-silkers are rare in the markets. Many are red-silked within an Ahn of their purchase. An interesting form of white-silker is the bred slave, raised in the sheltered gardens and housings of a gynaeceum, who is raised with no knowledge of men, until, say, unhooded, say, on an auction block, chained to a man's slave ring, cast amidst the tables of feasting warriors, or such. Such girls, of course, are quite expensive. Most men prefer red-silkers, as their slave fires have commonly been ignited. At frequent intervals they become painfully needful. One speaks of chains, ropes, thongs, and such, and they are lovely and instructive accessories, not to be overlooked or ignored, and are surely useful, as well, for inescapable custodial purposes, but it seems clear that the mightiest bonds, within which the slave is helpless, and forever ruined for freedom, are her needs, her slave needs, both physical and psychological, cruelly aroused by masters. Women, their master's properties, find their meaning, and their true self, in bondage. They are content, and whole, only at his feet. Sometimes slaves, before their vending, are starved of a master's touch for days. They then are desperately needful on the block, piteously supplicatory of purchase. I looked down from the platform and ring, at a particular slave, one I feared I was finding of interest, far below, Alcinoë. Already in her, I thought, even though she might as yet be white silk, there lurked a remarkable sexual latency, doubtless far greater than the naive slave now suspected. Doubtless she would be astonished at the transformation which would, as she was collared, eventually be wrought in her. Perhaps at first she might be terrified, or dismayed, to discover herself become so helpless, the victim and prisoner of needs so fierce and commanding, so uncompromising and uncontrollable, but later, though helpless in their throes, she, as her sisters, would rejoice in the thrashing ecstasies of the choiceless vessel of a master's pleasure. In her conquest and ravishing she is raised to the stars, if only to be scornfully cast again to earth, he finished with her, to sob her gratitude, and her hope that she might be again, at her master's pleasure, subjected to the enforced raptures of the conquered slave. Speak to such a woman of freedom? She has known bondage. She would rather die than leave her master.

From the platform and ring I looked down at the slave, in her work. She was not unattractive. How luscious are such nicely curved, worthless, meaningless, degraded objects! How men desire them! How different they are from free women, a thousand times inferior, a thousand times superior.

It is easy to understand how it is that men will kill for them.

Yes, I thought, she would doubtless be astonished at the transformation which she, the former Lady Flavia of Ar, would undergo. She would then find herself other than she had been, now irrecoverably different.

It is often amusing to see a woman who denies that she is sexual, and that she can be made so, and prides herself on her inertness, frigidity, and superiority to desire, put in chains, and, within Ehn, transformed into a begging slave. And that is the merest beginning.

Later, in her cage, she feels the collar on her throat, with both hands. She moves it about. It is well on her. It cannot be slipped. She then grasps the bars, kneeling. She squirms in the small cage, in which she cannot stand, naked, uneasy. She has begun to suspect what it might be, to be a slave. She wonders who will be her master.

I looked down again from the platform and ring on the slave, now, on its dangling, swaying rope, rinsing a wastes pail. I remembered her, at the foot of the second mast. Indeed, I recalled the view of the physicians, from long ago, early in the voyage. I had little doubt that slave fires might soon, when men chose, rage mightily and irresistibly in that lovely little belly. After a few days as a red-silker, I could imagine her crying out publicly, even before free women she had known, on an auction block, even in Ar, in misery and gratitude, at the deft, gentle, demonstrative touch of the auctioneer's whip. Her slave needs give a master much power over a woman. And it is pleasant, of course, to exercise such power. It is one of the pleasures of the mastery.

The girl, hand by hand, foot by foot, drew up the pail, swirled water within it, and cast the water back to the sea. She then undid its rope, and bent to fasten the second pail, emptied, to the rope, to rinse it, as well.

The other three girls had returned below decks.

The stem castle deck was empty. There was the helmsman, of course, on the helm deck. Two officers were on the stern-castle deck, but, at the distance, I could not identify them. Interestingly fewer officers were now in evidence than some days before, even after the stringing of the storm ropes. This was supposedly by order of the ship's governing lords, Nishida and Okimoto.

I had fastened the safety rope about my waist, as usual, but this precaution, day after day, seemed ever more unnecessary, if not foolish.

How could the sea be more calm?

Perhaps Thassa slept.

I saw no sign of her awakening.

There was no sign of the fleet of Lord Yamada. It had not followed us.

The sea was calm.

I did see, rather forward, on the starboard side, a dark cloud, far off. I had not noticed it before.

Two or three Ehn passed.

I sensed, suddenly that something was different, though I saw nothing. The girl, too, stopped in her work. I wondered if this strangeness was only felt forward. I saw no change aft, on the helm deck, or the stern-castle deck.

I suddenly cried out, in horror, "Seize the ropes! Seize the ropes!"

Before us, the sea had opened, and, before the ship, with steep sides, there appeared a valley, water pouring down its sides, as into a vast hole. "Seize the ropes!" I cried.

The bow of the ship paused, teetering, as though at the edge of a cliff, and then, suddenly, it plunged downward, and slid to the side of that steep, pouring, liquid valley, and went over to her side, and continents of water poured over her, and then engulfed her, and she spun about, for all her size, like a child's toy, and we were under water, turning, and I was swept from the platform and ring, and flung to the end of the safety rope. Then the great ship rotated, buffeted, in the sea, and was washed upward, and she righted herself, and her bow, like a breaching leviathan, the northern whale, broke the surface and I fell back against the mast, gasping for air. The great ship pitched and turned as might a straw in a maelstrom. The waters churned about her, and she was smote as with discordant, hurtling rivers in the sea, and I feared her timbers, though of mighty Tur wood, might be stove in. The ship leapt forward, as waves rose behind her, and then her bow again went under the water, and I clung to the mast, and saw the sea not feet below me. The ship rose from the water, water pouring from her, as from the back of an emerging sea tharlarion. I saw, far below, the small figure of the slave, on a storm rope, both arms fastened about it. Behind us I saw steam rising from the sea, and the water began to boil. The helm deck and stern-castle deck were empty. I feared the calking might be melted from the timbers. The bit of canvas we had flown was soaked, and heavy, and could barely move in the breeze which, but moments ago, had gentled us our course. The ship rocked, and, I feared, was turning back, toward the steaming sea. I saw a figure clamber to the helm deck, a hatch quickly sealed behind it. It was Tarl Cabot, the tarnsman, who threw his weight, as that of two men, against the helm pole. The ship, the breeze shaking in the soaked canvas, turned west. I saw another mighty trough before us, and tried to cry out, but no sound came from my throat, and I clung again to the mast. Twice more was the great ship submerged, and twice more, turned and buffeted, she rose to the surface. Steam rose from about us. Water churned, and the sea was as a cauldron, hissing and bubbling. And Cabot, struggling at the helm pole, held the course west, steadily. The sea, three times, had fallen away beneath us. It was as though the floor of the sea itself had shuddered and cracked, opening a world into which water had poured. But this was not what was most frightening, and I saw what many men know of, but few men have seen. Mighty Thassa would give berth. I saw rising, on either side, and before, mountains rising from the sea, mountains of fire, bursting alive, mountains moving, rising, run with molten streams of rock, some loose like flaming water, some patient and thick, dully red, and from these strange mountains, cast into the air were clouds of flaming rock, cinders, and ash. The air fumed and stung with particles, and I fought to breathe, and yet feared to do so. Ash clung about my face and mouth. My eyes stung. How could one live in such air? Surely one would suffocate, or strangle, and collapse, dying in such a fog of cinders and gas. The cracking noises of the angry, burning mountains, too, like thunder at one's ear, almost deafened one. A gigantic rock fell into the sea, hissing, to port. The sails, I feared, in the falling, flaming debris, would have been ignited, had they been dry. Cinders and ash rained on the deck. Cabot was screaming on the helm deck, for men to emerge, to see to the ship. There was fire on the stern-castle deck, and the bulwarks to starboard were aflame.

Coughing, eyes stinging, burned by cinders, I regained the platform and ring. I looked down to the deck.

Cabot had now been joined by Pertinax and Tajima, and a number of Pani and armsmen were emerging from the lower decks, forward. I saw Lord Nishida among them, gesturing, crying out. Men ran to smother flames. Buckets were cast, and heated water drawn aboard, to be splashed on the flames. Many men had put cloths about their faces.

I muchly desired to free myself of the safety rope, descend the ratlines, and aid in the protection of the ship, but I knew I would not do so. It was not that I feared to leave my post, or feared to be flogged, or killed, for doing so. Rather, it was my watch, and I was of the ship.

The deck was black, and pitted.

The heated air had dried the sails, and they now billowed, as the wind had risen. The course, now held by mariners, continued west, then west by southwest, taking its way amidst new-risen, flaming, towering mountains.

It became possible to breathe without pain.

Later, a light rain had begun to fall, for the first time in several days. This, I take it, may have been a result of the stifling, burning air ascending to the high, cold sky, familiar to jacketed tarnsmen, where, condensing, it fell as a soft, washing rain. Had we not been on the ship, I feared we might not have escaped death. Fixed in place, there would have been little to do but die.

I no longer saw the slave, but I knew that she had survived. Originally, I feared she might have drowned, her arms locked, desperately, frozen, about the storm rope, but, later, the ship righted and emergent, though cruelly pitching, I had seen her move, trembling, struggling to clutch the rope even more tightly. And later, as the ship had sought to effect its escape, I had seen her react, stung by the falling, fiery cinders. As she was no longer in view, she would have been conducted, or sent, below. Her body had been blackened in the soot and ash. I had seen her scratch cinders from her hair, slap frenziedly at the left side of her tiny tunic, where the material had caught fire. Then she had clung ever more tightly to the soaked, heavy rope. There would doubtless be marks on her body from it. I suspected that her hands and arms would have to have been pried from it.

So the slave had survived.

Excellent.

You must understand, of course, that there was nothing personal in this, nothing on the score of which I need castigate myself.

Surely one might be similarly pleased, and even legitimately so, at the survival of any other animal, as well, say, a verr or kaiila. The slave, as the verr or kaiila, and other such animals, has value. For example, she may, at one's pleasure, be sold.

Understand, clearly, that she meant nothing to me.

There was nothing personal in my feelings.

My concern was purely on behalf of the ship.

One does not care for a slave.

That is absurd.

She is not a free woman.

She is a slave.

Her purpose is to be mastered, totally, to be worked, commonly in the performance of repetitious, servile tasks, and to satisfy, obediently and unquestioningly, and helplessly, the lowest, most bestial, and carnal of her master's appetites. The free woman may be conducted to public readings and song dramas; the slave is to be at the foot of her master's couch, chained to his slave ring.

Of what value is a woman to a man if she lacks slave skills?

Even a brilliant woman, witty and articulate, learned, of the high Scribes, collared, her blue robes exchanged for a rag, must apply herself to new studies, the use of her lips and tongue, of her small fingers and glossy hair. Aside from homely tasks, she will be taught cosmetics and ornamentation. To the snap of a whip she will learn slave dance. If the master is cruel, earrings may be fastened in her ears. On the high bridges she will feel wind on her legs and arms, and in her hair, and on her unveiled features, on which men may look with impunity.

She is now a slave.

She belongs to her master.

Collared, she is freer now than she would have ever dreamed possible.

She hopes to prove a suitable slave to him, attentive, humble, grateful, zealous, and skilled.

Her errands done, she hurries to his quarters, to kneel before him.

Many men had now come to the deck, which swarmed with mariners and armsmen. I saw even Lord Okimoto.

About us were several of the fire mountains, less fearful now. We threaded our way amongst them with care.

The storm ropes were loosened and coiled, to be stowed below decks. The hatches, as the sky was clear, remained open. I did not understand it at the time, but the "ridge" had been passed. We were leaving the Raging Sea, the Sea of Fire.

I wondered why the slave, earlier, had not accompanied her collar sisters below, but had lingered on deck. Surely she knew she was risking a switching.

I trusted that she had been sent to the washing tubs, that her hair and body, and tunic, might be cleaned, and that physicians had tended to her burns.

Perhaps, by now, she was back in the Kasra keeping area, on her chain, run to its ring by her mat.

Though the hatches and portals had been sealed, I supposed that the great ship would have shipped some water. As I had heard no call for the pumps, I supposed it was negligible, and confined to the holds, where men might wade, and soon hand buckets from one to the other.

I saw Tersites on the stem-castle deck.

I thought him likely to be satisfied with the great ship.

She had come through the Raging Sea, the Sea of Fire.

I wondered if the slave, below, once cleaned, and salved, had been beaten. She had not accompanied her collar sisters back below decks. Her hair and body had been covered with soot and ash, her skin had been pelted with dust and scalding cinders, her tunic had been partly burned. Yes, I thought, she would doubtless have been switched. A slave is expected to care for herself, to keep herself clean, well groomed, and attractive, as she is her master's property.

The great hatch was rolled back. I gathered that tarns would be exercised. I also saw, for the first time, at the side of Tarl Cabot, as men drew back in fear, a large sleen, which dragged its left, hind foot. I had heard the animal a number of times before, but I had never seen it until now. Heeling Cabot, behind the lame sleen, was his barbarian slave, Cecily. She was attractive. I did not doubt but what she would bring good coin off the block. I wondered if the barbarian lands might not be rich with such women, ripe for bringing to the markets of Gor. By the morrow, I hoped that the *kajirae*, so long confined below decks, might be brought to the open deck, as before, for air and exercise. Alcinoë, I supposed, who would have incurred the displeasure of her keepers, would remain below, on her chain.

I scanned the horizon, that line below the sky, with the glass. Thousands of times I, and others, had done so.

How eager we were to see tiny irregularities in the distance, initially almost undiscernible, perhaps tiny, beckoning flecks of green or brown.

Sometimes, interestingly, particularly after long at sea, one sees such things when they are not there. It is well then to hold back, until one is sure, until matters are clear, at least to the glass. More than one watch had been flogged for crying out the sight of land, stirring crews, rousing jubilation, where there was no land.

It suddenly occurred to me that we must be at least two or

three days from land, else the tarns, the concealment of whose existence seemed a matter of such moment to Lords Nishida and Okimoto, would remain concealed. To be sure, perhaps we were months from land. I doubted that, however, if only because of the fire mountains. Might not such cataclysmic births herald a world or worlds similarly formed? Perhaps, I suspected, we were not far from the World's End, the Homeland of the Pani.

I sensed pressure on the ratlines to my right.

It was Leros.

"Tal," he said, looking about, clinging to the ratlines. The sight was indeed impressive.

"Tal," I said. "The jard flies swiftly."

"To where feasting may be found," he said.

He joined me at the platform and ring. "I will linger a moment," I said. I looked about. I had never before seen the formation of islands.

Chapter Twenty

**It Is Suspected That Land Is Nigh;
Many Slaves Are Allowed the Liberty
of the Deck; I Take the Opportunity
to Interrogate a Particular Slave;
No Cry of Interest Had Yet
Emanated from the High Watch**

Having passed the "ridge," and leaving the Raging Sea, the Sea of Fire, in our wake, we had turned north, and then north by northwest.

Though no word was spoken to the crew we suspected we were near land, that the long voyage of the great ship was almost done. Many were the looks cast forward. Some men, off duty, climbed the ratlines, and masts. The cry, "What, ho?" was now often addressed to the high watches, which were now maintained on every mast. On some decks there was singing. The wealth in the lockers, gleaned from the derelicts in the Vine Sea, was counted, and recounted. Many men, were they now in Brundisium, in Venna, in Ar, would have been rich in coin, in silks, in perfumes, and jewels. There was little fear now, even amongst the simplest of our armsmen and mariners, that the great ship might plunge from the planet's edge. The Pani were imperturbable. Lords Nishida and Okimoto seemed cheerful. We had the sense that some, if not us, found these familiar waters. They had known, for example, of the dangers of the Raging Sea, the Sea of Fire. The tarns were again housed below decks, which suggested the secrecy of their existence was again a matter of concern.

"You are often about," I said to her.

"I hope Master is not displeased," she said.

"You have many duties, it seems," I said.

"Yes, Master," she said.

"But not at the moment," I said.

"No, Master," she said.

It was not unusual now to see slaves on deck. I took it this was an additional indication that some change was nigh. It was only later that I began to suspect the rationale for this surprising liberty.

I had her on her knees before me. A slave commonly speaks to a free man only from her knees.

"Are you in need of discipline?" I asked.

"I trust not," she said.

The slave had often been in my vicinity, even when it seemed there was no cause for this proximity.

I wondered at this.

When I might glance in her direction, she would put her head down, shyly. Seeing my eyes clearly upon her, she would immediately kneel, her head to the deck. This behavior, of course, is not inappropriate in a slave. Whereas this sort of thing, frequenting the vicinity of a free man, is not unusual in an enamored slave, desperate to fall within the purview of a master's glance, hoping to be noticed, though she be only slave, it seemed unaccountable in the case of one who had once been the Lady Flavia of Ar. Did she not know that such behavior might be misunderstood, that it might be construed as a plea to be enfolded in a man's arms, to be purchased, to be put on his chain? The slave cannot choose her master, but she has many ways in which to plead that it will be she who is chosen.

The slave is not as helpless as she may seem. She has the weapon of her beauty, the tool of her desirability.

Could she be such a slave?

"It is fortunate," I said to her, "that in the Raging Sea, the Sea of Fire, you were not washed from the deck."

"Warned," she said, "I had time to seize the storm rope."

Seeing the suddenly opening valley in the sea before us, I had cried out a warning.

"Master saved my life," she said.

"The warning," I said, "was of general import."

"Even so," she said.

"But I am pleased," I said, "that you survived."

"The heart of a slave is gladdened," she said.

"Why?" I asked.

"Perhaps," she said, "a slave is of concern to Master."

"How could that be," I asked, "as she is a slave?"

"Were you not pleased?" she asked.

"Certainly," I said.

"I do not understand," she said.

"You are an item of ship's property," I said. "In saving you, I saved an item of ship's property."

"Is that all?" she asked.

"What more could there be?" I asked.

"I see," she said.

"You should not have been on deck in the first place," I said. "You dallied. You lingered. You did not accompany your chain sisters below. I trust that after you were cleaned and tended, the backs of your pretty thighs were kissed with the switch for that."

"They were!" she said.

"Why did you linger?" I asked.

"Can Master not guess?" she said.

This answer annoyed me. There is a fine line between deference and boldness, as between boldness and sauciness, and between sauciness and insolence. I considered cuffing her.

"Master?" she said.

How innocent she looked.

Yes, I thought, a cuffing might do her some good.

I recalled that she had proclaimed her love for me, the helpless love of a worthless slave.

What a liar was the collared slut!

Could she have truly risked the switch, that she might be longer in my view? That she might be longer in my presence, that she might be nearer to me, that she might, for a time, in effect, despite the breadth of the deck and the height of the high watch, be alone with me?

Even when the storm ropes were strung?

Did she think that I would be so much a fool that I would

take her for an enamored slave, the sort of slave who begs to be at a master's feet?

Doubtless she muchly feared that I might one day take her to Ar, for the bounty.

How clever she was in her collar.

Perhaps, I thought, I should take her to Ar, and cast her to the feet of the great Marlenus. She was no Talena, but she had stood high in the realms of treachery which had so beleaguered glorious Ar.

I had told her that I did not care for gold washed in blood, but I supposed she had not believed me. What might a man favor more than gold, a slave at his feet? Perhaps, I thought.

Could the slave, I wondered, be truly enwrapped in the toils of love?

How absurd that would be!

But I knew that no love could compare with the love of a slave for her master, the love of a vulnerable, helpless slave, who may be beaten or sold on a whim, for her master.

Is it not the most profound, the most helpless, the deepest, of all loves?

But the love of a slave, I knew, was to be scorned.

For she is a slave.

"Can Master not guess?" she asked, again.

"I think not," I said.

"I see," she said.

She was not the only slave who had been about me. Iole, too, had often been about, as had other slaves about other men. I saw the fellow who had been flogged on account of the blond slave, whom he had kissed with a might that suggested she might have been his, several days ago, and the blond slave who had been put under the slave lash for so provoking him. When he had not been looking, she had heeled him. When he turned, she knelt, her head to the deck. Then she had lifted her eyes to him, filled with tears. Twice he had cuffed her away, but each time she had returned to him, putting her hair about his feet. Once Iole had dared to brush against me, as though inadvertently, and had then, as though in contrition and terror, knelt before me, begging forgiveness. Shortly thereafter I heard men cry out and, turning, I saw her and Alcinoë rolling about on the deck, tearing at one another's hair, screaming, kicking, biting, and scratching. "Behold," laughed a man, "young, unmated she-sleen!" "Yes," said another, "in the late spring!"

I guessed it was not easy to reach into that turning, twisting, rolling, screaming, sobbing, hysterical, biting, scratching frenzy but one fellow managed to get one hand in Iole's hair and one in that of Alcinoë, and dragged them apart, and, as they shrieked with pain, held them apart, while they tried, sobbing, their bodies wracked with pain and frustration, to kick the other. Suddenly one fellow said, sharply, "Position!" Instantly, reflexively, Iole and Alcinoë, frightened, knelt, back on their heels, knees spread, back straight, head up, looking ahead, neither to the left or right, the palms of their hands down, firmly, on their thighs. Both slaves, in the presence of the other, tried to spread their knees as little as possible, while still maintaining position, as though each might thereby seem superior to the other, as being closer to the position of a free woman. Both were breathing heavily, gasping, and the cheeks of each ran with tears, of anger, pain, and frustration. Both were bloodied, and the brief tunic of each was half torn from her fair form. I had little doubt that both would be well attended to later. "Oh!" cried Iole. "Oh!" cried Alcinoë. The fellow who had put them in position with a single word had, first Iole, and then Alcinoë, kicked their knees apart, far apart. And thus each was reminded of, or informed of, the sort of slave they were. I saw a sudden look of surprise, and then understanding, manifest itself in the features of Alcinoë. Though she might be white-silk, she was a pleasure slave. Had she truly thought that she, and her some two hundred collar sisters, on their chains, so beautiful, so vital, so carefully selected, had been brought across the breadth of mighty Thassa, all the way from continental, known Gor, merely to be tower slaves? I did not think it likely she would soon forget the two booted blows which had publicly spread her thighs, and their import.

"Are you in need of discipline?" I had asked.

"I trust not," she had said.

"What was the business between you and Iole?" I asked.

Their fight had occurred two days ago.

Both were now cleaned and tended, both brushed and combed, and both now in a fresh, pressed tunic.

"It is only a matter between slaves," said Alcinoë.

"What matter?" I asked.

"If I may," she said, "I would prefer not to speak."

"Very well," I said.

I saw no reason to press her in this matter.

"Are you not ashamed," I said, "to have behaved as you did, to have made such a spectacle of yourself?"

"The Lady Flavia of Ar," she said, "would have been ashamed."

"But not you?"

"No," she said.

"What would the Lady Flavia of Ar have done?" I asked.

"The Lady Flavia of Ar had power," she said. "Were the woman a slave, I would have purchased her, had her beaten, put in earrings, and sold out of the city."

"I see," I said.

I thought the former Lady Flavia of Ar might look well in earrings herself. They are inflicted, of course, only on the lowest and most despicable of slaves. The common slave fears earrings more than the slave lash or shearing. To be sure, they are attractive on a slave, and, eventually, a slave is likely to become quite proud of them, even defiantly arrogant, for what they say about her, about what she means to men and what may be expected of her in a man's hands. She is special on a chain. Much may be expected of her. Pierced ears, too, tend to improve a girl's price. For that reason, even in the absence of discipline, slavers sometimes pierce a girl's ears, to her misery and horror, before putting her on the block, a pierced-ear girl.

"And if," said Alcinoë, "the woman was free, and even of high caste, I would have arranged for her to be in a collar by nightfall, and, chained, hurried from the city, to some mean and distant market, from which, after piercing her ears, she would be sold for a pittance."

Yes, I thought to myself, the former lady Flavia of Ar herself would look quite well in earrings.

Is it not the ultimate degradation of a female slave?

"But," I said, "you are not the Lady Flavia of Ar."

"No," she said.

"You behaved as a slave," I said.

"I am a slave," she said.

"I trust that you and Iole," I said, "were well punished for your altercation."

Normally masters do not much mix in the squabbles of slaves but, in this case, damage had been done, slaves bloodied, and tunics torn. Too, the slaves, in response to the command, "Position," had not knelt properly.

"Yes, Master," she said. "We were tied, side by side, and well lashed."

"Who wept first?" I asked. "Who cried out first for mercy?"

"I," she said. "I wept first. I was weakest. I first cried out for mercy."

I was not surprised at this.

"After what stroke?" I asked.

"The second," she said.

"So soon," I said.

"Iole cried out after the fourth!" she said.

"Still," I said, "the second?"

"Master may recall," she said, "that long ago I was lashed."

"Yes," I said, "for lying. You claimed I had raped you."

"I remembered the blows," she said. "I was terrified to feel another! I knew what it would be like! One stroke and I knew! I cried for mercy after the second stroke. Iole laughed, even in her pain, but she, too, soon, cried out for mercy."

I was not surprised. They were both lovely female slaves.

"You fear the whip," I said.

"We all do," she said.

"Some free women," I said, "think that slaves are weak, that they fear the whip."

"I did not fear it when I was free," she said, "for I had never felt it."

"Many free women," I said, "scorn slaves for their fear of the whip."

"Let them be stripped and tied, and put under it," she said, "and see how long they scorn it, and how quickly they beg for the surcease of its attentions."

"It is a useful device in improving a slave," I said.

"Doubtless," she said.

"Perhaps you would do much to avoid it," I said.

"Yes, Master," she said, her head down.

"You are quite sensitive to pain," I said.

"So, too, is Iole!" she said. "So, too, are we all!"

I saw little of Iole now. She must now respond to the snapping of fingers of Aeacus, who seemed somewhat taken with her, after she had been half stripped by Alcinoë.

The five-stranded slave lash, of course, is designed to punish, and keenly. It is also designed not to mark, for one would not wish to lower the value of a slave.

There are differences, of course, amongst slaves.

"You are not a strong slave," I said.

"No," she said, "Alcinoë is a small slave, a weak slave, a helpless, vulnerable slave. She cries easily, she has little control over her emotions, her skin is much alive. It is thin, soft, and sensitive!"

I was pleased to hear this, for the body of such a woman can become a burning tissue of awareness. It is, far beyond that of duller women, alive and helpless, aware of the tiniest differences of temperature and air, and acutely so if naked or in a tunic; it is aware of the smallest differences in textures and fabrics, in the feel of fur, in the weaving of a mat under bare feet, the coolness of a scarlet tile, the whisper of silk on a thigh, the coarseness of a rope bound about her body, a strap on her wrist, the clasp of slave bracelets, holding her small hands behind her body, the weight of shackles on fair limbs.

"I am pleased you fear the whip," I said. I was indeed pleased, for in such a case, it need seldom, if ever, be used. To be sure, it is occasionally useful, like a stroke of the switch, to remind a girl that she is a slave. It is well for a girl to never be in the least doubt about that. Even the most loving and kindest of masters will enforce a perfect discipline on his chattel, which reassures her, and to which she is helplessly responsive, sexually and psychologically.

Never let her forget to kneel appropriately, and obey quickly. Never let her cease to be pleasing to her master.

The least imperfection in a slave is not to be tolerated, for she is a slave.

"I do fear it," she said. "Muchly so, terribly so, dreadfully so."

"Excellent," I said.

This is common in a woman whose body is much alive.

"It scalds me, and burns me, and each stroke immerses me in fire," she said. "It shows me no mercy!"

"Then you would try to be a good slave, would you not?" I asked.

"Yes, yes," she said, "Master."

"Good," I said. "How many strokes did you and Iole receive?"

"Ten," she said. "And in the end we were helpless in the ropes, unable to stand, our weight on our bound wrists, shuddering, sobbing, our bodies afire, from the encircling tentacles of the lash, scarcely able to breathe."

"If one of you had seriously injured the other, cost an eye, or such," I said, "it might have gone seriously with you."

She shuddered. "Yes, Master," she said.

"Your discipline," I said, "was administered by an armsman."

"Yes, Master," she said.

"You were courteous enough to thank him, I trust," I said.

"Yes, Master," she said. "Suspended in the ropes, in our pain, as we could, we sobbed our gratitude."

"The common point of a whipping," I said, "is to improve the slave."

"I think, Master," she said, "that we both are now much concerned to be better slaves, and more pleasing to our masters."

"You were both foolish," I said, "to try to keep your knees more closely together than prescribed."

"Each wished to appear superior to the other," she said.

"Surely you were taught to kneel with your knees apart," I said.

"Yes," she said. "But I did not even know that I was a pleasure slave!"

"You know now," I said.

"But I am white-silk!" she said.

I found this of interest.

"For now," I said.

"When am I to be opened, who is to open me?" she asked.

"I do not know," I said. "Perhaps after your sale, by whoever buys you."

She looked at me, wildly.

How helpless are slaves, as other animals.

"The whip, then," I said, "after your beating, was pressed to your lips, to be kissed."

"Yes, Master."

"And you kissed it?"

"Yes, Master," she said, "fervently, piteously, hoping that it would strike us no more."

"I am curious," I said, "to inquire into a familiar distinction, but now, particularly, in the case of the slave, Alcinoë, a slave of the ship of Tersites."

"Master?" she said, puzzled.

"You fear the whip," I said.

"Terribly, Master."

"You are subject to it," I said.

"Yes, Master," she said. "I am a slave."

"How do you feel about being subject to the whip?" I asked.

"I fear the whip," she said. "I am terrified of its stroke."

"Of course," I said.

This is common with high-grade slaves, delicate, well-formed, finely featured women, women of high intelligence, profound emotion, and active imagination, irremediably sensate, tactually enlivened women, women keenly alive, women profoundly stirred by the floor beneath their knees, by leather thrust to their lips, profoundly responsive to the fingers of a man's hand on an ear lobe or thigh, women with helplessly sensitive bodies.

Such women, being so desirable, and alive, bring by far the highest prices off the block.

"I dread it," she said. "I will do anything to avoid its stroke."

"But," I said, "how do you feel about being subject to it?"

"Must I speak?" she asked.

"Yes," I said.

"I love it," she whispered.

"Speak further," I said.

"Must I?" she said.

"Yes," I said.

"It is hard to understand," she said. "I do not know if a man can understand it."

"Speak," I said.

"It is something I became aware of," she said, "when I first felt certain needs, and feelings, in my body. They were hard to understand. I looked about, and I saw the incredible, mighty differences between men and women, and understood that I, by nature or the will of Priest-Kings, was of that profoundly different sort, the woman. And I wondered why this should be, and what it might mean. How was I to understand it? What did it mean for my sex, and for me, who was of that sex? I felt myself somehow a part of that great difference, and union. Men were so aggressive, so possessive, so ambitious, so powerful, so strong, so proudly, so naturally, so unquestioningly, so intimidatingly so. We, on the other hand, were small, weak, soft, slight, and beautiful. Who was master, who was slave? Was nature to be denied? What of my feelings, my needs? Was I to pretend to be a man, in which sorry pretense I must fail, or should I listen to my heart, and acknowledge my difference? Nay, not only acknowledge this difference, but welcome it, celebrate it, acclaim it, rejoice in it! Is it not as meaningful, as glorious, as right, to be a slave as a master? Is one truly better than the other? Does the slave not need the master, and the master the slave? Is not each incomplete without the other? Of course, I tried to be as a man! I tried to live that mockery, that stunting lie. I sought to stand against them, rather than kneel gratefully at their feet! I flung myself, with like-minded women, into the games of power, exploiting my liberty to narrow and circumscribe that of men. How I thought I hated them, while I really wanted to be put in their chains. I used my sex, as I could, bestowing cordialities, hinting at favors, to influence men who, entrapped in the conventions of the cities, refrained from tearing away my veils and robes and putting me, as I deserved, in the bracelets of a slave. How natural then that they should seek the beauties of the paga taverns, that they should raid far cities to bring back women, much as I, naked, in coffles. How I, and my kind, hated slaves, women in their fitting place in nature, who, in radiance, and contentment, so joyful, were fulfilled by masters! How we envied those degraded, pathetic, despicable things in their tiny tunics, their bodies so bared, and collars, so unslippable, so closely encircling their throats, their thighs marked, as the animals they were, that all would recognize them as the properties of men. How cruel I was to my own slaves, making them suffer in proxy for my own self-hatred. How I kept them from men, that they might howl in anguish, and know something of my own unhappiness and deprivation. Then, to my horror, I found myself in a collar! How I fought the slave in me, until I met a man whose feet I yearned to kiss."

"You may continue to speak," I said.

"I am a woman," she said. "I suppose master cannot understand the rightfulness, the deliciousness, of the feeling that a woman has when she is dominated by a man. She responds, with her whole being, to his domination. In her subjection she feels most woman, most helplessly, most completely, most rightfully woman. She desires no choice. She rejoices to be put under his power."

I recalled a hundred slaves, a thousand slaves, on the streets of Ar, Jad, Brundisium, Temos, such places. I recalled the swaying hips of slave dancers, the proffering of paga, the extended hands of girls on the shelf, begging to be purchased.

"I want to be a slave," she said, "and love being a slave. I am a slave. I desire to be what I am. How can I be happy otherwise? To be sure, I am terrified, too, to be a slave. For I know what may be done with me, and how I may be treated. But I am content in a collar, for it is that in which I belong."

"You are destined to be a particular sort of slave," I said.

"I gather," she said, "—the pleasure slave."

"Like the others," I said.

"Even when I fastened myself in my own collar, as a ruse, as a disguise, long ago, in Ar," she said, "I felt sexual, alarmingly, troublesomely, disturbingly so. Master can well imagine then what it is to be fastened in that of another, one I cannot remove. My body, in its collar, is alive, and sexual. It tells me I am a woman, a slave, and a sexual being, a woman not her own but one who belongs to another, as a verr or tarsk might belong to another, one at the mercy of the master who may treat her as he wishes, and whom she must strive to please. Even white-silk, I can begin to sense something of what may become of me, how I will be transformed, how helpless I will be in the throes of passion, how I will be so much at a man's mercy, and will beg and cry out in need."

I had occasionally heard, even on the street outside a tavern's door, a girl cry out in relief and gratitude, the sound carrying from behind the leather curtain of an alcove itself.

"So, I gather," I said, "you love being subject to the whip."

"Yes," she said, "being subject to it. I do not want to feel it, of course, and will strive to keep it on its peg. But, knowing that it will be used on me, if I am not pleasing, thrills me. It reminds me that I am a slave, and must obey, and strive to please. It informs me that consequences will attend any laxity or slovenliness on my part, any imperfection in my service, any dissatisfaction on the part of my master. Is it not the symbol of the mastery? Does it not tell me I am an animal, that I am owned, and a slave? Perhaps my master will often have me kiss the whip, that I may thusly be reminded of my bondage."

"It seems," I said, "that you might enjoy being a pleasure slave."

"Better that than a tower slave, a laundress, a loom slave, a cooking slave," she said.

"You are a lascivious little beast?" I said.

"The pleasure slave in her master's arms," she said, "is the happiest, the most joyful, the truest of women."

"Or writhing in his bonds, his thongs, his chains," I said.

"Yes," she said.

A woman's helplessness, as is well known, is sexually stimulatory, sometimes almost unendurably so.

"It is my hope that my master will be kind to me," she said.

"He may," I said, "if he wishes, for amusement, bring you patiently to the brink of a yearned-for relief, one for which you are pathetically, beggingly desperate, and then abandon you, leaving you alone to thrash in helpless frustration."

"Surely not!" she said.

"You are a slave," I said.

"Master!" she protested.

"Perhaps you might beg prettily," I said.

"Yes, yes, yes!" she said. "Piteously, desperately!"

"He might be kind," I said. "Who knows?"

"I will try to be a good slave," she said.

"Do not think," I said, "because you are a pleasure slave, you will escape the common duties of slaves, cleaning, dusting, scrubbing, running errands, bargaining in the market, entertaining, cooking, sewing, laundering, polishing, perhaps spinning and weaving, such things."

"I was the Lady Flavia of Ar," she said.

"No matter," I said.

"No matter?" she said.

"No," I said.

"I see," she said.

"Who sees?" I asked.

"Alcinoë sees," she said, "Master."

"And at the end of the day," I said, "you may expect to be chained at your master's slave ring."

"Surely I would be permitted on his couch," she said.

"Such honor," I said, "for a slave?"

"Master?"

"Do you think you would be a free companion?" I asked.

"No, Master," she said.

"Expect to be chained to his slave ring, on the floor, at the foot of his couch."

"Chained?" she said.

"As any other animal," I said.

"Master?"

"By the neck or the left ankle," I said.

"I see," she said.

"If you are fortunate," I said, "you might be permitted a mat and blanket."

"So little?" she said.

"To be sure," I said, "you might have to earn them."

"Earn them?" she said. "How?"

"How do you think?" I asked.

"I see," she said.

"It is yours to serve and please your master."

"I would hope to do so," she said.

"Do you think you can kneel and belly, and crawl, and lick and kiss, and beg, and thrash and writhe?" I asked.

"A slave must obey," she said.

"A slave such as you," I said, "will not be able to help herself."

"Master?"

"She will beg to do so," I said.

"It is my hope that I will not be displeasing to my master," she said.

"You will heat, sweat, and mottle like fire, and juice like a fountain."

"I already sense such feelings in me," she said.

"You will be conquered, wholly," I said.

"I want that!" she whispered.

"It does not matter, one way or the other," I said.

"I understand," she said.

"You are willing, then, to be the most contemptible, the most hated and scorned by free women, the lowest, and most degraded of slaves, the pleasure slave?"

"Yes," she said, "more than anything. That is the slavery that is right for me!"

"For the former Lady Flavia of Ar?" I asked.

"Yes," she said. "That is the slavery she wants, the slavery fitting for her, the slavery her collar begs for!"

I regarded her form and face.

"Have no fear," I said, "that is the form of slavery which will be imposed on you."

"Yes, Master," she said.

Interestingly, almost every girl from the barbarian lands brought to the markets of Gor was brought as a pleasure slave.

I supposed, of course, as earlier suggested, that they were selected with care, that they were culled from the most delectable of slave stock. Not every girl from the barbarian lands, I supposed, would be worthy of being fitted with a slave collar in the pens of Gor; not every girl from the barbarian lands would be deemed fit to grace a Gorean slave block.

I wondered if, standing naked on the block, exhibited to buyers, hearing the bids on them, they realized their specialness.

"The pleasure slave," I said, "is the fullest and most helpless of slaves. As a pleasure slave you will be the meaningless possession, the toy, the plaything, the convenience, of your master. Your life will be one of obedience and passion. There is a wholeness of life in this. Even the simplest of servile tasks will carry an aura of sensuality about them, as they are performed for the master, by she who is his pleasure slave. She will live in radiance, within an erotic ambiance, and in anticipation of the caress of her master. You will experience a sexuality a thousand times beyond the comprehension of a free woman. You will belong to your master with a servitude and intimacy beyond that of other slaves. You will be a helpless animal with which he may amuse himself and on which he may slake his lusts. You will know his chains and ropes, his thongs and bracelets, his gags and blindfolds. You will be his, completely. You will be wholly helpless. You will be totally at his mercy."

"I understand," she said.

"Do you still think you might like to be a pleasure slave?" I asked.

"Yes," she said.

I had little doubt that the slave before me, on her knees, would be offered from any block, in any city, town, or village, as a pleasure slave.

It was difficult to conceive of her as anything else.

"But surely," she said, "much depends on the master."

"Nothing depends on the master," I said.

"Master?" she said.

"The slave," I said, "is to strive to please any master, to the best of her ability."

"But perhaps," she smiled, "a girl might hope that some master would have her in mind now."

"You may hope that," I said.

"I think," she said, "that some master may have me in mind now."

"Not to my knowledge," I said.

"No?" she said, startled.

"No," I said.

"But then," she cried out in dismay, almost daring to rise from her knees, "I might go to anyone!"

"Yes," I said, and then turned about, and left her.

This conversation took place on the last day of the fifth passage hand.

On the next day, the first day of the sixth month, the cry, "Land, ho!" was called from the foremast, by Leros.

Chapter Twenty-One

I Fear Disorder;
The Signal;
Slaves Are Returned to Their Mats

I stood at the rail, with many others.

Off the port bow one could see islands, far off, a part of what we would later learn was an extended archipelago, which extended for better than two thousand pasangs, only a relatively small portion of which was inhabited.

That we continued north, along these coasts, much displeased the men. Pani had interposed themselves between the great water casks and angry men with clubs and poles who wished to shatter the casks, that one must put ashore for fresh water.

I think there were few on board who did not voice their disgruntlement, if only privately, in their quarters, or about their work, when with agreeable confreres. Not since the mutiny had there been such seething ugliness beneath the veil of duty and discipline. When officers drew near, men grew silent.

Some of the minor officers had ordered floggings.

This seemed to me unwise.

"Please, noble lord," said Tyrtaios to Lord Nishida, nearby, "anchor, put forth the galleys. We have been long at sea. Meat and flour are short. There are many armsmen amongst us. They are not mariners, they are soldiers. They want to feel ground beneath their feet. Replenish the great casks with fresher water. Perhaps there is fruit on land. Perhaps there are forests. Might there not be hunting within them?"

"Such remarks," said Lord Nishida, "are best borne in private."

Tyrtaios was a clever man. I thought it no accident that he had addressed Lord Nishida within the hearing of others.

"Please ponder their worth, noble lord," said Tyrtaios.

"I have not seen the signal," said Lord Nishida. "It may not be safe to seek the shore. We are still days from the holding of Lord Temmu."

"It is well," said Tyrtaios, "that weapons were taken in. Else I would fear war."

Men glanced at one another.

"Not all weapons were recovered," said Lord Nishida.

"What shall we do?" inquired Tyrtaios.

"We shall await the signal," said Lord Nishida.

"May I implore Lord Okimoto," inquired Tyrtaios, "that he, as senior, may rule otherwise?"

"Certainly," said Lord Nishida.

Whereas Tyrtaios, as of the dismissal of Seremides, was no longer of the retinue of Lord Nishida, but of that of Lord Okimoto, at the latter's request, and was well aware that Lord Okimoto was of subtly higher station than Lord Nishida, he was also well aware, as were most of us, that Lord Okimoto, from the lofty pedestal of his seniority, commonly refrained from involving himself in the day-to-day activities and management of the great ship.

Tyrtaios then excused himself, and withdrew.

I glanced to the side.

The slave, Alcinoë, edged more closely to me. It was as though she did not know I was there. Her small hands were on the high rail, at her shoulders. She was looking forward. How lovely were her hands. Her long dark hair was back about her head, moved by the breeze. She wore a light, white, sleeveless tunic, slave short. She had exciting arms and legs. The metal collar encircled her neck. The rep-cloth of the tunic left few of her charms to the imagination. I was pleased that the brand had been put to her. Women such as she belonged to men. Let there be no mistake about it. Let them then be so imprinted, so designated. It was, appropriately, the common *kajira* mark. How right that was for her. How splendid that the former Lady Flavia of Ar should bear in her thigh, now that of a slave, the most common of Gorean slave marks, the tiny, tasteful, cursive *kef*, as did many thousands of others. The familiarity of this brand, of course, is no reproach, nor any indication of inferior merit. It is a very beautiful mark, enhancing a slave's beauty, and, as such, it is likely to mark not only the least of slaves but the highest of slaves, not only a pot girl or a kettle-and-mat girl but the pampered pets chained to the side of a Ubar's throne. Still, I was pleased that it was the common mark which had been put on her. That seemed appropriate. Too, it was one of my favorite brands. She wore the ship's collar, with the sturdy lock at the back of the neck. She had her head up, looking out, across the water. Surely she knew, the tart, that the collar increases the attractiveness of a woman a hundred fold. Is that not known even by free women? To be sure, the matter is not purely aesthetic, though that aspect is indisputable, but is also a matter of its meaning, that she whose neck it encircles is the most desirable of females, the female who is goods, slave goods. I found her incredibly beautiful, desirable, and exciting. I felt like seizing her, tearing away the tunic, throwing her to the deck, and putting her fiercely, impetuously, imperiously, to my pleasure. I looked to the side, with a studied lack of concern.

"What are you doing here?" I asked.

"Looking," she said. "The land is there!" She pointed, at a tiny line against the horizon.

"Are you not standing rather close?" I asked.

She looked up. "Does Master fear the closeness of a lowly slave?" she asked.

"Perhaps you should be behind me, to my left," I said.

"Master does not own me," she said.

"That is my good fortune," I said. "If I owned you, you would learn your collar a thousand times better than you know it now."

"Perhaps then," she said, "it is my good fortune that Master does not own me."

"Perhaps," I said.

Then, suddenly, she knelt beside me, sobbing, her head down to my feet.

"Own me, own me, Master," she begged.

"Who would want you?" I asked.

"I have seen many men look at me," she said. "Many men would want me!"

"Then let them buy you," I said.

"I want to belong to Master," she said. "Even from Ar, when I was the freest of the free, I wanted to belong to you!"

"You belong to the ship," I said.

She looked up, pleading. "Master!" she protested.

"Go to the Kasra keeping area," I said, "and beg to be put on your chain."

"Master!" she wept.

"Need a command be repeated?"

"No, Master!" she said.

"What are you going to do?" I asked.

"I will go to the Kasra keeping area, and beg to be put on my chain," she said.

"Go," I said. "Run!"

She leaped up and fled, sobbing, to the nearest open hatch.

"I see," said Lord Nishida, smiling, "you are fond of the slave."

I shrugged. "The little beast is not without her attractions," I said.

"Do not forget she is a slave, and only that," said Lord Nishida.

"I will not," I said.

"Lord Okimoto approaches," observed Lord Nishida.

Lord Nishida bowed first.

There is apparently a certain order to such things, who bows first, how deeply one bows, and such. On continental Gor, and the familiar islands, it is common to give the right hand, the usual weapon hand, to the other, though mariners sometimes clasp one another's wrist, in the mariner's grip, far more secure than the clasping of hands. Giving the weapon hand to the other is certainly a gesture of trust. Perhaps that is why one seldom shakes hands with strangers. The business of bowing seemed to me to make a good deal of sense. One exchanged a greeting with courtesy, and, at the same time, retained the freedom of the weapon hand. Hands, too, amongst the higher Pani, are often concealed in the broad sleeves of their robes. This makes possible the concealment, and the ready availability, of a sleeve dagger. The continental custom, on the other hand, makes it possible to draw the other off balance, and, obviously, if one is right-handed, one is more at risk from a fellow who might favor the left hand.

Lord Okimoto moved his larger bulk to the rail.

Both lords wore sandals.

The hair of each was drawn behind the head and fastened in a ball or top knot. This was the case with many of the Pani, not all.

Tyrtaios had returned with Lord Okimoto.

The warrior, Turgus, was nearby, who, as it may be recalled, had replaced Tyrtaios in the retinue of Lord Nishida.

Each lord seemed more comfortable, on the whole, dealing with the armsmen and mariners by means of an intermediary, Tyrtaios for Lord Okimoto, Turgus for Lord Nishida, though there was nothing rigid in this matter. Lord Nishida, for example, seemed somewhat more flexible in attending or not attending to this protocol. They both, for the most part, dealt openly with high officers. Lord Nishida, it might be noted, had spoken pleasantly to me, and I was not even an officer.

Lord Okimoto was handed a glass of the Builders by a Pani guardsman.

I heard a scratch and a tap, from my right, some feet along the rail, and saw Seremides bracing himself against the rail, shading his eyes. I saw men draw away from him. He was unarmed, as far as I could tell, in the ragged brown tunic. This was perhaps just as well, as there were more than a thousand men on board who could now, given his handicap, his helplessness on a single leg, his need of the crutch, easily best him with the blade, and perhaps a hundred or so would have been pleased to do so. Several had tried to goad him into seizing up a sword, placed before him, and entering into the games of steel, but he had not done so, enduring rather abuse and jeers, insults and ridicule, the raillery of many, and some, fools who, in his day of power, would have feared to speak before him, or come armed into his presence. How pathetically, with helpless tears, he would sometimes strike about him with the crutch, and then fall. How he would sometimes cringe, and weep, at his helplessness, begging to be left alone. How keenly, I thought, would so proud, and once so terrible, a man, have felt his reduction, its humiliation. To be sure, even in his ruin, there remained a sense of something formidable within him, particularly when others were not about him, and this, I thought, was primarily a matter of mind and will, of resolution. I did not doubt but what he might strangle a man with one hand, or, lunging, thrust his crutch through a body, but what I most feared in Seremides was something that had always been there, but had often been overlooked, something intangible, what I could not see, the sinister depth of his character, the danger of his mind, his capacity to hate, and remember. The *kajirae*, even more than the men, avoided him, fleeing at the sound of the tap and scratch of the crutch, hastening away, lest his large, awkward shadow fall upon them.

Lord Okimoto handed the glass of the Builders back to the guardsman.

He then turned to Turgus, subordinate to Lord Nishida. "Have Aëtius instruct the helmsman to bring the ship closer to shore, a half pasang."

I detected a subtlety here.

Lord Nishida, on the other hand, did not object.

"Is this wise?" asked Lord Nishida.

"Are we to put to?" inquired Turgus.

"No," said Lord Okimoto. "Continue our present course."

"Why so close?" inquired Lord Nishida.

"It is my calculation," said Lord Okimoto, "from the charts, that we have abeam the lands which were once those of Lord Temmu."

"The ancestral lands," said Lord Nishida.

"Lost early in the war," said Lord Okimoto.

"Fortunes wax and wane," said Lord Nishida.

"In any event, it is from this coastline that the signal is to rise," said Lord Okimoto.

"Secretly, doubtless," said Lord Nishida.

"Doubtless," said Lord Okimoto.

"I fear the war goes not well," said Lord Nishida.

"Something may be told from the signal."

"Or," said Lord Nishida, "if there is no signal."

"Yes," said Lord Okimoto.

"Why so close?" asked Lord Nishida.

"There will be no signal," said Lord Okimoto, "if our presence is unnoted."

"So close," said Lord Nishida, "any might note our presence."

"It is a risk," said Lord Okimoto.

"Surely," said Lord Nishida, "you will not put to, and risk a landing."

"No," said Lord Okimoto, "not without the signal."

I did not understand much of this conversation.

I did gather that some uncertainty attached to certain political and military matters.

In a quarter of an Ahn, we began to see more detail abeam, a steep, sandy beach, with hills and trees beyond it.

I estimated we were something like a half pasang offshore. Our course continued north.

That we were closer to shore, whatever might be its advantages or disadvantages, did increase the tension on board, and various crew members, acting as spokesmen for one group or another, from one deck or another, urged minor officers to petition for a landing. More Pani now appeared on deck, armed, as they always were. Lords Nishida and Okimoto had never disarmed their own men. The Pani, of course, were far outnumbered by the armsmen and mariners. Too, I had little doubt but what a number of weapons were concealed about the ship. Certainly several had never been recovered, for placement in the weapon rooms.

I muchly feared disorder.

When night came, we anchored.

I gathered this was a precaution, taken to minimize the chances of missing a possible signal.

It was now the next day, the second day of the sixth month, the day following the first sight of land.

We were still offshore, something like a half pasang, moving north.

As earlier, slaves had been freed of their chains, and many enjoyed the liberty of the deck.

I had seen Iole, Thetis, Alcmene, Pyrrha, Procris, and many others about. I also saw Alcinoë. I did not order her back to her chain. I enjoyed looking at her, in her tunic, the minimal tunic allowed to the Kasra girls. How amusing, I thought, that the former Lady Flavia of Ar should be so clad. To be sure, she did not seem to object, and was, often enough, in my vicinity. These were all ship slaves. Several privately owned slaves, too, were on deck, such as Lord Nishida's Saru. I also noted Cabot's Cecily, and Pertinax's Jane. 'Jane' is a barbarian name, like 'Cecily', but the woman herself, as I had learned, had had the benefits of civilization. Perhaps she had been given the name because it pleased her barbarian master, or, perhaps, as a punishment, that she would be thought of as, and treated no differently from, a barbarian slave.

I also speculated, as I had before, as to what might be the motivation of allowing so many slaves, mere ship slaves, such liberty.

Lords Nishida and Okimoto had been on the open deck, near the port rail, since the seventh Ahn. Each had at their disposal a glass of the Builders. Each had several guards at hand. I think they remained amidships not only to better monitor the fevers of the day, less accessible from the stem castle or stern castle, but to dispatch their guardsmen in case of need, perhaps to quell some disorder, or batten down hatches, keeping many below decks.

It was my impression, given the increasing restlessness of the men, which might approach the level of danger, given the excitements of the sight of land, that they thought it might be unwise, unless clearly called for, to order a clearing of the deck. We had been nearly a year at sea and the discipline of the armsmen, now that land was near, hung by little more than a thread.

Tyrtaios continued to urge a landing. I suspected he genuinely dreaded another mutiny.

"If a landing is made," said Lord Okimoto, "all treasure must remain on board."

"Of course," said Tyrtaios.

It was my understanding that a dialect of Gorean was spoken at the World's End, that the Priest-Kings had seen to this. By their mysterious power, and secret sky ships, it seems they had long ago placed Initiates amongst the Pani, perhaps centuries ago, who had taught them Gorean. These Initiates, as the legends went, had sought to exploit their prestige in an attempt to secure power, and had been done away with. The

Priest-Kings, on the other hand, by various manifestations of their power, doubtless the Flame Death, and such, had made clear the wisdom of retaining Gorean. It was written however, amongst the Pani, in an unfamiliar script, or set of signs, as it is, as well, I understand, in the Tahari. Whereas a variety of languages are spoken on Gor, Gorean, as you know, is almost universal. The common wisdom on such matters is that the Priest-Kings favor a common language, as a means to more easily communicate their views to humans, for example, with respect to the technology and weapon laws. It is apparently simpler to do this in one language than in several. Linguistic drift, at least on the continent, is managed by the standardization promulgated in scribal conferences held during the great fairs, held four times annually in the vicinity of the Sardar. I recalled that Lord Nishida had asked me, early in the voyage, if I could understand his Gorean. I could, though it was somewhat different. To be sure, there are many dialects of Gorean. I am told I have a Cosian accent, but I am not aware of this, or not much aware of it. But it is doubtless so. Certainly I would not deny it. One is seldom aware of one's own accent. As Alcinoë suggested, long ago in the cell, is it not the others who always have an accent?

Lord Okimoto clearly feared a mass desertion, particularly if the armsmen and mariners might depart with their packs filled with treasure.

The armsmen and mariners, however, as it later became clear, would not have been well advised to put such plans into effect, at least in the territories at hand.

Slaves, of course, another form of treasure, however desperate they might be to set foot on land, however pathetically they might plead, would remain on board, as well.

I then suspected the motivation for the unprecedented liberty that had of late been accorded to our shapely *kajirae*. Their display was to incite the interest of the men, and make their desertion less likely. Whereas I had no interest in desertion, had I any, I would not have wished to leave the ship without at least one of its slaves thonged and on my leash, perhaps Alcinoë, though I had no interest in her. To be sure, should I return her to Ar, I might collect a nice bounty on her, for she had once been the Lady Flavia, a traitress, once even the confidante of Talena, the muchly sought, false Ubara. I suspected that there were few slaves on board who had not caught the eye of one or more of the men. Aeacus, for example, I was sure, would not have minded having the lovely Iole squirming in his slave straps. There was something rather deceitful or meretricious in all this, of course, as the Pani had surely not brought these goods across the vast width of turbulent, green Thassa without plans for their disposition. Indeed, save for a brief time early in the voyage, these girls had been kept muchly away from the men, to the later annoyance of the men, and the misery and anguish of many of the slaves, pulling at their chains, tethered in place, their bodies denied the caress of masters, their hearts the ecstasy of the yielded slave.

It was in the late afternoon, shortly past the fifteenth Ahn, when a cry went up and I rushed, with others, to the port rail. Ashore, atop what appeared to be the left side of narrow defile, leading between hills into a wooded area, there was a narrow, ascending trail of reddish smoke. A moment later, near it, another narrow, ascending trail of smoke stood out against the sky, over the defile and woods. The second trail of smoke was yellow.

"Lord Temmu holds the shore," said Lord Okimoto, his glass of the Builders trained on the streaming smoke.

"His fortress stands," said Lord Nishida, his own glass trained, as well, on the smoke.

"Put to," said Lord Okimoto.

This was signaled to Aëtius.

We heard anchors rattling. Sails were slackened, and began to be furled.

"Look!" called a man.

"What is the meaning of that?" asked Tyrtaios.

A third spume of smoke rose now toward the sky. This column of smoke was clearly green.

Each of the streamers of smoke was now vanishing, drifting away.

On continental Gor, green is the caste color of the Physicians. I did not know its meaning here.

"Safety," said Lord Okimoto to Tyrtaios.

A cry of pleasure went up from men gathered about, and the motivation of this cry was quickly broadcast about the ship.

"Let us put forth the galleys, the small boats," said Tyrtaios.

Tarl Cabot, the tarnsman, commander of the tarn cavalry, had now joined Lords Okimoto and Nishida at the rail. Aëtius, who handled the daily management of the ship, was on the stern-castle deck, looking forward.

"I have seen three columns of smoke," said Tarl Cabot.

"We expected to see a single column," said Lord Nishida, "that of yellow, which would signify that the castle of Lord Temmu still stands, that it is not yet taken. To be sure, we did not know that even that would be seen."

"We feared," said Lord Okimoto, "that we were too late, that all was lost."

"The red column," said Lord Nishida, "we did not expect to see. It signifies that we hold the shore, that Lord Temmu has retaken ground. We rejoice."

"The third smoke," said Lord Okimoto, "that of green, of safety, means that a landing may be effected."

"That is what has so inspirited the men," said Lord Nishida.

Dozens of men had climbed on the rail, ascended the ratlines, or clung to the masts, that they might see the better.

"What I do not understand," said Lord Nishida, "is why there should be both a red and green column. If we hold the shore, it is safe, and the green column is unnecessary."

"It confirms the red column," said Lord Okimoto.

"Launch the galleys, the small boats," men cried.

"The green column," said Lord Nishida, "might indicate that an area is safe to approach, even though it might lie in the territory of Lord Yamada, no enemy being about, or that a passage has been cleared, or a castle may be approached, or such, and thus one might have green without red, but it would be unusual to have both green and red."

"Yes," said Lord Okimoto, "unusual, but scarcely a cause for concern."

"Yellow," said Lord Nishida to Cabot, "indicates that the holding of Lord Temmu stands."

"It would be difficult to take his castle," said Lord Okimoto. "It is a mighty holding."

323

"If we hold the shore," said Lord Nishida, thoughtfully, "it would seem quite likely that the castle of Lord Temmu would still stand."

"Thus," said Cabot, "it seems only one signal, the red, would suffice."

"Precisely, Tarl Cabot, tarnsman," said Lord Nishida.

"All signs," said Lord Okimoto, "are auspicious."

"It seems so," said Lord Nishida.

There was much clamoring amongst the men.

"I do not think they can be held longer," said Tyrtaios.

Turgus, who was liaison to Lord Nishida, looked about, with apprehension.

"Landing parties may be formed," said Lord Okimoto.

This decision was met with cries of approval.

"Order is to be maintained," said Lord Okimoto.

"Certainly," said Tyrtaios.

"Dispatch a scouting party," said Cabot.

"The smoke was red," said Lord Okimoto, patiently.

"Nonetheless," said Cabot.

"The signals are secret," said Lord Okimoto.

"We will not be able to restrain the men," said Tyrtaios.

Already men had rushed below decks, to obtain access to the three remaining nested galleys, and the numerous tiny, tiered, ship's boats.

Pani looked to Lords Nishida and Okimoto. Were they to use their swords?

To be sure, such an act would doubtless have cost dozens of men, and forever divided the Pani from the mariners and armsmen. As Tyrtaios had feared, war would betide the great ship. Too, the mission of the Pani, whatever it might be, would crumble.

"No," said Lord Okimoto.

"The men must be armed," said Lord Nishida.

"It is not necessary," said Lord Okimoto.

But Tarl Cabot had ascended the ratlines some ten feet, to where he might be clearly seen. "Open the weapon rooms!" he called.

Many were the cheers.

Men hastened to do his bidding.

He would not send men ashore unarmed.

Lord Okimoto was not pleased. His eyes narrowed, unpleasantly. "The commander," he said to Lord Nishida, "exceeds his authority."

"I shall reprimand him," said Lord Nishida.

"The commander," said Lord Okimoto, "is circumspect."

"He knows war," said Lord Nishida.

"The smoke was red," said Lord Okimoto.

"True," said Lord Nishida.

"The signals are secret," said Lord Okimoto.

"They were," said Lord Nishida.

"I see," said Lord Okimoto.

Men were hurrying below decks, to the weapon rooms.

"Who will disarm them?" asked Lord Okimoto.

"Many are secretly armed now," said Lord Nishida. "If we deny them arms, will they not distrust us, that we would send them so ashore?"

"Perhaps," said Lord Okimoto.

"A force of our men, fifty, divided between us, will go first," said Lord Nishida.

"Very well," said Lord Okimoto.

"We will keep a goodly force on board," said Lord Nishida. "As some return, others may go."

"No treasure is to go ashore," said Lord Okimoto.

"No," said Lord Nishida, "nor slaves."

The slaves, save some, kept below, were on deck, and this intelligence was received with dismay. "Please, Masters!" wept many. They knelt piteously, and extended their hands to mariners. They, too, longed to go ashore, to feel water about their ankles, to feel sand beneath their bared feet, to touch a stone, grass, a living tree. There were moans amongst them, and sobbing. Many stood by the rail, looking toward the land, their cheeks stained with tears. Those who had been kept below, even during the days of maximum liberty, had been mostly those who, when permitted on deck, had always been hooded.

It seemed unlikely to me that the hooded slaves, however beautiful they might be, would be that much more beautiful than their chain sisters, in either the Venna or Kasra keeping areas. The concealment of beauty, of course, might be only one motivation for hooding a slave. The usual motivation for hooding a slave is to increase one's control over the slave. A hooded slave, for example, is likely to be disoriented, confused, fearful, and helpless. Sometimes an unpopular, haughty free woman is surprised and hooded, and put by several young men to slave use, after which she is returned to her robes and freedom. Thereafter, she may speculate, encountering one young fellow or another, here or there, at one time or another, whether he is one, or not, who has enjoyed her. Can she live with this? Is that fellow smiling? What is the meaning of that look, by another, or does it have a meaning? When any fellow's eyes are upon her she seizes her veils and holds them more closely about her face. Do other free women suspect how she is now different from them? Could they possibly know? That she, though a free woman, has been subjected to slave use? How they would shun and scorn her, if they knew. Whose pleasure has she served? That of several, as might have a slave, but she knows not one of them. Can she endure this shame, this humiliation, this uncertainty, being the one who does not know, while others look upon her, and perhaps remember, and know? Is not a paga girl, in an alcove, serving her master of the Ahn, more fortunate? She is likely to be well aware of who it is who is putting her to use. Too, the fellow is likely to want the slave to be well aware of who it is who is seeing to it that she endures the lengthy and unspeakable raptures of her bondage. It is he whom she, helpless, clutching him, must beg for more. And, too, the free woman, to her chagrin, can recall the incipient feelings in her body, and her gasping, and how her small arms touched, and then held, and then clutched, gratefully, the body in whose power she lay. How they had laughed, when a spasm, to her shame, had rocked her. Then, having been given a taste, however brief, of what it might be to be subject to the mastery, she was returned to freedom, to live as she could, the life of a free woman. Such a woman, commonly, in her misery and loneliness, in her shame and humiliation, in her uncertainty and confusion, begins to roam the high bridges, frequent lonely streets, and wander unescorted outside the city gates. She courts the collar. She seeks it. She beseeches it. She weeps with rapture as she is stripped and bound.

Hooding may also figure in certain games, as when a hooded slave, or one fully concealed in a slave sack, is gambled for. What is the value? Is the stone in the box a pebble or a diamond, is the slave in the hood or sack a beauty or a she-tarsk?

Hooded slaves may also compete in various games, as in locating objects scattered about a room, arranging objects by size or weight, threading beads, fitting puzzle pieces together, a candy for the winner, a switch stroke for the losers, placing and tying sandals, plaiting binding fiber, braiding a whip, and such. Free women occasionally use hooded serving slaves on all fours, in crawling races, in which, walking behind them, they incite them to greater speed by the frequent monitions of a switch. Free women often delight in this game, as it gives them an opportunity to show what they think of female slaves. Free women hate female slaves; men, on the other hand, prize them, and seek to own them.

What man does not desire a slave?

Hooding has many uses; one might be, I thought, to conceal an identity. For example, a woman is sometimes hooded, and gagged, to be more easily transported from a city. Sometimes a woman is sold, hooded and gagged, but this is rare, as a buyer usually wishes to see all of a slave, before risking coin.

I heard a galley being placed in the water. Pani would be the first to board. I saw men moving about, now armed. Soon, a flotilla of small boats would be launched.

"Please, Masters!" wept kneeling slaves. And then others, from the rail, knelt about us, as well. "Please, Masters!"

"You have been long at sea, beauties," said Tyrtaios. "Perhaps you would like to go ashore."

"Yes, oh, yes, Master!" they wept.

There must have been some twenty before us, and I could see other such groups about the deck, imploring others.

Regarding them, kneeling before us, pleading, in their tiny, form-clinging tunics, and close-fitting collars, I was again impressed with the quality of the ship's *kajirae*. The Pani had made many excellent purchases. It occurred to me that perhaps they had not been bought to be sold, actually, but, rather, to be distributed, as gifts. Certainly there was not one but what would make a lovely gift.

I thought of Alcinoë, too, then, given as a gift.

She could be given to anyone, anytime, anywhere.

For a moment I was troubled.

Then I recalled she meant nothing to me.

Excellent, I thought.

She meant nothing to me.

Still, I thought, it might be pleasant to own her, such a slave, to own her completely, as one owns a slave.

"Perhaps you can beg prettily," said Tyrtaios.

"Master?" said more than one.

"Interest us," said Tyrtaios. "Show that you are worth owning."

"Do not be cruel to us," said a slave. "Have mercy on us. Do not make us show ourselves as what we are, slaves! Do not make us move so, as slaves! Do you not know what that does to us? To so perform before men! It arouses us, like slave dance, and teaches us we belong to men! It reminds us of what we are. Be merciful! Do not ask us to do that, unless you will subsequently fulfill us, according to us the caresses of the master. Please! Please! Else we will suffer the torments of the neglected slave! Please be merciful! We are already starved for the touch of masters!"

"You are slaves," said a man. "Move as slaves!"

"Please, no!" wept a slave.

"Move," said Tyrtaios.

The men began to laugh, and clap.

They moved well. How beautiful are women! I saw their eyes, their expressions, the needfulness in their movements, the subtleties. What fires men have set to burn in the bellies of slaves! Is it cruel, I wondered, to have done this to them, to make them the helpless victims of such powerful, frequently recurrent needs? I supposed not, as it makes them the richest and fullest of women, the most helpless and authentic of women, the most irreparably female of women, more a woman than a free woman, afflicted by her inhibitions, locked within her conventions, the prescriptions of her society, can dream. One cannot, of course, ignite needs which are not there, cannot set fires where there is nothing to burn, where there is nothing ready to burn, nothing eager to burn, nothing hoping to burn. One can free such needs, of course, order them forth, refuse to allow them to remain feared and denied, and their freeing is, essentially, what the woman, in her deepest heart, wants. On the other hand, as they are slaves, it does not matter. They are slaves. One does what one wishes with them.

The slaves now subsided, many on all fours, looking anxiously to the men.

"Now coffle us," said one of the slaves, "by metal, by wrist, neck, or ankle! Take us ashore, chained! We will not escape! We cannot escape! We are ready! You have made us so! We beg only haste! You need not take us to the grass, or the high, dry beach! Cast us to the wet, drenched sand, use us, if you wish, in the raging surf, but use us, Masters, use us!"

"That is enough whining and whimpering of the sluts," said Tyrtaios, addressing me, and several, who stood about. "Get them to their mats, and put them on their chains."

There were cries of lamentation from the slaves. Some, in frustration, and futility, struck the planks of the deck with their small fists.

I wondered if Tyrtaios cared for women.

He was, as I recalled, quite possibly of the Assassins.

Such men usually have more on their mind than slaves, such things as their kills, as wealth, as power.

One of the greatest had been Pa-Kur, whose horde had almost mastered Ar.

To be sure, the frustration of a slave is sometimes useful in the control of a slave.

And, I thought, Tyrtaios did little without purpose.

What in one man might seem pointless or gratuitous, in another, such as Tyrtaios, might be the result of sober calculation, a move on the kaissa board of advantage. On such a board slaves may be moved, as well as men.

And do they not make lovely pieces?

"Must whips be brought?" asked Tyrtaios.

"No, no, Master!" cried the miserable slaves, and they rose to their feet, many sobbing, to return to their keeping areas.

"Attend them," said Tyrtaios to me, and some of the others, who stood about.

I heard several of the small boats being put in the water. I supposed that some two thirds, or so, of the armsmen and mariners might make their landing, and others later, as they returned.

It was toward evening now.

Why, I asked myself, would Tyrtaios have us, several of us, attend the return of the slaves to the Venna and Kasra keeping areas?

It was only later that I understood, or thought I might understand.

Tyrtaios, I suspect, wished to appear to the men as one who might have much to give, to be perceived as a likely bestower of privilege, and power.

Nearby, standing near the rail, I saw a dark figure, that of Seremides, braced against the rail, the crude, narrow crutch beside him.

When Tyrtaios glanced at him, for Tyrtaios often apprised himself of his surroundings, Seremides looked away, as though concerned to watch the small boats, now about the galley, approach the shore.

I heard a soft, feminine voice at my side, one I would have recognized in the darkness, the pitch blackness, of a dungeon of chained slaves.

"Perhaps Master would like to put me to my mat," said the voice.

"Perhaps," I said.

"And see that I am well fastened there, on my chain?" said the voice.

"That would give me great pleasure," I said.

"I belong in the Kasra keeping area," she said.

"That for lesser slaves," I said.

"I am informed so," she said.

"Precede me, slut," I said.

"May I speak?" she asked.

"Yes," I said.

"I suppose," she said, "that not all sluts are slaves."

"Probably not," I said, "though doubtless they should be made slaves."

"But all slaves are sluts," she said.

"They had better be," I said.

"Good," she said, "Master."

Men were about us, hurrying slaves below. Some were conducted by the wrist, or arm. Others were put in painful leading position, one in each hand, their heads held at the hip of their keeper of the moment. Others were hurried on their way with a shove, or a stinging slap below the small of the back. Some cried out, hastened with the bow of a belt across the backs of their thighs. Most tried to hurry ahead, down the companionways, and through the corridors.

"Move," I told her.

"Yes, Master," she said.

I followed her. I wished I had her on a leash, if only that she might know herself leashed, and on my leash.

We were down three decks in a bit, and rather separated from the others.

"May I speak?" she asked.

"Yes," I said.

"I gather," she said, "that the men are to chain us."

"It seems so," I said.

"That is unusual," she said.

"Yes," I said.

"I am a slave," she said. "I prefer being chained by a man."

"I understand," I said.

This made sense as females know in their heart that they are by nature the property of males. This natural relationship, refined within, and expressed within, the enhancements of civilization, may be expressed in many ways, for example, by the brand, the collar, distinctive clothing, bracelets, a chain, and such. The chain, of course, is not purely symbolic. That is clear to any woman who finds herself on a chain.

"But why, now?" she asked.

"I am not sure," I said. Actually, it seemed very likely to me that, now that our voyage was much at its end, Tyrtaios, and doubtless others, would be anxious to enlist associates, for some end or other, to which end the prospect of a distribution of slaves might prove conducive.

Accordingly, in such a case, it might be useful to force, as he had, beautiful, half-naked slaves to prove their heat, and need, before virile males.

Who would not enjoy having one or more of them?

331

Similarly, it seemed that each might chain his choice.

I found that of interest.

Disputes in such matters are commonly adjudicated with the sword. The slave, in such a case, is usually stripped, bound, hand and foot, hooded or blindfolded, and thrown to the side. She must wait, to see to whom she will belong.

We had now approached the lower decks.

"May I speak, Master?" she inquired.

"Yes," I said.

"On our way," she said, "we will pass the Venna area."

"True," I said, "where the better slaves are housed."

"I am not sure of that," she said.

"You little she-sleen," I said. "How vain you are!"

"Have you ever been in the Venna keeping area?" she asked.

"No," I said, "nor the Kasra keeping area either, for that matter."

"I am curious to gaze upon these special slaves," she said, "particularly those who are always hooded when taken through the corridors, up the companionways, to the open deck."

"I doubt that you would be objective, in assessing your betters," I said.

"My betters?"

"Certainly."

"I am not sure of that," she said.

I did not respond.

"Are you not curious?" she asked.

"It is none of our business," I said. To be sure, I was curious.

"We may have few such opportunities," she said.

"We are near the Venna keeping area," I noted. The Kasra keeping area was on the deck below.

"The portal," she said, "is ajar."

The lock dangled.

It had been broken away, probably by a hammer.

We could hear the sounds of men, and slaves, and chains, within. There was much stirring. We could also see that lamps had been lit within. I heard nothing of the large women, so coarse, and gross, and their switches. How different they were from the slaves of desirability, the soft, beautiful, delicious, feminine slaves, the gems on a slaver's necklace, those for whom discerning men patiently wait to be put upon the block. Men, it seemed, on the word of Tyrtaios, had invaded this normally sequestered precinct. I suppose it was much the same below, in the Kasra area.

"Please!" begged the slave, Alcinoë.

In the light of the lamp in the corridor the collar, closely fitting, was lovely on her neck. She had not been given much to wear. It was a "Kasra tunic," so to speak, appropriate to the lower keeping area. She was lightly complexioned and her dark hair was soft about her head and shoulders. I myself wondered if the slaves who had been hooded could be much her superior. Certainly I did not think that those of the Venna keeping area who had been brought unhooded to the deck had been much her superior, if at all. Indeed, I suspected that she had been consigned to the lower area with aforethought, perhaps to suggest her unimportance. Seremides might have arranged that, I supposed. To be sure, there were some slaves from each keeping area whom I recognized would be likely to bring more off the block than Alcinoë, if sold as common meat, and not as an item of special interest, on which, say, a bounty might be collected. But, in spite of that, even considered as common meat, I thought one could do far worse than the slave, Alcinoë. Too, I thought her much improved from Ar. Always beautiful, always a female who disturbed dreams, who would be likely to occur in them naked, in a man's chains, she now seemed to me much more beautiful. And this was not, in my view, a simple matter of the carefully supervised regimen of diet and exercise routinely imposed on domestic animals of her sort, shaping, trimming, and vitalizing her figure, that it might be brought to the block as a superb stimulus to buyers. It was, rather, the fuller beauty of a woman, which is brought out by bondage, a tonicity, a softness, a femininity, an aliveness, a sensitivity, a vulnerability, an awareness, in which her wars are done, her conflicts resolved, her self-torments ended, her inhibitions vanished, her identity secure, the relief and welcome joy of a woman who accepts herself as what she is, and is content to be, and desires to be, a slave who hopes to be found pleasing by her master.

I recalled her from Ar, in her ornate, sumptuous robes, one of which might have cost a laborer a year's wages, sometimes so casual about the hem, lifting it up a bit, as to examine the heel of a slipper, but exhibiting an ankle, or drawing back, against her, or smoothing, about her, a garment, in such a way that one might speculate about the line of a figure, or the turn of a hip, but, much more often, the carelessness with which a veil might have been disarranged, adjusted, or loosened. Doubtless she had thought to torment a common soldier, one farther beneath her than the very dust beneath her slippers. But now, under the lamp light in the corridor, she stood before me, a slave, far less now the dust beneath the poor laborer's sandals, whose annual wages once might not have purchased one of her robes. I regarded her, collared, before me. There was no doubt now about her features, or her limbs, her rounded arms, her small hands, her thighs and calves, her ankles.

"Master views a slave," she said.

"Yes," I said.

"Does Master think of Ar?" she said.

"Yes," I said.

"I am different now," she said.

"Yes," I said.

"It sounds as though there are pleasantries within the Venna keeping area," she smiled.

"I think I will look upon these slaves," I said.

"May I accompany Master?"

"Yes," I said. "But stay close to me."

"I shall, Master," she said.

The great door, so often secured and locked, was now, the lock broken, swung back. I entered, followed by Alcinoë, close behind me, interestingly, on my left, but that is where a slave commonly follows a master.

I did not mind her behind me, on my left.

That was pleasant.

To be sure, sometimes a master has a slave precede him, that he may better observe her.

The area was low ceilinged, but not so low that a man could not stand upright. It was lit by several lamps. There were several fellows about, and several slaves. Some of the slaves had been put to their mats, and chained in place, but many were not yet secured. It seemed many fellows were reluctant to leave the area. Several dallied, even in the vicinity of the slaves who were already on their chains. "You are to secure them, no more," said a minor officer. "They are not to be used. Not yet. Difficulties with the Pani would ensue. Lords Nishida and Okimoto would disapprove. They are ship slaves. You do not own them. Pose them, examine them, feel them, delight yourself with their beauty, put them through chain paces, if you wish, but know that their bodies will be examined. These are not tavern sluts. Beware the wrath of Lords Nishida and Okimoto. Do not dally overlong. It is best to be quick. Secure them, and go."

"It seems," I said to Alcinoë, "the fellows are not eager to return to the deck."

Several of the slaves were standing, in examination position, legs widely spread, hands behind the back of their neck, or head. Others had been placed in the slave bow. Others, on their chains, were to react, as though struck, given a clap of hands. Some did so in terror. I gathered they had actually felt the whip. Others, to the rhythmic motion of a hand, writhed in their chains. Others endeavored to please the men, being put though slave paces.

"Do not dally overlong," pleaded the officer. "Their bodies will be examined. Secure them, and hasten away!"

There was much laughter.

But the men understood that the slaves were not to be used. Few cared to perish beneath the blades of the Pani.

I saw more than one rape the lips of a beauty with the kiss of the master, and then cast her, chained, to her mat, and depart, despite her extending her hands futilely after him. Well then did she jerk at her chain, again and again, in frustration, which held her in place.

"It will doubtless be the same in the Kasra keeping area," she whispered. "Will you protect me?"

"And who," I said, "will protect you from me?"

"I do not want protection from you," she said.

"You might make a nice armful of collar meat," I said.

I considered her, luscious, hot, aroused.

"I would hope to please you," she said.

Yes, I thought, she might be very nice.

To be sure, I must remember that she was nothing to me.

"You speak as a slave," I said.

"I am no longer free," she said. "I am a slave. Thus I may speak as I wish."

"If given permission."

"Of course," she said.

"It seems you are beginning to feel your collar," I said.

"Yes," she said.

"Next," I said, "you will be on your belly, begging to lick and kiss the feet of a master."

"May I so beg?" she asked.

"No," I said.

"That is a Kasra girl," said one of the slaves, a chain running from her ankle to its ring. "She does not belong here!"

"I am better than you!" said Alcinoë

"You are not!" said the slave.

"I am!" said Alcinoë. "If you are so good, why are there no men lingering about you? In the Kasra area, men would linger about me!"

"Slave!" hissed the girl.

"Slave!" hissed Alcinoë.

"Come away," I said to Alcinoë.

"I am better than she, am I not?" said Alcinoë.

"You are only a Kasra girl," I told her.

"But, am I not?" she said.

"Yes," I said, annoyed.

"Good," she said, "and I am only a Kasra girl!"

"That may be told from your tunic," I said. It was of low-quality rep-cloth, and, as noted, there was not much to it, not that I minded that.

"Beware the Pani!" called the officer.

Some two or three men left the keeping area.

"Where are the whip slaves?" I asked a fellow.

"Over there," he said, casting a contemptuous thumb to the side.

I went a bit to the side, and there I found, prone, naked, bound hand and foot, the five large, gross whip slaves who, as first girls, served to keep the smaller, softer, more beautiful, more desirable slaves in order. To be sure, their power rested on their authority, and not on their coarseness, or bulk. They had had behind them the power of men. Three or four smaller women, together, might have overcome, perhaps in her sleep, bound, and beaten such women.

"I trust the whip slaves in the Kasra area," said Alcinoë, "are similarly inconvenienced."

"Probably," I said.

"Good," she said.

She had doubtless felt their switches frequently enough.

I pulled the head of one of the whip slaves up a little, and back. She whimpered. She was afraid. To men, she was only another woman, and one unlikely to be of interest. Between the teeth of each was bound a switch.

"You tried to stop the entrance of men into the area?" I asked.

The woman, her head held up and back by the hair, whimpered once.

"Do you wish to be turned over to the slaves not yet secured," I asked, "to be lashed?"

She whimpered twice, pathetically.

I let her lower her head, stood up, and looked about.

The whip slaves doubtless feared the vengeance of the charges whom they had kept in such terror, over whom they had ruled with such cruelty.

Given their plainness, and grossness, they had something of the hatred of the free woman for the exquisitely feminine, muchly desired female slave, smaller and weaker, but so much their superior.

But once the slaves were chained, they had little to fear. When, later, they had been freed, by one officer or another, things would doubtless be much the same in the keeping area.

But perhaps not.

The men might come again.

The voyage might well be near its end, and, if that were the case, who knew what might ensue?

"Where are the hooded slaves?" asked Alcinoë.

It was quite unlikely they would be hooded now, in the area.

"They will be here, somewhere," I said.

"We may have seen them," said Alcinoë, "and, if so, they are not so extraordinary."

"You sound like a Kasra girl," I said, "a jealous one."

"Master!" she protested.

"There must be another area," I said.

Surely, somewhere, hoods would be stored.

I went toward the back of the keeping area. "There is a door here," I said. It was not a holding door, but a light door, more for privacy, I supposed, than anything else. I slid back the bolt, and swung the door open. It was dark inside.

"Master," I heard, from within, a woman's voice. They could see it was a man, as the light was behind me. "What is going on?" asked the voice.

"Curiosity," I told her, "is not becoming in a *kajira*."

"Yes, Master," said the voice, frightened.

"It is so dark," said Alcinoë.

"I will fetch a lamp," I said.

"You are curious, are you not?" she asked.

"Certainly," I said. "Are you not, as well?"

"Yes," she said. "I would look upon these allegedly fabulous creatures."

I unhooked one of the small lamps from the ceiling of the larger, general portion of the Venna keeping area, and, lifting it a little, entered the smaller area, followed by Alcinoë.

Lifting the lamp more we discerned some twenty women in the special area. Each was at her mat, and secured there by her chain. When the general liberty, recently, had been accorded the slaves, the freedom of the deck, these women had remained below, it seemed, in the darkness of their area, secured.

"Look, Master," said Alcinoë, pointing to a wall, to our left.

"Yes," I said.

There, suspended by their neck buckles, placed over hooks, were several slave hoods, each with a small padlock and key, the padlock about the buckle, the key on a string, dangling from the lock. Also, nearby, on another hook, a larger hook, were several loops of rope, by means of which the slaves, when brought to the upper deck, were belly coffled.

The slaves, who were naked, as one commonly keeps slaves at their mats, were huddled, crouched down, bent over, covering themselves, as they could.

"Master is not authorized," said one of the slaves. "Master must depart. We may not be looked upon."

"Do you wish to be lashed?" I inquired.

"No, Master," said the slave, hastily.

Though one of the slaves of the sheltered area, she was apparently familiar with the lash.

I looked about, as I could, in the light of the lamp. Some of the slaves had covered themselves completely with their small blankets; others gathered the blanket about their head and shoulders, and kept their heads down. Several, bent over, had brought their hair about their face, as a veil. Some, for whatever reason, perhaps discipline, had no blanket at hand. Their heads were down. Their small hands covered what they could of their beauty. Their knees were pressed firmly together.

Outside, in the larger area, I heard one or more men, perhaps apprehensive now, urging the others to make their departure.

I sensed some were leaving.

"I do not suppose they are so beautiful," said Alcinoë.

"It is hard to tell, as they are," I said.

"Should Master not consider departing?" said a slave.

"We are not to be looked upon," said another.

"And why," I asked, "are you not to be looked upon?"

"Because, Master," said a slave, huddled in a blanket, "we are of such extraordinary beauty."

"It seems," I said, "that that would be a reason why you should be looked upon, as Masters find it pleasant to look upon beautiful slaves."

"Please, Master," said one of the slaves, bent over, her hair held about her face.

"Is it true that you are all so beautiful?" I asked.

"Certainly, Master," said one of the slaves.

"We shall see," I said.

"Master?" said a slave.

"Position!" I said.

"Master!" protested several.

"Need a command be repeated?" I asked.

With cries of misery, and sobs, the slaves, or most, went to position.

"Hold the lamp," I said to Alcinoë.

She took the lamp.

"Please, no," wept slave after slave.

I drew away blankets, which had not fallen about the slaves.

"Backs straight," I said. "Lift your heads. Peer straight ahead. Shake the hair behind your shoulders."

I looked about, from one slave to another.

It was pleasant to do so.

"Shoulders back," I said. "Suck in your belly. Palms of your hands down on your thighs, firmly. Feel them there."

"Please, Master," sobbed a girl. "We are high slaves!"

"Many of us were once of high caste!" said another.

"Split your knees," I said.

"Master!" wept a girl.

"Wider," I said.

"Yes, Master," they wept.

"Better," I said, "better."

Yes, it was pleasant to look upon them.

I thought them quite nice.

Alcinoë followed me about with the lamp.

"What do you think, Alcinoë?" I asked.

"Average," said Alcinoë. "I see little that is extraordinary here."

Some of the girls gasped in indignation.

"There is some gold here," I said.

"Yes, Master!" said more than one of the slaves.

"Not much," said Alcinoë.

"Many are beautiful," I said. "But that is common with women whom men find worth putting on a chain."

"Beautiful enough, I suppose," said Alcinoë, with a toss of her hair which might have caused bids to surge. How right, I thought, how perfect, that women such as she were put in collars.

"It is true," I said, "that I see little justification for hooding."

"Master!" protested a slave.

"There is nothing special about high-caste slaves," I said. "They are often purchased to be put to lowly duties, and thrash at the slave ring."

"I wonder if any of these slaves are hot," said Alcinoë. I thought this was an interesting remark, considering that Alcinoë, at least as far as I knew, was white silk.

"If they are not now," I said, "they will soon become so, in the hands of masters."

"Please, Master," protested one of the slaves.

"As your beauty, while remarkable," I said, "does not seem all that unusual for slaves, I am supposing that there is another reason for your hooding."

"Master?" said one of the slaves.

"It is perhaps to conceal identities," I said. "Perhaps, say, in Ar, there is a bounty, for your return."

I heard a rattling of chain.

This reaction told me much of what I wanted to know. Hundreds of high-caste women, associated with the party of treason, must have fled Ar, many of whom, far from its Home Stone, might, as had the former Lady Flavia of Ar, fallen into bondage. Many may have had their hair shorn and begged retreating soldiers, of Tyros and Cos, and of the free companies, to take them with them, not as inconvenient, troublesome free women, but as begging, complaisant slaves. Others who had accompanied the retreat as free women might have found themselves eventually sold in the western ports, in particular, in Brundisium, where the Pani seem to have purchased most of their slaves for the voyage. The Pani, of course, would not have realized, in most cases, that there were bounties in the offing, and, had they realized it, they were, apparently, not much interested in such things. They were apparently more interested in what might be done with the women on the far side of Thassa. It was something there that they wanted them for. And, I supposed, not all of the women, and perhaps only a few, might be wanted in Ar. Of the women who had spoken, only two had had an accent which suggested Ar. Accordingly, it seemed clear to me that there must be a different purpose behind the hooding. Alcinoë, for example, whose identity might have been suspected by more than one fellow on the ship, had not been hooded. Too, if the Pani had any interest in bounties, and such, the last thing they would have done would be to transport such women far from Ar. The Pani wanted beauty, not gold, of which it seemed they had a good deal.

So why then, I asked myself, would these women, those of a particular group, housed in the Venna keeping area, have been hooded?

"Well," I said to Alcinoë, looking about, "what do you think?"

"Perhaps, Master," said Alcinoë, "they were not hooded for beauty, but, rather, to conceal their plainness."

"Master!" protested several of the slaves.

"Beat her, Master!" urged one.

"These are obviously beautiful slaves," I said, "high-grade merchandise, which would bring good coin off the block, but, as you have suggested, I see no particular reason for their hooding."

"Surely," said Alcinoë, "several of the other slaves, of the Venna keeping area, never hooded, are every bit as beautiful."

"Yes," I said.

I could remember that from the deck.

"And doubtless some of the Kasra keeping area, as well," she added.

"Yes," I said.

I could remember several of them, as well.

Alcinoë, I thought, was fetching in the Kasra tunic, what there was of it.

"Bring the lamp," I said to Alcinoë.

"Hold position," I said to the slaves.

"Perhaps we should leave, Master," said Alcinoë. "I think the men have left the outer area."

I looked about.

"Follow me," I said.

In the special area, that devoted to the slaves who would be brought hooded to the upper deck, there were twenty slaves, as I determined, arranged in five rows of four each. I went toward the back of

the special area, on the right.

Each slave was in position.

"Perhaps we should hurry, Master," said Alcinoë.

"Follow me," I said.

Alcinoë followed, with the lamp.

"Master?" said Alcinoë.

"I have not well examined this last row of slaves," I said.

I began with the one farthest to the right, drawing her head back, by the hair, that I might examine her features in the light of the lamp.

"She is nice, is she not?" I said to Alcinoë.

"Perhaps," said Alcinoë.

I released the girl's hair, that she might return to position.

I similarly examined the next two girls.

"Lovely," I said of each.

Of the first Alcinoë suggested that her value might be improved, if she could play the lyre. Of the second, Alcinoë wondered if slavers might be more interested in her, if she could dance.

"Can you dance?" I asked the girl.

"The flower dance of the free maiden," she said, frightened, her head held back, by the hair.

"Then you do not know the dances of begging slaves," I said.

"No, Master," she said. Such dances are often taught to the snapping of a whip.

"After you are in the hands of a master," I said, "you may beg to learn such dances."

"Master?" she said.

"To be more pleasing," I said.

"Yes, Master," she said.

I wondered if Alcinoë could learn slave dance. I thought so. Such dance is instinctual in a woman. I had little doubt that many lives had been saved, after the fall of a city, by a naked captive's supplicatory writhings before its conquerors.

We came then to the last slave, on her chain.

Oddly, she cried out in fear, broke position, and bent over, shuddering, covering herself, as she could, with her hands.

"Bring the lamp closer," I said to Alcinoë.

By the hair, I drew up the head of the slave, and she, interestingly, tried to turn to the side, and, neglecting her body, covered her face with her hands.

To be sure, many women fear face stripping more than body stripping. The face, after all, with its subtleties of expression, is uniquely personal, particularly revelatory, and especially revealing. A woman's face, exquisite, delicate, and beautiful, commonly so different from that of a man, unveiled, is vulnerable and defenseless, a window into her emotions and thoughts, into her heart and needs, a window that puts her ever the more helplessly in a man's power. A saying has it, bare the face, bare the woman. Another well-known saying is, remove the veil of a free woman and look upon the face of a slave. So it is no wonder that the free woman is concerned with her veiling. But this was a slave. Slaves are not permitted to conceal their faces. Their faces must be naked, and all are to be free to look upon them. Would it not be absurd to veil a verr, or kaiila? Such an inhibition seldom lasts past a girl's first switching. And soon a slave, the vain creature that she is, delights as shamelessly in the exhibition of her features as of her form. And perhaps more so. It is the whole of her, after all, marvelous and wondrous, that is collared.

So why would this slave have attempted to conceal her face?

"Position," I said to her, soothingly.

She then knelt.

"Split your knees," I said to her gently.

I released her hair, and, with a hand on each knee, widened them.

She still had her hands before her face. She was trembling.

"Lift up the lamp," I said to Alcinoë.

I then, gently, put a hand on each of her wrists.

"Please, no, please, no," she said.

"Master?" I asked.

"Please, no, Master," she begged. "Please, no, Master!"

I then, as she sobbed, pulled her hands away from her face.

"Aii!" cried Alcinoë, softly.

"Position," I said to the slave, soothingly, and she put her hands down on her thighs, looking straight ahead.

"Collared!" said Alcinoë.

I took the collar in both hands, turned it, examined the lock, and then, a bit roughly, turned it back into place, so that the lock was at the back of the neck.

"Yes," I said, "and perfectly."

It was a common ship's collar.

I then rose up, bade the slaves be as they would, and, followed by Alcinoë, left the special area, and, in a moment, the larger area, as well.

In a bit we had come to the Kasra keeping area, within which its whip slaves had been served similarly to those of the higher area, bound naked, hand and foot, prone, their switches tied between their teeth.

The other slaves of the Kasra area were on their chains, and most were asleep.

"This is your mat?" I asked.

"Yes, Master," she whispered, that we not disturb the others.

"Master!" she said, suddenly, frightened.

I cautioned her to silence.

"Strip, *kajira*," I said to her.

"Strip?" she said.

"Yes," I said.

She put aside the bit of cloth which had been granted her.

"Now," I said, "on all fours, on the mat."

It was a thick, well-plaited mat, narrow. I then picked up the chain, attached to its ring, and snapped it about her ankle, the left ankle.

"Now, turn around," I said, "and lie down, on your belly."

I stood up for a few moments, regarding her. Then, suddenly I crouched down beside her, pulled her up, turned her, rudely, and, with a rattle of chain, forced my lips to hers.

I then flung her back on the mat, on her belly, and exited the Kasra keeping area.

I then went to my quarters.

I was much troubled.

I had seen Talena, of Ar.

I recalled, too, we had come to land.

Chapter Twenty-Two

What Occurred on the Beach

"Slaughter!" I heard cry. "Slaughter!"

The alarm bar was ringing, frenziedly.

It was shortly after the first Ahn, and, when I raced up the companionways to the open deck, it was still dark, though there were dozens of torches on the beach. Some small boats were returning to the great ship. Some men were clambering up ropes, drawing themselves over the rail. I heard small boats, below, scraping against the timbers of the ship. Ropes and rope ladders were being cast over the side. Aeacus handed me a glass of the Builders. It was difficult to focus, and there was much movement. I twisted the glass into focus. There seemed madness on the beach, men crowded together toward the shore, trying to board small boats. I saw two founder. Some men were wading into the sea, trying to cling to small boats.

"What is going on?" I said, to anyone, for there were several about, trying to see the beach, perhaps as unclear as I was, as to the confusion, the motion of the torches.

Aeacus took back the glass, and then, in a moment, handed it to another.

"Tarnsmen," I heard, "to saddle!"

It was the voice of Tarl Cabot.

"No!" said Lord Okimoto, at the rail, barefoot, his robe awry.

I did not know the whereabouts of Lord Nishida.

I saw Tyrtaios, with others, on the ratlines, peering toward the shore.

I heard the poking noise of the crutch of Seremides.

"Roll back the great hatch!" called Tarl Cabot.

"Do not do so!" exclaimed Lord Okimoto. Men drew back.

"Lord!" protested Tarl Cabot.

"No," said Lord Okimoto.

The secret of the tarns, I gathered, was to be kept.

Some two thirds of the armsmen and mariners, following some fifty Pani, from the men of Lords Nishida and Okimoto, over several Ahn, beginning yesterday evening, had gone ashore.

"Launch the galleys!" cried Aëtius, from amidships.

I gathered then that the first galley had been returned to the ship, following the landing.

"No!" said Lord Okimoto.

I gathered that he was unwilling to lose another galley.

Tarl Cabot seized a fellow who was clambering aboard, from one of the small boats. "Go back!" he cried. "Go back!"

"No," said the man, wildly, shaking his head. "No!"

Cabot struck him to the deck.

"Go back," he cried to others, returning to the ship.

"The galleys must be launched," said Tarl Cabot.

"No," said Lord Okimoto.

Tarl Cabot turned on his heel, angrily, and rushed toward a flung-open hatch. He paused at the opening, looking about, in frustration. It was there I caught up with him. "You will need oarsmen," I said.

He clasped my hand. "Good Callias," he said. "Let us be fools together!"

"There will be several below decks," I said. "They are unclear, as I, as to what has occurred."

"Summon them!" said Cabot. "Send others about, as well, to summon others."

"To the galleys?"

"Any who can draw an oar," said Cabot.

"In whose name?" I asked.

"In the name of Lord Okimoto," said Cabot.

In a quarter of an Ahn three galleys had been lowered and, half manned, were about the ship, and moving amongst small boats, toward the shore.

I and the others were armed, as we had obtained weapons, in the issuance, hoping to go ashore in our turn.

I glanced back, to see Lord Okimoto, high above, at the rail of the great ship.

Cabot was at the helm of the galley on which I drew an oar. Across from me, alone on his bench, as I was, was Philoctetes. To starboard, back a bit, was another galley, also with a handful of oarsmen, it commanded by Pertinax, and to port, further back, was the galley of Turgus, more amply manned, as men, later gathered, had come to the last galley nest.

More than once the galley turned, and slowed, rocking, men from the water clinging to the oars. The other two galleys were similarly impeded. "Bring them aboard!" called Cabot. "Put them at an oar."

"Flee, Commander!" wept a man, drawn aboard. "To the ship!"

"We are going in," said Cabot.

"There are too many!" said the man. "It is hopeless! All will die."

"We are going in," said Cabot.

There was a cheer from small boats about us.

"Get to the ship, and then go back!" said Cabot.

There was another cheer.

Men clinging to oars came aboard, and took their places on the benches.

The galley's bow swung toward the beach, and Cabot, from the helm, called the stroke, and, water running from the lifted and dipping oar blades, the galley crested the night waters, and sped, like a gull, toward the torches and confusion on the beach. "Stroke!" called Cabot, "stroke!"

The fellow who had haplessly wept was now beside me at the oar, steady, and strong.

As we made our way through the small boats, most moving toward the ship, we began to hear the cries on the beach, the clash of metal.

It was now clear that quarterless war, red with blood, reigned upon the beach. Some hundreds of our men, in lines, were being forced back, away from the high beach, and the defile, toward the water. Glaives prodded them and struck at them. Swords flashed in the torches. Many, we had later learned, had perished in the defile, from concealed arrow fire, but arrows, now, save at short range, a yard or two, given the proximity of the combatants and the confusion, could scarcely find congenial targets. The arrow, ignorant of its purpose, might with equanimity bestow indiscriminate death.

Several yards from the torchlit, screaming, raucous shore, the clash of metal, the cries of enraged men, of frightened men, of dying men, Cabot turned the galley. "Back oars!" he commanded, and the stern of the galley, backing, pushed its way through small boats and wading men, and, a moment later, he cried "Hold!" and we lifted the oars, and we felt the keel of the galley grate on sloping, submerged sand, at the foot of the shore. We were some dozen or so feet from the beach. Dozens of terrified men rushed about us, wading in the water, seizing oars, trying to climb aboard. Shortly thereafter the galleys of Pertinax and Turgus, turned as well, lay to, at the shore, and were similarly subjected to clambering men. I saw several of the small boats returning to the shore from the ship. They had come back for their fellows. My heart was gladdened.

"Callias!" called Cabot to me, and I rose at the bench, amongst the swarming men.

"Commander?" I called.

"Prepare to command," he said. "I am going ashore."

"With commander's permission," I said, "I, too, am going ashore."

"Stay aboard," he said.

"I am coming with you," I said.

"You understand the danger?"

"Certainly," I said.

"I do not expect to return to the ship," he said.

"Neither then, commander," I said, "will I."

"You are indeed a fool," he said. He then called to Philoctetes. "Take the galley back to the ship. Return. Save whom you can!"

"Yes, commander," said Philoctetes.

"Let tarnsmen, armed, who dare, return with you," said Cabot.

"Yes, commander," called Philoctetes. There were now three or four men at a bench, which should hold two, and the galley was crowded amidships, and fore and aft. Then Cabot, I following him, leaped into the water amongst men trying to board the galley, and, water to our waist, we waded to shore. Once on the beach he paused only to issue similar instructions to Pertinax and Turgus.

"I am coming with you!" cried Pertinax.

"No, you are not," warned Cabot, with an unexpected ferocity that brooked no demur.

"Oars," called Pertinax, taken aback, his voice cracking with misery, "Stroke!"

The galley now captained by Philoctetes had already moved from shore, outside the light of the torches. I watched the galley of Pertinax, now crowded, low in the water, pulling away, toward the ship, dark in the distance. Small boats were about it, some coming, some going. In some of the small boats there were lanterns. A number of men were about, some back of us, in the water.

"Your friend wished to accompany you," I said. "Might his sword not have been of value?"

"He is a high officer," said Cabot. "He is not to be risked."

"Surely you are higher than he," I said.

"But I command," said Cabot.

"You would not risk him," I said. "You fear you will not return to the ship."

"Much depends on the tarn cavalry," he said.

"It may not be flighted," I said.

"It will not be," he said.

"I do not understand," I said.

"I have a plan," he said.

"Seek safety," I said.

"I will not abandon the men ashore," he said.

"Nor will I," I said.

He looked about himself, in the din, fatigued, frightened men, many wounded, moving past us, toward the water, the hope of a boat. He shook his head.

"It is worse than I feared," he said.

There were many torches high in the defile, above the beach. I sensed many men were there. He put his hands on my shoulders. "Good Callias," he said, "hurry to the galley of Turgus. There is time, a little. Board the galley, or a small boat, return to the ship."

"No," I said, "I am with you."

"I did not know the men of Cos had such courage," he said.

"Nor I those of Port Kar," I said.

"You are fearsome enemies," he grinned.

"And loyal friends," I said.

A man, bleeding, ran past us, toward the water, toward a small boat. Much was confusion. We were jostled in the press. Torches threw strange lights and shadows on the sand. Shouts, and the clash of weapons, seemed closer. I gathered our men were being forced toward the water. I turned about, and saw the galley of Turgus, oars striking the water, drawing away. I heard a weird cry behind us, in the water. In the light of a lantern, held by a fellow on a small boat, I saw a fellow's arm disappear beneath the water. I saw the lantern's light flash on a twisting fin, and then another. The tumult, the confusion, the striking of oars, the splashing of men in the water, had doubtless attracted the attention of marine predators, presumably sharks. The attack I had witnessed had taken place in less than three feet of water. The great ship lay some half pasang from shore, in the darkness. Some, of those who could swim, may have reached her. When I had been on the ship, I had, however, noted none who had reached her ropes and ladders from the water. In the distance up the beach, toward the defile, I heard a drum. It was not ours. Given the irregularity of the beat, I took it that its role was tactical, signaling orders. If this were so, the enemy, I thought, must be professional, disciplined, trained. One was not dealing with the disorderly frontal rushings of barbarians or savages, counting on the simple avalanche of numbers. Cabot, his blade now drawn, moved toward the front, while men continued to stream past him, toward the water. I saw his blade move quickly, and a fellow, mixed in with others, clad in black, the uniform of the night, staggered back, was buffeted, fell, and was trampled. Some fifty Pani from the great ship had preceded our hundreds of mariners and armsmen ashore. There were, facing the enemy, some seven or eight lines of our men, strung across an arc of the beach, some seventy yards in width, defending frontally and on the flanks. Behind this wall of steel, its interwoven columns seething forward and backward, giving way, and pressing back, the men at the beach were seeking flight. Had these lines of skilled, hardened men, selected with care by the Pani, veterans, mercenaries, killers, bandits, brigands, and pirates, from enlisted crews, rural gangs, disbanded cohorts, and scattered free companies, not checked the enemy, few if any of our forces would have escaped death. To be sure, these particular men were not so different from the others. That these particular men were where they were was, I supposed, as much an accident of battle as anything else. It doubtless depended on where the enemy had first struck. They knew that if they turned their backs, they would die. They constituted the fragile, dangerous wall behind which swirled panic-stricken rout, the wall without which our forces would be slaughtered, like penned verr, against the sea. I feared the defensive lines might break. A moment of panic, an unpredictable loss of nerve, can, in a moment, turn rows of desperate, brave men into disorganized, fugitive, vulnerable prey. One man in flight, followed by another, and another, can break a line. To be sure, it is reputed infamy to die with a wound in one's back. Indeed, in some cities, men returning with such wounds are put to death. I was at Cabot's side, to protect his left. And, as a man fell, he was at the left of a Pani warrior, with a large, horned, face-concealing helmet. The Pani warrior clutched a long, curved sword with two hands. A glaive struck at him, and one of the hands that bore it flew to the side, blood spurting from the severed wrist. Two foes lay at his feet, impeding the approach of others toward him. I thrust aside a glaive and tried to reach the fellow who wielded it, but it was drawn back. Another was striking downward and I managed to bend forward and catch it behind the blade, though I was forced down to one knee. I lunged upward and caught this darkly clad figure in the throat, below the black helmet. Blood ran upon the overlapping plates of leather mail. It was only later that I realized this was the attack of the doubled glaive, in which the first thrusts horizontally, and the second, on the chance that the defender's attention is distracted, strikes downward. I had a moment's respite. Such things oddly, intermittently, occur, inexplicable eddies in the crashing surf of war. I sensed the line a few feet to my right was, like an ebbing wave, washing back.

"Hold! Hold!" called a familiar voice and the wave held, and washed a bit forward, and I knew he in the great, horned helmet was Lord Nishida. Some Pani were about him, to his immediate right. I now have little doubt that it was his firmness, and leadership, and those of his fellows, Pani and others, which had organized and stiffened that resolute defense behind which the frenzied withdrawal of our primary forces, apparently ambushed, charged, and outnumbered, was in desperate progress. As the line had begun to constrict and hold, bodies, ours and theirs, had begun to encumber the immediate field. Four bodies, sprawled and dark, now lay between Cabot and Lord Nishida. I sensed that some of the dark figures before us were now reluctant to approach those two. Far off in the defile, above the beach, I could see, as before, a large number of torches. These, as it turned out, and as I feared, were lifted amongst ample reserves, not yet committed. A hundred yards or so, toward the defile, I heard the command drums of the enemy. Slowly, before us, facing us, the lines of the present enemy began to back away.

"Hold!" called Lord Nishida. I gathered he knew war, and would not permit his line to move forward, against a methodically retreating, ready foe. This withdrawal tactic is designed to encourage a line to break forward, in pursuit, after which its irregularity may be exploited by an even, frontal counter and pursuit. A similar danger is to pursue a broken foe, or an apparently broken foe, while the foe's marshaled reserves, ready at hand, or even hidden at hand, as in trenches, or amongst trees, are ready to strike from the flank. At this point, I might have ordered a careful, patient withdrawal, by means of which to tighten our line and more closely approach the sea, where lay our avenue of escape, if there were to be any such. But Lord Nishida did not order such a withdrawal. I shortly understood why. Availing myself of this lull, I looked back, toward the sea. I was pleased to see that the three galleys had now returned. They were being boarded by dozens of men. The apparent retreat of the enemy halted some twenty yards before us, toward the defile. If we had turned and fled, as I was tempted to do, we could have been caught against the sea and cut down before we could embark. I heard the drum again, now pounding with an intensity that literally suggested vexation, the drummer perhaps having caught the anger, disappointment, or frustration of whoever might be in charge of dictating the signals. For a few Ehn the two forces faced one another, in the strange light of the torch bearers. Shortly thereafter I understood why Lord Nishida had not ordered the seemingly judicious retreat I would have expected. The original ambush in the defile had begun with a rain of arrow fire, which had taken a heavy toll on our fellows, Pani and otherwise. Archery, later, as the forces had come together, had been substantially discontinued, save for occasional desultory fire, largely undirected, over the heads of the combatants, at generally unseen targets, often out of range, toward the beach. Now, however, to a new drum signal, hurrying between suddenly opening, evenly spaced gaps in the enemy forces, we saw what must have been one hundred to one hundred and fifty archers, with the large Pani bows. These men were not even in position when Lord Nishida signaled to his left flank and right flank, the left commanded by Tajima, of his retinue, whom I knew primarily as a Pani tarnsman, liaison to, or lieutenant to, Cabot, in the tarn cavalry, and the strange warrior, Nodachi, commanding the right flank. I now realized the reason for holding the line as it was, for the bodies with which the field in our vicinity, before us and behind us, was strewn were lifted up, held up, even piled on one another. A given body, held erect, constituted a post, barrier, or hurdle, behind which a column of crouching men might shelter themselves. A number of such bodies, aligned, constituted a set of palings between which it was difficult to find targets. The Pani archers took up their position some fifteen to seventeen yards before our line, some five to three before the infantry of the enemy. This would allow them to withdraw conveniently to the protection of their own forces before we could reach them, if charging. Four bodies were placed before Cabot and Lord Nishida, held by four men, and I, as they, took advantage of this shelter. The Pani bow is powerful but, like the common peasant bow, it, given the lightness of its missile, and that it is drawn by the strength of a human arm, can rarely tear its way through a human body, and its force, even if passing through an arm or throat, is largely spent in its passage. It is unlike an engine-driven shaft, as on a ballista, which might shatter a wall. The thrust spear, of course, impelled by the force of a strong man, may penetrate a four-layered shield or a human body, but then the spear is lost until its retraction. So deep a thrust, like the deep thrust of a blade, is foolish, unless intended to, say, encumber a shield, rendering it useless, preparatory to a blade attack. I heard, for the first time at this range, the sudden, unmistakable sound, so solid, so quick and frightening, of an arrow striking a body, and then its repetition, again, and again. Some of the arrows passed over us, the fletching streaking in the wind, like a darting bird, a whisper of light, almost invisible. Then, again and again, I heard the striking of arrows, one following on another, into the inert barriers, once alive, interposed between us and the Pani bowmen. Certain arrows skinned others, with a shaving, splintering sound. Few arrows found their desiderated marks; arrows bristled from the tragic barriers before us. I thought no single marksman, given the liberty of his judgment, would have continued to fire arrows with such little effect, but, I gathered, this action, with its largely futile waste of missiles, was in accord with the command of the drum, the captain of which, most likely, was well behind the lines, and ignorant, at least now, of the situation in the field. Training and discipline, and obedience to command, is usually, undeniably, of enormous military value. At other times, in altered situations, it is wasteful, unproductive, even stupid. Men who will lose their heads if they do not obey are likely to obey, even if the command is awry, uninformed, foolish, even dangerous.

Again I heard the drum.

Some sense of the situation at the front must have now been relayed to the rear echelons. A channel of communication, after all, is of little value unless it, like a road or river, can be symmetrically traversed.

Although I could not read the signal, its import was clear.

An archer charge is hazardous, of course, unless directed upon an inert enemy. The whole rationale of the war bow is to strike from the safety of distance.

The archers, many of their quivers almost emptied, now began to edge forward.

It would be difficult to elude the shafts at close range. Few had brought shields ashore.

There was a sudden cry from Lord Nishida and our fellows

cast aside the bodies, bristling with arrows, and leaped upon the startled, disconcerted archers, only feet away, few of whom could train or loose more than a single arrow before dying. I saw more than one quiver empty, a last arrow spilled beside a fallen bow in the moist, scarlet dust. Some archers fled back, but the ranks had now been closed against them. Some were slain with thrusts of glaives, others with swords. Several knelt docilely before their own men, shamed, and a headsman went from figure to figure, I gathered, restoring their honor.

By now it seemed, with the return and departure of the galleys, many of our men might have been returned to the ship.

I saw Tarl Cabot leave his position beside Lord Nishida, and move to the rear, where I sensed some stirring, doubtless amongst some of our men.

I did not understand the point of his departure.

I was more concerned with the Pani forces before us, presumably awaiting the issuance of its orders.

Cabot was shortly back, and I was aware of a message, or some form of communication, being passed throughout our lines, even to the left and right flanks.

"Be prepared to obey," said a fellow to me, and then repeated this message to others.

If that were the message, it seemed pointless to me. What soldier is not prepared to obey?

I stood up, and looked back. Some new fellows were behind us, almost as shadows, and, down at the beach, some others, I sensed, might have been approaching. I could see some lanterns, on small boats, and one on the stern of a galley. From torches I could sense, as well, a number of men at the water's edge. Our own position was precarious, but I was sure the defensive lines which Cabot and I had joined, commanded by Lord Nishida, had won the time needed for the withdrawal of most of our surviving forces.

They, at least, would return to the ship.

We waited in place, as did our foes, for the signal of the drum.

When it began to sound, we witnessed, as expected, the movement down the defile, marked by a hundred or more torches, of the mass of Pani reserves.

It did not seem likely we would return to the ship.

A fellow two or three men to my left, suddenly turned and fled toward the beach.

I felt much like following him, and a wash of panic and terror seemed to seize my whole body. Boats were at the shore. I could surely reach one in time. What was I doing here? This was not my war! It was no choice of mine! It was an accident that I was here, at all. It was not of my will that I was here. I was Cosian, not Pani. This was not my business. Too, I was only one man. What did it matter if one ran? The others would stay, and protect my back, my flight. I felt that I must move, run, flee, if only to do something. But I remained in place.

"Steady," I heard a fellow say, to someone, somewhere to my right, on the other side of Lord Nishida, who stood like a rock, unmoving, in the center of our line.

"They are coming," said a fellow beside me.

"Yes," I said.

I did not know why we were whispering. Too, was it not obvious that the enemy was massing, and approaching?

I heard a stirring to my left.

The fellow who had fled had returned.

He must have reached the water's edge, and then turned back, to take his place in the line. No one paid him any attention. He had never left.

The beat of the drum increased.

I supposed Lord Nishida, and the Pani, or some of them, might have read the drum. On the other hand, it was easy to read the movements before us, to see the torchlight on helmets and weapons, to hear, drawing closer, the rustle of steel, leather, and accouterments.

"Be prepared to obey!" called Cabot.

I thought the enemy before us, on the whole, had been directed rationally, its forces distributed intelligently, and applied judiciously, in such a way as not to crowd its attacks, or impede its own movements. In this way, one applies one's resources in a measured manner, conserving them as much as possible and maximizing their effectiveness. Similarly, timing the engagements of elements is important. On the other hand, I had the sense that the commander of the opposing forces had now come to the end of his patience, such as it might have been, and, contemptuous of care and delay, finished with military sobriety, and conscious of his numbers, intended to conclude matters with one crude, costly, irresistible, massive blow.

Men began to run toward us, some falling, stumbling, pushed from behind, jostled, some weapons down, some not lowered. In the torchlight I could see the almost random thicket of glaives, like bunched tem wood in the wind. In the darkness and torches it was almost like a flood of darkness on darkness, a storm of bodies. Some, from the sound, and cries, were trampled by others. The drum struck, again and again, wildly. I think many fell, thrust from behind, and many may have been the wounds inflicted by exposed weapons, edges run against, points buffeted, blades fallen upon. This mad, rushing wall of darkness, squandering men, swept forward.

"Tragic," said Lord Nishida.

"All tall," exclaimed Cabot. "Brace yourself for the impact!"

How could one brace oneself for such an impact? More easily might the talender resist the stamping boot. More easily might the stand of delicate Sa-Tarna turn back the scythe.

But is not deception the key to war?

Our standing masked what lay behind us, and our charging foes prepared to meet us, as we stood, tumultuous crowd to man.

The great flood of darkness, confused, proximate, rushing, pounding, imminent, was some five yards from our steel when Cabot cried out, "Down!"

We all crouched down, instantly, and, from behind us, over our heads, into the confused, rushing mass of men before us there poured a rain of arrows sped from the small, saddle-clearing Tuchuk bow. The leading, confused ranks of our foes probably did not understand what killed them, but they fell, and succeeding rows, four or five, stumbled over them, fell, rose, climbed over them, and met death. A mound of darkness began to form, hills of men. And as succeeding ranks surmounted their fellows, they, too, encountered the rapid fire of the small, powerful, swift bows, developed over generations of warfare amongst the Wagon Peoples of the Southern Plains. It was perhaps only the sixth or seventh ranks of the enemies, impelled by their fellows, who, in the light of the torches, some flung amongst us, realized they were facing archers, and of a sort with which they were unfamiliar. Some cried out, some turned, some stood, as they were, and died. They had no return fire. They had no cover. They could not reach the enemy with their glaives, or swords. Some, escaping arrows, rushed upon us, to fall amongst our blades. Many stood, confused, suddenly realizing they were defenseless, and doomed. The strike of the Tuchuk bow, short, of curved horn, requiring much strength to draw, is heavy, and, at close range, terrible, capable, like the thrust spear, of penetrating the typical four-layered shield. So hapless might be a shieldless swordsman viewing the crossbow, the ready quarrel leveled, set in its guide.

The flood stopped, and, like startled, turned verr, the enemy began to mill, and fearful words were carried to farther ranks, and men who could not even see us received reports so magnified that they must exceed the horror of reality. "Demons!" "Dragons!" we heard.

Had we had stakes and trenches before us, the trenches would have been filled, the stakes heavy with the impaled meat of death.

The enemy turned, and began to flee.

Some enemy officers struck about themselves with swords, trying to stop the rout, but these, too, were as often struck by terrified men who, in the darkness, were unclear as to their foe, his power, or even his nature.

Some of our bowmen climbed over bodies, and from the grisly height of such hills, formed of inert or bleeding men, plied their craft, playing, as it is said, tunes on the lyre of death.

I thought there would be much feasting here for Thassa's gulls.

Tor-tu-Gor, Light-upon-the-Home-Stone, began to rise in the east.

I looked back toward the water. There were now three galleys at the beach, and several small boats. Men stood about them, waiting.

"Honorable friends," said Lord Nishida, "let us return to the ship."

Chapter Twenty-Three

I First See the Castle of Lord Temmu;
Landfall Will Be Made

"It is there," said Tarl Cabot. "See?"

He pointed high, toward the mountains, their peaks soft with fog, off the port bow.

"No," I said.

"Higher," he said.

"No," I said.

"A moment," he said. "Wait."

"Yes!" I said, suddenly.

It seemed tiny in the distance, suddenly visible in the parted fog, and, then again, it was obscured. Small as it seemed now, I knew, given the proportion of the mountains, and the high cliff it dominated, it would be mighty in closer prospect.

"I am told," said Tarl Cabot, "that is the castle of Temmu, the holding, the fortress, of the *shogun*, Temmu."

Lords Nishida and Okimoto, each a lesser lord, or *daimyo*, had eaten of the rice of Temmu.

We had been coasting north for four days, perhaps a pasang offshore, this following the altercation attendant on the ill-advised landing.

It was, accordingly, now the seventh day of the Sixth Month.

I was now in attendance on Tarl Cabot, commander of the tarn cavalry. Though he did not so speak it, I think this may have had to do with the fate of the oarsman, Aeson, but more of that anon. In any event, in his service, I was entitled to be legitimately armed on board. None could then gainsay me a blade. I was pleased, though my swordsmanship was not unusual, to have steel at my hip. That endows one with a modicum of comfort, however modest might be one's powers. Surely, to have the chance of defending oneself is to be preferred to the lack of such a chance. Vulnerability is no virtue; it is peril for the vulnerable, and a fault for fools. Who will deny to the tiny ost the shield and threat of its venom, who convince the tarsk boar to put aside his short, curved tusks? How will the unarmed larl defend his territory, or life; how would the unarmed sleen defend its burrow, its brood, its life? Who most desires you to be disarmed? He who will himself be armed, secretly, or by means of another. Who, unarmed, is wise to dispute the will of the armed? Who wishes you to be most vulnerable, most helpless? He who will not make himself so.

Let slaves and beasts be disarmed, helplessly, and totally. That is fitting for them, as their collars and tethers. It is fitting for them, and perfectly, as they are slaves and beasts.

Let the slave, collared, and scarcely clad, know that she is at the mercy of men, at the mercy of masters—totally, and without recourse.

"There is a cove," said Cabot, "a harbor of sorts, protected from the sea, at the foot of a walled trail, leading upward, to the castle."

"You have not been there," I said.

"No," he said, "but others have."

"I have never seen such a castle, such a fortress," I said.

"I have seen representations of such structures, pictures of such structures," said Cabot, "but it was long ago, and faraway."

To me the slopes, the curves, the peaks, of roofs, and such, were profoundly unfamiliar, but, in their way, awesome, and beautiful. It was hard for me to imagine that so different and beautiful, so artistic, a structure, might be, in effect, a fortress, a place of harrowing might, a holding of formidable power, a housing for a hundred companies, a resister of sieges, a coign of vantage, from which might issue dragons of war, and a closed portal behind which they might, in security, withdraw.

"The men are uneasy," I said. "No longer are they eager to go ashore."

"Who could blame them?" said Cabot.

After the misfortune of the mutiny, we had retained something like one hundred and forty tarns, and seventeen hundred mariners and armsmen. Following that time, too, Lords Okimoto and Nishida had retained something like four hundred and fifty Pani warriors in their commands. Later losses in the Vine Sea and otherwise had not much affected these figures. Whereas we had lost no tarns in the recent tragedy of the ill-advised landing, we had suffered a severe loss of men, Pani and otherwise, in the fighting, in the defile, and later, on the beach. Had it not been for the stubborn rear-guard action of Lord Nishida and others, later reinforced from the ship, and the hasty, nocturnal, massive evacuation of our trapped forces from the beach, it seems clear that the enterprise of Lords Nishida and Okimoto, whatever might be its nature, would have been devastatingly crippled, if not precluded altogether. Proportionately the Pani, unflinching, ever foremost in battle, underwent the greatest loss. Few of the original fifty survived, and of others, of those landed, only some two hundred survived to return to the ship. Of common mariners and armsmen, who, over Ahn, had swarmed ashore, often without authorization, in greater numbers than I had originally conjectured, some twelve hundred had returned to the ship. I estimated our losses as one hundred Pani warriors and three hundred armsmen and mariners. That left us with some three hundred and fifty Pani warriors, and some fourteen hundred mariners and armsmen. These figures, of course, are partly conjectural, as the actual figures, in accord with common military practice, are not revealed to the men.

Some of our casualties, of course, had not taken place in the defile, or on the beach, but in the water, presumably at the side of the boats, or in an attempt to swim to the ship from shore. I had witnessed at least one attack, what I could see of it, of a marine predator, most likely a shark, within a few yards of the beach. One anomaly might be mentioned. Aeson, an excellent oarsman, was found in the water, at the side of the great ship, amongst the small boats, his throat pierced frontally, not laterally cut, a straightforward, cleanly inflicted wound. Obviously he could not have so swum from shore, and would not have been transported in such a condition. Moreover, interestingly, two of the fellows who had shared his boat, insisted that he had been whole at his oar, and that he had been the first to seize a rope, and climb toward the rail, far above. An accident, presumably, had somehow taken place in the darkness, somewhere above, perhaps at the rail itself, the stray movement of a weapon, a running against an anchored blade, or such. Perhaps he had been mistaken for an unwelcome boarder. Tereus, his fellow, who had found the body, drawing it from the water, in the half light of dawn, had howled with rage and demanded the apprehension and searching of the wretched cripple, Rutilius of Ar. This was soon accomplished. He was discovered on a lower deck. He was unarmed. The matter remained unresolved. I had seen such a stroke more than once, twice in the early morning, in a park in Ar, once shortly after dawn on the Plaza of Tarns. The next day Tereus, violent and distraught, had twice sought out Rutilius of Ar, or Seremides, as I better knew him, goading him, jeering him, apparently tempting him to seize up a weapon, or die. Finally the deck watch, disgusted at this bullying, this attempt to intimidate and threaten a substantially helpless man, castigated Tereus roundly and ordered him away, that he might desist in such unmanly, unseemly behavior, wanton abuse, inflicted upon an unfortunate who could not be expected to defend himself. When Tereus withdrew, storming away, in compliance with the instructions of the deck watch, it is said the eyes of Rutilius, glistening, followed him, and that he smiled, and then turned about, and hobbled away, poking at the deck with his makeshift crutch.

"I fear you mistake my meaning, commander," I said.

"I suspect not," smiled Cabot, "but speak."

"I am not an officer," I said.

"Neither are you a slave," he said. "Speak."

"Clearly," I said, "there is danger in this place, ashore, in these islands."

"True," said Cabot. "We received some hint of that at the beach."

"Would we not be outnumbered?" I asked.

"I think," said Cabot, "easily, muchly so."

"One gathers," I said, "the war has gone badly."

"True," said Cabot. "That is my understanding. It was

apparently only a tiny remnant of a once mighty force, driven about, harried, fought, defeated again and again, some seven or eight hundred men, perhaps a thousand, which, exhausted, bloodied, and starving, on a gray, cold morning, surrounded save for the sea, awaiting an onslaught they could not repel, awaiting death, in the Pani fashion, which reached the continent, in the vicinity of Brundisium, reached it somehow by the will of Priest-Kings, or perhaps others."

"Others?" I said.

"Not Priest-Kings," he said.

"And they have dared to return?"

"They are Pani," said Cabot. "I gather that it is to be expected."

"I gather it was expected, by the enemy," I said.

"That seems clear, from the false signals, the matter of the landing," said Cabot.

"Treachery seems to have taken place," I said.

"It seems likely that the signals were betrayed," said Cabot. "Surely they were falsely displayed, to invite the landing."

"Does one know whom to trust?" I asked.

"No," said Cabot.

"There may be enemies in the castle of Lord Temmu," I said.

"It is not impossible," said Cabot. "I gather from Lords Okimoto and Nishida that their movements in the war, in the fighting, were often anticipated. One fears their plans were often as clear to the enemy as to themselves."

"I see," I said.

"To be sure," said Cabot, "a brilliant strategist, an acute tactician, can often anticipate an opponent's moves. In the kaissa of steel such an opponent is quite dangerous."

"Perhaps one such as Lord Yamada?" I said.

"Perhaps," said Cabot.

"There may be enemies aboard, as well," I said.

"Quite possibly," said Cabot.

"Enemies even from the original camp?" I asked.

"Possibly," he said.

"What is the power here, the forces?" I asked.

"I gather," said Cabot, "that the forces with whom Lords Okimoto and Nishida are aligned are relatively few, and that little remains to Lord Temmu other than the great holding and, doubtless, some adjacent lands within its purview, which might be defended from the holding, and perhaps, as well, some obscure mountain valleys, or such, terraced, on which the holding may in part depend, valleys perhaps protected as much by the inaccessibility of the terrain as the castle's armsmen, its *ashigaru*."

"What hope is there of reversing the tides of war?" I asked.

"Very little," said Cabot.

"That may do for the Pani," I said, "but it is not likely to do for others."

"True," said Cabot, grimly.

"I would like to speak my mind clearly," I said. "I assume I may do so."

"Certainly," said Cabot.

"Most rational men," I said, "will be reluctant to commit themselves to a lost cause, to expend themselves in such a cause, particularly if the cause is not their own. Our men, who are mercenaries, and hired as such, save for the Pani, prefer to choose their wars intelligently, to weigh odds, to balance gold carefully against blood, to fight for a presumed victory, with loot and pay in the offing, not for defeat, not for the chains of a slave, not for a likely death in a strange land, amongst an alien folk."

"These things are clear to me," said Cabot.

"On the beach," I said, "they have met the foe, and have some sense of his prowess and numbers."

"True," said Cabot.

"Muchly then," I said, "have the odds shifted."

"Doubtless," said Cabot.

"Further," I said, "the lockers of the men, their kits, their sea bags, from the despoiling of a hundred ships in the Vine Sea, already burst with treasure, with silver, with gold, silk, pearls, and jewels."

"That is my understanding, at least substantially," said Cabot.

"Have they not then already been paid, have they not already acquired more loot than war might augur?"

"Particularly," said Cabot, "if the war seems foolish and dangerous, and the prospects of victory thin, if not hopeless."

"I do not think the men will fight," I said.

"They may have to," said Cabot.

"I do not understand," I said.

"They may have no choice," he said.

"I do not understand," I said.

"I think," said Cabot, "we can better see the holding of Lord Temmu now."

"Yes," I said. It was more toward noon now, and the fog had been largely dispelled.

"We should enter the cove by nightfall," said Cabot. "Lords Okimoto and Nishida will go ashore, to greet Lord Temmu, to gain intelligence, and prepare for the sheltering of tarns. In the morning, most of the men will follow, including the slaves, suitably coffled. Weapons and supplies will be also disembarked. Little will be left on the ship."

"The treasure?" I said.

"That is to remain on the ship," said Cabot, "at least for now."

"I see," I said.

Some men will betray a Home Stone before a tarn disk, being more willing to forsake the one than the other. So simple an arrangement can minimize desertion. To be sure, it is one thing to desert in Victoria, in Market of Semris, in Besnit, in Temos, in Ar, and quite another at the World's End.

"Tonight, under the cover of darkness," said Cabot, "the tarns will be flown."

"The treasure remains on board?"

"Yes."

"Our voyage then is ended?" I said.

"It seems so," said Cabot.

"Men will soon think in terms of another," I said.

"Lords Okimoto and Nishida," said Cabot, "are well aware of that."

Chapter Twenty-Four

We Have Made Landfall;
We Shall Approach the
Castle of Lord Temmu

The stone-set walls were high, on both sides of the steep, winding, cobbled trail, some ten feet in width, better than a pasang in length, leading tortuously upward to the castle of Lord Temmu.

Ashore the men were armed.

Some Pani folk, shuffling, heads down, ill-clad, had threaded their way past us to where lay the wharf, against which, last night, we had moored the great ship. These new Pani, so different from the aloof, proud warriors with which we had become familiar, seemed scarcely to exist. At the wharf, under the direction of higher Pani, in trip after trip, they would gather burdens, hundreds of bundles, bails, and boxes. These were lowered in nets, swung out by booms, to the wharf. These, shouldered, or hung on poles, or sometimes on yokes, they began to transport up the trail. The only paraphernalia we were allowed to carry were weapons and accouterments. The lower Pani, so to speak, were discouraged from touching such things. I had earlier shouldered a box, but one of the ship's Pani warned me to leave that for others. I gathered we were armsmen, and not the bearers of burdens. Perhaps Lord Temmu wished it to be clear that warriors had landed, and not porters. The Pani world was one of complex arrangements and degrees, and many proprieties, and formalities, at least to me, were mysterious. Whereas all natural societies are characterized by rank, distance, and hierarchy, acknowledged or not, I think there is no Gorean caste, from the highest to the lowest, which does not regard itself as the equal or superior, in one way or another, to that of every other. Where would society be without the Builders, the Merchants, the Metal Workers, the Cloth Workers, the Wood Workers, the Leather Workers, the Peasant, with the great bow, the ox on whom the Home Stone rests?

The trail upward was steep.

I was with the second contingent landed, some two hundred men, making its way down the ropes and rail nets.

Tarl Cabot, commander of the tarn cavalry, and his men, were not with us. Last night, under the cover of darkness, the tarns had been flown, to some undisclosed location.

We had seen no sign of the fleet of Lord Yamada.

I regarded the great ship.

Tersites had insisted, in the cove, that it come about, so that its bow might point toward the sea. This seemed to have met with general approval, certainly amongst the men. Treasure in hand, from the Vine Sea, what more was to be gained on a dangerous shore, at the World's End?

The orientation of the great ship, bow to sea, would allow it, should the fleet of Lord Yamada be sighted, to slip its moorings and escape the cove, to the security of the open sea. The orientation also, of course, would facilitate an expeditious departure at any time, independent of some emergency, perhaps one conducted at night, in haste, by stealth.

Did not the great ship, in its way, seductive and beckoning, constitute a temptation?

I lingered on the wharf, past the fourth and fifth contingents.

Interestingly, nothing was permitted to leave the ship through the galley nests, which, if opened, might have provided a convenient access to the wharf. The nests remained closed, almost invisible in the hull, and, I had little doubt, were fastened shut, and guarded, from the inside, by Pani. Opened, they would provide a breach into the ship, quickly and easily exploited. Aside from Tersites and Aëtius, who refused to come ashore, some officers, and a handful of mariners, only Pani were allowed on board, and their role, one supposed, was to prevent a general return to the ship, if not now, later.

I feared for the ship.

And, I suspect, I was not the only one. I saw Tersites at the high starboard rail, that of the stem castle, looking over the side. Then he had turned back, and I could see him no longer.

I feared for the ship.

Had it not served its purpose? Had it not traversed Thassa? Had it not vindicated the madness, the bizarre faith, the superstition and conviction, of its malformed master, half-blind Tersites, a jest amongst the islands, a joke in a hundred ports, who had sent it eyeless upon the open sea? I had long thought this omission, that he would not give the ship eyes, to the uneasiness of many, was cast down as a challenge to Thassa, that it was in its way a defiance, a boast that so mighty a structure had nothing to fear from mother Thassa, from whose womb the land was born, from her moods, her violence, her turbulence, and wind. But now it struck me, and eerily, that this seemingly fearful omission, the denial of eyes, was not so much a bold repudiation of common marine practice and lore as a concession to it deeper than was easily understood. She had been denied eyes that she might not understand how daunting were the long sea roads stretched before her, the perils into which she would be introduced. So, too, might a kaiila be hooded before being raced through the flames of a burning forest, in which arrested, it and its rider would perish.

I saw Tyrtaios stride by.

He was muchly independent now, as Lords Okimoto and Nishida were elsewhere, I supposed in attendance on the *shogun*, Lord Temmu.

"Tal, noble Callias," said he to me.

"Tal, noble Tyrtaios," I said.

He was followed by some eleven or twelve men. I did not know them. They hailed from more than one deck. This made me apprehensive. Tyrtaios, I suspected, was of the Assassins.

I looked up from the wharf toward the castle.

It would be a long, unpleasant climb.

The walls of the narrow trail, I had supposed, were to protect the passage from the castle to the water.

Certainly they would deter small groups, at least, from harrying, if not closing off, that passage, from impeding, if not cutting, the connection between the castle and the sea. On the other hand, such walls, serving to keep some out, serve as well to keep others within.

The most interesting cargo I noted being disembarked from the great ship, a cargo handled with great gentleness, and one not surrendered to the lower Pani, but to warriors, were the eggs of tarns. Each was given to a single warrior, who bowed to the egg courteously, wrapped it in silk, and then began to mount the trail to the castle. I would later learn there had been a much larger number of eggs, but many had perished on the vessel, and been cast overboard. Several had apparently been stolen or destroyed in the mutiny. Some had been broken into, for food. The Pani had slain more than one man for such acts.

A large cage, containing an enormous sleen, snarling and obviously discomfited, was slung over the rail, and lowered toward the wharf. It took eight of the lower Pani to manage the cage up the ascent to the castle. Whereas I had heard this animal from time to time, this was only the second time I had seen it. The first time it had been on deck, in the company of Tarl Cabot. As it moved, twisting angrily about in the cage, its left, hind paw dragged on the cage floor. Any sleen is a dangerous beast. Why would one keep one which was crippled? Slowed, less able to hunt, perhaps in pain, might it not be even more dangerous?

The slaves had been disembarked after the third contingent. They were put in left-wrist coffle, and, ten at a time, were lowered in nets. Once on the wharf, the first girl of one ten was fastened to the last girl of the preceding ten, and so on, until there was a single line of slaves, some two hundred, all joined by the left wrist. Interestingly, they were permitted clothing. Usually *kajirae*, weather permitting, are marched naked in their coffles. This is healthy, allowing the air to refresh their bodies. It also makes it easier to wash the stock, sponging it down, immersing it in local streams, ponds, and such. Too, it saves on garmenture, which might be soiled in a long march, perhaps in dust, or mud. Too, of course, when a woman is chained naked, it is difficult for her to forget she is a slave. The clothing permitted to the slaves, considering their status as livestock, was rather ample, as the tunics, their single garment, extended to the center of the calf, as opposed to being high on the thigh, and often cut at the hip. Further, the tunics were rather coarse, and opaque. They were sleeveless, of course, and their simplicity left no doubt that they were slave garments. As is common the slaves were barefoot. The generosity of the tunics, and their conservatism, had possibly to do with the introduction of such lovely beasts into a new environment, which they might find unfamiliar, and which might find them unfamiliar. Once such beasts would become familiar, and one could better assess how they might be received, with respect to the local populace, one could always display them, relate to them, and do with them as seemed appropriate. For example, they should not, at least initially, be so desirable, and exciting, that Pani free women might kill them. The Pani free women must come to understand that they are no threat to them, no threat to their beauty, prestige, station, and power, but only animals, and slaves, work beasts and toys for their men.

Having reached the wharf in the second contingent, disembarked, I, and some others, of both the first and third contingents, had waited about. It is pleasant to see the marshaling, chaining, and marching of beautiful slaves. Such helpless, lovely creatures, whom one might visualize on the block, whom one might buy, own, train, and master, fill the hearts of men with zest and unrestrained joy. To be sure, these were, on the whole, the livestock of the Pani, to be dealt with as they might please. Some of the fellows, of course, may have been waiting on friends. And others, one supposes, were not eager to essay a narrow, closed, walled-in path, which was clearly steep and long, and at the end of which lay a beautiful, but strange and mysterious structure, which might forebode we knew not what. But most, I think, were waiting to see the slaves. How marvelous that one might own such creatures, as one might own a verr or tarsk.

The slaves, being aligned on the wharf, each ten being fastened to the next ten, looked fearfully up the heights, at the rearing, surmounting castle far above. We were all apprehensive, at having come to the World's End, of course. But they were slaves, vulnerable, and utterly helpless. They were frightened belongings, soon to be fastened together. We were men; we were armed.

One of the girls was sobbing, her body shuddering. Perhaps she was frightened, apart from the security of her mat and chain.

Then the shackle was closed on her left wrist.

I had a special interest in these matters, other than the usual pleasures associated with the inspection and surveying of slaves. I wished to make sure that a particular slave, Alcinoë, was present, that she had not been kept on the ship. She was, after all, of some value. There was a bounty on her.

Accordingly, I had been pleased when I had detected her in the net, being lowered to the wharf with other girls, and had noted that she, the last of her ten, would be attached to the first of the next ten.

She was special to me.

I liked to keep my eye on her.

There was, after all, a bounty on her.

It was well that the slaves had been landed.

Some men, I fear, suspected that the great ship might depart the cove, with the treasure aboard, and the slaves, leaving the contingents then in a strange, hostile land. Thus they were reassured, at least to some extent, that the girls had been brought to shore.

Whereas the landing of the slaves might have been welcomed by the men, and might have well served the Pani by allaying some currents of suspicion amongst the men, it seems clear that, from the Pani point of view, the disembarkation of the slaves was no more than a disembarkation of cargo, no different from other forms of cargo.

That Alcinoë had not been kept on board, despite her value in Ar, pleased me. It suggested that this value might be unrecognized or, more likely, given the interest Seremides had expressed in her, that it was immaterial to the Pani who were seemingly in no need of economic resources, or, at least, of such a kind. She had been purchased in Brundisium as no more than another slave. Too, of what value is a coin which cannot be spent?

In any event, I was ashore, and much pleased that the slave, Alcinoë, was also ashore, and, obviously, for the time, at least, would be easy to keep track of.

Her left wrist was held, while the shackle was snapped about it.

She had been the lofty Lady Flavia of Ar, confidante of the Ubara herself. Now, no more than five yards from me, now almost indistinguishable amongst other goods, she was no more than a tunicked, barefoot, wrist-shackled slave at the World's End.

This pleased me.

Might it not be nice to caress her, until her body reddened and throbbed and her hips and haunches shook and she begged to serve my pleasure?

I thought of her squirming, begging, in my arms, helpless in the spasmodic, uncontrollable throes of a slave.

It might be pleasant.

Then I recalled that I had no interest in her, unless it be to return her to Ar. Still, there is more to life than gold, a girl, say, a slave at one's feet, in chains.

The last ten was attached to the coffle.

A cry rang out, and a whip snapped.

The first step is taken with the left foot.

They were instructed to walk as slaves, with their heads down, not looking to right or left, and, of course, keeping silent.

Women love to speak, and they do it articulately, and beautifully. It is a joy to hear them. It is a lovely part of their life.

Muchly then does it impress their bondage on them that this delight may not be exercised without the explicit, or implicit, permission of a free person. What a difference between the unquestioned prerogatives of the free woman who may speak if and when, and as, she pleases, and the helplessness of the slave who may be silenced with a word or gesture, and may not speak without permission.

Surely the nature of a woman much changes, once the collar has been snapped about her neck.

Men were about the wharf and the slaves' coffle must proceed between them. And, as is common, many were the remarks, comments, whistles, observations, sounds, and such, to which the shackled *kajirae* were exposed.

Such a coffle, in such a situation, such a display of goods, is sometimes referred to as a collar banquet, as though its contents might be something which men might seize and on which they might feast.

The coffle, interestingly, was accompanied by Pani youth, of the lesser sort, with switches. As I understand it, something similar is often done amongst the Red Savages of the Barrens, namely, that adult white females are placed in the charge of boys. In this way, controlled and herded as the animals they are, they are taught that they are inferior even to the children of their masters.

When Alcinoë passed me, I whispered to her, "Heat your thighs, slut," and she jerked at the chain, frightened, but kept her head down, and whispered, "Yes, my Master." That had surely been a mistake. She had been terribly startled. She had not thought. For such a mistake, a girl might be switched. I was not her master. She was a ship slave. I watched her proceed toward the end of the wharf, the walled-in trail. Normally, of course, that expression, 'my Master', is used only to one's actual master, the one to whom one belongs.

Almost all the slaves, of course, wore ship collars, as did Alcinoë, but some had lighter, lovelier collars, more common on the continent, and islands, but as securely locked, and as unslippable. I saw Pertinax's Jane and Cabot's Cecily. They had not been taken with the tarn cavalry, to whatever might have been its destination. Both seemed apprehensive. They were now with common slaves, public slaves, so to speak. Both were delicious sluts, with sweet love cradles. They were perhaps being confiscated. At the World's End, who could gainsay the Pani? The tarn cavalry had been brought, largely intact, to the holding of Lord Temmu. I wondered if Tarl Cabot, Pertinax, and some others, might not now be expendable. Surely they were not Pani. Did Pani now need them? Would Pani trust them? Slaves, of course, are in little danger. They are not likely to be slain, no more than other animals. They may, of course, as other animals, easily change masters.

The hatred and contempt of the free woman for the meaningless, despicable slave, so far beneath her, is well known. On the other hand, when a city falls, when walls crumble in flame, and the streets run with blood, the free woman, unlike the slave, has much to fear. Their freedom, commonly so estimable, is now likely to earn them the bloody blade, their heads as readily posted on pikes as those of others. There is none to defend them, none to save them. Where shall they hide, within the encirclements, away from the room-to-room searches, away from the snuffling sleen, searching for a scent? It is not unknown for them to tear away their clothes and prostrate themselves before mocking victors, covering their feet with kisses, and begging to be spared. "Are you a slave?" they might be asked. "Yes, Master!" they sob. "Whose slave?" "Your slave, Master!" Sometimes their own serving slaves, who have often been much abused, as is commonly the practice of the scornful free woman, set upon their former mistress, strip, and bind her, and lead her, leashed, to slave-gathering points, at a wall, or at major cross streets, throwing her to the feet of conquerors, that her thigh may be seared as theirs, and a collar put upon her. "I am a free woman!" might cry the shamed, affronted captive. "How dare you bring me a free woman?" might the slaves be asked. The free woman is then thrown to her belly, and a sword is put at the back of her neck, and the arm is then raised. Surely it is an honorable death. "Please spare me, Master!" cries the free woman. "Master?" "Yes, Master! Master!" The woman is rudely turned, so that she is supine. The eyes of men rove her. She trembles. Might she please a master? Would she do, as a slave, even minimally? "Take her away," says one of the men, "mark her, collar her. Perhaps she will do as a pot girl." The slaves laugh, as their former mistress is dragged to the side. In addressing the word 'Master' to a man, did she not confess herself slave? Her masquerade of freedom is then at an end. Many free women, it is said, and perhaps all, as is hinted, are merely slaves who have dared to conceal themselves for a time in the habiliments of the free. Better then, at last, that they will know the cage, the chain, the rope, the whip.

I saw the blond slave, Saru, pass.

I saw her, more than once, lift her head, slightly, and, with agonized eyes, whispering, interrogate some fellow to the side.

When she came to my vicinity, the chain had halted briefly, for some girls, ahead, had fallen, trying to ascend the steepness of the trail. It was not an easy climb. She whispered to me, plaintively. "Noble Master, where is Master Pertinax? Do you know him? Is he about? Tell him of me, please tell him of the slave, Saru!"

"Be silent," I told the slave. Surely she knew she was not to speak in coffle. I was entitled to strike her, but I did not. Any free person is entitled to administer discipline to an errant slave. It is, so to speak, a favor to the master. To be sure, I had no idea where Pertinax might be, save that I supposed him with the tarn cavalry, wherever that might be. Might not the slave have supposed as much? But perhaps not. Slaves are commonly kept in much ignorance. Would you, for example, spend time imparting information to kaiila, tarsks, and such?

Too, what was her interest, that of a slave, in the whereabouts of a free man? What might Pertinax be to her or she to him?

A bit later I gathered that her indiscretion had caught up with her, for I heard her cry out, in misery, several yards ahead, almost at the end of the wharf, near the beginning of the trail. One of the Pani youth had come up behind her, probably unnoticed, caught her speaking, and struck her, several times, swiftly, about the left arm and neck. She had her head down then. She looked neither to the right nor left. And I supposed she would now be silent, appropriately so, perfectly so, forbidden speech. And she might hope that she had not been noted in such a way that she might be whipped at the journey's end.

What might Pertinax be to her, or she to him?

I should mention one thing which I found of great interest, in the matter of the coffle. It may be recalled that amongst the slaves of the Venna keeping area, supposedly the area of higher slaves, there had been a certain number of slaves which, when brought to the open deck, had been invariably hooded. I had supposed, originally, as I saw no hooded slaves disembarked from the ship that those slaves were retained on board. On the other hand, I had heard a fellow remark, as one of the large cargo nets swung out from the rail again and once more began its descent to the wharf, "That is the last ten, the last of the slaves." "Surely not," I said. "How many are there?" he asked. "Two hundred, some two hundred," I said. "Well," said he, "when that ten is added, there will be twenty tens." "It cannot be all," I said. "There were hooded slaves." "I know fellows in the kitchen," he said. "They tell me two hundred, give or take two or three." "Where are the hooded slaves?" I asked. "Perhaps they have been cast overboard," said a fellow. There was laughter at this, so merry a jest, a form of humor likely to be less amusing to slaves than others. To be sure, who would jettison such lovely cargo, goods so pleasant to behold, and hold? "Mixed in," said another. "Yes," I said. "Mixed in!" "I do not see any who seem all that different from others," said a fellow. "No," said another. "Why were they hooded, anyway?" asked another fellow, scrutinizing the passing coffle. "Pani are strange," said a man. "It was a Pani madness."

I suddenly understood, or thought I understood, the rationale for the hooding. It was truly important to hood one slave only, the former Talena, of Ar. I had recognized her, to my astonishment, in the private area within the Venna keeping area. To hood several was merely to suggest that any particular one was not of paramount importance. A single hooded slave might have provoked a great deal of speculation. The nonsense of extraordinary beauty, though the slaves were clearly high-quality merchandise, was to conceal the identity of one slave, Talena, of Ar. If it was understood that she was on board, considering the bounty on her in Ar, the men might have become unmanageable, and insisted on putting about, and returning to the mainland. Pani, and some others, might have resisted, and the enterprise of the great ship, whatever it might be, would doubtless have come to an end. And the Pani, of course, would brook no temporary return to the mainland, no delay in their venture to the World's End. The outcome of the war might be soon decided, had perhaps already been decided. That Talena's presence on board might have been disruptive was clear, and that the concealment of her presence was prudent was also clear. What was not clear was why the Pani would have her on board, at all. I assume, given the precautions exercised, and such, that they were well aware of her political and economic importance. There must then be some additional reason for her presence, perhaps in the camps in the northern forests, of which I had heard, on the ship, and here, at the World's End. Indeed, why would she have been so mysteriously swept from the height of the Central Cylinder in Ar, long ago? She must have some importance to Pani, or to someone, or something, but what it might be, I did not know.

There had been twenty slaves in the private section of the Venna keeping area, those who had regularly been hooded. Alcinoë and I had seen them, even examined them, in the light of the lamp. It had been then that we had encountered amongst them, frightened, now only one slave amongst others, she who had been Talena, the Ubara of Ar, in the time of the Great Treason. I supposed that she had been given a name, as is usual with slaves, but I did not know what it was. I was sure that Seremides could recognize her, but I doubted that he knew she was about. I could recognize her, of course. And Alcinoë. But, as far as I knew, we might be the only three other than, presumably, some of the Pani, who could do so. I had no intention, of course, of revealing her identity. It might be worth one's life to do so. I envied many of my fellow armsmen, who could simply look upon her, as a man looks upon a slave, as merely another slave. To be sure, that was how she should now be looked upon, as that is all she now was. Let a woman be looked upon as a slave. She is then looked upon as a woman.

I saw whip slaves, in their turn, moving past.

They were wrist-shackled identically with the others, and were similarly clad, and were barefoot. Gone were their switches. Gone now was their authority. As slaves they were poor stuff. I doubted that, stripped and exhibited, they would bring much off the block. To be sure, some men might like them. Perhaps some Peasants might buy them, to hoe suls, to pick beans, to swill tarsks, to draw the plow, to warm their feet in the winter.

I did not expect to recognize all the slaves from the private section of the Venna keeping area, having seen them but once, in poor light, but I had little doubt I could recognize some of them.

The last ten had, as noted, been joined to the coffle.

"See the pelt on that one," said a fellow.

That was one, one from the private area, for sure. Her reddish hair, like a flame, burned to her very calves.

I then saw another I recalled.

Excellent, I thought. They are here, mixed in.

It was interesting to see them in the light. I remembered some six or seven.

Talena, I supposed, would be here somewhere.

"Keep your head down," said one of the Pani youth to a slave, and struck her, stingingly, once on each calf, below the hem of the tunic. "Yes, Master!" she said. "Forgive me, Master!"

I was pleased.

Slaves should well understand themselves as slaves, for that is all they are.

It was a great temptation, of course, for them to look up, and ahead, toward the castle of Lord Temmu, far above.

Curiosity may not be becoming in a *kajira*, but they are inveterately curious. How they will wheedle and plead for the least tidbit of information, kissing one about the knees, looking up, hopefully. Their curiosity reminds one of that of the tiny, agile, scampering saru, hurrying about amongst the branches of the forests of the Ua.

Then I saw her, rather toward the end of the coffle, perhaps seventeenth, or eighteenth, from the end.

She did not see me, of course, for she kept her head down, as the slave she was, and, I gather, now knew herself to be.

If she had any doubt as to the matter, a bout with the lash would soon convince her.

It is an excellent, and beautiful, moment when a woman realizes that that is what she is, a slave.

She is then whole within herself, content, and loving.

The pain is ended.

She is the property of her master.

Yet she had no private master. She was the property of the ship, which is very different. The Pani, of course, could give her to anyone. Perhaps she might even be given to Lord Yamada, among other gifts, in a petition for peace, or mercy, or as a token of esteem or good will.

I watched her approach.

It was interesting to me. She might be now struck, no differently from any other slave.

Who, at one time, would have dared to think of striking Talena, Ubara of Ar?

Now, a slave, she was subject to the whip of a child.

Had she had true power in Ar, had she been a true Ubara, and not a puppet of the occupation, her word might have created and destroyed fortunes, humbled generals and exalted common armsmen; armies might have been marched at her word, and tarn cavalries launched, wars begun and wars ended, but she had had, for the most part, only the trappings of power, not power itself. Yet she had sat upon the throne, presided on public occasions, issued the decrees prescribed, and made the appointments recommended. She had seemed to have power, and I do not doubt but what the unastute thought it hers.

Now she was approaching, coffled.

I had attended, as a guardsman, many of her fetes and banquets, and had attended her, and others, at the theater, at concerts, and song dramas. Her regalia had been complex and sumptuous, rich and colorful, the envy of every free woman in the city, each pleat and fold carefully arranged by slaves; her slippers had been laced with pearls, her veils had shimmered with jewels. Cast flowers and sprinkled perfumes, drummers and flautists, preceded her chair, borne by mighty slaves, flanked by liveried guardsmen.

"There is a pretty one," said a man.

"No, look at that one," said a fellow, indicating another.

Men may look upon slaves appraisingly, as upon other beasts. If one may admire the silken coat, the flanks, of a kaiila, one may, as well, admire the pelt, the flanks, the curvature of a calf, the trimness of an ankle, the roundedness of a forearm, the delight of a shoulder and throat, the lissome figure, the exquisite features, of a lesser animal, a slave.

Talena had been said to be the most beautiful woman on all Gor. There was no doubt she was quite beautiful. I thought she might bring as much as four silver pieces off the block. To claim however that she was the most beautiful woman on all Gor seemed absurd. A similar claim might have been made of thousands of free women, and with considerably more justification, given their revelatory garmenture, their total lack of veiling, and such, of tens of thousands of slaves. Who is to assess the complementarities, and mysteries, of such matters? A woman who is a pot girl to one fellow may be a dream to another, worthy of a diamond collar and a chain at the foot of a

Ubar's throne. There was no doubt that the traitress, the former false Ubara, Talena, was lovely. I myself, however, would have preferred to have the lips and tongue of another on my feet.

She who had worn the medallion of power in Ar now passed me, far from the city, far from her flatterers and servitors, far from the throne, merely another slave, wrist-shackled, tunicked, and barefoot.

The climb to the castle would be lengthy, and arduous.

Looking up toward the rail from the wharf, I saw Seremides, watching the Pani below.

I supposed that he would remain on the ship.

On the wharf, I saw Tereus. A mariner, assigned the wharf watch, in charge of order here, posted to discourage loitering and prevent pilfering, spoke to Tereus, and he began to ascend the trail.

I thought it wise for Seremides to remain on the ship.

Many were those who wished him dead.

Some of the lesser Pani were already returning to the wharf. Some bore sedan chairs, by means of which contract women might be carried to the castle.

I waited about.

A light rain began to fall.

Such rains, I would learn, are common in the area, and, not unoften, rains far more severe.

I supposed that Philoctetes had preceded me.

Licinius Lysias passed, and we exchanged greetings. I was uneasy in his presence. Early in the voyage, when a galley was launched, he had often been chained to his bench. As we had no bench slaves on board, such fellows usually found on round ships, I supposed him a recreant of sorts, spared for his strength at an oar. Later he had sat his bench not otherwise than the rest of us. More than once we had drawn oar together.

I was not eager to ascend the long climb alone.

Men passed me, and I thought of joining them, but one prefers fellows one knows.

Leros, and Aeacus, whom I knew from the high watches, had been in the first contingent and were doubtless already within the castle, or its walls.

I had turned about, finally, to join others, to make my way upward, when I heard my name called, "Callias!"

I turned about, and, to my surprise, one not pleasant, I saw Seremides hobbling toward me, the crutch striking on the wharf planks.

"Noble Rutilius," I said.

"You know me from Ar," he snarled.

"So who are you?" I asked.

"Rutilius, Rutilius, of Ar," he said.

"Of course," I said.

"There are no bounties here," he said.

"Clearly," I said.

"You saved my life," he said.

"I had not thought the matter through," I said.

"It is a life worthless enough, as it is," he said.

"It is worth what it is to you," I said.

"You protected me on the ship," he said, "from the sleen, Tereus, from the bullying urts, Aeson, Thoas, and Andros. I have never forgotten that."

"Thoas and Andros were slain on the ship, during the boarding, near the Warning Ship," I said. "Aeson was found in the water, near the ship, dead, the morning after the ambush, after the evacuation of the beach."

"Oh?" he said.

"Their deaths were not well understood," I said.

"I see," he said.

"You smile," I noted.

"Have you seen the oarsman, Tereus, about?" he asked.

"Surely you saw him from the rail," I said. "He was ordered from the wharf."

"He is gone?"

"Toward the castle," I said.

"He was waiting for me," said Seremides.

"I conjectured as much," I said.

"He intends to kill me," said Seremides.

"Do not be alone with him," I said. "Do not accept a challenge."

"In Ar," he said, "I could have cut off his ears and nose, and hamstrung him, before ramming my blade into his heart."

"You should have remained on the ship," I said.

"I was roped, raging, and lowered to the wharf, helpless, while they laughed, like a bag of sa-tarna."

"You are not of the Pani," I said. "Neither are you an officer, nor a mariner."

"They put me off to die," he said.

"Perhaps," I said. I thought that possible.

"Protect me," he said.

"Are you afraid?" I asked.

"Yes," he said, angrily.

"Seremides, afraid?" I said.

"As Seremides is," he said, "Seremides is entitled to fear."

"Certainly you have sent many before you to the Cities of Dust," I said.

"Never without cause," he said.

"Causes are easily come by," I said.

"Help me," he said.

"Why?" I asked.

"People pay me little attention," he said. "They ignore me. They do not know I am about. I do not matter. They speak freely before me. I hear things. I know matters which might be of interest to you, and others."

"I must be on my way," I said.

"How can I climb that hill?" he asked, angrily, gesturing with the tip of the narrow crutch.

"It will be difficult," I said.

"In Ar, we were brothers in arms," he said.

"In Ar," I said, "I was a fellow of the occupation, you were a traitor."

"We are of the ship," he said.

"You are a killer," I said. "And I think you are a murderer."

"You see me as one betrayed by fortune," he said. "Behold, I who once was formidable, mighty and feared, high in Ar, second only to Myron, *polemarkos* of Temos, am now reduced, am now no more than a mockery of a man, a helpless cripple, at the mercy of the meanest villain or rogue."

"I depart," I said. "Do not expect me to wish you well."

"Help me," he said.

"If I am with you," I said, "the same blade which seeks you may strike me."

"Are you afraid?" he asked.

"Certainly," I said.

"Who but you," he asked, "would protect me?"

"Cabot would," I said. "Tarl Cabot." I thought of him as perhaps as great a fool as I.

"Is he here?"

"I do not know where he is," I said.

"Protect me," he said.

"Seek another," I said.

"We are of the same ship," he said.

I cried out in rage.

"The same ship," he smiled.

"Give me your arm," I said.

As he lurched toward me, he brushed against me.

"You are armed," I said.

"Of course," he said.

We then addressed ourselves to the trail, in the light rain.

Chapter Twenty-Five

I Introduce Two Slaves to One Another

I had inquired the name of several slaves, now and then, casually, over the past few days, but was particularly interested in one name, that of one slave. Obviously I did not wish to signal her out, suggesting that she might be of special interest. Slaves, of course, as other animals, are named as masters may please. The name given to the slave was Adraste.

"It was you, in Ar, who threw me the rag of a slave!" hissed Adraste.

I had taken Alcinoë by the hair, bent her over, and thrust her into the same small kennel with Adraste, and had then swung shut the gate, it locking with its closure. In this way, the two former highest, richest women in Ar, both traitresses, both muchly involved in the Great Treason, both wanted in Ar, both now slaves, were forced to confront one another, in their current humiliation, shame, and degradation.

The thrice-walled grounds of the castle of Lord Temmu, all in all, must have occupied more than a full square pasang, extending broadly over a wide plateau, which, on one side, fell straight to the sea, and was accessible otherwise, as from the cove, by steep trails, one of which was walled, that from the wharf. The trails were narrow, fortified, and might be economically defended. An ascent otherwise, given the steepness of the plateau, almost vertical, accentuated by the work of Lord Temmu's military engineers, would have been not only difficult but extremely hazardous. A small group of skilled climbers, approaching at night, might have reached the foot of the walls, but it seemed that an ascent of the plateau by any large group, certainly undetected, would have been unlikely. Three additional precautions tended to militate against a practical ascent of the plateau, one of which was quite new to me. Comprehensible enough was the precaution of symmetrically placed, projecting guard stations built into the side of the plateau, each manned by two *ashigaru*. From each station arrow fire might rake the side of the plateau. No point on the plateau was not accessible to fire from two directions. Each station, too, was equipped with a drum, by means of which signals could be conveyed. A second precaution, sensibly enough, was the nightly illumination of the plateau, though dimly, by lanterns. A lantern which ceased burning would be noted and investigated. The most interesting precaution, at least to me, was the provision of nesting sites on the almost vertical slopes for the Uru, which is a small, winged, vartlike mammal. This mammal, which usually preys on insects and small urts, like several species of birds, is communally territorial. When disturbed, it shrieks its warning and it is soon joined by a clamoring swarm of its fellows. In this way, a natural alarm system is obtained. Moreover, if a nesting site is closely approached, the Uru is likely to attack the intruder. It is a small mammal, but, shrieking and flying at the face of a climber, one precariously clinging to an almost vertical surface, it is, I am told, at least in such a situation, something most unpleasant to encounter. In any event, the holding of Lord Temmu, if not impregnable, was redoubtable. It remained, at least until now, despite the woes of the war, secure and inviolable, one stubborn, mighty, obdurate impediment to the designs of Lord Yamada, *shogun*, as it was said, at least by his minions, of the Twelve Islands.

It was now the second day of the Sixth Passage Hand, three days before the autumnal equinox.

Pani continued to guard the great ship.

Training was extensive and exhausting.

I did not know when we would march.

I saw little of Cabot, but, from time to time, he appeared at the castle, arriving at night on tarnback, presumably to consult with the *shogun*, Temmu, and Lords Okimoto and Nishida. I gathered things proceeded apace with the tarn cavalry, surely so if they were as deep in training as we were.

I myself had never seen Lord Temmu.

I gathered this was not that unusual, given that he was a *shogun*.

We had seen nothing of the fleet of Lord Yamada. Were we in the vicinity of the continent, where the climate was less mild, I might have supposed the fleet had retired to its base, or port, for the fall and winter. Here, one did not know. It might, of course, have returned to port. One did not know. I did learn, interestingly, that Lord Temmu had possessed at one time a navy, but that it had been substantially driven from the sea. He had been, it seemed, no more successful at sea than on the land. To be sure, it had been a small thing, compared with the ships at the disposal of Lord Yamada. It consisted now, I had learned, of only three ships. They were much, presumably, like the ships of the Vine Sea, with their battened sails and high stem castles. One of these ships, to my great interest, had put in at the wharf a week ago, for water and supplies, and then, a day later, set out to sea again. I had learned much of these matters from some of the lower Pani after the wharfing of the ship, who, once they had overcome their diffidence, seemed pleased to speak with me, one who would speak with them, pleasantly, bow to them, show them respect, and such. They became silent when one of the higher Pani might approach.

Four days ago there had been much stirring, much agitation, amongst the men. Tersites, who, as Aëtius, his fellow, had never left the ship, had had eyes painted on its bow. In the morning, they were there, large, bright, patient, calm, stately. It was as though the wood had sprung to life. This produced alarm amongst the men, for it suggested the possibility that the ship might depart. Why else would eyes, after all this time, be given to the great ship? The anxiety of the men was somewhat assuaged when it was made clear to them that the Pani who guarded the ship were not mariners, and that the small number of officers and mariners who came and went upon her, from time to time, would not be enough to bring her to sea. I myself suspected that Tersites had at last given eyes to the ship because he was terrified for her, and hoped that she might now, moored at the wharf, be able to see her danger, danger more from men than the sea.

As long as the ship was there I knew that our men would see it as a symbol of the far world they knew, and remembered, would see it longingly, would see it jealously, would see it as their only likely passage home. Was their treasure not aboard? What had they to hope for here, other than uncertainty, danger, and possible death?

I sensed there was much secret speaking amongst the men.

The Pani, of course, would be well aware of this.

No wonder Tersites gave eyes to the great ship.

The slaves were muchly sequestered, in kennels here and there, these kept in sheds, within the compound, away from the frequent rains.

There were free Pani women in the castle, perhaps companions of officers, and several contract women. These women, demure in their kimonos, their tiny hands in their sleeves, would sometime, in their short, careful steps, visit the kenneled slaves. They looked upon them much as one would look on caged verr. Sometimes they spoke softly amongst themselves, laughed, and turned away.

Of what interest might such caged beasts be to anyone?

But men looked upon them and saw them differently, in terms of the uses of slaves.

There were fewer slaves now, as some fifty had been taken from the castle's grounds. Whereas certain things remained obscure to me, several of the lower Pani, who served in the castle, spoke to other Pani, and some of these spoke to me. A number of probes, reconnaissances, or inquiries had been conducted following our arrival. Doubtless some of these were intended to locate and ascertain the numbers and dispositions of Lord Yamada's forces in the vicinity, but others were apparently of a much subtler nature, some to instigate apprehension which might spread naturally to the enemy, with appeals to fear and superstition, and others of a more prosaic, diplomatic nature. Rumors were being spread by Lord Temmu's men, disguised as fishermen, herdsmen, and such, of new allies for Lord Temmu, strange warriors, arrived from far off, and, terrifyingly, of dragon birds, which might fly forth and destroy armies. I had no doubt that our mercenaries were formidable, but they were no more so, or less so, one supposed, than the forces likely to be arrayed against them. If nothing else, the ambush and fighting in the defile and at the beach would make that clear to the generals of Lord Yamada. The tarns were another matter. I gathered that these folk had never seen a tarn, and might not even, at first, understand such things to be a natural, vulnerable form of life. They might take it as a dragon bird, whatever that might be. Terror, of course, can be as dangerous a weapon as the sword or spear. Not only would tarns be new to these islands, but they were unfamiliar as well, as far as I knew, with the swift, lofty, silken kaiila, common in the Tahari, on the southern plains, in the Barrens, and such. An army could move only as fast as its slowest man could march. The Pani did have, however, one swift mode of communication. I gathered this from my friends amongst the lower Pani. To be sure, it was available only to a few. It was the swift-flighted, message-carrying Vulo, released, seeking its familiar cot and roost. The overtures of diplomacy were addressed to minor *daimyos*, of which there were many. The taxes of Lord Yamada were high, the agricultural confiscations were large, to feed his army, often leaving starvation in their wake. The contumely of his officers was oppressive, and their appropriations severe, enforced quarterings, sons impressed for the navy and army, daughters taken for training in the contract houses, or, as likely, simply caged for the girl markets. The rule of Lord Yamada was one of iron. Crucifixion was a common punishment, and might be inflicted for so small a cause as an indiscreet expression, a careless word, a bow deemed insufficiently prompt or deep, insufficiently ingratiating. A warrior might remove the head of a Peasant, to try the quality and stroke of a sword before its purchase. I did not know, were the situation reversed, if Lord Temmu would be much different. But the situation was not reversed. The fifty some slaves taken from the compound were an ingredient in these various diplomatic missions. They were apportioned, along with other gifts, among the *daimyos*.

In passing, one might mention the blond, barbarian slave, Saru. It may be recalled she was not a ship slave, but the personal slave of Lord Nishida. On the other hand, as far as I know, supposedly because of certain reservations pertaining to the nature and quality of her character, he had never deigned to honor her with slave use. It seems he regarded her as unworthy to be his slave.

In any event, she was stripped and danced before Lord Temmu, after which Lord Nishida, as was apparently his original intention, gave her to him. Lord Okimoto, then, perhaps not to be outdone, gave ten slaves to the *shogun*. Of our original store, or cargo, of slaves then, we retained something like one hundred and forty.

"It was you, in Ar, who threw me the rag of a slave!" hissed Adraste.

"It fitted you well!" said Alcinoë.

"I was naked, save for it!" said Adraste.

"I would not have given you so much," said Alcinoë, "despicable traitress!"

"I am Ubara!" said Adraste.

"Go back to Ar and claim your throne!" said Alcinoë.

"I am Ubara!" wept Adraste.

"You are a collared slave!" said Alcinoë.

Adraste clutched the collar on her neck, and shook it, as though it might be removed.

"See?" said Alcinoë.

"You, too, you slut," said Adraste, "are collared. You, too, are a slave!"

It may be recalled that I had taken Alcinoë by the hair, bent her over, and thrust her into same small kennel with Adraste, and had then swung shut the gate, it locking with its closure. In this way, the two former highest, richest women in Ar, both traitresses, both muchly involved in the Great Treason, both wanted in Ar, both now slaves, were forced to confront one another, in their current humiliation, shame, and degradation. I had thought this would be of interest, even amusing, to put the slaves together.

"Slave! Slave!" said Alcinoë.

"Slave, slave!" cried Adraste.

* * * *

I had earlier sought out Adraste's kennel, and stood before it. I had not spoken. Adraste, within, kneeling, in the rather generous tunic, given to the slaves by the Pani, looked out, through the bars. "Master?" she said, uncertainly.

"Do you know me?" I asked.

"No, Master," she said.

I thought it likely she had not recognized me in the private area of the Venna keeping area, some nights ago, for the light of the lantern had fallen full on her face, perhaps half blinding her, not on mine, and not on that of Alcinoë, who stood back, rather out of the light. Too, soon in position, she had scarcely dared to do more than stare ahead. Some masters do not permit the eyes of the slave to meet theirs, unless commanded to do so, or given permission. To me, that seemed absurd. Surely one of the pleasures of the mastery is to look directly into the eyes of the slave. Are their eyes not often beautiful, brown, blue, hazel, green, so delicate, so soft, so moist? Why should one not in all ways enjoy one's property? And is it not pleasant to hold her face in your hands, and look deeply upon it? Does her lip tremble? Has she committed a fault of which you might be unaware? Is she afraid of your switch? Or are her eyes pleading for the chains and fur?

"Look closely upon me," I said. I stepped more into the light.
Suddenly she shook with fear.

"You recognize me," I said.

"No, no!" she said.

"I recognize you," I said.

"I think not, Master," she said.

"Oh?"

"I am only a slave," she said, "only a humble slave. My name is Adraste! I am Adraste, Adraste!"

"If it pleases Master?"

"Yes, of course," she said, "if it pleases Master."

"It pleases me, muchly," I said.

"Thank you, Master," she said.

"You speak truly," I said.

"Master?"

"You are the slave, Adraste."

"Yes, Master!"

"And," I said, "once Talena, of Ar."

"No!" she said. "No!"

"You are no longer a free woman," I said. "You may now be punished for lying."

"Please, no, Master," she said.

"Have you ever felt the lash?" I asked.

"I?" she asked, disbelievingly.

"Yes," I said.

"No," she said.

"Some time with it would doubtless do you good," I said. Thousands, I supposed, would be pleased to think of the once-proud Talena, of Ar, now a slave, bound, and writhing under the lash, the slave lash, now appropriately to be applied to her. I had little doubt that the imperious and demanding Talena had put her own slaves under it, often enough. Now she, too, as they, a mere slave, was subject to it.

"I beg mercy," she said.

I did not deign to respond. Let her consider what might be done to her.

"Please do not punish a poor slave," she said.

"Have you not lied?" I asked.

"Forgive me, Master!" she said.

"The whip," I said, "is an excellent device for encouraging dutifulness in a slave, and a desire to please, a zealous desire to please. Surely you noted that in your own slaves."

"Please do not whip me, Master," she said.

"Why not?" I asked.

"I do not want to be whipped," she said.

"What is that to me?" I asked.

Tears suddenly sprang into her eyes, and her small, lovely hands clutched the bars, through which, pathetically, she peered up at me.

"You would have me whipped, would you not?" she said.

"More likely I would bind you, and do it myself," I said.

"Surely not!" she said.

"Know yourself recognized, slut," I said, "once Talena of Ar."

"No!" she wept. "No!"

"You are in need of correction, girl," I said. "I go now, to fetch the slave lash."

"Please, no, Master!" she said.

I turned back.

"Slave," I said.

"—Yes, Master."

"Who am I?" I asked.

"Callias," she whispered, "Callias of Jad, Cosian, spearman, first of nine, guardsman, the occupation, the Central Cylinder."

"Better," I said.

In her terror, and misery, she tried to rise up, but could not do so, as the kennel does not allow that. Then again she was on her knees. Tears now ran down her cheeks. She grasped the bars, tightly, desperately. She pressed her face, as she could, against the bars.

"And who are you?" I asked.

"You know!" she said.

"Speak it," I said.

"Once Talena, of Ar," she whispered.

"Yes," I said.

"Dear Callias," she said. "Please do not tell anyone!"

"'Master'," I said.

"Please, Master," she said. "Do not tell anyone!"

"You know the bounty on you?" I said.

"Yes," she whispered, frightened.

"Here is my hand," I said, extending it to the close-set, narrow, but sturdy bars, adequate to hold a female. "Kiss it, and lick it, first the palm, and then the back, reverently."

She put her face, as she could, through the bars, and carefully, with her small tongue, kissed it and licked it, first the palm, and then the back, reverently, and then drew back in the kennel, looking at me, but continued to grasp the bars. "Please do not tell anyone who I am," she said.

"Were I to do so," I said, "I would doubtless be killed, and others would fight over you, and there would be much bloodshed."

"We are far from Ar," she said.

"That, too," I said.

"As long as I am only Adraste," she said, "we are both more safe."

"How came you into the keeping of the Pani?" I asked.

"You, of Cos, well know of the insurrection," she said, "and its success."

"Indeed," I said, ruefully.

"I was betrayed in Ar," she said, "by the traitor, Seremides, by the hateful Flavia of Ar, traitress whom I had befriended, and others, who would turn me over to the forces of revolt, to bargain for their own amnesty or escape."

I knew something of this from Alcinoë.

"But on the roof of the Central Cylinder," she said, "there was sudden confusion, and darkness, and I was seized, and rendered unconscious. When I regained consciousness I found myself stripped and chained, with others, in a wooden stockade, somewhere in the northern forests, in the power of these strange, inexplicable men, Pani. I was collared, and enslaved, no different from the others, as though I might be no more than they."

"There is much in this that I do not understand," I said.

"Nor I," she said.

"I gather from keepers," I said, "that you bear in your left thigh, high, under the hip, not the common *kef*, but the mark of Treve."

She reddened.

"This is not the first time you have been a slave," I said.

"I was captured by Rask of Treve," she said, "a warrior amongst warriors, a man amongst men. I must wear a Trevan collar. I was tented with his women. Well did he humble me, and teach me how spasmodically helpless might be a slave in the arms of her master. I bathed him. He made me dance for him. I wore his silk, what he would give me of it."

"It is my understanding that women do not escape the chains of Rask of Treve," I said.

"He thought little of me," she said, "as I suppose is appropriate for a slave. And his interest in me, I gather, was primarily that I was the daughter of Marlenus of Ar, his mortal enemy, and the mortal enemy of Treve. It was doubtless primarily for that reason that he captured me, bound me naked before him, supine, over the saddle of his tarn, caressed me into need, and took me to his camp. It amused him, doubtless, to have the daughter of his worst enemy in his collar, an obedient, silked slave in his tent."

"You escaped?" I said.

"No, Master," she said. "As you noted, women do not escape the chains of Rask of Treve. I was given away, and, to show his scorn, to a woman, Verna, a Panther Girl of the northern forests."

"You would seem to be a prize," I said. "How is it that he would let you go so cheaply?"

"To humiliate me, of course," she said. "I, the daughter of a Ubar, given away like a pot girl!"

"Still," I said, "it seems surprising."

"There was another woman," she said.

"Of course," I said.

"It was a young, blond barbarian," she said, "blue-eyed, and shapely, who could not even speak Gorean properly, a meaningless slut, one named El-in-or."

"That is, I think," I said, "a barbarian name."

"I think so," she said. "Certainly she was a barbarian."

"She must have been very beautiful," I said.

"You can buy ten of them off any chain in a market," she said.

"You were then, it seems, deemed inferior to a girl, ten of whom might be bought off any chain in a market."

Her hands turned white on the bars.

How furious she was.

"She is now doubtless his companion," she said.

"Rask of Treve," I said, "does not free women. She is probably being kept as the most perfect of slaves."

Men desire slaves, women desire masters.

"I was taken to the northern forests," she said, "the slave of Panther Girls. Later I was sold, and eventually returned to Ar."

"It is my understanding," I said, "that you begged to be purchased."

"Of course," she said, angrily.

"You had compromised the honor of Marlenus," I said. "Accordingly you were disowned, made no longer his daughter. An embarrassment to the city, you were sequestered in the Central Cylinder. It is easy to understand your outrage, your bitterness, at such a reduction. Then something happened to Marlenus. He was long from the city. In his absence, with which you or others may have had something to do, you plotted with dissident factions and the island ubarates; you laid your plans carefully, and put them into patient and subtle execution; and then, eventually, by means of enemies without and treachery within, your schemes bore their ugly, dark fruit. You received the medallion. You were declared Ubara. The rest is well-known."

She was silent.

"So," I said, "you were adjudged inferior to a barbarian named El-in-or."

"By Rask of Treve!" she said.

"To be sure," I said.

"What does he know?" she said.

"What, indeed?" I said.

"He is only one man!"

"True," I said.

"I am the most beautiful woman on all Gor!" she said.

"Perhaps your slaves, and courtiers, told you that," I said.

"Certainly," she said.

"And you believed it?"

"Am I not the most beautiful woman you have ever seen?" she said.

"No," I said, "but you are quite beautiful. In a normal market, you might bring three, perhaps four, silver tarsks."

"Others might bring more?" she said.

"Of course," I said. "What I think you should understand, is that a woman might be the most beautiful woman in the world to one fellow, and not to another. A woman who is incomparably beautiful to one fellow might not be taken as a free pot girl by another. Perhaps the first fellow senses in her something the others have missed. There are mysteries in these matters. And often a fellow wants not the most beautiful woman, anyway, but the most desirable, the one he wants most, which is not necessarily the same thing. Who knows why one fellow wants one woman in his collar and not another?"

"You will keep my secret," she said.

"For the time being, certainly," I said.

"Do others know I am here?" she said.

"Doubtless some of the high Pani," I said, "or you would not be here, at all."

"Of what value am I to them," she said, "that I would be here?"

"I do not know," I said.

"Are there others?" she asked.

"I know of one woman," I said.

"What woman?" she said, frightened.

"You might be surprised," I said. "Perhaps I shall introduce you later."

"And others?" she said.

"Possibly," I said. "I do not know."

"I am afraid," she said.

"Seremides is here," I said.

"No!" she wept. "He had me bound at his feet, in the rag of a slave, to bargain with me in Ar!"

"He does not know you are here," I said, "though he may suspect it."

"Keep him from me!" she begged. "Do not let him know I am here!"

"He need only look into your kennel," I said.

"'Kennel'?" she said.

"Surely you know you occupy a slave kennel," I said.

"I am helpless," she moaned.

"At least," I said, "the Pani have given you a rather ample tunic."

"It is clearly the garment of a slave," she said.

"Perhaps it will protect you from the Pani free women," I said.

"They look upon me as though I were a beast," she said.

"That is all you are," I said.

She shook the bars.

"Are you hungry?" I asked.

"Very!" she said.

"Master?" I said.

"Very, Master," she said.

I took a small cake from my pouch, and she eagerly reached for it, but I drew it back. I gathered she was indeed hungry.

"Hands on the bars," I said, "face forward, open your mouth."

She complied, and I fed her by hand. Slaves may be fed that way. Sometimes they are knelt and their hands bound behind them. Sometimes they must take food and water from pans on the floor, without the use of their hands. Such homely practices are useful in reminding them that they are slaves.

It pleased me that the former Talena, of Ar, the former Ubara of Ar, was now before me, a kenneled slave. It pleased me that she had kissed and licked my hand, first the palm, and then the back, reverently. That is a common conciliatory act on the part of a slave, to lick and kiss, reverently, the hand by which she might be cuffed, first the palm, and then the back. In this way she might express her fear that she might be, and her hope that she will not be, struck. Commonly, however, this serves as a simple, lovely act of deference, by means of which the slave acknowledges that she is her master's beast, his owned, domestic animal. A similar act, perhaps more clearly symbolic, is involved when the slave, kneeling, licks and kisses the master's whip, held to her lips. Sometimes she must bring it to him in her teeth, on all fours, and then, on all fours, or kneeling, lick and kiss it, as it is held to her lips. In this way she acknowledges that she is subject to him, that she is his slave, his property. It pleased me, too, of course, that the former Ubara had fed from my hand. The hand-feeding of a slave, she not permitted the use of her hands, is, too, an act rich in symbolism. In this way it is signified that the slave is wholly dependent on the master, even for her food, and that it will be granted to her, if it is, only when, and as, he pleases. Domestic beasts, of course, are often fed by hand.

"Master well knows how to teach a girl her collar," she said.

"I know of someone whom you might be interested in meeting," I said.

"Not Seremides!" she said.

"No," I said, "a woman."

"Does she know me?"

"Yes," I said.

"And she is here?"

"Yes."

"Who is she?"

"I will introduce you," I said. "I think you will be surprised."

"Who is she?" she said.

"An old friend," I said.

"Who," she said, "who?"

I then turned away, leaving the slave, Adraste, in the kennel.

* * * *

"Slave! Slave!" had said Alcinoë.

"Slave, slave!" had cried Adraste.

"Is this any way for old friends to greet one another?" I asked.

"How is it that you are here?" asked Alcinoë.

"I do not know," said Adraste.

"What happened on the roof of the Central Cylinder?" asked Alcinoë.

"I do not know," said Adraste, "but you failed to sell me for your freedom in Ar!"

"You looked well on your knees, at the feet of Seremides," she said, "bound, helpless, waiting, in the rag of a slave!"

"You betrayed me!" said Adraste.

"You betrayed all of us, and Ar!" said Alcinoë.

"Do not pretend fidelity to the Home Stone," said Adraste. "You were eager, and much with me, each hort of the way! We were arch traitresses, we two, so vain and proud, so ambitious, so ruthless, each abetting and urging on the other. You would line your purse with gold and your station with power! No opportunity for wealth, for influence, for self-aggrandizement was neglected! We glorified our offices and despoiled the city, ruined our enemies and enriched our favorites, our pets and hirelings!"

"But all did not continue to go well," I said.

Both cried out with rage.

It amused me to see the two former high women of Ar, tunicked, barefoot, collared, kneeling, unable to stand, two slaves, crowded together in the small kennel.

How they, former conspirators, now helpless, hated one another!

It occurred to me that the occupants of that tiny enclosure were worth a fortune.

But I had never cared for gold washed in blood.

"You look well in a collar," said Adraste. "You should have always worn one!"

"I see a metal circlet on your neck," said Alcinoë, "slave!"

"How came you here?" asked Adraste.

"I escaped the city, but was captured, and collared," said Alcinoë. "I was purchased, honestly and openly, in Brundisium, by Pani!"

"As a common slave," sneered Adraste.

"And so, too, in similar straits," said Alcinoë, "would you have been purchased, as a common slave, and surely for no more than for a handful of copper!"

Alcinoë, as I recalled, had sold for forty copper tarsks, not even half a silver tarsk. Presumably the Pani had bought her on speculation, that she would improve. In my view, their investment was excellent, and the former Lady Flavia, dieted and exercised, and having come to some sense of what it was to be in a collar, had more than substantiated their judgment. The former Lady Flavia, her freedom behind her, was now considerably improved. She had become an excellent piece of collar meat, perhaps worth even two silver tarsks. I had seen several fellows, on the ship, and later, in the courtyard, while the girls were being exercised, usually five at a time, on tethers, assessing her, as men will assess slaves of interest. I wondered if slaves were fully aware of their superiority as females to free women. The most female of all women is, of course, the slave.

"I would have sold for a thousand pieces of gold!" said Adraste.

That was not at all likely, unless she was being purchased with an eye to the bounty, later to be collected.

Alcinoë laughed unpleasantly, scornfully. "Writhing naked in your chains, to the prodding of a whip, on a cement shelf, I do not think you would bring more than four or five tarsk-bits."

That estimate, in my view, was unrealistically low.

Alcinoë, incidentally, I had been given to understand, had been sold from such a shelf in Brundisium. Not every girl is publicly sold at auction. Indeed, some high slaves are exhibited privately to rich clients, in the purple booths. Even on the shelves, of course, as well as in the purple booths, a girl may be expected to perform to some extent, that some sense might be conveyed to the client of the possible value of the merchandise. It is only in the purple booths, of course, that a girl may be tried out by a prospective buyer, and woe to the girl, should she not prove satisfactory.

"I am the most beautiful woman on Gor!" said Adraste.

"I have seen tarsks better looking than you!" said Alcinoë.

"Do not strike one another," I warned.

"Am I not more beautiful than she, Master?" inquired Alcinoë.

"You are both nice looking," I said, circumspectly.

"Price us!" demanded Alcinoë.

"I would guess," I said, "that you would go for two silver tarsks, perhaps two and a half, and she for three, perhaps four, in a good market."

"See!" said Adraste.

"But there are many," I said, "who would be likely to go for far more."

"Surely not," said Adraste.

"Which of us would you prefer?" asked Alcinoë.

"That is a different question," I said.

"You prefer me!" she said.

"Oh?" I said.

"Yes," she said, "the girls have watched you watching me, and they tell me things. You look upon me as a master upon a coveted slave. As a slaver on a maiden of choice, unaware in the baths, as a hungry sleen on the grazing tabuk. Doubtless in your mind you have put your bonds on me many times! How many times, in your mind, have I lain naked before you, helpless, bound hand and foot?"

I began to suspect that there were networks of communication amongst slaves of which I had been unaware. No wonder one strives to keep such beauties ignorant.

"Is it not true?" demanded Alcinoë.

"It is true," I said, "that in a collar you are better looking than you were in your silks, in Ar."

"Yes!" said Alcinoë.

"But is that not true of any woman?" I said.

"I thought you were my friend, my closest friend," said Adraste.

"Ubars, and Ubaras, have no friends," said Alcinoë.

"No!" said Adraste.

"Who would be your friend?" asked Alcinoë. "You are vain, and pretentious, deceitful, treacherous!"

"You used me!" said Adraste.

"Yes, and hated you!" said Alcinoë. "It was with overwhelming pleasure that I, on the command of Seremides, hunted you down in your chambers, where you cowered, alone, unguarded, forsaken, and cast you the rag of a slave, demanding that you strip yourself naked and put it on!"

"She-sleen!" cried Adraste.

"How well it looked on you!"

"She-tharlarion, she-urt!" cried Adraste.

"How right bondage is for you!" cried Alcinoë.

"And for you!" cried Adraste.

"It is enough," I said to Alcinoë. "It is time to return you to your kennel."

I opened the door of the kennel, and Alcinoë backed out. My hand on her shoulder prevented her from rising. I then closed the gate of the kennel, which, with its closing, locked.

Alcinoë made again to rise, but, again, I prevented her.

"Master?" she said.

"Surely you do not expect to rise," I said.

"Master?"

"Return to your kennel," I said, "in the modality of the she-sleen, on all fours."

"Yes, Master," she said.

"And lift your garment," I said. "It is not to be soiled."

I watched her leave the shed, and begin to make her way across the courtyard.

"You well know, Master," said Adraste, "how to teach a woman her collar."

"Sometime," I said, "someone may teach you yours."

"No one can do that," she said.

"Rask of Treve did so," I said, "and the Panther Girls of the northern forests."

"No, no!" she wept.

I reached through the bars and drew her by the hair, tightly against the bars. "Remember the penalty for lying," I said.

"Yes, Master," she wept.

"You are no longer a free woman," I said.

"No, Master," she wept.

"Did they not?" I said.

Tears streamed down her face, some running on the bars. "Yes, Master," she said, "they taught me my collar."

"And well?"

"Yes, Master, very well!"

"You learned it?" I said.

"I was given no choice," she said. "I learned it well."

"And doubtless," I said, "you can learn it well, again, or better."

"Yes, Master," she whispered.

I then released her, and she drew back in the kennel, bent over, in its darkness, weeping.

Some free women think that they can never be taught the collar, but, when it is on them, they learn differently, and swiftly.

Chapter Twenty-Six

What Occurred in the Courtyard
of the Castle of Lord Temmu

It had been a good cast, from twenty yards, the javelin into the heavy post set in the courtyard.

"Well done, Philoctetes," I said.

There was general assent from the fellows about.

To one side Pani archers, with their large, unusual bows, were plying shafts into silk-covered straw targets.

I would not have cared to meet such fellows in the field.

"When will we march?" inquired Philoctetes.

"We must wait," I said.

A robust exploratory force of some five hundred men, a hundred Pani warriors of the men of Lord Temmu, and four hundred of our mercenaries, our armsmen, had been sent forth eight days ago.

Behind us we heard the striking of sharpened steel. Obviously one does the best to control the blade, but, even so, blood can be shed in such exercises.

"Many of the enemy, it is said," said a fellow, "are low Pani, impressed into service. The blast of a war horn should send them running back to their fields."

"Our fellows will harvest them like Sa-Tarna, split them like tospits, crush them like dried larmas," said another.

"Our fellows were well met at the defile, and on the beach," said a man, thoughtfully.

"We were taken by surprise, ambushed," said a man. "We were not ready."

"Those were prize troops," said a fellow, "gathered, and set."

"We stood up to them well enough at the evacuation," said another.

"Consider how heavily we were outnumbered," said another.

I was pleased to some extent, of course, that the morale of our armsmen seemed high. On the other hand, as far as I could tell, there was a serious likelihood that we might be seriously outnumbered in any pitched battle. The ideal, of course, is to engage the enemy only when it is to one's advantage, not to his advantage. Small units are likely to overcome smaller units. Thus, a smaller army, rapid and evasive, judiciously disposed and applied, may, in time, in a hundred actions, a hundred skirmishes, inflict much damage on a larger army, if its elements can be met seriatim, and divided. Statistically, two men are likely to vanquish a single man, one engaging, one killing, with the result that there is not likely to be one survivor, one of the two men, but rather two of the two men, the two who held the numerical advantage, slender though it might have seemed.

"Our fellows should be soon back, with trophies," said a man.

"And perhaps women," said another.

"They will be Pani women," said a man.

"What matter?" said another.

"How are they?" asked another.

"In the village," said another, "go to the slave hut."

I had no idea of how effective lower Pani, mostly peasants, impressed or enlisted as *ashigaru*, might be, as it was not their way of life, so to speak, as it seemed to be for higher Pani, such as the warriors of Lord Temmu, and Lords Nishida and Okimoto, but I was sure they could be trained, might be terrified not to fight, and, in any event, might be present in large numbers. And, of course, they would be stiffened by, and supplemented by, higher Pani, the sort who had, it seems, though doubtless in greater numbers, previously reduced and decimated the men of Lords Nishida and Okimoto, warriors for whom I entertained the highest regard.

In any event, I feared our fellows might underestimate the enemy. It is always preferable to anticipate the larl and meet the urt, than expect the urt and meet the larl.

Several men, in their turn, freed of duty for the day, had

issued from the courtyard, down various trails, to the local villages. I myself, in recent days, had visited two such villages. During the day, of late, the gates of the castle had been open. Lesser Pani were mostly barred entry, but higher Pani, and we, during the day, if not on duty, came and went rather as we wished. At night, the gates were closed, and access, and exit, it seemed, was carefully supervised. Probably secret signals were employed. The Pani, I had discovered on the ship, were familiar with such devices, and, as I later learned, with ciphers and codes, as well. When the men chose to leave the castle, they were given marked shells, rather like *ostraka*. These could be exchanged for things in the villages, fish, rice, *sake*, a fermented drink made from rice, and such, and, in the stalls, beads, cloth, trinkets, and such. These shells were not typical Pani currency, which, for the most part, consisted of metal coins, of silver, gold, and copper, of various certified weights, struck by various *shoguns*. As on the continent there is no common currency, but a variety of currencies, which often entails rumors, scales, bargainings, and such. Many of these coins, not all, were perforated in the center. One threads one or more such coins on a string, the string fastened about the bottom and top coin, or loops a string through several coins, and ties the loop shut above the top coin. In this way the coins are kept together, perhaps tied about one's waist, under the clothing, or put about one's neck, under the clothing, or simply dropped into a pouch, usually of silk. Lesser Pani sometimes, on errands, carry the coin or coins in the mouth, rather as slaves may on the continent, and on the islands, while marketing for their masters. The marked shells, then, I gathered, were rather in the nature of a form of script. I also gathered that if the villagers did not accept them they risked the loss of an eye, a hand, a foot, or a head. As long as they were unquestioningly exchanged, of course, at least in the local villages, the nature of the material made little difference. The marking on the shells, in part done in dots, presumably for our benefit, stipulated the value to be assigned to the shell. One bargained, of course, with such things, much as one might with pieces of metal, or, in the Barrens, with beads, strips of leather, furs, blankets, arrowheads, bowstrings, slaves, and such. In one village there was a slave hut, as alluded to, popular with the men, whose occupants I looked in on, but did not put to use. Their use cost a two-dot shell. The girls in the hut were not contract women but slaves, as the Pani keep slaves, as well as others, as is common in refined, advanced civilizations. The hut was lit by hanging lamps, and floored by a large, colorful mat, presumably to enhance the pleasure of the clients, for the Pani, at least the high Pani, refined, and civilized, tend to be quite open to the pleasures of the senses, such as color, textures, scents, and such. The girls, too, were given lovely silken sheets, which they might hold about themselves. Naturally they kneel humbly before the men, for they are not only females, but slaves. The Pani free women, incidentally, seem, except for the companions of high officers, and such, to have much lower status than the typical Gorean free woman, certainly one of upper caste. For example, an older sister, even a mother, must defer to a male child, bowing first, and such. When a client enters the hut, if he thinks he might find one of the slaves of interest, he has her stand before him, her head down. He then lifts away the sheet and considers her. If he is pleased, he instructs her as to how he wishes to be pleased. These slaves, with an exception or two to be noted, are Pani females. Many are captured in war, some are bought in the girl markets, to which I have hitherto referred, and some, it seems, are bred for the market. Each is chained by the ankle to a post which protrudes through a prepared aperture in the mat. Each, I was pleased to note, wore a locked metal collar, or a neck chain, with its attached slave disk, padlocked about her neck. In some Gorean cities slaves are put in the padlocked neck chain, with the slave disk, identifying her master, and sometimes noting her current name, but the locked metal collar is far more common, indeed, almost universal. It seems more secure, and is easily engraved. Some cities use the slave anklet on the left ankle, which is attractive. But as we recognize, and the Pani do as well, the ideal mounting site for a token of bondage is the neck. On the neck, the token is prominently displayed, for all to note. Too, on the neck, the collar is beautifully secure. It is absolutely unslippable, even a Turian collar. Too, with the loss of a foot or ankle, an anklet or bracelet might be lost. On the other hand, if one were to cut away the head, one has lost the slave. As noted, such slaves are almost always Pani females. On the other hand, when I looked into the slave hut, two slaves, Thetis and Iole, whom I recalled from the ship, and castle, were ankle-chained to posts in the slave hut. This was temporary, of course, for our slaves had not been brought across the ocean to be squandered in a village's slave hut, not even that of a rather large village, as was the nearest village, this village, which could be reached on foot in less than a quarter of an Ahn. They had been insufficiently prompt in service, or insufficiently deferent, I gathered, to a keeper, or a free person, and had thus been brought down to the village and put on their chains. "Master!" they cried out to me, from their knees, seeing me, extending their hands piteously to me. I supposed they had hoped that I had come to return them to their kennels on the castle grounds, but I had not. I had not even realized they were here, being disciplined. Their outburst earned them a cry of rage from the Pani woman in charge of the slave hut, who tore away their sheets, and gave them several stinging strokes of a bamboo switch. She apparently did not care for the two new slaves, with strange eyes, and light skin. Inquiries suggested, though, that the two new slaves were not unpopular with the hut's clientele. One supposes that novelty to some extent entered into the matter. To be sure, there were difficulties for the girls, as some of the commands they were given were unfamiliar, even unintelligible, to them. They simply did not know what to do. The Pani clients, of course, took it for granted that any slave in the slave hut would be obedient, prompt, and adept in a variety of performances. This innocent ignorance was not without its consequences, of course, and the girls were often subjected to castigation, scorn, kicks, slappings, and the stroke of the bamboo switch. Happily, I learned, Saru, the slave given by Lord Nishida to Lord Temmu, and the ten slaves given by Lord Okimoto to Lord Temmu, were more patiently and gently treated. One is not entitled to assume that a fair-skinned slave from abroad, one from a far different culture, is going to know what might be expected of her, the proper serving, for example, of *sake*, the appropriate temperature, and such.

The staple in the Twelve Islands, which is actually far more than twelve, is not Sa-Tarna, but rice.

Rice fields, or paddies, are associated with each village. A *daimyo* or *shogun* will have suzerainty over various villages, which he protects, and from which he obtains the means to maintain his men.

He who controls the rice, it is said, controls the islands.

Several rice fields were associated with the holding of Lord Temmu, most north and west of the castle. To reach such fields by land would mean to pass the holding of Lord Temmu. To reach them from the sea, from the north or west, one would have to put into shore, on the other side of the island, negotiate a difficult terrain, and thread one's way through guarded, easily defended passes. By the time one could reach the fields, it was likely the *ashigaru* of Lord Temmu would be in position.

"It is said," said Philoctetes, "Tarl Cabot is on the grounds."

"I have not seen him," I said.

To be sure, whenever it was thought he was at the castle, rumors hastened about. Certainly he was much in conversation.

This obviously had much to do with the war which, at present, seemed faraway.

As suggested earlier, it was not clear, at least to the lower ranks, when we might march.

It did seem clear that Lord Temmu had in mind carrying the war to the enemy. Certainly the reinforcement by foreign armsmen, and the acquisition of tarns, would suggest as much.

"Last night, on tarnback," he said.

"What is the meaning of that?" asked a man.

"I do not know," I said.

"A coordination is being envisaged," speculated a fellow.

That seemed to me likely.

"I think," said a man, "we are soon to march."

"The exploratory force," said another, "is still abroad."

"Look," said a fellow. "There is another."

"Ah!" said a man.

The fellow was pointing to a high storey of the castle, where there was a beating of wings, dark against the sky, and then the tiny bird disappeared, within. Though I had never been in that room, its window high, unshuttered, open to the sky, it obviously housed a number of the swift-flighted, messenger vulos, by means of which Pani might convey messages. These, it seems, were placed in tiny wrappers, and fastened to one of the bird's legs. Vulos who would seek this cot were carried about, for example, to the training area of the tarns somewhere back in the mountains, and, there, I had no doubt, in the mountains, were kept, in their tiny wood-barred cages, vulos which, if released, would seek as their cot and roost the very room above, high in the castle. Similarly there must have been vulos in that room which, if released, would seek a different cot and roost, perhaps, for example, one housed in the training area for tarns, back in the mountains.

There had been, of late, much traffic coming and going from that area, that mysterious room, high in the castle. This sort of thing had been given careful attention, obviously, by the men.

And this traffic had been much more frequent, of late.

I suspected we would march, upon the return of the exploratory force.

Interestingly, the number of Pani aboard the great ship, guarding it, had been recently increased.

This suggested apprehension on the part of the Pani, and suggested, as well, though not as clearly, that an order of march might be imminent.

A number of slaves, too, some twenty or thirty, fastened together by the neck, by a long rope, had been given bags of water, bundles of dried parsit, sacks of rice, and such, to convey to the ship.

They had made this laborious journey more than once, even today.

It seemed that the Pani aboard the ship were to be well-supplied.

As mentioned earlier, no easy access was to be had to the ship. The galley nests remained closed. Supplies were taken aboard by means of baskets on ropes, or by means of the nets, swung out on booms, and raised and lowered by pulleys. Even the slaves who brought the water and other supplies were not permitted near the baskets and nets, but must kneel on the boards of the wharf, until dismissed, to climb, roped together by the neck, the narrow walled-in path to the castle grounds. They were in the charge, of course, of youth, boys of the lesser Pani.

The gate to the wharf area, leading to the walled-in trail, was open, and the coffle, weary and footsore, neck-roped, their burdens delivered, were being herded within, by their young herdsmen.

Once within the gate the lads began to remove them, one by one, from the coffle. While the rope was being removed the slaves must kneel. Also, of course, they were in the presence of a free person, in this case, a boy, of the lesser Pani. Once free of the rope, the girls were permitted to rise to their feet, that they might seek their keepers, and be returned to their kennels.

The sun was high, and the day warm.

The burdens they had borne, while not heavy for a man, would have been heavy for a woman, and the climb back to the castle from the wharf, given its twistings and its tortuous steepness, would be time consuming and difficult for either a man or woman.

It was not an easy day for them.

I supposed they would be anxious to get to the shade of their housings, and a pan of water.

But one, I saw, seemed frightened; she was looking about, apprehensively. She was backed against the wall, the palms of her hands back, against the stone. She was breathing heavily, this stress marked by the lovely rise and fall of her bosom. I did not think this was entirely from the climb. She seemed apprehensive, even terrified. How appealing a beautiful woman is when helpless and frightened. One desires to reassure and comfort her, before taking her hands and braceleting them behind her back. She remained on her feet, I supposed, that she might the more seem ready, should she be questioned, to return to her kennel. I knew her, of course, even from across the courtyard, some forty yards, or so. One does not easily forget such a slave. One in every ten or so is such a slave. Alcinoë, for example, was such a slave. In any market, on any street, men would have looked after her. Her passage was such as might elicit soft whistles, the smacking of lips, explicit speculations as to her value off the block, or her worth in the furs. A slave is not a free woman. She must expect such things. Too, given the scantiness of her garmenture, such speculations can be more securely grounded than in the case of a free woman, wrapped away somewhere within the layers of her robes of concealment. The slave, of course, is intended to be a source of pleasure.

Her collar proclaims her such. She was looking at me. Why, I wondered. Then she sank down, half crouching, half kneeling. Her lips seemed to form the word, "Please!" She stretched her hand out to me, piteously. I did not understand her agitation. I did know she should be soon back in her kennel. Obviously she wished to speak to me. I did not understand this. What had frightened her?

I approached her, and when I had reached her, she knelt, bent muchly over, her head down. Did she fear to be recognized?

"May I speak, Master," she whispered.

As I did not respond to her, she looked up, frightened.

I pointed to my feet.

She bent down, and, the palms of her hands in the dirt, kissed my feet. "Thank you, Master," she said. She, a mere slave, had been permitted to kiss the feet of a free man.

"You may speak," I said.

Her concern, her agitation, her fear, was evident.

"I heard men speak," she said, "on the wharf. Is it true that there is one named Tarl Cabot here, at the World's End?"

"Yes," I said, "though he is not much about, is seldom on the grounds. He is Tarl Cabot, commander of the tarn cavalry, in the forces of Lords Nishida and Okimoto, and, I suppose, now, of Lord Temmu."

"A warrior?"

"Yes."

"A tarnsman?"

"Yes," I said.

"Of Port Kar?" she whispered, frightened.

"That is my understanding," I said.

She moaned.

"Do you know him?" I asked.

"I fear so," she said.

"He was on the ship when I was brought aboard," I said. "I take it he was on the ship from the beginning. He has, I take it, been with Lords Nishida and Okimoto even from the northern forests."

"So long?" she said.

"Yes," I said.

She began to tremble.

"You fear he might recognize you?" I said. I supposed that must be the source of her apprehension.

"He could recognize me," she said.

"I see," I said.

Surely she had enough to concern her, enough to fear, without learning that there was yet another about, by whom she might be identified as the former Talena of Ar, once the Ubara of Ar, now a tunicked, collared slave.

"You did not realize he was about?" I said.

"No," she said.

I supposed that this was quite possible. Slaves such as she, muchly controlled, largely sequestered in the keeping areas, not serving at the tables, not being privy to the casual discourse of masters, not being free in a city, to roam the streets, the shops and markets, and such, are likely to know very little of what is going on about them, even on board a ship. Certainly one would not be expected to furnish them with bulletins, crew lists, and such. Seldom would they be in a position to obtain such information. And who, possessing such information, would impart it to them? If they learn of such things, it would presumably be by inadvertence, or in passing, and she, given her keeping, would have had scant opportunity to obtain such intelligence.

"On the ship," I said, "you were aware of Pani?"

"Yes," she said, "but I knew nothing of their numbers."

"On the ship," I said, "who were the high officers of the Pani?"

"I know now," she said, "they were Lords Nishida and Okimoto."

"Did you know that on the ship?" I asked.

"No," she said.

I recalled that she, as some others, had been hooded when brought to the open deck.

"You fear Tarl Cabot?" I said.

"Yes, Master," she said.

"What have you to fear from him?" I asked.

"Everything," she whispered.

"I do not understand," I said.

"He would kill me," she said.

"Surely not," I said.

"Surely so," she said.

"You fear," I said, "that he would return you to Ar, to the justice of Ar, to the impaling spear?"

In the case of one of her importance, the impaling spear might be narrow, greased, and thirty feet in height, and, mounted on the wall, her slow descent, she writhing, trying her best to prevent it, unable to do so, might be visible for pasangs.

"No," she said, "I fear he would not be so kind."

"You fear more?" I said.

"Much more," she said.

"Perhaps your casual skinning, and salting," I asked, "prolonged for weeks, or months?"

"Perhaps more," she said.

"You are a well-formed, passable slave," I said. "Surely Tarl Cabot would have something better to do with such a slave than kill her."

"I think not," she said.

"Surely you are not unaware of the inordinate pleasure that a man may derive from a slave?" I said.

"You do not understand," she said.

"What do I not understand?" I asked.

"There are terrible things between us," she said.

"From when you were free?"

"Yes."

"I see," I said. I supposed there were many, a great many, who owed much to the former Mistress of Ar, who might adjudge the impaling spear an illicit, unwarranted mercy.

If she were one of the most desired, she was also one of the most detested, most hated, women on Gor.

"Do not make me speak further," she whispered.

"I have served with Tarl Cabot," I said, "on the ship, but I will not reveal your presence to him."

She put her head down, gratefully, her dark hair over my boots.

"But, like Seremides," I said, "he might happen upon you."

"How helpless are slaves!" she wept.

"But Seremides," I said, "can scarcely hobble about, and Cabot is much in the mountains, with the tarn cavalry."

"Perhaps I can be sold away from the castle," she said.

"Perhaps," I said.

"I am afraid," she said.

"Ar is faraway," I said.

"Tarl Cabot is not," she said.

"I do not think he would hurt you," I said.

"You do not know him," she said.

"Perhaps you do not know him," I said.

"You do not know what I did to him," she said.

"No," I said, "I do not know that."

"He would kill me," she said.

"It is time for you to return to your kennel," I said.

"Yes, Master," she said.

The slave had scarcely risen to her feet, backed away, head down, turned, and hurried toward the shed which housed her kennel, when I became aware of another figure near me.

"How homely she is," said Alcinoë. "I have seen tarsks more attractive than she. Surely you have no interest in so poor a slave."

"Have you been listening?" I asked.

"Certainly not," she said. "But I have been watching, from across the courtyard, over there."

She indicated a place, across the grounds, near some shrubbery, not far from the large, central portal of the castle, perhaps fifty yards away.

"She certainly kissed your feet well," said Alcinoë.

"She is a slave," I said.

"And she kneels well, too."

"Yes," I said.

"I wager," said Alcinoë, "that you enjoyed having her, slave, before you."

"Yes," I said. Indeed, what man would not? Indeed, every beautiful woman, indeed, every woman, should kneel before a man, his.

"I am far more beautiful than she," said Alcinoë.

"You looked well earlier, coffled, neck-roped, struggling under your bag of rice," I said.

"We had to make three trips!" she said.

"Excellent," I said, "that the former lady Flavia of Ar should be worked, as a common slave."

415

"So, too, was she!" said Alcinoë.

"I am well aware of that," I said. It had given me great pleasure to see the former two highest women in Ar, tunicked, collared, and neck-roped, portering for the Pani.

"Why do you share speech with so lowly, so worthless, a slave?"

"Do you object?" I asked.

"Master may do as he pleases, of course," she said.

"Are you barefoot?" I asked.

"Yes," she said.

"What is the garment you wear?" I asked.

"A tunic," she said.

"That is all?" I asked.

"Yes," she said.

"You are then naked, save for your tunic," I said.

"Yes," she said.

"What is that on your neck?" I asked.

"A collar," she said.

"What sort of collar?"

"A slave collar," she said.

"Then you are a slave," I said.

"Master?"

"Why are you standing?"

Swiftly she knelt before me.

"You must understand, Master," she said, looking up, "that she is cunning, deceitful, and clever."

"And you would warn me of her wiles?" I said.

"Yes," she said, "lest she cast the spell of her smiles over you, the magic of sparkling eyes, the sorcery of a trembling lip."

"The potency of such charms," I said, "however mighty in a free woman, are surely much reduced in a kneeling, tunicked slave."

"I, think, Master," she said, "they may rather be much increased."

I thought it quite possible that Alcinoë was not mistaken in this matter. Certainly the helplessness of the slave, that she is owned, and such, make her a hundred times more attractive to a male. She belongs to one. One may do with her as one wishes. One's possessions, of course, are always special to a fellow. Consider, for example, his sleen or kaiila.

"I take it," I said, "that you do not much care for the former Ubara of Ar."

"I hate her," she said.

"She doubtless entertains a similar regard for you," I said.

"Surely you do not like her," said Alcinoë.

"What is it to you?" I asked.

Tears suddenly flooded the eyes of the slave.

"I see," I said.

"No, no, no," she said. "You cannot see!"

"The conversation," I said, "which recently took place between a free man and a slave is no concern of yours."

"I understand, Master," she said.

"For what it is worth," I said, "I find you a hundred times more beautiful, and a thousand times more desirable, than the former Ubara of Ar."

"But she was Ubara!" she exclaimed.

"You are both now slaves," I said, "women reduced to their primitive essentials, women as slaves."

"Oh, Master!" she cried. "You care for me!"

"Care, for a slave?" I said. "Do not be foolish."

"Master?"

"I said that you were beautiful, and desirable," I said. "If you were stripped on a slave block, any fool could see that, and say as much. Beyond that, do not insult a free man! Do not insinuate that a free man might be so foolish as to care for a slave. Do not dare to utter such an absurdity! Slaves are beasts and properties. They are to be owned, and mastered, that is all. You are a slave. Only a fool would permit himself to care for a slave."

"Yes, Master," she said, happily.

If you were mine," I said, angrily, "you would learn your collar as few women."

"Teach it to me, Master!" she said.

"But I do not own you," I said.

She clutched at the ship's collar on her neck, and, two hands on it, jerked it against the back of her neck, again and again, and tears burst from her eyes.

"No," she said, "you do not own me!"

I think then she began to understand, more clearly than ever, what it was to be a slave.

"I want you to be my master!" she wept.

"Why?" I asked.

"Because," she said, "I—I—"

"Yes?" I said.

"Nothing, Master," she whispered.

"What a stupid little slave you are," I said, "but one well-curved."

"You dare to speak so," she said, suddenly, abruptly, eyes flashing, "to she who was once the Lady Flavia of Ar?"

"Certainly," I said.

"Yes, Master," she whispered.

"Have your keepers," I said, "in your training, not put you naked before a mirror, and bound, that you might look upon yourself?"

"Yes," she said, "and made me struggle in my bonds."

"Surely then," I said, "you are aware of your slave curves."

"I have known," she said, "since puberty, that I was a slave, and should be a slave."

"That is often denied," I said, "but it is not unusual."

"Are all women slaves?" she asked.

"I do not know," I said, "but surely many are."

"I am one such," she said.

"And such," I said, "will never be fulfilled, until they are at the feet of a master."

"I would be at your feet," she said.

"Any man will do," I said.

"Do you think," she said, "that a master makes no difference to a slave?"

"You speak of the feelings of a slave," I said. "Her feelings are unimportant. They are nothing. She is merely a slave. Let her kneel, and hope to please."

"Yes, Master," she said.

"One buys a slave for work and pleasure," I said.

"The slave seeks love," she said.

"What the slave seeks is unimportant," I said.

"How can a slave work for her master, know his domination, obey him, wear his collar, kneel before him, be put to his pleasure, squirm and kick, begging, in his chains, and not succumb to him, not fall in love with him?"

"Such things can take place without love," I said.

"We want our love master!" she wept. "Do not masters search for their love slave?"

"Speak of love," I said, "and you may be lashed."

"Yes, Master," she said. "Forgive me, Master."

I grew muchly uneasy, and angry. The slave is a work object and a pleasure object, nothing more. That must be kept in mind. She is a meaningless, purchased beast. See that you treat her as one. She is an animal. See that you train her as one. Dress her, if you do, for her exposure and exhibition, publicly and privately, and for your pleasure. She is to wear her hair, and such, as you please. Belittle and mock her, if you wish. Scorn and detest her, if you wish. Do not be easy to please. Never let her forget that she is a slave, only that. Command her. Master her. Yours is the whip. Hers is the collar. Do not let her forget this. Work her well, and derive much pleasure from her, inordinate pleasure. She is your slave.

"The slave is nothing," I said. "You must clearly understand that."

"Yes, Master," she said.

"Do not speak of love," I said.

"Forgive me, Master," she said.

"You are, of course," I said, "not displeasing to look upon."

"Master?"

"As an exciting, tender morsel of collar meat."

"Thank you, Master," she whispered.

"Excellent slave curves," I said.

"Thank you, Master," she said.

"It pleasant to have you on your knees before me."

"A girl is pleased, if she is found pleasing," she said.

"You kneel well," I said.

"Thank you, Master," she said.

"With one exception," I said.

"Master?"

"Your knees," I said, "split them,"

"Yes, Master."

"More."

"More, Master?"

"Yes," I said.

"Yes, Master," she said.

"How do you feel now?" I asked.

"I have known for years that I was a slave, and should be a slave," she said, "but until this moment, in this place, I did not expect these feelings, as they are now, which irradiate my body. I am enflamed, Master, helplessly enflamed."

"Describe your feelings," I said.

"I feel slave," she said. "I feel slave."

"You are slave," I said.

"Yes, Master," she said.

"A slave," I said, "yearns for her master."

"I would," she said, "that you would be the master of my slave, the slave that I am."

"You are not an unattractive slave," I said.

"Choose me!" she begged.

"As what?" I asked.

"As a mere slave," she said, "surrendering all, giving all, to her master, asking nothing, expecting nothing, of her master."

"I see," I said.

"Choose me, choose me!" she begged.

"Slaves do not choose their masters," I said. "Masters choose their slaves."

"Choose me!" she wept.

"I cannot," I said. "You belong to the Pani, to the ship."

She bent over, before me, her head down. Tears fell to the dirt.

After a time, she looked up, her face tear-stained.

I pointed to my feet, and she bent down, and kissed them. Tears were on my boots.

"Thank you, Master," she whispered, sensitive of the privilege which had been accorded to her, however unworthy she might be. She, a mere slave, had been permitted to kiss the feet of a free man.

"Master," she said.

"Yes," I said.

"All women are slaves," she whispered.

"Oh?" I said.

"Yes, Master," she whispered.

"I did not know that," I said.

"It is true," she said.

"Excellent," I said.

I smiled. I had thought that a secret shared only by strong free men, the sort who have women only as slaves, the sort before whom a woman can be only a slave, the sort before whom they remove their clothing and kneel.

She then looked up. "Perhaps," she said, "a free man may conduct a slave to her kennel."

"It will be so," I said.

Chapter Twenty-Seven

The Victory of the Exploratory Force;
There Will Be Feasting

I heard the drums, and emerged from the barracks.

It was early morning.

"The exploratory force returns," I heard, "in glorious triumph!"

I had heard nothing of them in the vicinity. Thus, I supposed they had marched all night.

"Let us see the trophies, and women!" cried a fellow, hurrying toward one of the plateau gates, surmounting a trail south of the castle grounds, that eventually abutting on the road leading to the largest of the three local villages.

I climbed the stairs to the parapet of the interior wall, of the three walls, which was the highest wall.

I had no glass of the Builders but one could make out the thatched roofs in the distance.

There were two Pani on the parapet.

There was a darkness on the road, in the distance.

"What is going on?" I asked the Pani.

One was shading his eyes.

"Tal," said the other, politely. They did not respond otherwise.

The courtyard below was beginning to be crowded, as men, our armsmen, and Pani, even some free women, or contract women, emerged from their respective housings.

Looking across the courtyard, I saw a vulo exit the castle. It seemed to circle, for a time, and then flew north, and west, toward the mountains.

Turgus and Tyrtaios both now joined me on the parapet,

Turgus, liaison to Lord Nishida, Tyrtaios to Lord Okimoto. Each bore a glass of the Builders.

Tyrtaios spoke neither to me nor to the Pani, but scanned the trail, the road, the village, the horizon, quickly, expertly. Then, in a moment, he had descended from the parapet, striding toward the castle. Turgus, too, put the glass to use, but more thoughtfully. Then he lowered it.

"The exploratory force returns?" I said.

"Yes," he said, and handed me the glass.

I looked down the trail. A column was indeed approaching. Before it were carried the narrow, vertical banners of Lord Temmu.

The order of march seemed ragged.

The column, as a whole, I conjectured, is separated from this column, a shorter column, on the trail, which must be the vanguard.

I turned the glass on the village, and its road. The thatched roofs swirled into focus, and the darkness on the road resolved itself into tiny figures, and several hand-drawn carts. Among these figures I made out what seemed to be a coffle, of some eight or ten figures, being moved northwest, toward the mountains.

I looked to Turgus.

"The village," he said, "is being abandoned."

Thetis and Iole had been returned to the castle grounds four days ago, following their disciplinary interlude in the slave hut. It was said their service was now humble, and zealous. It was also noted that now, before Pani warriors, they did not kneel, but prostrated themselves, putting themselves instantly, trembling, to second obeisance position, prone, hands to the sides of their head, eyes to the ground.

I returned the glass to Turgus.

He did not seem eager to report to Lord Nishida.

I suspected that Lord Nishida, perhaps from messages conveyed by vulos, had already sufficient reports in hand.

Down in the courtyard, now, in addition to the drums, there were soundings on the Pani's conch horns.

I made my way down to the courtyard, to welcome the returning troops, or, I trusted, the vanguard.

The plateau gate, the trail of which led most directly to the largest of the villages below, was swung open. I could then see, beyond it, the other two gates, already opened. I could see the tops of banners, approaching, up the trail, then helmets, then men. Blasts were blown on the conch horns. Drums rolled bravely. We in the courtyard moved to the sides, to clear a passage for the column.

None of the high Pani came to greet the column.

Several men began to cheer, but were then quiet.

The drums were silent; so too, the conch horns, or trumpets.

"Where are the trophies?" asked a man.

"Where are the women?" asked another.

The column, preceded by its bannermen, in rows of four, entered the courtyard.

The marchers were weary.

Given the Ahn, I feared they had marched all night.

They were drawn, and haggard, perhaps thirsting, perhaps hungry. Some men staggered, and some limped. Some men were aided by others. We saw some borne on litters. Many were in soiled, rent garments. Some wore bandages. A number were bloodied.

"How far behind is the column?" I inquired of a marcher.

He looked at me, vacantly, not responding.

Beside me now were Philoctetes, Aeacus, and Tereus.

"How far behind is the column?" I asked a second fellow.

"This is the column," he said, not looking at me.

"No speaking!" warned a Pani warrior, within, directing the bannermen, and their attendant troops, to follow him, away from the castle.

Turgus now joined me, come down from the parapet.

"There were a hundred Pani," I said. "I see almost none."

"Gone," said Turgus.

"There were four hundred armsmen," I said. "I do not think more than a hundred returned."

"The force, obviously," said Turgus, "was cut to pieces."

"I saw no Pani officers," I said.

"Probably most died in battle," said Turgus. "Others, I suspect, would not return and face Lord Temmu."

"They fled?" I said.

"That is not likely," said Turgus.

"Captured?" I said.

"I do not think so," said Turgus.

"What then?" I asked.

"It has to do with honor," he said.

"It is no disgrace to be defeated in battle," I said, "if one is outfought, if one has done one's best."

"I agree," he said.

"I do not understand," I said.

"We are not Pani," he said.

The first gate was then shut, and then the second, and then that near us.

"I do not think we will soon march," said Philoctetes.

"The village below," I said, "has been abandoned."

"It is likely to be burned," said Aeacus.

"Why do you say that?" I asked.

"I spoke to a fellow, who spoke to one, lower on the trail," said Aeacus. "The enemy is moving toward us."

"In what strength?" I asked.

"I do not think we know," said Philoctetes.

"It is speculated," said Aeacus, "that it is between five and seven thousand *ashigaru*."

"I would guess," said Philoctetes, "that the exploratory force encountered little more than its vanguard."

"We would then, I conjecture," I said, "be much outnumbered."

"Yes," said Aeacus.

I supposed Lord Temmu, who had furnished the hundred Pani who marched with the exploratory force, had some two thousand troops on which he might rely, most housed within the castle grounds. Lords Nishida and Okimoto, as I estimated their warriors, had some three hundred and fifty men. Of armsmen and mariners, I supposed we retained some eleven hundred men, after the apparent debacle of the exploratory force. All in all, as far as I could estimate these things, we must have something less than thirty-five hundred men at arms. Peasants might be impressed as *ashigaru*, but, I suspected, from what I had seen earlier, many of the local peasants might have left their villages and fields, and withdrawn to the mountains. We did have some one hundred and forty tarns back in the mountains, with their riders and auxiliary personnel. Whatever might be the initial psychological impact of the tarn on those unfamiliar with its form of life, it would be only a matter of time before it became clear to the enemy that the tarn, however formidable, was a natural creature, limited, and mortal, nothing dreadfully mysterious, no unnatural and inexplicable dragon bird, sprung from the clouds, gifted with the ability to blight fields, towns, and armies. Too, whereas a tarn cavalry can acquire intelligence, strike unexpectedly, cut supply lines, and such, it is of limited value against a distributed land force. In this way it differs from the crashing thunder of a tharlarion charge, or the swift attack of kaiila-mounted lancers.

"How close," asked Tereus of Aeacus, "is the enemy?"

"One gathers," said Aeacus, "its sighting may be imminent."

"Not necessarily," said Turgus.

"How so?" said Aeacus.

"I have learned," said Turgus, "from Lord Nishida, that this holding can withstand a siege of thousands, and has done so more than once."

"So?" said Aeacus.

"Thus I see no rush to be upon us," said Turgus.

"But the enemy is advancing," said Tereus.

"Yes," said Turgus.

"We will be penned here," said Tereus. "Waiting to be stormed, or to die, of thirst or starvation."

"The castle is equipped, of course," said Turgus, "with reservoirs, and supplies."

"We are muchly outnumbered," said Tereus. "Many will see little to be gained by huddling together in this place, without prospects."

"We are not Pani," said Aeacus.

"There is honor to be satisfied," I said. "Many of these men have taken fee."

"This is not our war, and not our country," said Aeacus.

"Fee has been taken," I said.

"I smell smoke," said Philoctetes.

"The village," said Tereus.

He looked across the courtyard, where Seremides, seeing him, quickly, awkwardly, hobbled away.

Tereus' hand went to the dagger at his belt.

He doubtless remembered Thoas and Andros, and Aeson.

At this point, a Pani crier began to cry out. A set of feasts were to be prepared, served in dozens of rooms, and barracks, and in the courtyard, at long tables, celebrating the victory of the exploratory force. I heard then the roll of drums once more, and the soundings of conch trumpets.

"It seems," said Turgus, "victory is ours."

"What victory?" said Philoctetes.

"The return of the exploratory force, some of it," laughed Tereus, and then he turned away from us.

I watched, to make certain he did not follow Seremides.

"Slaves will serve the feast, will they not?" asked Aeacus.

"One supposes so," I said.

"They are likely to know nothing of what has occurred," said Philoctetes.

"They will see it as a victory feast," said Aeacus.

"I suppose so," I said.

"I hope they will have tarsk," said a man.

I hoped that, too, as I was growing weary of rice and parsit. The Pani do raise tarsk, verr, and, of course, vulos.

"Perhaps they will break out paga," I said.

Some had been brought to the castle from the ship.

"Let us have a good time," said Turgus.

"Let us commemorate the beginning of a siege," laughed Aeacus, lifting his hand, as though it held a goblet.

"And," said a man, "let us celebrate the inviolability of the holding of dear Lord Temmu, and rejoice in our safety and security."

"Surely we dare not meet the enemy in the field," said a fellow.

"No," said Turgus.

"Excellent," he said. "So we will feast aplenty, and drink apace, whilst the enemy, should he invest this place, may freeze, wither, and starve."

"How long might a siege last?" asked Aeacus.

"One, I learned from Lord Nishida," said Turgus, "lasted four years."

"That would require a great deal of paga," said a man.

"Learn to savor *sake*," said a man.

I looked up to the parapet. I saw the warrior, Nodachi,

looking over the parapet, toward the village. He had his two swords with him. After a time, he began to turn about, and perform martial exercises, with a patient, unhurried grace.

Some of the Pani, I supposed, must know who he was, his background, his motivation to join us.

I, however, did not know. And I did not think that even his students, such as Pertinax and Tajima, the Pani tarnsman, understood the mystery of this unusually skilled, but enigmatic warrior.

I looked about. I had not seen Tyrtaios, after he had left the parapet.

This made me uneasy.

"So there will be feasting," said Aeacus.

"It seems so," I said.

"To celebrate the triumph of the exploratory force," he said.

"It seems so," I said.

"Some," said Aeacus, "will see things as they are said to be, not as they are."

"That is common, is it not?"

"I fear so," said Aeacus.

"So we will feast," I said.

"Will you sit at the long tables, in the courtyard?" asked Aeacus. "That might be pleasant."

"Let us fill our plates and lift our goblets privately," I said. "Let us seek one of the closed places. There are several. I will arrange one. Let it be only the members of the high watch."

"You have a reason for this?" asked Aeacus.

"More than one," I said.

"Where shall we meet?" he asked.

"Here," I said.

"What hall have you in mind?" asked Aeacus.

"That of the Placid Sea, or that the Three Moons," I said.

"Splendid," he said.

Both halls were small, and pleasant, each appointed with the spare taste, the lack of clutter, the movable, painted screens one expected in such places.

"You will arrange the food, the drink, the service," said Aeacus.

"Yes," I said.

"Hail the victory of the exploratory force," said Aeacus.

"Indeed," I said.

I saw Seremides, now again across the courtyard. I thought him wise to remain in public places.

"So," said Aeacus, "until this evening."

"Yes," I said, "until this evening."

We could smell smoke, coming from the village.

Chapter Twenty-Eight

In the Hall of the Three Moons;
What Is Seen from the Parapet;
I Descend from the Parapet

"Surely you have not forgotten the slaves," said Aeacus.

"No," I said.

Many were the savory odors which emerged from behind the screen, from sauces, stews, and soups, rich with shoots, herbs, nuts, spices, vegetables, and peppers, even tarsk and vulo, as well as parsit, crabs, and grunt, emanating from pots brought in from the central kitchens, which served the long tables, outside, the barracks messes, the larger halls, and the smaller halls, such as that of the Three Moons.

"And who will serve us?" asked Leros.

"These," I said, and, holding them bent over, in leading position, one on my left, one on my right, I produced two slaves, lengthily tunicked, as the Pani seemingly preferred.

"Show them to us," called one of the fellows.

I then straightened the slaves, and held them upright, each by the hair, standing, half on their tip toes, before the diners.

"Hands at your sides," I informed the slaves.

"Splendid," said a fellow.

The diners, at the small tables, some fifteen, those who had held the high watches on the great ship, sitting cross-legged, slapped their left shoulders with their right hands.

Both were beauties.

"First obeisance position," I informed the slaves.

Both then went to first obeisance position, kneeling, head to the floor, palms of the hands down on the floor, at the sides of their head.

"Speak," I said.

"It is the hope of this girl," said the first, "that her service will be found pleasing by masters."

"It is the hope of this girl," said the second, "that her service will be found pleasing by masters."

"Speak," I said.

"It is the hope of this girl," said the first, "that if her service is not found pleasing by masters, she will be well punished."

"It is the hope of this girl," said the second, "that if her service is not found pleasing by masters, she will be well punished."

"Kneel up," I said.

"Yes, Master," they said.

"Head up," I told them.

"Yes, Master," they said.

Sometimes masters have the girls in position keep their heads down, until given permission to raise them.

When the head is up, of course, the girls' features are well revealed.

They looked straight ahead, kneeling back on heels, back straight, belly in, shoulders back, hands palm down on the thighs.

"Well done, Callias," said a fellow.

"You must have looked through the kennels early, and well," said another.

"Pleasant vulos," said a man.

"Tastas," said another fellow.

"Master!" said one of the slaves.

"Do you object?" I asked.

"Please, Master," said the other slave.

"Perhaps you do not care to be so characterized?" I said.

"Consider, Master," said one of the slaves, and was then, suddenly, silent.

To be sure, a free woman, and particularly one of high station, would be outraged, and surely justifiably, to be so characterized, so familiarly, so intimately, so dismissively. Slaves, of course, as beasts and properties, to be looked upon with relish and objectivity, are accustomed to such appraisals. Indeed, they are indicative of interest and approval. Such things can warm the thighs of a slave. Do they not suggest that the object within her collar has come to the attention of free men? Do they not portend the possibility of eventual caresses, for which she hopes, which she is zealous to earn?

"Dear fellows," I said, "it is possible these two were once free women. Many slaves were. Thus, your words may not comport with the dignity of ones who were once such."

There was laughter at the tables.

"Thank you, Master," said the first slave, uneasily.

"Thank you, Master," said the second.

"Are you slaves?" I asked.

"Yes, Master," said the first slave.

"Yes, Master," said the second slave.

"Very well," I said, "pretty vulos, little tastas, split your knees."

"Master!" said the slaves.

"Now," I said.

A murmur of appreciation coursed through the men.

"How do you like them?" I asked.

"Superb," said a fellow.

"For such meat," said a fellow, "chains, and the block, were invented."

"Do you not think they might prove to be ready juicers, both of them hot little collar puddings?"

One of the slaves gasped. And, even in the lamp light, I thought both turned white.

"Yes, yes!" laughed the men. Some pounded their shoulders, others drummed on the small tables before them.

They had been spoken of as though they might be common slaves.

But, to be sure, they were now common slaves.

"They are ship slaves, of course," I reminded the fellows. "They are not to be put to slave use, without the permission of their owners, the Pani."

Moans greeted this announcement.

To be sure, the fellows were well aware of the restrictions involved. This was nothing new to them. Such slaves had not been brought from the continent, months away, to instigate rivalries, generate dissension, undermine discipline, raise issues, occasion brawls, if not killings, and foment disruption at the World's End. The fellows should have been grateful enough to the Pani that the slaves were made available for serving the general feast, in its several locations.

"What is your name?" asked Leros of one of the slaves.

"Adraste," she said, "if it pleases master."

"You are very beautiful, Adraste," he said. This was said with much the same objectivity with which one might have commended a kaiila.

"Thank you, Master," she said.

"And what is your name," asked Aeacus, of the other slave.

"Alcinoë," she said, "if it pleases Master."

"You are not a bad-looking slave," said one of the fellows.

"Thank you, Master," she said.

I thought I saw the trace of a smile on the lips of Adraste. And, if I am not mistaken, I thought I saw a flicker of annoyance course the features of the lovely Alcinoë, whom I, at least, thought quite nice.

I had two reasons for wishing a private supper, limited to a few, in this case the personnel of the high watches on the great ship, whom I knew and trusted. First, I was much afraid that if the two slaves would, for example, have been assigned to the long tables, those in the courtyard, one or another fellow might have recognized them. I did not think that Cabot was on the grounds, but Seremides surely was. Thus I was trying, for what it was worth, to conceal the identity of the two slaves. The fellows of the high watch, with the exception of myself, would know them, if at all, as only two slaves, to be sure, two rather attractive slaves. The second reason I wanted to have the small supper in a private area, was to give me the freedom to come and go, as I might please. For example, I was much afraid that the sorry return of the exploratory force, and the possible imminence of the forces of Lord Yamada, might further increase apprehension amongst the men, hasten the formation of reckless resolves, and lead to some rash action. If one were concerned to protect an endeavor such as our common enterprise, or forestall or thwart a conspiracy which might result in the ruination of that enterprise, whatever it might be, and perhaps the death of hundreds, subtlety seemed advisable. Certainly it would seem inadvisable to act openly, where one might fall within the purview of conspirators themselves, whoever they might be. One does not, if wise, arouse suspicion, and court a knife in the darkness. But, too, of course, what did I owe, really, to Lords Nishida and Okimoto, or to Lord Temmu, who, as far as I knew, might be as bad as, or even worse than, Lord Yamada. I was loyal, of course, to the ship. And I was reasonably clear that I owed my life to Lord Nishida, from long ago, and perhaps to Tarl Cabot, strangely enough, as he was of Port Kar, enemy to great Cos.

"Let the serving begin," I said, and the slaves sprang to their feet, and the men cheered.

"Is there paga?" inquired a fellow.

"Enough to keep you drunk for a month," I said.

This brought another cheer.

The slaves had now retired behind the screen, I think gratefully, to prepare for the serving. I found them bickering as to precedence, as to who might serve what dish, and when. Whereas I knew little or nothing of such things, decisions were in order, so I specified, very clearly, who should serve what, and in what order. I tried to distribute the best dishes, or what I took to be the best dishes, evenly between them. Both, of course, were to serve paga, but demurely, as one might serve another drink, not as it is commonly served in the taverns, or to a private master, in the privacy of his own quarters.

I heard some striking on the tables, in the dining area. The fellows were hungry, and growing impatient.

"Forgive me, Master," said Alcinoë, "but I am not a serving slave."

"Nor I," said Adraste.

"You chose us for this that we would be demeaned, did you not?" said Alcinoë.

"Doubtless it amuses the Master," said Adraste, "that I, who was Ubara, should serve men, as a serving slave."

"And that I," said Alcinoë, "who was second only to the Ubara herself should serve so, as well!"

"Perhaps you would prefer to serve the long tables, in the

courtyard," I said, "serve, say, Tarl Cabot, if he is there, and Seremides, who may well be there, and others?"

"No, Master," said Adraste, quickly.

"No, Master," said Alcinoë.

"But that we should serve, at all," said Adraste.

"At all," added Alcinoë.

"It does amuse me," I said, "that the former Talena, the former Ubara of Ar, and the former Lady Flavia of Ar, her confidante, now slaves, should serve common fellows, as might any other slave."

"Very amusing," said Adraste.

"And I will tell you, pretty Adraste, how you will serve them," I said.

"Master?" she said.

"Remove your clothing," I said.

"Excellent!" laughed Alcinoë, delighted. She clapped her hands with pleasure.

"There are no free women out there," I said.

"Surely you cannot be serious," she said.

"Get it off," I said.

Frightened, Adraste drew her tunic off, over her head.

"How wonderful, how splendid," said Alcinoë, "she who was Talena of Ar, now a stripped serving slave!"

"Men," I told Adraste, "find it pleasant to be served by naked slaves."

"Master," moaned Adraste.

Alcinoë laughed.

"It improves the appetite," I told her.

"Take that, haughty, vain, deceitful slut!" said Alcinoë.

Tears ran down the cheeks of the former Ubara.

"Naked slave!" laughed Alcinoë.

"Alcinoë," I said.

"Master?" she said.

"Remove your clothing," I said.

Her eyes regarded me, wide, startled.

"Now," I said.

"Yes, Master!" she said, and hastily drew off her garment, over her head.

"Slave!" said Adraste to her.

"Slave!" said Alcinoë.

The slaves now wore only their collars. How beautiful are women, so!

"I hate you, Master," said Adraste.

"I hate you, Master!" said Alcinoë.

"I was Ubara!" said Adraste.

"I was second to the Ubara, her confidante," said Alcinoë.

"Pick up your plates," I told them.

They did so.

"I only regret," I said, "that your rivals, other free women, your enemies, women loyal to Ar, are not out there."

The slaves moaned, softly.

It is very pleasant, of course, for a free woman to come into the ownership of a former enemy, or rival, and have her serve her guests naked, as the lowest of serving slaves.

I picked up a cloth. The slaves' hands were occupied, each holding a dish which they might serve. "Let us wipe away these tears," I said. I wiped the tears from the cheeks of Adraste, and softly touched the eyes of Alcinoë, that her eyes not sparkle with her distress, and shame.

I then went to the men's side of the screen.

"Two slaves," I said.

The slaves, miserable, trying to hold themselves erect, each holding a dish, emerged from behind the screen.

"Excellent!" cried men.

Some struck their left shoulders with the palms of their right hand. Others pounded on the small tables with pleasure.

"Now," said Leros, "we shall have a proper supper, even at the World's End!"

There was much assent to this.

I then fetched a slave whip which I had earlier put to the side. "Pass the whip about," I said. "Each slave, when she first serves you, is to kneel and kiss the whip, and then place the plate before you."

Let them learn well, I thought, what they are, the former Talena of Ar, once Ubara, and the former Lady Flavia of Ar, once her confidante, that they are now slaves, only that.

I tossed the whip to Aeacus. Adraste knelt beside him, at the edge of the small table, bent forward, and kissed the whip, which he extended to her. She then put the plate before him, humbly. He handed the whip to Leros, and Alcinoë knelt at his place, and leaned forward, kissing in her turn the whip proffered to her lips, and then, as Adraste before her, placed the plate humbly before the free man. Soon Adraste would return, with another plate, and the whip would be passed to the next fellow. "Fellows," I said, and loudly, that the slaves might hear as well, "if the service is not fully pleasing, or is lacking in any respect, use the whip on them."

"Yes," said more than one man. "Yes!"

The slaves, I was sure, would be zealous to please. I did not doubt but what they would do their best to serve well.

For the men, of course, it is pleasant to be served by naked slaves. I supposed that free women speculated that private dinners amongst free men, to which they were not invited, were often so served. Let the mother, the aunt, the sister, and such, familiar with a son's, a nephew's, or a brother's quiet, refined, demure, tastefully attired slave not speculate on how she serves his guests at a private party nor, more interestingly, what occurs later at his slave ring.

I went behind the screen, where the slaves were preparing to continue serving.

Now that the feast was in progress, I felt I might slip away, unnoticed.

Alcinoë was standing at the edge of the serving table. She was lovely in the lamplight. She turned, to look at me. Then she fled suddenly to my arms, and I held her to me. Tears coursed her cheeks. Words rushed out of her, as though a stream had broken forth from behind some obstruction, sweeping debris to the side, and, released at last, it rushed forth, threatening its banks, in a churning, grateful torrent. "Thank you, oh, thank you, Master," she sobbed, "thank you for making me serve naked! I feel so female, so slave, serving men, so exposed, my masters! I am thrilled. I am a different form of life, I know that now, I am now fulfilled. Let them look upon me! It is such as I who belong to them! I am now as I should be! I would serve all your feasts, Master, naked, as a woman, and slave. It is so right, and I am so happy!"

I crushed her to me. She was slave, and in my arms!

"Thank you for giving me no choice, for making me do what you will have me do," she said. "Thank you for your command, your power, your uncompromised, unqualified domination! Be ruthless with me, be severe. It is what I want! I respond in a thousand ways! I revel in it. I need it, I am a woman, I am incomplete without it! Yes, make me serve men naked, or as you wish! I love it! It is what I am for!"

I held her tightly.

She could not have begun to free herself.

She was slave.

"My body is so different from that of men," she whispered, "a body designed by nature for their pleasure. To look upon it, do they not know it was made for them, and is such that it belongs to them! That they find it different and beautiful, and desirable, excites me. How meaningful, and warm, and real it makes me feel! I want them to look upon it, with zest and pleasure. As the body of a woman is it not theirs, a fitting belonging, like the whole of a woman, of men? I have always wanted to show it, to display it, and I am grateful that I must now do so. Must we always be content with a disarranged veil, the hem of a skirt, lifted about an ankle? Better the slave in her collar, given no choice but to be bared before masters! Does not the free woman, in her heart, yearn to cast aside her robes, and show herself as what she is, woman! Does she truly wish to bargain with the promise of her beauty, dangling it before her like a closed purse, whispering its hints from behind an opaque screen? Are not such mercenary ones better put on the slave block, in chains? The beauty of a woman is not a thing of shame. Who could think so? Does she truly think it a thing of shame? Surely her beauty is not a thing of shame, not a blemish, or crime, to be concealed from view. Does she truly wish to conceal her beauty? Does she not rather, in her heart, desire to reveal it? How different is it, truly, from that of a thousand other beauties, that of grass and wine trees, that of tabuk, of sleen, or kaiila? Is it not a thing with which to be pleased? Let the slave, brazen in her sex, be proud. Let her say to the free woman, 'Here I am, a female, found pleasing by men, and collared, for their pleasure. Are you so much? I am helpless, and theirs. I must be obedient, and fear the whip! Would you not be so ? Abuse me, and hate me, if you wish. I am content. I am happy. Are you so?'"

My lips drank from her the wine of her bondage.

She gasped, her small arms clutched me.

"Oh!" she said.

When I would thrust her from me, the mark of my buckle would be in her body.

"Own me," she begged. "I am your slave! You know that!"

That one could own such a thing as she much pleased me.

She was slave in my arms.

"I love you," she said, "I love you, I love you, my master!"

"Beware," I said.

"Do not have me sold!" she said. "Do not put me on the block! I am so helpless!"

"I do not own you," I said.

"It is your collar I would beg to wear!"

"Surely you wish to be free," I said.

"No, no, no!" she wept. "I want to be a slave!"

"Why?" I asked.

"Because I am a slave," she said. "It is in my heart to love and serve! I want to give all. I want a master! I want to be owned! Chain me, tie me, master me! I want to be so desired, so wanted, so lusted for, that it would not occur to a man to keep me other than as what I am, as a slave, even to the whip! That is how I want to be kept! Oh, I would strive to be found pleasing!"

"Surely you want freedom," I said.

"I am not a man," she said. "I am a woman!"

"Even so," I said.

"No," she said, "a thousand times no! I have known the emptiness, the loneliness, of freedom, the pretensions, the selfishness, the uncertainties of freedom, the confusions, the lack of place, the opacities and ambiguities of freedom, the lack of purpose, the lack of meaning and identity!"

"It is true," I said, "that a slave has her purpose, and her meaning. Such things are quite clear. It is also true that what is expected of her is clear, and that there is no doubt as to what she is. That is as clear as the collar on her neck."

"It is in my sex and my heart," she said. "It is an ancient and needful thing in my body, to belong, to be owned, to kneel, to revere, to submit, to serve, to please, to find myself at a master's feet, where I desire to be!"

"Surely freedom is precious," I said.

"So, too," she said, "is bondage."

"I have heard so," I said.

"What woman does not wish to be owned," she said, "what woman does not wish a master?"

"Some, I suppose, free women, would deny it," I said.

"Such expressions are expected of them," she said, "even required of them. How they would be ostracized and scorned, put from society, if they did not say such things! Indeed, they might be remanded to slavers."

"Some," I said, "might suppose themselves, honestly enough, if naively, to subscribe to such expressions."

"Then," she said, "let them find themselves at the feet of a man, stripped, and in his collar. Let them find themselves mastered, and then let them examine their feelings anew."

"Might they not cover their chains with tears?" I said.

"Yes," she said, "and then kiss the chains that bind them, so helplessly, so securely!"

"Many free women," I said, "fear the collar."

"And long for it!" she said.

"Perhaps," I said.

"Many were the civilized women, educated and refined, and barbarian females, illiterate and primitive, not even able to speak Gorean, brought, shackled, to the markets of Ar, lamenting their fate," she said, "but before *Tor-tu-Gor* had run half his course, they had only one thing in common, their submission to masters, the love of their collar, and the fear that they might be freed."

"Would you impose your views and values on all?" I asked.

"I leave that to others," she said.

"I see," I said.

"Do you speak for all women?" I asked.

"Yes," she said.

"Perhaps," I said.

"Whatever might be the truth in these matters," she said, "for those of us who are slaves, and know we are slaves, and would be slaves, and are complete only at the feet of men, do not be cruel, do not begrudge us our collars!"

"You would be owned?"

"Wholly, and helplessly!"

I regarded her, not speaking, not releasing her.

"Is it wrong for one who is a slave to want to be a slave?"

"No," I said. "It is not wrong."

"Keep me in a collar!" she said. "I belong in it, I want it."

"I do not own you," I said.

She sobbed, pressing herself against me.

I looked to the former Talena of Ar, once Ubara.

"And perhaps you, Adraste," I said, "would be pleased, in your collar, to serve naked, at another's feast."

Swiftly, she turned away.

I thrust Alcinoë from me, and she slipped to the polished floor, of dark wood, and knelt there, holding my leg, pressing her cheek against it.

"Master, Master," she said.

I disengaged her hands and held them apart, looking down on her, she on her knees at my feet. Then, holding her hands, I put my right foot against her left shoulder, and then spurned her to the floor, as the slave she was, and she turned, tears on her cheeks, and looked up at me. "I love you," she said. "I love you! Care for me, care for me, just a little, Master!"

"You are a slave," I said, turning away.

She sobbed.

At the exit, I turned, again. "Continue serving," I said.

"Yes, Master," said Adraste.

"Yes, Master," said Alcinoë.

I then left the small dining area, the Hall of the Three Moons.

It was dark outside now, but, under torches, there was still feasting at the long tables in the courtyard.

What a glorious victory had been that of the exploratory force!

I would ascend to the parapet.

When I reached the height of the wall, the inner wall, the highest wall, I looked over the wall, down, toward the village. Near me were two Pani, guards, on the parapet, as well. The village, or where it had been, was dark, but, as far as I could see, scattered about, to the south, were a great number of campfires.

The force of Lord Yamada, or his generals, was in place.

I stayed sometime on the parapet, for the most part, however, not looking over the wall, but looking back, down to the courtyard, where I might observe the tables.

As I feared, later, near the nineteenth Ahn, a number of men withdrew from the tables, and I saw them gather in a corner of the courtyard. Others were now joining them, from various barracks, and halls.

I thought of Alcinoë.

I attempted to scorn and detest her. Did I not know she was a slave? Was I not a free man, and a warrior? Why then, I asked myself, would I die for her.

What a weakling and fool I was!

I wondered if she should be freed?

Did I hate her so much?

Were her soft lips not made to be pressed to the feet of a master?

I laughed, and the two Pani guardsmen regarded me, puzzled.

Free her, I thought. Never!

How absurd such a thought, for such a woman!

If I owned her, I thought, she would well know herself slave. Her collar, as it is said, would be well locked.

Women such as Alcinoë belong in a collar.

Accordingly, they are to be kept in one.

They do constitute a danger, of course.

They are appealing, desirable, helpless, and owned.

One must thus be careful lest one begin to care for them, lest one begin to succumb to their charms.

What curvaceous, cunning little brutes they are!

Take no chances with them!

Keep them in the strictest and most perfect of bondages. Do not let them forget they are slaves. Let them fear the whip. If necessary, they may be taken to the market and sold. Such women, after all, however delightful in their collars, are nothing. They are only slaves.

I hastened down the steps from the wall.

Many had now left the tables.

I saw Seremides hobble out of the darkness. "They are going to take the ship!" he said.

"I know," I said.

Chapter Twenty-Nine

What Occurred at the Gate

Four Pani, in defensive stance, glaves at the ready, stood before the innermost gate.

"Stand aside!" commanded Tereus.

The Pani did not budge, though, obviously, resistance would have been useless.

"Stand aside!" said Tereus.

Behind him were a large number of armed men. Later, as they would be counted, there would be eight hundred and seventy men, precisely.

"We may not do so, honorable one," said one of the guards politely.

Clearly Tereus did not wish to force the gate, but, as clearly, he was prepared to do so.

"We are going to the ship," said Tereus.

"Have you permission?" inquired the guard.

There were cries of rage from several of the men. "Kill them," I heard.

I pressed through the crowd.

I had thought the instigator of this action would have been Tyrtaios, but I did not see him. Tereus was a fine oarsman, and, in his way, an honorable fellow. I did not think he had managed this business, though, at present, it seemed he was its spokesman.

I suspected that those who were most behind this matter were in the background, waiting to see how matters might proceed.

Shedding the blood of others is easy; parting with one's own is much more difficult.

Personally, I did not blame the men for wishing to withdraw.

Much treasure had been gathered in without much difficulty, from the derelicts in the Vine Sea. This treasure was aboard the ship. The men were mostly mercenaries, fee fighters, and they had already riches. What more could they hope for here, at the World's End, in a war amongst strangers for strangers, a war from which they had little to expect and, presumably, a good deal to fear. They had encountered the enemy in the ill-advised landing and the exploratory force, to their sorrow, had encountered him more locally. These events augured no simple and speedy route to victory. The ship, on the other hand, was the means to return, rich, to continental Gor. They might have no other opportunity. It was not surprising, then, particularly given the apparently decisive defeat of the exploratory force, that fellows would think of escape, think of taking the ship and putting to sea. It had reached the World's End from the northern forests of continental Gor. Why then might it not return? Too, who knew if the fleet of Lord Yamada might not soon appear on the horizon, and close the mouth of the cove, closing the door to escape and precluding the eventual exploitation of the hitherto garnered riches?

I continued to press through the crowd, trying to reach the gate.

Most of the men knew me, directly or indirectly, by accounts, from early in the voyage, my retrieval from the *Metioche,* and the test by Lord Nishida, early in the voyage, with Philoctetes, and later, from my attendance on Tarl Cabot, my actions in the Vine Sea, my role in the evacuation, my frequent participation in the high watches, and such.

I was not, of course, an officer, but, in this situation, I thought I might have more influence on them, being one of their own, so to speak, than an officer.

I broke through the crowd, I think a moment before the four Pani guardsmen would have been rushed, and the first of the three gates swung open.

I put myself before Tereus, and the fellows at his side.

"Hold, friend Tereus!" I cried, putting out my hands.

"Rescuer of Rutilius, the murderer," he said, "stand away!"

Men growled beside him.

Tereus had unsheathed his sword. I had kept mine sheathed, of course, not so much because I wanted my intervention to be peaceful, though I surely wished that, as because, drawn, it would have done me little good. I might, with fortune, have slain one or two men, but then I would be swept aside, probably trampled, probably bleeding from a hundred wounds.

"You are all of the ship," I cried to the men. "Do not betray her! Do not insult her! You have taken fee! Honor is due! You have come to serve, so serve! Do not desert your fellows, the Pani, and others, who have fought with you! You have been treated fairly by Lords Nishida and Okimoto. They have sought your service, paid for it with good coin, which you accepted, and brought you here, in trust, across vast, green Thassa, to the World's End, that you may prove your worth and earn your pay, that you may teach those of these islands the honor, the prowess, and might of the archers, spearmen, and swordsmen of Ar, Jad, Brundisium, Temos, Kasra, Tor, and a hundred ports and cities."

Men wavered, and looked to one another.

"He is Cosian," said a fellow of Ar.

"You cannot stop us with words," said a fellow, "you and four behind you."

"You may stay here to die," said a fellow. "We will not!"

"We came for gold, and we have it," said another. "There is nothing to keep us here."

"Honor!" I cried.

"Do not speak of honor," said a fellow. "Many here have betrayed Home Stones."

"Or been cast from our gates in the name of Home Stones," snarled another.

"You cannot take the ship," I said. "The galley nests are not open. The bulwarks are high. The ropes and nets will not be lowered."

I saw more than one fellow in the crowd with loops of rope. I saw more than one grappling iron, and, I supposed, there were others, which had been smuggled from the ship. I knew, as well, that mooring ropes might be climbed, and that spikes might be hammered into the side of the ship, by means of which men might climb the sides. Even so I doubted that the assault on the ship would be successful. Although the Pani on the ship would be much outnumbered, they would have the advantage of position. Arrow fire would flow from the ship to the wharf, and from the wharf to the ship. Hundreds might be slain.

"Go back," I begged the men. "Go back! There will be much killing. Remember the mutiny! Nothing will be accomplished. Much will be lost. The wharf will run with blood. Go back!"

"Step aside, friend of Rutilius," said Tereus, "or meet our steel."

"Kill him!" said more than one man.

"We are going to open the gate," said Tereus.

"That will not be necessary," said a quiet, polite voice, but one which somehow carried.

"Lord Nishida," said men.

This high officer had approached, unnoticed, from the side.

Not one Pani warrior was with him.

I thought he must be a fellow of great courage. Surely he must understand the men were frightened, resolved, and desperate.

As Lord Nishida turned, benignly, toward me, I bowed, not knowing anything else to do, which bow he returned, politely. His hands were in his sleeves.

"Noble Callias," he said, "your effort at the gate is commendable, if somewhat foolish. Nonetheless, it is appreciated, and it will not be forgotten."

"Noble Lord," said Tereus, "open the gate."

"You are the oarsman, Tereus, are you not?" inquired Lord Nishida.

"Yes," said Tereus.

"I find it surprising," said Lord Nishida, "that you, an oarsman, should be the captain of this enterprise."

"Open the gate!" called a man.

"There must be men here from several decks," said Lord Nishida. "Something like this must have taken careful planning, thorough preparation, and meticulous organization. The expeditious marshaling of the men here, from diverse locations, and the timing of their confluence at the gate is also impressive."

"Lord Temmu will be mustering Pani!" said a fellow.

"Not at all," said Lord Nishida, quietly.

"Open the gate!" called another man, frightened, angrily.

"I request," said Lord Nishida, "that you Tereus, and your friends, return to the feast."

"Lord Nishida," said Tereus, "open the gate."

"Certainly," said Lord Nishida, indicating that the Pani guards open the gate. I stood to the side, bewildered.

I was more startled when I saw the other two gates between the courtyard and the steep, downward trail to the wharf already stood open.

The men, led by Tereus, rushed past us, through the opened gate. In moments Lord Nishida, the four Pani guards, myself, and two or three armsmen in the vicinity, were alone, by the gate.

"There will be terrible bloodshed on the wharf," I said to Lord Nishida.

"I think not," he said.

Chapter Thirty

How the Desertion Failed of Its Purpose;
I Realize the Danger Which Is Not Spoken

Not one man had been killed.

We counted them, eight hundred and seventy of them, as they returned in the morning, making their way up the steep path, to the inner courtyard gate.

They were admitted one at a time through the narrow opening in the barricade which had been set up at the gate. Each man, as he entered, cast his weapons in the pile to the right of the barricade, as he passed through it, was searched by Pani, relieved of any unsurrendered weapon, had his left forearm stained, and was then conducted to one of the barracks which had been reinforced that it might serve as a prison.

"Lord Okimoto is generous," said Tyrtaios to the superior with whom he was liaison, Lord Okimoto. "On the continent the desertion of a single man is usually punished by his death, the desertion of a unit, its impermissible flight from the field, not routed, its refusal to engage, or such, by decimation, putting to death every tenth man, this determined by lots."

"It would be pleasant to crucify them all," said Lord Okimoto, "but, unfortunately, that is impractical, for several reasons. They retain value. It is difficult to replace them. Too, their fellows, those who did not join them, those who remained loyal, questioned, object strenuously. The application of appropriate measures, thus, might precipitate a new mutiny. Too, of course, there is fear abroad, and, should customary measures be inflicted, it is recognized that the strength of our force would be considerably reduced by the elimination of these men, this in the face of the enemy, whose attack may be imminent. Too, unfortunately, several of our officers, Turgus, Pertinax, Cabot, and such, have made clear their opposition to such things. We do not know how serious they are, but we cannot risk the loss of the cavalry."

"Lord Nishida recommends clemency," said Tyrtaios.

"It is his way," said Lord Okimoto.

"It is perhaps wise," said Tyrtaios.

"It seems," said Lord Okimoto, "that you wish to preserve the men, as well."

"Surely they may prove useful," said Tyrtaios.

"That will be our hope," said Lord Okimoto.

"What is the view of Lord Temmu?" inquired Tyrtaios.

"Those who would desert have been marked," said Lord Okimoto. "Records will be kept. Lord Temmu is patient."

"I see," said Tyrtaios.

"It would be pleasant, of course," said Lord Okimoto, "to know who were the captains of this business, those who planned and organized it."

"Surely Tereus, the oarsman," said Tyrtaios.

"We think not," said Lord Okimoto.

"Oh?" said Tyrtaios.

"Others," said Lord Okimoto, "remain in the shadows."

It will be recalled that the trail to the wharf was walled-in.

It will also be recalled that Lord Nishida had had the gate opened, rather as though he recognized the futility of defending it, as though, perforce, he recognized that the desertion could not be forestalled. Those who would desert, then, rejoicing that they were unopposed, hurried down the trail. Apparently they did not question that the two further gates lay open. When they reached the foot of the trail they found it barricaded, before the wharf, a barricade manned by several Pani, drawn from the ship, a barricade, given the narrowness of the passage, easily defended by a few against many. Outside the trail walls, Pani archers had been stationed, lest any, held inside, attempt to scale the walls. When the deserters had sped down the trail, Lord Nishida had had a similar barricade erected at the height of the trail, similarly easily defended. In short order then those intent on desertion found themselves trapped in a steep, narrow, tortuous passageway, without food and water, from which they could not easily extricate themselves. At best, from the trail, they might see the wharf, and the great ship moored there, on a dozen lines, the ship they were unable to reach. Then, presumably to make more clear the hopelessness of their position, several barrels of oil were poured onto the stone flagging flooring the trail, oil which, obviously, if desired, might be ignited. Other inflammables, pitch, and such, were cast over the walls from the outside, which, by a flung torch, a cast, flaming bundle of straw, or such, might be as easily ignited. In such a way the walled-in trail might, at selected points, as desired, be transformed into a blazing furnace. The principle points in question were the approaches to the entrance and exit of the trail. Any concerted attempt to storm the barricade at either end then, in addition to its dubious prospects at the outset, might also find itself forced to proceed through a wall of fire. Similarly, if the deserters should congregate in any part of the passage, or be forced to do so, say, by Pani entering the passage, they might be similarly discomfited. Accordingly, by morning, well apprised of the desperateness of their situation, the deserters had surrendered. Whereas the surrender was unconditional, the deserters realized, as well as others, first, that the Pani would not be likely to accept a grievous loss of armsmen which would be likely to jeopardize, if not ruin, their cause, and, second, that their brethren, their fellow armsmen, and their fellows of the ship, would not be likely, particularly under the circumstances of the desertion, to accept their wholesale slaughter, or even decimation.

When Tereus emerged from the trail, to surrender his weapons, and have his arm stained, Seremides was waiting for him, leaning on his crutch, grinning.

"Sleen," hissed Tereus, as the stain was spread upon his left forearm.

"You would not take me with you," said Seremides.

"Had you been with us," said Tereus, "you would not be alive now."

"How fortunate then," said Seremides, "that I was not with you."

"Treacherous tarsk," said Tereus.

"Here, noble lord," said Seremides to Lord Okimoto, indicating Tereus, "is the leader of the desertion."

Seremides, prior to his crippling in the Vine Sea, had been liaison to Lord Okimoto, a post now held by Tyrtaios.

"If so, Rutilius, half of man," said Lord Okimoto, "what should be done with him?"

"I resign that matter cheerfully, noble lord," said Seremides, "to your judgment, or that of the great Lord Temmu."

"It is our view," said Lord Okimoto, "that the leader of the desertion did not participate in the desertion, but would have appeared shortly, had it proved successful."

"Lord?" said Seremides.

"If that is so," said Tyrtaios, "the true leader would not have been Tereus."

"He led, clearly," said Seremides.

"Perhaps another," said Tyrtaios.

"Another?" said Seremides.

"Perhaps you," said Tyrtaios.

"I?" said Seremides, startled, turning white.

"Did you not inform Lord Nishida of the conspiracy?" asked Tyrtaios. "How would you know of it, had you not been involved in the matter?"

"If I designed the matter," said Seremides, "why would I betray it, and thus preclude its fruition?"

"Perhaps that one you fear might be thereby slain," said Tereus.

"Ah," said Tyrtaios, thoughtfully.

"Would it not have been simpler to strike him in the night?" asked Lord Okimoto.

"I am loyal!" said Seremides.

"To whom?" asked Tereus, his left arm dark with stain.

"If the matter carried," said Tyrtaios, "I expect you would have profited from it."

"You do me too much credit," said Seremides. "How could I, no more than a worthless cripple, ridiculed and scorned, manage so great an affair?"

"Your wit is not crippled," said Tyrtaios. "Who knows what venom you might brew?"

"I am innocent!" said Seremides.

"Perhaps," said Tyrtaios.

"Tereus, Tereus!" insisted Seremides.

"One does not know," said Tyrtaios.

"The matter was cleverly done," said Lord Okimoto, "and moved from man to man. Where it began may remain unclear."

"Somewhere it must have begun," said Tyrtaios, "and from somewhere been monitored and directed."

"Doubtless," said Lord Okimoto.

"Consider the perfidious Tereus, Lord," said Seremides.

"Do you think, upon reflection, good Tyrtaios," asked Lord Okimoto, "that our friend, Tereus, a simple oarsman, could have managed so much, so well?"

"He spoke for the desertion, he led the flight, he was first through the gate," said Seremides. "His guilt is obvious!"

"Too obvious," said Lord Okimoto.

"I do not think so, Lord," said Tyrtaios.

"Nor I," said Lord Okimoto.

"Then Rutilius," said Tyrtaios.

"No!" said Seremides.

"I think it would have been difficult for Rutilius," said Lord Okimoto.

"Then, who?" said Tyrtaios.

"Yes, who?" said Lord Okimoto. He then gestured that the disarmed, weary, disconsolate Tereus be conducted, his arm stained, his steps slow, in his turn, to a prison barracks.

Seremides, angrily, turned and hobbled awkwardly away, the crutch poking at, and dragging in, the dirt.

Various times, in the last few days, he had importuned me to kill Tereus for him.

I had, of course, refused.

"I will come again to power," he said. "You are my only friend. You protect me. You saved my life. I will not forget that. I will come again to power. You will stand high."

"I will not kill Tereus for you," I said.

"Get him drunk," said Seremides. "Provoke a quarrel. Strike. It will not be difficult."

"No," I said.

I thought that Tereus might be more safe in the prison barracks than free on the castle grounds, particularly at night.

It is dangerous to be feared by Seremides.

I had then turned away from him.

"Callias," said Tyrtaios.

"Noble Tyrtaios," I said.

"We owe you much," he said. "Had it not been for your intervention, at the gate, the time taken, the desertion might have proceeded apace."

"I do not think so," I said. "I think the desertion was anticipated, and prepared for."

"Betrayed by Rutilius?" he said.

"I suspect it was independently anticipated," I said. "The Pani are not fools."

"In any event," said Tyrtaios, "it is clear you were not with the desertion."

"That is true," I said.

"That will be remembered," he said.

"How so?" I said.

"Perhaps I may find a way for you to be rewarded," he said.

"You?" I said.

"Yes, I," he said.

"I need not be rewarded," I said.

"That is for me to say," he said.

"You have friends?" I said.

"Of course," he said.

"Where?" I asked.

"Here and there," he said.

"And they might arrange my reward?"

"Quite possibly," he said.

I recalled seeing Tyrtaios in company with several fellows, the past few days, fellows from various decks. Some of them had been amongst the deserters, and were now incarcerated in a prison barracks.

If a snake could take human form, and the form of a warrior, I thought, would it not be much like the form of Tyrtaios?

I suspected that the machinations of Tyrtaios lay behind the abortive desertion. It would not do to say so, of course, for he stood close to Lord Okimoto.

I did not think that Seremides had planned and organized the desertion. As he had suggested, few would take him seriously, now, as a leader. I did suppose that he, unobtrusive, scarcely noticed, might have overheard revealing remarks, and thus come upon the matter. He may well have conveyed his intelligence to the Pani, particularly had he inveighed with Tereus, or others, to permit him to accompany the flight, and had had his request refused. Why should others escape the World's End, if not Seremides? I speculated, of course, that the Pani had independently anticipated, and prepared for, such an exigency. Its likelihood would have been much increased given the miserable return of the exploratory force and the arrival of enemy troops, in force, in the vicinity. Seremides had, of course, attempted to use the failure of the desertion, naturally enough, as an opportunity to embroil Tereus, whom he feared, with the Pani.

I wondered, of course, if Lord Okimoto suspected Tyrtaios, as well. Certainly Lord Okimoto, despite his ponderous bulk, his measured, graceful movements, and such, was, like Lord Nishida, a very clever man. I supposed that one neither easily attained, nor easily retained, the status of *daimyo* in these strange, warlike islands. And too, I wondered, what must then be the nature of a *shogun*?

I was troubled by the events of the past ten Ahn or so. Much moved in my mind that I did not understand. It seemed formless, and yet on the verge of form. I think now, in retrospect, that it was clear enough to me, but that I was unwilling to let it stand before me, but that I rather kept it to one side, knowing it was there but refusing to look upon it.

I went to the inner wall, the high wall, as I had the previous night, and, standing on the parapet, again surveyed the countryside. I had seen campfires last night; this morning, or early noon, I saw a great number of tents. Where the village had been there was now debris, and darkness, and ash. When the wind shifted a bit, a hint of smoke still reached the parapet.

Some Pani were on the wall, as well, and some were equipped with a glass of the Builders. There was a drum in view, and, if there was movement below, massive movement, as opposed to tiny parties, scouting, I had no doubt a muster would sound, and the walls might be manned.

I did not know if Lord Yamada, or his generals, contemplated addressing the castle, or had come largely to destroy villages, and fields. I knew, at least according to report, the castle had never been taken. Clearly, as it was manned, and provisioned, it would be costly to attack. It seemed to have little to fear, at least for months, unless it be treachery.

I thought of the disarmed men, more than eight hundred and fifty, indeed, precisely, eight hundred and seventy, now held in the three prison barracks, hot, windows boarded, guarded by Pani. It would not do, of course, to keep them there indefinitely. At some point they would have to be released and rearmed. And then, I thought, would not the same prospects and dangers confront them as before, prospects and dangers which once encouraged them to think of flight, and might well again?

On the parapet I suddenly felt sick, and cold.

I was of the ship.

I knew what the Pani would do.

I turned about and hurried down to the courtyard. I must seek an audience with Lord Nishida.

Perhaps I would be slain, or put in the prison barracks with the fellows I had sought to deter from the rashness of desertion.

Or, perhaps there would yet be time to flight a messenger vulo to the mountains, to contact Tarl Cabot.

I knew what I must do, as I was of the ship.

Chapter Thirty-One

I Fail to Satisfy the Curiosity of Seremides

"Surely you know what they plan to do!" said Seremides.

"Yes," I said, "but I do not think they will act until night."

The eight hundred and seventy men were still held in the prison barracks. They would not interfere. They would be kept there until afterward, at least until tomorrow, when it would be too late.

A weapons inventory had been ordered for the loyal armsmen, and all weapons more serious than daggers were to be put into the great *dojo*, or training house, to be counted.

I did not think that most of the armsmen suspected what was afoot.

All morning and into the afternoon coffles of slave girls, ours, those brought on the great ship, and local girls, lovely, but of a low-Pani sort, kept in the castle for the pleasure of the Pani warriors, roped together, had descended to the wharf and then, laden with treasure, had been conducted up the trail, not by boys now, but by Pani warriors, to the high wharf gate. More than one such trip had been made. It was made clear to our men, our armsmen and mariners, that this action was intended to be one much to their benefit, that it was intended to secure and safeguard the treasure. Most of the men, given the identificatory markings on sacks and boxes, carefully checked and recorded, accepted this explanation, and even welcomed the removal of their wealth from the ship, and its storing closer at hand, under conditions of greater security. Given the harrows of the night of desertion, it was no longer accepted, at least uncritically, that the ship constituted an impregnable, unassailable refuge or depository for one's riches. Better that they be guarded, and by our own armsmen, within the grounds themselves. Were they not vulnerable, outside the walls? Might there not be bandits? Might not the fleet of Lord Yamada appear, unexpectedly, or might not forces be landed from it, somewhere in the vicinity, which might raid the ship? Indeed, did not soldiers of Lord Yamada even now camp within sight of our walls?

It was late afternoon.

Our girls had been returned to their kennels, in the sheds, and the Pani girls to their housings within the castle.

The treasure, I gathered, was now on the grounds.

Interestingly, the Pani girls, though slaves, and of low-Pani origin, had been much distressed that they had been neck-roped in the same coffle with our ship slaves. Some had dared to voice their objections, and had been well switched, across the backs of the calves and ankles, by the Pani warriors charged with the care of the coffle, in this instance, as indicated, a treasure coffle, one used to transport carefully sealed, and marked, sacks and boxes from the ship, containing wealth derived from the derelicts of the Vine Sea. Were some slaves, truly, as might be suggested by the protests of the Pani slaves, objections promptly rebuked by the sting of switches, so appropriately despised, and so obviously inferior to others, that it was humiliating to share a coffle with them? Certainly there were differences amongst the slaves, with respect to the nature of their eyes, the color of their skin, their accents, and such. Who could, or would wish to, gainsay that? On the other hand, beyond that, what would remain to be said? Surely they were all attractive. This is not surprising. If a woman is not attractive, she is not likely to be enslaved. Let the homely, plain ones be as free as they wish. Surely the Pani slaves and our ship slaves, despite obvious differences in appearance, had much in common. Each was attractive. Each was a purchasable beast, a domestic animal. Each was a slave. Thus, despite the concerns of the Pani collar meat, how could they be more equal? On the other hand, our ship slaves, with their generally fair skins, were neck-roped at the end of the coffle, which is often taken as a position of inferiority. This, I gather, pleased their Pani chain sisters.

One additional point might be noted with respect to the treasure coffle. The boxes, on straps, and the sacks, on cords, were slung about the slaves, two to each slave, a balanced load, one strap or cord running from the left shoulder to the right hip, and the other from the right shoulder to the left hip. This was because the hands of the slaves were not free, as is common in a coffle. The hands of the Pani slaves were tied together, and fastened about their collar, either in front, or behind the neck, and the hands of the ship slaves were thonged together behind their back. The reason for this was to preclude any possible attempt to rifle the contents of a box or sack. To be sure, as these containers were sealed, and marked, it was unlikely that any such tampering, or pilfering, would take place, certainly without being eventually detectable. This arrangement also made it unnecessary, at the journey's end, to examine the bodies of the slaves, or, for the next day or two, their wastes.

"They will not act," said Seremides, "until the ship's garrison is withdrawn, to the wharf, or trail."

"That will be after dark," I said.

"The trail, the wharf, will be guarded," he said.

"Doubtless," I said.

"Should it not be taken to sea first?" said Seremides.

"I do not think they will risk that," I said. "Too, these Pani are not mariners."

"Do you have a plan?" asked Seremides.

"How is it that I, one such as I, should have a plan?" I asked.

"What is to take place?" he said.

"Much is uncertain," I said.

"Take me with you," he said. "Do not leave me here!"

"How is it that I should go, anywhere?" I said.

"Take me with you," he said.

"Stay with your treasure," I said.

"We must seize it, and take it," he said.

"It is guarded," I said.

"I know a slave," he said, "who would be worth gold in Ar."

"What slave?" I said.

"You know," he said.

"Perhaps not," I said.

"She may be abducted," he said. "We can break the locks on her kennel, and take her with us."

"What slave?" I asked.

"I will reveal her name," he said, "if you will take me with you."

"I have no intention of going anywhere," I said.

"Do not jest," he said.

"I do not jest," I said.

"Her name is Alcinoë," he said, angrily.

"Interesting," I said.

"Some will go!" he said.

"Some may try," I said.

"I have seen mariners converse," he said.

"On what subject?" I asked.

He turned away, angry, and swung his body, a stride at a time, from my presence.

I had spoken truly to Seremides.

I was not going anywhere.

She was worthless, of course, and I was weak, but I would not leave her behind, no more than my heart.

Fool, I said to myself, fool!

Do not care for her!

Use the whip on her!

Teach her she is a slave!

Do not let her forget it!

But I would not leave her behind.

Chapter Thirty-Two

Lines Are Severed;
Torches Fall into the Sea

Dust was roiling in the courtyard from the beating of wings. I feared it was too late.

The great birds did not land, but hovered, some yards from the ground; long knotted ropes, fastened to their saddle rings, spilled to the earth. Each bird could carry, for a short way, some seven or eight men. In such a way men may be borne over the walls of a city, in a raid, to set it afire, to attack a Ubar, to free a fellow, to fight to open a gate. In a city, of course, one risks swaying, almost invisible tarn wire, capable of disemboweling or beheading a bird, cutting away a wing in flight.

I, and others, including Leros, Aeacus, and Philoctetes, seized a rope, and, elsewhere, others of the high watches, and several mariners, did likewise.

Already the Pani with their vessels of oil, and their torches, had begun the descent of the wharf trail. Too, at its end would be other Pani, who would let them pass, but not others.

"Aii!" I said, as I felt the tearing jerk on my hands, anchored behind one of the knots, as I felt my feet pulled away, upward, away from the courtyard, and, for a sickening moment, I saw the ground dropping away below me.

I heard cries below, and sensed Pani rushing out from the barracks, to the courtyard.

Something went past, like a bird, a fierce whisper of wind, the rushing of a fletched shaft toward the starlit sky.

Then we were over the walls.

A drum began to beat. I heard alarmed blasts, twice, the second more distant, on one of the Pani's conch horns, perhaps kept on the parapet.

The trail, with its tortuous twisting, taking advantage of the side of the mountain, was better than a pasang in length, but, it seemed in a moment, I saw the wharf. Almost at its end the Pani, with their flammables, and lifted torches, looked up, startled.

A fire bowl was ignited, I think by the rider of the lead tarn, it flown, I suspected, by Tarl Cabot himself, and the bowl, trailing its tiny flag of fire, descended gracefully toward the stone flooring of the trail, before the defensive barricade, and splashed into the combustibles put there on the night of the desertion, to deter a rushing of the barricade. Suddenly the entire width of the trail, within its walls, for better than forty yards, began to roar with flame. The Pani, descending the trail, arrested in their descent, by angry sheets of fire, backed away, for the heat, and could not proceed. The Pani at the barricade looked up, startled, crying out, in futility. A moment later, the birds hovering over the deck, men loosed their grip on the ropes, and dropped to the planking.

"Hurry! Hurry!" cried the high, wild voice of Tersites, from the stem castle.

I felt the deck beneath my feet, and was sliding across it, and then released the rope.

I was conscious of mariners rushing to the ratlines on each side of the ship.

Angry Pani were shouting below.

They had no way to climb to the deck. No Pani were on the ship, having been withdrawn in the afternoon.

"Cut the mooring ropes! Cast off!" I heard. I recognized the voice. It was that of Aëtius, apprentice to Tersites, who had captained the ship in its lengthy, incredible, unprecedented voyage.

I remembered that the great ship now had eyes.

"Hurry!" cried Tersites.

Mariners rushed about me.

An ax was thrust into my hands, and I rushed to one of the long, mooring lines, cutting it, even striking sparks from its broad cleat, anchored in the deck.

The sound of drums reached us, from afar, probably from the walls, far above.

"Good fortune to you!" cried a voice. It was that of Tarl Cabot. Then his tarn lifted away from the vicinity of the ship, the ropes dangling behind it.

I heard a flood of canvas loosed from a yard, with a great, snapping noise, and then another.

I rushed to another mooring line, and then another.

Four more tarns flighted from the ship.

"Wait!" I called. "Wait!"

"You," screamed Aëtius to me, pointing, "that line, the last! Cut it, now!"

I cried out with rage, but rushed back, along the broads, toward the stern. It was the last line. The ship moved a bit from the wharf at the bow, moving to port, but there was a jerk and a vibration of line, and the ship was stopped, pulling against the line. I saw a number of Pani rushing toward the ship with torches, hurrying through scattered, subsiding flames.

An arrow sped past.

Two mariners were at the helm.

There was an odd tension on the last line, not adjusted to the motion of the ship, as it might ease from its berth.

Men were climbing the line.

I struck down, frenziedly, at the line, sparks flashing from the cleat, and the line parted, and jerked away. Men, clinging to it, Pani, climbing it, had fallen to the water, between the wharf and the ship.

Much canvas had now been spread, but it hung slack.

"Well done, fellow," screamed Aëtius.

I looked about, wildly.

The last tarn, unnoted, had flown.

"I must go back!" I said.

"They will not burn my ship!" screamed Tersites. "Blow, wind, blow!"

The Pani, of course, would wish to burn the ship, that our armsmen would be stranded, here, at the World's End, without recourse, that all hope of escape would fade, and that their eyes must now turn perforce to undesired, unwelcome war. Here, escape precluded, they must stay. If they would survive, they must fight. The Pani had seen to it that they would discharge their fee. No longer had they a choice.

I ran to the rail.

"Alcinoë!" I cried. "Alcinoë! Alcinoë!"

I heard a creaking of the foremast.

There was a cheer from a dozen mariners.

"She lives! My ship lives!" cried Tersites.

I saw the opening of the cove before the bow. The tide was with the ship. A soft breeze from the shore swelled the sails.

The wharf was now yards away.

One or two torches were flung toward the ship, but fell short, and struck the water, hissing.

"What are you doing?" exclaimed Philoctetes, at my side.

"I am going back!" I said. I tore away my cloak.

"You will be killed!" said Philoctetes. "Aeacus!" he cried. "Leros, Leros!"

"Let me go!" I cried.

We struggled. Then, in a moment, I was held, as well, by Aeacus and Leros.

"Let me go!" I said. "Let me go!"

I felt rope being looped about my body. I struggled. "Alcinoë!" I wept. "Alcinoë!"

"She is only a slave," said Leros.

"Yes," I said, helpless. "She is only a slave."

A light rain, one such as is common in the islands, began to fall.

"There are lights ahead!" called a fellow, partway up the ratlines to starboard.

"It is the fleet of Lord Yamada," said a man.

"We will clear the cove," said Philoctetes. "We will run without lights."

"I think we have time," said Aeacus.

"They will not catch us," said Leros.

I felt the rain on my face, and was aware, too, of the taste of salt.

Chapter Thirty-Three

It Is Now Morning in Brundisium

The tharlarion oil had burned low in the lamps, and, outside, we could hear the sounds of the morning, the roll of carts, men calling to one another.

The bar signifying the fifth Ahn had rung.

The Sea Sleen is a small tavern, not particularly well-known, even in Brundisium. Those near the southern piers, however, are likely to be aware of it. It was to this tavern the stranger, haggard, destitute, in his rags, in his soiled mariner's cap, had come, and regaled us with a story, however far-fetched.

He had been fed, and given paga.

Surely that is payment enough for a story.

"You are a liar," said the proprietor to the stranger.

"He wheedles paga and a free meal cleverly," said another fellow.

"Beware of mariners," laughed another.

The stranger smiled, as though discovered.

"Clever fellow!" laughed another.

The stranger took no offense. The comments of those about the small table were uttered in the way of good-natured raillery, and were not designed to disparage or affront a fellow, but, rather, to let him know they were not the sort to be taken in, not the sort to give credit to the absurd, the wild, and incredible, that they were aware astute fellows, and not fools.

I saw, clearly, that the stranger had not expected to be believed, and was not concerned that he had been found out, had he been found out.

"Have you a place to stay?" I asked him.

"All Brundisium," he said.

"Do you have money, for food?" I asked.

"I need it not," he said. "Garbage troughs are at hand."

"You need not compete with pier urts," I said. "I will give you a tarsk-bit."

"For what?" he said.

"For hearing your story," I said.

"I have been paid for that," he smiled.

"Are you a liar?" I asked.

"Perhaps," he said.

"Was there a Cabot, a Tersites, an Alcinoë?" I asked.

"Perhaps," he said.

To the side, there was a small sound of slave bells. They were fastened, with cord, about her left ankle. She had been brought to the table, last night, to serve the stranger paga. He had then had her reveal herself, removing the thin, clinging, camisk of yellow rep cloth. He had later had her bound, hand and foot, it had been done by the taverner's man, and it was thus that she had begun to hear the story, as a helpless, kneeling, nude slave, her wrists bound behind her, her ankles crossed and fastened together. In such a way a woman is well apprised that she is bond. Later in the evening, he had permitted her to recline, beside the table, but still bound, hand and foot. She hung upon the story, as did we. And when slaves were mentioned her breath quickened, and she leaned forward a little, that she might the more clearly sense the feelings of women such as she, far away. And how far away must her former reality have seemed, the former reality of this small, luscious barbarian, a brunette, nicely breasted, narrow waisted, and invitingly hipped, with small hands and feet, from her present reality, lying bound on the floor of a tavern, at the side of a table of masters. Although she had reportedly not been long in the collar, her slave fires, following a remark of the proprietor, were already causing her the restlessness and agitation so familiar to the occupants of the collar.

"Is this not an attractive barbarian?" I asked the stranger.

"Lift her up," he said, "your left arm beneath her knees, your right hand supporting her, behind the back."

I did as he asked, and turned her, so that he might see her, so held.

Commonly a slave is not so held, but she may be held so, to be the better displayed. Commonly a slave is held on her belly, over the left shoulder, her head to the rear, rather as other goods might be conveyed, sacks of sa-tarna, and such. A free woman, held so, can do little other than squirm, and strike futilely with her small fists, on the back of he who carries her. To be sure, a free woman would not be likely to be so carried, were she not being carried to a slave pen.

She looked down and back at him, helpless, and frightened, and so looked up to me, from my arms, as well.

What a nice bundle a slave makes, so held, so tied.

"Yes," he said. "She is attractive." He pointed to a place on the floor, near the table. "Kneel her there," he said.

And the small barbarian *kajira* was so knelt.

"I understand," said the stranger to the slave, "that you have not been named."

"No, Master," she said. "I have not been named."

Sometimes one holds off on the naming of a slave, for the naming of a slave, as of any other animal, is a matter which may call for thought. To be sure, as with any other animal, names may be withheld, or changed, at will, at the master's will.

"You are a paga slave," he said.

"Yes, Master," she said.

"That is quite different," he said, "I take it, from your former reality."

"Yes, Master," she said, "I was what is called a graduate student, a student of certain classical languages, Greek, and Latin, languages unfamiliar to you."

I saw they were indeed unfamiliar to the stranger. "Like archaic Gorean," I said.

She looked at me, suddenly, startled. "You know of such things?" she asked, eagerly.

"A little," I said.

"He is a Scribe," said the stranger. "You can tell from his robes."

"You know something of Earth!" she cried.

"I am familiar with the second knowledge," I said. "The

languages you refer to are little, if at all, spoken on that world now."

"No," she said.

"Why would you concern yourself with them?" I asked. To be sure, this question was a test, as much as anything, to help me ascertain her depth, and worth. One hopes for such things, obviously, in a slave. One does not buy without care, one does not own without circumspection.

"They are beautiful," she said, "and they speak of distant, different, exciting worlds, worlds in many ways natural and beautiful."

I was pleased with this answer.

Would not such a one look well, bound before one? Would the lips of such a one, on her belly, not be pleasant on one's feet?

"Surely you have noticed," I said, "that words from those languages, along with those of many other languages, are found in Gorean."

"Yes, Master," she said.

"She seems to me quite intelligent," said the stranger.

"I expect so," I said.

To be sure, high intelligence, sometimes quite high intelligence, was often found in barbarian *kajirae*, as masters preferred it in their slaves. Few men wanted a stupid slave. The intelligent slave is more likely to survive her training, and, once trained, is likely to sell for better prices. She is also likely to be considerably more sensitive to her condition, and is likely to be far more prompt in understanding what is expected of her, the devoted and zealous service of the interests, inclinations, and pleasures of her master, than a less intelligent woman. She tends, as well, to be more vulnerable, and more sexually responsive, than her simpler sister. How easy it is, in so soft, nicely curved, and vital a property, astonished, reveling in her newly discovered profound and radical femininity, which she is no longer permitted to suppress or deny, to ignite slave fires. How helpless she will be, now the property of men, once they flame in her belly. Once they burn, would she then trade her collar for a shallow deceit, the denial and falsification of her most profound reality, that of female, for the betrayal of nature, for the repudiation of her deepest self, for the inertnesses and tepidities of freedom? She has found herself, and is content. How secure she is now, having found herself at last to be what she has always wanted to be, and has always been. Is this not the life she has secretly dreamed of living, now put upon her, as securely as her collar, as securely as her chains? She is attentive to the master, for she fears his whip, but she is inventive, as well, for she desires to please him, and be found pleasing. It gives her joy to be found pleasing. As she learns Gorean, too, her high intelligence well serves her, for her master delights in her lyrical capacity to express herself, delights in learning of her feelings and thoughts, and delights in the joys of her intellectual companionship, though she may be chained naked at his slave ring. In bondage, many such women learn their beauty, their sex, their nature, their meaning, and their identity. They learn they are not men, but women, and are content, and whole.

"Intelligence is often associated with the intensity of slave fires," said the stranger.

"Yes," I said.

It is well known that the most intelligent slave is often the most helpless in a man's arms. So often are conjoined intelligence, vitality, sensitivity, and imagination with uncontrollable, inevitable responsiveness. The more intelligent woman swiftly comprehends what is being done to her, recognizes her vulnerability as a female, that she is defenseless, powerless to resist the inescapable ecstasies to which she will be subjected, that she will be mastered, as a female in the order of nature, and will soon be a gasping, begging, pleading, yielding slave. Then, in her mind and heart, she surrenders, as she knows she will, and must, and wants, rejoicingly acknowledging herself as her master's slave. She is now herself.

There are two sexes, and they are not the same.

"Touch her," said the stranger.

"Ai!" sobbed the slave, squirming.

"See?" said the proprietor.

It was clear to all.

"In your studies," I said to the slave, "doubtless you learned of certain aspects of those worlds you described as different, distant, and exciting, those worlds in many respects quite different from that which you knew, worlds in many respects natural and beautiful."

"Yes, Master," she said.

"Perhaps it was such things," I said, "which attracted you to such worlds."

"Doubtless, Master," she said.

"Were you aware that in such worlds there were slaves?"

"Certainly," she said.

"And that among these," I said, "many would be female?"

"Yes, Master."

"And did you ever imagine yourself as a female slave?"

"—Yes, Master."

"You spoke of yourself as a 'graduate student'," I said.

"Yes, Master," she said.

"Touch her," said the stranger.

"Oh!" she cried.

"See her press herself against his hand," said a fellow.

"Yes," said another.

The slave pulled back, as she could. Tears sprang to her eyes.

"Do not be upset," I said to her. "Being unable to help yourself, hoping to be touched, begging to be caressed, responding helplessly, is a sign of vitality, of health."

"Yes, Master," she whispered.

"And it will improve your price," said a fellow.

"When you were engaged in your studies," I said, "I would suppose you did not anticipate your fate, that you would one day find yourself a slave on a far world, one you had perhaps heard of, but had not realized existed."

"I thought it was only in books," she said.

"You think differently now," I said.

"Yes, Master," she said. "I find myself kneeling, naked and bound, collared, before masters, in a tavern in Brundisium. I think differently now."

Many of my world, of course, did not accept the existence of her Earth, as another world. They thought it the name of a remote place on Gor, from which lovely barbarians, illiterate, somehow, unbelievably enough, not even capable of speaking the language, were harvested for the markets. Such goods, for example, must have some place of origin.

"Perhaps," I said, "my lovely graduate student, as you call it, your current reality is not so different now from that which you occasionally imagined on Earth, when you thought of yourself as a slave in one or another of those different, ancient worlds."

"No, Master," she said, squirming, "but now it is real."

I thought her quite beautiful.

But what woman is not, naked and bound?

"Master," she said, "I think you understand me!"

"A little, perhaps," I said.

How piteous she seemed!

"I have waited so long for one who might understand me!" she said, tears in her eyes. "You are the first who has done so, on this world!"

"He is privy to the second knowledge," said the stranger. "See his robes. He is a Scribe."

"Perhaps," I said, "you would like a private master?"

She leaned forward. "Oh, yes, yes, Master!" she wept. "I want a private master, a private master!"

This is not unusual amongst slaves. It is a common dream of public slaves, tavern slaves, brothel slaves, the girls of the laundries, the public kitchens, the mills, and such, that they should have a private master. And, of course, the dream goes far beyond this, for usually the dream is to be the single slave of a private master, to be the only slave in her master's household. For example, there is often much misery, much grief, even lamentation, in the pleasure garden of a rich man, who is assuredly a private master, where slaves may often constitute little more than another adornment, much as the colored grasses, the trimmed shrubberies, the beds of flowers, the exotic trees, the unusual fruits, to enhance the beauty of the garden. Perhaps no more than two or three preferred slaves are ever called to the slave ring of their master. Indeed, he may often bring in rent slaves from the party houses to sing and dance for him, and his guests, to play the kalika, to accompany with flute music the measuring of wine and the cutting of meat. Indeed, as the stocking and tending of such gardens is often managed by independent companies, staffed with professionals, he is likely to have several girls in his gardens whom he, personally, has never seen.

"You are looking upon me, Master," she said. "Would that I might find favor in the eyes of Master."

I wondered if she, as a graduate student, whatever that might be, had ever thought that she might one day kneel naked and bound before a man, a slave, and speak so.

Certainly she was beautiful. And she was clearly of high intelligence, and her background, I thought, though of Earth, was of a sort which shared certain affinities with that of my caste. Too, she impressed me as a girl who might soon, in the throes of her need, belly and grovel for the caress of a master. Already, I had understood, from the proprietor, she had begun to feel slave fires in her belly. Certainly that had been suggested by her responses to my touch. And had not her belly, as that of a slave, pressed beggingly against my hand, until she, suddenly, realizing what she had done, that she had betrayed her need, and vitality, had withdrawn it, with tears of shame?

She must, of course, learn the absurdity of shame, and that it was not permitted to the slave. If nothing else, let the whip teach her so. Such indulgences and frivolities are not permitted the slave; they are permitted only to free women, who might be foolish enough to cultivate them. The slave is an animal, and is to be as wild, and open, and free, and appetitious and sexual, as any other animal. What a pathological world from which she must be derived, I thought, to be ashamed of her health, her vitality, and womanhood. What purposes could be served, and whose purposes, I wondered, on such a world, to instigate such suspicions, such conflicts and contradictions, to set one part of a body against another part, one part of a mind against another? How ill or insane the society which might find profit in such divisions and treacheries! Why should she not be tutored in other betrayals, as well? Why should she not be taught to fear the dictates of her hereditary coils? Why should she not be terrified at the movement of a tiny corpuscle in her lovely body, not be ashamed, as well, of the beating of her heart, the circulation of her blood?

The slave is not to be ashamed of her needs; she only need fear that the master will not satisfy them.

Yes, it was clear that the slave fires had begun to burn in the belly of the fair slave before me.

And once she had bucked and writhed in the slave orgasm, helpless in her ropes or chains, she would be spoiled forever for freedom. What had freedom to offer a woman which might compare with the caress of her master?

"Does a master not look upon me with desire?" she said. "Does a master not look upon a slave with lust in his eyes?"

I was silent.

I wondered if, in her former world, when she was clothed, and free, she had ever been looked upon with lust, with thoughts of stripping, with thoughts of the rope, and leash.

And had she ever, even, I wondered, thought of herself as such a woman, one who might one day be so looked upon, and who might be purchased?

Yes, I thought, for she had imagined herself a slave.

"Buy me, Master!" she said. "I beg to be bought!"

And thus, irremediably, she acknowledged herself as that which could be bought, as slave.

"Three silver tarsks," said the proprietor. "No less!"

The stranger laughed. Clearly the slave did not begin to be worth so much. She was barbarian, she was a mere paga girl, and from a low tavern, her accent was unusual, she had not been much trained, she was new to her collar, and she was just beginning to sense the heat of slave fires, in the grasp of which, perhaps even in days, she would find herself helpless. She was certainly beautiful, and would not have been purchased had she not been, but I did not think she would be likely to be the first pick of many of the tavern's customers. I suspected the proprietor had not paid more than a quarter of a silver tarsk for her, in a pier market. I thought she might bring a silver tarsk, or one and a half, but not two. And I could not afford even a silver tarsk. I could, of course, afford the tarsk-bit which, in a low tavern, such as *The Sea Sleen*, might purchase a cup of paga, accompanying which, if I chose, might be her use.

"I cannot afford one silver tarsk," I said.

"It is morning," said the proprietor.

We struggled to our feet, stiff, from the night.

"My thanks," I said to the stranger, "for your unusual tale."

He grinned.

I looked down at the table, where the two quarrels, fired

by the Assassins, had struck the wood, piercing it, scattering splinters about, when the stranger had interposed it between himself and their missiles.

"Why, friend," said I, "were you sought by those of the black caste?"

"It was doubtless a case of mistaken identity," he said.

"Or, perhaps," I said, "Tyrtaios, who wished to reward you for your opposition to the desertion, had a colleague, or agent, aboard the great ship."

"But then," said the stranger, "the tale would be true."

"Where is the great ship?" I asked.

"I do not know," he said. "Tersites is mad, and the ship had eyes, and could now see her way. Thassa was vast before him. A hundred horizons beckoned. There are shores that have not yet been seen. I, with others, desiring to return to civilization, were put ashore at Daphna, of the farther islands, and we made our way severally, as we would."

"And you came to Brundisium?"

"Those who draw the oar," he said, "do not set the helm."

"You were followed, it seems," I said.

"Seemingly so," said he.

"The arm of Tyrtaios was long," he said.

"Not long enough," he said. "Thassa, last night, received two of the black caste."

"I believe your story," I said.

A couple of the fellows laughed.

"Then," said the stranger, "you are a fool. Had I heard my story I would not have believed it. Why should you?"

"True, true," laughed a man, good-naturedly.

"Return the slave to her cage," said the proprietor to his man.

The slave looked up at me, wildly, piteously, and squirmed a little. Her lips formed the word, 'Master'.

I said nothing.

Why should one deign to acknowledge a slave?

The slave was then freed, and, stood. "Oh," she said. Her footing was a bit uncertain, as her ankles had been crossed, and tied, for some Ahn. There was a sound from the bells fastened about her left ankle. Then she, unsteady, and rubbing her wrists, was taken by the hair, by the proprietor's man, was bent over, at the waist, and, in standard leading position, was conducted to the back of the tavern, and drawn through a thick curtain of layered, dangling, colored beads. A moment later I heard a last flash of bells, and the closing of a sturdy metal gate.

"You found the slave attractive," I said to the stranger.

"Of course," he said.

I went to press a tarsk-bit into his hand. "This is for her use," I said.

"For the story?" he said.

"Surely," I said.

"No," he said.

"Why not?" I asked.

"She is not Alcinoë," he said.

"I see," I said.

"Keep it, pay for her use, for yourself," he said.

"I do not wish to share her with others," I said. "I do not wish to pay for her use. It is her, the whole of her, I want."

"You have seen her before?" he said.

"Surely," I said, "and with interest, but never as this night."

"She is quite beautiful," he said.

"And never so beautiful as this night," I said.

"Clearly the meaningless slut, the worthless chit," he said, "wants you for her master."

"And I," I said, "want her for my slave."

"She is a true slave," he said. "She will be hot, and helpless."

"I read her so," I said.

"She is on the verge now," he said. "Did you not see her respond to your touch?"

"That is why," I asked, "that you had her subjected to the touch of a master?"

"Yes," he said, "and twice, that she would understand herself to be what she is, and that you could see, without mistake, what she is."

"A slave," I said.

"Yes," he said.

"I see," I said.

"There is an affinity here," he said. "Strange it is how a slave, transported, might find her master on a new, unsuspected world, one far different from her own, on which she must kneel and wear a collar, and a master might find his slave, placed at his feet, brought to him from a far-distant, scarce-realized world."

"You realize there is such a world, a different world," I said, "from which she was harvested."

"I have gathered so," he said.

I thought of men and women, of masters and slaves.

A word is spoken, a glance registered.

How mysterious are such things, I thought. There is nothing, and then there is everything. Who can understand such things?

How piteously, how zealously, I thought, the girl had begged to be purchased!

And how well, I thought, would my collar look on the neck of that slave!

"And how would you keep her?" asked the stranger.

"As she should be kept," I said, "absolutely and totally, without the least recourse or qualification, without the least concession or compromise, as a complete slave, how else?"

"Even to the chain and whip?" he asked.

"Of course," I said.

"Excellent," he said.

"Noble fellows," said the proprietor. "It is morning. The tavern must be vacated."

We, all of us, moved toward the door.

Several of us, who had listened through the night, bade the stranger a hale farewell.

"You are a liar amongst liars," grinned a fellow.

"Would you believe your story?" asked a fellow of the stranger.

"No," he smiled, "not if I heard if from another."

"And if you heard it from yourself?" laughed another.

"Probably not then, either," said the stranger.

"I wish you well, fellow," said more than one.

I think the fellows had been pleased enough by what they had heard, but that few, if any, would take it seriously, with its talk of the World's End, of the great ship, of the mad Tersites, of Tarl Cabot, the tarnsman, of the much-sought fugitive, Talena of Ar.

Who could believe such things?

And from a derelict and vagrant, from a wanderer and

vagabond, from a drifter, and wayfarer, worn and soiled, without a tarsk-bit in his wallet.

"Out, out!" said the proprietor, and closed the door, and bolted it, behind us.

The stranger and I were then alone, on the street, before the tavern.

"Come with me," I said to the stranger. "I will get you some breakfast."

"The garbage troughs are at hand," he said.

"I work in the harbor office," I said, "at the high piers, where the great ships dock, in the registry."

"Few dock now," he said, "the season is late."

"The work is light," I agreed.

He began to turn away.

"Come along." I said. "You need money. I may be able to find you a day's work, on the high piers, in a warehouse, if not on the dock."

He looked at me, and I felt tested.

"Leave the garbage troughs for the urts," I said.

"I am of Cos," he said.

"You are more welcome here," I said, "than those of Ar."

"Ar is dangerous now?" he said.

"Marlenus is again on the throne," I said.

We then, together, began to make our way along the waterfront, to the high piers, so called, those which might, by depth of water, levels of platforms, varieties of lading devices, and proximity to shops and warehouses, accommodate and service round ships. It is in this district that is located the harbor office, where I worked, in the registry.

"I hear the bar," said the stranger. "Why is it sounding?"

"Do not be concerned," I said. "It is coming from the high piers."

"Is it an alarm?" asked the stranger.

"No," I said, "it is the signal of a new docking, a round ship, doubtless."

War galleys were not announced, and, shallow-drafted, commonly used the low piers. When a new round ship docks its arrival is usually announced by the bar. At such a time, those with business, or who hope for business, as well as the idle and curious, may visit the piers. One might see docksmen there, as well, looking to pick up coin. If it were later in the day, paga girls might be sent to the wharves, to solicit custom for their master's establishment. There are often boys about the docks, too, in ragged tunics, who love to see the large ships, and hope, one day, to learn the trade of the sea.

"Is the signal commonly so vigorous?" asked the stranger.

"No," I said. "I do not understand."

The sound of the bar carried over the port, even to the land walls. It suggested an intensity, or agitation.

"Surely it is an alarm," said the stranger.

"No," I said. "The sound is different, the tone, the strokes. It is not the bar of alarm."

"It sounds like no simple announcement to me," said the stranger.

"Nor to me," I said.

"It is something unusual?" he said.

"Clearly," I said. "Let us hurry!"

"Ho!" cried men, running past, come up from the docks, hurrying toward the high city. "A strange ship! A strange ship!"

Other men were rushing toward the high piers.

A number of boys, shouting to one another, ran past.

Many citizens, from their windows, looked toward the sea. I saw several on the roofs, pointing toward the high piers.

The stranger and I were jostled.

He caught my arm, once, and kept me from falling.

Two free women joined the crowd.

I heard a fellow call out to his slave. "Go, see what is going on! Come back, and tell me!"

"Yes, Master," she cried, and, barefoot, in her light tunic, sped toward the docks.

"I have never seen anything like it!" said a fellow, standing on a ledge, shading his eyes.

"Could it be the ship of Tersites?" I asked the stranger, though he, of course, was in no position to see better than I, from our current position.

"I cannot think so," he said. "I do not think Tersites would risk her east of the farther islands, because of Cos and Tyros, and it would be madness to bring her as far as Brundisium. Too, if the ship is at the piers, I do not think it could be that ship, given her draft. It is no common round ship. She would lie a quarter of a pasang offshore, or seek a harbor of unusual depth."

"What ship, then?" I asked, as we hurried on.

"Aii!" cried the stranger, as we surmounted a small rise, and then had the piers below us, and before us.

We stopped.

Men with us, too, stood in amazement.

"I have never seen such a ship," I said.

"I have," said the stranger.

"It is so large," I said. "How could it be at the pier?"

"It is shallow-drafted," he said. "It can manage rivers. It maintains stability in the high seas by the descent of a dagger board."

Men were pointing at the ship.

Boys continued to run past us.

The ship had a high stern castle, and four masts. Most unusual to me were the large, strange sails, tall, and rectangular, and ribbed, divided into lateral sections.

"That," I said, turning to the stranger, "is a ship from the World's End."

"It is," said the stranger.

"How can it be?" I asked.

"Tersites," he said, "showed the way. He proved that such a voyage was possible. For those at the end of the world, we are the World's End. What can be done by sailing west, can be done, as well, by sailing east. The voyage of Tersites has made the world different. Because of him men will never again think of the world in the same way."

"You have seen such ships," I said.

"Yes," he said, "many, in the Vine Sea, but few as large."

"It is a strange, and beautiful, ship," I said.

"I know its lines, its markings," he said.

"You have seen it before?" I said.

"Yes," he said, "briefly, at a wharf, at the foot of a walled-in-trail, in a sheltered cove."

I regarded him.

"It is, or was, one of the three ships," he said, "of the *shogun*, Lord Temmu."

Chapter Thirty-Four

A Scribe's Interlude

"Have you finished your work?" I asked my slave.

"Yes, Master," she said, kneeling beside me, placing her right cheek softly, lovingly, on my knee. I brushed aside her hair, and touched her collar, fingering it idly.

What pleasure can compare with having a slave at one's feet?

To be sure, the mastery of her, and the enjoyment of her.

"Your slave begs to be caressed," she whispered. "Would master be pleased to caress his slave?"

How much she was a slave!

And how perfect she was in her collar!

"Please, Master," she whispered.

At one time I supposed she had never dreamed that she would one day be a slave, and on a world far from her own.

How far she was today from the noise, the pollutions, the lies, the corruptions, the hypocrisies, and falsifications of her world!

"Please, Master," she said. "Your slave begs your caress. She would be touched."

"I take it your need is on you well," I said.

"Yes, Master," she whispered.

"You will go to the market," I said, "and buy tur-pah, tospits, suls, and a bottle of ka-la-na."

"Yes, Master," she moaned.

I watched her rise, and go to the chest at the side of the room, kneel there, and count some coins into her hand.

She turned, on her knees, to face me, the coins clutched in her hand.

"May I wear a tunic?" she asked.

"Yes," I said. "The blue tunic, the short one, with the ragged hem, of rep-cloth."

"Thank you, Master," she smiled.

I thought that would turn some heads in the market. It is pleasant to witness the admiring glances which might fondle one's slave, as she busied herself on my business in the market. Sometimes I took her out, leashed, on the promenade, her hands braceleted behind her. Occasionally on such outings I permitted her a tunic. The tunic I had prescribed for her today was the tiny one, of blue rep-cloth. It would not hurt for idlers and passers-by to guess, from the color of her scrap of clothing, that she was a Scribe's girl.

"Hold," I said, she at the door, and I rose to walk about her, and inspect her. "Stand taller," I said, "lift your head, and put your shoulders back. Be proud. You are not a free woman. You are a slave. A female found worth being collared by men."

"Yes, Master," she said.

"And remember," I said, "you are a reflection on me."

"Yes, Master," she said.

She stood nicely, lissome, and appealing.

Her feet were small, and bare.

I unhooked the switch from its peg, and, returning to her, standing behind her, slapped it twice in the palm of my hand.

She winced each time, but the useful, supple implement had not touched her.

"Bargain well," I told her.

"I will try, Master," she said.

"If you do not, in my view," I said, "you will be well stung upon your return."

"I do not know your world," she said. "And the market is different, day to day. Perhaps suls will be in short supply. And some in the stalls will attempt to cheat a slave, who would dare no such thing with a free woman!"

"And particularly," I conjectured, "one whose accent might betray her as a barbarian."

"I fear so, Master," she said.

"Linger about," I said, "sense the prices, the market, see what goods go for, question other slaves, ones who might speak to you, perhaps another barbarian, if you can find one, do not be afraid to thank the Merchant, respectfully, and prepare to leave. If your offer is reasonable, you will be hailed to return, however begrudgingly. Do not then pretend to victory, but be deferent, and grateful, that mercy has been taken on you."

"I have done well with smiles, too, Master," she said.

"That is one of the few advantages you have over free women," I said.

"Yes, Master," she said.

The face of the slave, by law, must be naked. Free women insist on that. They are not to be confused with animals, with collared beasts. The features of free women, presumably so exquisite, precious, and marvelous, are not to be exhibited to common view. Accordingly, given the depth of their veiling, and the opacity of the common street veil, they cannot well prevail upon, or influence, the peddler or merchant, the fellow sitting behind his goods, spread upon a rug or cloth, or the stallsman, behind his counter, with the loveliness of a woman's smile. To be sure, they do their best to smile with their voices, banter pleasantly, and hint with a deft word or two how astute is the tradesman, and how attractive he is, and how grateful they would be, mere weak, defenseless women, and possible beauties, should he unbend a bit and relax his adamancy by a tarsk-bit or so. And sometimes, it must be mentioned, a veil might slip a little, or require some hasty, furtive, readjustment. They, too, as the *kajirae*, are women, and, accordingly, not above wheedling a favor, pleading a cause, or improving an occasion, by means of their sex. It is such considerations which influence many a tradesman, in his imagination, to pierce the robes of so cunning a creature and imagine her before them as what she should be, a stripped, collared slave. One wonders if the free women sense that. One supposes not. Else they might hurry from the market to their domicile, remove their robes, stand before a mirror, touch their throat, and wonder what it might be, to belong to a man. One is reminded of the saying that a free woman is but a slave without a collar.

"So," I said, "you use your smiles?"

"Certainly, Master," she said.

Many men would do much to win a smile from a beautiful slave. How cunning are the delicious brutes.

"That is less easy for a free woman," I said.

"It is not I who veil them," she said.

"Surely you, or such as you, historically, have had something to do with the matter, however indirectly," I said. "They are muchly concerned that they not be confused with such as you."

"—a mere beast," she said.

"In the view of some," I said, "you are less than a beast."

"Master?"

"—a slave."

"I see," she said.

"But have no fear," I said. "In my view, and in that of most, and certainly in the eyes of the law, your status is clear."

"Master?"

"You are an animal, a beast."

"But no more?" she said.

"Certainly not," I said. "You are collared, you may be bought and sold."

"I see," she said.

"You would sell for far less than a tarn, and much less than a sleen or kaiila, but more, usually, than a tarsk or verr."

"I see," she said.

"To be sure," I said, "much depends on the market."

"Doubtless," she said.

"Of course," I said.

"So I am a beast," she said.

"Yes," I said, "and only that."

"On Earth," she said, "I did not think of myself as a beast."

"On Earth," I said, "you were not a beast."

"But here I am such," she said.

"Yes," I said.

"And only such," she said.

"Yes," I said.

"But I am a pretty beast, am I not?" she asked.

"Certainly," I said.

There was no gainsaying that. There were few men who would not want one or more, such as she. Who would want an empty slave ring at the foot or one's couch? And there are many in the market, assuredly, and affordable, whose trim ankle would fit well within the ring.

"On your world," I said, "you were free, were you not?"

"Yes," she said.

"Interesting," I said.

"'Interesting'?" she said.

"Yes," I said, "as you obviously belong at a man's feet, as a slave."

"I assure you," she said, "I was free."

"What is wrong with the men of Earth?" I asked. "Why would they not take their most desirable women and collar them? Do they not want them?"

"It seems," she said, "they do not want them that much."

"Perhaps some women are slaves, even there," I said, "and wholly, but the matter is kept from public view."

"As the relationship seems quite natural," she said, "and seems embedded in the human psyche, I suppose that is possible."

"But let us leave that unusual world to its own devices, its own prevarications, inhibitions, and deceits," I said.

"You think I am a natural slave, do you not?" she said.

"You are a female, of course," I said.

"I feel I am a natural slave," she said.

"And in your feeling," I said, "is found the truth."

"My world," she said, "does not even permit me to entertain such thoughts."

"But you did entertain them, and do entertain them, do you not?" I asked.

She lifted her head, boldly. "Yes, Master!" she said.

"Put your head down," I said.

She lowered her head.

"Your body is rich with the curves of a natural slave," I said. "Consider what you are, your softness, your thoughts, your hopes, the most secret of your secret dreams, your desire to be owned, your desire to belong to a master, your desire to kneel and serve, your desire to be found pleasing, your desire to be uncompromisingly possessed, yes, possessed, and to be treated as, and ravished as, a slave, your femininity."

"Yes, Master."

"Think carefully," I said. "Are you a natural slave?"

"Yes, Master," she whispered.

"Then," said I, "you should be a slave, and it is right that you should be a slave."

"Yes, Master," she said.

"And on this world," I said, "what is fitting and right for you has been imposed on you."

"Yes, Master," she said.

"So here on this world," I said, "you are a slave, and choicelessly, a well-collared slave."

"Yes, Master," she whispered.

"You have pretty legs, slave girl," I said.

"Thank you, Master," she whispered.

"Were you, and such as you, veiled on Earth?" I asked.

"No, Master," she said.

"Really?" I said.

"No, Master," she said.

"That must make things quite easy for slavers," I said.

"Doubtless," she said.

"You must have been scouted, reviewed, considered, entered on a slave list," I said.

"I know nothing," she said. "I was returning one evening from a library, sensed something behind me, was held, so tightly, found it difficult to breathe for a moment, and lost consciousness. When I awakened, I found myself nude and chained, in a slave pen."

"I find it difficult to believe that you did not veil yourself in your world. Did you not know you were attractive?"

"I had hoped I might be," she said, "but I struggled to put such thoughts from me, as unworthy of a woman. We are not supposed to think of such things in my world."

"Doubtless," I said, "that is a prescription of those who are unattractive."

"Many of my fellow female students," she said, "made clear to me the unimportance of beauty."

"It is quite important on the block," I said.

"And they lost no opportunity to scorn and disparage it."

"And so," I said, "the lame might denounce the swift, and the weak the strong."

"I do not know," she said.

"Were you popular?" I asked.

"Certainly not with my fellow female students," she said.

"That is because you are beautiful," I said.

She was silent.

"On this world," I said, "we do not object to beauty. Too, on this world, beauty is abundant, and well exhibited, and well owned. That makes things pleasant for men."

"I am pleased to be on a world," she said, "where one is not expected to neglect or ignore beauty, nor pretend that it is meaningless, nor apologize for it, nor belittle it, nor treat it as some flaw, or defect."

"Perhaps," I said, "they hated you not simply for your beauty, but because they sensed in you the ancient, natural woman, the yearning, needful woman, who cannot help but respond to men as a slave to her master, something they much feared in themselves, something that terrified them, something they would struggle to resist with informative, betraying ferocity."

"You think they sensed in me," she said, "that I should most appropriately be a belonging of men, a female slave?"

"Yes," I said, "and I think what they sensed in you was what they most feared in themselves."

"I wonder," she said, "how they might fare in the collar."

"Most, I conjecture," I said, "would not be adjudged worthy of a collar. Forget them. And I suspect that those on whom it was found fit to be placed would soon learn the vacuity of their former views, the artificiality and poverty of their previous ideology, and hasten to press their lips fearfully upon the feet of masters."

"It is my hope," she said, "that they would find happiness."

"It matters not," I said, "as they would then be slaves."

"Yes, Master," she said.

"So you did not veil yourself?" I said.

"No, Master," she said, "and, in my part of the world, in my civilization, it is not customary to do so."

"Truly?" I said.

"Truly," she said.

"What slaves!" I said.

"But few have masters," she said.

"That is remedied on Gor," I said.

"Yes," she said, "—my Master."

"You had best be on your way," I said.

"Yes, Master."

"Bargain well," I said.

"I trust," she said, "that I will not be switched, if I have done my best."

"You will be," I said, "if your best is not good enough."

"I see," she said, uneasily.

I had scarcely ever used the switch on her. Like the whip, it is commonly most effective on its peg. When she realizes that she is subject to the whip, truly, and that it will be used on her, if she is not pleasing, it is seldom, if ever, necessary to use it. Knowing it is there, she will commonly do her best to avoid its stroke, will commonly do her best to be pleasing, fully pleasing. Usually, of course, the girl, after a bit of time at the slave ring, does her best to be pleasing not to avoid the whip or switch, which is a rather prudential, mercenary motivation, after all, but, rather, because she wants to be pleasing to her master. She is, after all, a slave, and he is her master.

I did switch her well, once.

The little she-sleen had wished to reassure herself that she was truly a slave, and had dared to be lax in her duties, and, when questioned, had unwisely been curt, even insolent. I think she was surprised at the force with which she was seized and bound.

"Forgive me, Master!" she wept, at my feet, alarmed. "It is not necessary to strike me! I will mend my ways! I will be good!"

It had doubtless been a test on her part, to ascertain permissions, latitudes, limitations, and such, but I thought it well for her to comprehend what might be the consequences of such a test.

She had, after all, been lax in her duties and, when questioned, had been curt, even insolent, and so, whatever might have been the motivation for these unwise hazards or indulgences, they would have their predictable outcome. In moments, startled, disbelieving, she had rolled, twisting, and miserable, sobbing, crying out for mercy, under the blows of the switch.

"You have been displeasing," I informed her.

"Forgive me, Master!" she wept, her fair skin flaming with pain.

I then put the switch again to her, and, after a time, as she shrieked for mercy, I desisted, and left her, blubbering on the tiles, bound, behind me.

"Master," she wept. "Master!"

I left her there, bound, for better than an Ahn.

Before I untied her, I put the switch to her lips, and she kissed it, fervently.

Thereafter I had revoked her general permission to speak, for several days. She must then ask permission to speak, before daring to do so. Too, instead of the normal protocol of her kneeling when entering my presence, or being addressed, I forced her to do such things on her belly, to crawl on her belly into my presence, and remain on her belly before me, unless given permission to assume a different attitude. Too, for some days, I kept her in the bondage of the she-quadruped, or she-tarsk, not permitting her to rise to her feet, but she must go about on all fours. Too, her food and water must be taken from pans on the floor, without the use of her hands. More than once, afterwards, I had caught her pressing her lips to her fingertips, and then pressing her fingertips against her collar. More than once, as well, I had seen her lift her slave-ring chain to her lips, and kiss it.

Her little test was then over and done.

She now realized that she was truly a slave, would be treated as one, and, if appropriate, would be punished as one.

If she had entertained any doubts as to the matter, I gathered they were now dispelled.

She had, some days ago, been returned to the normal parameters of her bondage, had been given a general permission to speak, was permitted to walk about, was permitted to use her hands to feed herself, though I sometimes hand fed her, and was permitted a slave's normal modalities with respect to entering a room, being addressed, and such, being allowed to kneel, rather than belly.

She became ever more affectionate, ever more eager to please.

Sometimes, as though for good measure, I gave her a stroke of the switch below the small of the back.

I wagered that those who had known her on a far world, when she had been free, might have enjoyed doing so, as well.

I wondered what those who had known her on her own world would think of her now.

I thought the females she had known might envy her, and I thought the males she had known, if they were men, would not be displeased to own her.

I found her, all in all, despite her limitations, and what I had paid for her, an excellent property. Certainly she was a pleasant little beast to have in one's collar. She would require more training, of course, but I would give her that. One of the pleasures of the mastery is seeing to the improvement of the slave, training her, and such.

"Do the best you can, in the market," I told her.

"Yes, Master," she said.

She had wanted to be caressed, but I had thought it best to send her to the market first. Her slave fires, which had begun periodically to roar apace, made her now more a slave than she had ever been.

Those flames would bring her periodically to a man's feet.

Do they not put her in bondage more than her brand, her collar, and chains?

I opened the door, and watched her go down the balcony, and descend the stairs, leading to the street.

I thought of her, in her way, as being also of the Scribes, though, in her world, I gather that that caste is unknown, despite the fact that it is one of the five high castes. I had spoken to her for many Ahn, telling her of Gor, for what is a paga girl likely to learn of Gor, serving paga, serving pleasure, in an alcove? And she, in her turn, often nude at the slave ring, or before me, stripped, kneeling, hands braceleted behind her, had told me much of her world. It seemed to me a complex, but sorry world, one crowded and polluted, one of noise, fumes, and smoke, of pushing and shoving, one of haste with few places to go, or worth going, one without much love, and one, clearly, without Home Stones, if one can conceive of such a world. Too, it seems those of her world, incredibly, do not much care for their own world. Are they not like animals who would soil their own nest, like madmen who would poison their own air and water?

Given a garden of loveliness, would they not burn it, and turn it to ash?

She had now disappeared down the stairwell, on the way to the market.

How beautiful she was!

And how fetching she was, barefoot, in the brief, ragged tunic of blue rep-cloth.

She had clutched the coins in her hand.

Had she been natively Gorean she would probably have carried them in her mouth.

When the fellows in the market saw the color of the tunic they would guess, I supposed, and correctly, that she was the property of a Scribe.

Chapter Thirty-Five

The Wharfing of an Unusual Ship

From the bulwarks of the large, unusual ship men strangely clad threw down ropes to docksmen, who fastened them to mooring cleats.

The sea end of the pier had now been cleared by guardsmen, that the ship might be attended to, but the land end of the pier, and the adjacent waterfront, even to the warehouses, and the streets leading up to the city, were still swarming with people, men, and women, and boys.

Brundisium is one of the world's largest, busiest ports, with one of the finest harbors on the planet, host to a hundred traffics, headquarters of a hundred Merchant houses, but never, until now, had there been seen such a ship.

"Yes," had said the stranger. "I have seen that ship! It is, or was, a ship of the *shogun*, Lord Temmu!"

"Come from the World's End?" I said.

"Yes!" he said, pressing forward.

"Stop!" said a guardsman. "Go back!"

A lowered spear barred our way, and that of others.

"Wait!" I cautioned the stranger.

We then stood back, in the crowd.

"Make way, make way!" called a herald.

Making their way to the pier were members of the port's administration. I knew several, from my work in the harbor office, in the registry.

How would one record the arrival of this ship, I wondered.

What would be its registry, its port of origin, who would be its master, what would be its business, its cargo?

We waited behind the line of guardsmen, while the port's delegates approached the ship.

A gate in the bulwarks of the ship swung back, and was fastened open. Through this opening, several men began to thrust forth, foot by foot, a loading plank. They were short, sturdy men. They were barefoot. They wore short, hitched-up robes, with short sleeves.

"They are from Schendi," said someone near us.

"Too light," said another.

"See the eyes!" said a man.

"Tuchuks," said a man. "I saw one once."

"Yes!" said a fellow.

I looked to the stranger.

"Pani," he said.

"Do they speak the language?" I asked.

"Yes," said the stranger.

I recalled that last night the stranger had alluded to this matter. It had had to do with the will of Priest-Kings.

"What is such a ship doing here, in Brundisium?" I asked the stranger.

"I do not know," he said.

"Should you not, at the first opportunity," I said, "seek to make contact with the ship?"

"No," he said.

I recalled the two Assassins, of yesterday evening.

"It is that ship," said he, "which is, or was, of the much-diminished navy of Lord Temmu, but the war was going badly. The fleet of Lord Yamada was approaching the cove, when the great ship slipped away."

"You think," I said, "it may be a prize, taken by the ships of Lord Yamada's admiral?"

"I think it unlikely," he said, "quite improbable, but, in any event, caution is advised."

"Why unlikely, why improbable?" I asked.

"It was not in the cove when the fleet of Lord Yamada made its appearance," he said.

"It could have been overtaken and seized elsewhere," I said.

"That is possible," he said. "But one wonders why Lord Yamada, rich with resources, with many *ashigaru*, with many ships, with many villages and rice fields, with his war well in hand, on the brink of victory, would send a single ship to Brundisium, or even, say, to Kasra or Telnus."

"It is then likely," I said, "that it is still of the forces of Lord Temmu."

"Almost certainly," said the stranger. "But let us see how matters unfold."

"What are you talking about?" asked a fellow.

"Of far and strange things," said the stranger.

"Pani, I gather," I said, "have been in Brundisium before."

"I have gathered so," said the stranger, "long ago, by the intervention of Priest-Kings."

"For what reason?" I asked.

"To hire men, to buy women," he said. "To establish camps, to secure timber, to obtain tarns, to prepare a resistance, to ready themselves to wage a war anew."

"Why would they come again?" I asked.

"I do not know," said the stranger.

"Look," said a fellow pointing. "It is Demetrion!"

"Who is Demetrion?" asked the stranger.

"He is the harbor master," I said.

Demetrion had taken time to don his formal robes, lengthy and abundant, of white and yellow. He was approaching the lowered gangplank, one end resting on the pier, the other fastened, roped, to the bulwarks, on each side of the opened gate. With Demetrion were his aides, also of the Merchants, and two Scribes, one of which was Phillip, my superior in the registry.

The guardsmen had rather followed Demetrion's party, for which, I gathered, they had been waiting, and this permitted the stranger and myself, and the crowd, generally, to proceed several yards further down the pier. The guardsmen did, however, maintain an open space about the gangway.

Demetrion paused at the foot of the gangway and lifted his hand in greeting. "Tal," he said.

"Tal," said a thin, angular fellow, in an unusual, sashed robe, in which were two curved swords, a larger and a smaller, who stood at the bulwarks, to the right of the gangway, as one would look toward the ship.

"Be welcome, noble friends," said Demetrion, "to the great port of Brundisium."

The fellow on the ship bowed, slightly, presumably acknowledging this salutation. His hair was drawn back on his head, and fastened in a knot, behind the back of his head.

"I am Demetrion," called out Demetrion. "Harbor master in Brundisium."

Demetrion looked up to the bulwarks, but there was no response. The fellow on the ship did not exchange greetings, identify himself, or the ship, or state his business.

"Permission to come aboard," called Demetrion.

"No," said the fellow on the ship.

"No?" said Demetrion.

"No," said the fellow.

Demetrion had placed one foot on the gangplank, in anticipation of boarding the ship. Two of the Pani, at the height of the gangplank, had instantly removed the longer of their two swords from their sash, and, two hands fixed on the long, tasseled handle, drew back the weapons.

Demetrion stepped back, on the pier.

"The great port of Brundisium is a neutral port, open to all shipping," said Demetrion. "I trust you come in peace."

"We seek one Cineas," said the fellow on the ship, who seemed to be its captain, or, in any event, in a position of some authority.

"I know no Cineas," said Demetrion.

"I know him," said the stranger to me. "He is a mariner, who went ashore with me, and others, at Daphna. We arrived in Brundisium, together, oarsmen, some days ago. I soon spent my coin. But he seemed well supplied with silver."

"Enough," I asked, "to hire Assassins?"

The stranger looked at me, startled. "Yes," he said.

Four Pani rapidly descended the gangplank, passed Demetrion and his party, and threaded their way through the crowd.

The stranger pressed back, unwilling, I gathered, to be noted. He did, however, scrutinize the four Pani who, intent on some mission, looking neither to the left nor right, moved quickly past.

"Do you know them?" I asked, when they had passed.

"I know one," he said, "Tatsu, who was on the voyage west to the World's End, to the Twelve Islands."

"Then the ship sails still for Lord Temmu?" I said.

"I think so," said the stranger.

"What is your business here?" called Demetrion to the fellow by the bulwarks, who seemed in authority.

That individual, however, made no answer.

"I know not your people, your land, your city, your ship, your family, your caste, your clan," said Demetrion, "but whoever you be, if anyone, there is wharfage due in Brundisium."

Many were about, and I fear that Demetrion sensed he had been affronted, and that his office, and station, had been too little recognized, let alone respected.

The man above Demetrion, on the deck of the strange ship, near the height of the gangway, the presumed captain or officer, drew forth from his sash a small sack and tossed it to the pier. It stuck the planks of the pier, at Demetrion's feet, with an unmistakable sound.

This drew a response from the crowd.

"Pick it up," said Demetrion to one of his aides, unwilling to do so himself. He was a personage of dignity, harbor master in Brundisium, perhaps the most important single person in Brundisium, or, at least, the best-known and most prominent. Brundisium has no Administrator and no Ubar. It is ruled by a Merchant Council, with its day to day affairs managed by an executive committee, chief of which is the harbor master.

Demetrion's aides were as reluctant as he to stoop to retrieve the small, but weighty sack. The two Scribes, as well, looked away. Little love is lost between the Scribes and Merchants. The Scribes is a high caste and the Merchants is the richest caste. Each therefore regards itself as superior to the other, and each, then, would be reluctant to seem to lower itself before the other. I would have been quite willing to retrieve the sack and deliver it to Demetrion, but Phillip, my superior, was in his party, and there is, of course, the dignity, and the prestige, of the caste to maintain.

To my surprise, the stranger left my side, and slipped, unprevented, between the guardsmen, retrieved the sack, assured himself, it seemed, of its weight, which was apparently impressive, and climbed up the gangplank.

Neither of the Pani warriors at the top of the gangplank lifted their swords.

The crowd began to murmur, in astonishment.

The stranger, at the head of the gangplank, held out the sack of coin to the angular fellow, who had cast it to the feet of Demetrion.

"If this coin is what I think it is, from its weight," he said to the spare, angular fellow, presumably the captain, or a high officer, "it is too much."

"Give me the coin!" called Demetrion, from the pier.

Perhaps he then regretted that he had not stooped to pick up the sack himself.

"This sack, I take it," said the stranger, "contains ten tarn disks, of double weight."

"Fifteen," said the angular fellow, "certified with the stamp of Ar."

The stranger then removed one such disk from the sack, and held it up. "This," he said, "is far too much."

"What are such things but pieces of metal," said the Pani.

The stranger then handed the sack, less the single tarn disk, to the angular warrior, who replaced it in his sash. The stranger then tossed the single coin which had been extracted from the sack to the planks at the feet of Demetrion, who swiftly reached down, and snatched it up.

He and his party then forced their way back through the crowd, some of whom had been close enough to see what the coin had been. "Festival!" called more than one man. "Set the public tables!" called another. "For a week!" cried another. "Free ka-la-na!" called a man. "Free paga!" cried another. "No, no!" cried Demetrion. "Only silver, only a tarsk!" But that single, weighty coin had been yellow, like *Tor-tu-Gor*.

"I am Nakamura," said the angular fellow, presumably an officer, certainly a warrior, to the stranger.

The stranger bowed, which gesture of greeting was returned by the officer, Nakamura.

"I do not know you," said the stranger.

"I am captain of the *River Dragon*, ship of the navy of Lord Temmu."

"You have come to Brundisium," said the stranger.

"I am pleased to see that you are alive," said the officer.

"You thought I might not be?"

"One did not know."

"You know me, then," said the stranger.

"I think so," said the officer. "I think you are Callias, of Jad, a Cosian, he who prevented the destruction of the great ship, he who plotted its escape, he who set designs in motion, he who engineered its flight."

"Scarcely by myself," said the stranger.

"Then you are he," said the officer.

"I fear so," said the stranger.

"Lord Okimoto was not pleased," said the officer.

"I regret his displeasure," said the stranger.

"For far less," said the officer, "men have perished most unpleasantly."

"I am sure of it," said the stranger.

"I am charged with seeking you out," said the officer.

"You have been successful," said the stranger.

"Do you know why I have come?" he asked.

"I would suppose," he said, "to kill me."

"Not at all," said the officer. "Rather, I bring you greetings from Lord Nishida and from Tarl Cabot, tarnsman, commander of the tarn cavalry of Lord Temmu."

Chapter Thirty-Six

**The Warehouse;
The Encounter with Cineas,
the Agent of Tyrtaios;
The Gift of Lord Nishida and
Tarl Cabot, Tarnsman**

It was now four days following the docking of the Pani ship, the *River Dragon*, and the stranger and I, invited by Captain Nakamura and the harbor master, Demetrion, who now seemed on splendid terms with the captain, perhaps because commerce fosters affability, were in one of the great warehouses adjacent to the high piers. Its light was dim, but it was natural light, flowing in through a large number of high, narrow, barred windows. Slaves in transit are often kept in places with such windows, that they cannot see outside. Such windows, too, of course, are more difficult of access, both from the inside and outside. In the warehouse, on several long tables, set in rows, stretching back, toward the rear of the room, were spread varieties of goods, and such goods, indeed, overflowing, found their way to mats and cloths spread on the floor, amongst the tables. The Pani had brought much with them, for selling and trading, taken from the many officially sealed, watertight compartments of the *River Dragon*, and local Merchants, who swarmed about, within, moving from table to table, and to the floor displays, were interested, as well, in buying and selling. I had gathered that the movements of the forces of Lord Temmu were much restricted in the islands, with the result that an overseas trade, as it might slip through the blockades of Lord Yamada, might provide an access to goods otherwise less available, in particular, weaponry, missiles, cloth, leather, hemp, siege stores, tarn tackle, and such. For example, exquisite Pani ceramics, intricate carvings, and dyed silks, produced in the castle shops of Lord Temmu might bring silver in Brundisium, and be sold for gold in Ar and Turia, and the silver from Brundisium, in Brundisium, of course, might be exchanged for sinew, arrow points, fletching, larmas, tospits, sa-tarna, and such. The voyage of the *River Dragon* then, I took it, was a pioneer voyage, which might inaugurate routes of trade and perhaps open conduits of diplomacy. When land roads are closed, Thassa's roads beckon. What cannot be secured locally may be fetched from abroad. It was a small thing, of course, a single voyage, but it is not unusual that the explorer is followed by the Merchant, just as it is not impossible that the Merchant might be followed by the soldier. Such a voyage may take several months for a single ship, but if a hundred ships are making such voyages day by day, one may well arrive daily in one port or another. One supposed that Lord Yamada, in his less-straitened circumstances, would be less motivated to seek foreign goods, but, too, one supposed, if he were once apprised of tarns, as presumably he soon would be, and might now be, he would be eager to supply himself with so valuable a military arm. One could conceive then, eventually, of the navies of warring *shoguns* extending their concerns beyond their embattled local waters, and beginning to compete for trade routes and access to distant ports.

Another commodity the Pani were interested in buying, I learned, was women. Apparently fair-skinned female slaves were rare in the islands, and often figured, amongst other gifts, in the attempts to woo political alliances. Too, one supposed they would not do badly off the block, as well. For example, a girl who might go for less than a silver tarsk in Brundisium might, presumably as something rather in the nature of an exotic slave, certainly a rare one, bring the equivalent in local currency of two or three such tarsks in the islands.

"The most beautiful of all female slaves on all Gor are sold in Brundisium," Demetrion assured Nakamura, the captain of the *River Dragon*. Certainly this was false, as the captain doubtless surmised, but that is not to deny that some very fine slaves, the equals of any anywhere, are occasionally purchased from Brundisium blocks.

"Ahh," said Captain Nakamura, politely.

This boast of Demetrion, on behalf of shapely, quality merchandise available in Brundisium, brought to my mind, naturally enough, a particular slave, one whom I would have liked to purchase, but could not afford. To be sure, she had not been bought in Brundisium, but in Market of Semris. On the other hand, the sales barns of Market of Semris are not far from Brundisium, and some fellows from Brundisium like to frequent them, looking for bargains, in particular, paga girls, dancers, and such.

The stranger and I, it may be recalled, had been invited to the warehouse by Demetrion, the harbor master, and Captain Nakamura, captain of the *River Dragon*, now wharfed nearby. I have little doubt that this invitation, though issued in the name of both the harbor master and the Pani captain, came about as a result of the captain's request. Demetrion knew little more of the stranger, the Cosian, Callias of Jad, than the fact that he may have cost the harbor, or, better, its administration, a number of golden tarn disks, of double weight. But, even so, a single such disk had been welcome. Demetrion knew me by sight, but by little more, from the registry. The captain, for some reason, had wished for the stranger to stay on board the *River Dragon*, but, as I would not be allowed to do so, as well, the stranger declined the offer.

"He offered me money, when I had no money," he told the captain, "he offered me lodging, when I had no lodging."

"He is not Pani," said the captain.

"Neither am I," said the stranger.

"But," said the captain, "you were of the ship."

"He has been seen with me," said the stranger. "If I am in danger, so, too, is he."

"That is possible," said the captain.

"Give me a sword," said the stranger.

A blade was brought, with its shoulder strap and sheath. It was not a Pani sword, but a *gladius*, a weapon with which, I took it, the stranger would be familiar.

"Do not sell it," said the captain.

The stranger smiled, and turned to me, who stood at the foot of the gangway. "Would you have a guest?" he asked.

"Welcome," I said.

My name was given to the captain. "The harbor office will know his residence," said the stranger.

"Stay on board," said the captain.

But the stranger had already descended the gangplank.

"My quarters are near," I told him.

"Excellent," he said, looking about himself.

Demetrion, the harbor master, had been with the captain, the stranger and myself, on the floor of the large, crowded warehouse, but Demetrion now excused himself, being anxious, one supposed, to do some looking about, and trading himself.

"You wished to see me?" said the stranger to Nakamura, captain of the *River Dragon*.

Captain Nakamura glanced to me, politely, but the stranger encouraged him, saying that he might speak in my presence.

"I am pleased that you are armed," said the captain.

"I have not sold the blade yet," said the stranger.

"I would not do so, if I were you," said the captain.

"I have remained in seclusion for four days," said the stranger, "and am now invited to the warehouse."

"We cannot remain indefinitely in Brundisium," said the captain. "Each day may be important in the islands. The first day we docked, I sent four men forth to locate the oarsman, Cineas. Unfortunately, he has eluded them."

"Eluded?" asked the stranger.

"Yes," said the captain. "They were sent to kill him."

"Why?" asked the stranger.

"You will recall the attempted desertion, which you did something to delay, and may have fatally impaired, at the gate. Its leader or leaders were not in evidence. The oarsman, Tereus, was a figurehead in the matter, if that, and probably more of a dupe than anything else, though one willing enough, one supposes. Surely he was not alone. Many armsmen were eager to escape the islands. Suspicion, in our search for the leaders and organizers of the attempted desertion, fell naturally on armsmen, and, in particular, on those who were, or had been, high armsmen. Inquiries were conducted, contacts investigated, relationships noted. Of five groups what man had they all in common, and of those men held in common, who, in turn, had they all in common? Some seeming patterns began to emerge. More than a hundred armsmen who had attempted desertion were questioned, several unpleasantly. Most professed to know little, but many littles, compounded, may become large. Shortly, within two or three days, suspicion began to fall on a particular armsman, one named Tyrtaios, who was the liaison officer of Lord Okimoto."

The stranger did not seem surprised at this report.

"Indeed, he was later denounced explicitly by the cripple, Rutilius of Ar, who had been succeeded in his post as liaison for Lord Okimoto by the same fellow, Tyrtaios. Too, it seems that Lord Okimoto himself had begun, days before, to suspect him, as well."

"A personal enmity, or resentment, may have been involved there," said the stranger. "At one time I saw them as allies, Tyrtaios and Rutilius. But Rutilius was repudiated, cast aside by Tyrtaios, after his crippling, as he was, as well, by Lord Okimoto. Rutilius, whole or incomplete, has a long memory, and is a dangerous enemy. It is possible, too, that Rutilius wished to accompany the deserters, but had not been permitted to do so. His inability to move with agility might have slowed the flight. Too, he was not popular with many armsmen. His betrayal of Tyrtaios may have been his vengeance for being discounted, and neglected, by Tyrtaios, and perhaps others, as well."

"Although the progress of the investigation was putatively confidential," said the captain, and largely confined to the various prison barracks, where the would-be deserters were held, this Tyrtaios seemed, somehow, to have been well apprised of how matters were proceeding. It is suspected that he was kept informed by some individual in a high place, perhaps a well-placed spy, some individual secretly in the service of Lord Yamada. In any event, on the eve of his planned arrest, he disappeared from the castle grounds, abetted in his escape by an unknown party or parties. One supposes he was given a letter of safe conduct by means of which he would make contact with, and be received by, the forces of Lord Yamada, those in the vicinity of the castle."

"His loss could be grievous," said the stranger, "as Tyrtaios was a high officer in the resistance, knows much of its organization, and is familiar with the defenses of the castle of Lord Temmu. He is also familiar with tarns and their possible military applications. Thus, much of the surprise value of tarns will be lost, something on which Lords Temmu, Nishida, and Okimoto have doubtless heavily counted. Perhaps most serious is the fact that many of our armsmen respect him as an astute leader, and surely favored, with him, the cause of desertion. In certain circumstances, then, it seems not unlikely they might once more look to him for leadership, and once more follow him."

"And such a possibility," said the captain, "would not be likely to be overlooked by Lord Yamada, or his advisors."

"I would suppose not," said the stranger.

"In one matter, a subtle one," said the captain, "Tyrtaios may have erred. One suspects it is a matter connected with his vanity. Before his disappearance he left a note in his quarters, obviously intended to be discovered. It seems he had earlier anticipated that Lord Temmu would wish to have the great ship destroyed, to preclude its possible employment in an armsmen's flight, and that some, sensing this, might attempt to save the ship, by removing it from danger. Accordingly, given this possibility, he planted one of his minions amongst the great ship's most likely mariners, those most likely to be recruited in any attempt to save the ship."

"This was the man, Cineas?" said the stranger.

"Yes," said the captain. "He was to see to your death, for your role in foiling the desertion."

"That," smiled the stranger, "was to be my reward."

"Your enemy," said the captain, "the minion of Tyrtaios, was frequently at your side."

"He seemed amiable enough," said the stranger. "He went ashore with me at Daphna. We took ship together to Brundisium."

"It was he, then," I said, "who hired Assassins."

"My men," said the captain, "went to the Court of Assassins

in Brundisium. Two had been hired, but they did not report back."

"Nor will they," said the stranger.

"That is known to me," said the captain. "Their bodies were washed ashore."

"You are in danger," I said to the stranger. "The Assassins will come to avenge their own."

"No," said the captain, "at least not those of the Court of Brundisium, unless more coin is put forth. Vendetta is not their way. Their fellows took fee and failed to earn it. They are not to be avenged. They failed. They are disgraced. They are no longer of the Court."

"Cineas," said the stranger, "may not even know they failed."

"He must know," I said.

"In any event," said the captain, "my men, amongst whom is Tatsu, perhaps known to Callias, for he was on the great ship, arranged certain matters with the Court of Assassins."

"I know him," said the stranger.

"What matters?" I asked the captain.

"Two of the black caste were hired to seek out Cineas, and slay him," said the captain. "I do not think they have yet found him."

"What was the fee?" asked the stranger.

"A silver tarsk, each," said the captain.

"Why would Tyrtaios leave such a message in his quarters, pertaining to these things?" I asked.

"Gloating, one supposes," said the captain.

"But he warned us," I said.

"He did not think so," said the captain. "He thought merely to inform us, too late, of his cruel scheme. The great ship was gone. How could word reach Callias in time to warn him? The engine was in place, and irremediably in motion. The missile was in flight, and beyond interception."

"The cove was empty," said the stranger. "He had no way to anticipate, nor would he later to forestall, the voyage of the *River Dragon*."

"We feared we would be too late," said the captain.

"Assassins now seek Cineas?" said the stranger.

"The dagger has been painted," said the captain. "Inquiries are being made."

"It seems then," I said to the stranger, "that you have nothing to fear."

"My men, as well," said the captain, "still seek Cineas."

"He is doubtless now well beyond the gates of Brundisium," I said.

"He may not know he is pursued," said the captain.

"When one learns that," said the stranger, "that one is sought, by the black caste, it is often too late."

I recalled the Assassins, at the tavern, some nights ago.

"In any event," said the captain to the stranger, "I would not yet sell my sword."

"I understand," said the stranger.

"The profit involved in such a transaction," said the captain, "may be considerably outweighed by a possible loss."

"True," said the stranger.

"The war goes not well abroad," said the captain. "Each day may be important. I must thus soon finish my business here."

He looked about, at the tables, at the goods, the swarming crowd, some idlers, some guardsmen, and listened, for a time, to the murmur of bargainings. Men came and went. There were occasional shouts. Things were placed in bags, and things were removed from bags. Cases were opened, and closed. Many were the bulging wallets, and sleeve purses. Porters, too, were there, some with boxes, full and half-full, attending Merchants. Much was done with ink and paper, deliveries arranged to the ship, the coin to be paid at her side. The warehouse was a large one. I thought there must be more than six or seven hundred fellows here, coming and going. The place bustled. I thought that Demetrion would be much pleased. Seldom did a trove of such magnitude, on a single ship, as opposed to a convoy, come to Brundisium. In a couple of places on a platform, there was a harbor praetor, now indoors, in the warehouse, on his curule chair, as opposed to on the docks themselves, their usual station, who might clarify the Merchant Law, interpret it, adjudicate disputes, and make rulings. There were many caste colors in the crowd, but clearly predominating were the yellow and white, or white and gold, familiar to the Merchants. I saw two in the yellow of the Builders, and several in the blue of the Scribes, some assisting Merchants; the guardsmen, as they were on duty, were in red. I saw two Initiates in their snowy white, with their golden pans held out, to receive offerings. Commonly they do nothing for coin received, but, occasionally, they agree to bless the giver, and commend him to Priest-Kings. Among their many services, for a sufficient fee, they assure success in business, politics, and love, which successes are unfailing, it is said, unless they not be in accord with the will of the Priest-Kings. On the docks, also for a sufficient fee, they sometimes sell fair winds and clear skies, which also never fail, it is said, save when not in accord with the will of the Priest-Kings. The Pani, discovering that the Initiates were not marketing their golden pans but expected to receive something for nothing, as it were, or nothing tangible, asked them to step aside, as they were impeding the way of honest tradesmen. Many fellows, of course, do not wear their caste robes about, except when on caste business, and some don them only on formal occasions or holidays. Many free women, for example, and some men, concerned with respect to their appearance, do not care to limit their wardrobes as narrowly as their castes might seem to recommend. Several in the warehouse were in nondescript garb. I did note, however, the brown and black of the Bakers, the black and gray of the Metal Worker, the brown of the Peasants, and several others. I saw nothing which suggested the Physicians, but that, of course, did not rule out the presence in the room of those of the green caste.

"I would like, if possible," said the captain, "to sail with the morning tide."

"So soon?" I said.

"It would be my preference," said the captain.

"I am pleased," said the stranger, "to have had conveyed to me the greetings of Lord Nishida and Tarl Cabot, commander of the tarn cavalry."

"Both wish you well," said the captain. "Lord Nishida expresses his appreciation for your work at the gate, at the time of the attempted desertion, and both he and Tarl Cabot, the tarnsman, salute you, in the matter of the ship."

"The matter of the ship?"

"Surely," said the captain, "you understand that without your concern, and your initiative, without the actions which you set in motion, in particular having Lord Nishida contact Tarl Cabot, the tarnsman, in the mountains, the ship would have perished. As it was, it barely escaped the torches of Lords Temmu and Okimoto. Both Lord Nishida and Tarl Cabot, the tarnsman, were fond of the ship. It served them well. Neither wished to see it destroyed, wise though might have been its destruction to deter desertion, to convince armsmen that flight was impossible, and that they must now reconcile themselves and their fortunes to our cause."

"But why would they have had the ship destroyed?" I asked. "Why were they not willing to merely send it away? Let it depart. Escaped, it can berth no deserters."

"Finality, assurance, definitude, putting an end to things, the assertion of authority, the clarification of command," said the captain.

"Still," I protested.

"What if it should return?" said the captain.

"I see," I said.

"As long as it existed somewhere," said the captain, "might there not be hope of its return? Might the men not be uncertain, might they not wait, might they not keep watch, might they not be divided, might they not be unwilling to commit themselves wholeheartedly to the war?"

"I understand," I said.

"And, if it returned," said the stranger, "would it not again face the torches of the castle?"

"Of course," said the captain.

That seemed obvious.

"A ship destroyed," said the captain, "is a ship no longer to be feared."

"True," said the stranger.

"There would be the danger, as well," said the captain, "that the ship might fall prize to the fleet of Lord Yamada."

"Yes," said the stranger. "That would be a danger."

"I trust you now understand the motivation for its destruction, the rationality of doing away with it."

"Of course," said the stranger. "That is clear."

"Very clear," said the captain.

"What would you have done?" asked the stranger.

"I?"

"Yes."

"I would have saved the ship, of course," he said.

"I see," said the stranger.

"One is of the ship," said the captain.

"Yes," said the stranger. "One is of the ship."

"Friends," I said. "I see one in the robes of the Merchants, but muchly hooded, who has entered, who looks about, but who does not seem concerned with the tables."

"I have seen him," said the stranger.

"You have just now noticed him?" inquired the captain of me.

"A bit ago," I said. "I have watched him."

"We have been waiting for him," said Captain Nakamura.

"We put out word in the city," said the stranger, "here and there, that Callias, of Cos, would frequent these premises sometime today."

"This is the reason we have been summoned from my quarters?" I asked.

"Yes," said the captain. "Forgive the precipitancy, but we have waited four days now, in our attempt to locate Cineas, and protect Callias, and time is short."

"I am pleased," said the stranger. "I would have it done with."

"It is a ruse to draw Cineas forth?" I said.

"Assuming," said the captain, "that he is still intent upon his dark mission."

"If that is he," I said, "it seems he is so intent."

Captain Nakamura drew his longer blade from his sash. His feet were slightly spread; two hands were on the hilt of the weapon.

"No, my friend," said the stranger. "I shall greet him."

As I watched, uneasily, the stranger began to thread his way amongst the tables. He had scarcely moved, when the hooded figure, he in the robes of the Merchants, saw him, and stiffened, reacting as might a hunter, catching sight of a sleen in the shrubbery, a larl amongst rocks of the Voltai, not yet expected, yards away, just noticed. The stranger had removed his sheath and belt from across his body, and held these in his left hand.

The sword, the *gladius*, given to him on the *River Dragon*, was in his right hand. I trembled, for I had seen that simplicity, that ease of grip before, neither clenched nor tight, neither loose nor careless, in a guardsman's blade, moving toward a fellow backed against a wall. No words had been exchanged, nor needed there have been. The stranger's blade was like an extension of his arm, seemingly as natural, and as thoughtless, as uncalculating, as the now-exposed claws on the paw of a stalking larl. The buyers and sellers, and lookers-on, the dealers, the idlers, the porters, the curious, the men in the warehouse, I think, noticed nothing of what was passing amongst them, no more than trees, or rushes bending in the wind, might have noticed the passage amongst them of some silent, patient, sinuous, stealthy form, almost invisible, certainly unnoticed, intent on its own business, which had nothing to do with theirs.

"I take it that is Cineas," said Captain Nakamura.

"Doubtless," I said.

"Do you not think he would have been wiser to move differently amongst the tables, to feign interest, here and there, approaching ever more closely?"

"I would suppose so," I said.

"Too," said the captain, "I suspect he would have done well to hood himself less closely. It would have been simpler merely to keep his face averted."

"Until he would strike?"

"Certainly."

"Were I he," I said, "I would have fled the city."

"That he has not done so," said Captain Nakamura, "is significant."

"How so?" I asked.

"He knows he could not reach the gate," said the captain.

"I do not understand," I said.

"Note two who have entered," said Captain Nakamura, "just within the door, in shabby garb, each with his forehead obscured, by the talmit."

Such bands are usually signs of authority, worn by foremen, leaders of work gangs, first slaves, and such, though they may serve, too, simply to keep hair back, in place, away from the eyes, protect the eyes from the running of sweat, and so on.

They might, too, of course, serve to conceal any mark or sign which might be placed on the forehead. It would be rare, given the common meaning of the talmit, that of authority, to see two together, both in the talmit. To be sure, ranks can be signified by color, markings, and such.

The stranger paused some four paces from the figure in the white and gold.

The figure then threw back the hood.

"Tal, Cineas," said the stranger. "You may withdraw. I shall not follow you. Let all be forgotten. Seek a gate. We have been of the ship."

Cineas discarded the white and gold he had donned.

Seeing this, men suddenly began to withdraw from the vicinity. The trees, the rushes, so to speak, had suddenly become aware of what might be amongst them.

The blade which had been concealed beneath the robes of white and gold was now in evidence.

"Let all be forgotten," said the stranger. "Go, leave the warehouse, leave the city. Seek a gate."

"Noble Callias," smiled Cineas, "there is no time to reach a gate."

Cineas then lifted his sword to the stranger, in a salute, which salute was returned by the stranger.

Men backed further away.

I saw the two fellows, in the talmits, approaching.

Cineas, then, with a wild cry, rushed toward the stranger.

What happened then happened very quickly. Whereas I had gathered from the tale of the stranger that he did not much credit his skills with the blade, I now realized that they were far from indifferent. In that quick moment I understood how it was that he had held the rank of First Spear, and had been assigned duties, long ago, in the Central Cylinder of Ar itself.

He stepped away from the body.

The two fellows in shabby garments had now approached, the talmits no longer bound about their foreheads. I saw on each forehead the simple mark, the sign of the black dagger. One of them rolled the body over, and then looked to the stranger.

"You have killed him," said the man, straightening up.

The stranger shrugged.

"Therefore," said the man, "the killing is yours."

Each of the men then, from their purse, removed a silver tarsk, and placed it in the hand of the stranger.

"I want no money for his blood," said the stranger. "I would rather he had found the gate, and fled the city."

"Still," said one of the fellows, "the killing is yours."

"Consider it yours," said the stranger, "as you hurried him onto my sword."

The two members of the Black Court of Brundisium regarded one another.

"Suppose," said the stranger, "one in fear of you, dreading discovery each day, unwilling to accept such misery longer, or to frustrate you, put himself upon his own sword, or, in fleeing, drowned, or fell from some cliff, would the killing not be yours?"

"It would," said one of the fellows, "and the fee might be kept."

"Keep it then," said the stranger, and returned the two coins, first one, and then the other.

Each returned the coin to his own purse, and then wiped from his forehead the dagger.

More than one man breathed then more easily, for those of the Black Court no longer wore the dagger.

I saw now the four Pani who had originally left the ship, the man, Tatsu, amongst them.

"We followed the fee killers, Captain," said Tatsu, to Captain Nakamura. "We knew not the city. They did. We gave them hire. They found the quarry. Had they failed to earn their fee, our swords would have spoken."

The long, curved blade of Captain Nakamura was still free, held in two hands.

"I think it safe, now, to sell your sword," said Captain Nakamura to the stranger.

"I think, nonetheless," said the stranger, "I shall keep it."

"Good," said Captain Nakamura. "He who surrenders the means to defend himself delivers himself into the hands of his enemies."

"I regret the death," said the stranger.

"Do not do so," said Captain Nakamura. "It is unwise to leave a living enemy behind one."

"Prepare the body," said Captain Nakamura, to Tatsu.

"What are you going to do?" asked the stranger.

"You do not want the head, do you?" asked Captain Nakamura.

"No," said the stranger.

It took a single, measured stroke, delivered at the base of the neck.

Men cried out, in dismay.

Captain Nakamura straightened up, holding the head in his left hand, by the hair. "The women," he said, "will not perfume this head, nor comb its hair, nor paint its teeth black, for beauty, nor add it to the collections. This head, rather, is for Tyrtaios. It will be mounted on the wall of the castle of Lord Temmu, for ten days, and it will then be cast amongst the soldiers below, of the forces of Lord Yamada, with instructions that it be delivered to their man, Tyrtaios. He is entitled to learn the fate of his emissary, and thus we, too, will have our small joke."

"What is going on here?" inquired Demetrion, harbor master of the port of Brundisium, followed by two guardsmen.

"An accident," said the stranger. "This fellow fell upon my sword."

"He was attacked," said a man. "He but defended himself."

"His neck fell upon your sword, as well?" said Demetrion.

"My sword," said Captain Nakamura, "fell upon his neck."

"You took his head," said Demetrion.

"That is true," said Captain Nakamura.

"Why?" said Demetrion.

"He no longer had any use for it," said Captain Nakamura.

"Assassins are involved in this," said a man. "We saw the daggers."

"Aii," whispered Demetrion, softly.

"Fee was taken," said a man. "We saw the coins."

The two guardsmen looked at one another.

The two of the Assassins were no longer in evidence. They had withdrawn from the warehouse.

"If there is a concern here," said a man, "it is to be taken up as a matter between you and the Black Court."

I saw that this did not much please Demetrion. The business of the Black Court was not one in which men lightly dabbled. In many cases one was not even sure who was, and who was not, a member of the black caste. I recalled, from the tale of the stranger, that some evidence had suggested that Tyrtaios, who may have had much to do with the attempted desertion, and who had disappeared from the castle of Lord Temmu, might be of the Assassins.

The two guardsmen now withdrew.

"It is over now, is it not?" said Demetrion.

"Yes," said Captain Nakamura. "But, if you wish, we will conclude all trading, return to the ship, and take to the sea, and then perhaps this ship, and none like it, will ever again come to the piers of great Brundisium."

"No, no," said Demetrion, hastily, and then, raising his voice, he called out, "It is over! It is done, all done. Return to business! To business! The house remains open late this night!"

This announcement was met with pleasure.

"I will have the body delivered to the pool, by garbage slaves," said Demetrion.

Supposing this allusion might be obscure to the stranger and Captain Nakamura, I explained it to them. For any who might come upon this manuscript and are not familiar with Brundisium, the pool, when the grating is raised, is accessible from the sea, and may be entered by sharks, and grunt. It serves several purposes. It tends to draw predatory fish away from the piers, and it provides a convenient way of disposing of large forms of garbage, the bodies, say, of dead animals. It is also used as a place of execution, in particular, for minor offenses, such as theft. The grating is raised, which is a signal to fish in the vicinity that a feeding is at hand. If the victim is alive, a limb is severed, which distributes blood in the water, and then the limb and the victim are cast into the pool.

The head which had been removed from the body, with the apparent intention of bringing it eventually to the attention of Tyrtaios, was given into the keeping of the Pani, Tatsu, who accepted it, and, holding it by the hair, bowed, and then withdrew, with his three fellows, presumably to the ship.

"I will have warm water and dry cloths brought," said Demetrion, "that you may wash and dry your swords."

"My thanks," said the stranger.

The captain bowed, slightly, acknowledging the courtesy.

One seldom sheaths an unclean sword, and, one supposes,

one would be reluctant to return such a blade to a clean sash, as well. In the field, leaves, and grass, may be used. Some use the hair and clothing of the fallen. Others carry a soft cloth for such a purpose. When the blade is clean and dry, it is often given a thin coating of oil, which protects against rust, and, some believe, facilitates the flight from the scabbard.

The body of Cineas, headless, was removed by two garbage slaves, short brawny men, kept by the harbor office.

Shortly thereafter a lad, employed in the warehouse, brought the stranger and Captain Nakamura two small vessels of heated, colored, scented water, and two soft, brightly white, deeply napped, scarflike cloths.

Captain Nakamura, one gathers, a man of refinement, if not the stranger, appeared to recognize and appreciate the nature and quality of this homely amenity. Many of the high Pani, I am told, are sensitive to beauty, to matters of artistry and grace, even in small things, such as the serving of tea, the arrangement of flowers.

The two blades were soon cleaned and returned to their respective housings. The stranger, being right-handed, ran his sheath strap from his right shoulder to his left hip, so the blade was at his left hip. Before he met Cineas he had removed both the strap and sheath, for such things may be seized. When danger is imminent the strap is usually, for a right-handed swordsman, simply put loose over the left shoulder, where, in a moment, the blade drawn, the belt and sheath may be held, as the stranger did, or, as is often the case, discarded altogether, to be retrieved later, this being permitted by the outcome of the encounter.

"We have accomplished much, successfully, noble Callias," said Captain Nakamura. "We have journeyed to the World's End, Brundisium, we have founded a trade route, we are in the process of obtaining much needed goods for our *shogun*, Lord Temmu, we have foiled, or meddled in, the plot of the traitor, Tyrtaios, have perhaps saved your life, and, in any event have deprived him of his agent, Cineas, and we have conveyed to you greetings, those of Lord Nishida and Tarl Cabot, the tarnsman."

"I wish you well," said the stranger, Callias, to the captain, Nakamura, of the ship, the *River Dragon*.

I would have thought they might then have clasped hands,

hand to hand, or, perhaps, exchanged with one another the mariner's clasp, hand to wrist, wrist to hand, but, instead, the stranger bowed to Captain Nakamura, and he, in turn, returned the bow. This seemed to me rather cool, rather formal, but in it was clearly expressed, I sensed, much respect.

"What will you do now, noble Callias?" inquired Captain Nakamura. "What are your are your plans, when we sail?"

"I would sail with you, of course, to return," said the stranger.

"That is not possible," said the captain.

"I must!" said the stranger.

"You have enemies amongst those who would have deserted," said the captain. "Your interference at the gate will be recalled. We could not guarantee your safety from such men, even at the castle."

"It is a risk I accept, a risk I welcome," said the stranger.

"I fear," said the captain, "matters are far more serious."

"I do not understand," said the stranger. He was much agitated. I had not understood the gravity of his determination to return to such a far, strange, and dangerous place, the World's End.

Would one not rather strive to avoid a resumption of that perilous journey, at all costs?

What sort of men would dare to journey to the World's End?

"You would be killed," said the Captain. "Lords Temmu and Okimoto would see to it, for your part in stealing the great ship."

"They would have destroyed it!" said the stranger.

"Yes," said the captain, "and you were instrumental in foiling that design. Do you think that would be forgotten?"

"I was not alone!" he said.

"Tarl Cabot is important to the tarn cavalry," said the captain. "I fear his men would die for him. It would be very dangerous to dispose of him, and, worse, presumably unwise. He may be needed. And Lord Nishida is a *daimyo*, with villages, rice fields, peasants, and *ashigaru*. He is respected by a hundred minor *daimyos*, and important in significant diplomacies, maintaining precarious neutralities amongst those who might lean to Lord Yamada, and perhaps, eventually, he might prove significant in the enlistment of allies."

"And Callias," said the stranger, bitterly, "has no such weight, no such power."

"Certainly not," said the captain.

"One who steals a sul may be mutilated, crippled, or killed," said Callias, "whereas one who steals cities may be gifted with the medallion of a Ubar."

"Or the throne of a *shogun*," said the captain.

"I must go, in any event," said the stranger.

"I will give you no berth," said the captain.

"Why?"

"I have given my word on the matter," said the captain.

"How so?" asked the stranger. "To whom?"

"To Lord Nishida, and Tarl Cabot, the tarnsman," said the captain.

"But you have conveyed their greetings!" he said. "Are they not well disposed toward me?"

"More so than you realize," said the captain.

"I do not understand, I do not understand," said the stranger.

"Why is it so important to you?" inquired the captain, politely.

The stranger seemed about to speak, but he did not speak. He turned away.

"I fear," I said, "Captain, that the matter has to do with a slave."

"No, no!" said the stranger.

"A slave?" said the captain.

"I fear so," I said.

"Ah!" said the captain, suddenly. "I had forgotten."

The stranger turned to face him.

"Forgive me," said the captain. "It had slipped my mind, doubtless in the press of circumstances, arranging matters with the harbor master, renting space, organizing goods, supervising trading, and such."

"What had you forgotten?" asked the stranger.

"Lord Nishida and Tarl Cabot, the tarnsman," said the captain, "have included with their greetings to you, a gift, as well."

"I need no gift," said the stranger, ruefully, bitterly.

"Do you refuse it?" asked the captain.

"I thought they were my friends," said the stranger.

"Is it to be returned?" asked the captain.

"Certainly not," I said.

"No," said the stranger, wearily. "I am not so boorish. If they are not my friends, yet I am theirs. I would not so insult them."

"I would like to sail with the tide, in the morning," said the captain, "if our business can be finished here tonight."

"The warehouse will remain open, until late," I said. "And surely another day or two will not matter."

"A day may matter," said the captain. "One does not know."

"You wish to sail as soon as possible?" I asked.

"As soon as is compatible with our business here," said the captain.

"You hope to sail tomorrow?" I said.

"With the tide," he said.

"Time is short, then," I said.

"We will have it so," said the captain.

"Accept then the gift, and have done with it," I said to the stranger, "for the captain is much engaged."

"I do not want it," said the stranger.

"But you will accept it," I said.

"Yes," said the stranger, looking toward the tables.

"Where is the gift?" I asked.

"It," said Captain Nakamura, pointing, "is in a back room, there, behind that door. We did not put it on the floor as it is a gift, and not for immediate sale."

"But perhaps for later sale?" I said.

"Of course," said the captain.

"I would return to the World's End," said the stranger. "That they, Lord Nishida and Tarl Cabot, whom I have served, and well I trust, in whose regard I putatively stand, would deny me that, is unconscionable."

"They do not want you to die," I said.

"They deny me the world, which they could easily grant, and send me instead, the sop of a gift," he said, angrily.

"I do not think they meant you harm, nor insult," I said. "Accept it, and then, if you wish, rid yourself of it, in anger."

"I do not want it!" he said.

"They sent you greetings," I said, "from the World's End."

"I do not want it!" he said.

"You may dispose of it, sell it," I said.

"I do not want it!" he said.

"Very well," I said. "Look upon it, and then leave it."

"Follow me," said Nakamura, captain of the *River Dragon*, who then began to move amongst the tables, toward the back of the room. In a moment, he had reached the door he had earlier indicated, opened it, and stood beside it, not entering.

"Captain, noble captain," called Demetrion, harbor master in Brundisium, from several yards away, lifting his hand. "Your mark is required."

"Will you excuse me?" said Captain Nakamura to the stranger and me, and, after bowing, went to join Demetrion.

Many Goreans, particularly of the lower castes, and some of the Warriors, a high caste, cannot read. Literacy is accepted in the lower castes, but not encouraged. There are Peasants who have never seen a written word. Some Warriors take pride in their inability to read, regarding that skill as unworthy of them, as being more appropriate to record keepers, tradesmen, clerks, and such, and some who can read take pains to conceal the fact. Swords, not words, rule cities, it is said. And some Goreans feel that reading is appropriate only for the less successful, those too poor to have their reading done for them, their letters written for them, and such. Slaves, unless formerly of high caste, are often illiterate. And barbarian slaves are seldom taught to read. This produces the anomaly that many barbarian slaves, who are generally of high intelligence, will be literate in one or more of the barbarian languages, but illiterate in Gorean. Indeed, they are often kept so, deliberately, that they may be all the more helpless, as slaves, and know themselves all the better as mere slaves. Needless to say, all members of my caste, even from childhood, are taught to read. How can one be fully human without the dignity, glory, and power of the written word? Is it not to the world what memory is to the individual? By its means words spoken long ago and faraway may once more be heard. By the magic of such marks, the sorcery of small signs, we converse with those we have never met, touch dreams we could not otherwise share, at a glance rekindle flames which first burned in distant hearts. How else might one hear the tones of distant trumpets, the tramp of vanished armies, ford rivers where now lies cracked earth, witness distant sunsets, and stand wondering on the shores of vanished seas? Pani warriors, those of the high Pani, so to speak, I learn from the stranger, are almost all literate. It is not regarded as demeaning for them. Indeed, some take great pleasure in reading, as others might in music, or conversation. Indeed, it is not unusual for a Pani warrior to compose songs, and poetry.

Demetrion had spoken of Captain Nakamura's "mark," as though he might have been illiterate. This misunderstanding was based on the fact that the Pani transcribe their Gorean in their own way, with their own characters, as do many in the Tahari region. There is a single Gorean language, but it may be transcribed in different ways. A consequence of this is that two individuals might converse easily, while, at the same time, finding one another's written discourse unintelligible.

As the captain had indicated the door, and opened it, I took it that one was free to enter the room. Curious, I did so.

The room was perhaps some twenty-feet square, with a smooth flooring of dark, polished wood. The walls were white. Two narrow, barred windows, set some eight feet from the floor, admitted light, rather as the windows in the general trading area.

There was only one object in the room.

I turned about, toward the door, for I had expected the stranger to be behind me, but I did not see him.

I went to the door, and looked out, into the general area. He was a few feet away, his back turned.

When I had entered the room, the object had stirred, as it could, aware that the door had been opened, and that someone had entered the room.

"Ho!" I called to the stranger, from the door.

He did not turn, though he had doubtless heard me.

I turned back, to the room.

I had seldom seen a woman tied more pathetically, or helplessly. The Pani, I gathered, well knew how to bind a female. I wondered if, in some sense, she could be important. There was not the least possibility of her escaping. She would remain as she was, wholly helpless, at the mercy of any who might find her. I moved the long Pani tunic up, on her left side, to the hip. I saw then that I was mistaken; she was not important. She was well marked, with the *kef*. She was then only a slave. I replaced the tunic so that, as before, the hem was across her ankles. I myself liked a shorter tunic on a slave, as the legs and thighs of a chattel are exciting. Also, the shorter tunic helps her to better understand that she is a slave.

I regarded Callias' gift.

The Pani had tied her kneeling, and bent tightly over. Her head was down, to the floor, and was held in place, in slave humility, by a short, taut cord which ran from her collar back, under her body, to her small, crossed, thonged ankles. In this way any pressure is at the back of the neck, away from the throat. Her small wrists were also crossed, and thonged together behind her back. She was, thus, cruelly and tightly bent over, a small, compact, nicely curved, well-tethered, attractive bundle of slave meat. She had also been blindfolded and gagged.

I again regarded her.

She was totally helpless, and unable to either see or speak.

I went again to the door, and again addressed the stranger. "Ho!" I called. "Come and see your gift!"

He then turned, though I fear reluctantly. Indeed, I had feared he might have left the warehouse.

"What is it?" he called.

"I fear it is negligible," I said. It was, after all, only a slave.

"Good," he said.

He had been denied passage on the *River Dragon*, which had been of desperate importance to him. What then might compensate him for a loss so grievous? A valuable gift would have been, under the circumstances, cruel, or insulting. A negligible gift thus, at least, demonstrated that Lord Nishida and Tarl Cabot understood and respected his feelings, acknowledging, in this way, the accepted disparity involved, that the values involved were incommensurable.

He approached the door, and I stood aside.

He stopped within the threshold. He stood still, there, as though shocked, as in disbelief. He put a hand to the door jamb, on his right, suddenly striking it, to steady himself. He wavered. I feared, for a moment, his knees would buckle. Was this the man, I asked myself, who had faced mutineers, who had stood before a gate at the World's End? He trembled. He tried to speak.

No words emerged. He shook his head, twice, as though to assure himself that what he saw was real.

"Are you well?" I asked. "What is wrong?"

He did not respond to me.

"You need not accept it," I said, "but I think it would be churlish not to do so. When the ship is gone, which will apparently be soon, sell it. It is your right."

"Can it be?" he said. "Can it be!" he cried.

"No one would blame you," I said. "Not Lord Nishida nor Tarl Cabot."

"Aii!" he cried out, suddenly, and flung himself on his knees, beside the object, his dagger free.

"Do not kill it!" I cried, alarmed.

I seized his arm, holding it.

"Do not be enraged!" I said. "Do not take your disappointment out on the slave. She is innocent! She is only a slave. See, she is bound! She is blindfolded! She is gagged! She can help nothing!"

I struggled to hold his arm.

I could not determine if he were laughing, or crying.

"Innocent?" he cried. "A slave, innocent! See her beauty! You say she can help nothing! Every movement, every wisp of her hair, is guilty! Her ankles, her wrists, her bosom, her eyes, her lips, her feet, her hands, each quarter hort of her, each bit of her, each particle of her is guilty! Innocent? A slave, innocent! Does her beauty not wrench the heart of a man! Might not her smile slay with the swiftness of a quarrel? Is her touch not more dangerous than that of the ost? Does she not make a man helpless! Might she not conquer with a whisper, a caress? A kiss might breach the walls of a city, overturn the thrones of Ubars! What net, what web, can compare with her laughter?"

"Do not be concerned," I said. "They are animals, she-sleen! Keep them in collars. Hold the whip over them. They understand the collar, the lash! It is a question of who will be master. They crave strength, not weakness! Freed they are the bitterest and most frustrated, the subtlest and slyest of enemies. In their collars, they are content, appetitious, desirable, grateful, and fulfilled. They find the wholeness of their joy only when they are choiceless, and mastered. Men seek their slaves, and women their masters."

He pulled his arm away from me, and the dagger swiftly parted the cord that held her head down, fastened to her feet.

Her eyes must have been wild, open, but unable to see anything, blocked in the darkness of the blindfold. She made tiny, helpless, piteous, desperate noises, scarcely detectable outside the sturdiness of the gag, its tight, encircling leather perimeters.

The Pani had done their work well.

The slave could neither see nor speak.

"Kneel her up," I said. "What does her collar say?"

As the collar was light, it seemed to me likely that it was a private collar, not a public collar, not, say, a ship's collar.

"Read it," he said.

"I cannot read Pani script," I said. I had seen samples of it amongst the trading tables.

"You can read it," he said.

"Ah!" I said.

I could indeed read it.

"It is in familiar Gorean," I said.

"Tarl Cabot," he said.

"But the gift, surely," I said, "is from Lord Nishida."

"Yes," said the stranger. "He is a *daimyo*."

The collar read as follows: "I am Alcinoë. I belong to Callias, of Jad."

"It was for this," I asked, "that you would have ventured to the World's End, for this, a mere slave?"

"Yes," he said, "for this, a mere slave."

Chapter Thirty-Seven

A Scribe Concludes an Account

"Wine, Master?" said my slave.

"Wine, Master?" said the slave of the stranger.

"Yes," I said.

"Yes," said the stranger.

They served the wine well, kneeling beside the two small tables, behind which we sat, cross-legged, touching the goblet softly, tenderly, appropriately, to their body, then lifting it, and licking and kissing the goblet's rim, as they looked over the rim, into the eyes of their masters, then lowering their heads humbly between their extended arms, both hands on the goblet, proffering the goblets to the masters.

My slave had done well in the market, and I was quite pleased. The ka-la-na, for example, was excellent. I was impressed as she was a barbarian. I wondered if the slave of the stranger would have done as well. For example, when she had been free, given her station, she had probably had few experiences making her way amongst the stalls and baskets.

The ka-la-na was indeed excellent.

I wondered how much that had to do with her market skills, and how much might have had to do with her smiles and the brevity of her tunic. To be sure, for a slave, one supposed a sharp distinction amongst such things might not be warranted.

It had taken Callias only a moment, in the back room of the

warehouse, at the side of the slave, to cut away her bonds, and tear loose the blindfold and gag.

"Master! Master! Master!" she had wept, joyfully, clutching him, melting against him.

"Oh!" she cried.

"Do not break her back," I warned, for he held her with possessive address, with ferocity.

I supposed few free women had ever been so held, unless they were on their way to the marking iron, the collar.

She drew back for a moment and her lips were reddened, and bruised, and the lower lip bleeding, and then she thrust them, again, wildly to his.

"Stand," I said to Callias. "She is a slave. Put her to your feet!"

But, both kneeling, they clung to one another, kissing, each weeping.

I stood to one side, embarrassed, if not dismayed, at this demonstration.

"It is only a slave," I said.

"Yes!" he gasped.

"Are you going to keep it?" I asked.

"Yes," he said, "yes!"

"For a time, at any rate," I said.

"Yes!" he said. "Yes!"

I feared he was not attending much to me.

"I take it," I said, "that that is Alcinoë. That was the name, at any rate, on the collar."

"Yes," he said.

"I gather you do not need now to journey to the World's End, as it, so to speak, has been brought to you."

He mumbled something, but the words were blurred, as he had his mouth on the side of her neck, under her hair.

"I suppose Lord Nishida, and perhaps Tarl Cabot, suspected you had some interest in this slave. Otherwise, certainly her presence here would seem fortuitous. Are you listening to me? She is a well-formed slave, but you could probably trade her in, at a slave house, for a better, given an extra coin or two."

"No," I think he said.

"I do not much care for that tunic," I said, "it is too long, too heavy, too opaque. A scrap of silk would better remind her that she is a slave."

He then put her at arm's length, and looked upon her, enraptured.

"What color are her eyes?" I asked.

But I received no answer, for they were again in one another's arms. Her eyes, as I later ascertained, were brown. It seemed difficult to communicate with Callias at the time.

"Is she white silk?" I asked.

"I do not know," he mumbled.

"Surely you are interested," I said. To be sure, a white-silk slave is quite rare.

I was having not much fortune in conversing with Callias, and so I thought I might try it with the slave. "May she speak?" I asked Callias.

"Yes," he said. "Certainly."

I was alarmed for Callias. Apparently he had given the matter very little thought. In any event, it seemed he accorded her a standing permission to speak. Many masters do, but, of course, with the understanding that that permission is revocable at any time. He had not even made the slave wait, in unsettled apprehension, for a time, to see what might be his decision in the matter. Whereas many masters do accord their girls a standing permission to speak, many others do not, but expect the slave, under normal conditions, at least, to request permission to speak, before speaking. Fewer things make it clearer to a woman that she is truly a slave, than that she may not speak without her master's permission.

"Slave," I said.

"Master?" she said.

"Are you white silk or red silk?"

"White, white, white!" she said, continuing with her kisses, then licking at the shoulder of her master, thereby confessing herself the more his loving, begging beast.

That answer, it seemed to me, was clear enough. I supposed that she had been kept white silk deliberately. I would not have guessed, however, from the sheen of sweat on her body, her avidity, the eagerness of her kisses, the wetness of her hair back against her neck, that she was white silk. As mentioned, white-silk slaves are rare. Often there is not one in a slave house.

Given the look of this slave, who was quite beautiful, though I had seen many better, it seemed unlikely she was truly white silk. Her body, its deliciousness, its vitality, its movements, its pressings and brushings, its piteous closures with, and its desperate touchings against, the master, its pleadings, did not suggest white silk. To be sure, there is a simple test for such things, often conducted by slavers. If she were truly white silk now, it was interesting to speculate on what she might be if red silk, if become the victim of irresistible slave fires. How easily a slave may be managed, and controlled, by such things! Must she wait? Will one choose to satisfy them, and how often, and in what way, and to what extent? A red-silk slave is often deprived of attention for some days, say, four or five, before being brought to the block, that she may writhe in the sawdust, extend her hands pathetically, and howl her need to the buyers.

"Have you had your slave wine?" I inquired.

I thought this a judicious question, and one that might not occur to Callias, and the slave, given the reckless pitch of their activities. A sober head is not amiss in such matters. It also seemed a good question to ask, too, as the slave, if white silk, did not seem destined to long remain in that condition.

"Yes, Master," cried the slave, gasping, "that horrid stuff was forced down my throat shortly after my first collaring, and when I first came aboard the great ship, that of Tersites, and before I was landed, at the World's End, and again, here at Brundisium, before I was brought ashore."

I was well satisfied in this. Indeed, given improvements in slave wine, dating back some years, brewed from the sip root, the first administering of the wine would be sufficient indefinitely, until the administration of a releaser, which removes its effects. The releaser, I am told, unlike slave wine, which is quite bitter, is quite pleasant, rather like a sweet wine, or fruit liqueur. It is usually administered when it is decided that the slave is to be bred. Sometimes slave wine is administered more than once. There could be several reasons for this, for example, one might not know if it has been administered before, and one might wish to make sure of the matter, or one might simply wish additional security in the matter, which seemed to explain the dosage at the World's End, or that before bringing the slave ashore in Brundisium. Too, one might administer it as a punishment, rather like a whipping or a night in close chains. Needless to say, if the slave comes with papers, a certification with respect to slave wine, and the date of its most recent administration, will usually be included in the papers.

"She seems a passionate little thing," I said. "Are you going to breed her?"

"Yes, breed me, breed me, Master," she wept, kissing him.

"I do not think she understands," I said to the stranger, Callias. "Are you going to put her out for breeding?"

"Put me out for breeding?" she said, startled.

"It is a way of increasing one's stock of slaves," I said. "To be sure, there would be a fee for the use of the male slave."

"I could be bred?" she said.

"Of course," I said, "you are slave stock."

This sort of thing, on the whole, however, is usually done by fellows who have many female slaves and do not know them, often the proprietors of large farms. The slaves, then, are bred with the same attention to lines, and properties, as other domestic animals, tarsk, verr, hurt, kaiila, tharlarion, and such. This sort of thing is independent of the sort of thing practiced on the great slave farms. Some bred slaves have pedigrees going back several generations.

"Master, Master," she wept, "do not breed me. Keep me for yourself!"

"He will do as he wishes, slave," I informed her.

Usually, in slave breeding, both the male and female slave are chained in a breeding stall, and hooded, that neither may know the other. The breeding takes place under the supervision of masters, or their agents, and the slaves, of course, are forbidden to speak to one another. If the breeding is successful, the mother is hooded during labor, and never sees the child, which is taken from her, to be tended, and cared for, elsewhere.

"I am so a slave, so a slave!" she said.

I frankly doubted that Callias would put her out for breeding. Indeed, I was beginning to wonder if he would release her from his arms.

"It may be done with you, *kajira*," I assured her.

"Yes, Master," she whispered, frightened. It seemed I had suggested to her a new dimension of being a slave, to which she had hitherto devoted little thought.

"Keep me, keep me for yourself alone," she begged Callias. "I would be yours alone!"

"Do you think you could be a good slave?" I asked her.

"Yes, yes," she said, "Master!"

I supposed this was possible. Most private slaves, after a time, are hopelessly devoted to their masters. Doubtless this has to do with the collar.

It is hard to be in a man's collar and, after a time, not come to be his slave, not merely in law, but in heart. And it is hard to have a woman in one's collar without noticing, after a time, how well she looks on her knees before you.

"I fear, dear Callias," I said to the stranger, "that you are weak."

"I?" he said.

"Do not forget that this curvaceous little thing you have in your arms is not a free woman, nothing warranting respect and dignity, but a beast, a worthless slave, only that."

"Is she not lovely," said Callias.

"I have seen many better," I said, "on the shelves, in the cages, on the block, even in secondary markets."

"Surely she is the most beautiful woman in the world," said Callias.

"Not to everyone, surely," I said.

"Who better?" he asked, annoyed.

"Thousands," I said.

"Do you have an example?" he asked.

"Certainly," I said. "What of the barbarian in *The Sea Sleen*, the slender brunette, the exquisite paga girl, whom you had decamisk herself before you?"

"She cannot even speak Gorean properly," said Callias.

"She can learn," I said, now myself annoyed.

"Let her be whipped, regularly," said Callias, "until her diction becomes passable."

"Perhaps your Alcinoë could do with a bout with the whip," I said.

"Master!" protested Alcinoë.

"Did I hear a slave speak without permission?" I asked.

"No," he said, "she may speak as she will, until such permission might be revoked."

"It does not seem to me that she has had the time to earn such a privilege," I said.

"I grant it," he said.

"Too quickly, too easily," I suggested.

"Surely you see," he said, "how lovely she is!"

"There are many better," I said, "for example, the barbarian at *The Sea Sleen*, who heard your story."

"She cannot even begin to compare with Alcinoë," he said. "And she is not even Gorean."

"I think she is Gorean now," I said. "She is now no more than another collared Gorean slave girl."

"You admit she is beautiful," he said.

"Yes," I said. From the tone of his voice I thought it well to concede this. Besides, I supposed she was beautiful.

"Very beautiful," he said.

"Perhaps," I said, "but now she is sweaty and heated, and her hair is wet, and there are still thong marks on her ankles and wrists."

I noted, too, that her body was imbued with desire. To be sure, this adds to the appeal of a slave.

"Perhaps," I said, "you are thinking of freeing her."

"No," cried the slave, frightened. "Do not free me, Master! Keep me! I am your slave! I belong to you! Your collar has been put on my neck! It is locked on me, and I cannot remove it! But I do not want to remove it! I want it there for all to see, that all may know that I am a slave, and that you are my master! I love my collar! I am proud of it! I want to be owned! I want to be possessed, utterly, and without qualification. I know myself, by beauty, by blood, by thought, by dreams, by needs, to be naturally the property of men, and it is your property I wish to be!"

He held her out, again, from him, both of them on their knees, on the planks of the dark, polished floor.

"What do you see?" she laughed.

"A slave," he said.

"Yes, Master!" she laughed, and leaned forward, as she could, straining to reach him with her lips.

"I am not a fool," he said.

"No, Master!" she said.

This was doubtless an allusion to the well-known proverb, that only a fool frees a slave girl.

"All my life," he said, "I have waited for such a slave."

"All my life," she said, "I have waited for such a master."

"So why, then, should I free you?" he asked.

"You should not," she said.

"I will not," he said.

"A girl is grateful," she whispered.

"Some women are too beautiful, too desirable, to free," he said.

"It is my hope," she said, "that I am such a one."

"The collar proclaims you such," he said.

"The heart of an eager and willing, but choiceless, slave rejoices," she said.

"You understand," he said, "the meaning of your condition?"

"Yes, Master," she said.

"Unquestioning and instantaneous obedience?"

"Yes, Master."

"Subjectability to discipline, even to the whip and chain?"

"Yes, Master."

"The slave is not a free woman," he said.

"No, Master."

"What, then, is the duty of a slave?"

"Master?"

"To be a dream of pleasure to her master."

"I will strive to be pleasing to my master," she said.

"And if you fail?"

"Then I trust that the master will better train me, will correct my behavior, and see to my improvement," she said.

"It will be so," he said.

"I will do my best," she said.

"No one can ask more than that," he said.

"Such words fall delightfully on the ears of a slave," she said.

"But it will be I, and I alone," he said, "who will decide whether or not you have done your best."

"I understand, Master," she said.

"Beware, my friend, dear Callias," I said. "I suspect you are in danger."

"How so?" said he.

"I do not claim, of course," I said, "that you are subject to this danger."

"What danger?" said he.

"Some men, doubtless fools and weaklings," I said, "are particularly subject to this danger, the danger of becoming enamored of a slave. It is quite enough to lust for them, desire them, master them, and rule them, quite enough to rope and chain them, and pleasure yourself with them, as frequently and variously, and as inordinately, as you wish, and derive from their conquest, their helplessness, and submission the thousand satisfactions and delights, the triumphs, of the mastery, of owning and governing such a property, of enjoying such a vulnerable, shapely beast, but it is quite another to care for one."

"Do you think," he asked, "that I am a fool and weakling?"

"In general, no," I said, "but men wiser and stronger than you, I am sure, and men perhaps wiser and stronger than I, have succumbed to eyes bright with tears, a strand of hair brushed piteously aside, a faltering syllable, a trembling lip."

"But she is Alcinoë," he said.

"And Tula is Tula, and Lana is Lana, and Iris is Iris, and Lita is Lita, and so on," I said. "They are all soft, subtle, cunning, dangerous beasts."

"You feel I am in danger?"

"That is my surmise," I said.

"Surely I am not uniquely in danger?"

"Doubtless not," I said. "But see that the stern resolution which takes the beast from the block does not melt when it lies at your slave ring. Deprive the she-sleen of her domination and she will become confused, and bitter, denied her coveted meaning as your beast. She will turn on you. She will scorn your weakness, and mock your frailty. Unmastered she is an angry leaf in the wind, without direction, no better than a free woman, flung about, tormented and unfulfilled. She longs to obey, to love and serve. Deny her this and you deny her to herself. She understands will, and the whip. See that she is never in doubt as to either. The slave is never content until she lies naked at the feet of a man."

There was then a knocking at the jamb of the open portal, and Captain Nakamura appeared in the opening. He carried with him a small package.

The stranger rose to his feet.

Doubtless he was embarrassed to be found on his knees, a slave in his arms. Certainly I trusted so.

"Do you accept the gift?" asked Captain Nakamura.

"Yes," said the stranger.

"I am sure I can find others, who will buy it from you, if you wish," he said.

"No," said the stranger.

"Lord Nishida and Tarl Cabot, the tarnsman," he said, "have included some tokens with the gift, which, as you are accepting it, I may present to you."

"My thanks," said the stranger.

"One is a slave garment," he said, "which seems more locally cultural than her current tunic, and the other is a coiling of chain and rings, which, I am told, is a sirik."

The stranger accepted the small package, a slave tunic, within which was wrapped a sirik.

"Do you wish her current tunic back?" asked the stranger.

"No," said the captain, smiling, "though we have purchased some local slaves, for transportation to the islands."

I did not understand the smile of Captain Nakamura, as he seemed, on the whole, a rather undemonstrative, reserved fellow. To be sure, I am informed by the stranger that these fellows are much freer in emotion, teasing, joking, and such, when amongst one another.

The slave, who had her head down, I thought was smiling, as well.

I did not understand the meaning of this, either.

The first thing I would have done was discard the long, heavy, opaque Pani tunic, which seemed quite inappropriate for a slave, at least in good weather, given what a slave was.

Let it be cast away!

Captain Nakamura then bowed, excusing himself, but paused, at the door. "It is my understanding," he said, "from a cripple at the castle, a man named Rutilius of Ar, that the slave, Alcinoë, may have value in Ar."

"Oh?" said the stranger.

The slave, on her knees, turned white.

"It is his claim that she is the former Lady Flavia of Ar, a fugitive, one for whom a sizable bounty would be paid. I was to arrange for her delivery to Ar, collect the bounty, and divide it, on my return, with him."

"Interesting," said the stranger.

"In any event," said the captain, "the slave is yours."

"Yes," said the stranger, "she is mine."

The tone of his voice, I conjectured, would leave no doubt in the slave's mind but what she was indeed his.

It would be up to him, whether or not she would be taken to Ar.

With another short, courteous bow, Captain Nakamura withdrew.

I was apprehensive.

The attitude of the stranger seemed to have changed.

Outside the tall window a cloud must have passed before *Tor-tu-Gor*, and the room seemed suddenly, ominously dark, and the slave little more than a shadow between us.

But the simple words of Captain Nakamura, I thought, even more than a darkening cloud, had engloomed the chamber. It was as though they had enkindled a mysterious lamp, a lamp of memory, which, when lit, emitted not light, but darkness, fear, and cold. Where there had been warmth, light, joy, touching, and love, there was now a dampness, as of the dungeon, a darkness as of caverns, a polar chill, the coldness of fearful order, of propriety, of a vision of justice, as unwelcome as the touch of a snake at night.

The stranger handed me the scrap of cloth, which would be a typical slave tunic. He retained the sirik.

I myself had no doubt that the slave, appropriately on her knees before her master, the stranger, had once been highly placed in Ar, and perhaps a conspirator in the treason that had betrayed that city into the hands of Cos, Tyros, and several of the free companies.

The stranger looked down on the slave, and she shrank

small before him. I sensed then that his memory swept him back to Ar, and that, for a moment, he saw before him not a loving, eager, precious possession, who might be sought even at the World's End, but a traitress and fugitive, one vain and treacherous, one who, when free, had betrayed her Home Stone, abused power, and turned even on her supposed friend, whom she had honored as her Ubara.

"Strip," he said to her.

"Master?" she said.

"Instantly," he said.

"Yes, Master," she said, frightened, and hastened to pull away, over her head, the Pani tunic.

He then dangled before her frightened eyes the loops of chain, with its rings.

"I am no longer she whom you despise," she said. "I am different! I am now in a collar! I am only a collared slave, and yours, my master! I am contrite! I am penitent! I have learned softness, deference, humility, vulnerability, giving, truth, honesty, kindness, caring, service, awareness of others!"

She looked up at him.

With a movement of his foot, he brushed the Pani tunic to the side. I thought it made an unusual noise, sliding on the boards.

"Stand," he said.

"Surely you care for me, a little!" she said. "And know, Callias, of Jad, that I am yours, not just to the collar, but to the heart."

He reached down, and struck her twice, sharply, first by the palm of his right hand, and then by the back of his right hand.

"The slave," he said, "does not soil the name of a free man by putting it on her slave lips."

I supposed she had been aware of this protocol, that the slave does not address a free person by his name, but, perhaps, in the stress of the moment, this simplicity had escaped her. In any event, such lapses are not permitted in a slave.

"Forgive me," she said.

He motioned for her to rise, and she did so, and stood before him, though I feared she might fall.

"Prepare to be siriked," he said.

She put her hand, frightened, before her face, and then, suddenly, turned, and fled to the opposite wall, against which she stood, the palms of her hands at the side of her head, her belly to the wall.

"Return," he said, evenly.

Numbly, she turned, and retraced her steps, and then stood before him, head down, small before his size and power.

Then she raised her head, and said, "Sirik me."

The neck ring was snapped about her throat first, rather like a Turian collar. Next her small wrists were clasped in the wrist rings, each at the terminus of the short, horizontal chain, attached to the vertical chain dangling from the collar, which vertical chain, continuing, looped down to the floor where, attached to it was the second horizontal chain, each end of which terminated in an ankle ring. Two snaps, and she was ankle bound. The sirik is a lovely and practical chaining arrangement. The two horizontal chains may be used in conjunction with the vertical chain, or independently, in which case one might have wrist shackles, in which the wrists might be confined before or behind the slave, and ankle shackles. Her wrists, now confined before her, were some six inches apart, and her ankles were something like a foot apart, permitting her to shuffle, or walk with small, careful, measured steps, but not allowing her to run. The vertical chain may function independently, as well, as a chain leash, or a tethering device, by means of which the slave might be secured to a slave ring, a tree, a stanchion, or such. The length of the vertical chain, which may loop to the floor when the slave's hands are lowered, is also long enough to permit her, her hands lifted, to feed herself.

He regarded the slave before him, small, naked, siriked.

"The visage of Master is terrible," she said. "Is Master angry? Does Master despise his slave? How different he is now from but moments before. She would that Captain Nakamura had not spoken of past things, of fearful things, of things long since regretted. I am not different from what I was, but moments ago, in Master's arms."

He was silent. His fists were clenched.

"It seems Master has recalled another woman," she said, "the vain, deceitful, greedy, traitress, Flavia of Ar."

"Yes," he said.

"She who once was that woman now stands before you," she said, "naked, and siriked."

"It is thus," said the stranger, "that Marlenus prefers to have his captives brought before him, naked and chained, then to be flung to their knees before his throne."

"Yes, Master," she said.

He regarded her, I fear, with ferocity.

"I am naked and chained," she said. "I am helpless. You can do with me as you wish. I cannot escape. I cannot prevent you from taking me to the restored Marlenus now, and putting me before him, if you will, my knees on the tiles, before his throne."

"Cry out now," he said, angrily, "with all the pride, fury, and rage of the free woman.

"Were I free," she said, "I would not do so, but would rather beg to be shown mercy, and beg instead that you would make me your slave."

"You are such?" he said, scornfully.

"Yes, Master," she said.

"Slave," he sneered.

"Yes, Master," she said, humbly.

"Cry out," he demanded, "angrily, loudly, insolently! Threaten me! Denounce me!"

"Do you not understand, Master," she said. "I cannot do so. That is all behind me. See my collar. See my mark! I am now a slave!"

"Yes," he said, "it is true. I doubt then that you, now a slave, would be impaled as high as a free person, for that might demean them, you, say, some seven or eight feet, not twenty or thirty, as they, to show your lowliness."

"I am sure," she said, "in the end, it makes little difference."

He folded his arms, and regarded her.

"Despise me if you wish," she said, "but despise me not as the Lady Flavia of Ar, for I am no longer she. Despise me then, if you must, as a slave, the slave that I am."

"You should be taken to Ar," he said.

"Take me to Ar," she said.

"I do despise you," he said, "but not for your collar; rather for what you once were."

"And no longer am," she said.

"But were once!"

"But no longer!"

"You should be taken to Ar," he said.

"So," she said, "I am to be taken to Ar?"

"Perhaps," he said.

"Are there no better things to do with a slave?" she asked.

She was cuffed, sharply.

"Forgive me, Master," she said.

"Ar would be too easy for you," he said, "for one who was once the Lady Flavia."

"Master will not take his slave to Ar?" she said.

He was silent for a time, regarding her. Her head was down. Then he said, "No."

"Master?" she said, looking up.

"There are better things to do with a slave," he said.

"That is my hope," she said.

"Long ago, on the ship," he said, "I told you that I did not care for gold washed in blood."

"That pleases me," she said.

"And thereby I lose myself a fortune," he said.

"But obtain thereby," she said, "a much greater fortune, that of being yourself."

"Slut, slave, vile thing," he said.

"I will try to please my master," she said.

His eyes were hard.

"Be kind," she said, frightened.

There was a small sound, as the links of the sirik rustled.

Not every man, of course, will accept bounty, particularly on a woman. Callias, of Jad, was a warrior, an oarsman, at one time an officer. Bounty hunters are commonly low warriors, men without Home Stones, brigands, assassins, villains, thieves, reprobates, the recklessly impecunious, gamblers, the dishonored. I had not thought that Callias was such a man, and my judgment was now vindicated. To be sure, what now stood stripped and siriked before him had once been the Lady Flavia of Ar. Nothing could change that.

The stranger did not care for gold washed in blood.

Should he then return her to Ar, that she might suffer at the hands of an alien justice?

What good could be served by such an act?

Many are the masks of justice, and behind those masks there may be no face, only a choice of masks.

He who has power chooses a mask to his liking.

How fiercely the masks scowl at one another.

I thought the slave was right, that the Lady Flavia of Ar was gone, that she had vanished, with the snapping of a collar. What remained might be named, and dealt with, as one pleased.

Still the lovely slave between us had once been the Lady Flavia of Ar. That could not be gainsaid.

"May I kneel?" she asked.

The stranger nodded, and she sank to her knees, gratefully. I did not know if she could have managed to stand much longer.

"At least," I said to the stranger, "you have recalled the nature of the slave."

"Yes," he said. "She was once Flavia of Ar."

"And more broadly, and to the point, and more importantly, I trust, putting aside her past, which we may ignore for the moment," I said, "you have recollected the nature of a slave, as a slave."

"Yes," he said.

"Good," I said. "Now, I trust, you have overcome your foolishness, or weakness."

"What foolishness, what weakness?" he asked, not pleasantly.

"At least," I said, "the remote possibility of caring for a slave."

"Have no fear," he said. "I have eluded that danger, if ever it was a danger, which very thought seems absurd. All such risks, however unlikely or tenuous, are put aside."

"Good," I said. "Then you will see her, and treat her, as what she is, a slave."

"Yes," he said. "As worthless, meaningless collar meat."

"Precisely," I said.

"But, in her case," he said, "there is something in addition, that will add to my pleasure."

"What?" I asked.

"That she was once the Lady Flavia of Ar."

The slave, head down, siriked, moaned in misery.

"The Lady Flavia of Ar," I said, "—who is now mere collar meat."

"Yes," he said.

"Do you hate her?" I asked.

"I must try," he said.

"For what she once was?" I asked.

"Yes," he said.

"Do not hate me, Master!" she wept. "I love you! I love you!"

"Liar!" he said, angrily.

"I may not lie!" she cried. "I am a slave!"

He drew back his hand, and she shrank down, but he did not strike her.

He placed his boot on her shoulder and thrust her to the floor, on her side. She crawled back to him, on her belly, and, putting down her head, kissed the boot which had spurned her to the floor.

"You have been white silk long enough," he told her.

"Master?" she said.

"On your knees," he said, "former Lady Flavia of Ar, facing away from me, your head to the floor."

With a rustle of chain the slave obeyed.

"So, Master?" she said.

"Yes," he said.

"Master well humbles the former Lady Flavia of Ar," she said. "But Alcinoë, the slave, hopes that she will be found pleasing by her master."

"Return shortly," said the stranger to me, and I left the room. I heard a jerking of chain, and heard the slave cry out, startled. Then I heard her cry out, "Master! My Master!"

I walked about the trading area, which, if anything, was even busier than before. Against one wall there was a coffle of stripped, kneeling slaves who, I supposed, had been brought in by a dealer, for the inspection of the Pani. From something Captain Nakamura had said earlier, I gathered they had already made certain purchases. The girls were in neck coffle, and had been placed in the position of pleasure slaves, which seemed to be the sort of slaves in which the Pani, for their various purposes, were interested. When a girl was regarded, she would lift her head, and say, "Buy me, Master." I suspected, however, that few of the girls were interested in being bought by the newcomers, so strange and unfamiliar to them, within whose purview they found themselves scrutinized.

I returned to the open portal of the back room, and entered. "It is as I feared," I said.

"Oh?" said Callias.

He was seated near a wall, that in which the portal was, cross-legged. The slave was lying near him, lovingly, on her side. I noted blood on her leg, which suggested that, however unlikely it seemed, the Pani had actually kept her white silk. In that I suspected the hand of Lord Nishida and Tarl Cabot, the tarnsman. I noted that she was no longer confined in the sirik, and its coils lay to one side, near the cast-aside Pani tunic. Her head was against one of his legs. She looked at me, but dreamily. It was almost as though I were not there.

"Does it hurt?" I asked.

"Very little, Master," she said. She drew up her legs more.

"I am not too pleased," I said.

"Oh?" said Callias, seemingly distracted.

"Next," I said, "I suppose you will grant her a tunic."

"I suppose so," he said. "That should make it less likely she would be stolen."

"Am I likely to be stolen?" she asked Callias.

"You are that beautiful," he told her.

"Master," she said, kissing his knee.

"Not the Pani tunic," I said.

"Certainly not," he said.

The small slave tunic brought into the room earlier by Captain Nakamura, in which the sirik had been wrapped, lay to the side.

"You will, at least, I trust," I said, "see to it that she works for that tunic, perhaps for several weeks."

As an animal, a slave is not entitled to clothing. If permitted clothing, it must be understood as a gift from her master. To be sure, most slaves are clothed, particularly in public. Free women are quite adamant on that point. If it is appropriate to speak of a compromise in these matters, presumably it would be that the slave is clothed, but as a slave. Here we have something of an agreement, or compromise, between free women and masters, namely, that the garmenture of the slave must be clearly indicative of her bondage, and, secondly, that the slave, as she is usually the property of a man, may be dressed for his pleasure. The usual outcome of this interaction is the slave tunic. The camisk is less acceptable to free women, but they reconcile themselves to the camisk on the grounds that the female slave is so worthless that it is acceptable for her to be camisked. The female serving slave of a free woman is likely to be modestly tunicked, whereas the slave of a free man is likely to be tunicked in such a manner as to make it clear to other men that she was worth buying.

The stranger glanced down to the slave, lying at his right knee. "Would you like a tunic?" he asked.

"Oh, yes, Master," she said, "very much."

"You," I said, "as far as I know, do not even have a slave whip."

"That is true," he said.

"I assure Master," said the slave, "he does not need a whip."

"No," he said. "One must have a whip."

"But for what possible purpose?" asked the slave.

"Guess," he said.

"Yes, Master," she said. "What is Master doing?"

The stranger was removing his dagger belt, from which he removed, as well, the dagger and its sheath. He then buckled the belt, so that it constituted a closed loop.

"Master?" said the slave.

"This will do," he said, "until I obtain a proper whip."

"I see," she said, uneasily.

"And now," he said, "I think I shall begin your training."

"My training?" she said.

"Surely you know that slaves, as many other sorts of animals, are trained."

He then tossed the looped, buckled belt across the room, to the far wall.

"Fetch it," he said, "on all fours. Do not touch it with your hands. Bring it back in your teeth."

"Yes, Master," she said.

It pleased me to see the former Lady Flavia of Ar cross the room on all fours, bend down, pick up the belt in her teeth, and then turn about, and return, on all fours, to her master, the belt dangling from her teeth.

He removed the belt from her teeth. "You may now," he said, "show the belt deference."

"I do not understand," she said.

"We do not yet have a whip," he said. "Lick and kiss it."

This was an analogy to the simple ceremony of kissing the whip, wherein the slave demonstrates her bondage and submission, acknowledging and accepting her subjection to the mastery, a common symbol of which is the whip. Similar things may be done with rope, the chain, slave bracelets, and such.

The former Lady Flavia of Ar addressed herself to the belt of her master.

"She seems tentative," I said.

"I think you are right," he said.

The slave looked at me, angrily, but then her master's hand was in her hair, twisting it, and she cried out in misery, and his other hand was up, the looped belt in it. "No!" she cried, her head held in place. He then gave her two sharp strokes with the looped belt.

Tears sprang to her eyes.

He then put the belt again to her lips, and she began to kiss and lick the belt more seriously.

"I hate you!" she said to me.

"I think she does not understand what is required," I said to the stranger.

She then received two more strokes of the looped belt.

Then, fervently, desperately, the frightened slave, Alcinoë, the slave of Callias, of Jad, a Cosian, addressed herself to the belt of her master.

"That is much better," I said. "I suspect you are beginning to comprehend."

"Thank you, Master," she said.

"Now," I said, "with your lips and tongue, as the most helplessly needful of all women, as a slave, make love to the belt of your master. In kissing it, tenderly, you express your gratitude that you, only a slave, have been permitted to touch a belonging of your master. Too, in this way, you express your devotion for the master, your reverence for him, perhaps unnoticed by the master, by tenderly and gratefully kissing even a belt, even a tunic or sandal, of the master. In licking it, slowly, you express yourself, and your bondage, that you submit yourself to him wholly, without reservation. In licking it slowly, and sensuously, you express your passion, and need, your desire, that you would serve him intimately, as the least of slaves, as the readiest of aroused, owned beasts."

She suddenly looked at me, with recognition, with understanding in her eyes. "Thank you, Master," she whispered. "I think I understand! Perhaps I was ready for such things. Perhaps I wanted them, and longed for them! Is that possible? I change! I have changed! Such acts change me! No wonder they are forbidden to free women! How they make us slaves! How right they seem! So right, so right! Inwardly I am different! How can one do such things, and live so, without becoming a slave? How close I am now to myself! In such acts I am changed! They show me to myself! They open doors to my secret heart! How can I understand these emotions, their depth? How happy I am, and how helpless! How helpless I am in their grasp! I feel so slave! I am so slave!"

She turned her head, wildly, to Callias, her master. "I heat, Master," she said. "I am heated! I flame! Please, please, Master!"

With a great cry, he seized her in his arms, turned her, and flung her beneath him, across the scrap of tunic which had been brought to the room earlier by Captain Nakamura. I thought it well, then, to exit the room. I left the door open, behind me, however, as she was not a free woman, but a slave.

Eventually the eighteenth bar sounded.

I secured one of the public lamps, and reentered the room.

"I do not think," I said, "that the *River Dragon* will make the morning tide. Commerce proceeds apace, and ever new Merchants, now even from Market of Semris, arrive each Ahn. The warehouse will be closed soon, to reopen at dawn. I think a day or so more will secure such supplies as Captain Nakamura never anticipated, and would not choose to leave without. Yet I expect him, still, to leave as soon as matters are well concluded."

"I would see him sail," said the stranger.

"Perhaps the day after tomorrow," I said.

"What do you think of my slave?" he asked.

I lifted the lamp.

She was now tunicked, but not in the lengthy tunic of the

Pani, but now, rather, in the tunic which had been brought in earlier by Captain Nakamura, that within the folds of which had been the coils of the sirik.

Alcinoë twirled before me.

What a vain thing she was, but are not they all? Surely, given their beauty, their desirability, they are entitled to a little vanity, or, indeed, I suppose, to a large measure of that sometimes annoying, but generally endearing, charming quality. Free women have their vanity, sometimes extravagantly so, so why not a slave, as well? And, indeed, is not a slave even more entitled to vanity than a free woman? She, after all, has been looked upon by men, and found fit for collaring. To be sure, the slave is well advised to conceal her vanity in the presence of a free woman.

"She is quite pretty," I said. "The tunic is a bit long, is it not."

"I think so," said Callias.

This would not be unusual, of course, as few tunics are tailored to an individual slave. Given the common looseness, and drapery, of a tunic, a number of different slaves might wear the same tunic, which would be indifferently fetching on most of them. Many slaves, of course, once they have a tunic, will do their small, mysterious things to the garment in such a way that it seems designed for themselves alone. Some masters, too, of course, will take their slave to one of the Cloth Workers, and have one or more tunics altered to, or even made for, the particular slave.

Alcinoë looked at me, startled. I gathered it had not occurred to her that the tunic might be too long.

"Many Merchants," I said, "have frequented the warehouse since morning. If I were the harbor master I would put them out. Why should they hold a position that long at a table? Others clamor for their turn. One would think they were doing kaissa, or stones, not buying and selling. In any event, venders of comestibles, biscuits, candy, fruit, and such, with their carts and trays, have been about, and doing their business, too. I suggest we leave this room, if you two can manage that, buy something to eat, I will pay, as you have no money, and then go to my domicile, get some sleep, and return, if you wish, in the morning."

The stranger rose to his feet.

"What have you two been doing all this time?" I asked.

"Waiting for master," laughed Alcinoë.

I saw this as an excellent argument not to give a slave a standing permission to speak.

"What do you think?" said Callias.

"One thing, I see," I said, lifting the lamp higher, to the better view Alcinoë, "she has spent at least some of the time becoming more beautiful."

"Yes," said Callias.

The slave looked down, bashfully.

Happiness makes a woman more beautiful. Even a plain woman who is happy is beautiful.

"I think we had better go," I said. "Gather up the sirik, and I will discard the Pani tunic, wretched garment, in the garbage, as we leave."

"I would not do so, if I were you," said Alcinoë, who knelt, understandably enough, as she was addressing a free person.

"You do not like the garment, I hope," I said.

"I think it is horrid," she said.

"Good," I said, and bent down to pick up the tunic.

"Please wait, Masters," she said. "Perhaps you should examine the tunic."

I suddenly recalled some puzzles I had had, pertaining to that distressing garment, its thickness, its opacity, its length, long and heavy, even for a Pani tunic, a smile on the face of Captain Nakamura, and a smile on the features of the slave, the sound it had made when it was brushed across the floor by Callias' boot.

"It is my conjecture," she said, "that Lord Nishida and Master Tarl Cabot, who commands the tarn cavalry of Lord Temmu, would not have been likely, as an expression of their esteem and gratitude to my master, to send him so negligible a gift as a mere slave, and one untrained, too."

"No!" said Callias. "You are a thousand times more than enough. They must know that. You are the world to me!"

Beware, Callias, I thought, beware.

"A slave is grateful to be so esteemed by her Master," she said, "but Alcinoë is well aware that she is only a slave, and that her monetary value is determined only by what masters will pay for her."

"She is right," I said.

"I would pay the world for her," he said.

"You do not have the world," I told him. "And, unless you have not been candid with me, you do not have even a tarsk-bit."

"And poor Alcinoë," she said, "as a gift, may be worth but, say, five silver tarsks."

"Closer to two," I conjectured.

"Oh?" she said.

"Yes," I said.

"And thus, if such things are so, five, or perhaps two," she said, "the gift of Lord Nishida and Tarl Cabot, the tarnsman, would seem surprisingly modest, particularly for those who have much they might bestow."

"No matter," said Callias.

"Thus," she said, "perhaps masters might examine the tunic, before disposing of it."

We looked upon the tunic, lying crumpled on the floor, to the side.

"Close the door," said Callias. "Bring the lamp closer."

I closed the door, and brought the lamp to where Callias sat, putting it on the floor beside him.

Alcinoë fetched the Pani tunic, knelt before her master, spread the tunic before her, lifted it in two hands, and then, her head down, between her extended arms, proffered it to her master.

"Now a gift of true worth," she said, "is presented by a slave to her master, with the affection and regard of Lord Nishida and Tarl Cabot, commander of the tarn cavalry of Lord Temmu."

"You are the gift of true worth," said Callias to the slave.

"Yes, yes," I said, "I am sure of it, but let us examine the tunic."

"It would be well," said the slave, "to open the lining carefully, and examine every inch of the tunic."

"Have no fear," I said. "Friend Callias, loan me your dagger."

"What is here?" Callias asked the slave.

"Some coin," she said, "tiny golden tarsks, almost like beads, which are light and consume little space, but mostly pearls, and jewels."

"How much is here?" I asked.

"Slaves are not told such things," she said. "But I do not think masters will be disappointed."

"Callias," I said, freeing a pearl from the garment, "I think you are a rich man."

"Even if it is nothing," he said, placing a hand on the arm of the slave kneeling beside him, "I am already a rich man."

The slave kissed his hand.

"Be serious," I said. "Here is another!"

"How much did you know of this?" asked Callias of the slave.

"I knew, of course, that the garment contained such things," she said, "but I did not know how many or of what worth."

"Curiosity is not becoming to a *kajira*," I said.

"But not unknown, I assure you," she said.

"True," I said.

"I was, of course, to guard it with my life," she said.

"What if you were taken to Ar, as I suspect you deserve," I said.

"One supposes," she said, "that the garment, if handled, would betray its secrets."

"It might have been cast aside," I said.

"I prevented that this evening," she said, "and, in any case, would prevent it."

"Even were you on your way to Ar?"

"Of course," she said.

"Why?" I asked.

"I love my master," she said. "It was intended for him, and it was my charge to see that he received it. I wanted all that was good for him. He might thus add it to a fugitive's bounty. Of what value is wealth to one on the impaling spear? And if my master does not want me, what matters the manner of our separation? Why not the impaling spear?"

"I want you," said Callias, "more than all the wealth in the world. I would never let you go. I would die for you!"

"Do not forget I am only a slave," she said. "That is what I am. And I would be kept as one."

"And you will be," he said, "even to the chain and whip!"

"I will try to be pleasing to my master," she said.

"Fully pleasing," he said.

"Yes," she said, kissing him, "fully pleasing."

"From the first moment I saw you," he said, "I wanted to own you."

"And from the first moment I saw you," she said, "I wanted to belong to you."

"You do," he said.

"Yes, Master," she said.

"Love slave," he whispered.

"Love master," she said.

"I could slip half of this into my purse," I said, "while you two are carrying on, as it is said, dizzy on the heights of desire, wandering on the roads of delight, lost in the forests of rapture, drunk on the wines of love, swimming about in one another's eyes, and such. Repulsive. Offensive!"

"Perhaps," said Callias, "you, too, one day, will as gladly lose your way."

"You are fortunate," I said, "that my caste codes discourage robbing armed warriors."

"How does it proceed?" asked Callias.

"I am not of the Street of Coins," I said, "but I think it is clear that you are a wealthy man. I have a hundred golden tarsks here, a hundred pearls, a hundred jewels, of various sorts and sizes."

"That is a great deal," said Callias.

"This one pearl," I said, "I would estimate at a dozen silver tarsks."

"So much?" he said.

"It would buy six slaves such as Alcinoë," I said, "on the open market."

"She is much better than that," he said. "Perhaps four," he speculated.

"Master!" protested the slave.

I spread the tunic on the floor, between myself and Callias, the slave to the side.

"I think that is all," I said, "as I have opened and removed the lining, shaken it, fingered every square hort of the garment, and bitten and chewed each square hort as well, to make doubly sure. On the other hand, the tunic is yours, as is she who was its occupant, and if I have missed anything, it should turn up eventually, when it is unraveled into its least threads."

I thrust the sorted objects across the floor toward Callias, and he scooped them up, and placed them in his wallet.

"I am hungry," he said.

"Let me buy from the vendors," I said. "The smallest tarsk here, the smallest pearl or jewel, would attract attention."

"I think not," he said, "given the trading."

"Exchange no more than one," I said, "and let it be as though it were your last, your only one."

"Very well," he said.

"I, too, am hungry," I said. "What of you, girl?"

"I, too, Master," she said.

I opened the door. Outside the floor was still crowded.

"What of the slave?" I said. "Are you going to put her in the sirik?"

"No," he said. Then he turned to the slave. "You will not attempt to escape, will you?" he inquired.

"No, Master," she said. "And Master well knows," she said, as she touched her collar, and then her left thigh, and lifted, a little, the hem of her tunic, "there is no escape for the slave girl."

"True," he said.

"And she wishes no escape," she said.

"I am famished," I said.

We then left the back room, and, a bit later, Callias had exchanged one of the tiny beadlike golden tarsks for nine silver tarsks, ninety-nine copper tarsks, and a hundred tarsk-bits, at one of the changing tables maintained in the warehouse by the harbor administration, to facilitate trading.

I might have been concerned here, but the warehouse seemed filled with bulging purses, and the counting boards on several of the long tables were so filled that coins lay loose, spilled beside them.

At that point the nineteenth bar sounded.

The house would close at the twentieth Ahn, to open in the morning, with the first light. Several Merchants, I did not doubt, would arrive well before dawn.

"As I recall," said the stranger, "you were going to buy us some food."

"Yes," I said.

"That should be easy, as there are still several vendors about."

"Yes," I said. I did have some tarsk-bits in my purse, and I had certainly volunteered to buy something to eat. On the other hand, that was at a time, as I recalled, when I thought the stranger had not a tarsk-bit to his name. He was now a wealthy man, quite possibly the most wealthy man in Brundisium not of the Merchant caste. I suddenly began to suspect something of the economic dispositions, calculations, and shrewdness of the extremely wealthy, which shrewdness, and such, apparently, it did not take long to acquire. After all, I thought to myself, too, he is a Cosian, and everyone knows what Cosians are like, though to be perfectly honest I had never given much thought up to that point as to Cosians in general. Still, he was not a bad fellow. And some fellows are changed by a single tarn disk, so there was some excuse for him.

"Wait here," I said.

In a few moments I had made my way to a vendor's cart and purchased some wrappings of food. I spent a bit more than I had intended, an extra tarsk-bit or two, but, in this manner, I thought, I might demonstrate the munificence of the Caste of Scribes, apparently a munificence well beyond that of warriors, mariners, the common oarsman, the newly rich, and such, a munificence, to be sure, commonly exercised within judicious limits.

"Where is your master?" I asked Alcinoë.

She was kneeling where I had left her and the stranger.

"I do not know, Master," she said.

"You are not secured," I said.

"No, Master," she said.

Usually one does not leave a good-looking slave alone, unless properly secured. There were, at the wall, for example, some slave rings, to which more than one slave was chained.

"What is going on?" I asked. "Was there trouble?"

"I do not know, Master," she said. "I do not think there is trouble. My Master said for me to wait here, and we might begin to eat."

"Is he coming back?" I asked. "The warehouse will close shortly."

"I am very hungry," she said.

I gave her one of the wrappings of food, and took another.

After a time, as the stranger had not returned, and the warehouse was to close in a bit, we divided the last wrapping of food between us.

Let Callias take that, I thought.

Still I was uneasy.

"I fear for your master," I said.

"He is armed," she said.

"What business would take him from your side?" I asked.

"I do not know," she said.

"It must be of great importance," I said.

"I would like to think so," she said, licking her fingers.

"The closing bar will ring shortly," I said. "It will be the twentieth Ahn. We will be expelled."

Already some of the tables were closing.

Some men were exiting the warehouse.

"Where is he?" I asked. "I am concerned. I am apprehensive. The streets may be dangerous."

Actually I did not have too much concern along these lines, as the night lamps would be lit, and, given the warehouse, the exiting Merchants, and such, there would be a number of guardsmen about, private guards, city guards, and guards in the employ of the harbor administration. Too, I had little doubt there would be a sufficient number of Pani about, as well, some to assure the safe conduct of their goods, gains, and such, back to the ship, and others outside, to guard the warehouse, and the abundant stores still within.

"I trust he had something to eat," I said.

"I would suppose so," she said.

"He was to return, and meet us here, was he not?" I asked.

"He did not say so," she said.

"It seems he has been detained," I said.

"He is armed," she reminded me.

"On what business was he embarked?" I asked. "Did he say nothing?"

At that point the trading bar began to ring.

"It is the twentieth Ahn," I said.

"I think we must leave," she said.

That was very clear, as goods were being covered, lamps were being extinguished, the praetors had left their platforms, and attendants were marshalling folks out. To dally was to invite the intervention of guardsmen, impatient for the conclusion of their day's duty. It is well to follow the requests and instructions of such fellows punctually. The pounding of spear shafts and butts produces serious bruising.

"I still do not see him," I said, looking about, outside the large portal to the warehouse.

The street was darker than I had anticipated. I could see lights on the *River Dragon*, moored at the nearby wharf. The crowds were thinning out, and, I feared, the streets would be soon deserted. I did see a pair of guardsmen at the land end of the wharf, and a number of Pani were taking up stations near the now-closed warehouse.

That much was surely to the good.

I supposed it was safe enough in the vicinity of the warehouse.

I was not at all sure about some of the nearby streets.

Where was Callias?

If he had not met us in the warehouse, should he not, at least, meet us here, outside the warehouse?

The bar had rung.

It was clearly past the twentieth Ahn.

"Should I not be bound and leashed?" asked the slave.

"Your master retained the sirik," I said.

"You have no binding fiber, no leash?" she asked.

"I am a Scribe," I said.

"Do not Scribes have slaves?" she asked.

"This one does not," I said.

"If you had one, you would doubtless have such things," she said.

"Doubtless," I said.

"Poor master," she said.

I could think of a slave I would have enjoyed having in my binding fiber, and on my leash, a slender brunette, a barbarian paga slave, whom I knew from *The Sea Sleen*.

I looked down the dark street, about the right-hand corner of the warehouse, as one faced it.

"I would rather have you free," I said, "so that you can scream, and run for guardsmen."

"But men might emerge from a doorway," she said, "and subdue and gag me before I could do so."

"We will keep to the center of the street," I said.

"The streets seem to be quite narrow," she said.

"Ho!" called a cheery voice.

"Callias!" I cried.

"Here you are," he said, genially. "Let us make our way to your domicile. As Alcinoë and I have no other lodging, and it is rather late, I take it you will put us up, give us breakfast, and charge us nothing."

"Certainly," I said. "Who but a boor could deny one as needy as you so trivial a boon?"

"Good fellow," he said.

He then took some time to embrace and kiss Alcinoë.

"It is past the twentieth Ahn," I said. "It is rather dark."

Callias unsheathed his sword and led the way, followed by myself, and, lastly, heeling us, Alcinoë.

People of means commonly do not frequent the streets at night, and, when they do, they often hire a lantern bearer and a pair of guardsmen to attend them.

My domicile was not far away, but it always seemed farther than usual at night.

"It is a pleasant night," said Callias.

He was in a good mood, which, given the events of the day, was not inexplicable.

"Do not sheathe your sword," I said.

"Just smell Thassa, the salt, the wind from the sea," he said.

"Watch the doorways," I said.

My domicile was reached by an external stairway, leading to a long balcony, off of which were several common-wall dwellings in a single long, elevated building, on pilings, facing the harbor. It is within walking distance of the registry. Two lamps were posted at the head of the stairwell, and, in their light, one could negotiate not only the stairs but, though with more difficulty, the balcony, which tended to the left of the stairwell.

We ascended the stairway, went left, and, a few doors later, were before my domicile.

"Wait!" I said. "That is not my signature knot."

"No," said Callias, "it is mine."

Many doors in Brundisium, particularly in the more impecunious quarters, are tied shut, often by a leather cord tied about two staples, one on the door and the other on the jamb. To enter the door, one simply unties the knot and frees the door. Whereas anyone may untie the knot the tying of the knot is a secret, difficult to duplicate except by one familiar with the knot. If, say, the proprietor returns to the dwelling and discovers the knot is missing or different, that suggests that the area has been entered without authorization. Doors may be secured from the inside, usually by two bars. In some dwellings, of a somewhat better sort, such as mine, the signature-knot fastening is combined with a latch or bolt arrangement, in which the drawing of a latch string, put through a small hole in the door, moves the latch or bolt. When one is absent, or within and, say, expecting company, the latch string may be left free, outside the door. When one wishes, one draws the latch string within, which prevents the door from being opened, except from the inside. In more prosperous areas, generally farther from the waterfront and the warehouse district, metal locks, answering to metal keys, are more common. Some of these locks are massive, with corresponding keys. Indeed, the keys might function as weapons.

Callias undid his knot, drew the latch string, freeing the latch, and opened the door.

"After you," he said.

"The lamp is lit," I said.

"I left it on," he said.

"I will see if I can find you something to eat," I said.

"Do not bother," he said. "I had a pleasant supper at a tavern."

"Good," I said.

"I trust you fed well," he said.

"The vendors had something left," I said.

"Splendid," he said.

"It is late," I said. "I shall arrange some bedding."

"When I am finished with Alcinoë," he said, "she shall sleep at my feet."

"Of course," I said.

"Friend," said Callias.

"Yes," I said.

"You have treated me well," said Callias. "You were kind in the tavern. You offered me money. You befriended me. You gave me lodging. I am grateful."

"It is nothing," I said.

He pressed into my hand a tiny beadlike object.

"No," I said.

"Yes," he said.

"Low Scribes do not have such things," I said.

"Be the first," he said.

"I cannot accept this," I said. My view of rich men, and, in particular, of Cosians, was in the process of being suddenly and radically transformed. They were, after all, were they not, generous and noble sorts?

"Would you dishonor me, by refusing?" he asked.

"No," I said.

"And there will be more later," he said. "Where are you going?"

"To *The Sea Sleen*!" I said.

"Hold," said Callias, "it is late, and dark, you are unarmed."

"No matter," I said.

"You would carry a golden tarsk through the streets of Brundisium, at this Ahn?" he inquired.

"Who would know?" I asked.

"One need not know," he said. "You could be robbed for a copper tarsk, for a tarsk-bit."

"I wish you well!" I said. "You, too, Alcinoë!"

"Thank you, Master," she said.

"I take it you have a sudden craving for paga," said Callias.

"A sudden craving, yes, dear friend," I said, lifting my clenched fist, holding the tiny, beadlike coin, a golden tarsk, "but scarcely for paga."

"What then could you possibly have in mind?" he asked.

"Come now, dear friend," I said, "can you not recall something which I could not hitherto afford, something in a yellow camisk, with bells on her left ankle?"

"The paga girl," he said, "the slender brunette?"

"Of course!" I said.

"She is a barbarian," said Callias.

"One I want in my arms," I said.

"You would do that, you would buy her, a barbarian?" he asked.

"Yes," I said. "Yes!"

"Why?" he asked.

"Be serious," I said.

"Barbarians are not that rare," he said, "not in the larger markets. They are brought from that place called Earth."

"Surely you have noted," I said, "that they are generally of extremely high quality."

"They are selected with that in mind," he said.

"It is not simply that she is beautiful, that she is exquisite, that she is delicate, that she has deep, profound eyes, lips made for kisses, small wrists and ankles, that her body is rich in slave curves, in the many turnings and planes which the auctioneer's whip calls to our attention. It goes mysteriously beyond such things, eluding calculations and measurements."

"To you," said Callias, "she is different, and special."

"So tamely put," I said, "such words manage only to point, only to hint, at ineluctable, mysterious matchings, and sensings."

"Perhaps," said Callias.

"And what does Alcinoë mean to you?" I asked.

"Ah!" smiled Callias.

"Master," breathed Alcinoë, softly.

"To all fours," he said to her.

"Yes, Master," she said.

This position can be igniting to a female slave, being so positioned by a master. At the least, they are well reminded, so positioned beside a man, that they are slaves.

No free woman, of course, would be so positioned.

It makes clear that the slave, legally, and otherwise, is an animal, her master's animal.

"Surely," I said, "you could detect her intelligence, her sensitivity, her emotional depth, her readiness, her softness, her femininity, her needs, the incipience of her passions?"

"I gathered something of that," he said.

"Consider," I said, "such a one, with all her beauty, intelligence, and depth, and how helpless she will be when slave fires burn in her belly!"

"I saw her look upon you," he said. "I suspect they burn there already."

"She is perfect," I said.

"How so?" he asked.

"Consider the studies to which she was drawn, studies of a world much different from her own, a simpler, more natural world."

"And she a female," he said.

"What would be the most, on such a world, for which she, an alien female, might hope, and what, on such a world, might be what she truly desired, wanted, and would hope for?"

"As she is a desirable female, and might bring a decent price on a block, that seems clear," he said.

"She must have understood," I said, "that she, in all likelihood, if found on such a world, would be captured, and would soon find herself stripped and in the chains of a slave, awaiting her sale."

"I would think so," he said.

"Do you think she did not know herself, even on her own world, as suitably a man's slave?" I said.

"What woman does not, on any world?" he asked.

He looked on Alcinoë, and she, on all fours, put down her head.

"Why then should she be denied, as her own world would deny her, submission to the mastery, ropes on her ankles, her wrists pinioned behind her back in slave bracelets, a collar on her neck, her lips pressed obediently to a master's whip?"

"I, for one," he said, "would have no interest in denying her such things, particularly if she would look well at a man's feet. It is cruel to deny to a woman her nature, and, as well, to a man his."

"She would be a delicious, perfect slave," I said. "I want her! I want her, wholly! I want to own her, completely! Let herself then discover herself, and know herself, as that for which nature has designed her, a man's slave!"

"And if you owned her," he said, "and she writhed in her chains before you, miserable in the throes of slave fires, and begged for the attentions commonly bestowed on a slave, would you show her mercy?"

"Perhaps," I said, "if she begged well."

"I see," he said.

"Master," said Alcinoë to the stranger, looking up at him, "I am needy!"

"Kneel," he said.

"Yes, Master," she said.

"Bedding is there," I said, pointing to a side of the room. "And in the locker, at the back, you will find ka-la-na, and food. I am off now to *The Sea Sleen*!"

"Do not go," said Callias.

I paused at the door.

"You advise me to wait until morning?" I asked. Surely there was much to be said for such counsel.

"No," he said.

"You wish me to wait, a bit," I asked, "and you, armed, would accompany me? I would be grateful, and that is thoughtful, but it is not necessary. Too, I suspect there must be guardsmen about. I will keep to the wider, better-lit streets."

"No," he said.

"I do not understand," I said.

"It is too late," he said.

"I do not understand," I said.

"I stopped by *The Sea Sleen*, after leaving the warehouse," he said. "It is there I had supper."

"So?" I said, apprehensively.

"The slave whom I suppose you mean," he said, "the slender brunette, who heard the story of the voyage, she of the yellow camisk and belled ankle, is no longer there."

"No!" I cried.

"I assume she is the one you had in mind," he said.

"She is no longer there?" I said. "Are you sure? Perhaps she was not on the floor at the time."

"No," he said. "She was sold."

"When?" I asked.

"Does it matter?" he asked.

"No," I said.

"Recently," he said.

"Aiii!" I moaned. I sank to my knees beside the door, my head in my hands. My body shook with sobs.

"Master!" breathed Alcinoë, concerned.

"Please," said Callias, embarrassed.

"Forgive me," I said.

"It is only a slave," he said.

"Of what value is this?" I said, looking down at the tiny golden tarsk in my hand.

"Something like a hundred silver tarsks," said Callias.

With a cry of anger and frustration I cast the golden tarsk to the end of the room.

It was retrieved by Callias.

Alcinoë had not stirred. A slave, commonly, may not touch money without permission.

Callias thoughtfully placed the coin in my purse.

"Thank you," I said.

"These things are not to be thrown about," he said.

"No," I said.

"Forget her," said Callias.

"No," I said.

"You can buy another," said Callias.

"I do not want another," I said. "All my life I have waited for one such as she."

"And then," said Callias, "you found her."

"In one brought from a far world," I said.

"A mere barbarian," he said.

"What is a barbarian," I asked, "other than one whose native tongue is not Gorean?"

"Oh, much more than that," said Callias. "One lacking civilization, or derived from some civilization which is unnatural and inferior, perhaps one which is complex, selfish, polluted, crowded, and uncaring, one unfamiliar with suitable customs and proprieties, with codes and castes, with literature, music, and poetry."

"Gorean literature, music, and poetry," I said.

"I knew a barbarian once," said Callias, "who not only lacked a Home Stone, but did not know what a Home Stone was."

"That is more serious," I granted him. "I am sure she knows now!"

"But a slave is not permitted one," he said, "no more than a verr, a tarsk or kaiila."

"True," I said.

"There are places, I am told, on the world, Earth, where free women do not veil themselves."

"Shameless," I said.

"You know why that is, do you not?" he asked.

"No," I said.

"Because they are slaves," he said. "They bare their features that men may look upon them, and scrutinize them, and ponder them, and assess them, and consider them as what they are, as slaves."

"Perhaps," I said.

"And do you not think their men do not strip them in their minds, imagine them naked in collars, and consider what they might pay for them?"

"Perhaps," I said. "I do not know."

"Do you not do the same with free women," he asked. "Do not we all, perhaps glimpsing an ankle, a bared wrist, a fluttering veil, the turn of a hip within the robes of concealment?"

"Master!" protested Alcinoë.

"Be quiet, girl," said Callias.

"Yes, Master," she said.

"You are attractive in your tunic," said Callias, "but I think we may shorten it, considerably."

"As Master wishes," she said.

"Also," he said, "there are many of these slaves brought to Gor who do not even know how to please a man, are ignorant even of the dances of slaves."

"They may be taught," I said.

"I would conjecture that your little barbarian," he said, "knows nothing of the dances of slaves."

"She could be taught," I said.

"Do you think she might look well, writhing before you, hoping to please her master, fearing your whip did she not do so?"

"I would think she would look quite well," I said.

"Has she not in her imagination, many times, naked and in a collar, so danced, danced as a slave before men, fearing their whips?"

"I do not know," I said.

"She has," said Callias. "That was clear in her expressions, in her movements, in the tavern. She is a slave."

"You think so?" I said.

"She is a slave to the core, awaiting her master."

"And she is gone, sold!" I said.

"Poor, dear Master," breathed Alcinoë.

"There will never be another," I said.

"And there need not be another," he said.

"What?" I said.

"Alcinoë," he said, "are your thighs hot?"

"That is not all that is hot, my Master!" she whispered.

"I take it you are well lubricated," he said, "and are oiling nicely?"

"Yes, Master!"

"Are you ready to squirm as the slut you are?" he asked.

"Yes, Master!" she said.

"Do you beg to do so?" he asked.

"Yes, Master," she said. "Yes, Master!"

"My dear friend," said Callias to me, "as I recall, you mentioned you might arrange some bedding."

"It is at the side of the room," I said.

"Perhaps you might spread it for us," said Callias.

"What?" I said.

"We are your guests," he said.

"It is right there," I said, pointing.

"And you are our host," he said.

"You have spent several nights here," I said. "Is it suddenly so inaccessible?"

"Please," said Callias.

"Very well," I said.

I moved toward the bedding.

"Wait!" I said.

"What?" he said.

"We shall learn her fate," I said. "In the morning, we will venture to *The Sea Sleen*, find out to whom she was sold, contact him, and buy her back!"

"She had no papers," said Callias. "The transaction was informal. She is nameless. It would be difficult to trace her.

Moreover, it seems she was not purchased by one of Brundisium, but by an itinerant, one bound abroad."

"Surely there is a name," I said.

"Apparently," said he, "no name was given."

"We must watch the gates," I said, "the piers!"

"All of them?" he asked.

"What shall we do?" I asked.

"I would think about retiring," he said. "Is there not the matter of the bedding?"

"I trust that you will enjoy Alcinoë," I said.

"I intend to," he said.

"Please, hurry, Master," said Alcinoë.

"Do not be bitter," he said. "Remember that your paga girl is only a slave."

"So, too, then," I said, "is your Alcinoë."

"Yes, yes," said Alcinoë. "Please, Master."

"You are quite right," he said. "Alcinoë is, of course, only a slave, but one must note, as well, that she is different, perfect, wonderful, unique, special, and incomparable, unparalleled, and the most desirable woman on all Gor."

"Please," said Alcinoë, "please, Master!"

"To you," I said.

"Surely you acknowledge she is quite nice," he said.

"Yes," I said, "she is quite nice."

"The bedding, the bedding," he said.

I reached down, angrily, seizing the first covering to hand, one of the down-filled comforters, for I could not afford furs, and lifted it back.

"Aii!" I cried.

"I expect to be leaving in a few days," he said. "I do want to see the *River Dragon* sail."

"You are an itinerant," I said, "one bound abroad!"

"Yes," he said, "one soon bound abroad."

"You gave no name," I said.

"No," he said, "but I suppose some might have recollected it, from before."

The large, soft eyes of the girl were frightened, looking up at me. She squirmed a little, but was helpless. She was naked, of course, and bound, hand and foot. I turned her quickly, exposing the left thigh, high, just under the hip. She was kefed, the letter nicely entered into her thigh. How beautiful is the *kef*! And how meaningful, recognized on all Gor. I then put her to her back. She pulled at her bound wrists; her small ankles were crossed, and thonged closely together, as had been her wrists. She was not collared, but such an oversight may be remedied quickly, at the shop of any Metal Worker. I already had one in mind, he closest to my dwelling, scarcely yards away. I would have to have a slave ring put in, and buy some chains, rope, binding fiber, slave bracelets, perhaps ankle rings, and, surely, an attractive leash. In time, if she proved satisfactory, I might even consider a tunic, or two, the sort of tunic men choose for owned women. I doubted if, when on her own world, her old world, that no longer her world, as she was now of Gor, she had anticipated her present helplessness, and the absoluteness of her new condition, that of a Gorean *kajira*.

She looked small, half concealed in the bedding, that within which she had been placed.

I held up the lamp, and, in its light, examined her, from the smallness of her thonged feet, to the curves of her calves, and thighs, the sweetness of her love cradle, the narrowness of her waist, the delights of a small but ample, well-proportioned, exciting bosom, which would be so vulnerable to the caresses, the lips, and kisses of a master, to her rounded forearms, half pulled behind her, her soft shoulders, the white throat, yet to be closely clasped in a signet of bondage, her exquisite features, her lips, and eyes, her wide, frightened eyes, and her dark hair, which I supposed had not been cut since her arrival in some slave pen, as Gorean masters commonly like long hair in a slave. She presumably did not even know the pen, or its location, in which she had first learned that she was now a property, goods, to be disposed of as men might see fit.

"I trust," said Callias, "she is the right one."

"Yes," I said. "Yes, yes, yes, yes!"

"Good," he said.

"You bought her!" I said.

"For you," he said. "The barbarian is yours."

"I can never pay you back," I said.

"You could," he said, "as the tarn disk in your wallet, which you were so careless with a moment ago, would buy several such as she."

"Allow me to recompense you," I said.

"No," he said. "She is a gift. And one of not much importance."

"She is the world to me," I exclaimed.

"Continue her examination," he said.

"'Continue'?" I said.

"Turn her," he said, "put her on her belly."

I did so.

"A bit slender," he said, "but lovely lines."

"Yes," I said.

"Sit up, girl," said Callias, and the slave turned about and struggled to a sitting position before us. Her hair was partly before her face. She drew back a little, from my hand, frightened. I brushed the hair to the side.

"I did not allow her to speak," said Callias.

I nodded. She had been then, as it is said, gagged by the master's will.

"Perhaps she has heard more than we might like, words which might frighten her, or go to her head," he said, "but I did not wish to leave her lying about, just anywhere."

"Certainly, Master," said Alcinoë, "it will not hurt her to know that she has been found of interest by free men, and is desired."

"No," said Callias, "so much is known by any woman who is bought off the block or pulled by the hair from her cage."

"Even muchly desired?" smiled Alcinoë.

"You will need a whip, of course," said Callias.

"Of course," I said.

Fear showed in the slave's eyes. I gathered she had been whipped, perhaps in the slave pen, long ago, to help her understand she was a slave, and perhaps in the paga tavern, to assist in her training. She impressed me as a frightened, timid, bashful slave, who well knew herself a slave, and would be muchly concerned to be found pleasing by her masters. Such slaves scarcely ever feel the lash. There would be no point to it. The slave is to be worked, mastered, and enjoyed. If one is not interested in relishing and cherishing a slave, why own one?

"To be sure," said Callias, "she may have heard too much, but if she is wise she will not attempt to grow bold, or presume on a master's indulgence. It is a simple thing, when she is in your collar, to correct such mistakes. Let her be in no doubt that when she is in your presence, she is, so to speak, to be on her knees. Too, perhaps, we overspoke ourselves, or your mind may change, and the whim of one day be unknown to the whim of another day. Keep her as the slave she is, and all should go well."

"I see," I said.

"Besides," he said, "you have not owned her before. Perhaps you have overestimated her. Perhaps she will not prove to be satisfactory."

"She is so beautiful," I said.

"Then you could sell her," he said.

"Master!" said Alcinoë.

"So let her rejoice, hope that all will go well, and tread softly," he said. Then he turned to the seated, bound slave, who shrank back. Callias, when he wished, could be intimidating. "You are no longer a paga girl," he told her. "You have been purchased. I bought you. You are a gift." He then indicated me. "I bought you for him. You are now his. You belong to him," he said. "Do you understand?"

The slave nodded.

"I have not given her permission to speak," said Callias.

"I see," I said.

"You are in the presence of your master," said Callias. "Get on your knees, and put your head down, to the floor."

The slave struggled to comply.

How beautiful she was, so before me.

"Step back," said Callias to me.

I moved back, a few feet, across the floor.

"Now," said Callias to the kneeling girl, bent over, her head down to the floor, "to your belly, and wriggle across the floor, to your master, and then put your head down, and lick and kiss his feet, until you are permitted to stop."

I stood back, and watched this dream of pleasure, bit by bit, struggling, approach me, as a bound slave, and then that beautiful dark hair was about my feet, and I felt her lips and tongue, those of this beautiful animal, a slave, my beautiful belonging, caress my feet.

There are many gestures of submission.

The common submission of a free woman, usually rendered in terror of her life, as amidst the flames of a burning city, is to kneel before the male, and lift her crossed wrists to him, her head bowed between her arms. In this way her submission is clear, and she is hoping to buy her life with her beauty, the crossed wrists, ready for binding, indicating that she is pleading to be accepted as a slave. If she is accepted, the wrists are usually bound, and she is expected to follow her captor docilely. Sometimes, of course, after this gesture, she is put to her belly, her wrists are bound indeed, but behind her, and a rope is put on her neck, or, sometimes, a nose ring, on a cord, is affixed, such things functioning as a leash or tether.

She continued, on her belly, bound, to tender a slave's deference to a free man.

Looking down upon her, I thought how strange it was that she, from a far world, be here, thusly. I wondered what her fellow students, from her own world, those supposedly so superior to beauty, its naturalness, and purpose, might think of her now, she to whom they had regarded themselves so superior, on the grounds of ignorant doctrines, labored concealments, and falsifications of nature, as she now was, a frightened, bound slave, understanding herself subject to the uncompromising domination of a male. Could they understand the needs, the joy, the readiness, the responsiveness, the passion, of a woman mastered? Perhaps they would be indignant, offended, outraged. Or perhaps they would be amused, and think her fate one well deserved, a fate well deserved by one whom they suspected did not share their views. But then, at night, would they dream of themselves so, at the feet of masters?

"It is enough," I said.

I then lifted her to her knees, before me.

I then went behind her, and, with some difficulty, undid the knots binding her ankles together, and then those confining her small wrists.

She moved her ankles, and rubbed her wrists, looking up at me.

"Position," said Callias, sharply.

Instantly, frightened, she went to position. I noted, interestingly that Alcinoë, reflexively, had also gone to position.

She seemed nonplussed for a moment, but remained in position. I did see that this pleased her master.

My slave seemed apprehensive. This night she had changed hands. She may well have been unaware of the transaction, until she was called forth, and delivered into the hands of Callias.

Callias scowled at her, at the gift he had made me. I gathered he wished to make sure that it was a good one.

"Your knees," he said. "Widen them. What sort of slave do you think you are?"

Obediently she spread her knees more widely.

I supposed she had no doubt now, but what she had been purchased for a pleasure slave. To be sure, this should have been anticipated by any paga girl. I forced myself to remember that she was a barbarian, and, as I recalled, had not been long in bondage. Indeed, on her own world, I supposed she had been free, as free, at any rate, as such women could be, in such a world, where, I gathered, their values, views, attitudes, dress, behavior, and such were dictated, as nearly as I could tell, by lunatics who, in fear of themselves, lived in hiding, walled away from nature, and her fulfillments. One gathered they somehow supposed that nature was a mistake, the foe of happiness, rather than its foundation and truth. How such an aberration might come about seemed inexplicable. Doubtless there had been cultural turnings, misdirections, roads wrongly taken. Doubtless there were historical reasons underlying this phenomenon, reasons by means of which a suitably informed scholar might intelligently speculate on the matter.

She was before me, in position, kneeling back on her heels, her back straight, her head up, looking ahead, the palms of her hands down on her thighs, her knees spread, this making clear the nature of her bondage. Alcinoë, too, to the side, was in position.

Both were lovely slaves.

I regarded my slave, rapt.

I wondered if women could begin to understand how they appeared to men, and what they meant to men.

I supposed not.

How could they?

They were not men.

They could know, of course, that they were desired, sought, hunted, captured, bound, chained, bought and sold, owned, and mastered.

Perhaps that would give them a sense of things. Free, of course, distracted, confused, uneasy, restless, discontented, suspicious, and unhappy, and not knowing why, their beauty was extremely dangerous, and could easily be misused to torment and divide men, to influence and manipulate them, to discomfort and afflict them, for not all wounds and bruises, blows and goadings, are the results of steel or leather. The question then is a simple one, which is "Who shall be master?" The man is mightier, and, in his heart, wishes to own the female. The female, is weaker, smaller, softer, and, in her heart, longs to be owned, and mastered. She is content only at the feet of a strong male. Accordingly, the relationship of the male master and the female slave is appropriate, a relationship in which nature is fulfilled, to the benefit of both. The female responds to the master, as his slave, and the master revels in the possession and mastery of the female, his slave. The war is done. She kneels before him, wearing his collar.

I looked upon my slave, and my slave knew herself looked upon, and as a slave.

She trembled, but retained position.

"Slave," I said.

She looked at me, frightened. Her lips trembled a little, but formed no sound. She looked wildly, frightened, to Callias. I recalled she had been forbidden to speak. Clearly she did not wish to feel the lash.

"It is I who now own you," I said. "Do you understand, female?" So addressed, as "female," the woman, whether free or slave, is forcibly reminded of what she is, radically and basically, and that it is quite different from something else, that of being a male. And this recollection, on the part of a slave, who is vulnerable, helpless, and owned, is even more devastating, for she is not only a female, but a female who is a slave.

The slave swiftly nodded, frightened. Her hair moved about her shoulders as she did this. I wanted to seize her in my arms, fling her to the floor, and cover her with kisses.

"You have, as of now," I said, "a standing permission to speak."

"Thank you, Master," she whispered.

"Revocable at any time," I added.

"Yes, Master," she said.

"You may speak," I said. "Speak."

"I am afraid," she said.

"We will have to improve your Gorean," I said.

"Yes, Master," she said.

"It is reasonably fluent at present," I said.

"That is my hope," she said, "Master."

"I am going to be about for bit," said Callias. "In that time, Alcinoë will work with her."

"She is a barbarian, Master!" said Alcinoë.

"No matter," said Callias, touching his belt.

"Yes, Master," said Alcinoë, quickly.

Callias then seized up one of the heaped comforters, spread it a bit, and then slung it to the side, on the floor.

"Lie there," said Callias to his slave, Alcinoë, pointing to the comforter.

Quickly she hurried to the comforter, and lay upon it, I thought rather seductively, considering that she has recently been white silk.

"It is late," announced Callias.

"It is my hope," she said, "that I may be permitted to give pleasure to my master."

Callias drew off his belt and tunic, and took his position on the comforter, and Alcinoë crawled eagerly to his side, but his hand, in her hair, held her for a time at his thigh, which she licked and kissed hopefully, and then, after a bit, he put her to his pleasure, with patience, until, at last, wild-eyed, looking toward the ceiling, gasping, she begged to be permitted to yield, as his slave. She then cried out with the sobbing joy of the well-ravished slave. I did not think he was so quickly through with her, but, as Callias had noted, it was late.

"Master?" said my slave.

I took another comforter, and then another, and arranged them on the floor, rather off from where Callias and Alcinoë were still tangled together.

No, I thought to myself, he is not yet finished with her.

I removed the Scribe's satchel, my purse, the Scribe's robes, and lay upon the comforter and, on one elbow, regarded the slave.

"Am I to be whipped?" she asked.

"Do you wish to be whipped?" I asked.

"No," she said, "no, Master."

"I do not have a whip," I said.

"A slave is pleased," she said.

"I shall obtain one shortly," I said.

"Yes, Master," she said.

"I am of the Scribes," I said.

"I know," she said.

"Do you know much of Scribes?" I asked.

"Only that they make me serve well in the alcove," she said.

"But that is not unusual, is it?" I asked. "With fellows of any caste?"

"No, Master," she said.

"You," I said, "have an affinity with the Scribes."

"Master?" she said.

"I think you are the sort of female who would appeal to a Scribe," I said.

"I will try to please my master," she said.

"You were a student, of sorts?" I said.

"Yes, Master," she said, "one spoken of as a graduate student. I was in what is called a university. I was in what is called a department, for in my old world knowledge is often put in departments, its wholeness, doubtless of necessity, being ignored or neglected. My department, in which I studied, was one devoted to classical studies. One attended classes, one heard lectures, one participated in what are called seminars, smaller courses, more informal courses, where students might participate in discussions, commonly held about tables."

"Interesting," I said.

"It is a way of doing things," she said.

"One gathers then, that many might be in such places."

"Yes," she said.

"Would there be more than one, or, say, two students, with a teacher?"

"Often several," she said.

"They do not live together?"

"No," she said. "They meet at appropriate times and places, according to schedules, beginning when clocks strike or bells ring, and ending when they strike or ring again."

"As hiring space on a passenger wagon?" I asked.

"Perhaps," she said.

This account seemed strange to me, but I supposed she had no reason to lie to me. I had spent several years in the household of my teacher, who would accept no pay, because, for our caste, knowledge is priceless. One day he had said to me, "You may leave now," and I knew then that I was of the Scribes.

"Are there many students at these places?" I asked.

"Sometimes thousands," she said.

"There are so many," I asked, "who hunger so for knowledge, and so avidly seek it?"

"Not at all," she said. "By far the greatest number have little or no interest in learning whatsoever."

"Why then are they there?" I asked. "What are they doing there?"

"It is expected of them," she said. "It is something to be done."

"Why?" I asked.

"One supposes there are many reasons," she said. "If one does not perform certain actions, enact certain rituals, spend time in certain places, and obtain legal evidence that one has done so, one may be culturally disadvantaged."

"And what do these actions, these rituals, or such, have to do with learning?"

"In most cases," she said, "very little, if anything."

"Might they not just as well do other things for the same amount of time," I asked, "jump up and down, or sing songs, or such?"

"I had not thought about it," she said, "but one supposes so."

"It is a cultural thing?" I said.

"Yes," she said.

"Is there not some sort of monstrous mistake, or deceit, or fraud, involved in all this?" I asked.

"It is a way of doing things," she said.

"Is this not a misunderstanding of learning, a disparagement of learning, an insult to learning, a cheapening of learning, a prostitution of learning?" I asked.

"Some care," she said.

"Even there?" I asked.

"Yes," she said.

"You were interested in far worlds," I said, "ancient worlds, ancient to your former world, their culture, their languages, their way of life, their beliefs."

"Yes, Master," she said.

"I approve of that," I said.

"I am pleased," she said.

"Who is pleased?" I asked.

"A slave is pleased," she said.

"Perhaps, someday, you will speak to me, at length, of such things."

"Surely Master is not interested in my interests, my feelings, my mind?" she said.

"In that question," I said, "I detect the pathology of your world."

"Master?"

"A Gorean," I said, "wants all of a slave, and owns all of a slave."

She looked at me, startled.

"All of her is in his collar," I said.

"A slave is pleased," she said, "that a master would lock his collar on the whole of her."

"Few men would want less," I said.

"I did not gather that," she said, "from the alcove."

"You did not have a private master," I said.

"No, Master," she said.

"As a student, a graduate student, or such, on Earth," I said, "I would suppose you did not anticipate that you would one day be on Gor, kneeling naked before a man, his slave."

"No, Master," she said, "but in secret moments I dreamed of such things."

"Did you know of Gor?" I asked.

"I thought it only in books," she said.

"What do you think now?" I asked.

"I have felt the thongs of a Gorean master on my limbs," she said, "I have been collared, I have served on the floor of a Gorean tavern, I have striven in the alcove to be found pleasing by my master's customers, I am no longer of the opinion that Gor exists only in books."

"You are very pretty," I said.

"Thank you, Master," she said.

"Of your fellow female graduate students," I said, "I wonder if you were the only one found worthy to be put in a Gorean collar."

"Perhaps," she said. "I do not know."

"So," I said, "you were a student, a graduate student?"

"Yes, Master," she said.

"Spread your knees more widely," I said.

"Yes, Master," she said.

"You obey promptly," I observed.

"I hope to please my master," she said.

"What do you think of dancing naked?" I asked.

"I would have to obey my master," she said.

"But what do you think of it?" I asked.

"I would hope to please my master," she said.

"Do you know how to play the kalika?" I asked.

"No, Master."

"You do not know slave dance, I take it," I said.

"No," she said.

"You may be taught such things," I said.

"Yes, Master," she said.

"Slave dance," I said, "is very attractive in a woman."

"I doubt that I could be so beautiful," she said.

"One does not expect every woman to bring a hundred pieces of gold as a dancer," I said.

"No, Master," she said.

"I have seen many dancers, even public dancers, brothel dancers, street dancers, tavern dancers, who were not as beautiful as you."

"I do not know how to dance," she said.

"Perhaps, with the encouragement of the lash, you could learn," I said.

"The slave who desires to please her master," she said, "does not require the encouragement of the lash."

"You would do your best?" I said.

"Certainly, Master," she said.

"Would you like to dance—*as a slave*?" I asked.

"On Earth," she said, "I dreamed of such things."

"Speak," I said.

"I thought of myself, frequently enough, as a property, as owned, as a girl who must unquestioningly, fearfully, obey masters, who might dance for their pleasure, about campfires in lonely places, on streets in shabby districts, to a master's flute, on the decks of galleys, to the clapping of hands, on the floor of taverns, to music, silks swirling, bangles clashing, to shouts, to hands reaching for me, to the clash of goblets and the spilling of drink, to the cries of aroused men, pleased to look upon me as I would then be, a vulnerable, helpless slave, desperate to be found pleasing."

"And did you dream of yourself helpless in the chains, or arms, of a master?"

"Yes, Master," she said, putting down her head.

"Where were you sold?" I asked.

"In Market of Semris," she said.

"In what pen, or slave house, were you first marked?" I asked.

"I do not know," she said. "I, with other slaves—"

"Barbarians?" I asked.

"Yes, Master," she said. "—were transported naked and collared in a closed slave wagon, with blue and yellow silk, our ankles chained to a central bar, it run the length of the wagon bed. We traveled for days. At night, in camps, we were chained in the open, to trees or the wagon wheels. One or another of us were hooded and removed from the bar in one place or another. We were, I take it, distributed amongst various markets. Only three were left in the wagon when the hood was buckled about my head and I was lifted from the wagon. I felt the dust of a road beneath my feet. My hands were braceleted before me, and I was tethered by the bracelets to the stirrup of some large, four-footed beast, which I later learned was a kaiila. After some weary hours on the dusty road I was brought to a sales barn, where my tether was freed of the stirrup, and I was unhooded and debraceleted. Shortly thereafter, I was fed, watered, and rested. Later I was processed, washed, brushed, combed, and such, preparing me for my sale."

"Which was in Market of Semris," I said.

"That is my understanding," she said.

"Did you enjoy your sale?" I asked.

"I was terrified," she said. "I found myself turned about, and positioned, delicately, expertly, by the auctioneer's whip, exhibited as merchandise, displayed, as a slave, while men cried out, and called bids on me."

"I see," I said.

"And then," she said, "the auctioneer touched me, unexpectedly, and I leaped with a cry of misery, in piteous response, which delighted the men. I could not help myself! 'Pleasure slave,' I heard call. 'To the taverns with her!' I put my head in my hands, and bent over, and sobbed. I could not help myself. Then I was apparently sold, for I was conducted from the platform."

"What did you go for?" I asked.

"I do not know," she said. "But I gather it was for less than a silver tarsk."

"You were purchased for a paga slut," I said.

"Yes, Master," she said.

I was interested in this information not simply because it pertained to the slave, but because it seemed not untypical of certain mysteries commonly obtaining in the case of barbarian slaves. Many things seemed obscure about such barbarians, or reasonably so, for example, the location of their first acquisition, apparently a far world, the means by which they were brought to Gor, where they were initially housed on our world, why they seemed to be distributed about, almost tracelessly, and such. As nearly as I could determine they were derived from several places on the far world, and brought by different ships, or by some method of conveyance, at different times, to many different locations on Gor. Subtleties or secrecies seemed to be involved. In any event, I knew little of these matters, and, if others knew, they were apparently less than communicative.

"I have never had a private master," she said to me.

"I have never owned a slave," I said.

"Master must have seen me many times in the paga tavern," she said.

"Yes," I said.

She put down her head, shyly.

"Did he find me of slave interest?"

"Certainly," I said.

"If he found me of slave interest," she said, "why was it that he never snapped his fingers, summoning me to his table, why did he not bind me, and thrust me before him to an alcove?"

"I did not want you thusly," I said, "a girl for a coin, to be relinquished after some Ehn or an Ahn, or so, to be ceded in her turn to another, to be surrendered at the closing of a tavern's portal. I wanted you whole, and mine, indisputably, legally, in every way. I did not want to rent you for the price of a drink. I wanted more. I wanted all. I wanted everything. I wanted to own you, completely, every strand of hair, every bit of you."

"You sensed something in me?" she said.

"Yes," I said.

"I noticed your eyes upon me," she said, "as one would look upon a slave one would own."

"Perhaps," I said.

She lifted her head.

"Surely you noted me putting myself before you often enough," she said.

"Yes," I said. How tormenting had been that flash of thigh, that whisk of a camisk as she turned, the flash of the bells tied about her left ankle.

"In my cage," she said, "I hoped you would bid on me."

"I am a poor man," I said, "a low Scribe, one who labors in the registry. I could not afford you."

"I thought that you might understand me, as others could not," she said.

"Do not expect to be too much understood," I said, "as you are a slave."

"Yes, Master," she said.

Surely she knew that her feelings, her thoughts, her hopes, her desires, her dreams, and such, were meaningless, and of no consequence, as she was a slave.

"I saw you look upon me," she said, "as a master looks upon a slave, and I trembled, and shivered, and wondered, and I feared, and hoped, that you would be my master."

I did not respond.

"I may be from Earth," she said, "but I have learned here, as

I suspected on Earth, that women are slaves, and that I am a woman, and a slave. I want to be what I am, a slave. I will try to serve you well, and please you so."

To the side Callias and Alcinoë were asleep, in one another's arms.

"It was with joy," said the slave, "that I, my presence unknown to you, heard you speak of ineluctable, mysterious matchings, and sensings."

"I did not know you were there," I said, annoyed.

"I understand," she said. "I only want to say to you that I, too, in the tavern, on different nights, looking upon you, felt such things."

"Have you eaten?" I asked.

"Yes," she said. "Has Master?"

"Yes," I said.

She looked at me. "It is strange," she said. "I have come from far away, to find my master."

"Strange, too," I said, "that I should so find my slave, in one come from so far a world."

"Do you think you might care for me, eventually, a little, Master?" she asked.

"I will buy a whip in the morning," I said.

"Yes, Master," she said.

It was hard to take my eyes from her. How beautiful she was, kneeling before me, in the light of the lamp.

"I am marked," she said, "as Master determined, the common *kef*. I am thus well identified as a slave."

"So?" I said.

"And," she said, "I think that Master may like me, forgive me, Master, as I could not help overhearing words which gave me such hopes, and surely he knows my antecedents and origins, my affinities, as he will have it, if he is correct, with the Caste of Scribes, so lofty a caste, and my former station and position, as a student in a university, and thus, in a sense, my prestige, dignity, and such."

"I do not understand," I said.

"So," she said, "it will not be necessary to put me in a collar. I am above a collar."

"You were collared in *The Sea Sleen*," I said.

"I was a paga girl," she said. "They did not know my

specialness. I am now the slave of a Scribe, and the Scribes is a high caste."

"Look to the side," I said. "Do you see that slave, she, Alcinoë?" I asked.

"Certainly," she said.

"Well," I said, "she was once a free woman in imperial Ar, a high lady, a woman of importance and power, of wealth and station. What is on her neck?"

"A collar," said the slave.

"What sort of collar?" I asked.

"A slave collar," she said.

"Precisely," I said.

"But she is Gorean," said the slave.

"And you are a barbarian," I said, "a thousand times less."

The slave touched her throat, lightly, tentatively, apprehensively.

"Master will collar me?" she asked.

"Yes," I said. "Tomorrow you will wear a collar, a slave collar, and it will be locked on your neck."

"I will not be able to remove it?"

"No," I said.

Relief, to my surprise, flooded her features.

"Thank you, Master," she said. "That is what I want. I want your collar on my neck, and I want it there, locked, as on the neck of any other slave, for I am only another slave. No more! That is what I am, and want to be. How happy you make me! I am grateful! I will try to be worthy of wearing your collar. Thank you, Master. I will love my collar."

I then lay back on the comforters, which I had spread on the floor.

"Master?" she said.

"Please me," I said.

She crawled to my side. "I will try, Master," she whispered.

"Wine, Master?" had said my slave.

"Wine, Master?" had said the slave of my friend, Callias.

"Yes," I had said.

"Yes," had said Callias.

As noted, the slaves had served the wine well.

I thought the supper was nicely prepared.

Too, as noted, the ka-la-na was excellent.

This morning we had all ventured to the high piers, bid farewell to Captain Nakamura, and watched that unusual ship, the *River Dragon*, unusual, at least for Brundisium, take its leave.

We watched it, until it could no longer be seen from the high pier.

"I wish them a good journey," said Callias.

"I, too," I said.

"Tersites," he said, looking out to sea, "had eyes painted on the great ship."

"I recall that, from your story," I said. "It pleased me. Now she can see her way."

"A day out from the cove of the castle," said he, "we heaved to, and Tersites himself, with his own hands, poured wine, oil, and salt into the sea."

"I am pleased to hear it," I said. It seemed then, at last, that Tersites had made his peace with vast, mighty Thassa.

"Where is the great ship now?" I asked.

"I do not know," he said.

"One wonders what transpires at the World's End," I said.

"Yes," he said, "one wonders."

"You need not have shared so much with me," I said, "the coins, the jewels, the pearls."

"Have no fear," he smiled. "What you received is small, compared to what I retain."

"I suspect," I said, "that you would have been more than content with no more than a mere slave."

"Yes," he said, "that would have been more than enough."

"But, surely," I said, "the gold, the jewels, the pearls, and such, were welcome."

"Do you not think it would have been boorish, not to have accepted them?"

"Quite," I said.

We turned about, to join the slaves, one in a scarlet tunic, one in a blue tunic, waiting at the land end of the pier.

* * * *

The slaves now, at our supper, brought forth the Turian liqueurs.

"These are expensive," I said.

"One wishes to make his contribution," said Callias.

"You have done far more than that," I said.

"Alcinoë," he said, "knows of such things. She used to approve the menus for banquets, for state dinners, for private suppers, and such."

"A valuable slave," I said.

"In many ways," he said.

Alcinoë smiled. "After supper," she said, "with master's permission, I will show him how valuable a slave can be."

"And I trust," said my slave, "that I may convince my master that a mere barbarian is not to be despised in the furs."

As the reader, if such there be, may apprehend, I could now afford furs. To be sure, expressions such as 'serving in the furs' are rather general.

Whereas the girls prepared and served the meal, we had them share it with us, as well, they kneeling at the small tables, at which we sat cross-legged. This is not that unusual in small households, where informality is common. We did, of course, take the first bite of the various dishes, the first sip of the various beverages, and such.

"Your vocabulary and grammar," I told my slave, "is much improved."

"Alcinoë has been very helpful," she said.

"Beware her accent," said Callias. "It is of Ar."

"It is a beautiful accent," said my slave.

"Doubtless," said Callias, "but there are places where that accent might earn you a blow."

"I listen carefully in the market, on the streets, and about the piers," she said, "and do my best to speak as those about me."

"I have a western, coastal accent," I said. "Callias, not surprisingly, has a Cosian accent."

"East Cos, Jad, I am told," said Callias.

"It seems then," said Alcinoë, "that I am the only one without an accent."

"That is the vanity of Ar," said Callias.

"Someone must speak correct Gorean," she said.

"I trust," I said to Alcinoë, "that your kind efforts to assist my slave with her Gorean are not completely unrequited."

"No," she said.

"Perhaps she does some of your chores for you?"

"No," she said.

"What then?" I asked.

"She has informed me of certain tricks of the alcove," said Alcinoë, "unlikely to lie within the repertoire of the average free woman, which I once was."

"Good," I said.

"Interesting," said Callias. "That explains much."

Shortly thereafter the slaves rose to their feet and, a bit later, I could smell the fumes of freshly brewed black wine. It shortly made its appearance. Alcinoë, as she was Gorean, had the honor of bringing forth the vessel and cups, and my slave, as she was a barbarian, and thus subordinate, unless it was otherwise specified, brought forth the small pitcher of cream, the tiny spoons, and the small, flat bowls of sugars and spices. Later, each slave brought forth, as well, a tray of assorted cakes and pastries.

I thought the slaves served well.

Both wore only their collars.

This is not that unusual, at small suppers, and such, in the absence of free women.

It is pleasant for a fellow, of course, to be so served, by naked, beautiful slaves.

The mastery is characterized by many such delights.

After supper, and the slaves had cleared, and then washed, dried, and stored the dinnerware, and such, we addressed ourselves, each with his own slave, to the pleasures of the furs.

Later the slaves slept, lying beside us.

"Callias," I said.

"Yes," he said. He was not asleep either.

"There is interest in many of these things," I said, "in Tersites, the great ship, in Talena, of Ar, in Tarl Cabot, the Pani, the World's End, and such. Would you mind, if I might, as I could, tell your story?"

"No," he said. "But no one will believe it."

"There was Captain Nakamura," I said, "and the *River dragon*."

"A strange ship," he said, "from faraway. What might that have to do with the things you mention?"

"It came from the World's End," I said.

"All people will know," he said, "is that it is an unusual ship, and it is not clear from whence it came."

"Is it important," I asked, "whether people believe it or not?"

"Not at all," he said.

"You do not mind," I said, "if the story is told?"

"No," he said. "I would like for it to be told."

"You will be leaving in a few days," I said.

"Yes," he said.

"I shall not ask where," I said.

"I am not as yet sure myself," he said.

"I conjecture that names, and such, will be changed."

"Quite possibly," he said. "That would seem judicious."

"I will wish you well," I said.

"And I, too," he said, "will wish you well."

I now conclude this tale.

It may be recalled that my slave had long been nameless. For example, she had had no name given her in *The Sea Sleen*, and had been purchased by Callias as a nameless slave, much as one might purchase any nameless animal. Still slaves like to have names, and it is convenient that they should be named, obviously, for a variety of reasons, for ease of referring to them, instructing them, and such. Her collar, in *The Sea Sleen*, had simply identified her as a paga girl of that tavern, to be returned there if found strayed, or fled. Her name now, with mine, identifying me as her master, appeared on her collar. It seemed she had hoped to be given a beautiful name, and had long hoped that a particular name, one which much appealed to her, would be given to her. It was with fervency that she had knelt before me, her head to my feet, and timidly asked that she might be given a name, and informed me of the one she hoped might be hers. I thought her choice lovely. It is a name not unknown in Brundisium, and one often encountered amongst the islands. It is 'Helen'.

So let this tale be concluded.

I wish you well.

> Calisthenes,
> Office of the Registry,
> Harbor Administration,
> Port of Brundisium,
> Scribe.

About the Author

John Norman, born in Chicago, Illinois, in 1931, is the creator of the Gorean Saga, the longest running series of adventure novels in science fiction history. Starting in December 1966 with *Tarnsman of Gor*, the series was put on hold after its twenty-fifth installment, *Magicians of Gor*, in 1988, when DAW refused to publish its successor, *Witness of Gor*. After several unsuccessful attempts to find a trade publishing outlet, the series was brought back into print in 2001, and after *Witness of Gor* (2002), *Prize of Gor* (2008), *Kur of Gor* (2009), *Swordsmen of Gor* (2010) and *Mariners of Gor* (2011), they are now preparing the 2012 release of *Conspirators of Gor*. Norman has also produced a separate, three installment science fiction series, the Telnarian Histories, plus two other fiction works (*Ghost Dance* and *Time Slave*), a nonfiction paperback (*Imaginative Sex*), and a collection of thirty short stories, entitled Norman *Invasions*. The *Totems of Abydos* was published in spring 2012.

All of Norman's work is available both in print and as ebooks. The Internet has proven to be a fertile ground for the imagination of Norman's ever-growing fan base, and at Gor Chronicles (www.gorchronicles.com), a website specially created for his tremendous fan following, one may read everything there is to know about this unique fictional culture.

Norman is married and has three children.